OF
LOVE
AND
LIFE

OF LOVE AND LIFE

Three novels selected and condensed
by Reader's Digest

CONDENSED BOOKS DIVISION

The Reader's Digest Association Limited, London

The Reader's Digest Association Limited
11 Westferry Circus, Canary Wharf, London E14 4HE

www.readersdigest.co.uk

ISBN 0-276-42734-3

For information as to ownership of copyright in the material of
this book, and acknowledgments, see last page.

CONTENTS

A Married Man

Catherine Alliott

For four years Lucy has grieved for her husband, Ned, who died in a car crash on the way to the birth of their second son. Ever since that tragedy it has taken an enormous effort of will for Lucy to get through each day.

Then one afternoon she catches a glimpse of an attractive man in the street and realises that her emotions are coming alive again—she is no longer just existing. As Lucy embarks upon a mission to learn more about the compelling stranger, the consequences for her and her sons are far-reaching.

Chapter One

'SHE'LL HAVE YOU for breakfast,' observed Jess tartly, rubbing a bit of grime off a Spode jug and setting it down on the trestle table in front of us.

'Who will?' I broke from my contemplation of the assorted bric-a-brac and antiques before us to glance up defensively.

'Your mother-in-law, of course. Talk about strolling back into the lion's den. You didn't actually say you'd go, did you?'

'Of course I did,' I said hotly. 'Christ, Jess, if someone offered you two scts of school fees and a converted barn over your head in a picturesque, rural idyll, don't tell me you wouldn't leap at it too. Anyway, she's my *ex*-mother-in-law—that makes all the difference.'

'Rubbish,' she scoffed as she arranged a fistful of silver spoons on our faded velvet tablecloth. 'Not in her eyes. As far as she's concerned you'll always be the mother of her grandchildren and that, my dear Lucy, is entirely the point. That is precisely *why* you've been offered such a mouth-watering package down in Netherby-sur-la-ancestral-pile. It has absolutely nothing to do with your well-being or your undoubted charms.' She beamed past me as a customer loomed.

'Yes, madam, it *is* Royal Worcester and it's in wonderful condition for such a rare piece, don't you think?'

She bestowed a radiant smile on Madam who, swaddled in ethnic knits on this flaming cold June day and with all the hallmarks of a seasoned Portobello Road aficionado, was peering doubtfully over her spectacles. She ran a practised eye over the rest of the collectibles on our stall, sniffed, and put the teapot down. She looked far from convinced.

'No,' she snapped. 'I think it's in rather ropy condition actually. And I also think that all these tags you've put on everything are very misleading. Who are you to tell me that's a very decorative piece of early Meissen? Surely I should be the judge of whether it's decorative or not?'

'It's to help some of our less discerning customers,' purred Jess obsequiously. 'To point them in the right direction, antiquarily speaking, so they don't feel foolish asking. Clearly you don't need any pointers, but, golly,' she rolled her eyes expressively, 'you should see some of the types we get round here.'

I smiled, reflecting that Jess's labels had indeed got more outrageous as the weeks had gone by. We'd temporarily taken over the antique stall from my mother, Maisie, who'd had a stall in the Portobello Road since I was a little girl. In the last couple of weeks, though, her chronic arthritis had almost forced her to give it up, so I'd stepped into the breach to keep it going until she was better, roping my oldest friend Jess in with me. For Jess it made a welcome diversion from changing her small son's nappy at the weekend, and for me—well, antiques were my passion, so I was happy. Happy just soaking up the atmosphere of this famous street, gazing at the stalls crammed haphazardly along it, silver next to clocks and yellowing books, starched Victorian christening gowns billowing in the breeze beside pop memorabilia, and, of course, my mother's own eclectic offerings, which included anything from exquisite porcelain to faded sepia postcards. I'd even added a few choice pieces of my own, which I'd priced ridiculously high and watched like a hawk, hoping that they wouldn't sell, but knowing I needed the money.

I needn't have worried. As we'd sat there, three Saturdays in a row now, surrounded by what we thought were the most delicious and interesting bits of other people's domestic history, we'd sold very little. Today, business was disastrous.

'Come on,' muttered Jess, 'let's pack it in.'

'How did we do?' I asked, as she shook the little velvet bag of money onto the table.

'Twenty-two pounds and . . . six pence. That's our worst yet.' She sighed. 'Oh well,' she said grudgingly, 'I suppose at least you'll be taken away from all this. But I still think you're selling your soul.'

'Oh, don't be so melodramatic,' I snapped. 'What option have I got? I can't afford to send Ben to a good school—and he hates the one he's at—and I can't stay in that tiny little flat any longer, either. Even if I could afford it, which I can't, the three of us are bursting at the seams. And anyway, Jess, what could be nicer than living in the country? The children walking across the fields to school, ponies to ride,' I said wistfully, 'streams to dam, daisies to, um, you know . . .'

'Chain,' she said drily, 'prior to rattling them. Come on, Lucy, you're a city girl through and through and you know it. You'll miss the buzz. Fresh air is wonderful for the cheeks but it doesn't do much for the brain. You'll stagnate down there.'

'Jess, I have to cut my cloth,' I warned tersely.

'Yes, to go and live on your parents-in-law's estate, *completely* beholden to them, and absolutely at their beck and call. There you'll be with Lady Horse-face lording it over you, always surrounded by the memory of your dead husband who'll stalk in and out of the plot like Banquo's ghost!'

I blinked at her in silence.

'Sorry,' she said abruptly, hoisting a sackful of china onto her back and picking up one end of the table we'd speedily collapsed. 'But you must admit, Luce, it's going to set you back about three years, and you were doing so well. You've got those four mornings a week in your beloved porcelain department at Christie's, you've got this stand—'

'This stand,' I said witheringly, swinging another sack onto my shoulder and picking up the other end of the table.

She swept on regardless. 'The kids are doing well, and *you're* so much better. You're finally out of the loop.'

We plunged into the Portobello Road, dodging through the crowds.

'I mean, OK, the money's tight,' she yelled back at me, 'but give it a couple more years and you'll be through it. But to go down there, to be *swamped* by that wretched family again . . .'

'The money's not tight, Jess.' I stopped suddenly in the street, jolting her to a standstill. 'It's bloody non-existent! Christie's pay a pittance—'

'But you love it!'

'Yes, *and* I can keep on doing it. People do commute from Oxfordshire, you know. And I'm going to change it to two full days,' I said confidently. 'And anyway,' I sighed, picking up the table and moving on again, 'I told you, even if I wanted to stay in that flat, I can't. I can't afford it. Even the council tax is crippling.'

'So why don't Lord and Lady Po-face offer to pay it for you?' she demanded. 'Or set you up somewhere else in London? Why do you have to be down there with them?'

'Because Ben starts prep school and they've offered to pay the fees. And because he needs somewhere that can cope with dyslexia—'

'And because they want him to go to the Right One. The school of their choice, where they can mould him. They want control, Luce, control of you for a start—but more importantly, control of the children. Of *course* they want you down there in their tastefully converted barn!'

'You're so cynical, Jess,' I said hotly. I stopped and made her face me

11

again. 'OK, Ned's mother can be,' I hesitated, 'a bit tricky at times . . .'

'Tricky!' she scoffed. 'Needs smothering with a pillow, you once said.'

'But you know recently,' I hurried on, 'well, Rose and I have sort of,' I licked my lips, 'bonded.'

'What!'

'And even if we hadn't,' I went on defiantly, 'there's simply no way I'd look this gift horse in the mouth. You don't know what it's like, Jess, eking out a widow's pension. I've been beside myself with worry. When I got Rose's letter I wept, I was so relieved. So just back off, OK?'

She made a face but looked slightly contrite. We walked on in silence.

'Sorry,' she mumbled, scuffing her toe. 'It's only 'cos I care. And I'll miss you. Selfish really. But I can't help feeling . . .' she puckered her brow and wrestled with herself for honesty, 'that there's nothing *down* there for you.'

'No man, you mean,' I said darkly, as we picked up our load and dodged through the crowds again.

'Well, you can bet it's a social wasteland where they live, stuffed full of aged old retainers. God, you'll be lucky if you run into anyone under eighty. I suppose you might meet the odd blacksmith or two,' she conceded grudgingly. 'All red-hot irons and rippling biceps, but you'll never meet anyone cerebral, whereas here—hey!' She broke off suddenly. 'Whatever happened to that guy you mentioned last week, Charles or something. Fantasy man in the office?'

'Charlie.' I coloured instantly, glad she couldn't see. Crikey, had I said in the office? Perhaps I had.

'Ah, you see! Charlie. Well, you won't see him, will you?'

'I might. He's got a place near Oxford,' I said, unable to resist it.

She halted suddenly, obliging me to stop behind her.

'Right,' she said slowly, watching me carefully. 'And did you know that when Rose asked you to go and live down there?'

'Well, I . . .' I hesitated. Oh God, I knew I shouldn't have mentioned Charlie. 'Forget Charlie,' I said quickly. 'The truth is, Jess, I don't even know him, and even if I did, he'd be out of the equation, because . . . because he's out of my league.'

'Bollocks. No one's out of your league, Lucy, you're flaming gorgeous! It's just you got married so young no one else ever got the chance to tell you. You were snapped up by Ned at university in about ten seconds.'

'Nonsense.' I gazed past her.

'Oh, yes, waist-length blonde hair, blue-green eyes and a voluptuous figure to die for, *very* unattractive. Do me a favour!' She peered at me. 'God, you're *still* red. Purple! Who is this guy, anyway?'

12

'I told you, Jess,' I snapped. 'He's no one. Just leave me alone, can't you?' I made to move on but she stuck firmly to the pavement.

'So what's wrong with him then?'

'There's nothing *wrong* with him.'

'Oh yes there is. You're being really cagey, and I know you, Luce.' She narrowed her eyes thoughtfully. 'He's married, isn't he?'

'Of course he's not married!' I blustered. 'Would I mess around with a married man?'

'You bet your sweet life you would, and you know why? He's not *quite* available, so no real emotional output. You don't have to commit yourself, don't really have to take the plunge. Ooh, yes, ideal.'

'Just get off my case, Jess,' I said angrily. 'I told you, there's nothing in it. I have a harmless, long-distance crush on him, OK? Like sitting in the hairdresser's and gazing wantonly at Hugh Grant's picture in *Hello!*. He's just someone who makes my heart beat faster when I walk past him in the stree—office,' I said quickly. 'That's all.'

'Well, it'd bloody better be,' she said darkly. 'You know how I feel about married men. It's a sacred institution, Luce, and don't you forget it.'

'I'm hardly likely to with you ramming your perfect marriage permanently down my throat, am I?'

Suddenly we stared at each other, aghast.

I swallowed. 'Why are we fighting?'

'I don't know.' Jess scratched her head sheepishly. 'My fault, I think. Anyway,' she shrugged, 'you know as well as I do my marriage isn't perfect. Jamie would love to be your man in the office, love to have women gaze open-mouthed at his chiselled features as they stand beside him at the photocopier, but because they don't, he stares at their tits instead.'

'All men look, Jess,' I said generously, knowing she was magnanimously knocking her own life now in the hand of friendship. 'And you know jolly well he doesn't touch,' I added staunchly, as we picked up the table and trudged on.

Jess sighed, and I knew she was wondering what might have been. Bright as a button, she had been on the brink of a partnership in a merchant bank when—oops! She was pregnant. Unfazed, she'd swiftly married the perpetrator—who, happily, she was in love with—and lined up a nanny, determined she'd be back at work nine months later in her size ten Armani suit. But then, when the baby was born, Mother Nature roared in too, and amid many tears and much heart-searching, Jess had been unable to do it. Jamie, who was understandably alarmed at this sudden loss of her income, had nevertheless taken it on the chin and gone off to work, only that much harder, and that much later, it seemed, now that he was the sole breadwinner and had a wife and child to support. Jess, though, having lived the life, was unable to look at his long hours rationally. She was plagued with doubt as to her lovely, twinkly-eyed journalist husband's fidelity.

As we finally turned the corner into my parents' road, she sighed again. 'All I'm saying, Luce, is don't forget this Charlie character has a wife.'

I dropped the table with a bang, hopefully on her foot. She swung round. 'Could we please get this into perspective, Jess! I told you, he doesn't even know I exist, for crying out loud, that's how close I am to wrecking his marriage. Forget it, OK? God, I wish I'd never told you.' I tore my hair briefly, hopelessly. 'Why did I tell you?'

'Because,' she said as we picked up the table and lobbed it expertly over the small wall and into my parents' front garden, 'until you tell your friends your dreams, they lack an important dimension. They're not real.'

I was about to protest but she swiftly leaned forward and gave me a quick, conciliatory peck on the cheek. 'Bye. Give my love to Maisie and Lucas and—listen, sorry if I banged on a bit.'

'Forget it. You were just flexing your argumentative muscles because you don't get to use them at work any more.'

She laughed and turned off down the street, giving me a brief, backward wave. I puffed on up the steps with the two sacks of loot, barging through the bright blue front door of 36 Burlington Villas. Shut your eyes and push was the only way to squeeze down the dark, narrow hall stacked floor to ceiling with Maisie's accumulated antique clutter. Battling on through the darkness, arms outstretched, one eventually stumbled left into a sitting room and yet more clutter. Ancient chandeliers, Georgian commodes and Art Deco girls holding balls of light aloft jostled for space with three-legged Victorian balloon-back chairs, enamel pitchers and ancient mixing bowls. Any conceivable floor or table space was taken up with these assorted curios.

Here Maisie was, despite her arthritis, on all fours with her youngest grandson on her back. A light flex had been slung round her neck for reins, and an old lampshade was on her head, since, clearly, this neddy wore a hat. Her bright copper hair was now a faded gold, the Celtic blue eyes which she turned on me now were a little misty, but still huge— eyes that, four years ago, without her having to utter a word, had informed me that my husband was dead.

Max, my youngest son, squealed with delight as I came in now, and Maisie sat up on her haunches to let him slide off her back.

'You're back early, love—no luck? How was business?'

'Terrible,' I groaned, collapsing into an armchair. Max grabbed my handbag and proceeded to disembowel it, searching for sweeties with all the thoroughness of the Drugs Squad.

'Here, Smarties.' I delved in and handed them to him. 'No, it was just a really, really bad day, Maisie. Probably the weather. But thanks for having them for me. Were they OK? Where's Ben?'

'Gone to the new Howard Hodgkin exhibition at the South Bank with Lucas,' she said. 'But Max didn't want to go, did you, love?'

'I seen a picture before,' he informed me importantly.

''Course you have, my darling,' I said, giving him a cuddle. 'Seen one picture you've seen them all, haven't you?'

'Cup of tea? There's one in the pot.' Maisie got to her feet.

'Please,' I said gratefully, following her into the hallway.

As we reached the kitchen, the back door flew open and in came my eight-year-old son, at a run. He was followed by his grandfather; tall, slightly bowed, and, as usual, sporting his rather dashing felt hat.

'Mum! Guess what? We went to the National because the other one was shut—and we saw loads of fat naked ladies! Didn't we, Lucas?'

'We did, my love, although sadly not in the flesh.' Lucas winked at me and dropped a National Gallery catalogue onto the table as he sank into a chair with a sigh. 'Ahh, cup of tea,' he murmured, his Polish accent still faintly discernible. 'Lovely.'

'And some of them had huge, *huge* bottoms.' Ben seized the catalogue and riffled through to show me. 'Really white and flabby, Mum, and bosoms as droopy as yours—look! And it was really fashionable then. Just think, you'd have been cool, Mum, in the old days.'

'Born just a couple of centuries too late then, eh?' I smiled as Maisie set a cup of tea in front of me. 'Ooh, thanks. I'll drink this and then we'll be out of your way.'

I was all too aware of how exhausting small children could be, particularly as my parents were not young. Having had two children in their twenties, brought them up and sent them out into the world, they must have been somewhat aghast when I'd appeared when Maisie was forty-five. If they were, I never knew it. To me they were the most loving, laid-back parents and the envy of all my friends as I was growing up. So relaxed were they, in fact, that when my brother had referred to them by their Christian names as a joke, Maisie and Lucas, it had stuck.

Seventy-five-year-olds, though, in my opinion, need to see their grandchildren in short, sharp bursts. 'Come on, you two.' I began bundling Max into a jumper. 'Back to the flat. But only for a few more days, and then, my darlings, we're away!'

'Oh.' Maisie clapped a hand to her head. 'That reminds me. Rose rang.

Said she's expecting you on Thursday, and something about a nanny.'

'A *nanny*? What? What about a nanny?'

'Oh, just something about how she thought it would be much nicer if you took your evening meal up there with them, rather than sitting all alone in the barn,' said Maisie vaguely. 'So she's organised a girl—a lovely girl, she said—to come and baby-sit the boys.' She frowned over at her husband. 'That was it, wasn't it, Lucas?'

Lucas slowly raised his brown eyes from the newspaper he'd picked up. They met mine. 'Yes, love,' he said softly, 'that was it.'

His gaze was steady, but I slid my eyes away. Down towards my tea. I took a hasty gulp. It was colder than one would wish.

Ned died in childbirth. Mine, of course, not his. It happened while I was giving birth to Max. While I was straining and sweating, swearing and cursing and yelling, where *was* my wretched husband? Digging my nails hard into Maisie's hand, shrieking, 'Just *get* him here someone, please! I don't want him to miss this!'

And then, suddenly—suddenly it didn't matter. Suddenly a computer beside me, the one that had been monitoring the baby's heartbeat throughout, started beeping urgently. I remember urgent mutterings about the baby being distressed, about the cord being round its neck, perhaps, and a no-nonsense hand thrusting up to sort things out.

Sheer panic, now, on the faces around me. It *was* round his neck. Had he lost precious oxygen? Should they rush me down to theatre for a Caesarean? No, too late, the baby was coming, the head had crowned and—oh God, that sheer, white pain as the head emerged. That ghastly, final push—and out he slipped, like a seal.

I leaned back weakly on the pillows, eyes wide with shock to the ceiling, the agony over. Someone scooped him up joyfully.

'Look, dear, you've got a baby boy.'

I gazed up expectantly, a weak smile forming on my lips, awaiting my precious moment, longing to hold him in my arms. 'Is he OK?'

'Fine,' one nurse chuckled, 'just fine. A very bonny boy.' She took off her mask and handed him to me, a huge grin splitting her face.

'I'll go and tell Lucas,' Maisie muttered, coming forward, taking my hand, fighting tears. 'He's outside.'

'Yes, yes—and Ned,' I urged, as she made to go. 'Maisie, did you get hold of Ned? Try his mobile again or—'

And that's when I knew. As she turned back to face me. Knew something truly horrendous had happened, when her eyes met mine. Full of foreboding, full of fear.

She shook her head. 'No, well, no. But, yes. I'll—I'll try again.'

A terrible fatalism rose up from my soul and stilled me. Something too horrific to contemplate had happened. Something she couldn't tell me about, not now, not with this newborn baby in my arms. I lay there, paralysed with fear, thinking the unthinkable, so that when it happened, I was almost, ridiculously, prepared.

Half an hour later, they wheeled me into a private room and whisked Max away to the nursery. Maisie and Lucas came in. They sat, side by side, white and harrowed, and Lucas told me. Twisting his felt hat in his hands, ashen-faced, he told me how Ned had lost control, it seemed, rushing to get here. How, mobile phone in hand, he'd taken a bend too sharply, colliding with a lorry. No belt on, he'd gone straight through the windscreen and had died instantly.

Memory, kindly, becomes something of a blur after that, but I do remember uncontrollable shakes, and someone whisking a blanket around me, swaddling me like a small child. I remember, too, that Maisie kept a constant vigil; a constant grip on my hand, never letting go.

People say to me now, 'Oh, it must have been so much worse for you with a new baby,' but actually, that made me cope. That, combined with an overwhelming incredulity that numbed my mental processes, slowing them almost to a halt. In those early days I felt detached from my life; I had no thoughts, made no plans, I just existed, disorientated. I didn't have the luxury of going to pieces, either, because I had Max and Ben to look after.

My parents were my lifeline at that time, but friends were extraordinary too. Some steered clear 'until she's ready'—and I haven't seen much of them since—while one or two, like Jess, got it spot-on. Not overdoing it, but nevertheless wading in when I needed her; getting drunk with me into the small hours, crying when I cried.

I had grief counselling too, on a Monday night, just like an upholstery class or something, when I'd sob and rant at a perfectly sweet, middle-aged woman with a twitch. I even punched her walls on one occasion. She didn't seem to mind, but she didn't seem to help, either, and it was after that occasion that one of my neighbours said, 'Well, for God's sake, come and punch *our* walls instead!' So I did.

I had five neighbours: Teresa, Carlo, Theo, Ray and Rozanna, who were all, to a man or woman, spectacular. In fact, in those early days, when their walls took quite a battering, I'd swear I could hear Ned's delighted voice saying, 'See? Look who I found for you, Lucy! We made the right decision, didn't we?'

'The decision', taken just before he died, had been where to live. At the time we were living in a basement flat in Fulham, which was small, dark and all we could afford, but light was beginning to filter through in the form of a promotion for me at Christie's, and the promise of an art-house film for Ned to direct at his production company in Soho. Since there was another baby on the way, we decided to move.

In the wake of all our friends, we dutifully trekked south of the river, to find 'a bit of space'. Putney, Clapham and Wandsworth beckoned, along with rows of Victorian terraced houses in tree-lined streets. One of them, a four-bedroomed semi, held our attention. It had a large knocked-through drawing room and an airy kitchen billowing onto a huge garden.

'It really is one of the nicest roads around here,' our vendor confided. 'And full of *such* lovely people. I mean, next door, for instance, he's with Morgan Stanley, and she's a solicitor, and then on the other side, he's at Goldman's and she's in advertising. You won't be short of friends.'

'Right. And everyone,' Ned glanced up and down, over the fences, 'has the same climbing frame.'

'I know, isn't it uncanny?' She laughed. 'We call ourselves the Tommy Tonka set.'

Once outside on the quiet pavement, Ned gazed around at the rows of tastefully draped windows, at the terracotta pots on the doorsteps. 'I suppose we'd better take the plunge.'

I scuffed my toe. Nodded. 'Yep. You're right, we should.'

'I mean,' he struggled, 'it's easy to mock, to call it suburban, all pro-fessionals in a row, brolly and *Telegraph* under the arm, but—' He broke off, considered. 'Well, for Ben, and the baby? Cricket stumps in the garden? Bikes? Bit of conforming for a change?'

I glanced up. Smiled. 'I agree. Time to grow up.'

The next morning he rang me at work.

'Meet me in your lunch-hour,' he said excitedly. 'I've found a flat.'

'A flat! But I thought—'

'Twenty-four, Royal Avenue, SW3. Twelve thirty. Just be there, Luce.'

And I was. Running hotfoot from work, which, from South Ken, wasn't far, towards the Royal Hospital and the river. My pace slowed as I approached, and I seemed to be walking into the most perfect London square imaginable. It was broad and long, and lined with tall, white, wedding-cake houses, all with glossy black front doors and brass knockers that glinted in the sunlight. I stopped and caught my breath. The square itself had an almost Parisian feel to it, with gravel instead of grass, and some Chelsea Pensioners, complete with medals and sticks, sat on a bench in the sunshine. At one end, crowds of people thronged, but the shops of the King's Road held them in thrall. At the other end, the Hospital Gardens formed a warm, tranquil pool of green.

A cab drew up and Ned jumped out, bright-eyed.

'You're mad,' I called, as he flashed me a grin. 'What is it? A shoebox?'

'Practically,' he said cheerfully, 'but look at the location.' He swung his arm around demonstratively. 'Come on.'

Keys in hand, he dragged me, protesting, up the grand stone steps and into the communal hall. On we went, up the wide stairs, up and up until we eventually arrived, panting, at the fourth floor.

'With small children?' I gasped. 'Prams? Bikes?'

'Good exercise,' he grinned. 'I'd leave the pram at the bottom.'

'Oh, would you. And the oxygen cylinders?'

'Don't be wet,' he scoffed, and put the key in the door. He led me into a white, tiny hallway, which in turn, led into a corridor.

'Down here,' he insisted, leading the way into a bedroom.

I looked around. Shrugged. 'Not a bad size, I'll give you that.'

He ushered me out, across the passage, and into another bare room. 'Boys' bedroom,' he breezed. 'Bunks here, in the corner.'

'Boys?' I said, hand on the bump of my stomach. 'How d'you know?'

He grinned. 'And then back here—' He disappeared. 'A bit of a kitchen.'

'A bit is right.'

'*Very* neat and tidy and, Luce, look—no, *not* the window, Luce, not yet.' He put a hand over my eyes and hustled me away, to face a pair of double doors. 'Ta-da!' he grinned, opening them with a flourish.

I gasped. Because I had to admit, this room was a joy. Large, lofty, and with acres of pale wooden floor. Tall sash windows marched all the way down one side, except in the middle, where the windows went right to the floor and issued onto a balcony. And then, of course, there was the view. I stepped out onto the balcony, gazing over the rooftops. A fair old chunk of London town looked back at me, with the King's Road to the right, and, to the left, the river and the hospital gardens.

'Perhaps they could ride their bikes in there,' I mused. 'If it's allowed.'

'Of course they could. And in the square—which we have a key to. And look, come and see this.'

He led me out of the front door and across the hallway and banged on the green front door opposite.

'Ned!' I drew back in horror. 'What the hell are you doing?'

The door opened almost immediately, and a pretty, continental-looking girl stuck her head round.

'Aha!' She swung the door open wide. 'You back. You say you be back and you are.' She beamed delightedly at my husband. 'And you bring your lovely wife too.' She beamed at me. 'And pregnant! Lucky you.' I smiled back. Impossible not to like her.

'Lucy, this is Teresa,' Ned introduced us, 'who has a shop in the King's Road which sells . . .?'

'Oh, you know,' she waved her hands about airily. 'Lovely beady scarves and belts and silky bits and bobs which I buy for nothing back home in Italy and sell for a fortune over here!' she said cheerfully. 'And thees,' she swung her arm back, 'is my husband Carlo.'

A small, swarthy man got up from a table where he'd been playing backgammon with two older men. He gave a small bow.

'And thees,' went on Teresa, 'is Theo and Ray, who live on first floor.'

They got to their feet politely; a pair of immaculate, well-preserved, elderly gentlemen, with pressed jeans, pastel Polo shirts, and cashmere jumpers slung artfully round their shoulders. Clearly an item. They shook hands.

'We gather you're moving in. How absolutely marvellous,' boomed Ray in a theatrical, John Gielgud voice.

'Well, I—'

'And so much more marvellous because you have a Ben, and I have a Pietro!' broke in Teresa. 'Four years old together, see?' She lunged for a photograph on a crowded sideboard. A little dark-haired boy with mischievous eyes smiled back at me. 'So they be matey, yes?'

I smiled. 'Well, obviously, though, Ned and I will have to discuss—'

'Of course! So many things.'

I glanced at Ned, who was looking inordinately pleased with himself.

'And soon,' went on Teresa, 'you meet Rozanna. She come up for a sharpener most days, but she not here today. She live on first floor and—'

'What d'you mean, she's not here today,' purred a silky voice behind us. 'She's very much here. My usual, please, Carlo, there's a love. Sorry I'm late, darlings,' she breathed as she whisked by, 'but I got waylaid by a ghastly prospective client. He wanted to relive his toddlerhood, but I told him my days of dressing up as Little Miss Muffet were over, and he could take his eyes off my tuffet. I lost him eventually. Hello, my dears,' she drawled, turning deep blue eyes on us. 'Teresa told me you were moving in, and I couldn't be more pleased. Heterosexual *and* English. Such a rarity round here, surrounded as I am by foreigners and poofters.' She rolled her eyes as her friends laughed. 'And a baby!' she beamed, looking down at my stomach. 'What heaven.'

I blinked at this very beautiful girl, blonde, tanned, and swathed from head to toe in silk and suede. She rolled her eyes again. 'God, I love babies, when's it due?'

20

'In May.'

'Lovely. A spring baby, so we can all take turns to push it round the square. Stopping for a game of backgammon, my dears?'

'No, no we really must be going,' we said, and finally we made our exit and clattered downstairs.

'Bastard,' I muttered. 'You stitched me up.'

'Not at all!' Ned laughed. 'I simply wanted you to see some local colour. And you must admit, it's a bit more vibrant than Clapham.'

More vibrant, definitely, but it was the warmth that really knocked me out. I'm quite sure the stockbrokers south of the river would have been equally kind, but all I know is, when the shit hit the fan six months later, these people weren't just kind, they were my family.

In those dark, early days after Ned's death, I'd take to my sofa in that lofty, airy room for hours at a time; a tiny baby asleep on my tummy, a sea of screwed-up tissues around me. And left to my own devices, that's where I'd have stayed. All day. Until Ben came back from school. Except that, around mid-morning, there'd be a soft tap at the door and it would be Teresa, wondering if I'd like to see her new collection of scarves, or Theo, saying no pressure, but they needed a fourth for whist. They were kind, never pushy, but also, immediate. I didn't have to make arrangements; I'd just force a smile, heave myself off my sofa and totter downstairs. Then an hour or so later, I'd totter back up. It was enough.

No one was ever asked to Rozanna's flat. Ben and Pietro, who'd become inseparable, once knocked on her door, giggling, but she'd shooed them away, carefully shielding the Cabinet Minister in his dressing gown from view. 'Not in here, my darlings,' she'd said gently. 'Not in Rozanna's little *salle d'amour*.'

True to her word though, she regularly took the baby to the park. When she returned him, she'd linger, concerned, making tea, chattering gaily, until she was sure I could take over the reins again.

And so there I was, surrounded by my parents and Jess on one side of London, and my new friends in Chelsea on the other. All of them were magnificent, and all of them did their damnedest to assuage my grief. And then, of course, there was Ned's family, the Felloweses, who, as far as I could tell, did their damnedest to augment it.

I didn't meet Ned's family until just before we were married, and a whole year after we'd been going out together, as students, at Oxford. Too long, I'd decided, one bright April morning as we cycled to lectures together. Crikey, I reasoned, he'd met Maisie and Lucas loads of times, been to stay with my sister Dee in Florence—my brother in India was somewhat harder—so how come I'd never set eyes on any of his lot? Was he ashamed of me?

'Of them,' he'd assured me firmly as he wedged his front tyre in the bicycle stand. 'They're not like me, Lucy, and they're not like you. Or Maisie and Lucas. They're not normal.'

I laughed. 'Why—how so? Hairs on palms of hands? Eyes in the middle of foreheads? In what way not normal, Ned?'

He smiled wryly. 'Trust me. You're going to get a terrible shock.'

'Try me,' I said defiantly. 'Let's go and see them this weekend.'

'Big mistake,' he said, shaking his head ruefully. 'Really big mistake.' But I was insistent, so we went.

Two days later, I emerged, wide-eyed and reeling. Hairy palms would have been lovely. Cyclops, perfect. Instead, it transpired that, far from dating a bog-standard member of the proletariat, as I'd rather assumed, I was actually dating Prince Charles. Ned's father was Lord Fellowes, ennobled for services rendered during the Thatcher government, and his mother, naturally, Lady Fellowes, but actually, as the daughter of an earl, Lady Rose, too. So far so scary. Secondly, 'home' was Netherby Hall, a majestic Georgian mansion surrounded by 2,000 acres of prime farmland. And there they all lived. The entire Fellowes clan, with the exception of Ned, under one roof. A ménage I'd previously only encountered in a popular eighties TV drama, based on an oil baron's family.

Ned's father, Archie—Eton, Oxford, Grenadier Guards—was pop-eyed but amiable and quiescent. Lady Rose, by contrast, was gimlet-eyed, had a smile that could freeze the marrow in your bones and a tone of voice similar to that employed by our first lady prime minister. She certainly scared the pants off me. Hector, the elder brother and heir apparent, was flaxen-haired, pink-faced, and easily embarrassed, while his sister, Lavinia, was formidable, forthright and liked a drop. Pinkie, the indulged younger sister, was flighty and oversexed. Finally, there were two maiden aunts who shuffled on- and off-stage periodically, neither of whom were the full shilling. Phew.

'I see,' I'd said faintly to Ned, in the car on the way home.

He grinned across. 'Still fancy me?'

'Ask me again in the morning,' I said as I leaned my weary head back.

He did, and asked me to marry him too, to which I happily agreed, and then he accused me of gold-digging because I'd seen his house.

'It's that family crest that's got you all excited, isn't it, you little hussy,' he hissed, as we rolled around giggling on his futon in his Oxford bedsit. 'You can't wait to get your hands on my motto.'

'That's it,' I squeaked. 'And you'd better get the family vaults prised open pronto. I want a socking great rock for my finger, too!'

Instead, he decorated it with a dear little garnet which we found together in Bermondsey Market the following weekend. I can still remember smiling uncontrollably at it, admiring it on my finger.

The wedding, we decided, would be at my parents' local church in London, with a quiet lunchtime reception in their back garden. A few mutual friends from Oxford would be there, Jess, of course, all my family, naturally, but apparently none of Ned's.

'Ned, this is crazy!' I said. 'Write to them. Ask them to come. They can always say no.'

'But that's just it, they will say no. It's hardly the Guards' Chapel and a reception at the House of Lords, and that, my dear Luce, is what they'll want. Either that or something equally grand with a sodding great tent in the grounds at Netherby, and I don't want that. It's not my style.'

It wasn't mine either, but I couldn't help feeling we were sneaking around, which I wasn't comfortable with. I bit my lip for a couple of days, then steeled myself and wrote to them. I told them where and when it was happening and invited them. It sparked our first row.

'Don't ever interfere with my family again,' he seethed, as I told him what I'd done. 'You know nothing, Lucy, nothing. They've had a damn good crack at messing up most of my life, but they're not going to balls up this bit, OK?' I'd never seen him so angry.

'OK, OK,' I whispered. 'I'm sorry.'

Nonetheless, Rose wrote back immediately, clearly touched. '. . . *you were so sweet to let us know. Of course it was a shock, but I always had an idea that Ned would get married like this. Quietly, privately, and to a clever, bright girl like you. Thank you so much for writing to us, my dear . . .*'

I showed it to Ned, waving it triumphantly in his face as he woke up.

'You see? Couldn't be nicer. And she approves of me, too.'

'Oh, I knew that wouldn't be a problem,' he muttered sleepily. 'Can't help noticing they're still not coming though.'

I blinked and read the letter again. Oh. No. Clearly not.

And so the wedding went ahead, quietly and simply, as planned, and aside from a lovely cousin of Ned's called Jack, we didn't trouble the Felloweses. In fact, we didn't trouble the Felloweses again for—ooh, the next couple of years.

Periodically, though, as time went by, I felt guilty. When Ben was born, I insisted we go and see them, just occasionally, to show them their grandson. These forays were never a great success. Ned was mute and stony-faced as we ate lunch in the huge panelled dining room at Netherby, with its pendulous chandelier and array of dazzling silver, and I was always terrified that Ben would misbehave. Often there'd be scores of other friends and family too, because Rose, it seemed, being terribly social, couldn't sit down without at least twenty people around her. Or maybe she felt that it diluted a potentially tricky situation. Either way, we'd finally drive home exhausted, with Ned, after one such occasion, vowing, 'Never, *never* again.'

Ironically, we never did go again, because six months later, he was dead. Rose was beside herself, naturally—her son, her beloved boy—and wept so loudly at the funeral she had to be restrained by Archie at the grave. I couldn't help wondering why she hadn't shown more emotion when he was alive. Then she was on the phone constantly, day and night—mostly night, my worst time. How was I coping? Didn't I miss him dreadfully? How was I finding the strength to carry on?

Finally, I realised she was doing me no good. I was trying my damnedest to be strong, and she was breaking down my defences. Gradually, guiltily, I let things slide. I left the answering machine on and I rarely returned her calls. Cruel? Perhaps, but I knew it was for the best.

At first she persisted, but then she, too, went quiet. I heard nothing for months, by which time I was too nervous to ring out of the blue, and she, I think, was too proud. I kept meaning to write, but I never did. Four years went by. Christmas cards were exchanged, presents arrived in the post on the boys' birthdays, but no contact. Until I got her letter.

My dear Lucy,

Forgive me for writing to you after such a long silence, but this letter has been written and rewritten many times. So much to explain, and so hard to know where to begin. Firstly, my unshackled behaviour at the time of Ned's death must have unnerved you, and I feel I should go some way to explaining what must have seemed like a disproportionate outpouring of grief. You see, my dear, despite all the differences Ned and I had in later life, as a child, he and I were inseparable. Until he was fifteen, he and I would fish for salmon most weekends, walk the dogs together, read the same books, enjoy each other's company.

One should never admit to having them, of course, but he was my favourite, my darling boy. Perhaps that goes some way to explaining why, when he had a classic teenage rebellion, it came as such a terrible shock to me. He wore such strange clothes, became obsessed with music and the film world, smoked and drank—all natural progressions, of course—yet instead of accepting them as such, I felt as if I'd been slapped in the face, and told him so, too. We rowed horrendously and some terrible things were said, mostly by me, for which I'm sure he never forgave me. The memory makes me go hot with shame. But perhaps you now understand the depths of emotion only shimmering on the surface, and how hard it was for both Ned and me.

Still, the years have gone by, and I'd like to make it up to Ned's memory. I gather from Maisie that money is tight, so here it is: would you do me the honour of letting me help? Archie and I would love you and the boys to have Chandlers Barn—you know, the pretty old timbered one at the top of the meadow where the Jacob sheep are. It's been beautifully converted and would make a wonderful home. We are close by, of course, but your privacy would be respected and paramount. The barn would be made over in your name, and we'd also like to pay for the boys' education, at schools of your choice. Do let us know if you feel you could accept our offer, we would so love to have you among us.

With best love, Rose

I showed it to Maisie. 'Lovely,' she said, finally. 'I always thought there was a heart lurking in there somewhere. What are you going to do?'

'I don't know,' I said quietly, taking the letter back.

But I think I did, even then. I think I'd made up my mind the moment I'd read it. Ben was unsettled at school, Max was riding his bicycle around our minuscule flat and driving me insane, and Netherby was only a couple of miles away from Hexham. Hexham? What difference should that make to anything?

Oh. Well. Hexham was the village where Charlie lived. And I had to do something about Charlie. It was just getting ridiculous.

I first met—no, saw—Charlie, about six months ago. He was standing at the end of my road talking to Ricky, the flower-seller, newspaper under one arm, dark head thrown back, laughing loudly. He had an athlete's physique, tall, broad and powerful-looking, and I just remember thinking, what an attractive man. When I came out of the newsagent's, he was still there. He caught my eye, smiled, and I smiled back.

When I reached home, I ran straight up our four flights of stairs without pausing. I went to my bedroom and sat down at my dressing table, heart pounding. I stared at my reflection. My cheeks were pink, but no pinker than they'd be under normal circumstances if I'd just run up four flights, and my eyes sparkled a bit, but there was something else, too. Something stirring within me that was making me glow, that I recognised as pure sexual attraction. Something I hadn't experienced since Ned.

And not for want of trying. Oh, no, I knew what was expected of me. 'Can't mope for ever, Lucy, life goes on,' et cetera—and so I'd been out with one or two guys, mostly at Jess's instigation. Nice guys, too. I'd been to the theatre, out for dinner, and once I'd even asked a guy in for coffee and gone for a full-blown snog on the sofa. We'd almost got to the bedroom door, when—

'God, I'm so sorry, it's me, I just can't seem to . . .'

'No, no, don't worry. It's fine. I'll go.'

And he had. Whoever he was. Nothing, you see. Not a spark, not a flicker of interest. And yet, just now, after the briefest of moments on a pavement . . . something.

I picked up my brush and swept back my hair—hair Ned wouldn't recognise now with its honey-blonde highlights—and gave a sudden smile. Well, whaddya know, Lucy. Progress. Definitely progress. Perhaps there's hope for you yet?

After that, I kept an eye out for him. Only on a terribly casual basis, you understand. I certainly wasn't tailing him or anything creepy, but I was alert. I checked on the corner shop, for instance, walked slowly past Ricky with his flowers—any sign? No. But then a few days later—bingo. As I walked into Mr Khan's Seven-till-Eleven, there he was, wire basket in hand. It was summer, so khaki shorts and a blue sailing sweatshirt, bleached and worn. His black hair was a little damp around the edges, particularly at the back of his neck, indicating a recent shower. I could hardly breathe, I was so excited. Joyfully I snatched a basket and scurried over to the chilled cabinet where he was browsing.

'Ooops, sorry!' I said, as our hands clashed over the semi-skimmed.

'Here,' he laughed, handing me a carton. 'You're obviously in need.'

'Thanks.' I flashed up a smile.

'Thirsty work, this weather, isn't it?' he grinned.

'It certainly is.'

And that was it. Two seconds later he'd paid and left the shop, and I was still standing there. Must follow, must follow, I thought desperately, scurrying to the till. But Mr Khan was on the telephone and I had to watch, helplessly, as my man strode past the plate-glass window, disappearing into the crowd. By the time I'd emerged, he'd gone.

The next time I saw him nip into Mr Khan's I had Max with me.

'Come on!' I seized Max's hand. 'Sweeties, Max, we need sweeties, don't we? Come *on*!'

Max looked startled, but rose magnificently to the occasion, and we were in that shop in seconds. I grabbed a magazine from the rack and nipped in behind my man in the queue, elbowing an old lady out of the way in my excitement.

Sanjay, Mr Khan's son, was serving behind the counter.

'Orright, Charlie?' He chewed gum unceasingly.

Charlie! Now I knew. I gazed rapturously at Charlie's back.

'Not bad, Sanjay, and you?'

'Yeah, orright. Thrashing you in the test. A hundred and three for four. There you go.' He handed him some change. 'Yeah?' This, to me, because Charlie was walking away from the counter while I gazed, slack-jawed, after him. I snapped to.

'Oh! Oh, yes. Come on, Max, hurry. What d'you want, fruit gums?'

The door was opening. God, he was going. Quickly, I swung round. Smiled, as if surprised. 'Oh, hi there!'

Almost out of the shop, he glanced back. Blinked. Clearly didn't recognise me, then either did, or pretended he did. 'Oh, hi.'

Sanjay cleared his throat. 'Just the fruit gums and *Caravanning Weekly* then, luv?'

I glanced down at the magazine, horrified. Charlie looked too, then up at me in surprise.

'Oh! Oh, no, I thought it was . . .' I dropped it hurriedly. When I glanced round, Charlie had gone. God, what was I *doing*, picking up men in corner shops? I rooted miserably in my purse for some change.

'Charlie not with it today.' Mrs Khan smiled kindly at me, elegant in her sari as she came forward to take over from her son. 'He lost in his work. He not recognise anyone when he like that.'

'Oh!' I stared. 'No, that's right. He does get very involved, doesn't he? Um, does he say how it's going?'

'Oh, he nearly finish, he say. But then, he also say he can play with it, you know?'

And that was that. I walked slowly back to the flat, wondering what on earth it was Charlie was playing with.

The next day I breezed back in again. Oh good, Mrs Khan. I smiled at her as I handed her a *Daily Mail*.

'Charlie looks well. I've just seen him in the street. Says he's finished.'

'Oh, good.' She smiled. 'So he can go home soon. He like that.'

'Home?'

'Yes, somewhere near Oxford. He only here to work, and he miss his wife, I know. Forty pence, please.'

I left, shattered. In pieces. *Married*. Oh well, that was it. Definitely it. Married. Hopeless!

Except that it wasn't it. Two days later, without even looking for him at all, I was in the deli with him. Only this time, he was behind me, and I was at the front of the queue, choosing some cheese.

'That,' he said, leaning past me and tapping on the glass cabinet, 'is delicious.' He pointed to the Epoisses.

'Oh!' I breathed as his shoulder brushed mine. 'Is it?'

'Strong, powerful, really mature, and it just oozes . . . everywhere.'

Well, I nearly lost control of my legs.

'I'll take the Epoisses!' I gasped, holding on to the counter.

'How much, madam?'

'All of it!' I squeaked.

I made my purchase and turned to thank him, but found he had turned to someone he was with, an older man, and continued his conversation. As I left, I was just lucky enough to hear—

'Yes, sir?'

'A piece of Epoisses, please.'

'Oh, I'm awfully sorry, that lady just bought the lot.'

I stopped, horrified. Shut my eyes and groaned.

This is absurd, I thought, a few minutes later as I headed down the road to Safeway's, to do the proper shopping. I hadn't behaved like this since I was about sixteen. And not with Ned, certainly, because he'd chased me. So had I ever—I thought back . . . no, I decided. Never. Never chased a man in my life. So this was what it felt like, eh? I smiled. I felt invigorated; better than I had done for months—'Damn!'

A jar of Branston slipped from my distracted grasp, smashed on the supermarket floor, and splashed up, all over my jeans. I appeared to be up to my knees in pickle. Was this symbolic? I wondered.

Was this all getting out of hand? I asked myself, as I finally lugged my carrier bags home. And if so, did it matter? After all, I was happy, and in some ways, it was so uncomplicated. So much easier than having a real man. In my head, he was already mine. Yes. Mine. I could see why people did it. I stared at my reflection, horrified. Did what, Lucy? Stalk? Clutching my Safeway's bags, I bolted upstairs, aghast.

Teresa was at the top, just trying my door handle.

'Ah, you back! Good. I brought you a present, see?'

She drew a beautiful blue-green scarf from a plastic bag. 'See, it go with your eyes.' She wrapped its silken swathes around my neck.

'Thanks, Teresa, it's lovely, and lovely to see you, too. I think I've been on my own too much recently. Going quietly crazy. I've got a present for you, too. Here.' I handed her the Epoisses.

'For me?' She sniffed. 'Aahhh! Proper cheese.'

'Well, you know I can't take anything stronger than Dairylea, and I was . . . talked into buying it. Come on, come in. I need a drink.'

'But it only five o'clock, Luce. Bit early, no?'

'It must be six o'clock somewhere. The boys have got football club, so we've got at least half an hour.'

I poured a glass of wine from the fridge and handed it to her. She walked with it to the window.

'Teresa, d'you think it's healthy to daydream?' I asked tentatively. 'I mean, constantly? As if . . . well, as if reality's some kind of unwelcome intruder.' I frowned.

'Lucy, these past few weeks, I never seen you look so well,' she said softly. 'Your eyes, they sparkle now, and your face has lost that defeated look.' She smiled. 'If I didn't know better, I'd say you were in love.'

I laughed nervously. 'No, not in love, because there's nothing real about this, and never will be. You see, it's all in my head.' I must have looked anxious, because she came across and hugged me.

'It's got to start somewhere. It's fine, let it grow, work with it. It's good, you know? You're coming back to life.'

The weeks went by and the summer blossomed. I saw Charlie—ooh, probably once a week. He'd hop on a bus and I'd spot him and hop on too. God knows where I was going, but I'd sit behind him for a few euphoric minutes, then get off at the next stop and walk home, smiling. It was ridiculous. I felt—possessed, almost—but I loved the feeling. Hugged it to myself, and told myself it was harmless.

I was learning more about him, too. I knew which paper he read, which brand of cereal he liked, but I still didn't know where he lived. I hadn't actually had the courage—or the audacity—to tail him home, though I have to admit, the opportunity had never really presented itself. One of the peculiarities of the King's Road is that it can bustle to bursting point, with people literally jostling one another off the pavement, but pop down a side street and wham! It's empty. He'd know I was following him. I had to be so careful.

One day, I had a thought. I borrowed Theo and Ray's dog.

'He's had a walk today already, Lucy,' Ray insisted in the hallway, as I put Bob on a lead. Bob was a rather scrawny Yorkshire terrier who wore his fringe in a bow, poor chap.

'And he does get awfully puffed,' added Theo.

'I'll carry him if he gets tired,' I promised with a smile. 'Trust me, boys, I grew up with dogs, he'll be fine.' And with a tug of the smart tartan lead, we were off. Off to wander those smart, slumbering backwaters where Bob, I reckoned, was my perfect excuse, as looking—hopefully—rich and nonchalant, I searched for the most fragrant lampposts, the most manicured squares, in order for Bob to do, what was for a small dog, quite a bit of business.

We trailed for miles, Bob and I. Up and down those discreet, bleeding backwaters, and yes, one day—we did see Charlie. Just as I was bending down to scoop the poop. Just as—as luck would have it—a pair of sunglasses fell out of my shirt pocket, and plopped right into it.

'Arrrggh!' I screeched. 'Oh God, now it's all over my hands!'

Naturally, Charlie didn't linger. He gave a brief, nervous smile of recognition, neatly sidestepped my crouching form, and walked smartly on.

At times like this, as I straightened up from my pile of ordure, I'd swear I could hear Ned laughing at me. 'You idiot, Lucy,' he'd hoot. 'What on earth are you doing?'

I didn't feel guilty about chasing a man in the presence of my husband's ghost. You see, I was thirty-one years old. Would he want me to be alone for ever? No. Did he want the boys to have another daddy? Oh harder, much harder. He would always be their daddy. And he'd loved Ben so . . .

But there. Enough. He was laughing at me now. God, what a *mess*, Luce, I could hear him sigh.

'Yes, I know,' I muttered, trying to wipe my hands on the grass. 'I know, Ned, and I know he's married too. But I'm not actually interested, OK? I'm just interested in the way it's making me feel better, that's all.' I hoped I could sense him nod approvingly, but I couldn't be sure.

And then, one day, Charlie disappeared. A week went by and I didn't see him, and then another. After four weeks, I was distraught. I could feel myself sinking down again. Saw those dark pools of despair rising up to meet me. And I didn't want to go down that black alley again. I felt like a junkie desperate for a fix.

Mrs Khan at the corner shop couldn't help.

'Golly, I haven't seen Charlie for absolutely ages, have you?' I breezed brazenly one morning, no pride now.

She frowned. 'No, no, I not seen him. Maybe he go home.'

'Yes! Yes, maybe,' I agreed, raising speculative eyebrows, as if this thought hadn't occurred to me every waking moment. 'And that is?' I asked shamelessly, out of control now. 'Charlie's . . . home is?'

She blinked. 'No idea. Like I say, he say Oxford but—ah, Rozanna, she know. Rozanna, where Charlie Fletcher live?'

I swung round to see Rozanna behind me, holding half a bottle of gin and looking gorgeous as usual, swathed in lilac cashmere.

'Charlie Fletcher?' she drawled. 'Oh, some farmhouse near Woodstock, I believe. Why?'

'Because Lucy was—'

'No reason,' I interrupted, flushing. 'How—how d'you know him, Rozanna?'

'I shag him, darling.'

I stared, horror-struck.

She gave a throaty laugh. 'No, no such luck. No, everyone knows Charlie, he's quite famous. Writes TV scripts. Wrote that arty little film—*Coming Up for Air*. It was on Channel 4.'

My mind was assimilating all of this greedily.

'And married to a lovely girl called Miranda, who runs a very successful business from the country but I can't quite remember what it is.' She frowned. 'Catering, I believe, or something domestic. I was at school with her actually. She's awfully nice. Stunning too. You've gone terribly pale, Lucy. Why d'you need to know all this?'

'Oh, because I—need—to send him some mail. For some reason it got sent to me. So I need to know his address.'

She frowned. 'How bizarre. At your flat?' She regarded me for a moment. 'Oh well, here, darling. I've got it in here, somewhere.' She rooted around in her Gucci bag and found her address book. Flicked through to the F's. 'This . . .' she showed me, pointing, 'is where I presume he's hanging out now. In Oxfordshire.'

'**H**ave you got everything, boys?' I yelled, clattering downstairs with a box full of saucepans.

'Can I take this?'

I swung round to see Ben at the flat door, dragging an ancient wicker chair with exploding arms out onto the landing.

'Oh, darling, no, not really. I thought we'd leave it. I did say I'd leave it fully furnished and I won't have room in the trailer.'

'But it's my special chair, where all my animals sit, and where I read and things. Where am I supposed to sit and read in my room then?'

'Granny will have masses of chairs, you'll see, lovely ones.'

'I'll take it,' said Teresa, quickly coming to the rescue from across the hallway. 'And when you come and see us, you take it then.'

He gave it up sulkily, then went trudging back inside, slamming the door behind him.

I caught Teresa's eye and she smiled sympathetically. This wasn't going quite as smoothly as I'd hoped. Ben, who initially had been thrilled to bits at the idea of the move, was suddenly getting very cold feet. Catching the vibes, Max was rapidly coming out in sympathy.

When I went back up to collect the pair of them, they were sitting on the top bunk together, eyeing me resentfully.

'Come on, boys,' I cajoled softly. 'It'll be great when we get there, you'll see. You'll be tickling trout and whittling sticks and wondering why on earth we didn't go sooner.'

31

'No, I won't,' said Ben, jumping off the bunk but snapping his Walkman firmly to his head. 'I'll be wondering why I can't go to Peter Kelly's party on Saturday, and why you always decide things without thinking about us.'

'Yeah,' added Max for good measure, glaring at me. 'Finkin' 'bout us.'

As Ben brushed past me with his henchman beside him, I caught my breath at the injustice. Did I deserve this? Did I? As they stamped out to the landing I walked around that tiny flat one last time.

A company had bought it, and paid me a fairly decent whack, but perhaps I should have rented it, I wondered nervously. Perhaps I shouldn't have burnt my boats entirely, because what if Oxfordshire . . . No. It *would* work out, and anyway, this home had too many memories. I had to make a new life for myself, elsewhere.

'Come on then, Pickle, let's go,' I said, forcing a smile as I encountered Max, staging a last sit-in on the landing. I picked him up. Ben trailed miserably down the stairs behind us.

I'd said my goodbyes to everyone else in the block last night and, as requested, only Teresa was hovering helpfully.

She hugged me hard on the pavement. 'You'll come back?'

'Of course I'll come back, you idiot. I'm only in Oxfordshire. Anyone would think I was going to the moon! And you'll come and stay?'

'Maybe, but I worry about you, stuck down there. And no job now.'

I sighed. Teresa had a happy knack of not pulling her punches and this one caught me low. She was right, of course. Last week I'd finally plucked up the courage to ring my head of department at Christie's to find out what sort of headway he'd made in changing my four mornings a week to two full days. There'd been an awkward pause and then, 'Well, Lucy, it's all been a bit tricky. You see, I've been instructed by the powers that be to cut down on all the part-timers. They're being a bit all or nothing about it. A bit sort of total commitment on all fronts. Which means five days a week plus overtime and trips abroad if necessary.'

'But I can't possibly do all that with two children and a commute.'

'Er, no. Quite.' Silence.

'So it's the nothing option, is it? Is that it, Rupert?'

'Sorry, Lucy,' he muttered.

I felt sick as I put down the phone. My lovely job. My slice of London, my *money*. But I turned a brave smile on Teresa, aware of Ben's anxious, knowing little face turned up to me now.

'Oh, I don't mind about that,' I lied breezily. 'It would have been such a slog, coming up from the sticks. I'll find something down there.'

She hugged me hard. 'You being brave,' she muttered in my ear.

'What choice do I have?' I muttered back. 'I've made the decision now.'

I gave Teresa one last hug and snapped Max into his car seat. Ben got in beside him and I hopped into the front. Then, beeping my horn, I took off. With the trailer piled high behind us we headed for the M4.

It didn't help, of course, I thought, that I was grotesquely hung over this morning. Yes, last night had been send-off night in Royal Avenue. In the first-floor flat the usual suspects had gathered: Theo and Ray, the hosts, together with Rozanna, Teresa and Carlo, Jess and Jamie, Lucas and Maisie. Theo and Ray, being the most marvellous cooks, had prepared a feast fit for kings. A mountain of ceps risotto, together with bowls of salad had appeared. We'd fallen on it ravenously, and then had happily frittered the night away and drunk their cupboard dry. Lucas, Maisie, Ray and Theo had talked music and theatre. Teresa, Jess and me were predictably on schools, while Jamie (in thrusting *Daily Mail* mode) had cornered Rozanna, probing her for a scoop on her latest liaison with a well-known captain of industry. Their heads were close and their voices low, and Jess, naturally, got the wrong idea.

'You see?' she'd whispered furiously in my ear. 'Just look at him flirting with her, Lucy. And look at her, too, smouldering away under those heavily made-up lids. She looks like a high-class tart, for heaven's sake!'

'But that's exactly what she is,' said Teresa.

Jess's jaw dropped to her chest. 'No! God, how gripping! Is she really? Why didn't you tell me, Luce?'

I shrugged. 'Because she's always wanted to maintain the fiction, I suppose. So I have too, for her sake. Rozanna's quite vulnerable, you know, for all her supposed toughness.'

Rozanna turned. Smiled fondly. 'All right, darling? Lovely party. Did you manage to get that stuff off to Charlie, by the way?'

Jess's ears pricked up. 'Charlie? The guy in your office?'

Rozanna frowned. 'In your office? At Christie's? But—no, I told you, darling, he writes film scripts and things. He—'

I caught my breath. 'Yes, yes, I know,' I gabbled, 'but he—just came in one day. To view an auction. English furniture, I think.'

'Hang on.' It was Jess's turn to frown. 'You said he worked with you. I thought you said he was in your department or something.'

'Oh, *that* Charlie!' I said quickly, wondering why on earth I hadn't killed Jess months ago. Stabbed her to death on our stall with an antique letter-opener, popped the body in a black bin liner and dropped it in the Thames. 'Rozanna's talking about a completely different Charlie. One who lives round here.'

'Ah.' Jess shut her eyes in mock exhaustion. 'Lordy, silly me. I'm losing track of all the Charlies. Not the one you've got the hots for then.'

I coloured dramatically and could feel Rozanna's eyes on me. 'I haven't got the hots for any Charlie, actually, Jess,' I spluttered.

'Just as well in Charlie Fletcher's case, daahling,' purred Rozanna. 'Because, believe me, you'd be going down an awfully blind alley there.'

As I gripped the steering wheel now, steaming down the M4, I knew just how blind she meant. He wasn't just married, he was happily married. In my head, I'd always entertained dreams that it was otherwise. Imagined that his wife was perfectly ghastly, vile. Much older than him, probably, forty-five at least, and I imagined she drank heavily and had indiscreet affairs. The marriage was a sham and he was miserable. It was only a matter of time before I cruised in and saved his bacon. But no, according to Rozanna, she was lovely. Beautiful, talented, successful and he loved her dearly, as Ned had loved me. I swallowed. And imagine if it *were* Ned and me, I thought in sudden horror. Imagine some predatory hussy prowling around Soho with a ridiculous dog under her arm, waiting for my husband to emerge from his editing suite, waiting to hustle him downstairs and pin him to the cutting-room floor.

Suddenly I felt dirty, cheap and low. As I sped off at the motorway exit, I resolved not even to look up Hexham on the Ordnance Survey map when I got there. No, I'd find someone else, I determined, squaring my shoulders. Someone single and available. Find a bloody blacksmith, if needs be, bonk the living daylights out of him.

I swept a despairing hand through my hair. What sort of a madness had gripped me? I'd followed my hotheaded instincts and now here I was, hurtling down country lanes with two unhappy boys in the back, no job, no prospects and destined to live with my mother-in-law . . . Christ!

Ben removed his earpiece for a moment and looked at me in the rearview mirror. 'Mummy, why are you banging the steering wheel?'

'Oh, was I? Well, because I'm so excited, I suppose. Just look at all this lovely scenery, Ben. All that lovely—grass.'

He sat up. 'Are we nearly there, then?'

'Nearly there? This is Granny's lane, Ben. Don't you recognise it?'

'I'm not sure, it's ages since we've been.' He sounded nervous. 'Is that their house?' He pointed to a little lodge as we swept through the gates.

'Um, no, darling. That's the gatehouse.'

The car purred slowly up the long drive, through the parkland, rattling periodically over cattle grids, and we all fell silent as we took in the well-tended acres that spread to either side of us, the trees neatly encircled by deer protectors, the sheep that grazed contentedly.

'So . . . where's the house?' asked Max, at length.

'It's right round this bend, I think,' I tinkled merrily.

As we turned a corner, Netherby finally unfurled itself, rearing up at us in all its Palladian glory. Banks of windows glinted in the sunlight from the golden, sandstone façade, and balustrades and porticoes frowned down. Halfway up, a front door loomed, and from it, a huge bank of steps swept down and then divided into two, to meet the sweep of gravel below. Beyond the house, beyond the parterres, the lavender walks and the rose gardens, immaculate parkland rolled to a glassy lake, then up again to wooded hills in the distance.

'Oh! It's like a castle!' breathed Max, suddenly excited.

'Isn't it,' I agreed, crunching to a halt on the gravel. And there, I thought, with a gathering sense of dread, was the Queen.

Rose, who'd clearly been waiting, came out of the front door and tripped dramatically down the steps to meet us. Behind her, slowly, came her eldest son, Hector; gangly and blond, corduroys billowing in the breeze, blinking away behind his glasses, clearly under orders to attend.

Rose came towards us across the gravel, beaming; a tiny spry, energetic figure, neat in a lovat-green twin-set and smart trousers. Her navy shoes had horse bits on the front, and her immaculate grey hair was swept back and curled neatly round her ears.

'Darlings! You're here!' she called, still from some distance.

I clutched my two boys by their hands and steeled myself. Then I strode confidently towards the welcoming committee, a smile fixed firmly in position. 'Hello, Rose.'

'Lucy! Ben! Max!' Rose called lightly. She gave me a swift kiss. 'Isn't this wonderful?' She crouched down between the boys. 'Isn't this perfect? Here we all are, together again. At long last.'

Chapter Two

'COME IN, COME IN!' she cried, leading the way towards the steps. 'I'm sure you'll want a cup of something after your journey,' she said, striding on, 'and then I'll show you Chandlers Barn. Follow me, Lucy.'

I paused to greet Hector, whom she'd brushed past rather dismissively. 'Hi, Hector, how are you?' I bestowed a quick kiss on his cheek.

He blushed predictably. 'I'm well, thank you, Lucy,' he muttered, as he glanced nervously at his mother's back. 'Shall we . . .?'

I took the point and we obediently fell in behind the great lady. As we crossed the threshold and went through into the vast, vaulted, black and white flagstone hall, Rose paused—for effect, I couldn't help thinking. We dutifully gazed about us. Above the magnificent stone fireplace a stag's head bore down with dead eyes, and from the walls, yellowing, faded faces gazed out from the ancestral oils. Dotted about sparingly was the sort of furniture one normally only views from behind a rope, and, in the distance, I heard the stately ticking of an ancient clock.

'Wow,' said Ben, shortly.

Rose said nothing, but smiled, a proud gleam in her eye. Timing it to a nicety, her daughter chose that moment to trip lightly down the grand staircase. One hand brushed the rail and her dark, straight hair bobbed and shone behind her, held back by an eighties velvet hairband. She was wearing a sensible Liberty print shirt and skirt.

'Lucy! You're here at last!' she cried. 'How marvellous! We've been absolutely dying for you to come.'

'Have you?' I said. 'Gosh, how sweet of you, Lavinia.'

Poor Lavinia, jilted two years ago by Piers, the fiancé whose feet had frozen solid just as the invitations were going out. She'd gone into a steep decline, unable to eat or sleep for months, poor girl. Her whole life had been a preamble to getting married to the right man, living in the right house, and in the right county. Never mind that her suitor brayed like an idiot and had all the prepossession of a duck, he was also in possession of a pile which, while not comparable to Netherby, was still 'a house one wouldn't be ashamed to entertain in,' she'd once confided breathlessly to me. Lavinia was devastated by her loss. I wondered, then, if she'd ever get over it, but looking at her now, her hazel eyes shining, I thought with relief that she had.

'And look at you, you great big boys!' She bent down to greet them. 'My, you've grown—haven't they grown, Hec?'

'They certainly have,' said Hector. 'And may I say, Lucy, how pleased we all are that you decided to come and live here. We couldn't be more delighted to have you and the boys among us, and we hope you'll be very happy.' This was quite a speech for Hector, and his glasses all but steamed up with the effort.

I was touched. And, suddenly, thoroughly ashamed of my misgivings. I looked at the three faces smiling anxiously at me and realised that, actually, they were all perfectly sweet and it was all going to be fine.

'Thank you, Hector,' I smiled. 'That's so kind of you.'

'So.' Rose clapped her hands happily. 'Come on, then, let's take you boys through to the sitting room for an orange juice and a biscuit, and we'll get Mummy a cup of coffee.' She led off down the corridor. 'Here we are,' she hung a left. 'In here, I thought, it's cosier.'

I followed her into the sitting room. A stool in front of the fireplace was laden with coffee, juice and biscuits, which the boys fell on instantly.

Rose had indeed chosen one of the few cosy rooms in this vast mausoleum of a house for our induction, and Jaffa Cakes out of a packet with the boys kneeling on a rug and patting the dogs while they ate, would never have been allowed when I'd first met Ned. I had a feeling Rose had planned the consciously casual ambiance rather meticulously, but so what? That in itself was considerate, designed to make us comfortable. Perhaps, too, they had relaxed a bit.

'What's this one called?' asked Ben, hugging a huge shaggy lurcher.

'That's Hoover, and you can see why,' remarked Rose as he licked the carpet clean of crumbs. Ben laughed. 'And that,' said Rose, pointing to the one sitting in front of Max, 'is his daughter. She's called Dyson.'

The boys were delighted with this. 'Is she going to have puppies?'

'Yes, if we can find a suitable mate.'

Ben instantly ransacked his memory bank for more household suction appliances to cover this eventuality. 'Electrolux! If she had puppies you could call one Electrolux! Or—or just Vacuum, that'd be good.'

'Or Dildo,' said Max thoughtfully.

'Max!' I gasped, horrified. 'Where did you hear that word!'

'Pietro told me. Rozanna's got one in her flat. You turn it on and it shakes.'

'Well, that's not a Hoover then, is it?' demanded Ben. 'That's no good, it's got to be a sucky thing.'

'More juice, boys?' murmured Lavinia, shooting me a faintly hysterical look. Rose looked thoughtful. 'Hmm, Dildo. Pretty name. I'll put it to Archie.'

'How—how is Archie?' I managed.

'Fine,' she beamed, 'in peak condition, as he would say. Fishing, naturally, at the moment, but longing to see you. You'll see him at supper. I thought we'd have an early supper, incidentally, so that the boys could join us. Or,' she added anxiously, 'or maybe you'd prefer to be on your own the first night?'

'An early supper would be fine,' I soothed. 'Thank you.'

'Excellent. So, let's go and see the barn.' She rose abruptly.

'Oh! Right.' I startled. Threw a cup of hot coffee down my throat.

The others jumped up too, and it dawned on me that this was quite an event. I prayed the boys would react well, enthuse madly, that we could all come up with some kind of reciprocity of scale.

I needn't have worried. As we trooped out of a side door, followed a gravel path past a number of formal beds, and headed for the most parklike fringes of the place, I suddenly spied it across the lake.

'Oh!' I stopped in my tracks. Shaded my eyes. 'Is that it?'

Where once had stood a dilapidated barn on the far bank, now stood a very smart, timbered and whitewashed affair, complete with a reclaimed slate roof, a weather vane on top, and surrounded by a riotous jumble of cottage garden.

'Oh, but it's gorgeous. Look, boys, isn't it heaven!'

But they were off already, running down to the water's edge, thundering across the wooden bridge that crossed the narrowest part of the lake, and up the bank towards the little picket fence that surrounded it. It was closer to the main house than I'd remembered, I thought, glancing back at Netherby with a secret qualm, but at least we were separated by the water, I consoled myself rather guiltily.

By the time we'd got there, the boys were throwing back the front door. 'Look, Mum, it's huge!'

I peered inside. Blinked. It was. True to the natural aesthetics of a barn, it had been left open and cavernous inside with no obvious partitions. The floor was of seasoned wood, the walls whitewashed and beamed but hung with Navajo-style stripy blankets, and the sitting area, a square of colourful, squashy sofas and armchairs covered in kilim tapestry; all flowed effortlessly into a dining area, with a small wooden kitchen beyond, facing the garden. Up above, and running all round, was a gallery, where huge exposed rafters supported the roof.

'Oh, Rose, it's wonderful,' I breathed, meaning it.

'Do you like it? Do you really like it!' Lavinia was beside herself with excitement.

'It's fab, Lavinia. Really fab.'

'Up here, Mummy! Look!'

The boys had clattered up to the gallery and were leaning over. 'There are some rooms up here, Mum, bedrooms, and—ooh, look!' They disappeared into one. 'This is ours, because it's blue with two beds in it.'

'I put them in together because I knew that's what they were used to in London.' Rose sounded anxious. 'There *is* another bedroom, only it's much smaller and I didn't know if Max might feel aggrieved.'

'No, together is perfect,' I said. 'Thank you, Rose. Thank you so much.'

As Rose dispatched Hector to supervise the bringing round of my luggage, I wandered round touching everything, taking it all in.

Running my hand along the granite work surface that divided the kitchen, feeling the soft, thick curtains, unpretentious, expensive.

'But the money,' I breathed, 'I mean, to convert this place, and all these furnishings!' I knew it was unutterably vulgar to mention the subject in this family, but I simply couldn't help myself.

'Now don't you worry, Lucy,' said Rose, quickly coming over and putting a hand on my arm. 'I wanted to do this for you and the boys, but . . .' she hesitated. 'Well, I wanted to do it for Ned, too. Anyway, it's given me an aim, a project. Don't quite know what I'm going to do with myself now.'

'I'm not sure I do, either,' I said nervously. 'You see, I'm afraid they've ditched me at Christie's. I'll have to look for something round here.'

'Oh, what a shame.' Rose looked genuinely concerned. 'You loved that job.'

'But you're not exactly desperate to work, are you?' ventured Lavinia.

'Well, I'll need the money, obviously.'

'Oh, but, my dear, I intend to pay for everything here,' said Rose in surprise. 'You know that, surely? All your bills, your gas and electricity, telephone—you won't actually need much money.'

'I couldn't possibly let you do that!' I said, horrified.

'Nonsense, I do it for all the other children. It would be quite wrong of me not to,' she added firmly. 'What with the money you got for the flat in London—well, you won't need to work.'

They regarded me squarely. If all I had to do was find the wherewithal for food and clothing for me and the boys, the Royal Avenue money would easily cover it. I was grateful, overcome even, but panicky too.

'But I will have to do something, Rose,' I said carefully. 'To satisfy myself. You've all been so kind, but I do feel I'd like to do something.'

'Prison visiting,' Lavinia said. 'That's what I do. Honestly, Lucy, it's marvellous, and so spiritually uplifting, I can't tell you.'

I had an idea it was the prisoners' spirits that were supposed to be lifted, but I let it pass.

'Er, yes, well, prison work would be lovely, or—'

'NSPCC?' Rose swooped. 'I always did the NSPCC when I was younger, remember, Lavinia? And we had a super committee. Hugo Ashworth was chairman then, of course.' She looked wistful. 'He had the most marvellous balls.'

'Oh!' I blinked.

'Yes, huge. In his old barn. We used to get at least three hundred in there, plus a jazz band.'

'Er, yes, maybe. Or,' I ploughed on bravely, 'or, you know, perhaps something in an office? Proper work. Like a career,' I said desperately.

'Oh!' Rose looked startled.

'Like I had before. Something for me.' I flushed. 'But you're quite right,' I mumbled. 'I could do some charity work as well. It would be . . . terribly good for me.'

'Excellent!' beamed Rose. 'I'm sure Lavinia can think of something suitable. And there's always the church flower rota, of course. Mimsy Compton-Burrell usually does the altar, but you could take the pews. And don't forget, it's not all work and no play around here. There's always a tennis four somewhere, isn't there, darling?'

Lavinia nodded enthusiastically. 'Oh, absolutely. And masses of girlie lunches and dinner parties galore. You won't be short of things to do.'

'Super,' I breathed faintly.

'Now. Hector's gone to make sure that your luggage is brought straight round,' said Rose. 'We're going to leave you in peace now to unpack, and we'll see you for drinks at six, when I'll introduce you to your new au pair. Toodle-oo!'

And off they both scurried, out of the barn.

I watched them go, leaning rather feebly on the door frame. I felt exhausted already. Faint, even. This vile hangover didn't help, but— something else, too. Something to do with turning over a new page in my sketchbook, expecting to see a fresh sheet—only to find someone else had already started a picture.

Later, as we walked up through the park on what was turning out to be the most blissful summer's evening, I noted with surprise that everyone was gathering on the huge balustraded terrace at the back. It was well known that Archie loathed eating outside, but a table under a vast umbrella had been laid.

'How nice,' I said in surprise as Rose came scurrying across.

'I thought the boys would prefer it out here. It's much less formal.'

'It's perfect,' I assured her. 'And the boys will love it. Oh, Archie.' I turned. 'How lovely to see you.'

Archie, a huge man with bristling eyebrows, was bearing down on me, brigade tie strangling him in an uncompromising knot. As Rose slipped away, his rheumy brown eyes roved over me lasciviously.

'Lucy, my dear. Looking quite ravishing as usual if I may say so.' He kissed me, quite close to my mouth, and then quickly rubbed his thigh with the palm of his hand, which he did when he was excited. 'I can't tell you how delighted we are to have you here among us, and with these young whippersnappers too! Grrrrr!' He ruffled the boys' hair so energetically Max nearly fell over. 'So! Quarters all right? Rose has been fannying around down there for months, so it should be up to scratch. Obsessed, she's been. Sliding off at a moment's notice to iron napkins or some such rot—so much so that I thought she might have a lover down there. But no such luck—*haw-haw*!'

I joined in nervously. It had long been tacitly accepted that relations had fizzled out years ago between Rose and Archie. Rose, after four children, had determinedly hung up her negligee, leaving Archie to 'sort himself out' as she delicately put it, as if he was simply fixing his own breakfast. The 'sorting out' involved a mistress in the next county, who hunted hard with Archie twice a week, before tumbling into bed with him for some energetic sex, with Rose, one assumed, happy enough to turn a blind eye. It was clear that this didn't entirely satisfy Archie, though. There were rumours of liaisons in London.

This evening I noticed his brown eyes were focused on a very pretty girl with auburn curls, a wide smile and a Gap T-shirt strained across her ample bosom, talking to Hector, who looked flummoxed by the attention. Her antipodean accent drifted across the York stones, and I guessed she was the au pair. As I talked distractedly to Archie, it occurred to me to wonder if Rose had selected her deliberately. There had long been some frustration in the Felloweses camp at Hector's inability, at thirty-six, to produce a girl. He went to dinner parties and met plenty of women, but never brought anyone back. 'And he's got so much to offer!' Rose would lament, waving her arms around to indicate, one felt, rather more than just his personality.

'Have you met Trisha yet?' Archie hissed, dragging me across the terrace. 'Hell of a filly. *Hell* of a filly. I say, Trisha!'

She broke off from talking to Hector, which gave the poor boy a chance to mop his brow and rearrange his trousers. Just then, Rose came bustling up.

'Oh, Lucy, have you met Trisha yet?'

'Well, no, but Archie was just—'

'Only I simply wanted to say that I don't want you to think I'm arranging everything without consulting you, but, my dear, we've been *so* lucky. Trisha here is over from Australia for a year, and although primarily engaged to help Joan in the kitchen, she's also agreed to look after the boys, if and when you need her. No pressure at all though, Lucy. It's just—well, if you want to—I don't know, get your hair done—'

'It would be marvellous,' I broke in, 'to know I could leave them in capable hands. Thank you, Rose.'

Rose beamed in relief as Trisha and I shook hands.

'Hi!' she grinned, flashing perfect pearly whites at me. 'And these are the boys? Ben and Max?' She crouched down. 'We're going to have such a good time. D'you know how to play canasta?'

'No, I don't,' said Archie eagerly as the boys blinked shyly. 'Sounds fun. Cana—?'

'It's a card game, Archie,' she laughed, straightening up. 'And you're probably a bit old for it.'

'Rubbish!' he snorted. 'Not too old for anything. Fit as a fiddle, me. Keep going for hours—I mean, miles!' He rubbed his thigh feverishly.

I smiled and left them to their cross-purposes. I'd spotted Pinkie, tripping across the terrace to greet me, resplendent in kitten heels and cropped jeans.

'Hi, darling,' she squealed. 'God, I'm delighted to see you. We simply must have a goss, I'm dying to hear all your news. And that fab barn! What d'you think?'

'Amazing,' I agreed, kissing her.

'Tell you what, why don't I come down tomorrow? We'll sink a bottle of Chardonnay between us and I'll tell you all about Ludo.'

'Ludo?'

She rolled her eyes. 'Heaven. Sheer, unadulterated heaven. Daddy will hate him, of course, and call him a filthy dago, but I don't care, he's the most terrific lover. But it's much more than that. He's terribly talented, has the most marvellous hands.'

'A pianist?'

'No, a plumber. He can mend anything. You'll adore him.'

'I'm sure I will.' I found it hard not to like Pinkie. 'So—what are you up to these days, Pinkie?'

As her eyes went blank, I wished I hadn't asked. Opening gambits of this nature were generally a mistake in this household, I'd found.

'Up to?' Pinkie repeated.

'Well, yes, you know. Um, courses, or anything?' I helped.

'Oh! Oh, yes, well I did do the most marvellous Pilates course a couple of months ago. Sweet local girl. I'll give you her number.'

'Thanks,' I said faintly. 'I'll bear that in mind.'

We all seemed to be drifting towards the table. Joan was bringing out plates of melon and Parma ham, which, luckily, the boys loved, and Archie was marshalling Ben and Max to sit either side of him. We'd been in our seats some minutes, when Lavinia finally appeared through the French windows. She held a large tumbler in one hand—ice and lemon clinking at a dangerous angle—and a rolled-up magazine in the other.

'Am I late?' she sang loudly, staggering about a bit, I noticed.

'No, darling, not a bit,' said Rose, with a touch of ice in her voice.

Ah, I thought, picking up my fork. So the little problem still existed. Even if it only materialised in the evening.

'I'll sit next to you,' Lavinia murmured, slipping into a spare space beside me. 'Because I've got something to show you,' she slurred, stabbing a finger at the magazine she'd hustled under the table. 'I have to tell you, Lucy, there are some dreamy ones in here this month. Absolute whoppers.'

I swallowed a bit of Parma ham whole. 'Really?' I coughed.

'Massive,' she trembled. 'Mummy gets totally livid, of course,' she confided, 'so I have to be really careful. But when I say *now*, glance across.'

Sure enough, my mother-in-law's glacial eyes were firmly upon us.

'Um, Lavinia, maybe later,' I said nervously. 'I really think—'

'*Now*,' she insisted, her voice horribly loud.

Against my better judgment, and to shut her up, I shot terrified eyes down into her lap and found myself gazing at a double-page spread—of a huge, Jacobean mansion.

'Look at the gables on that one,' she purred. 'Pure Grade One Elizabethan, and with all the original features. And look . . .' She flipped feverishly through the pages of *Country Life*.

'That'll do, Lavinia. Put it away, please.' Rose's silken tones cut icily across the table.

'I'll show you later,' Lavinia promised.

'Now why,' her mother went on smoothly, 'has poor Lucy still got a spare place on the other side of her? And—oh heavens, look over there, another one next to Ben! That wretched girl Joan's laid too many.'

'No, no,' Archie explained to Rose. 'I invited the aunts, my dear. Saw them this morning in the village and asked them to come for supper, seeing as how it's a family do.'

Rose opened and shut her mouth. 'The aunts!' she squeaked. 'Oh, good grief, Archie, you might have said!'

I smiled into my plate. Archie's aged sisters, Cynthia and Violet, lived in a cottage on the estate. Cynthia retained some of her marbles, although it was a bit hit and miss when she paraded them, while Violet, the younger, had surely lost most of hers years ago.

'Oh God,' Rose shut her eyes. 'Hear that? Talk of the devil.'

There was the distant roar of a car travelling very fast. It appeared to be roaring up the front drive, with the speed and accompanying gear changes that one would normally associate with Formula One racing. We waited, spellbound, as seconds later an ancient red Fiesta shot round the side of the house and careered towards the fountain below us, performing a hair-raising handbrake turn in the gravel. As it lurched to a halt, we held our breath, waiting for the doors to open. Seconds later it lurched backwards, though, into an ornamental box hedge. The doors opened and the sisters squeezed out through the hedge, nonchalantly brushing bits of box off themselves.

Cynthia, the elder, was looking immaculate in a silk Jacquard dress and pearls, very Knightsbridge, until one looked down and realised she had woolly socks and slippers on. She marched purposefully towards us, a handbag in one hand, a packet of sausages in the other.

Violet, her sister, followed behind. She was more casually dressed in a red and black silk jockey's cap; a shirt that had lost most of its buttons and revealed a black bra; and a pair of trousers so covered in mud they practically stood up by themselves.

As they walked up the flight of terrace steps, Archie found Ben's ear.

'Not quite like other budgerigars,' he murmured.

Poor Ben's eyes widened as, totally unfazed, the sisters sat down at the two empty places. Cynthia put the sausages in the middle of the table. 'Thought we'd make a contribution,' she said firmly.

'Thank you, my dear,' said Rose faintly. 'And . . . how lovely to see you. I hope you don't mind, we started without you, so you've missed the first course. We'll move on to the duck if—ah. Thank you, Joan.' Joan materialised to clear the plates and a brief silence ensued.

'Now,' Rose smiled, regaining her composure. 'Cynthia, I don't know if you remember Ned's wife, Lucy? And my grandsons, Ben and Max. They're going to live in Chandlers Barn.'

'Of course I remember Ned,' snapped Cynthia. 'He was my nephew, for crying out loud. The only one of you lot that had any sense.' She narrowed her eyes at me. 'Ned's wife, eh? I remember, you're Lucy. So that makes you Hetty's girl, doesn't it?'

'Er, well. No, I—'

'*Violet, it's Hetty's girl!*' she yelled across the table at her sister. 'Bit deaf,' she muttered to me. 'How is that trollop of a mother of yours? Still whoring her way around Cadogan Square?'

'Oh! No! No, she—'

'Terrible business with Roddy McLean, eh? His poor wife ended up falling on a fish-knife she was so distressed.'

The duck appeared and the evening lurched on. I struggled to eat, coping with Lavinia, who was muttering on about porticoes, and trying to keep an eye on Ben, who was making a valiant effort to eat his food, while Max was falling asleep in his plate.

I was just clearing my throat to suggest that the boys were awfully tired and could I possibly hustle them away, when Cynthia roared across the table, '*Do your shirt up, Violet! No one wants to see your tits!*'

Rose gave a nervous little laugh. 'Cynthia dear, language. *Pas devant les enfants, n'est-ce pas?*'

Max sat bolt upright, eyes snapping open. 'I know what that means. It means not in front of the children. And I know what tits are, too.'

''Course you do,' said Cynthia briskly. 'Every woman's got them, for God's sake, just as every man's got balls.'

'And a willy,' added Max. 'And mummy's got a string.'

There was a startled silence. I stared, horrified, at my plate.

Archie frowned. 'A string . . .' he said thoughtfully at length. 'Interesting. Let me have a little chat with you later, eh, young fella? Set you straight on a few things.'

'Come on, Max,' I said, lowering my burning face. 'We'll have to go. Rose, everyone's exhausted. You know, first night, and everything. Would you mind awfully excusing us?'

Rose inclined her head graciously. 'Of course. *A demain.*'

'And tomorrow,' said Lavinia, suddenly coming to from her drunken slumber and snatching my arm, 'we'll see about those committees.'

'Well, actually, Lavinia, I've decided I'm not really committee material,' I said bravely, getting to my feet.

'Not?' She looked up, horrified. Pissed, but horrified.

'I don't mind helping out in some small way for the church, or—'

'Flowers?' she pounced. 'The second Sunday of the month?'

'Flowers,' I agreed. 'Once a month.'

'Perfect,' she beamed, satisfied. 'Mimsy and I will be in the church from about three tomorrow, so pop down any time after that. OK? We'll show you the ropes. She'll be thrilled to have you on board.'

'Fine,' I said faintly, thinking even I could shove some dahlias in a jar once a month. 'See you tomorrow.'

The following morning the boys and I were in the car on our way to Oxford, to have a look at their new school. If I'd had one clear thought as I'd crawled out of bed, it was that we needed a plan. We needed to look busy, and not as if we were waiting for the Felloweses to come and organise our lives.

This gracious old city, where I'd spent three happy years, never failed to work its magic with me, and, as we approached, I couldn't wait to show my sons my alma mater, their father's too. Unfortunately, the traffic was so heavy and the sun so fierce, we were all but melting by the time we reached the centre.

'Look,' I gasped. 'That's where Daddy went. See, through the archway.'

'Can we get out?' moaned Max, clawing at the door.

'No, darling,' I said, looking desperately for a space. 'I can't park. But maybe down here . . .' No. Chock-a-bleeding-block. Disastrous.

'And—oh! There's my old college.' A pretty blonde girl dismounted from her bike. 'And that could have been Mummy,' I added boldly, 'off to a lecture!'

The horror and disbelief on the two faces in the rearview mirror was shaming. That I could *tell* such craven lies. I had, of course, always been a desiccated thirty-one and always would be.

'Mum, we're dying in here!'

'I know, I know,' I muttered, 'but if we could just find somewhere to flaming well park . . . Jesus, this place is a nightmare.'

It occurred to me that in London we'd walked to school, and that this drive was going to test our nerves every morning. Finally we parked, miles away, and trudged back, mostly uphill.

We teetered to a standstill beneath a redbrick building in a busy street with lorries thundering past; tall and towering with bars on the windows.

'Looks like a prison,' said Ben.

'Nonsense, darling, it looks lovely. Look at the playground.'

'That's a paving stone, Mum.'

'Well, perhaps there's more round the back.' I rattled the gates. 'Shall we see if we can open these? Maybe we could—'

'No, come on, Mum. Let's go.' Ben bit his nails nervously.

I glanced at him. 'All right, my love.'

We walked silently down the street, Max trailing behind.

Food and drink were crucial now, and Brown's would be lovely, I decided, with its palms and cooling fans. I headed eagerly in the direction of Woodstock Road. Naturally, the queue to get in went all the way down the street, as, naturally, it did at the next watering hole of my choice. We ended up in a dismal McDonald's, too tired even to talk, the boys draining Coke after Coke in silence.

What were we doing here? I wondered on the way home. Where were my friends? And once the boys had started school, what then? They'd make friends, but what about me? If I couldn't find work? Christ! I came to a sudden halt in a country lane. Stared up at the signpost.

'Why have we stopped?' asked Ben, who was map-reading in the back. 'It's straight on here.'

'Yes, I know, it's just . . .' I licked my lips, then suddenly, on an impulse, shot off down a tiny lane.

'No! No, Mum, this is totally, totally wrong! This is miles out of our way.' Ben frowned down at the map.

46

I breathed deeply and gripped the steering wheel, wishing he wasn't so flaming smart. He was supposed to be dyslexic, for God's sake. Why couldn't he behave like any other educationally challenged child, instead of navigating like a demon?

'Oh well, never mind. I'm pretty sure we can get back to the road this way.' I was beadily scrutinising the signs at every junction now. 'I wonder where this little road goes?'

'It goes to Bartwood actually,' he said sulkily. 'Followed by Hexham.'

'Really?' I breathed. 'Hexham.' Oh God, I needed to say it. I rolled it around in my mouth, savouring it. Charlie Fletcher territory. And I needed my fix. Needed to breathe again.

'D'you know, you're quite right.' I feigned surprise. There was a stony silence in the back as we cruised along. 'Here we are, in Hexham.'

I peered over the wheel excitedly. We purred slowly through a pretty village and I glanced feverishly from left to right, scanning the names on the gates. *Apple Tree House. Tudor Cottage* . . .

'I'm hungry, can we get some sweets?' whined Max.

'We could, my love, although there doesn't appear to be a shop. There is a church though.'

'That's no good.'

'So Church Farm,' I muttered under my breath, 'must be somewhere down . . . bingo.'

I slowed right down. Stared. It was a long, low, ancient-looking farmhouse, seventeenth century perhaps, whitewashed and beamed, and with what looked like a carefully tended garden at the back and a duck pond at the side. Comfortable, but not grand and imposing, and utterly, *utterly*, charming. I gave a groan of pleasure.

'Lovely,' I breathed, coming to a stop on the opposite side of the road.

Ben shrugged. Looked around. 'It's all right. Why have we stopped?'

'Oh, because I have to post a letter, darling.'

Handy. *Very* handy, I thought, spotting the red box across the road. I wondered if he was here. It was amazing how just knowing that he lived here sent the blood racing round the old arteries. Hello, the front door was opening. A young woman was coming out.

I ducked my head down and peered. Yes, a slim, attractive young woman in a denim dress, clutching a purse, with long blonde swinging hair was turning back to talk to someone in the doorway, who—shit! It was him. I watched, frozen with guilt and fascination, as he put an arm round her shoulder, giving her a quick squeeze, before she turned and went down the drive to her car. I knew, deep in my soul and without a shadow of a doubt, that it *was* his wife.

She started the engine, then negotiated the gravel drive, turning in a circle and driving towards me. I instantly shot my head down further.

'I thought you said you wanted to post a letter?' said Ben.

'Yes, yes, I do. It's just these shoes have come undone . . .'

'Mum, you've got espadrilles on. Where is this letter?'

I sat up and reached for my bag, realising that even though she'd gone, Charlie was still in the doorway, looking curiously at our car.

'Quick, Ben, here.' I shoved a letter into his hand. 'Run across and post it, quick.'

He stared. 'But it's already got a postmark. This is addressed to you.'

'Just post it, Ben, post it!'

God, Charlie was *really* peering at us now. I went hot. He mustn't recognise me, or think, Gosh, how odd, I used to see her in London, and now here she is, lurking outside my house.

'It's open, too, Mum. This is just an old gas bill you've had in your bag.'

'Just post the sodding thing, Ben, or I'll sodding well kill you!'

There was a deathly hush. After a moment Ben slid out of the car, posted the letter and got back in again. We sped off down the road.

There was a horrible silence. Even Max was stunned.

'Sorry, darling,' I croaked finally. 'Really sorry.'

'You swore at me,' he said in a small voice.

'Said sodding,' added Max importantly. 'Twice.'

'I know, I know. I said I'm sorry.'

'And you deliberately posted an old letter just to give the postman more work,' he said coldly. 'I'm ashamed of you.'

I was ashamed of myself. Thirty-one years old and stalking a man. Christ. And I'd sworn I wouldn't *do* it. But, oh God, it gave me such a rush. Ah well, I thought, letting out a huge sigh. Off to church now to meet Lavinia. How appropriate. Off to atone for my sins.

As I drew up to the little Norman church I swivelled round in my seat and bestowed a conciliatory smile on my travelling companions.

'I've promised to pop in here to see Aunt Lavinia, OK?'

'I'm staying here,' said Ben, staring stonily out of the window.

'Me too,' added Max.

I shrugged, then got out and went up the path to the main door and on into the delicious, dark cool. I spotted Lavinia in the aisle, talking nonstop and stooping, collecting armfuls of greenery from a huge heap on the floor. Her voice echoed around the place, gushing, ingratiating.

'Oh, so *pretty*, Mimsy—enchanting, in fact! I don't know how you do it. I end up with short ones at the back and tall ones at the front. I'm all over the place.'

She scuttled ahead of me carrying armfuls of flora and singing 'Bread of Heaven' in a breathy contralto, her attention firmly fixed on a pretty girl with short blonde hair, up at the altar, arranging flowers in vases.

'Sorry I'm late, Lavinia,' I called as I approached. 'And I can't stay long, I'm afraid. I've left the boys in the car.'

'Lucy, hi.' She turned round looking hot and overexcited. 'Lucy, this is Mimsy Compton-Burrell, a *very* dear friend of mine,' she beamed.

'Hello.' I smiled.

'Hi,' said Mimsy. 'Come to join the workers?'

'Well, I'm not sure I'll be able to do anything like that,' I said, gazing in awe at a truly beautiful and elaborate arrangement of lilies, white roses and greenery.

'Oh, don't worry,' Mimsy told me. 'Any help is much appreciated, and it really doesn't matter what you do.' And as Lavinia hurried off to the pile by the door again, shrieking, 'More gypsophila!' Mimsy muttered, 'Don't let Lavinia talk you into doing too much. She'll organise the pants off you if you're not careful.'

'Oh, I'm well aware of that,' I muttered back, thinking how nice Mimsy was. She looked nice too, with her wide-apart, merry green eyes, floppy blonde fringe and huge toothy smile.

'More ferns, too?' cried Lavinia musically, from down by the door.

'I rather thought I'd finished, Lavinia.' Mimsy raised her voice. 'What d'you think?' She turned the vase round to show her.

'Perfect.' Lavinia came scurrying back, clasping her hands sycophantically. 'Just perfect. Got the idea, Lucy?' she panted. 'Couple of large displays either side of the altar, a few little dinky ones at the end of the pews, and then a nice big fronty one by the door. I'll put your name down for two weeks on Sunday, OK?'

'Fine,' I said meekly, 'only I must dash now, boys in hot car and all that. It was lovely to meet you, Mimsy. Perhaps I'll see you around,' I added hopefully, recognising a possible kindred spirit.

'Oh, but I will. I'll see you on Saturday, up at the house, surely?'

'Really?'

'Yes, didn't Mummy tell you?' Lavinia turned to me with a frown. 'She's having a big drinks thing for you. You know, to welcome you to the neighbourhood, introduce you to everyone. Half the county will be there! Such fun.'

'But I've made plans for this weekend. Teresa, a friend of mine and her son might be coming down and—'

'Well, that's wonderful,' she purred, 'the more the merrier. I'm sure Mummy won't mind a bit.'

Rose rang the following morning. 'I gather you've got a friend for the weekend?'

'Er, yes,' I said, struggling into a dressing gown, somehow feeling she could tell I was nibbling toast in bed and that the boys were downstairs watching cartoons. 'I was going to ring you, Rose. Lavinia said you were having a party, so—'

'For you, my dear, so you can meet people,' she interrupted. 'Of course your friend must come too. Her name is?'

'Teresa. Teresa Carluccio, and Pietro, her little boy.'

'Foreign?'

'Well, yes, Italian. But listen, Rose—'

'Hmm . . . better not mention that to Archie. Just in case. How long is she staying, your Italian friend?'

'Oh, just the night.'

'Oh, just the night! Oh, fine, fine, not a problem. We'll see you both up here at about seven then, shall we? Just drinks in the rose garden for about fifty, OK? Bye now.'

Not a problem? I thought, putting the phone down. Of course it wasn't a problem, it was my flaming house Teresa was coming to, wasn't it? Surely I could invite who I liked? As I sat glaring at the phone, nostrils flaring with annoyance, it startled me by ringing again.

'Hello!' I barked, snatching it up.

'God, you sound cross.'

'Oh, Jess, sorry. Hi.' I held my forehead.

'What's eating you so early on a beautiful morning, then? Not that hagridden old mother-in-law of yours, I hope?' she said gleefully.

'Oh, no, no. She's . . . fine. How are you, Jess? I've been meaning to ring you, honestly, but I just haven't had a moment. I've been absolutely up to my eyes down here.'

'What, in clover or cow poo?'

'Oh, clover, definitely clover. It's really lovely down here,' I enthused. 'So pretty, and the barn's amazing.'

She sniffed. 'I hear Teresa is coming for the weekend. I bumped into her in Harvey Nicks.'

Bugger. 'Did you?' I panicked. 'Yes, yes, she is, actually, and I was going to ask you too, only I thought you'd like to come with Jamie, and isn't he still covering that European conference?' I said lamely.

'That finished weeks ago. And why would I want to come with him? We had a huge row last night, actually, about him always going away and me never going anywhere, and at the end he said, "OK, so why don't I look after Henry this weekend, and you go and see Lucy?"'

'Oh, how sweet,' I said faintly. 'Yes, lovely, well *do* come down, Jess. The only problem is, there's a party on Saturday night at Rose's. Quite a smart do, I gather, which may not be your sort of thing—'

'Nonsense, I love parties. And I do possess a posh dress, Lucy, and can be relied upon to behave in a civilised manner.'

'Of course.'

'So I'll be down at about lunchtime on Saturday, OK?'

'Fine, fine. Look forward to it, Jess.'

I put the phone down and held my head. Oh God, what was I going to say to Rose? I went to take a shower, and was just working out my plan of action, when Ben popped his head round the door, distraught.

'It's Teresa on the phone. She says they can't come on Saturday after all because Rozanna's got crabs or something. It's not fair, Mummy, please make her come. I want to see Pietro!'

Tears began to stream down his cheeks, as dripping and swearing I grabbed a towel and ran to the telephone again.

'Teresa, I'm counting on you,' I hissed. 'Ben's desperate for some company. What d'you mean, she's got crabs?'

'Cramps, not crabs. Rozanna's been getting these terrible cramps, you see, Luce. I don't think she should be left on her own. I mean, I could bring her along with me, I suppose, she love that, but it's a lot for you . . .'

I looked at Ben's white, tear-stained face beside me. 'Oh Christ, bring her,' I said resignedly. 'God knows where we'll all sleep, but if we put the boys on Lilos in the sitting room . . .'

After I put the phone down, I paced around the house dithering about what to say to Rose. Finally, I seized the phone, ready to brazen it out. Pinkie answered and it dawned on me I could just leave a message.

'Oh sure, Lucy,' she said airily, 'that's not a problem. The more the merrier. I'll let Mummy know when I see her.'

I didn't hear from Rose, and a day went by, and then another, and so after a while I breathed again and wondered what on earth I was worrying about. Come Saturday, I was so excited to be seeing the old crowd, I simply didn't care.

Ben and Max gave a shriek of glee as the car approached. We all went outside to meet our visitors as they tumbled out of Teresa's car. The boys fell on Pietro and instantly disappeared into the barn, then Jess emerged, all in black Lycra and looking very London in her dark glasses. She was followed by Rozanna, swathed in cream silk and looking gorgous but pale, a huge bunch of lilies in her arms.

'Darling, how lovely,' she murmured, embracing me affectionately. '*So* sweet of you to have me.'

'It's great to have you,' I assured her. 'How are you feeling?'

'Better,' she smiled. 'Teresa forced me to go to the doctor, who assured me I have mild rheumatism and not Parkinson's as I rather feared.'

'Oh, Rozanna, that's a relief. You must have been worried.'

'Wow, it's huge!' said Teresa admiringly, getting out of the car and gazing up at the barn.

'Look inside.' I swung the door right back and they gaped.

Jess gazed around wistfully. 'Seems you've really fallen on your feet this time, Luce.'

I grinned gratefully and settled them all in their rooms; Rozanna and Teresa sharing, Jess in with me, and the boys downstairs. Later we ate huge bowls of pasta and salad in the garden and drank far too much wine, roaring with laughter. The boys played happily the while, proudly showing Pietro the lie of the land, while the rest of us frittered away the afternoon in a soporific haze.

That evening, when we'd all changed into our party gear, we strolled up to Netherby. The rose garden was thronging with people, everyone chattering away at the tops of their voices, champagne glasses clinking.

'You know, secretly, Lucy,' Jess confided in my ear, 'I adore Queen and Country and all that regalia, but this place makes me want to leap on the nearest chair and sing "The Red Flag".'

'You were going to behave. For my sake, resist that temptation,' I begged grimly as we moved forward and muscled our way in.

I'd deliberately timed our entrance rather late, so that, hopefully, most people would have assembled and my few extra guests could mingle with the crowd and not be too noticeable. The garden was indeed awash with people, but none, perhaps, quite so gorgeous as Rozanna, in a simple white linen shift dress, slim arms and legs golden brown, her blonde hair tumbling down her back. Rose was upon us in seconds.

'Who, my dear, is that beautiful girl?' she murmured, as I took a glass of champagne from a passing waiter's tray.

There was no escape. 'Oh, that's Rozanna,' I said. 'She's staying with me.' I called Rozanna over. 'Rozanna, this is Rose Fellowes, our hostess.'

Rozanna said hello, and Rose inclined her head, just a fraction. She gave a tight little smile and looked like she'd swallowed a lemon.

'My dear, you didn't say you had other guests,' she murmured.

'Oh, just one or two,' I said brazenly. 'And this,' I went on, as Archie ambled up, 'is our host, Archie Fellowes. Rozanna Carling.'

Archie's eyes inexplicably popped. 'Rozanna!' he gasped.

'Archie, how lovely to see you,' purred Rozanna.

'Oh, er, yes. I—er . . .' Archie spluttered as he took her hand, his face quite purple now. Sweat was beginning to bead on his brow.

'You've met?' Rose frowned. 'Where?'

'Oh. Now. Let me think. Where was it? Um . . .' Archie stuttered.

'House of Lords,' said Rozanna quickly with a smile. 'A reception there, back in May. I was with my father. Lord Belfont.'

'Was it?' He looked startled. 'Oh, yes, yes, that was it. House of Lords.'

'Really?' Rose eyed her suspiciously. 'Well, how lovely to meet you.' She collected herself. 'Do excuse us if you would though. Archie, come.' She called him sharply to heel and he followed sheepishly.

'Oh, please don't tell me,' I groaned as they disappeared, shutting my eyes. '*Please* don't tell me, Rozanna . . .'

'That he was one of my clients? Prospective, actually, but I turned him down. Much too old.'

'You realise Rose has beetled straight off to the library to look you up in *Debrett's*?'

'Which is precisely where she'll find me,' she said sweetly.

'Oh!' I blinked. 'Really?'

'Really.' She glanced around. Sighed. 'Rather a lot of people I know here, actually. I must say, it's a novelty to see them with their wives. Amazing really,' she mused. 'I could clear this place in seconds.'

'Well, please don't,' I said nervously. 'Oh, look, here's one you won't know, hopefully. Hector, this is Rozanna Carling.'

Hector sidled up, blushing, and shook hands, his enlarged Adam's apple bobbing up and down in his throat. Rozanna, spotting a gauche *ingénu*, smiled gently and engaged him in conversation, while I took the opportunity to wander off. Jess and Teresa, minus their husbands thank you very much, appeared to be having a whale of time, being thoroughly chatted up by a couple of older, hearty-looking hunting types, and flirting their little socks off.

I jumped as Lavinia suddenly seized my arm from behind. 'I think you should meet Simon,' she hissed urgently, teetering to a standstill beside me. 'God, Mummy's invited some real duffers this evening, I can't *tell* you how shocked I am at the standard, Lucy, and I'm so sorry, but Simon's sweet. You'll like him. Bit of a rectory.'

'Sorry?' I glanced across as she jerked her head in the direction of a pallid, narrow-headed man in a shiny dinner jacket.

'That's what he's got. Wouldn't do for me, of course, you'd be pushed to even call it imposing.' She sniffed. 'Handsome though.'

I peered. 'D'you think?'

'No, no, the rectory.'

'Ah, right.' I recovered. 'Oh, I see. Oh, well, he wouldn't do for me at all. You see, unless it's Grade One Georgian and moated, with four thousand acres and a safari park, I'm afraid I'm simply not interested.' I bestowed a sweet smile and moved on.

God, this *family*. No wonder Ned had avoided them like the plague.

A few minutes later, the aunts arrived, having roared throatily up the drive—momentarily scaring the party in the rose garden into silence. They were resplendent in matching floral frocks of an eye-searing pink and yellow combination, emblazoned with a bird of paradise design. It came to me that these were their old curtains.

As I watched them march determinedly into the middle of the party, I heard Rose whisper to Archie, 'We'll have to get the doctor to order them to give up driving. They'll kill someone one day.'

'Actually, it wouldn't make much difference,' said a dry voice in my ear. 'Most of the residents round here are half dead anyway.'

I spun round. 'Jack!' I said delightedly, as I was swept off my feet in a huge bear hug. 'Oh, Jack, how lovely! What are you doing here?'

Jack was Ned's cousin, a lovely, irreverent, dissolute man; tall, and with the Fellowes blue eyes, but with dark chestnut curls and a disreputably handsome face. 'I thought you couldn't bear these bashes!'

'Oh, I'm here in a professional capacity, in anthropological mode. Come to watch another world go by. A dim and distant one.' He grinned. 'And anyway, I'd heard you were here, so I thought I'd come and pester you.'

'You're staying?'

'Oh, yes, most definitely. Most definitely on the scrounge for some hospitality, but unlike you, not for ever. No, I'm just here for a month or so while my house is being renovated.' He regarded me mischievously.

'Jack, I am not on the scrounge,' I said furiously. 'I was kindly offered the barn by Rose, and for the boys' sake, simply for the boys' sake—'

'Quite right too.' He grinned. 'Don't worry, Luce, I'm just seeing if you still rise as spectacularly as you always did. Just reeling you in.'

'Ah, the Compleat Angler,' I observed drily.

'Absolutely, and keen to do a bit of the real thing too, while I'm here. The river looks perfect. Still,' he mused, 'be interesting to see if you can stay the course. They haven't driven you to drink then yet?'

I groaned. 'No, but I have a feeling it's only a matter of time. I'd forgotten—well.' I stopped, guiltily.

'How ghastly they all are? Ah, no, not me,' he said shaking his head, lips pursed. 'I only have to walk through that front door and it all comes flooding back in glorious technicolour. Still, needs must, and I have to say, I am a bit needy at the moment.' He drained his glass cheerfully.

I smiled. Jack taught English and Theatre Studies at London University. He was a bit of a poet, too, but as he rather ruefully observed, poetry wasn't quite merchant banking, and he always seemed to be lurching from one financial crisis to the next.

With an appalling reputation for unsuitable dalliances with beautiful women, Jack, nonetheless, was terrific company. He radiated vitality, and was the only member of the family Ned had ever had any time for. The first time I'd met Ned, years ago, at a dance here in Oxford, he'd been with Jack. The pair of them had been propping up the college bar and Ned had bought me a drink and the three of us had chatted. After that, Ned and I danced the night away—eyes locked in recognition of something wonderful—and I didn't see Jack till the end of the evening.

'And you, Luce. Are you better?' he enquired gently.

'Oh, yes, much better, thanks.' I blushed. Poor Jack had been party to some miserable evenings with me after Ned had died. I'd sobbed all over him, and not just at the time, either. Up until relatively recently he'd been subjected to some very maudlin company in Royal Avenue. 'It took me a long time,' I said ruefully. 'But you know, Jack,' I glanced up, 'I think I can safely say that I'm as well as I'll ever be.' I smiled. 'And you? Unusual to see you unaccompanied, I must say. What happened to that pneumatic Brazilian beauty I met you with last time?'

'Two Planks?' His eyes widened.

I giggled. 'Oh, come on, she wasn't that bad.'

'Oh, no, not that bad. But actually'—he mused—'these days, well, I'm a changed man. I've decided to abandon the predatory sexual role. I've grown weary of it, you see.' His blue eyes widened innocently.

I chuckled. 'I don't believe that for one moment!'

'Ah, but it's true.' He sighed. 'I'm too old for all that.' He shook his head ruefully. 'In fact, I sometimes think . . . Hello?' he said suddenly. 'What have we here?'

I followed his gaze to where Trisha, who was supposed to be handing round canapés, was roaring with laughter in the middle of a clutch of male guests, dressed in a low-cut top and a sarong skirt.

I laughed. 'You see? You *see*! Always on the prowl!'

'Not at all,' he said quickly, 'I'm merely continuing the anthropological study I mentioned earlier. And speaking of study, young Lucy, what do you intend to do with yourself down here? Thinking of going back to work at all?'

But I wasn't listening. I was still watching Trisha, who was pulling the arm of a man who had his back to us. I caught my breath, tightening my grip on the stem of my champagne glass. The man turned his head and looked in our direction. My heart leapt up into my throat. They were coming towards us now and the man Trisha had by the sleeve of his jacket—was Charlie.

Chapter Three

THE PAIR OF THEM came across the lawn towards us. Charlie, looking even more devastatingly handsome than I remembered, was wearing an elegant, biscuit-coloured linen jacket. His head was slightly cocked to one side as he listened to what Trisha was saying; his dark eyes, though, were bright and focused. Principally on me. I felt the blood drain right through me, down my legs, and away into my witty little Italian shoes.

'Lucy,' Trisha called. 'Hey, Lucy, listen!' She halted breathlessly in front of me. 'This guy's called Charlie Fletcher, right, and you won't believe this, but I was like, prattling away to Charlie just now about all your antiques and stuff in the barn, telling him how it had been your thing in London, and he told me that he's got this friend, right, who's got an antiques place near here, and he's looking for some help.'

She glanced back at Charlie, but he was staring intently at me. He didn't appear to be listening to her at all.

'But how extraordinary,' he said finally. 'It's you. We know each other, don't we? Please tell me I'm not going mad.'

I could feel my cheeks burning up now. 'N-no,' I stammered. 'You're not. I mean, you're right, we do. Know each other. From London.'

'From London,' he said. 'That's it. How peculiar.' He blinked. 'D'you know,' he said, turning to Trisha, 'it was the weirdest thing. Up until a few weeks ago, I used to see this girl practically every single day. Everywhere I went in London, every shop I went into, every bus I got onto—there she was! It was quite extraordinary. And now—well, bugger me,' he turned back. 'Here you are again. Lucy, is it?'

'Yes, Lucy,' I gasped, horrified. Oh, come *on*, I thought. Not *every* day, surely, and not *every* bus, and *every* shop! I was aware of the deep blush spreading down my neck now, and of Jack's eyes upon me.

'And always with your dog!' persisted Charlie relentlessly. 'You used to walk up and down my street *endlessly* with him. You were always staring around, wild-eyed. What were you looking for?'

They were all looking at me expectantly.

'Grass,' I croaked finally.

'Grass?' Jack looked startled. 'Well, stroll on down. I didn't think you indulged,' he drawled. 'You were always such a goody-two-shoes.'

'No, no, for the dog! He couldn't do it on the pavement. Had to have a bit of soft stuff for, well . . .'

'Anti-splash?' offered Jack. 'Don't we all, my love, don't we all. How very fascinating, Luce—ooh, hello.' He broke off to gaze down appreciatively at Trisha's bejewelled navel. 'Someone's had a tummy job.'

'What dog's this then?'

I turned to find Jess at my elbow. Oh God, she was all I needed, although I was relieved to see that Trisha was leading Jack away towards the shrubbery.

'Oh, um, Theo and Ray's Yorkie,' I mumbled. 'You remember, I used to take it for walks a lot. In London.'

'Did you?' She blinked. 'I didn't know that. Hi there.' She directed this last at Charlie, flashing him a dazzling smile. She shot me a look and waited expectantly.

'Oh, um, this is Jess O'Connor, and this . . .' I stalled suddenly. Panicked. Oh bugger. 'This . . . is Charles,' I concluded lamely.

He raised his eyebrows in surprise. 'No, no, Charlie's fine. I haven't been called Charles since I was at prep school.'

'Charlie,' said Jess thoughtfully. Her eyes narrowed. 'Really. And how do you know Lucy, Charlie?'

'Well, we don't actually know each other,' Charlie was saying, 'but as I was just explaining, we used to bump into each other an awful lot in London. We—'

'Look, this job,' I blurted out, desperate to turn the conversation away from chance meetings in London streets and Jess's beady gaze. 'Trisha mentioned an antique shop?'

'Oh! Oh, yes, quite right. We got sidetracked. Yes, well it belongs to a mate of mine called Kit Alexander. It's in this amazing old manor house in Frampton, takes up about three floors. He's always run it pretty much single-handed, but now he's looking for some help. Is that the sort of thing you'd be interested in?'

'Oh, definitely,' I breathed. 'My mum has a stall in the Portobello Road, so I know all about selling antiques. Jess and I used to help her with it, didn't we?' I said eagerly.

'We did, but that was just a lark on a Saturday morning.' Jess turned to Charlie. 'Lucy's not giving you the entire picture here, I'm afraid. She used to work in the porcelain department at Christie's. She's a specialist in eighteenth-century European china, hardly a shop girl.'

'But this would be a start, Jess,' I hissed.

'Yes, but you don't want to take this job as "a start" and then leave the poor chap in the lurch, do you?'

And you don't want to find arsenic in your cornflakes.

'Perhaps the thing to do is to be honest with him,' suggested Charlie. 'Say that you'd like the job, but you might well move on at a later date.'

'Oh, absolutely,' I agreed, nodding earnestly.

'I was going to pop in and see him on my way to Bristol on Friday, actually,' said Charlie thoughtfully. 'Why don't I pick you up and take you with me?'

I nearly fainted with pleasure. Those glorious words. Pick You Up And Take You With Me. What, in his arms? Naked but for a wolfskin?

'That would be marvellous,' I croaked.

'Trisha pointed your barn out to me earlier, Lucy. I'll come by at about ten o'clock, shall I? Would that be all right?'

'Perfect,' I smiled happily. 'Oh, look, here are the boys!' I went on, as at that moment, Teresa appeared with Pietro, Ben and Max.

'They were getting a little out of hand,' called Teresa, keeping a tight grip on various small hands. 'I thought maybe we take them back. Max—he been a real monkey. Keep asking waiters for Bacardi Breezers!'

Jess laughed. 'The little love. So killing at that age. Do you have any children, Charlie?' Out it flicked, faster than a serpent's tongue.

'A daughter, Ellen. She's eight.'

'How lovely,' smoothed Jess, not done yet. 'And is your wife here tonight?'

'She's got a filthy cold, so she decided to give it a miss. And are these yours, Lucy?' He grinned down at Ben and Max.

'We saw you the other day,' Max said suddenly. 'I remember you. You were outside that white house. The one with the pond at the side.'

'That's it!' Charlie exclaimed. 'Exactly! God, I was trying to remember where I'd seen you, and you were parked outside my house.'

Was it my imagination, or had the world gone a little darker?

'Yes, because Mummy wanted Ben to post a letter,' went on Max. 'And then they had a fight and Mummy said she'd sodding well kill him if he didn't sodding well put it in.'

'Ah ha ha!' I tinkled merrily. 'Yes, well, I'm sure Mr Fletcher doesn't want to hear all our domestic trials and tribulations. Come along, boys.'

Charlie chuckled. 'I believe that's what's known as a bit of a handful?'

'Oh, no, much more than that,' I admitted. 'More like a truckful. In fact I'm not sure I contain him at all, sometimes.'

'Ah. So, it's "wait till your father gets home", is it?'

'No, no, his father's dead. Ned died four years ago.'

'Oh. I'm sorry.'

He looked at me for a long moment and I believe he meant it. His eyes were warm and sincere, and it seemed to me that something unspoken passed between us.

'Right, let's go then,' said Jess, breaking the moment. She turned to Charlie and gave him a sweet, but dangerous smile. 'Goodbye. It was lovely to meet you.'

'Lovely to meet you too.' Then he turned to me. 'Bye, Lucy.' He leaned forward and brushed my cheek with his lips. 'See you Friday, then.'

'Yes!' I gasped. 'Super.'

We walked through the park towards the lake in uneasy silence.

'Race you back, boys!' Teresa cried suddenly, knowing the air had to be sliced. The boys yelped and raced off as she ran on ahead of them.

Jess folded her arms and dredged up a great sigh.

'Oh, Lucy. Be careful. Be very, very careful.'

'Hmmm?' I didn't look at her. My heart was thumping.

'Jesus, even I felt the heat back there.'

'Did you?' I stopped. Touched her arm. 'It wasn't just me then? Wasn't my imagination? You could sense something too?'

She laughed drily. 'Oh, yeah. Something with a few thousand volts attached to it, but, Lucy,' she struggled. 'I know you've had a rough time and deserve some happiness, but you *know* what I'm going to say.'

I tilted my hot face up to the cool blue vault of the heavens. 'I know. He's married. But, Jess—surely, if there was something electric going on back there, there's something wrong with the marriage?'

'What, because a man looks at a pretty girl like that at a party? Do me a favour, it can be the most blissful of domestic set-ups and lightning can still strike if circumstances allow it. Just means that temptation is in the way. A boozy party, a conference abroad . . . that's what's so frightening.'

'You're talking about you and Jamie now,' I muttered.

'Yes,' she sighed. 'Maybe I am. Part of me believes he is faithful, actually. It's just—well, OK, suppose he was at a party, right, and some single girl starts making goo-goo eyes at him like you've just done to Charlie, well, in a way, what's the poor sod supposed to do? He's only a man, for Christ's sake. But where does that leave me? And where does it leave Charlie's wife? Alone, at home, unaware that some predatory hussy is eyeing up her husband and arranging a date.'

'It's not a date,' I muttered. 'It's to see about a job.'

'Which under normal circumstances you wouldn't even consider,' she scoffed.

I struggled to be honest. 'Maybe not, but, Jess, something about this whole situation makes me want to—well, just peer round the corner. I can't stop now.'

'If you can't stop now, you'll be totally out of control later,' she observed sourly. 'This is the best time, Lucy, believe me. On this first corner. This is the time to ring him up and say, "Actually, forget it, mate."'

We'd arrived at the garden gate now and Rozanna, who'd got back earlier, was opening the barn door for the others.

'The awful thing is, I know you're right. It's just—'

'It's just you're still basking in the afterglow of your titillating conversation, longing to go to bed and hug it to yourself.'

'Yes!' I breathed, turning to her. 'That's it.'

'And because no one's ever come remotely close to making you feel so alive and excited since Ned died, you want to know if this feeling is for real. See if you really *can* unfurl your dry old roots and drink again, but of course, you wouldn't do anything silly. Wouldn't go the whole hog with this guy, nothing naked and horizontal.'

'That's it exactly, Jess! I wouldn't. Really I wouldn't.'

'Bollocks,' she scoffed. 'You're a lost cause, Luce, sunk without a snorkel. Because take it from me, my friend, in that quaint little country pub, where you'll undoubtedly end up, the moment your eyes lock over that bottle of Chablis—'

'Coo-eeee!'

We swung round together in surprise. As we peered down the bank in the half-light, I saw Rose coming up behind us, waving wildly.

Suddenly I felt awful. God, I hadn't thanked her for the party! I hurried down to meet her as she came panting up towards me.

'Oh, Rose! I'm so sorry, how awful of me! I didn't come and find you to thank you. And it was such a lovely party, really it was, but the boys were a bit tired, so we thought we'd slip away without breaking it up.' I took her arm anxiously as we walked to the barn together.

'Oh, absolutely,' she panted. 'Quite right, you had to get the boys back. But what I actually came to say is that you can't possibly all squeeze in here tonight, when we have so much room up at the house. Ah, here's Ted.' She turned. 'He's come to take the bags back. Ted! Quickly now.' She beckoned him and he shuffled obediently towards us.

'But, Rose, we're perfectly happy,' I objected. 'We like being together.'

'Don't be silly, Lucy. Now, Ted. Get Lady Rozanna's bag from upstairs, please, she'll show you where, and, Jess, where are your things?'

'My God, she really has looked me up,' muttered Rozanna, as she and Jess filed past me to beat Ted to their belongings.

'And I, of course, will stay here with my son,' smiled Teresa firmly.

Rose looked at her as if she were something nasty that had crawled out of the woodshed. 'Yes, yes, of course. Right. Come along, then, my party. Rozanna, can you manage?'

Rozanna, carrying the tiniest of handbags, shot me a hysterical look as she came out of the barn, while Jess, emerging with her canvas sack over her shoulder, shot me one of horror.

'Must we?' muttered Jess.

'I think it might be politic,' I muttered back helplessly.

Teresa and I sat in the sunny front garden the following morning, enjoying an extremely late breakfast as the boys played in the woods. Suddenly Rozanna and Jess appeared, struggling up the bank towards us, dragging their bags and giggling wildly.

'Couldn't you get your batman to bring those for you?' I called.

'No time,' gasped Jess. 'Had to escape. God, it was like Colditz up there, with Kommandant Rose in full swing.'

'She certainly takes a bit of laughing off, doesn't she?' panted Rozanna, flopping down into a chair. 'Anyone would think she'd had a sniff at something, she's so fizzed up. Ooh, yes, please.' She sat up and took the coffee I offered her gratefully. 'Thanks, Lucy.'

'Lovely croissants,' said Jess greedily, reaching across for the basket. 'God, you should have seen our morning fare. We had to present ourselves at the sea of polished mahogany and wade through mountains of kedgeree. And then listen to Lady R berating poor old Hector, because he hadn't talked to some girl called Sophia Lennox-something, who'd come all the way from Cirencester to see him, and who was in possession of, and I quote, "the most marvellous seat I've ever seen!"'

'What, ancestral, or on a horse?'

'Who knows, either way it was all Greek to me. Anyway, clearly Hector is firmly in the doghouse.'

'To which he crawled, apologising profusely?'

'No, he didn't actually. It was really rather surprising. He told his mother to shut up and keep her bloody nose out of his personal life. Then he stormed out of the room.'

'Blimey! That's a turnup for the books. Completely out of character.'

'Oh dear,' said Rozanna. 'Such a bizarre family. If one didn't know better, one could swear they were terribly aristocratic, they have all the hallmarks. But you know, Lucy, they're really frightfully parvenus.'

I put my coffee cup down. 'How d'you mean?'

'Well, I looked *them* up while I was having a bath—and I don't know what Ned told you, but they're only first generation. Quite the arrivistes. Archie's a self-made man. Made his fortune marketing frozen pies—very definitely trade. And Rose is actually only entitled to call herself Lady Fellowes by virtue of her marriage to Archie, and not Lady Rose, which she appears to have affected.'

'How strange,' I pondered. 'I'd always heard that she'd . . . well. Rather married beneath her, as she would say. I wonder who she was before she met Archie?'

'Word has it,' said a low voice in my ear, 'that she was a topless lap dancer in a night club.'

I swung round in horror. 'Jack!' I gasped. 'You made that up!'

'Of course I did,' he said cheerfully, swinging an elegant denim leg over the bench beside me. 'No, if you really want to know, according to my aged pa, she was just a rather ordinary, tennis club type who hung about on shooting weekends until she got her hooks into Archie.'

'I prefer the lap dancing,' giggled Teresa.

'Oh, mè too,' agreed Jack. 'And that's why rumours start, you know, Luce, because they're far more entertaining. You have to be very, very careful, particularly when you get into strange men's cars, for instance. People will construe all sorts of things.' His blue eyes twinkled at me.

I stared. Strange men's cars? What the . . . oh, for God's sake! Jess went pink and hurriedly attended to something crucial deep in her handbag. Clearly a briefing session had gone on over breakfast.

'I see,' I said evenly. 'Do tell me, how is the erotic alternative to *Mary Poppins* shaping up?'

'Now, now, no need to be catty.' He grinned. 'She's training to be a nurse back home, I'll have you know. But since you ask, she's shaping up very nicely, thank you. I've been helping her perfect her bedside manner. As a matter of fact, we've just spent a very happy half-hour with a box of sticky bandages and a blood pressure kit.'

'What you do with the blood pressure kit?' Teresa asked curiously.

Jack turned full circle to face her. 'I'd be happy to show you any time. No pain, I promise. We simply do some really rather strenuous exercises. And then we have a cosy ten minutes comparing pulses.' His eyes widened. 'Trisha enjoyed that bit very much.'

'I see.' Teresa grinned and waggled her wedding ring at him.

'Oh, that wouldn't stop Jack,' I sneered.

'True,' he swung round. 'But it would normally stop you.'

A silence unfolded. God, what was this, a bloody conspiracy?

Jess glanced at her watch. 'Actually, I must go and ring Jamie. Check how he's getting on with young Henry.' She shot Jack a look as she left.

'Lucy,' Rozanna said into the silence, 'couldn't this supposed hell-raiser of a man make himself useful in the gin and tonic department?'

'Of course he could, Rozanna,' I agreed staunchly.

Jack grinned good-naturedly and got up to oblige. As he disappeared into the barn, Jess suddenly materialised, her face as white as a sheet.

'What is it?' I leapt up.

'It's Henry,' she breathed. 'He's got chickenpox.'

'Chickenpox!' Teresa and I exchanged stifled smiles. 'Oh, Jess, that's not serious. A bit of calamine lotion, a few quiet days at home.'

'Yes, but Jamie won't know what to do,' Jess hissed. 'Oh gosh, Teresa,' she turned anguished eyes on her. 'I'm awfully sorry to drag you away, but, I wonder, would you mind terribly if we . . .'

'No, no, ees fine.' Teresa got quickly to her feet.

As they hurried into the house to pack, I got up and headed inside to help. Jack had reappeared, armed with drinks, and his voice drifted back to me in the air.

'Pleasant evening, Rozanna?'

'Lovely, and actually it got better as the night went on. An unexpected visitor dropped into my suite last night . . .'

Days passed and Friday dawned bright, clear and full of delicious portent; Charlie was due to arrive at ten o'clock. Having crept out of bed at eight, so as not to wake the boys, I took a long, hot soak in a steaming, rose-scented bath. I then settled at my dressing table, surrounded by eye shadows, foundations and blushers, which I'd read in *Vogue*, if subtly applied, could take years off me and make me look a dewy twenty-six.

Another half-hour was then spent with the hair dryer, which, of course, should have been done *before* achieving the dewy twenty-six, as my make-up, disastrously, began to melt in the heat. By nine thirty, I was gazing at my reflection in despair.

'Bugger!' I shrieked, reaching for a scrunchy. I scraped my hair back with it and ran to the sink, washing it all off. 'Bugger!' I wailed into a towel. 'Oh God, it's twenty to ten already and I look bloody awful!'

Ben put his head round the door. 'You don't,' he said thoughtfully, picking his nose. 'You look nice. Go like that.'

'Like this?' I peered in the mirror. At least my face looked clean and fresh. I added a spot of mascara and a touch of lipstick.

'Better?' I smudged my lips together anxiously.

'Yeah, fine. You look great, Mum, like you normally do. And anyway, what's all the fuss? It's only to see about a job working in a shop, isn't it?'

'Yes, darling, quite right. Now listen. Trisha's coming up any minute and she'll either stay here with you this morning or take you up to Granny's. Oh, look, here she is.'

'Hi, guys! Hey, you look nice.' Trisha strode into the bedroom.

'Thanks. Um . . . so do you,' I added nervously.

It was, admittedly, a warm day, but Trisha was dressed for the Caribbean. Her denim shorts showed at least half her bottom, her top was actually not a top at all but a bikini, and she'd wrapped a bandanna round her head, warrior style. Her long limbs gleamed.

'Jack and I thought we'd take the boys fishing today. Is that OK?'

Jack *and* Trisha, I thought nervously. 'Ah, well, actually—oh! He's here!' I yelped, at the sound of a car drawing up outside.

'Yep, that's your lift,' said Trisha, sticking her head out of the window. 'Yoo-hoo! Up here, Charlie!' I winced as she waved extravagantly. 'She'll be down in a minute,' she yelled. 'Just fixin' her face!' I winced again. Trisha turned back. 'It's OK, you've got a mo. Jack's chatting to him.'

I snatched my bag from the bed and flew downstairs. As I got to the open door, I stopped. Outside, Charlie was leaning against a pale blue convertible, talking to Jack. He was wearing cream trousers and a faded blue shirt. Tall and broad, he threw back his head and laughed at something Jack said. Then he turned and saw me.

'Hi!' He smiled, and it seemed to me that the whole of my front garden lit up like a Hollywood set.

'Hi,' I breathed back. There was a moment's silence as I gazed at him, hopefully not too wantonly.

'Hi!' gasped Jack breathlessly, in a direct parody of me.

I regarded him coldly. 'Hello, Jack. What are you doing here?'

'Well, I was thinking of taking my young nephews for some trout tickling today since you're otherwise engaged. All right by you?'

'I'm not sure that it is, actually. I'm not too keen on Max being near the water when I'm not around. He's only four and he can't swim yet.'

'Aw, come on, Luce. I'll keep an eye on him. And anyway, I've promised them. They'll be so disappointed.'

This much was true. There'd be uproar if I refused. 'Well, OK. But listen, Jack.' I led him away out of earshot. 'I want you to give me your solemn word there won't be any funny business in front of the boys. Just see that you—you know, behave responsibly.'

'Aye, aye, miss, will do. Will do my very best. Dib dib dib. But when you're back, I mean later on, when the children are all tucked up in bed and it's after the nine o'clock watershed—all right if I give her one then?'

'Oh, for God's sake, Jack. You can do what you damn well like! It makes no difference to me!' I hissed.

He laughed as I stormed off to the car, desperately trying to rearrange my expression.

'Sorry about that,' I purred as I slipped into the passenger side. 'I'd forgotten how obnoxious Jack can be. Anyway,' I beamed, 'enough of him, how are you? This is so kind of you to take me to see Kit. Are you sure it's not out of your way.'

'Well, Bristol was cancelled,' he grinned, shifting into gear, 'but it's not out of my way at all. If I wasn't doing this I'd only be sitting at home trying to write another wretched, ill-fated TV drama. I'd much rather take you up to Frampton instead.'

He smiled and I glowed with pleasure, waving to the boys as we took off down the drive.

'Is that what you do then?' I raised my voice above the roar of the engine. 'I mean, write for TV?' Oh, cunning, Lucy, cunning. Pretend you don't know.

'When I can. There's so much bloody competition, though. In the old days I used to just submit a script and they'd say, "Thanks very much, Charlie, that'll be on air next autumn."' He grimaced. 'Now there's a fair amount of um-ing and ah-ing and muttering about difficult schedules. Anyway, I'm not complaining. I tick over.'

On we drove. The noise of the engine didn't necessarily make for smooth conversation, so I contented myself with sneaking sidelong glances at his profile. Lovely straight nose. Square jaw, too. He caught my eye. Probably my slack jaw, too.

'So what's he like then, this Kit fellow?' I yelled.

'Lovely chap. Bit older than me, I suppose, but full of energy. When he bought that house it was in a terrible state. He did it up himself. It was a hell of a project, and I think he slightly lost interest at the end when his wife ran off with the plumber.' He grinned.

'Oh God, how awful! Poor guy.'

He shrugged. 'She had a very roving eye. It would have happened sooner or later, and probably better for Kit that it was sooner. Gave him some time to get on with his life.'

'And has he? Got on with his life?'

'Well, he was some time getting over it, but that's when he started selling the antiques, and it's been a huge success. But if you mean is there another woman, then no. And you?' he asked, glancing across. 'Have you got on with your life since your husband died?'

'Oh. Well, for years, no. I mean, I held down a job and looked after the children and didn't go to pieces in the supermarket or anything, but in private . . . well. It hit me pretty hard. Took a while. I'm much better now, though,' I said brightly. 'I've—you know, moved on. Had to really. I was just clinging to the wreckage, as they say.'

He nodded. 'One does. Sometimes it's all one can do.'

I narrowed my eyes in the wind, tucked back my hair. 'You know?'

'Yes, in a slightly different way. We had another child. A boy, Nicholas, a year older than my daughter Ellen. He was killed four years ago.'

'Oh God, how awful!' My hand flew to my mouth. 'How did he—no. Sorry.'

'No, no, it's fine. He was walking home from school. Just the little village one across the road from where we live. My wife was with him, saw him across. But he still got knocked over. He was four at the time.'

'Oh, how ghastly!' I breathed inadequately. 'You must have been devastated. All of you. How did you cope?'

'Cope? Well, I threw myself into my work.' He shot me a wry look. 'Grief doesn't do much for one's marriage, as I'm sure you can imagine.' He sighed. 'I bought the flat in London so we could have some space from each other. Sometimes we couldn't bear to be in the same room, let alone the same house. That worked, in a sense.' He paused. Considered. 'Of course, I haven't *coped*, not completely. I've just got by.'

'And,' I took a very deep breath, 'your wife?' There. I'd said it.

'My wife? She found solace with someone else.'

'Oh! You mean . . .'

'Yes, there are three of us in this marriage, as Princess Diana once famously said.' He smiled. 'But not another man. No, my rival is God.'

'God!'

'Yes.' He smiled. 'You see, Miranda was saved. Lucky devil. That's how she coped. She saw the light, found salvation. Came home from Waitrose one day, dumped the shopping bags down in the middle of the kitchen floor and said she'd been reborn.'

'In Waitrose?'

He shrugged. 'Apparently. Marvellous really.'

'Oh. Yes, of course.'

'But awfully difficult to live with, nonetheless.'

'What—because she's quite committed?'

'*Quite* committed. Ha!' He gave an explosive laugh. 'Just a bit. And she's frightfully keen to recruit me, too. But since I'm something of an unbeliever, we've reached a bit of an impasse.'

He stopped at some red lights and glanced across at me. 'Why have I just blurted all that out? I've only known you ten minutes.'

I felt my mouth go dry. I held his gaze . . . until we were tooted from behind. The lights had changed and we took off again.

We drove the rest of the way in silence. I was lost in heady thought. She was a religious maniac. The marriage was unhappy, they made it work for the child. Quite right, admirable actually, and yet . . . to live an empty life like that? To endure such a hollow marriage?

'Here we are,' he said suddenly.

He swung the car round some towering gateposts and we swept up a gravel drive. A beautiful, stone manor house unfurled, Gothic and splendid, with arched, mullion windows. 'Oh! It's lovely,' I breathed.

'Isn't it just,' he agreed, coming to a halt.

We got out and walked up the drive together, circling a moss-encrusted fountain. We then entered a lobby, which led us into a hall about the size of a football pitch. A vast stone fireplace took up most of one wall. Positioned on either side of it, and sitting on a beautiful old Aubusson carpet, were two supremely elegant sofas, lavishly carved, with curled backs. Two Georgian sofa tables stood behind each one, crowded with photographs.

'Oh.' I was surprised. 'It's not a shop at all. It's like a home.'

'It is a home,' agreed Charlie. 'Kit lives here, you see. It's just that everything is for sale. Ah, the man himself!'

I glanced up, as down the sweeping oak staircase came a tall, elegant man. His swept-back hair looked faintly prewar, and he had a thin, intelligent face. It broke into a radiant grin when he saw Charlie.

'Charlie! Good to see you. How've you been?'

'Really well.' Charlie pumped Kit's outstretched hand enthusiastically. 'Kit, this is Lucy Fellowes.'

'Delighted,' he beamed as we shook hands.

'I've been admiring your house,' I said shyly. 'It's beautiful. All these lovely things.' I gazed around.

'Thank you. Yes, they are lovely, although I suppose I notice them less these days. I used to be forever shifting things around and trying to get it absolutely right, but now I just sort of live in it.'

'But that's what's so wonderful. It makes it so uncommercial. And if something sells . . .?'

He shrugged. 'I just replace it. We got through five dining tables recently, and I must say, I felt like shouting, "Stop! I've nowhere to eat my bloody supper."' He grinned. 'But most of the time business is slow enough for me to replace at leisure. Go abroad and find unusual things, which is what I like to do. Come on, come and have a proper look.'

He ushered us into the drawing room. It was decorated unashamedly in the style of a French chateau. The windows were ornate with heavy silk drapes, and gesso moulded mirrors reflected back at each other from either end of the room; Louis Quinze needlepoint chairs were grouped around delicate, tripod tables. Marie Antoinette could have fanned herself by the fire without anyone batting an eyelid.

'I think it's marvellous,' I enthused. 'And you sell . . .' I hesitated. 'Well, surely not to passing trade?'

He laughed. 'No, much too pricey. No, it's mostly interior decorators from London or New York who come by appointment. But there *is* a little passing trade, which is why, my dear, I'm looking for help. Charlie did say you'd be keen to do a couple of days, maybe?'

'Oh, I'd love to!' I trilled. 'This is *far* better than I ever imagined. I mean, I just thought—well, that you had a shop,' I said hastily. 'But nothing has a price tag on?'

'No, I have an inventory, and if someone is interested in—say, that, for instance,' he pointed above the fireplace, 'I simply go to the list and look up . . .' He paused.

'Early eighteenth-century delft figurine?' I suggested.

'Exactly, or?' He pointed.

'William and Mary balloon-back chair, Hepplewhite?'

'Spot on,' he grinned. 'You clearly know your onions. Would it suit you, Lucy? A couple of days a week? So I can go on my treasure hunts?'

'Oh, yes,' I said. 'Definitely. Although . . .'

'Lucy may not be here for ever,' Charlie put in. 'I said you'd understand that.'

'Oh, absolutely! But until you sort yourself out?'

'Perfect,' I beamed. 'Trisha can fill in for a couple of days a week. The boys will love it, actually.'

'Excellent,' Kit looked relieved. 'And the dog?'

'Ah, yes,' said Charlie, 'I forgot to mention that. But Lucy loves dogs, used to look after one in London. I'm sure that'll be fine.' He smiled.

'Dog?'

'Rococo,' explained Kit. 'I'll get her. Rococo!' he called.

Instantly, an Irish wolfhound bounded in, as if from nowhere. She bounced across the room, and stuck her head straight up my crotch.

'Ooof! Lovely!' I gasped, backing away. I'd seen smaller ponies.

'A bit of a brute,' said Kit, seizing her head away and wrestling it playfully from side to side. 'But a complete softy, as you can see. So.' He straightened up, smiling. 'Sunday morning, then?'

I blinked. 'Oh! Yes. Why not?'

'We haven't mentioned money,' he said awkwardly. 'So shall I give you a ring about that, when I've had a think?'

'Fine. Oh, and I'd better ask too—is everything for sale? I mean, I don't want to find I've inadvertently sold the family silver or anything.'

He shrugged. 'Yes. It is all for sale. All these possessions, much as I love them, are actually very easy to give up. It's other things one can't afford to lose. Can't replace, either.'

He looked beyond me, abstracted for a moment. Then he came to. He smiled and shook my hand warmly as we took our leave of him.

'He's still sad,' I murmured as I got in the car beside Charlie.

'Hmm. Well, he lost his two boys for a while, too. She got full custody.'

'Oh! How awful. Didn't he see them at all?'

'Hardly. Now, they're old enough to choose. And they spend a lot of time with him. But you can't make up for those lost years.'

I thought of the son that Charlie had lost, the years that he had imagined. Just as I'd often imagined the years the boys had lost, the ones they should have had with their father.

'No,' I agreed soberly, 'you can't.'

We drove home in silence, and I was curiously grateful for the roar of the engine.

At length, we purred up the back drive to Netherby and drew up outside the barn. The front door was shut, as were the windows. It looked empty, deserted. Trisha, Jack and the boys were clearly still out fishing. Charlie turned off the engine. We didn't look at each other, but in the silence I could almost hear my heart beating.

'So. Here we are,' he said quietly. I detected a faint tremor to his voice. 'And now, I suppose, Lucy . . .' He swallowed. 'We're going to have to decide . . . what on earth we're going to do.'

'Do?' I echoed stupidly. My heart still racing, I turned to face him.

'Well, clearly something bigger than both of us is going on here, don't you think?' he said softly. 'I mean, I don't think it's entirely coincidental that we kept tripping over each other like that. In fact I'd say it was something of a sign.'

'It was extraordinary, wasn't it?' I agreed, looking bewildered.

'And the fact is,' he turned to face me fully for the first time, 'I can't stop thinking about you, Lucy.'

'Oh!' My limbs twitched convulsively.

His dark eyes were bright and sparkling, fixed intently on me. I could feel my nostrils flaring back with excitement, my heart pounding.

'I know you feel it too. I can sense it,' he urged. 'Please tell me I'm not going completely mad?'

'You're not,' I murmured, glancing nervously about. The desire to collapse into his strong, brown arms was almost overwhelming, but here? With the windows of Netherby glinting away over there in the sunlight?

'What about a cup of coffee?' I gasped nervously.

'Excellent idea.'

I leapt out of the car and scuttled up the garden path. I was aware of him following, at a more sedate pace. Christ, what's the matter with you, Lucy? I thought furiously. This is what you wanted, what you've dreamed about for months. So why are you acting the nervous ninny now? As he came through the front door, though, I knew why. I turned.

'You're married,' I said abruptly.

He looked back at me steadily. 'Quite right, there's no arguing with that.' He came towards me, stopped in front of me. 'Lucy, nothing like this has ever happened to me before, I swear it. I mean, not since I met Miranda. I've never looked elsewhere. But I just know that I'd like to spend time with you.'

'I'd like that very much too,' I breathed.

'And equally,' he went on, 'there's nothing I can do about my marital state. In time, who knows. I think you get the picture about how Miranda and I live, fairly separately, but what I'm saying is—well. This is me, warts, marriage, baggage and all. It's up to you, Lucy.'

'That's a pretty full-on way of putting it.'

'It's as honest as I can be.' He thrust his hands deep in his pockets. Frowned down at the floor. 'My only other problem is that, having said all that, the fact of the matter is that I find you so utterly, dangerously, irresistibly,' he looked up, 'desirable.'

I put the kettle I was filling down with a clatter. It seemed to me that the barn whirled. I gripped the work surface hard. Slowly, his hand crept across and covered mine.

I glanced up. Fatal. Our eyes collided and in an instant he was round that counter. In another, I was in his arms. His lips came down to meet mine, urgently, desperately—and then his hands were in my hair and then all over my back, his lips pressed hard against mine. I felt weak. Not weak enough not to respond enthusiastically though. Kissing him madly, I felt his body respond, hard against mine, pressing into me. I shut my eyes, letting desire wash over me, as a familiar voice said, 'God, it must be over a foot long!'

My eyes snapped open. Through the window, I saw Ben, coming up the path, rod in hand, holding up a fish for Jack to inspect.

'Probably more like nine inches,' Jack said, 'but anglers always lie about length.'

'Shit!' I squeaked. We flew apart like deflecting magnets. Frantically, I smoothed down my hair and wiped my mouth as Jack and the boys came barging through the door.

'Oh, hi, boys!' I trilled.

Ben stared. 'You're all red in the face.'

'Have you been running?' asked Max.

'Yes, I have. For the phone. I was upstairs. N-no, downstairs! Anyway, darlings, have you had a good day?'

I crouched down to Max, hiding my confusion in his little face. I didn't want to meet Jack's eye. I couldn't look at Charlie either.

'We caught two really big ones, but we put them back,' said Max. 'Ben was allowed to keep that one, and I caught this wiv a net.'

He took his hand from behind his back, and presented me proudly with a jam jar. A huge toad stared back at me, bug-eyed with terror.

'Lovely, darling,' I breathed. I glanced up, finally. 'Thank you, Jack.'

'Pleasure,' he drawled. 'They're great boys. A credit to you.' He deliberately sounded surprised, as if 'amazingly' somehow hung, unspoken, in the air. As if I was already a fallen woman. I straightened up, flushing.

'I really must be away,' smiled Charlie, looking really remarkably composed. 'Good to see you again, Jack. And you too, boys.'

'I'll come out with you,' I muttered, scuttling after him to his car.

'When will I see you again?' I asked, a trifle desperately perhaps.

'I'll ring you,' he promised. 'But maybe,' he tilted his head back towards the house, 'in London.' He took my hands and I held on tight. 'There are too many distractions here, but in London . . .'

'Ooh, yes!' I said greedily. Glorious, glorious London, where I could breathe again—and of course, where his flat was.

'Yes, and I could tell everyone I was going to see Maisie and Lucas, my parents,' I said excitedly. 'Come up for a night, even.'

It seemed to me that all the birds in the trees, the squirrels on the branches, paused, poleaxed by my brazenness.

He smiled gently. 'Great. I'll ring you,' he promised again, as he got into his car.

I could feel myself flushing. A night? You fool! Why don't you just calm down, not act like a girl who hasn't been kissed for four years.

I watched him go, hating the moment when I'd have to face Jack. I prolonged it, standing in the front garden. As I began deadheading the roses, something caught my eye. A scurrying figure was tottering precariously across the bridge. It was Rose, and for once I was glad to see her. I waved, and went to greet her at the garden gate.

'Lucy! Oh, I *am* glad I've caught you, I wasn't sure if you'd be in,' she panted, eyes shining. 'Tell me, have you and the boys had lunch yet?'

'No, not yet. Been, er, job hunting,' I added guiltily.

'Well, do please come up and have a bite with us. I've got such exciting news.' She beamed. 'Hector,' she paused importantly, 'and Sophia Lennox-Fox are—what do you young people call it now—an item!'

I frowned. 'Really?'

'Yes!' She clasped her hands. 'Apparently he *did* spend time with her at the party, and then he slipped away on Sunday morning and followed her up to London. He's *completely* smitten, the dear, *dear* boy!'

'Really? Golly. Well, that's wonderful. Who told you all this?'

'He told Pinkie, on the telephone. We'll all have a glass of champagne to toast the happy couple.'

'Oh, Rose,' I cautioned. 'Bit soon, wouldn't you say?'

'Well, let me tell you, Lucy, this is *it*, I can feel it in my bones. I know that boy like the back of my hand, and I knew full well that one day he'd just shut his eyes and leap. Impulsively. So, please, *do* come up.'

I smiled. 'I'd love to. Boys!' I yelled back over my shoulder. Ben stuck his head round the door. 'Darling, wash the river off your hands and faces please, we're going up to lunch with Granny.'

'Oh, OK.' He popped back in, then his head came out again. 'We're just gutting this fish. We'll come up with Jack, in a minute, OK?'

'Fine, darling,' I said coolly.

Rose linked my arm. 'So, now, tell me what you think,' she gushed on excitedly. 'Obviously the reception will be at her parents' house, which is desperately ugly—we'll have to positively drip it with flowers—but I did wonder . . . d'you think we could host a dance here as well? Or d'you think that would be treading on their toes?'

'Well, no, as long as that's what Hector and Sophia want.'

'Oh, my dear, I feel I could faint away with happiness!'

'I'm glad,' I smiled, meaning it. Finally one of her children had come up trumps for her.

As we strolled across the rolling parkland, we were met by Lavinia, running down the terrace steps.

'Isn't it exciting!' she shrieked. 'Pinkie told me!'

'Oh, my darling, you are so sweet to take it like this,' said Rose, clutching her arm anxiously. 'I rather thought—'

'Not at all, Mummy, I'm thrilled to bits. A wedding! Think of all the parties there'll be!'

Think of all the men to trawl, she meant. Behind us, out of the corner of my eye, I could see Jack and the boys coming. I stuck to Lavinia like glue and followed her up the terrace steps and round the table, which, yet again, had been laid outside for lunch. Archie was grinning broadly as he sat down beside me.

'Well, what a to-do! Your ma-in-law is in a perfect twitter, eh?'

I grinned. 'It's what she's been waiting for. This is her big moment.'

Ben and Max appeared and scuttled in between me and Pinkie, which left Jack—oh God—opposite.

'So,' he eased himself in, 'I gather old Hector's spilled some girlie beans. Bad move. But then he's new to this game. And frankly I'm surprised. I had an idea the object of his affections was someone entirely different, that's what a little bird told me, but never mind.' He glanced around the table. 'I don't suppose there's any danger of you lot letting him conduct this love affair in private, is there?' He grinned and reached for a bread roll. 'All love affairs need room to breathe, you know, to flourish. Especially sexy new, illicit ones, eh, Lucy?' He winked. I flushed angrily. 'Give the boy a break, that's what I say!'

'Of course we'll give him a break,' said Rose, bustling through the French windows, still smiling, and carrying a bowl of Caesar salad. 'We'll give him whatever he wants, won't we, darling? If he needs space, he can have the dower house.' She beamed at her husband.

Archie blinked. 'Steady on, old girl. And I do think, my love, that Jack has a point. Give the lad five minutes' peace, eh? Don't interrogate him the moment he walks through the door. And don't scare the poor girl away, either. No waggling *Brides* magazine under her nose or mentioning family tiaras.' He got up as the telephone rang.

'Mummy, I meant to say,' Lavinia leaned across the table, 'Mimsy Compton-Burrell has just done the most *delicious* flowers for the church. If we wanted to keep it simple and un-Londony, then we couldn't do better than her. She does the most heavenly things with cow parsley.'

'I agree. I must talk to Angela Lennox-Fox. Not to—you know, foist our opinions on her or anything, because she is after all, in pole position, but just, you know, to *guide* her. She has got the most frightful taste.'

'Which at least means you won't clash at the wedding, Rose,' Jack pointed out naughtily. 'Since you'll be in the most tasteful ensemble imaginable.'

'Oh, heavens, no, we won't clash! She'll be in some ghastly fuchsia pink affair, much too short, whereas *I'll* be in—'

'Lilac?' suggested Jack, head on one side, index finger pointing camply to the corner of his mouth. 'Lilac's very à la mode this year.'

'P-oss-ibly,' nodded Rose, unaware she was being wound up, 'or maybe pale lemon. I saw a divine lemon suit in Peter Jones recently.'

'Oooh, lemon!' Jack shut his eyes ecstatically. 'Heaven!'

'Yes, it was heaven, actually,' Rose went on excitedly. 'And—Archie! Good Lord. Whatever's the matter?'

Archie had appeared through the French windows. His normally ruddy face was pale and his lips, thin and compressed.

'That was Hector,' he announced. 'Ringing from London.'

'Oh!' Rose got up happily. 'Is the dear boy coming back soon?'

'Sit down, Rose,' he snapped. 'No, he rang about the wedding.'

'Oh! So there *is* going to be a wedding!'

'Oh, yes, there's going to be a wedding. But he's not marrying Sophia Lennox-Fox at all. He's marrying Rozanna Carling,' he said grimly.

The blood left Rose's face. 'Rozanna? You mean Lucy's friend?'

'Exactly.'

'Oh!' Rose's hand flew to her mouth. 'So why did Pinkie say . . .' She turned in a daze to her daughter. 'Pinkie, why did you tell us . . .?'

'Because that's what *he* said,' squeaked Pinkie indignantly, colouring up. 'He said Sophia Lennox-Fox!'

'What, with no prompting?' asked Jack.

'Well,' she blustered, 'I suppose I did rather, you know, press him. But not much. When he said he was with someone, I just sort of teased him. "Ooh, Hector," I said, "it's Sophia, isn't it?" And finally he just sighed and said, "Oh God, Pinkie, whatever you want to think."' She went a bit redder. 'I didn't know he was palming me off, did I?'

'Well. Rozanna!' Rose's face was still pale but her eyes were suffused with a curious brightness. 'I thought she was delightful, actually. I mean—her father's Lord Belfont, isn't he?' You could see the frantic thought processes at work as she turned to Archie. 'And she was awfully pretty, don't you think?' She swung round in her chair to face me. 'She's a friend of yours, isn't she, Lucy? You brought her down here.'

I swallowed, feeling faintly sick and wishing I were another form of life. An earthworm would be ideal. 'Um, yes,' I muttered eventually.

'And, Lavinia, you liked her, didn't you, darling?'

'I thought she was a complete poppet,' gushed Lavinia, clearly not to be done out of her party. 'So elegant and sophisticated.'

The colour was rapidly returning to Rose's cheeks as she warmed to her theme. 'And, Lavinia, did you see the way she knew everyone? Obviously *extremely* well connected, and—*oh*!'

We all jumped as Archie slammed his fist down hard on the table. 'There isn't going to be a wedding to Rozanna Carling!'

'B-but, Archie. I thought you liked her! I thought you knew her, you introduced me to her. Why on earth—'

'Because she is . . . a tart.' He enunciated it, through clenched teeth.

'What's a tart?' piped up Ben.

'You know, like Pinkie,' offered Max helpfully.

'Max!' I swung round, appalled.

'But you said so, Mum. To Teresa, I heard you.'

'No, no,' I blustered, 'not *this* Pinkie, darling.' Christ, how many Pinkies could there be? 'Pinkie Jameson—the one I was at school with.'

'Oh, *that* Pinkie,' muttered Jack drily. I glared at him and avoided Pinkie's eye, flushing madly.

'But—but surely you don't mean,' Rose was still struggling to get to grips with this preposterous proposition. 'You surely don't mean a *proper* one—well, like a call girl?'

'That's exactly what I do mean, Rose,' said Archie. 'Rozanna Carling is a high-class courtesan. Very expensive, very select, but a courtesan, nonetheless. A prostitute.' There was a silence.

'How do you know?' Rose gasped, at length.

Archie ground his teeth savagely. 'One . . . just . . . does,' he hissed.

Although she wasn't beside me, I felt Rose stiffen.

'So there will be no wedding,' Archie went on quietly. 'And if there is, if Hector persists in seeing this woman, and going through with this ridiculous charade, he'll get nothing from me. Not this house, this land, nothing. He forfeits everything.'

With that he marched back into the house, slamming the French windows behind him. There was a shocked silence.

Rose put a trembling hand to her bosom, her face white. 'Oh God, he means it,' she whispered. 'Oh, my poor Hector. He'll turn Hector out on the streets. It'll be the end of him. Oh dear God, that'll be two of my sons gone. First Ned, and now Hector. Oh, where will it all end!'

At this point she was ambushed by tears. Lavinia and Pinkie instantly got up and moved smartly into action like a pincer movement, one at each shoulder, hugging and squeezing hard. This only served to make her sob louder. My boys were transfixed and it occurred to me to wonder if they'd seen enough street theatre for one day.

'Ben, Max, help Joan to clear the table, please,' I asked them. Neither child moved, damned if they were going to miss a moment.

'I'll go and talk to him,' Lavinia announced importantly, straightening up from her mother's shoulder. 'I'll go and see him, make him see reason. Tell him he'll be ruining the family name.'

'Yes.' Rose brightened perceptibly. Looked up with a sniff. 'Yes, darling, do that. Stress the family name. Good idea.'

'D'you think you're the right person, Lavinia?' enquired Jack. 'Only, with all due respect, you and Hector have never exactly seen eye to eye.'

'You're absolutely right, Jack,' answered Rose. 'She's not the right person to go. *You* go. He'll listen to you. And, Lucy,' Rose turned to me, 'you go with him.'

'Me?'

'Yes. Both of you go, and *talk* to him, please. Make him see reason.'

I swallowed nervously. 'You know, Rose, I can't help thinking this may not be the best course of action. I just wonder if perhaps the thing to do would be to leave well alone for the moment, and let the affair run its course. Then perhaps it'll fizzle out naturally.'

'Hear, hear,' agreed Jack.

'No!' Rose got to her feet, eyes blazing. 'No, I insist you go and talk to him. I know Hector, and given half a chance he'll get hitched on some Jamaican beach, barefoot with flowers in his hair, with this—this two-bit *whore*,' she screeched, 'standing beside him!' At this truly terrifying scenario she caught her breath, sat down abruptly, and then suddenly slumped forward, headfirst into her Caesar salad.

There was a horrified silence.

'Is she dead?' Ben whispered.

'No, no, darling,' Lavinia swooped to lift her mother's head, wiping lettuce off her cheek. 'No, not dead. Angina. She gets it occasionally. Pills, Pinkie, quick!' she snapped. 'In her cardigan pocket.'

Pinkie hastily found them and wrestled with the lid.

We watched as the two sisters helped their mother sit up at the table, simultaneously popping pills in her mouth. Rose seemed to know the ropes and gulped obediently at the glass of water.

'Better?' barked Lavinia.

'Much, darling. Thank you,' Rose muttered bleakly. Some colour did indeed appear to be returning to her cheeks.

'Come on, then,' ordered Lavinia, 'upstairs to beddy-byes for a little rest.' Adopting a tone normally reserved for the mentally subnormal, she hauled her mother to her feet. 'Upsy-daisy!' Jack got to his feet too, but Lavinia shook her head firmly. 'No, Jack, we're fine. I'll tell you what you could do though. Ask David to pop over.'

'Right.' Jack got to his feet and made to go in, to ring David Mortimer, Archie's oldest friend and the family doctor.

'Yes, get David,' Rose muttered as she was manoeuvred off. Suddenly her head swung round like a machine gun. 'And you'll go?' She gazed at us both. 'To see Hector?'

'Yes, we'll go,' agreed Jack, his foot inside the French windows.

'Tomorrow?' she pleaded. 'Please say you'll go tomorrow, Jack?'

'We'll go tomorrow,' he soothed.

When they were out of earshot, I stood up. 'We will *not* go tomorrow, Jack. We'll think about it, and go when we choose! God, why should we ruin Hector and Rozanna's fun the second it starts, because you are too wet to say no to her?'

'Right, fine.' Jack held up his hands. 'Though I'd like to help Hector. I'd like to make sure a wedge isn't driven between him and his family. He is, after all, my cousin, and Rose is my aunt and I actually feel rather sorry for her, right now. You see, however much you deride this family, Lucy, we seem to be affiliated to them. Let me know when you do feel the time is right. No pressure.'

He put his hands in his pockets and walked calmly into the house.

'Ooooh . . . bloody man!' I seethed after him. I unballed my clenched fist and stuck it out to Max. 'Come on. We're going home.'

And with that we set off down the terrace steps.

'Why are you so cross?' panted Ben, trotting to catch up with me.

'Because Jack thinks he's right all the time, that's why.'

Max and Ben looked at each other. 'Stre-ssy,' murmured Ben.

Yes, stressy. Principally because I had a nasty feeling he *might* be right, damn him. I watched the boys run on. He'd shamed me with his talk of duty and family, and who in God's name would want their son to marry a call girl? What the hell was Rozanna up to? I wondered. Clearly something had happened when she'd stayed the night at Netherby. I'd give her a ring. Find out what the devil was going on. I strode determinedly up the path to the barn.

As I flung open the front door with a flourish, a chaotic scene met my eyes. The fish had obviously been gutted by the boys on the kitchen floor in a bowl of water. There were bloody knives and pools of rank water everywhere.

'Aaaarrgh! *Bloo*dy man!' I yelled. 'Clean this place up *now*, boys.'

At that moment the telephone rang. I snatched it up with irritable emphasis. 'What!' I shrieked furiously.

'Oh! Um, Lucy?' It was Charlie.

My heart leapt right out of my mouth. All around the room, in fact. 'Charlie.'

'Gosh, Lucy. Didn't sound like you.'

'No! No, no, sorry, I was . . .' I put a hand to my forehead. Shut my eyes. 'Oh, well, never mind. How are you?'

'Fine. Really fine. I feel . . . well, I just feel rejuvenated, Lucy. Can't stop thinking about you.'

'Oh!' I clutched the receiver with two hands. 'Yes, me too.'

'And, Lucy,' he lowered his voice, 'guess what? I suddenly have the most amazing excuse to go to London tomorrow. The BBC have just rung to say they'd like to talk to me about a new series. I'd be busy for much of the morning, but I'd be free after that. Is there *any* chance of you getting away? I'm desperate to see you.'

My knees buckled and I sat down hard on a convenient sofa.

'Not impossible,' I croaked. 'In fact, really rather possible.' My head whirled. 'Oh, Charlie, I'm desperate to see you, too!' I whispered.

'Oh, Lucy, that's brilliant. Listen, I should be at the flat from about twelve onwards. I have to be back here by teatime, but we should have a couple of hours . . . OK?'

I shut my eyes and tried not to think of all the things that could happen in a couple of hours. 'OK,' I murmured.

'I must go, my love. I'll see you tomorrow then, my darling. Oh, and by the way—twenty-two Langton Villas!' The phone went dead and I threw myself headlong onto the sofa, pressing my mouth ardently to a kilim cushion. 'Twenty-two Langton Villas, twenty-two Langton Villas,' I whispered passionately. 'Oh, shit! Tomorrow!'

I dialled Netherby and, luckily, Jack answered.

'Um, listen, Jack,' I ran an uncertain hand through my hair. 'Er, I was thinking. You know, you're probably absolutely right about wanting to go up to London tomorrow. To see Hector. I mean—we are a family, aren't we? Terribly important to stick together, don't you think?'

'Oh? You've changed your tune.'

'I know but—well. You know. I've had time to think.'

'What, two minutes? I've just walked in.'

'Yes.' I ground my teeth and shut my eyes. 'That was literally all it took, Jack, to see that you were absolutely right. As usual. I'm sure Trisha won't mind having the boys, so I'll pick you up at the house at nine o'clock tomorrow, OK?'

'Whatever you say, Lucy,' he said with weary indifference.

The following morning Trisha was ostensibly waiting for the boys at the back of the house when—late, naturally—I roared up the drive to Netherby, although what she was actually doing, I noticed, was flirting outrageously with Jack. He was balancing on the wall round the fountain, arms outstretched, and she was shrieking with laughter, goading him on, rushing up to whisper something in his ear as he jumped off.

'Stinks in here,' muttered Ben as Jack opened the passenger door for him. 'And watch your p's and q's, Jack. She's really hyper this morning.'

'I am not hyper, Ben,' I hissed, running round to help Max out. 'It's just you're making me late!'

'There's no rush,' said Jack easily, lowering himself into the vacated front seat. 'I mean, they don't even know we're coming, do they? Blimey, Ben, you're right, there is a terrible pong in this car. What is it?'

'It's Chanel Number 19, actually,' I snapped, getting back in. Damn, had I overdone it? 'And the point is, Jack,' I said, letting out the hand-brake and reversing at speed, 'I've got other things to do in London today besides seeing Hector and Rozanna, and I don't want to be late, OK?'

I ran a harassed hand through my hair and turned back to wave at the boys. As I did, I saw Trisha blow Jack a kiss.

'What things? And why are you all made up?' He peered at me.

I flushed and declined to answer.

'Ah right,' he nodded, 'don't tell me. Plan A is for you to go in all hot and vampy and steal Hector right from under Rozanna's nose, is that it?'

'I do not look hot and vampy!' I tugged desperately at my, admittedly, rather short skirt.

'Nothing wrong with hot and vampy,' he mused, eyeing my legs. 'Depends what it's all in aid of. Or who. What other things?'

'Oh. I'm, um, going to see Maisie and Lucas.' I felt my colour rise.

He regarded me quizzically. 'Right. I, too,' he gave a secret smile and folded his arms, 'have things to do this afternoon.'

'What?' I asked lightly.

'Oh, this and that,' he winked. 'Concluding unfinished business.'

'Ah. I see.' I smiled knowingly. 'You don't change, do you, Jack? Trisha know about this unfinished business?'

He frowned in mock alarm. 'Why on earth would Trisha want to know? Now, Lucy, please don't quiz me any more. I'm not used to get-ting up at this unearthly hour. I'm a poet, not a Eurobond dealer. I need my shuteye.'

He leaned back on the headrest with an equable smile, and shut his eyes. I glanced across, envying him his totally relaxed disposition. I wondered, nervously, if I wasn't a bit old for all this. I sighed and turned to Classic FM for comfort while I drove.

Later, as I wove off the main A40 into London, through the streets of Fulham, and into the narrow roads I knew so well, I really did relax. I turned into the bustling King's Road, crowded as ever, kicking with vitality, and felt a rush of love for the place. Pulling up in my old road, flicking my just-about-valid parking permit into the window, I felt over-whelmingly nostalgic. I swallowed hard and willed myself to buck up.

'Jack—wake up! Listen, we're here. What are we going to say?'

'Hmmm?' Jack opened his eyes. He yawned and stretched. 'Oh, I'd say we pretty much play it by ear, wouldn't you? We can't drag him

79

home by the scruff of his neck. He's thirty-six, for goodness' sake.'

I got out of the car and followed Jack nervously up the steps. I no longer had a key so we had to press the buzzer. As we stood on the step, Jack smiled at me.

'How does it feel to be back?' he asked gently.

I shrugged nonchalantly. Pulled a face. 'OK. A bit weird, actually,' I lied. It felt safe. Like home.

'Oh!' Rozanna squawked through the intercom after we'd announced ourselves. 'It's you. Well, you'd better come in.'

We pushed the heavy black door and then walked down the long corridor. Rozanna was standing at the entrance to her flat, arms folded in her blue silk dressing gown. She smiled ruefully.

'Well, I suppose we should have expected this. Hey, Hec,' she threw over her shoulder. 'It's the Seventh Cavalry. They've come to rescue you.'

'Idiot,' I said, kissing her as she let us in. 'We're not rescuing anyone. Just came to see you, that's all.'

Hector, who had been reading in the window seat, stood up indignantly. 'Bloody cheek. She sent you up here, didn't she? Well, I'm not going back, you know.' He blinked hard, fists clenched by his sides.

'We just wanted to talk to you, that's all,' I soothed. 'See—'

'How the land lies,' interrupted Rozanna. 'Well, get on with it, then.'

'You can tell her that I love Rozanna, and I'm not giving her up. I'm going to marry her, and that's the end of it, OK?' Hector's face was flushed with emotion.

'Good for you, old boy,' said Jack quietly. 'That's all we need to know. No doubt about your feelings, we'll report back immediately. Rozanna?' He turned quickly, smiling, but regarding her carefully. 'Do you have anything to report?'

She wrapped her blue robe around her with a smile. 'You think Hector is the innocent here, don't you? And that dear old Rozanna, well, I mean, she's knocked about a bit, hasn't she? She's a tart. How can she possibly have feelings about anyone?' There was a silence as she went to stand beside Hector. 'Except that, actually, Jack, despite all those men, I've never met a guy like Hector. One I'd like to keep. But, then,' she turned fondly to Hector, 'like I said, I never met one like this before.' Their eyes seemed to collide. 'A decent, kind, straightforward man, who isn't afraid of his emotions, who tells me what he's thinking the moment he thinks it. A good person.' She turned back. 'Prior to that, I'd only ever met men who couldn't get over themselves. Men like Archie.'

I blanched. Glanced quickly at Hector. Rozanna smiled wryly.

'Oh, it's OK, he knows. In fact, he knows everything about me now.'

Hector put his arm protectively round her. 'But that's all going to stop now. It's all going to change, isn't it, Rosie?' He looked down at her.

I caught my breath. It seemed so unfair to say it, but—

'Rozanna, his family. Hector's family. They're obviously very upset.'

'Of course,' she agreed, 'and so would I be if I were them. And that's why I've told Hector to ask me in a year's time. I've told him to forget it for at least as long as that. To ask me then.'

'Seems sensible,' nodded Jack.

'But, actually,' broke in Hector quietly, 'I'm not waiting a year, whatever she thinks. I'm going to ask her every day. Every morning when I wake up with her, watch her blue eyes open. And one fine day, she's going to say yes.'

There was a silence. Jack and I regarded them, standing there before us. Hector seemed to have grown in stature overnight, tall and protective, while Rozanna looked smaller, softer.

Jack cleared his throat. 'Well, Hector,' he strode forward and stuck out his hand. 'All I can say is good on you, mate. More power to your elbow!' He pumped his hand enthusiastically.

I hugged Rozanna. 'Congratulations,' I whispered. 'Lucky you.'

After that, it seemed only natural to have breakfast with them, and listen, in slack-jawed wonder, as Hector told us exactly what his father could do with his Oxfordshire pile and that he intended to make his own way, and that for the first time in his life, he was going to get a job.

An hour or so later, after we'd finally said our goodbyes, we headed off down the corridor and I shook my head in disbelief.

'Startling enough for you?' murmured Jack as he opened the heavy front door for me.

'Totally,' I sighed. 'It is rather romantic, isn't it?'

'Oh, I agree. But not without its problems.' We stood thoughtfully for a moment, side by side on the chequered steps.

'So . . . what do we do now?' I asked.

'What can we do but report back accordingly?'

'Rose will kill us,' I said.

'Well, we'll see.' He glanced at his watch. 'Coffee? Or even—God, no, wine. It's nearly twelve o'clock.'

I gazed at him in horror. 'It can't be. I said I'd *be* somewhere at twelve!'

He frowned. 'Only Maisie and Lucas's, surely?'

'Yes,' I gulped, hastening down the steps. 'Yes, they'll understand.'

I hovered on the pavement, wishing he'd go. I had a parking place, and Charlie was only round the corner. I didn't want to have to go through the rigmarole of pretending to drive off to my parents.

'If you're going via the King's Road, I'll cadge a lift,' he said.

I stared. 'No. No, I'm not going via the King's Road.'

'Ah. Tower of London, perhaps? The scenic route?'

'Of course not,' I blustered. 'It's just—well, I thought I'd pop in on Teresa. For a moment. Since I'm here. See you later, Jack.'

'Ah. Sorry, my mistake, I thought you were late. I'll be at 69 Upper Cheyne Street, Luce, when you're ready.'

I waited, just to make sure Jack had gone. Then I started running, very fast. Down to the end of my road I scampered, then left, along a bit, and up the second turning on the right. Oh, I knew precisely where Langton Villas was, had trudged up and down it many a time, with that wretched dog, all hot and bothered just as—well, I was pretty hot and bothered now, wasn't I? I slowed down abruptly. Good grief, Lucy, so what if you're a few minutes late? D'you really want to appear on his doorstep in a complete lather? And apart from anything else, I thought, I'd break my ankle in these ridiculous, kitten-heeled mules if I wasn't careful.

I stopped in front of number 22, then teetered up the mountain of stone steps, my heart hammering. I scanned the doorbells nervously. Mr Charles Fletcher was on the ground floor, apparently. I pressed the bell and prepared my most dazzling smile. As the door opened and he appeared, I bestowed it on him, and happily, got an even more dazzling one in return. It came streaming off his face, and, for a moment, I just bathed. He looked heavenly, naturally, in slightly faded black jeans and a white T-shirt, with an open, checked flannel shirt over the top.

'Hi.'

'Hi.'

With these brief words did we salute each other. He, too, gazed appreciatively. 'Lucy, you know, you really are . . . so very lovely.'

I gulped, as tears unaccountably welled up inside. It had been so long, you see, since anyone had said anything like that to me. I must hold myself in check, I thought desperately, as I went inside. I must be cool and dignified. Except that surely, I thought, gazing up at him now, rather as a cat contemplates a saucer of cream, surely a kiss of some sort was more or less due? After all, I'd been here nearly a whole minute.

'Would you like something to eat?' he asked tentatively.

'Oh!' I was momentarily nonplussed. 'You mean, out?' I mean full marks for chivalry and all that, but I couldn't help feeling that Out was a retrograde step. Away from whatever sumptuous, king-sized delights lay behind one of those white panelled doors.

'No, no, I just meant here, in the kitchen.' He led the way. 'I threw a few things together earlier, just a bit of salad and cheese . . .'

'Oh! Lovely. Yes, good idea.'

Golly, we had time for a bit of bread and cheese, surely, here, in his flat. I followed him into the kitchen, but we didn't stop, we bowled right on through, and out into the garden. French windows issued onto a tiny paved area, surrounded by raised beds full of leafy green foliage, and a wrought-iron table laid for lunch.

'Oh, how lovely!' I exclaimed.

Yes, and how extremely civilised, I decided as he pulled my chair out for me. He wasn't rushing me, wasn't treating me like some two-bit floozy he'd picked up at a party, he was doing this properly. I felt a rush of warmth for him. As I sat down, I smiled up, and simultaneously felt my skirt ride up to somewhere around my pants. Oh God, why had I worn it? It must look like such a come-on, as if I was desperate.

'Remember how desperate you were for it in that shop?' He grinned, sitting down opposite me.

My jaw dropped, and I was about to protest when suddenly I realised he was nodding towards the cheese, an oozing, evil-looking affair with a colossal whiff.

'Oh, yes!' I tinkled a merry laugh. 'Of course. Espouse, isn't it?'

'No, no, Epoisses,' he said, helping me to a great soggy dollop.

'Ah. Right.' I flushed, realising that espouse meant something entirely different, something I hadn't meant to mention at all. The more I thought about it, though, or her, or spouses in general, the more compulsive it became.

'And, and how, how is your . . . your daughter?' I finished.

'Ellen? She's fine, thanks. Came up with me this morning, actually. She's staying with her cousins for a couple of days over in Chiswick. They're all great mates, and with Ellen being an only, it's quite fun for her. And your boys?'

'They're fine too,' I said shortly, and strove to change the subject.

'Mmm . . .' I shut my eyes and popped a dollop of cheese in my mouth, thinking it really couldn't be that bad. It was much worse. Oh God, it was putrid. I lunged for my glass, took a big gulp, and miraculously, the cheese went down with it.

He grinned. 'Quite cheeky, isn't it? Have some salad.'

'Thanks.'

I helped myself to a huge mound of greenery to cover its cheekiness and chomped away like a happy rabbit to prove how delicious it was, when—oh Christ. Vinegar. In the dressing! The only other one of my all-time greatest hates . . . I put my fork down miserably. Oh hell. I looked up and realised that he was watching me.

'You can't eat,' he breathed, really rather excitedly.

'N-no!' I admitted, spotting a convenient loophole. 'Can't even swallow.'

He pushed his plate away. 'I'm not sure I can, either.' Then, 'Sod it,' he declared impulsively. 'It's no good,' he whispered, in tones I'd previously only ever encountered in pulp fiction, 'I can't resist you any longer, Lucy.'

In an instant he was on his feet, and I was in his arms. His lips met mine, our eyes shut, and we slipped into an endless kiss. Oh my, it was passionate. His hands explored me and I felt the excitement surge through me like a torrent, as if with a deafening crack of melting ice, the spring floods had burst down through the parched old valleys, taking with them everything in their path.

Welded together by various vital organs, we started to inch our way inside, moaning with excitement. Movement was difficult though, but finally we were there, and inching slowly through the kitchen. His hands slipped quickly up my shirt as we made for what I presumed was the bedroom in this ground-floor flat, except that the kisses were getting more and more intense and we seemed in danger of never actually leaving the kitchen. In fact, we seemed to be heading irrevocably for the kitchen table. Keen to be more comfortably installed, I led him decisively by the lips, and the shirt collar, down the passage.

At the first door we came to, I felt behind me, turned a handle, and leaned determinedly against it. It flew open and we landed in the cupboard under the stairs.

'Oh God, sorry!' I gasped from beneath him.

'Fine, no, it's fine,' he panted back, wrestling with my shirt.

What, fine as in—This Will Do? I wasn't convinced myself, but as I spat out a bit of feather duster and manoeuvred a vacuum cleaner nozzle out of my back, I reasoned that, actually, it was quite spacious, and dark enough to hide any cellulite or stretch marks. He was all over me now, anyway, convinced I'd found the perfect spot, and d'you know, as pleasure overtook me, I was beginning to think I had, too, when there came a sudden, shrill ringing in my ears. We froze, mid-caress.

'What was that?' I gasped inanely, knowing full well.

'The doorbell,' he panted back.

We stared at each other, horrified, in the gloom.

Then it came again. A shrill, persistent summons, accompanied, this time, by a sharp rap on the glass pane at the top of the door.

'Bloody hell,' muttered Charlie. Then, 'Hang on, I'll have a peek.'

Charlie stuck his head round the cupboard door and peered down the hallway. 'It's my sister. What the hell's she doing here?'

I stared. How the dickens would I know.

'It's probably nothing, but I'll have to go and see. Then I'll get rid of her. Wait here and I'll be back in a tick.'

He quickly did up some shirt buttons and smoothed his hair down.

'Is there a light?' I squeaked, as he made to shut the door behind him.

'Oh, yes. Here.' He flicked it on, and left me in the 100-watt glare of what transpired to be a very dingy, unattractive cupboard. Crouched there, in among the Hoover and the squeegee mop, horror and shame rose within me. God, what was I *doing* here? Shirt up around my armpits, like some cheap floozy? And suppose that had been his wife? How awful would that little scenario have been?

Suddenly I realised I could hear voices, more than two, and that they were coming this way. I shrank back in horror and quickly flicked the light off. The voices seemed to be fading again now, and I waited, rigid with fear, until the door opened softly.

'She's gone,' Charlie whispered, 'but Ellen's not very well, so Helen brought her back here. I've settled her in front of a video in the sitting room, but, my darling, I really don't think we can—well, prostrate ourselves, with an eight-year-old girl in attendance.'

'Of course we can't,' I said, horrified. 'No, no, I must leave at once! Do I have to go past the sitting-room door? On the way out?' I said, frantically tucking in my shirt.

'You do, but it's shut. She won't see you. Come.' He made to lead me by the hand, then turned and kissed me very thoroughly on the mouth. 'But, Lucy,' he whispered urgently, 'we have unfinished business here, my darling. I'll see you very, very soon.'

I nodded, gulped. Unfinished business. The very words Jack had used to describe his liaison just south of here. So I'd joined the gang, eh? No time to consider the implications of that. Right now I had to concentrate on tiptoeing down that hallway, shoes in hand.

As I turned to say goodbye on the steps, the sitting-room door opened.

'Dad, where's the remote control? I can't—oh!' She stopped. Saw me, and stared. A small, blonde girl with little round glasses, wearing jeans and a T-shirt. She blinked at me, then turned to her father.

'Ah! Ellen, darling, this—this is Laura. Laura works with me at the BBC. She's just popped round to collect some papers.'

'Hello!' I quaked cheerily.

'Why haven't you got your shoes on?'

'Oh! Blisters. It's tearing all over those—those wretched fields,' I gabbled nervously.

'Fields?' She frowned. 'What—at the BBC?'

'Oh, well, I do—you know, out-of-studio productions. On location. Animal shows, that kind of thing.'

'Oh, cool. What, like *Pet Rescue*?'

'Mmm. Sort of.'

'I love that programme. There was a really, *really* lovely hamster on the other day, with only one leg, that *badly* needed a home, but Mum said no. Do they mostly end up with good homes, though?'

'We . . . try to place them as best we can,' I croaked. 'You know, depending on suitability.' I nodded.

She nodded too. 'Ah, right. So—you wouldn't let a pony go to someone who lived in London, for instance?'

'No-o,' I agreed, swallowing. Chatty little boffin-like child, this.

'Come on now, Ellen,' broke in her father, and not before time in my view, 'back to the sofa, before you catch your death.'

When she'd disappeared and the door had closed behind her, I leaned, weakly, against the door frame and slipped on my shoes.

Charlie took my face in his hands. 'I'll ring you, my precious,' he whispered. '*A bientôt.*'

It's fair to say I wasn't in the best of humours a little while later. I drove down a quiet, leafy backstreet just off Cheyne Walk, gazing up at a row of tiny mews houses and stopping outside the requisite one, a rather dear little pale blue affair. At the top of some smart, well-scrubbed steps, a gleaming white front door with a large, shiny brass knocker rose up; on either side of the door, two square, Versailles planters frothed over with a delightful abundance of ivy and petunias, and in the window boxes, lacy lobelia blossomed. I stared up in grudging admiration at this exquisite doll's house, small, but on three floors. It was the sort of house I would cheerfully have killed for.

All the same, I thought, glancing back enviously as I purred past, trying to find a parking space, it was typical of Jack to have a floozy in such an exclusive location. For all his irritating, libertine ways, the man had some style, even if I couldn't park in this wretched, stylish road—

'*Arrggh!*' I finally gave up and screeched backwards until I was bang outside the house again. I sounded the horn impatiently.

Two seconds later, an upstairs sash window flew up. A pretty, auburn-haired girl stuck her head out. ''Ello?' she cooed.

'Oh, hello, is Jack there, by any chance?' I yelled.

'Jacques? Yes, he here, hang on. Ja-acques!' she called in a heavy French accent. She popped back in.

A moment later she was back at the window with 'Jacques'.

'Oh, hi!' He looked surprised. 'You're early.'

'Something came up,' I said coolly. 'Not too inconvenient, I hope.'

'No, no, it's fine. We'd pretty much finished here, hadn't we, Pascale?' He turned to his French pal, who giggled. 'I don't zink so!'

'Oh, come now, Pascale,' he grinned. 'Can't go on all day. Well, I know you can. This is Pascale De Maupessant, by the way,' he called, turning back to me. 'Lucy Fellowes.'

'A pleasure,' she beamed, prettily. 'Won't you come in?'

'I can't park,' I yelled. 'Jack, I'm sorry, but could we—you know . . .'

'Give me five minutes,' he called down.

He winked broadly at me before shutting the window again. Their figures moved out of sight. I imagined them, though, moving back towards the bed; her trying to cajole him duvet-wards, covering him with kisses, while he reached for his jacket, simultaneously murmuring that he'd see her soon, but the old tartar was waiting outside and clearly in a filthy mood . . . mmmmm . . . OK, just one last . . . kiss . . .

A sour and angry feeling of uncontrollable jealousy flooded through me. God, it should have been me having the saucy afternoon, not him. I hadn't chauffeured him up here to get his rocks off while I had an unsatisfactory grapple in a broom cupboard, for heaven's sake!

He sauntered casually down the steps, jacket nonchalantly slung over one shoulder, looking, I had to admit, rather attractively rumpled and post-coital, as he glanced up to the top floor and blew Pascale a beguiling kiss. She blew an equally coquettish one back.

'For pity's sake.' I reached across and flung open the passenger door with a flourish. 'Get in, can't you. This isn't the bloody balcony scene.'

'Ahh . . .' he sighed happily, settling himself down beside me and ignoring my evident irritation. 'Lovely girl that, absolutely lovely. You must meet her properly, you'd love her. How about you, little Luce? If you don't mind me saying so, you look a bit down in the mouth. Like the cat who didn't quite get the cream, am I wrong?'

I swallowed. 'Not at all,' I said lightly. 'I had a lovely time with Teresa.'

'Ah. So, you didn't get to see your parents, then?'

I licked my lips. Damn. I'd forgotten about that little lie. How awful.

'No, I—well, you know. Teresa and I had so much to catch up on. We just sort of curled up on her sofa and gossiped. Lost track of time.'

'Really?' He frowned. 'How extraordinary. I popped out for a bottle of wine at one point. Could have sworn I saw her in her shop.'

I flushed and stared straight ahead. 'Are you spying on me, Jack?'

'Good heavens, no,' he said in mock horror. 'Why on earth would I want to do that?'

'I have no idea,' I said, between clenched teeth. 'But I don't take kindly to having my private life scrutinised. I'm a grown woman, you are not my keeper, and what I do in my own time is my own affair, got it?'

'Message received and understood,' he grinned, tugging his forelock. 'If it's all right by you, I intend to spend this return trip in precisely the same way I spent the outgoing one. It's been an exhausting afternoon.' And so saying, he rested his head back and shut his eyes.

When we finally made it back to Netherby a couple of hours later, Joan was in the front drive, trying to pull a rug out of the boot of a very twisted and mangled red Fiesta.

'Oh God—it's the aunts' car!' I gasped, getting out in horror.

'They're fine,' Joan assured us. 'Escaped with a few cuts and bruises, but the car's a write-off, as you can see. Wrapped it round an oak tree in the park. Anyway, they're both in there now,' she jerked her head towards the house, 'with everyone gathered in the morning room.'

'Ah. I wondered if we'd have a reception committee,' murmured Jack.

Sure enough, Archie, Rose, Lavinia, Pinkie and the aunts were all assembled. Also in the room was Sir David Mortimer, a small, dapper man with a quick, bright smile. I'd noticed, since my marriage to Ned, that he tended to be present at most important family gatherings. I'm not sure in what capacity his presence was deemed necessary—perhaps to be on hand if Rose had another attack of angina—but he was a calm, sensible man, and his presence was welcome.

Archie was pretending to read the *Telegraph*, Rose was sitting opposite him on the other sofa, bolt upright, and Lavinia and Pinkie were at a little table, playing Scrabble with Cynthia and Violet.

'Darlings!' Rose got to her feet, eyes bright with anxiety. 'How was it?'

Archie, too, stood up, bushy brows furrowed. 'Well?' he barked. 'What did he have to say for himself?'

Jack held up his hands as I quaked in behind him. 'Look, I'm afraid it's no go. I'm sorry, but his mind's made up, and he wants to marry her. I must say they appear to be very much in love, and I think there's damn all anyone can do about it.'

There was a silence at that.

'Rozanna is acutely aware of the hurt she's causing,' Jack went on, 'and also that Hector is something of an innocent, so she's asked him to wait a year. Hector wants her now, and he's going to ask her every day until she says yes.'

'Oh,' breathed Pinkie. 'How romantic!'

'Shut up, you stupid girl!' Rose rounded on her furiously. 'There's nothing remotely romantic about a scheming, manipulative whore who's got her claws into my only boy!' Her voice cracked slightly at this and a hanky came out of her sleeve.

'Steady, Rose,' said David quietly.

'Well, it's true!' she sobbed.

'Maybe so, but David's right, no point getting hysterical,' said Archie tersely. 'Hector's clearly made his mind up and he's a bigger fool than I thought he was. I said it yesterday, but I'll say it again. He'll get nothing from me, and he'll never set foot in this house again, not on that woman's arm.' With that he turned and left the room.

There was a silence. 'He doesn't mean it,' piped up Pinkie, at length, in an unnaturally shrill voice. 'He's upset. I can talk him round, I always can. After all, this is the twenty-first century! So what if she's a tart? Golly, we've all been around, haven't we? OK, she does it for money, but that's the only difference. I mean—'

'We're playing for money?' Cynthia glanced up, startled, from her Scrabble letters. 'You didn't tell me that.'

'No, no, we're not playing for money,' soothed Lavinia.

'I wouldn't have let you have "dyke" if I'd known. It's in the dictionary as "derogatory", you know.'

'Hector's girlfriend's a dyke?' enquired Violet.

'No, dear, she's a whore.'

'What?' Violet cupped her ear.

'*She's a whore!*' yelled Cynthia.

'Stop it!' Rose's voice rang out shrilly. She got to her feet, trembling. 'Doesn't anyone have any idea what I might be going through, how I might be feeling? I've just heard that my only boy, my—'

'Rose, you're upset,' David soothed, taking her arm. 'Lavinia, I think your mother should lie down.'

'Of course I'm upset,' Rose shrieked, rounding on me suddenly. 'And you're the cause of it.' Her eyes glittered with rage.

I stepped back, stunned. 'Me?'

'You brought that girl to my lovely party,' she trembled, 'knowing what she was. You let me introduce her to all my friends. And then you introduced her to Hector. Not content with taking one son from me, you wanted to take another.'

'Now, Rose,' David said gently. 'I don't imagine Lucy—'

'Quiet, David,' she ordered. He pursed his lips. Frowned at his shoes. 'And now,' she went on in a quavering voice, 'he's lost to me for ever.' She gave a strangled sob. 'I'll never forgive you for that, Lucy, never!'

Her pale blue eyes were huge as they fixed on me, her face, bloodless. She gave me one last, defiant stare, then turned and ran from the room.

Chapter Four

I WOKE UP the following morning and immediately felt sick as the full force of Rose's invective came flooding back. I glanced at the clock. Nine o'clock. What? I peered incredulously. No! Crikey, it was. I must have overslept. And the boys must have had their breakfast already and gone out to play, because it was awfully quiet.

After Rose's walkout, everyone had been terribly sweet, rushing to ply me with drinks, making me sit down and telling me how she was just upset and it didn't mean anything, really it didn't. I have to say, I'd felt genuinely shaky and gulped down all the gin and sympathy they could offer. David had been very kind, bustling off to see Rose first and giving her a sleeping pill, but then coming back and sitting beside me, explaining that Rose had secretly hoped for a much better outcome from our mission to London, and that her diatribe was just disappointment talking. 'Don't hold it against her,' he'd advised.

I shivered now in the shower, even though it was warm, remembering Rose's glacial blue eyes glaring at me. And how on earth were we supposed to carry on, I wondered, in such close proximity to each other now I knew she despised me? So stupid, I thought, with awful, dawning realisation, to get myself into this situation in the first place. Hadn't it occurred to me I might fall out with my in-laws? Jess had warned me, and—oh God, now that was the bloody *telephone*!

I rushed out to answer it. 'Hello?' I gasped, grabbing a towel en route and wrapping it around me.

'Lucy? Hi, it's Kit here.'

'Kit?' I went blank for a second. Suddenly I felt horribly hot. Christ—my job! 'Oh! Oh God—Kit!'

'I just wondered, only I was sort of expecting you at about a quarter to nine and it's five past now.'

'I'll be there. It's just, well one of the children was sick this morning. I should have rung, but—well, I'm on my way.'

'Oh, that's great,' he said with evident relief. 'It wouldn't matter, normally, it's just that I need to go to Cheltenham today. There's an auction I want to get to, but I don't have to be there until lunchtime, so . . .'

'Kit, I am *so* sorry. I'll be there. I promise.'

I put the phone down, horrified. My first day at work—how could I have forgotten? '*Max!!! Ben!!!*' I shrieked, rushing wildly to the door. '*Where the hell are you?*'

I charged downstairs like a maniac and tripped over a dumper truck Max had kindly left on the bottom step, landing smack on my forehead on the wooden floor. I lay there for a moment, gasping with pain. Then I got up, and abandoning the towel, limped, wincing in agony, towards the ironing basket.

'Please let there be clean pants,' I moaned, riffling through it, my head hurting like hell. Oh, pants, please be here, but, actually, I knew they wouldn't be, because I'd spotted them all in the dirty washing yesterday. I panicked. Could I recycle some? I wondered. Or—hang on. I seized a pair of Ben's. They were—I peered at the label—aged nine to ten, and he was quite a big boy, so . . . I stood up and put my feet into them. J-u-s-t about squeezed them up past my knees and up to my thighs. I wriggled hard. There was no way they were going to—'*Aarrgghh!!*'

I nearly fell over with fright. Coming up the garden path, with a boy on each hand, was Jack. I froze, naked but for the vicelike grip of my World Cup knickers. Horrified, I grabbed a Royal Horticultural Society tea towel, and, with my top half covered in herbs and spices and my bottom by David Beckham, I fled upstairs.

'What the hell are you doing here?' I hollered, behind the safety of my bedroom door.

'Sorry,' he said mildly, from the bottom of the stairs, 'but I found these two down by the lake. One's a bit wet.'

It took a moment to sink in.

'Oh!' I threw on a dressing gown and flew downstairs. 'Oh God—Max. Darling, did you fall in?' I rushed to him, sinking to my knees to hold him. 'Oh God, you're sopping. You are *not* to go down there alone.'

'I didn't really fall, Mum. I saw a trout, and was just sort of reaching for it, but Jack grabbed me and made me come out. Mum, can we fish today?'

'No. No, absolutely not, I've got to go to *work* today! I completely forgot, should be there already. I need Trisha, I need her *now*! Max, go and change. Ben, pass me the phone, quick.'

He narrowed his eyes. 'Why are you wearing my pants?'

'What? Oh, because I'd run out.'

He threw the phone at me. 'God, you're weird.'

I was aware that I was panicking and that Jack was watching me. I took a deep breath. Turned to him and smiled.

'Thank you so much for bringing the boys back,' I purred, hoping to convey the right amount of gratitude and dismissal.

He inclined his head. 'Pleasure. Listen, I'm fishing today, so if you're stuck for someone to look after them—'

'No. No, thank you, Jack. I'd like Trisha to have some quiet time with them.'

While I talked to Trisha, I turned my back rather pointedly on Jack, and when I'd finished talking and turned back, I saw with relief that he'd gone.

'Oh, great,' murmured Ben. 'Quiet time with Trisha, instead of fishing with Jack. Really great, Mum, thanks.'

'Yes! Because you know full well, Ben, that I absolutely forbade you to go to that lake on your own, and you went. With Max! So a few quiet hours won't hurt you. Life is not all beer and skittles, you know.'

'Oh, really? Seems like it is for you. You're just jaunting off again, leaving us. Just like you did yesterday, and the day before that. So much for family life.' And with that he stormed upstairs.

Oh God. Kids. And I still wasn't dressed.

Twenty minutes later I was driving fast down the A41; wet hair, no pants. At half past nine, precisely forty-five minutes late, I performed an emergency stop outside Frampton Manor.

I flew inside to find Kit, clearly ready to leave, jingling his car keys in his hand, jacket on. 'So sorry, Kit!' I gasped.

He grinned. 'It's OK, I'll just quickly show you a couple of things.' He moved across to a desk. 'Phone is here, should you need it, and if anyone buys don't forget to give them a receipt. There's a book of them over there.' He pointed. 'But I have to tell you, sales are unlikely. Most of your time will be spent taking telephone enquiries and sending photographs of stock, a pile of which are in here.' He pulled out a drawer.

'Right. Brilliant.'

'So. That's all fairly straightforward. It's Rococo that's the problem.'

'Not well?' I queried.

Kit shrugged. 'Just not herself. I took her to the vet yesterday and he said it may be that we have to adjust her insulin. She's diabetic. What I would like you to do, and what the vet suggested, is to test her urine. You just syringe some up with this pipette, three times a day, drop a bit on here,' he showed me a piece of litmus paper, 'and record what colour it goes. D'you think you could handle that?' He looked at me anxiously.

'Of course,' I said. 'Now, Kit, you'll be late, so just go. Rococo and I will be fine.'

'Great.' He relaxed and smiled with relief, and I thought how attractive his slim, intelligent face was when he smiled. It quite lit up.

'Thanks, Lucy. It's wonderful to leave the place with someone I trust.'

'What have you got your eye on today, by the way?'

'Oh, the most wonderful console table. Napoleonic, and in fabulous condition. Look.' He whipped a catalogue out from inside his jacket.

'Oh,' I drooled. 'What heaven. Actually, this reserve isn't bad . . . How exciting,' I said. 'I wish I was coming with you.'

He turned at the door. Regarded me for a moment. 'D'you know, so do I.' There was a silence. 'Anyway,' he collected himself, 'I must be away. Have fun, Lucy, and don't work too hard. See you at about six.'

What a nice man, I thought as I shut the door behind him. I walked back through the huge, empty house, my fingers trailing thoughtfully over the exquisite furniture. So many treasures here, really quality antiques. He had the most fantastic eye.

As I sat down at the desk in the front hall, I realised what a relief it was to have time to collect my thoughts in the peace and quiet of this vast old house. No children, no Felloweses. Except . . . except that, sadly, my thoughts were full of Rose and her accusations last night.

I walked to the window. Outside, it had started to rain. 'Buck up, Lucy,' I muttered. 'It's not that bad. You've got the boys, you've got a roof over your head, and right now you've got a diabetic dog who needs her urine tested in the pouring rain.

'Come on, Rococo,' I muttered, striding purposefully out of the front door. 'Let's go. Get it over with.'

She leapt to her feet and followed me joyfully as I led her to a patch of grass. She regarded me a moment, then suddenly turned her back, and bounded off down the garden. I dashed after her. By the time I reached her, she was in the depths of the shrubbery. Damn. Why hadn't I put her on a lead?

Suddenly I had an idea. Over in the yard, I spotted a tap.

'Quick, Rococo—come!'

She bounded after me. I hastened into the yard, and turned the tap on. Rococo gazed at it for a moment, head on one side. Then, lo and behold, she turned, sauntered languorously across to a patch of grass, lowered her hindquarters and . . . ahhh . . .

Oh God, the syringe! I'd forgotten to bring it out. I looked around wildly. A flowerpot, perfect. I ran across to a tottering pagoda, seized the top one—happily no hole in the bottom—ran back, and shoved it underneath. *Yesss!* Oh joy. The obliging Rococo was filling it to the top—hang on. Was that a car? On the gravel?

Carrying the pot carefully, I strolled nonchalantly round the front of the house, where—oh! Instead of a matching pair of indignant Americans in Burberry macs wondering where the hell the patron was—there stood a familiar figure.

'Charlie!'

Smiling that lovely, sexy, tigerish smile that made his face crease up and his eyes slant, he sauntered over to meet me. 'I was surprised to find the door open. Thought maybe you'd done a bunk already.'

'No. No, I had to pop out for a moment, but—oh, I'm so pleased it's you. Oh, Charlie, it's *so* lovely to see you!'

I knew it wasn't cool, but it was. So lovely. It seemed to me that in that one moment, my angst about Rose just melted away. None of it mattered. I smiled, basking contentedly in his warm, appreciative gaze. His eyes seemed to smoulder with desire.

He glanced down. 'What's that?'

'Oh,' I murmured, still gazing up, mesmerised by his deep, choco-latey eyes. 'Just a urine sample.'

'Oh.' He looked surprised.

'Come on, come in.' As I carried the brimming pot, he followed me.

'That's very impressive,' he said, eyeing it nervously. 'Cystitis?'

'Oh, no, diabetes.'

'Golly! Poor you.' He looked startled.

'Yes, such a pain. Has to be done three times a day.'

'Right.' He swallowed. 'And always . . . alfresco?' He gestured towards the flowerpot nervously.

'Well, she'd make a terrible mess *inside*, Charlie,' I laughed.

'She?'

'Rococo. The dog.'

'Ah!'

I frowned. 'What did you—'

'No, no! Nothing,' he interposed, beaming. 'Excellent. No, excellent news.' He flung the door open for me with a flourish. 'Now. An empty house. Lock the door,' he whispered, holding my eyes.

'No, Charlie,' I croaked feebly, 'I can't possibly. What if Kit—'

'Kit won't be back for hours.' He turned the key. Then he turned the OPEN sign around to CLOSED, with the naughtiest of smiles.

'Charlie,' I protested desperately, 'this is—*mmmmmm!!!*'

Suddenly the breath was being squeezed out of me and he was kiss-ing my mouth, my throat, back up to my mouth to quell my protests. I tried to resist, but, oh hell, it was so delicious, I appeared to be joining in. The next moment I found myself being lifted in his arms.

'No!' I squealed in horror. 'You can't possibly carry me, I weigh a ton!'

And—shit! I had no pants on! I went rigid in his arms, horribly aware that a struggle at this point could prove deeply embarrassing. Galvanised by my lack of resistance, he strode on, and before I knew it, I was being carried up the sweeping staircase and into a bedroom.

The room whirled as he deposited me on the four-poster bed and lay down on top of me; everything whirled, in fact, my senses, the tapestries, the Old Masters on the walls, the plush violet canopy overhead, blurring madly as he enveloped me in his arms. Charlie launched an attack on my top half but I'd chosen to wear a sort of crossover top, with ties that poked through holes at the sides and knotted at the back. He was just about getting to grips with it, when somebody snored.

We froze, mid-caress. Stared at each other.

'There's someone in the bed!' I shrieked, sitting up in horror, pulling my top around me.

We glanced about frantically. It was a huge bed, to be sure, and we'd only, in our haste, occupied one small corner of it, but still, there were no ominous lumps to be seen. And then it came again. A deep, sonorous, long-drawn-out snore.

'Christ! Who is it?' I leapt off the bed.

'It's coming from underneath!' Charlie hissed, scrambling off, too. He bent down, cautiously lifting up the bed-skirt. He peered. There was a horrible hush. Then: 'Rococo! OUT!' he roared.

'Oh! Oh God, Rococo!' I gasped with relief.

'She's not waking up,' Charlie reported. 'Seems dead to the world. D'you have any real objections to having her there, or—'

'Yes, I do. I'm not—mmm . . . well, maybe just a little kiss and—'

Already he was stopping my mouth. I could hear Aphrodite whispering in my ear, telling me to let sleeping dogs lie. He lay me down on the bed again and golly, where were we? Oh, yes . . . lovely, except—God. Bugger. There it was *again*. Only louder. It didn't even sound like a proper snore. It was too harsh, too sort of disjointed.

'Hang on.' I sat up, pushed him off. 'Charlie, why didn't she wake up? You called her, and she just didn't move, did she? Suppose she's ill?'

'Don't be silly,' he told me. 'She's not ill, just asleep.'

'No, but she has been ill, you see. Recently, Kit said so, and—listen.'

It came again. Long, drawn out, with a slight whimper at the end.

'That's not a snore, that's a death rattle,' I said. 'Charlie, get her out!'

Swearing, Charlie dutifully rolled off the bed, reached underneath, and grabbed Rococo by her back legs. I grabbed the front, and together, we slid her out across the wooden floor. Her breath was coming in tiny, sharp gasps, eyes worryingly half open, her tummy going up and down quickly, almost in spasms.

'Oh God, Charlie, I know what this is,' I said, trembling suddenly. 'It's a diabetic coma. You must get her to the vet because I can't leave the shop. I'll ring and say you're coming. Let's get her in the car.'

Between us we lugged, dragged and carried Rococo down the stairs—eyes rolling, tongue hanging, paws flailing—and out to the car.

Charlie got resignedly into the driver's seat. He buzzed down the window. 'It must be love,' he said bitterly. 'There is no other woman on the face of this earth I would do this for.'

'I think it's love too,' I whispered, leaning in and kissing him warmly on the mouth. 'And I think you're a lovely, lovely man. Now go!'

He pulled off, and I dashed back inside to call the vet. I also called Kit, on his mobile, and gave him the bad news, but I told him not to rush back, because Charlie was quite happy to stay with Rococo at the vet's. He didn't ask what the devil Charlie was doing at his shop in the first place, and I made a mental note to smooth down the bedspread before his return.

An hour or so later, Charlie rang me. Rococo was coming round, and was 'comfortable' now, apparently.

'I tell you, I can't take any more of this coitus interruptus, Lucy, I'm too old for all this. It's got to be a good old-fashioned dirty weekend in a cosy country hotel, with no sick children,* no dogs, no broom cupboards, so I can ravish you to my heart's content. What d'you say?'

I giggled, but hesitated. 'A whole weekend might be a bit tricky, Charlie. The boys, you know.'

'But a night?' he persisted.

'A night,' I agreed, 'would be very acceptable.' I imagined a cosy old pub, a drink in the bar, huge log fire burning; then a table for two in the tiny, candlelit restaurant, faces glowing, then later on, off up the rickety staircase to a cosy feather bed, away from the world and its prying eyes . . . 'Ooh, yes,' I breathed. 'In fact, it would be perfect.'

'Right,' he warned dangerously. 'You're on. I'll book it.'

Having called in at the vet's, Kit finally walked through the door at about seven o'clock. I was only supposed to stay until six, but decided, under the circumstances, that I'd better wait to debrief him on the day.

'It was a reaction to the insulin,' he said, flopping wearily onto a sofa. 'They're going to test her over the next couple of days. Thank God you were here, Lucy. This is exactly why I need someone responsible.'

I cringed, recalling my fairly irresponsible exploits upstairs.

'I hope you don't mind that Charlie popped round, Kit.'

'Mind? Of course I don't. I'm delighted if your friends pop in, makes it much less boring for you. I mean, it's not as if you're a teenager, sneaking your scruffy boyfriend in for a quick one on my sofa!'

Crikey. What the hell was I up to? Not for the first time, a wave of shame washed over me.

Kit interrupted my thoughts.

'Any customers at all, or was it a totally disastrous day all round?'

'Er, well, no. But there were a couple of calls.'

'Excellent. You'll join me for a drink, won't you?'

I glanced at my watch. It was almost the boys' bedtime and I felt I hadn't seen them properly for a few days, but it did seem rude not to. He handed me a whopping great gin, and then settled himself down beside me on the sofa.

'God, bloody long day. And the console went for an astronomical sum.'

'Ah. I was going to ask.'

'Yes, well, don't. Total waste of time. But no matter. Someone told me about a gem of a house clearance sale going on in Paris next week, so I shall whiz across for that and, once again, leave the reins in your capable hands. This is working out *so* marvellously, Lucy, I'm so glad you're here. You weren't bored, I hope?' He turned his head anxiously.

I sipped my drink nervously. 'Er, no. Not at all.' Heavens no. Not with a diabetic dog and a red-hot lover.

I shook my head in disbelief as I drove home later that night, having actually shared more than just the one gin with him, and having had quite a giggle, too. We'd realised we knew pretty much the same people in the antiques world and had roared away at their idiosyncrasies. A charming, erudite man with a cosmopolitan, interesting life, so why on earth, I wondered, had his wife left him for the *plumber*?

As I drew up outside the barn, I saw that the boys' bedroom was in darkness, so hopefully they were fast asleep. It occurred to me that I should have rung, warned Trisha I was going to be late, but actually, she was sensible enough just to put them to bed and wait. When I walked in, she was sitting on the sofa with her back to me. She stood up and turned round, except that it wasn't Trisha at all, it was Rose.

'Oh! Rose, what on earth—' It appeared she'd made herself a cup of coffee, read my magazines, settling herself down in *my* home . . .

'Sorry to startle you, Lucy.' She smiled.

'No—no, it's fine. Are the boys—?'

'Up at the house. We popped them into bed in the spare room. I'm afraid Joan needed some help in the kitchen. I've got a big dinner party tomorrow, so Trisha's working for me this evening.'

'Oh. Right.' I flushed, embarrassed. Yes, how presumptuous of me to assume she'd work for me all the time, but actually, that's what I'd been led to believe. And I wasn't sure I liked the boys not being here when I got back, but then again, that was my fault too, I supposed.

'And, my dear, the reason I'm here is to apologise.' She smiled graciously. 'It was quite shameful of me to accuse you like that last night. I wanted to ask you to forgive my ridiculous outburst.' Her blue eyes widened anxiously, appealing to me, as she twisted her rings nervously.

'Of course,' I said. God, I'd almost forgotten. Only yesterday, but it seemed so long ago. So much had happened.

'I can't think what came over me. Of course I was upset. But what I don't want, Lucy, under any circumstances, is for it to get in the way of our relationship. We have such a close friendship now, don't we, and I don't want it to come under any sort of threat.'

I found myself taken aback once more. Close friendship? Did we? But then, Rose was so cold, maybe this was her idea of mateyness. In any event, I decided firmly, she was quite right, we couldn't have carried on with such an atmosphere hanging over us. I smiled.

'I quite agree. It would be awful to live cheek by jowl and be under any sort of strain.'

'Precisely,' she agreed. 'And even worse would be, if you felt so uncomfortable, you decided you couldn't live here. I was up all last night worrying about it, but you wouldn't think that, would you, Lucy?'

Ah. So that was it. I knew that this was a key question, and I had to answer it carefully.

'No, I'm not thinking of moving out of here, Rose.'

'Oh, I'm so pleased!' She beamed.

'But,' I hesitated. 'I can't, either, give you a rock-solid guarantee that I'll be here for ever.'

'Well, no, obviously not for ever!' She laughed nervously.

'What I'm saying is, I don't know what shape my life will take. I don't know where I'll eventually work, for instance.'

'Oh, but your job at the manor! Ideal, all those antiques.'

'Yes, ideal for the minute, but it's not a career. Anyway, who knows, there might be other factors to consider. I might meet someone,' I added brutally.

Her eyes clouded at this, and her chin shot out, almost as a defensive reflex. She collected herself. 'Well, yes, of course you might. You're young, no one expects you to be a widow for ever, but this place is plenty big enough for a family, and you know, you could always add on at the back.'

I caught my breath at this. How much she'd already thought through.

I picked my words carefully. 'Rose, if you're looking for a guarantee that we'll stay here long term—I can't give you one. I truly don't know which way my life will go. I suppose what I'm saying is, I can't make promises.'

Her eyes glittered dangerously for a moment. Then she raised her chin. Smiled. 'Of course you can't, and who can. Golly, even those of us with the most settled of lives can't tell what's round the corner.'

At that moment, headlights shone in the barn and a car came to a halt outside.

Rose got to her feet. 'That'll be Archie. I told him I was popping down here; he probably thought it was too dark for me to walk back.'

I walked her to the door, struggling with my emotions, hoping I hadn't been too harsh. 'Rose, we *do* love it here,' I began, 'the boys and I. Don't get me wrong, it is idyllic, it's just—'

'I know.' She stopped me with an unexpected peck on the cheek. 'You just don't know yourself, that's all.' She gave a wan smile.

I watched her get in the car, but as they turned round and purred back past me, I realised it wasn't Archie driving, but David Mortimer.

When I went up to Netherby the following morning to collect the boys, they weren't there. Nobody seemed to be there, in fact, but I finally ran Archie and Pinkie down, in the pale blue breakfast room, lingering over breakfast and buried in the *Telegraph* and the *Mail* respectively. Archie looked up, surprised, when I asked.

'Ben and Max? No, my dear, they've gone into Oxford with Rose. There was some talk of a puppet show, I think, at the Bloomsbury. Didn't she mention it?' he muttered, going back to his paper.

'No! No, she didn't. So, did she say what time she'd be back?'

'Hmm?' He glanced up abstractedly from the depths of Court and Social. 'Didn't say, my dear,' he muttered.

Nice of Rose, I thought, as I stalked angrily down the oak-panelled passage, to take the boys without asking me. I mean, yes, sure, a puppet show with Granny was terrific, and I was determined not to overreact, but she might have mentioned it.

As I headed off towards the back door, I passed the kitchen and was halted by a sob. I peered in. Trisha was sitting with her elbows on the kitchen table, forehead propped up in her hands, while Joan, a plump arm round her, patted her shoulder awkwardly. Trisha swung a tear-stained face round at my approach.

'What is it? What's wrong?' I hastened over and sat beside her. Joan, relieved to be able to abandon her post, hurried away to the boiling vat of water on the stove.

'Boy trouble,' Joan muttered darkly, snatching a tea towel from a rail to drag the cauldron off the heat. 'I told her, right from the start, Lucy: it ain't no good hankering over someone like Jack Fellowes. He'll never settle. I'm not sayin' he's a bad lot, but I've never seen him more than five minutes with a girl and that's a fact.'

I squeezed Trisha's hand. 'Oh, Trisha, Joan's right, I'm afraid.' I sighed. 'God, I wish I'd warned you too, but I had no idea you were in so deep.'

This prompted a fresh outburst of tears.

'I can't help it. I—just love him so much! And, Lucy, he had absolutely no idea! Thought it was just a bit of fun, until I mentioned yesterday that it might be nice to get away from this place, stay in a nice pub or something, just a weekend, but he was like, "Oh my God, a relationship!" I tell you, you've never seen anyone retreat so fast in your life.'

I grimaced. 'Yes, well, I can imagine one might not see him for the dust on the soles of his trainers. God, he makes me cross sometimes.'

'And the thing is,' Trisha sniffed, 'I'm sure there's someone else. The other day he went to London—you know, with you, Lucy—and when he came back, he was really—oh, I don't know—distant. Distracted.'

I swallowed, recalling the svelte and beautiful Pascale as they'd cooed out of her bedroom window.

'Ye-es, well, possibly,' I conceded, not wanting to twist the knife. 'One never quite knows with Jack. But even if there is someone else,' I hastened on, 'it's absolutely no reflection on you, Trisha. He's just that kind of man. He is what I believe used to be called a bounder.' I grinned and squeezed her shoulder, trying to buck her up.

She gave a weak smile in return. 'He's also the nicest, kindest, most generous, funniest man I've ever met in my life,' she said in a low voice. 'And I can't help loving him. I can't help it, Lucy! And what's worse is I have to see him every bloody day! And I just don't know how I'm going to bear that.' With another strangled sob she jumped up and, blinded by tears, knocked her chair over backwards and fled from the room.

I reached down slowly and picked up the chair, setting it upright. I felt my blood rising. 'Where is he, Joan?'

'In the library, as usual. Writing those poems of his, no doubt.'

'Right. I'll give him something to write about.'

I got up and marched out, heading off to the library. As I crossed the front hall, I could feel fury mounting with every step. The door was closed. I raised my hand to knock, but then turned the handle and strode in. It was a large room, and with the sun in my eyes, it took me a moment to see Jack at the far end, behind a mahogany desk in the bay window, a paperback, with a lurid red and black cover, propped up in front of him. He looked momentarily annoyed. Then his face cleared.

'Oh, Lucy, hi.' He quickly shut the book and put it in a drawer.

'Don't you "Oh, Lucy, hi," me,' I snapped, striding across to him. 'What have you done to that poor girl?'

He looked bewildered. 'Which poor girl?'

'Trisha, of course! My God, you've only broken her heart and you can't even remember which girl it is. What's wrong with you, Jack? Haven't you got any sense of responsibility? Any heart, for crying out loud? Don't you know when a girl is falling in love with you? Or is it that you *can* read the signs, but couldn't care less?'

He regarded me across the desk. 'Actually, it wasn't like that at all,' he said carefully. 'I had no idea she was "in love with me" as you put it, until she sprang this weekend break on me, and I didn't encourage her, unless you count passing time with her and the boys. I'm sorry if she's upset, genuinely, but—'

'Oh, spare me that bollocks,' I spat. 'I've seen you in action and I know the routine. This isn't the first girl I've had sobbing on my shoulder over you, and to be honest, I'm getting just a bit fed up with it. You're not a teenager, for heaven's sake, you're just a sad, ageing Lothario, a serial shagger who can't keep a grip on his trousers for ten minutes.'

I could feel myself shaking with rage. I was also vaguely aware that quite a lot of pent-up anger, which might have been better directed at my mother-in-law, was winging Jack's way.

'I see,' he said quietly. 'So what does that make you?'

'What? We are not talking about me,' I said, 'we're talking about you, and your irresponsible behaviour. A young girl is sobbing her heart out and do you care? No!'

'Well, I do, but then again,' he paused, 'she's not married, is she?'

'What?' I narrowed my eyes incredulously at him. 'Oh, that's pathetic, Jack,' I said at length. 'Truly pathetic. And cheap too.'

'Is it?' He got up and came round to my side of the desk. He seemed very tall all of a sudden. 'Cheap to suggest that before you come marching in here talking about responsibility, you take a look at your own glasshouse? To suggest that before you start lobbing stones in my direction, you do a little reinforced double glazing to ensure against the effects of your own actions?'

'Oh, you're so clever, Jack,' I said between clenched teeth, 'with your English tutorial metaphors, but I know what you're talking about. Yes, he's married. OK? But the marriage is not mine, and it is not my duty to maintain it.'

Even as I said it I knew I was shot to bits.

'You don't believe that for one minute,' he scoffed. 'That's just cowardly cant. That's someone small, weak and deceitful talking. That's unworthy of you, not like you at all.'

'Oh, really?' I flushed, furious I'd let myself be cornered. 'And if you're trying to tell me you've never fallen for a married woman you're a hypocrite and a liar.'

He paused. 'Only once. And it was unrequited.'

'Rubbish,' I scoffed. 'You've been nipping in and out of marital beds for years—oh, you've been there all right, and what you don't like is that now *I'm* there too. You don't like the fact that I'm finally getting out and having a good time. You want me in widow's weeds for ever!' I turned and walked angrily to the door. When I looked back, his face had paled.

'That's a despicable thing to say,' he said in a low voice, 'and you know it.'

'Oh, do I?' I retorted.

I slammed the door behind me and stalked off down the corridor, a mixture of fury and guilt rising within me like a surging torrent as I made for the open doors onto the terrace and back towards the barn.

My parting shot had been below the belt, I knew that. No one had tried harder than Jack to help me get over my grief. No one, except perhaps Jess, had spent more evenings in my flat just being there, sitting with me at my kitchen table, as I let rip, sobbing into old photograph albums while he mopped the photos dry with kitchen towel. I remembered the endless bowls of spaghetti carbonara—the only thing he could cook. I remembered his patience, his kindness, his total lack of compassion fatigue. I'd been wrong to . . . well. I swallowed.

But then again I'd been provoked, I thought quickly, anger rising self-righteously. I'd lashed out because he'd preached to me like some wise old paternalistic sage, and yet everyone knew he conducted his life like a randy old mongrel, sniffing out every bitch on heat in the county. That was what had goaded me, I decided angrily—his hypocrisy.

I marched up the hill in the heat, the sun burning down on my forehead now, the beginnings of a monumental headache throbbing away. As I went up the little brick path to the barn, I knew that nothing other than a handful of painkillers and a darkened room would do.

Inside, making slowly for my bedroom and the painkillers, the telephone rang. 'Hello?' I whispered.

'Lucy?'

'Oh, Charlie, hi.'

'Sound a bit faint, my love. Can't you talk?'

'No, no, I can, the boys aren't here. Thumping headache, I'm afraid.'

'Oh dear, poor you. Now, listen, my love,' he hastened on, 'I'll be brief, because she's only popped to the shops, but could you possibly get away on Saturday night? An old schoolfriend of Miranda's is coming to stay and I know she'd like me out of the way, so, under the guise of "working in London", I've taken you at your word and booked *the* most idyllic retreat imaginable. It's in a tiny village somewhere near Bicester, complete with romantic four-poster bed and the most stunning views imaginable. What do you say, my darling?'

My heart pounded. My head too. I tried to think. The machinations involved in getting away for the night made me feel quite sick.

'Lucy?'

'Yes, yes, I'm thinking, Charlie. It's just I've got to come up with some sort of excuse. The boys, you know.'

'What about your friend in London? Jess?'

'Oh, yes, Jess. Yes, I could, I suppose . . . I haven't seen her baby for ages, and he is my godson.'

'Good.' He sounded relieved. 'Oh, Lucy, I can't wait.'

'Neither can I,' I breathed, as a rush of love kicked in. 'Oh, Charlie, I know this is right,' I said. 'No matter what anyone says!'

'Anyone?' he repeated, sharply. 'Who's anyone?'

'Oh, no, just Jack. Ned's cousin. He was sounding off about people who have'—I faltered in the face of the word 'affairs'—'our sort of rela-tionship,' I finished lamely.

'He doesn't understand,' he said soberly. 'He has no idea. If he did, my God, he wouldn't be so quick to judge. This sort of love, the sort that we have, is blind to all obstacles.'

Was it? 'Yes, you're right. You're right, Charlie. And I can't wait for Saturday. Can't wait to walk into that pub, see you standing at the bar, take our drinks over to the cosy inglenook fireplace—'

'Could do, or take them upstairs.'

'Then a meal in the restaurant—'

'Yes, or apparently they do room service.'

'And then up the creaky stairs to the sumptuous feather bed.'

'Don't,' he groaned. 'Now I shall have to have a cold shower! I—Oh, she's back,' he said in a low voice. 'I hear the car. Till Saturday, then, my darling. The Hare and Hounds, Little Burchester, seven o'clock.'

The line went dead as he hurriedly put down the phone.

Saturday dawned bright and promising. As I drew back my bedroom curtains and leaned out into the sweet morning air, a broad grin spread uncontrollably across my face, and my tummy leapt with excitement.

Tonight then, was most surely the night, and considering the ease with which the logistics had fallen into place, the omens were good. Trisha had readily agreed to baby-sit, on the basis that she certainly didn't want to be in the same house as *him*. All the same, I decided, I'd better just nip up and confirm the arrangements with her. I didn't want anything scuppering my plans at the last minute.

My plan was to take the boys out for the day, before delivering them back here to Trisha, where she would oversee pizza, ice cream and crisps in front of a new video. I wasn't too proud to buy my way into my children's good humour, to silence that mutinous 'we see less of you now than when you worked in London' malarkey. I, meanwhile, would whiz upstairs to begin my devotions, anointing my body with lotions and potions, then pour the body beautiful into my black jeans and a cream, antique lace camisole top, over which I planned to throw my favourite beaded cardigan. There. I laid it all on the bed and stepped back. Oh, and some black suede boots. I dragged them out from under the bed. Perfect.

The boys were still asleep, so I left a quick note to tell Ben where I was, and scuttled up to Netherby. I clattered through the kitchen door with a cheery 'Morning, all!' expecting to find Joan and Trisha finishing their breakfast chores—only to find Rose behind the huge oak table, unrolling bundles of silver from grey felt cloth.

'Oh!' I stopped, startled. 'Rose, I—'

'Didn't expect to find me in this part of the house?' she finished smoothly. 'Oh, I do venture out here occasionally, if only to check everyone's doing their best, which, judging by the terrible state of the silver, they're not. Can I help?'

'Oh, well, no, not really. I was just looking for Trisha. She's going to baby-sit for me tonight, and I wanted to check that she was still OK.'

Rose frowned at me. 'Then it's just as well you came up, Lucy, because I'm afraid she is not "OK". I have a luncheon party for twenty-two tomorrow, and both Joan and Trisha will be spending their evening polishing all this silver. Fancy putting it away like this.' She held a fork up to the light and peered critically at it. 'Is that a problem?'

I gazed at her in horror, all my dreams turning to dust and ashes.

'Well, I promised to go and spend a night with Jess in London. Her—little boy hasn't been well.'

'Oh, really?' She eyed me steadily. 'But of course you must go, if she needs you. The boys can stay up here.'

A mixture of relief and uncertainty filled me. 'Or I might be able to get another baby sitter.'

'What, at such short notice?'

I gazed into her steady blue eyes. She was right. I was being silly.

'You're right,' I said timidly. 'They'll love it up here. I'll go back to the barn and tell them.'

'Oh, I don't think you'll find them there,' she said, slotting spoons and forks back in felt pockets. 'I saw them pottering around in the greenhouse with Archie a moment ago.'

I started. 'Really? But—'

'It's already nine o'clock, Lucy,' she said patiently. 'They quite often pop up and have breakfast here while you're having a lie-in, you know. Now, if you'll excuse me, I must get on.' She swept past me and disappeared down the corridor.

The boys were already up here? But their bedroom doors had been shut, so I'd assumed . . . but I hadn't looked, had I? I flushed. How *awful*. And they came up here for breakfast on a regular basis? I frowned. No. Well, maybe a few times.

I walked out across the stable yard, and down towards the walled garden. Sure enough, Ben and Max were in the long Victorian greenhouse that leaned against the huge, crumbling, kitchen-garden wall, picking tomatoes with Archie.

'Listen, boys.' I said to them brightly. 'If Grandpa can spare you, I thought we might drive into Oxford today, take a boat down the river. Would you like that?'

'Oh, cool!' Max jumped into my arms and Ben smiled.

'Can we go for the whole day?' he asked suspiciously.

'Sure, why not? I need to be back at about five though.'

'Go on then, boys,' said Archie, passing Ben the bowl. 'Take those up to Joan for me, then get out in the sunshine with your ma.'

'I'll make some egg sandwiches,' I promised, as we strolled back across the lawn to the terrace. 'And we can pack some peaches and some biscuits and put it all in a rucksack.'

'And sweets?' added Max hopefully.

'And sweets,' I agreed. 'So. Why don't you take those tomatoes round to Joan, and I'll see what Lavinia's getting all excited about.'

Up on the terrace, Lavinia was flapping and waving her arms at us like someone guiding in a 747.

'What is it, Lavinia?' I called. The boys scampered off to the kitchen.

'Oh, *there* you are, I've been looking for you everywhere! You haven't forgotten it's the second Sunday in the month tomorrow? You're supposed to be doing the flowers for the church today.'

I gazed at her. My mouth opened. 'Oh, gosh, Lavinia, I'd completely forgotten. And—well, I've promised to take the boys out today.'

'Do them tonight then, that's fine.'

'Damn.' I bit my lip. 'I can't, I'm going out. Oh, look, Lavinia, I couldn't do it next week, could I? Would you be an angel and step in for me?'

'Well, normally I would, of course, but I'm off out for lunch today! Roddy's taking me to Brown's,' she said proudly.

'Roddy?'

'Roddy Taylor. Met him at the Rochester-Clarkes' the other night. Sweet, actually.'

'Ah. Bit of a rectory?'

She giggled. 'Sadly not. In fact, desperately mock Tudor, and on the edge of a golf course, but,' her face softened, 'he's terribly nice. Seems rather fond of me too, actually.' She went a bit pink.

'Oh, Lavinia, that's great.' I was genuinely pleased for her. 'Well, of course you can't do it, so that's that then,' I said resignedly. 'I'll do the flowers, it's just—oh dear. The boys are going to be so disappointed.'

'About what?' Ben appeared at my elbow.

I licked my lips. 'Darling, I've made the most ghastly boo-boo. I completely forgot, I promised to do the flowers for the church today.'

He stared. 'What, so we're not going?'

'Well, Ben, how can I? I promised you see, so—'

'Yeah, and you promised us too!'

'I know, Ben, but it's not so bad. We'll pick the flowers here, together, and then we can have a picnic in the buttercup field, and then take the flowers up to the church. You can help me arrange them.'

'A poxy flower-arranging day instead of a boat on the river? No, thanks,' he said angrily. With that he turned and ran back to the barn.

I bit my lip anxiously as I watched him dash across the bridge, forge on up the hill, charge up the path and dart inside. A moment later his curtains drew upstairs, and I knew he was sitting on his bed in the dark, a Walkman clamped to his head.

In the event, Max and I picked the flowers. Ben didn't appear, but his brother and I were told by Granny that yes, we could gather from her garden, as long as we picked carefully and sensibly. But on no account, she eyed me sternly, was I to go anywhere near the hot bed.

'What's the hot bed?' I asked Lavinia as she showed us where to pick.

'It's over there behind the shrubbery. Everything in it is red or orange. You know, flaming azaleas, red asters, that type of thing.'

Lavinia scuttled away to meet her man, but she'd rung Mimsy and she would be at the church to show us the ropes.

'Oh, thanks, Lavinia,' I breathed. 'That'll be a great help.'

I concentrated on the herbaceous border, trying to keep it tasteful, with plenty of white and, oh—lots of foliage. Then, straightening up, I wondered idly how Max was getting on. I gazed around. I couldn't see him anywhere. Well, he wasn't in the hot bed, that was a relief, but was that him . . .? Oh, no!

I dropped my secateurs and ran towards him. He was struggling across the terrace, puffing and panting, and dragging ten, maybe fifteen even, of Rose's two-foot-tall, majestic, rare amaryllis plants.

'I found them growing in the conservatory.' He beamed proudly. 'I picked all of them, Mum. They're wicked, aren't they?'

'Oh, Max,' I groaned, gazing horror-struck at the beautiful, rosy, trumpet flowers on truncated stalks. 'Oh, darling, not inside the house, just the garden!'

'But Granny didn't say that! I thought you'd like them.' Tears welled.

'Oh, I do, I do,' I said, meeting David Mortimer's horrified eyes as he came out of the study onto the terrace to see what was going on.

'But so did Granny,' he finished grimly, eyeing the huge plants. 'Nurtured them for ages. Pride and joy, as it were.'

'Oh, David, she'll go insane,' I whispered fearfully. 'What are we going to do!' I wailed, wringing my hands.

'Come clean, I suppose. All we can do.'

'We?' I yelped hopefully.

He grinned. 'Well, she'll flay you alive, that's for sure. Come on, young Max.' And so saying, he gripped Max's shoulder, turned him firmly round and marched him off.

I gulped and watched them go. Thank goodness for David, I thought. I hopped through the French windows into the study. I didn't, actually, want to be too associated with those plants when Rose came out to inspect. Instead I slipped behind the heavy green curtains, not exactly hiding, but, well . . . skulking.

I waited for ages for David to come back. Finally I heard footsteps. I peeped round but—it was Jack. Striding across the gravel, towards the stable yard where the cars were kept. I ducked back. He looked all set to go somewhere. A leather bag was packed, a linen jacket slung through the handles. Heading back to Pascale, maybe? Or was he leaving Netherby entirely? That would be a relief after yesterday, but, ridiculously, I felt something like regret wash over me, too. I bit my lip as I watched his tall, erect figure, russet curls gleaming, stride confidently towards a car in the yard.

As I leaned against the glass, wondering why on earth I should feel unsettled, David appeared with Max. 'Not too bad,' he said, loosening his tie. 'I mean, ranted and raved for a bit and all that, but seeing as it was Max, well . . .' He grinned. 'It seems your boys can do no wrong.'

'Oh, thanks so much for bailing us out.'

Not for the first time it occurred to me to wonder what David saw in this family. But, then again, with no family of his own, perhaps he relished these little dramas. The ups and downs of family life.

'Pleasure. But don't waste them now, will you, those huge great triffids. Now you've got them, may as well put them in the church.'

'Oh, d'you think?' I gazed down doubtfully.

'Why not? At least that way Rose will get something out of it. Imagine, the whole village will think she's kindly donated three dozen amaryllis, grown especially for the church. Come on, I'll give you a hand.' And so saying, he scooped up an armful.

Half an hour later I was hurtling down to the church. I'd been unsuccessful in my attempts to get the boys to accompany me, but in view of my increasingly skippy excitement about this evening, it was probably just as well. As I mentally scurried through my itinerary, I reached for my mobile to ring Jess. It had suddenly occurred to me that it would be just like Rose to flaming well ring and check I was there.

'Jess? Hi, it's me. Listen, I've been meaning to ring and ask about Henry's chickenpox, but—'

'Oh, he's fine, *so* much better,' she gushed. 'Yes, no, completely over it, thanks. He's lovely at the moment actually. It's such a sweet age.'

'Oh! Good.' Blimey, she sounded chipper. 'And, um, Jamie?' I asked tentatively. Still away? I wondered. Still a bastard? It had to be gone through, this ritual. She had to get some ranting off her chest.

'Divine,' she purred. 'Completely yummy actually.'

'What?' I frowned into the phone. 'How come?'

'Well, I overheard him talking on the phone the other day. He was pouring his heart out in a most un-Jamie-like way to his mate from work. About how he thought I was having an affair, because I was so cold and funny towards him—can you imagine? The prat!'

'And the *reason* you were all cold and funny,' I sighed, 'was because you thought *he* was the one having an affair. You're the prat, Jess.'

'I know,' she agreed. 'We don't communicate, you see, that's our problem. But—oh boy, are we making up for lost time now!'

'Oh, Jess, how wonderful.' I meant it. So why did I feel a pang of jealousy? Surely my life was wonderful too? Of course it was. I had my Charlie! I told her the wheeze.

'What—so you want me to lie?' she asked coldly.

'No! Not lie, Jess, no one's going to ask you, for heaven's sake. I'm just covering my back here. Just in case.'

'This isn't like you, Luce. Sneaking around. Being deceitful.'

'Oh, for God's sake, Jess, don't go all pi on me! It's just—well, you know, if the boys rang, you could say I'd just popped out or something, that's all.' I felt hot, sweaty. Awful suddenly. Why had I rung her? All she was going to do was throw cold water on my lovely plans. 'Never mind, Jess,' I said hurriedly. 'I can see it puts you in a difficult position.' I drew up outside the church. 'Forget it.'

'Of course I won't. I wouldn't let Ben be scared and upset and wonder where you are. If he rings, I'll say you've popped out. But, listen, Luce . . .'

I listened. But held the phone quite a long way from my ear. Didn't actually hear too much. When she'd finished, I brought it back. 'OK?' She was reasoning. 'You do see that, don't you?'

'Of course I do,' I agreed. 'Speak to you soon, Jess, OK? Lots of love.'

I snapped the mobile shut and walked up the narrow gravel path to the church door. Inside, up near the altar, Mimsy Compton-Burrell was already busy, collecting vases of nearly dead flowers and bustling across with them to a side room.

'Sorry I'm late,' I called. I followed her into the little whitewashed vestry with its long table, laden with vases and green foam. 'This is just so sweet of you to come and give me a hand.'

She grinned. 'It's not a problem, I wasn't doing anything today so— good grief.' She stopped short. 'Whatever have you got there!'

'Oh,' I grimaced. 'Rose's entire collection of amaryllis plants. Max picked them. Thought he was being helpful.'

'Oh!' Her hand flew to her mouth. 'Rose must have gone bananas!'

'Don't,' I groaned, shaking my head wearily.

'Where is Lavinia, by the way?'

'Hot date,' I said wryly, watching admiringly as she arranged the towering plants in a crystal vase.

'Oh!' She stopped. 'Not that ghastly Rochester-Clarke buffoon?'

'No, someone called Roddy Taylor?'

'Oh, Roddy Taylor! Actually he's rather sweet. Rochester-Clarke's ghastly. I made the mistake of going out with him. Ages ago, I invited him round to the flat one evening and I think we both tacitly understood there might be some action. Anyway, he appeared, complete with an overnight bag, which I thought was a bit rich, and inside it was a pair of pyjamas, a toothbrush, slippers, a packet of All Bran, and—I kid you not—a disposable loo-seat cover.'

'No!' I laughed. 'For a night of passion?'

'Well, of course it never happened. I simply couldn't face it. I think it was the combination of the All Bran *and* the loo-seat cover that did it. As if one would inexorably lead to the other. Not a sexy thought.'

We shrieked with horror, then hastily covered our mouths. It sounded wrong, somehow, laughing like drains in a church, but lovely, too. The familiar, cosy, companionable sound of women's laughter. I glanced at her as she deftly aimed long stems at the back, short at the front, making it look so easy. Her blonde hair flopped into her merry eyes as she worked. It was good to see her again.

'So what do you do down here for entertainment then, Lucy?' she said. 'I heard you were working up at Kit Alexander's place, but that's not going to offer much in the way of a social life, is it?'

'Well, I can see that it might—well. Be on the quiet side.'

'I tell you, Lucy, you'll never meet a man down here. You'll have to dash back to London periodically, to ferret.'

'Oh, but I already have,' I said happily, unable to resist. 'I mean, met somebody. And he's absolutely gorgeous, but I must admit, I did meet him in London first.'

'Really?' She gazed at me admiringly. 'Quick *work*. I'm impressed. And when I know you better I'll probe a little more,' she teased. 'But please tell me it's not Kit Alexander?'

I stared. 'No, it's not,' I said slowly. 'But what's wrong with him?'

'Oh, nothing,' she said hastily. 'He's lovely. And a complete sweetie. It's just . . .' She hesitated. 'Well, he has a little personal problem, which I'm afraid, being a mate of Julia's—his ex—I probably shouldn't divulge.'

'Oh. Right!' I put my flowers down, rapt. 'God, I always wondered about her. Did she really leave him for the plumber?'

'Oh, yes, she really did, but only after years of trying not to. You see,' she wrestled with her conscience, 'well, the thing is—Kit's impotent.'

'Oh!' I gazed at her. 'Oh dear.'

'Having said that though, they did manage two boys in the early years. But in the later years . . . no sex. Poor Julia moved hell and high water to become a sex kitten and steam Kit up. She went to the gym, got all toned up, acquired an all-over tan and was always out, riffling through the negligee rails. Baby doll, vamp, Miss Whiplash—you name it, she wore it, and then she'd shimmy out of the en suite bathroom, with Kit in an agony of anticipation on the bed, and—oh. Oh dear.' She held up a crooked little finger.

I suppressed a giggle. 'So it never actually happened?'

She sighed. 'Oh, no. But they both went to terrific lengths to save that marriage. Ten out of ten for creativity.' She narrowed her eyes into the distance. 'Yes, naked croquet was a big theme, as I remember, at one time. Kit insisted that the stance, and the swing of the mallet, did wonders for his libido.'

'It's no wonder she opted for some boring straight sex with a blue-collar worker then.'

'Well, quite. Oh—hello.' She paused as a car horn tooted urgently from outside. 'That'll be for me.' With her hands full of greenery, she kicked the vestry door wide open so we could see into the church. Outside, a car door slammed. 'My daughter at last.' Mimsy looked at her watch. 'She's been to a party,' she explained, 'and I asked one of the mums to drop her off here.' The church door flew open and a moment later, a child's running footsteps echoed noisily on the flags, as hurtling down the aisle, pigtails flying—came Ellen.

Chapter Five

'HI, DARLING, HOW WAS IT?' Mimsy smiled as Ellen ran into the vestry.

'Really cool, actually.' She skidded to a halt on the other side of the trestle table. 'We had a totally brilliant conjurer and then Polly's dad did a barbecue.' Then she looked at me. 'Oh, hi!' she said, surprised, blinking behind her spectacles.

'Hi,' I breathed back, wanting to vomit. She'd recognised me, and here I was, trapped in the vestry with her and—oh my God. I turned horrified eyes on Mimsy, or should I say *Miranda*. I stared. Was this woman with the merry green eyes and infectious giggle really her, then? The sanctimonious religious fanatic?

'You two know each other?' Mimsy said, surprised.

I gazed stupefied. Opened my mouth, but couldn't speak.

'Yes, we met in London, with Daddy. She works with him, don't you?' Ellen's beady eyes peered up at me.

'That's right,' I breathed, finally finding my tongue. 'But—I, I hadn't made the connection,' I faltered. 'Lavinia said you were Compton-Burrell, and Ellen's father is—'

'Fletcher, yes, that's right, but I hardly ever use my married name. Compton-Burrell's my professional name.' She grinned. 'It gets me far more bookings at smart weddings than Fletcher ever would. They like the Mimsy bit too, frightfully U and nursery, you see. Charlie can't bear it, though, so he's always called me Miranda. But I still don't quite understand. You met Ellen in London?'

'Yes. It was—a research meeting.'

'Research? Golly, Charlie is getting highfalutin. I remember the days when he just sat down at the kitchen table and scribbled out a script. What sort of research material did he need?'

'Oh, Mum, it's totally cool, she does animal stuff, don't you?' Ellen beamed up at me eagerly. 'Works on a sort of *Pet Rescue*-type thing.'

Mimsy's eyes widened, as well they might. 'Really! Gosh, I had no idea. Lavinia said antiques, and you're working at Kit's, so I assumed . . .'

'It's a sideline,' I broke in breathlessly.

'What, the antiques? Or researching for the BBC?'

My mouth dried. 'The antiques. I mean—the research. Well, they're both about the same, really. You see, I could never decide which I preferred, so I sort of troubleshoot, between the two.'

'Troubleshoot?' She laid down an amaryllis in wonder. 'Heavens, how glamorous. But I wouldn't have thought that was possible. Antiques and animals don't seem to mix, do they?'

'Oh, you'd be surprised,' I croaked. 'Some things make the strangest bedfellows.' I almost fell over with fright as that came out. *Bed*fellows. But Mimsy had moved on, captivated by my scintillating career.

'How does that work then? Are they somehow connected?'

Fear was filling every vein now. Yes. Yes, perhaps they were connected. 'What, you mean . . .' I faltered, seizing a handful of greenery and busily arranging it. 'Oh! *Antiques Roadshow*?'

'Sorry?'

'Well, you know, antique animals,' I gabbled with relief, trying not to sound as if I'd just thought of it. 'You see, if, for instance, Hugh Scully, or one of the other presenters, comes across a, I don't know, Chinese lion from the Ming Dynasty, they come to me for advice.'

'Do they really? Gosh, and I always thought they knew their onions on that programme. But—so hang on. How does Charlie fit into all this? Antiques sounds a bit stuffy for him, and he never writes animals into his scripts. Says the actors curse him for it, hate working with them.'

'Yes.' I felt faint. 'Yes, I can imagine.' I swallowed. 'Well, Charlie comes into it because'—I was interested to hear how my voice would go on—'because, well . . .'

'I know!' Ellen suddenly seized my arm. 'It's prehistoric animals, isn't it? Really antique ones!'

Mimsy laughed. 'Oh, Ellen, don't be silly!'

The trouble was, I didn't have a better idea. 'No,' I hastened, 'not so silly, actually. But the thing is, I can't really say anything at the moment.' Why hadn't I thought of that earlier? 'It's all a bit, you know, hush-hush.'

'Oh, cool! You mean Dad's writing one of those *Jurassic Park*-type scripts? With dinosaurs? Oh, Mum, we'll be rich!'

'But how extraordinary.' Mimsy's brow puckered. 'He never mentioned it.'

'Well, as I said, it is a bit—you know. Under wraps.'

There was an exhausted silence as they took all this on board. I'd floored them, finally, with a baffling litany of career moves, and they were grappling now with the implications. Visions of me on my hands and knees, fitting dinosaur bones together, perhaps at the *Antiques Roadshow*, perhaps in the *Pet Rescue* studio, perhaps at Kit's—all scenarios were doubtless springing, bewilderingly, to mind.

'Gosh, Lucy, what a fascinating career you've had,' said Mimsy at length, with evident feeling.

'Yes, I suppose I have,' I conceded, equally exhausted. 'So. Two big vases either side of the altar, d'you think?' I grabbed one and made to take it away, my heart pounding. I'd had a lucky escape.

'Lucy?' echoed Ellen, suddenly. 'I thought Dad called you Laura?'

I froze, the vase in my hands. A terrible hush fell over the church. A ghastly, sickening silence. Finally, Mimsy spoke. I couldn't look at her. But I had a feeling her face was pale.

'Ellen, wait for me in the side room, would you?' she said quietly. 'There are some colouring pencils and books in there. I won't be long.'

Her daughter went without a word, perhaps sensing in her mother's voice something serious. I put the vase back down on the table.

'Are you having an affair with my husband?'

I breathed in sharply, then I forced my eyes up. Her face was indeed very pale, and the green eyes no longer sparkled but were flat, defeated, vulnerable. I saw the face of a woman who'd already had her share of grief, and who was now enduring more, heaped on her, by me.

'I . . . well. No. I mean . . . not quite. But we . . . were going to. We . . . we haven't actually got round to it yet,' I muttered miserably, my eyes slithering away from hers in shame. I felt despicable, dirty, cowardly. 'I was going to meet him tonight.'

'And he'd told me he had a meeting up in London,' she said flatly.

'I'm so sorry,' I gasped. 'I had no idea he was your husband.'

'And that would have made a difference? If you'd known?'

'I don't know. I mean . . . yes. You're so nice, and so totally not what I expected. You see, I almost felt like I had an excuse,' I blurted out, 'because he'd said you were so . . . oh, I'm so sorry!' To my utter horror and shame, I burst into tears. In an instant she was round the table and, to compound the shame, had put her arms round me.

I sobbed into her shoulder, quite unable to stop myself. 'It should be you in tears, not me! You should be the one having the breakdown.' I gulped between hiccups, pulling away to wipe my face with my sleeve.

'Oh, don't worry,' she smiled sardonically. 'I've had too many in the past over this kind of thing. Haven't got the energy.'

'You mean, this has happened before?'

'Oh, yes, quite a few times,' she sighed.

'A few!' My eyes dried dramatically, and I stepped back, horrified. So appalled was I, in fact, that I had to lower my bottom onto the little wooden pew against the whitewashed wall. She sat down beside me.

'But I thought I was the only one!' God, how naive it sounded. How familiar, out there in the open. 'Good God,' I said humbly. 'I had no idea.' I thought back to Charlie's protestations of love; of deep, true and meaningful love, all, if I'm honest, though, couched in rather physical terms of endearment. 'So,' I said tentatively, 'so, in fact, you're not really very surprised?'

'No. But disappointed. You see, when he's not seeing anyone I always think, Oh good, he's better. But then it happens again.'

'Better?'

'Yes.' She gave a sad smile. 'He's only been like this these last four years, you see. Before that, we couldn't have been closer.'

I struggled. 'Four years? But why—'

'That's when Nick died.'

'Oh.'

'And this is his way of coping, trying to forget. To distract himself.'

I frowned. 'You think?'

'Oh, I know. He's desperate, Lucy. Because he knocked Nick over.'

I stared, horrified. 'No!'

She nodded. 'He was coming out of the driveway. Too fast, in his car, just as I was walking round with Nick. I'd picked him up from school and had hold of his hand, when Charlie's red Mercedes came swinging round the gatepost. Knocked Nick flying.'

'Oh God!' I clutched my mouth, froze. Slowly I lowered my hand. 'How *aw*ful! He never said—'

'No, of course not, how could he? He can't accept it himself. So, when he meets new people who don't know, he tells a slightly different story, because he feels so terrible about it. And how do you get over a thing like that, Lucy? It's bad enough for me, losing a child, but far worse for him. He can't forgive himself, so he tries to lose himself. Tries to reinvent himself. Then lots of frantic sex to make it all go away.'

'He's not well,' I said soberly.

She shook her head. 'No, that's too strong. And too easy. As I said, it's his way of coping. We all have to find a way.'

I looked at her. 'And you found God?'

She smiled. 'Is that what he told you?' She pushed her fringe out of her eyes. 'In the beginning, yes, it was true. I *was* desperate, so I did turn to God. And I was infatuated to start with, fanatical, evangelical, sure. But like any new passion, it can't go on at that rate for ever. That frenetic pace has to settle down, find some balance. So now . . . well, now I've got it more in perspective. I still have a very strong faith, it's still my rock, but now it's not my whole life.' She smiled. 'So, sadly, I'm not the mad, breast-beating zealot that Charlie would like me to be. Not the convenient excuse he needs. Maybe I was once, four years ago. I was quite mad then. Mad with grief. I know that.'

I nodded slowly. 'Four years ago, I was mad too.'

She nodded. 'I know. I knew that. Grief does crazy things. I don't know you very well, Lucy, but I'd hazard a guess you're not the type to sleep around with married men.'

I swallowed. 'Now you're giving *me* an excuse,' I muttered. 'Letting me off the hook.'

She shrugged. 'Maybe, but your life was shattered, just as mine was. When we're forced to take a completely different route, who's to say, as we're groping in the dark, which side lane we might inadvertently slip down, when we're at our most vulnerable, at our lowest ebb?'

'But I thought I *was* better,' I said. 'I thought Charlie was my salvation, my compensation, even, for all those ghastly years. I couldn't see it was still the wrong lane.'

'Because you wanted to be better. I've done that so many times. Seen so many things as a miracle cure. It's only now I'm realising it has to come from within. That no outside influence can cure you.'

We sat silently together, side by side, on that low wooden pew, in that tiny, vaulted, whitewashed room. A single shaft of sunlight streamed through the high, mullion window and fell on discarded stems on the trestle table. I thought how marvellous she was. How strong and brave, and I wondered if I would have shied away from Charlie if I'd known earlier. I hoped so.

'I'll ring him,' I murmured, getting to my feet.

She stopped me. 'Please don't. Please go to him, go and meet him as planned. Tell him gently. Or even,' she hesitated. 'Even, carry on.'

I stared down at her. 'What! You can't mean that!'

'I just don't want him to be hurt, to suffer any more.'

I felt humbled by her strength. Her compassion. 'Oh, Mimsy, I—I couldn't,' I mumbled. 'I mean, I just don't feel the same way about him.'

'No, I can see that,' she conceded. 'But he's not a bad man, Lucy. One day, I know he'll come back to me. And I so badly want him back in one piece. Be gentle with him, won't you?' She fixed me with her sea-green eyes, unblinking, clear and true.

I gazed at her. Nodded. 'Of course I will,' I whispered. 'Of course.'

I arrived at the Hare and Hounds some time later with a heavy heart. Inside, the pretty, whitewashed pub was softly lit and muted, but as I glanced around in the gloom, I saw Charlie immediately.

He was sitting at a table by the far wall, over by the fireplace, both arms stretched along the back of an old oak settle. My heart lurched as he swept a hand back through his dark hair, brown eyes dancing. I swallowed hard. Charlie. My Charlie. But it was not to be. He saw me and raised a hand. 'Lucy! Hi, darling—over here!'

'Hi.' I made myself walk over.

'I'll get us some drinks,' he smiled, as I sat on a bench opposite him.

I stared hard at the beer mats on the table, my cheeks flushed, until Charlie came back from the bar with the drinks.

'I've been up to check out the room,' he said, squeezing in on the bench next to me. 'And I promise you, you are not going to be disappointed. Just what the doctor ordered. A long, low-ceilinged attic affair with beams you're guaranteed to bonk your head on at every step. The only answer, I've decided, is to spend the entire evening horizontal in the feather bed. What d'you say we have a couple of sharpeners down here first and then have supper in our room?'

I swallowed. Gripped the stem of my glass hard. 'Charlie, I don't think I can stay for supper.'

He paused, a frothing pint at his lips. 'What d'you mean you can't stay?' He swivelled on the bench to look at me properly, brown eyes bewildered. 'Lucy, what's happened?'

'Charlie, I met your wife this afternoon. Actually we've met before. Because we're on the church flower rota together. It's just, I never made the connection.'

'I see,' he said quietly, carefully. 'And now that you've made that connection, suddenly this whole shooting match is off, is that it?'

'Charlie, look.' I struggled. 'It changes everything! In the first place, she's nothing like you described. Icons and genuflecting—it's not true.'

'It used to be,' he said obstinately. 'In the beginning.'

'Yes,' I nodded, 'and she admitted as much. But, well, she's come a long way since then, Charlie, you know she has, and—'

'And in the second place,' he interrupted, in a deathly quiet voice, 'she told you what really happened, is that it? Told you about Nick.'

I took a deep breath. Let it out slowly. 'I'm—so sorry.' My hand closed over his on the table.

He stared down at our hands for a moment. 'Sorry for me, for what I did to my son, or sorry that you can't be with me? Can't love me. Even though we haven't given it a chance?' He looked up, beseechingly.

'Both,' I said softly. 'So sorry for what happened, for your terrible, terrible loss—God, any words sound trite—but'—I struggled to explain— 'I can't be part of your healing process, Charlie. I can't be with you for that reason.'

He paused to take this in. 'I see. I suppose she told you that this is how I forget, the only thing that takes away the pain.'

'Did you know that she was aware? I mean, of all your affairs?'

'I suspected,' he muttered. 'But nothing's ever said. Oh, Lucy, it's almost worse that she *lets* me, doesn't confront me.'

'She doesn't want to stop what helps you.'

'Because she's so good, and kind!' He banged his fist on the table. 'I can't *bear* her kindness sometimes, and the fact that she's actually forgiven me, for what I've done to Nick, is almost too much to endure.' He turned agonised eyes on me. 'Christ—would you forgive someone who killed your precious four-year-old? Wouldn't you rant and rave, blame, recriminate? Well, not Miranda. Not once. Not even in the beginning. No guilt whatsoever, Lucy, has ever been laid at my door, and believe me, that makes it far, far worse.' He shook his head. 'How can she forgive me, Lucy?' he cried.

'Because she has to. It's the only way forward, otherwise she'd go mad. And she'd lose you, too. You'd part, the two of you, and that would be too much for her to bear. She's lost her son already, don't you see? She doesn't want to lose the rest of her family. She loves you!'

'She has lost me,' he said bitterly. 'She's become too good, and I became too bad. She scurries off to Bible classes, and I scurry off to the flat for a night of lust. We've drifted too far apart. There's no going back.'

'Of course there is,' I insisted. 'There's always middle ground. Meet her there, Charlie, talk to her, tell her what you've just told me.'

He shook his head. 'We wouldn't know where to begin,' he said sadly. 'It's been going on too long. There's too much crap to sift through.'

'But you have to sift through it, for Ellen's sake.'

He sighed. It was a sigh that seemed to come from the depths of his soul. 'We had a fantastic marriage, Miranda and I. Everyone said how lucky we were. I was mad about her, loved her so much.'

'Of course you did,' I urged, 'and I did too, Charlie, I loved like that, and I'd give anything to have it back, to have Ned back. And the thing is, you *can* have it back. If I were you, I *know* I'd make it work.'

'Yes, but that's easy to say when you haven't killed anyone.'

I stared at him. Took a very deep breath. 'How d'you know?'

'What?' He looked at me blankly.

'As far as I'm concerned, I killed my husband, Ned.'

He frowned. Tucked his chin in, sharply. 'What? Hang on, I thought he died in a car crash? While you were in labour?'

I nodded. 'He did, and I was. But at the time he died, he was on his mobile phone, talking to me. I'd rung him, you see, furious that he wasn't with me.' My eyes filled up with tears as I remembered.

'And that's when he crashed?'

'Yes,' I said, blinking hard. 'I was in such a state at the time, I didn't really register anything. Just a hell of a noise, and then the line going dead. And it didn't even click when my parents came to tell me what had happened, that the lorry driver had said he was on the phone. It was only much later, days later even, that I realised. If he hadn't been distracted, talking to me, trying to pacify hysterical me, he'd have seen that lorry coming. He'd still be here!'

Charlie looked at me for a long moment. Finally he shook his head. 'You don't know that. You can't possibly torture yourself with that.'

'I don't,' I hissed, leaning forward. 'Too much, at least, which is precisely my point. Oh sure, in my darkest moments there have been times, definitely, when I've beaten myself up over it, but not continually. Because, Charlie, there is no point. It's like pressing the self-destruct button, not to mention being totally destructive to your loved ones. Don't you see? Accidents do happen, tragic ones, and there's nothing we can do about it. Bad things happen to good people all the time, but it doesn't make them bad people. It doesn't make *you* a bad person!'

Charlie didn't answer. Our eyes were still locked, and for a second or two, neither of us flinched. Then he looked away.

Another silence prevailed. At length he spoke. 'I know you think I'm just a terrible old philanderer, Lucy, but I felt—still feel—very deeply about you. Even though we've never . . . well. You know.'

I smiled. 'I know.'

He smiled ruefully and I felt him retreat back into his past. It was the same sort of road I'd been on. A road filled with loss, and pain, and grief, but I knew he'd been further down it than me. At length, I stood up. I bent down to kiss his cheek. He squeezed my hand tight, but he didn't speak. Didn't look up at me, either. I think maybe he couldn't.

'Bye, Charlie,' I whispered.

I drove away, spent, exhausted and full of our collective sadness. The injustice of it all enraged me. Who was Mimsy's God, who let things happen in milliseconds that would shatter lives for ever? A child thrown in the air, a husband through a windscreen—it didn't make sense, any more now, than it had done when Ned had died.

I knew how terrible the pain had been, but Charlie, who had undoubtedly been to hell and back, could surely now, four years on, face up to it, start again, start a new life with Miranda? I felt there was new tissue there, and that it might not tear as easily as the old. I hoped so, for both their sakes.

Looking back, I wondered if what Jess had said, about deliberately picking a married man, now held a ring of truth? Because now that he wasn't available, was I beside myself with grief over the man I'd loved— and lusted after, I added guiltily—and had now lost? If so, why the dry eyes? Could I have loved him? Or had I just been going through the motions to get back on track?

I sighed and glanced at my watch. Nine o'clock. I didn't want to go back to the barn. Didn't want to drive past Netherby, where no doubt the Fellowes would all be having supper on the terrace, amazed to see my car drive past when—hang on, wasn't she supposed to be in London for the night? No, I decided. I couldn't go back until it was quite dark and I could slip in quietly.

As I drove along, I realised I was driving through Frampton and approaching the manor house gates, and . . . yes. Yes, Kit was in his front garden, a glass tumbler in his hand, strolling among his box hedges and lavender parterres. Kit, a friend, surely, albeit a new one, but would he want to be bothered? I raised my hand, tentatively, and at the same moment he saw me and he waved back. I grinned with relief and slowed to a stop as he strode down to swing open the gates, smiling broadly.

Oh, *yes*, I thought with a rush of relief. Dear, kind Kit; dear, kind, *safe* Kit, more to the point, particularly after what Mimsy had told me. *What a good idea.* I jumped lightly out of my car, smiling.

'Well, *what* a pleasant surprise,' he called. 'I was just thinking, What a glorious evening, and no one to share it with. No one to escort round my garden, glass in hand, admiring my borders and my wild-flower meadow, and now here you are! What'll you take for it, my dear?'

'I'll take exactly what you're having. A large gin and tonic by the looks of it.'

He ushered me inside to collect a drink. For a while we stood chatting in the dark hall, and then, clutching drinks we sauntered round the back of the house to the terrace. It issued onto the glorious wild garden where the musky scent of nicotianas mingled with cowslips, and beyond that, the apple orchard, with its ancient gnarled trees.

I sighed with relief, settling down on a bench in the shade of a huge canvas umbrella, Kit sitting beside me.

Rococo padded up the terrace steps from the garden below, and put her huge head in her master's lap, tail slowly wagging.

'Fully recovered?' I asked, reaching across to stroke her.

'Completely. And all thanks to you and Charlie.'

I sighed, remembering that strange, funny day. Charlie scooping me up in his arms in this very house, passion dancing in every vein. A deep melancholy rose within me.

'Ah,' said Kit softly, seeing my rueful face. 'Have I mentioned the wrong person?'

'No, not at all,' I said quickly. 'As a matter of fact—well, I'd like to talk about him.' I glanced across tentatively. 'You knew . . . I take it?'

'About you and Charlie? Well, I suspected, certainly, and in the past my suspicions about Charlie have been pretty well founded.'

I paused. Licked my lips. 'Lots of . . . other women?'

He hesitated. 'Well, a few. Although, no one ever quite of your calibre, Lucy.'

I smiled. 'You're very gallant, Kit, but it's OK, you don't have to be tactful. It's all over now, so you can tell me what a shit he really was.'

'He wasn't a shit,' he said slowly. 'Just a guy with problems to sort out.'

'I know.' I flushed dramatically.

'And let's face it,' he went on, 'no one really knows the truth about a marriage, do they? No one knows the real nuts and bolts, except the two sharing the double bill. Everything else is just rumour and speculation.'

I swallowed. 'Well, quite,' I said slowly. 'Quite. No one else really *does* know.' I was thoughtful for a moment.

'Another drink, Lucy?' He stood up with a smile.

I gazed up at him. His eyes reminded me of a bird's egg. Speckled, with little flecks of hazel and green. I came to. 'Please,' I said, handing him my glass. 'Thanks, Kit.'

'Oh, and while I'm gone,' he reached across to another chair and threw a glossy auction catalogue at me, 'Gregorio de Conquesca's private collection. It's up for grabs in Venice next Thursday. Take a look.'

'Oh. Thanks.' I took it, still miles away. I flicked distractedly through the pages, but eventually a Jacobean pitcher and bowl got the better of my abstraction.

'Oooh,' I groaned, 'just look at this pitcher! *Beautiful* condition, and look at all this early Meissen,' I marvelled.

'Exactly,' he called from inside. 'There's going to be the most almighty scrum, of course, dealers from all over the world will be going, but it'll be great fun. Come with me, if you like.'

I glanced up quickly from the book. Come with him? What, to Venice? I blinked. Golly, well . . .

'Beautiful roses,' I smiled, as he reappeared a few moments later.

'Aren't they just,' he agreed, ducking under the umbrella to hand me my drink. As I took it, I could have sworn he'd undone another button. On his shirt. Quite a lot of chest was showing. But maybe not. I looked away quickly.

'Ahh . . .' He sighed happily and settled back on the bench, stretching an arm along the back. 'It's been a good year for the roses.' He turned his head and looked at me very directly for a moment. 'In fact, it's been a very good year all round.'

I met his eyes, surprised. Then I flushed and looked away. I was aware of his hand on the back of the bench, a millimetre from my hair. It seemed very important, all of a sudden, to carry on staring at the roses.

'Tell me, Lucy,' he murmured at length. 'Do you play croquet?'

I choked violently. 'Sorry,' I croaked, coughing noisily, trying to catch my breath. 'Gin and tonic went down the wrong way.'

'Golly, poor you.' He got up and patted my back in consternation. Waited for me to recover. 'Better?'

'Yes, fine now, thanks,' I gasped. 'Absolutely fine.'

'No, I was just wondering,' he went on, undeterred, 'what d'you say we have a little round before the sun completely disappears?'

I wiped my mouth and put my drink down carefully on the table.

'Actually, d'you know, Kit, I've just realised I really ought to be getting back. Only, the thing is, Rose is baby-sitting so I shouldn't be late.' I stood up, quickly. 'Sorry.'

'Not to worry,' he said easily, getting to his feet. 'We'll do it some other time. The croquet, I mean.'

'Y-yes, lovely.' I faltered, blushing furiously.

Oh, how awful. How *awful*! I gripped the wheel and bombed through the dusky countryside, desperate to distance myself from the whole embarrassing episode. Had he really thought I'd be interested in a little . . . had he imagined me a desperate, thirty-something woman, jumping from one man to the next? Good grief, it was unthinkable. And I certainly couldn't handle a predatory employer chasing me around stark naked, a mallet swinging between his legs.

Well, I'd have to make it plain, I thought, driving through Netherby's gates defiantly. Have to—Jesus Christ, what was that? Away, in the distance, just behind Netherby in fact, and lighting up the night sky, was a huge, blazing, orange glow. As I drove along, my eyes hooked on the horizon, a terrible knowledge began to squeeze my heart. My hand shot to my mouth as the flames blazed high into the night sky. The barn. The barn was on fire.

Chapter Six

I ROARED UP THE HILL and skidded to a halt. Flames were licking out of the top windows, and part of the roof was blazing, the timber frame crackling and burning. For a moment I was transfixed with horror. Oh, thank God the boys were up at the house!

Archie, David, Pinkie, Lavinia and the aunts in their dressing gowns were standing on the lawn, staring up. I ran towards them.

'Oh Jesus, Archie—what happened!'

'Lucy!' He swung round, white-faced, fear blazing in his pale bulbous eyes. 'Lucy, you're not to—they'll be all right!' He held my arm in a vice-like grip as if to stop me hurling myself at the flaming building.

'Who'll be all right?' I stared at him in horror, terror rising fast as I saw it in his own eyes.

He gripped my other arm. 'Jack's in there,' he breathed. 'He's getting them out. It'll be all right, Lucy, he's getting them out!'

I gazed at him, appalled. Then—'*Nooo!!!*' I screamed, pulling away. 'No, they can't be! Oh God—*Ben, Max!!!*' I struggled to escape, as he held on tight. '*Ben!!!*'

At that moment, a figure appeared. It was Jack, running from the blazing house, a child in pyjamas in his arms.

'*Ben!!!*' I finally wrenched free of Archie as he let me go, and hurled myself towards them. 'Ben! Are you all right!'

'He's fine!' yelled back Jack, black-faced, as Ben collapsed, coughing in my arms. 'He's just full of smoke. Take him away, Lucy, back there.'

'But where's Max?' I shrieked, dragging Ben away from the heat.

'Keep her out!' roared Jack, as he went running back in. But there was no need. I was paralysed with fear now. Frozen with shock.

'Oh dear God,' I prayed, as Ben clung on round my waist.

David was beside us now, encircling us, a tight arm round both of our shoulders. 'He'll be fine. Jack'll see to it. It's all under control.'

'It is *not* under control,' I gasped. 'My baby's still—*oh, thank God*!'

I lurched forward as Jack suddenly reappeared, this time with Max in his arms, blinking, eyes streaming. I snatched him to me, sobbing.

'Oh, darling, my poor darling—are you all right?'

Max nodded, eyes huge.

'He's fine,' croaked Jack, 'but find something to wrap him in.'

'Yes! Oh God, in the car, a rug, but, Jack—where are you going!'

'One more,' he said grimly, turning back.

'Rose is still in there,' said David quietly, beside me.

'*Rose*? But why? And why were the boys in there?' I ran desperate hands through my hair. 'And where's the fire brigade?'

'Coming!' sobbed Lavinia, running up. 'But—oh God, Lucy, they're taking for ever, and she'll die up there, won't she? She'll die!'

She clung onto me, trembling. We were being beaten back all the time now, pulling the boys with us, wrapping Max in a rug, the heat seeming almost to take the skin off our faces as we gazed, petrified, at the top floor.

My mind spun like a top as the seconds ticked by. Oh God—Jack and Rose . . . I felt sick to my stomach. Oh, please, God, don't let them die.

Suddenly, glass shattered and a face appeared at an upstairs window. 'Staircase has gone—catch this!' yelled Jack. 'And hold it out—taut!'

He threw down a blanket. David and Archie grabbed a corner each. I seized another and Lavinia the fourth.

'Now—don't let go!' Jack ordered. We stood beneath him, bracing ourselves. He was poised up at the window, a small, limp body in his arms. Rose. 'Now—catch her!'

He let her go, and down she came, fast, spiralling through the air like a tiny rag doll. As she hit the blanket, Archie scooped her up, cradling her in his arms, dragging her away from the flames. Her head lolled and I saw her eyes, wide with shock, her mouth wide open, the inside of her mouth very pink against her black face.

'Jack! Oh God. Jack, jump!' I screamed, but he'd disappeared back into the furnace.

A moment later David yelled, 'Jack's coming over the gallery on a rope!' As the fire engines and ambulance came roaring into view, Jack's figure stumbled out of the front door, coughing. David threw a blanket round him, pulling him away. Finally, they made it to the bank and sank down on the grass. I flew to his side.

'Jack—are you all right?'

He couldn't speak. Raised a slow hand to show he was fine. Then he sat, hunched, his shoulders heaving with exhaustion.

'Boys?' he croaked finally, looking up, his face blackened.

'Absolutely fine,' I breathed, 'thanks to you.'

'Rose?'

We both looked across. Her family were gathered around her, as she lay still on the grass. The ambulance came to a halt beside them.

'Not sure,' said David quietly, as he went across to join them.

We watched as the back door of the ambulance flew open, and two men jumped out, swiftly followed by a stretcher. Rose's tiny body was lifted onto it. She was carried inside. Archie and the girls followed, all sombrely climbing in, and the doors slammed. Before the driver got in the front, though, he ran across to us.

'Rest of you all right?' he shouted. 'Was anyone else inside?'

'My boys!' I said, standing up and pushing them forward.

He took a quick look. 'Well, they look OK, but there's another ambulance coming. Make sure they get in it. They should be checked over.'

The ambulance roared off down the drive, siren wailing, and hoses gushed into life, as the fire brigade, running back and forth, took their water from the lake and shot great jets at the flames. Jack and I watched from the bank, each holding a wide-eyed child in our arms.

'A timber-framed barn—no way. God knows what happened in there,' said Jack.

'God knows,' I echoed, numbly. 'Ben, what—'

'No, not now,' said Jack quickly. He got to his feet. 'Look, this ambulance won't appear for hours. David can look at the boys. We'll go up to the house. Come on.'

I realised I was shaking. David came back and I felt a blanket being gently put round my shoulders.

He looked at Jack. 'Let's go,' he said quietly.

I don't remember much, but I think Jack and David carried the boys inside. David and I took them up to the bedroom they normally slept in. I washed their hands and faces in a blur, dimly aware I was functioning on automatic pilot as I dipped flannels in hot water, wrung them out, wiped away soot and grime.

Joan bustled in, her face white and shocked. 'Poor lambs,' she muttered as she put down some warm milk. 'How are they?'

'They're fine, Joan,' I whispered.

'We could have died,' Ben informed her solemnly, his face a pale mask as he sat bolt upright in bed. 'We nearly burned to death in there.'

'Did we?' said Max, the full horror dawning in his big blue eyes.

'Nonsense,' I soothed. 'Jack got you out in bags of time.'

'You're shaking, Mummy,' said Max.

'She's cold,' said David quickly, making them lie down. 'And it's all been a bit of a shock. Now, come on, boys, Joan will sit with you until you're asleep.'

'Oh . . . no . . .' I started. 'I'll do that, David. I'll—'

'You'll do nothing of the sort. I want you downstairs by the fire with a brandy.'

I suppose I must have looked awful. No good to the boys at all, evidently. As I followed David to the door, though, I turned.

'Ben, what were you doing in there? You were supposed to be up at the house, with Granny.'

'You didn't tell us that. We thought Trisha was baby-sitting at the barn, so we just went down there and went to bed. We thought she'd come.'

I stared at him, horrified. God—hadn't I told them? Was that right?'

'But—but surely . . .' I faltered.

'Come on, now,' interrupted David gently, taking my arm. 'We can sort it all out in the morning.'

In the small sitting room a fire was blazing. Jack was sitting beside it, cradling a brandy and staring into the flames. He'd wiped most of the grime off his face but there was still a dark tidemark round the edge. He reached for the decanter on the table beside him as we came in.

'One for each of you, I presume?'

'Certainly one for Lucy.' David pulled the other armchair right up to the fire. 'But I'm going on to the hospital now, so I won't.' He stood still for a moment, his face white. He looked all in.

'You'll let us know?' I said, moving gratefully to the chair and sitting down. God, my legs were wobbly. 'I mean, how she is?'

'Oh, of course,' David said.

A curious stillness seemed to fall on the room as he left; it was as if Jack and I, alone in front of the fire, were in some kind of limbo. I looked at the amber liquid someone had put in my hand. I took a great gulp and stared into the flames. I saw Jack, running out of them, with Ben in his arms.

'Jack, how can I ever thank you?' I trembled. 'If you hadn't—'

'If I hadn't, the fire brigade would have got them out,' he interrupted firmly. 'The fire hadn't got a proper hold.'

I knew this to be a lie. I remembered watching the huge jets battling to put out the flames. We hadn't stayed to watch the fight, but I knew it had been in vain.

'Everything that we owned was in there,' I quavered. 'Photos, all my pictures of Ned . . .' I put a hand over my eyes, horrified as I realised. 'Letters—everything!'

'I know,' said Jack quietly, 'but that's all you can't replace. Everything else, you can.'

His face was pale, his blue eyes unnaturally bright in the firelight. He'd been in and out of a burning building three times to save lives, and I was talking about possessions.

'Of course I can,' I breathed. 'And what do all those things matter, when Rose is in hospital—oh, Jack, I'm sorry.' I covered my face with my hands. 'I—I don't seem able to handle this.' I was shaking violently again. 'Oh God, I was just so frightened!'

To my horror, tears were streaming down my face. In a second he was beside me, kneeling, his arm tight round my shoulders.

'It's fine,' he said firmly, 'you shouldn't have to handle it. You're in shock, that's all.'

'My *children*!' I gasped, all control gone now. 'Coming out of those flames! White-faced, in their pyjamas. And me not there. Me not with them. But, Jack, what were they *doing* there? I left them here with Rose, I did!' My voice rose shrilly.

'Of course you did, my love,' he soothed, scooping me off the chair now, pulling me down onto his lap, holding me close.

'I didn't leave them alone, I swear—Oh, Jack, they could have died.'

'They didn't die though, did they? They're alive and well and asleep upstairs, OK?' He searched my face with his eyes.

I nodded. 'OK!' I gasped, finally.

He was stroking my hair off my face now, holding me close. It was so lovely, such a comfort. His warm body close to mine by the fire. I felt I wanted to stay there on his lap for ever, curled up like this, and that if I did, everything would be fine. I felt a weight lifting from me and a warm, submissive feeling spread from my stomach to my limbs. His face was still close to mine, bright blue eyes watching me intently.

'Are you going to kiss me?' I whispered.

He looked startled. Gave a slight smile. Regarded me quizzically for a moment. 'Do you want me to?'

'Very much.'

For several seconds we continued to look at each other. Then he leaned the last few inches necessary for his lips to meet mine, and his arm in the small of my back pulled me gently close into him. I could feel my heart pounding against my ribs. At length we drew apart. His eyes searched mine.

'Lucy,' he said softly.

That was all. But as we regarded each other, it seemed to me that here was a face I knew so well, and yet—I almost hadn't known was there. It was as if I'd been close up to something so large, so huge, I couldn't see it, had been unable to focus. Until this moment, when he ceased to be the boy I'd met in a bar in college, Ned's cousin, a friend to my sons, and became a stranger, with whom I longed to be on intimate terms. I saw his eyes recognise this too, and in another moment his lips were on mine again. In a silken movement, he deftly lifted me off his lap, and laid me down on the carpet, and then he was beside me, so that we were lying together. As he drew me into his body I arched my back and inadvertently sighed. Then I felt his body harden and respond.

When we heard the telephone ringing, our eyes flickered open at each other. 'Leave it,' I ordered breathlessly, as for a moment, we parted. We listened. Motionless, we stared at each other.

'We have to get it,' said Jack suddenly, drawing away from me and kneeling up. 'It might be David.'

'Oh! Yes, of course.'

I sat up as he left the room. My head was spinning incoherently, but through the blur, through the confusion, the only clarity of thought I had was that I wanted him back, now, beside me, by the fire.

And he was back, a moment later. As he came through the door though, his face was ashen.

'That was David,' he said. 'Rose died ten minutes ago.'

When I awoke the following morning, it wasn't that I didn't know where I was, it was just that I couldn't work out why. I appeared to be in bed, in the green room at Netherby, but—I struggled up onto my elbows—God, I felt so groggy. But then . . . yes, of course. Jack had given me something to make me sleep. My mind reeled back. Jack, white-faced, helping me up that sweeping staircase, getting me into bed, then pulling the covers up, and telling me to sleep.

I sat up, and realised that, apart from my shoes, I was still wearing my clothes. I swung my legs out of bed and immediately felt sick. Whether it was the aftereffect of a pill, or Rose's death, or my home burning to the ground, or perhaps the full implications of my behaviour the night before dawning, I don't know, but I ran to the bathroom and threw up.

Slowly, I washed my face, and wiped it numbly with a towel. Then I sat on the edge of the bath for a bit. Eventually I got up and tentatively made my way back to bed. And then, from the next-door room—I heard voices. The boys. Oh Christ, the *boys*! I flew out onto the landing and darted into their room.

Max was standing at the end of Ben's bed in his Harry Potter pyjamas, shouting at Ben, who was pale and wide-eyed, sitting up in bed.

'Mum! Ben says I'm fibbing, but it's true, Joan told me! Granny's dead, isn't she?'

'Yes, yes, it's true,' I breathed, going towards them both, encircling Max with my arm and drawing him over towards Ben in the bed. I took his hand. 'Ben, listen. Granny, very sadly, died last night.'

'No!' he yelled, snatching his hand away. 'Not in that fire! Not burned to death, that can't be true!' Horror filled his eyes.

'No . . . no, not like that,' I said quickly. 'Not burned at all. It was the smoke, you see, and the shock, and her age too, you know. It was all too much for her. Her heart wouldn't—'

'*No!* I don't believe it. Granny can't be dead, she can't be!'

He was screaming now, tears pouring down his cheeks, grief buckling his pale face. I let him cry for a bit and drew him close.

'But he's right, the barn did burn down,' insisted Max. 'Look!' And with a four-year-old's zeal and enthusiasm for all things dramatic, he ran to the window and swept back the curtain.

I caught my breath. There, perched on the soft, rolling hills that swept up from the lake, rose up the jagged, blackened shell of our home; sodden, from the fire brigade hoses, and minus a roof and most of the top floor.

'Wow!' breathed Max. 'You can still see sofas and tables and every-thing, 'cept they're all black! But—our rooms have gone. Look, Ben!'

But Ben was not finding it nearly as enthralling as his brother. 'I can't bear to think of us in there, of Granny struggling to get out . . .'

'Draw the curtain,' I ordered Max. '*Now!*'

He hastily obeyed.

'Now, listen, Ben. Max, you listen too.' I pulled Max back from the window and put my arms round their thin shoulders on the bed. 'What has happened here is,' I struggled, 'horrendous, yes. And desperately sad. But Granny *didn't* die a violent death, Ben, she died peacefully. In hospital, surrounded by the people she loved. You saw her come out alive, and I don't want you rewriting history, OK?'

Ben nodded. 'But why us again?' he asked, turning his face up to mine.

Max frowned, confused, but I knew Ben was talking about his father.

'I don't know,' I admitted. I felt fury rising up within me that once again my precious boy had been damaged.

'Can we go home, Mum?'

I stared. Had he not completely taken it in?

'He means to London,' put in Max.

'But, darlings, the flat's gone! I sold it, you know that.'

'But you could ask the man who bought it if we can buy it back?'

I licked my lips, marvelling at their simple faith, their trust in the consummate ability of grown-ups.

'I know,' I said suddenly, 'we'll go to Lucas and Maisie's.'

'Yes!' they both gasped, and, for the first time that morning, the dull fear lifted from Ben's eyes.

'Can we?' said Ben, clinging to it. 'Can we go?'

'I don't see why not,' I said carefully. 'Wait here and get dressed.'

'We can't!' Ben's face was suddenly panic-stricken again.

'Yes, you can.' I pulled open a drawer. 'Remember, Granny kept these in here, in case you stayed.' I dragged out shorts and T-shirts. 'See?'

'Oh, yes. She did,' Ben said slowly. He fingered the clothes reflectively, remembering Granny again. Nothing could be fixed that rapidly.

'Oh, and hop in the bath first. I'll be back in a moment.'

It was surely mid-morning, but all was silent. The huge house was deathly quiet as I passed down the long passage, and it struck me that it felt more like a mausoleum than ever. But then, Rose had been its lifeblood, its force. Her tiny presence had been the pulse of the place.

I finally found the shattered remains of her family in the morning room. Archie was slumped in a wing chair by the fireplace, with Pinkie and Lavinia perched on either arm. His eyes were blank and glazed. The girls were talking across him in low voices. They stopped talking when I came in, and stood up.

'Lucy,' sobbed Pinkie.

I quickly crossed the room to hug them both.

'Pinkie, Lavinia, I'm so sorry,' I whispered, holding them both tight.

They nodded, gulping. Their clothes smelt of smoke and I realised nobody had been to bed.

'Archie . . .' I crouched down in front of him, the better to see his face. My hand closed over his. He squeezed it.

'She . . . had a good life, you know,' he murmured softly. 'A full one. Children, grandchildren, the garden, and so on . . . Committees and what not. And she wasn't in any great pain, when she went. It was all . . . very peaceful. Quiet. And thank God the lad came.'

'Hector? Was Hector there?'

'Lavinia rang him. Came immediately. They had time together. Alone.' He looked at me directly for the first time, his swimmy brown eyes childlike. 'That's important, don't you think?'

'Oh, yes. Yes, very,' I breathed.

'And she had such sadness, too, of course. Ned, you know. Never got over that. Never. Thought that the boys, Ned's boys . . . well, thought the world of them, what?' His voice was vague, distant, and he seemed confused. 'Filled a gap, I suppose. But she dreamed too much. Didn't know it could never happen . . . I couldn't let her have that, however much she'd been hurt. You do see that, don't you, Lucy?' He turned to me again. Eyes wide, appealing. 'Wouldn't have been fair.'

I wasn't sure I had a clue what he was talking about, but I nodded. 'Yes, Archie, I see.'

'But, thank God those boys got out. Thank God . . .'

'Yes,' I gulped. 'Thank God.' I knew I'd have my own nightmares about that, for years to come. 'And, Archie, you know, the boys. They're—well, Ben is desperately sad and distressed, about Rose, and—disturbed, almost, about the fire. I'd like to take them away, to my parents, to get them away from it all. Of course I'll be back,' I added quickly, lest anyone should think I was deserting a sinking ship.

'Lucy's right,' said Lavinia. 'They must have some space.'

I looked at her gratefully and Archie nodded.

'Good plan. Quite right. No need for you to be here. Police have been up already, of course,' he glanced at me, 'while you were still asleep. They believe it was some electrical fault. Some cockup at the hands of those cowboy builders Rose got in to wire it up.' His chin wobbled at this, and a tear trickled down his papery cheek. Pinkie swooped.

'Oh, Daddy, don't!'

They clung to each other as Pinkie sank to her knees beside him.

'Go,' Lavinia whispered. 'I know where you are if we need you.'

We hugged each other hard and then, with one last look at Archie, I darted gratefully away to get the boys.

I made for the back corridor, to take the quicker, backstairs route. As I approached the gunroom, I heard voices. I moved quietly towards the open door and saw David, pacing up and down by the window. He stopped abruptly the moment he saw me, and glanced warily at someone sitting in the huge leather chair that had its back to me.

'Lucy!' He quickly crossed the room and came out to the corridor, shutting the door firmly behind him. His face was terribly drawn, and white with fatigue. 'How are you? How are the boys?'

'Well, Ben's so upset and . . . oh God, what a ghastly mess.'

'Take them away, Lucy. This is no place for them. Not at the moment.'

'I'm going to,' I breathed. 'We're going to my parents.'

'Good, good,' he interrupted, 'fast as you can, good plan.' He dropped his voice. 'And listen, Lucy, ring when you get there, OK?'

'OK,' I said slowly, staring at his shattered face. I felt David was hurrying me along, or was it just the shock playing tricks with my emotions?

'And don't worry,' he said kindly, 'children are very resilient. Particularly yours. They've been brought up with so much love, they've a wealth of resources to fall back on. They'll be fine.'

'Thank you,' I said, flooding with relief, so glad he'd said that.

He gave a sad smile and went back in. As he made to shut the door, I saw a pair of khaki-clad legs stretched out in front of the leather chair. I recognised the shoes. So Jack was in there with David, I thought, as I walked slowly away. But he hadn't wanted to be seen. Least of all, by me.

I walked heavily upstairs and a lump came to my throat. I told myself not to think about what had happened last night. That there were far more cataclysmic events to consider this morning. But my mind refused to behave. It seemed full of Jack; his tenderness last night, his kisses, his kindness, so much so that when we drove out of Netherby ten minutes later, I hardly even registered the police car coming up the drive in the opposite direction. Didn't stop to consider it at all.

So—why hadn't Jack acknowledged me then? I wondered feverishly, incapable of letting it drop. Why hide? I swept a bewildered hand through my hair. Glanced in the rearview mirror. Max was nodding off on the back seat, his head on Ben's shoulder. Why hadn't Jack got up the moment David had said my name? Was he really so embarrassed?

It was almost as if he was hiding behind that chair because I'd thrown myself at him or something. Christ, maybe I had. Shamefully I recalled my 'Are you going to kiss me?'—and the surprise on his face. And not just surprise, either, but amusement, I decided, going hot. I cringed. How *could* I have said that, and to Jack, of all people! Jack, the practised seducer—no wonder his eyes had danced so uproariously. Oh, terrific, Lucy, really terrific. Another unsuitable candidate. Another serial philanderer. Look at the way he dropped Trisha like a cup of cold sick. The man has the moral sensibility of an alley cat—he's downright fickle!

Or was it me that was fickle? I asked myself with a sudden, secret qualm. My reaction to Kit's veiled proposition yesterday came back to haunt me. So soon after Charlie—why, it was insulting! And yet hours later, there I was, down on a rug, with . . .

And why was I suddenly so attracted to him now? I wondered desperately, when I'd known him for—well, for ever. Well, I'd never considered him attractive because—well, he was too flippant. Too wayward. Not a man to be taken seriously. But, then again, wasn't it true that he'd always had the power to unsettle me? That a cold look from Jack could rattle my cage, unnerve me? I recalled his censorious eyes following me as I'd chased after Charlie.

And another thing, I thought suddenly. Jack was practically the boys' uncle. Naturally he'd thought that through—hang on, Lucy and I are friends, related by marriage. The boys adore me, but when I dump her they won't, so do I want that sort of mess on my doorstep? No, thanks.

So. He was finishing it before it had even begun, was he? Of course, sensible. And that's what I'd be, next time I saw him. Friendly, of course, but distant. Forget it ever happened. I tried desperately not to think about lying in his arms by the fire, his breath on my neck . . . I moaned, gave a little shudder, gripped the wheel. Then I shot nervous eyes in the rearview mirror. Max was almost asleep, but Ben was watching me.

'All right, my darling?'

'Yes, thanks,' in a small voice.

'Ben,' I smiled into the rearview mirror. 'About last night. You went to bed in the barn because you weren't sure where you were sleeping, is that right?'

He stared at me in the mirror, silent.

'And Granny came down and baby-sat down there,' I persevered, 'presumably because you'd already got into bed?'

'Mummy, I really don't want to talk about it.' His voice wobbled.

'All right, darling, no. No, fine, of course not,' I said quickly.

I licked my lips, worried. He seemed so incredibly buttoned up. No small boy goes to bed voluntarily. He'd have stayed up with the adults, at Netherby, until told to do otherwise, wouldn't he? Something didn't quite ring true here, but I couldn't probe further. Not yet.

'So!' I said cheerily. 'Lucas and Maisie's for a bit. That's cool, isn't it?'

He smiled and a spot of colour came to his cheeks.

'Adults don't say cool, Mum. It sounds sad.'

'Ah.' I nodded. 'Sorry.'

'So, do they know? Maisie and Lucas? Have you rung them?'

'I have, and they're thrilled to bits, darling.'

Sort of true. I'd briefly had a word with Maisie, in the ten minutes or so we'd had at Netherby before David had come upstairs to hustle us down to the car, which he'd kindly brought round to the back door. I could imagine her worried face, though, as she put the phone down, went to find Lucas, to tell him. Lucy in trouble again. Oh dear. Coming home. And they had good cause for concern, too, because—what on earth was I going to do? I couldn't stay with them for ever, could I, so where would we live?

'And are we going to live there for ever? At Lucas and Maisie's?'

More wheel gripping. 'Ben, what we're going to do is, we're going to play it by ear. Which is so exciting, isn't it? Not make any firm plans yet, but make plans—oooh, I don't know. In a day or two, say. OK?'

He glanced at me. Gave a worried half-smile. 'OK.'

When we arrived, Maisie was waiting at the front window. She hurried out when she saw us. I fell on her, hugging her hard, tears brimming as I blinked into her faded gold hair. Maisie. My mum.

'Now, come on, Ben, Max, my chickens,' she bent to hug them. 'My, how you've grown in a few short weeks! Come in!' She led the way.

'You boys are in your usual room at the top of the house,' she called as she weaved ahead down the hall, crowded as usual with her precious wares, to the kitchen, expertly avoiding the flotsam. 'So take your things up and then come down for cake and tea.'

'We don't have any things,' said Ben flatly.

Maisie turned, flustered. 'But of course you don't,' she said, rallying. 'How exciting! Golly, I wish I could start again from scratch, get rid of all this rubbish. Just think of the fun you'll have buying it all.'

'Oh, cool!' Max's eyes lit up. 'Can we buy lots of stuff tomorrow, Mum?'

'Er, I think we'll wait and see what the insurance company has to say first,' I said nervously. 'Why don't you bags your beds, though?'

'I'm by the window!'

'No—I am!'

They thundered upstairs, happy to be back on familiar territory.

'*Everything's* gone?' whispered Maisie incredulously as she led me into the kitchen. Lucas was settled in an old Windsor chair, reading.

'Everything.'

'But you and the boys are all right,' said Lucas, standing up and putting his book down, embracing me. 'And that's all that matters.'

'Exactly,' I agreed, raising a weary smile. I felt exhausted suddenly, now that I could relax, now that I was here, and headed gratefully for a chair. I flopped down and a great wave of fatigue broke over me.

Maisie and Lucas bustled around putting the kettle on and getting cake out. I gazed about, noticing that Lucas's book was the same one Jack had been so engrossed in. I recognised the name, Jason Lamont. Slightly trashy I'd have thought, for Lucas.

I heard someone clatter down the stairs and turned to see Ben, in the hall, picking up my car keys from the table, opening the front door and heading to the car, probably to get the few remaining books and toys that happily had been in the boot and escaped the fire.

'Good cake,' I affirmed, biting into it.

'The usual Dundee, but I might try one of those Nigella ones now the boys are here. They like to help if it's chocolate.'

'Help lick the bowl, you mean,' I said, grateful we were not talking fires or Felloweses yet. I knew they were waiting for me to tell them in my own time.

I glanced down the passage to the front door. Ben had been gone for a while and I began to feel nervous. Presumably he *had* just gone out to the car. He wouldn't go off or anything, would he? The doorbell rang.

'Ah!' I breathed, with relief. 'Coming, darling!' I called, as the bell went again, with typical eight-year-old impatience.

When I opened the door, there he was, flanked by a young couple. The girl was pretty and sweet-looking, with curly blonde hair, and the man, slightly older; tall, slim, with a narrow, intelligent face. He smiled.

'We found this little chap in the road. I believe he belongs to you?'

'Oh! Thanks.' I drew Ben in quickly and grinned. 'Playing with the traffic, was he? I'll have the law onto me. Come on, Ben.'

'We are the law.'

I suddenly realised I'd seen the man before. In the back seat, being driven fast up the gravel to Netherby, as I left in the opposite direction.

'Well—you'd better come in,' I flustered, standing back to let them through as Ben ran off down the passage.

'It's just a few routine questions. Won't take a minute.'

Maisie's anxious face appeared round the kitchen door. 'Ben says the police are here.'

'It's all right, Maisie, just a few questions.'

I led them into the sitting room, clearing piles of books from the sofa to give them room to sit down.

'So! Any further on? Archie said the fire was probably caused by an electrical fault, dodgy wiring, is that it?'

The man had an impassive, watchful face and his hazel eyes were trained on me, thoughtful, contemplative.

'Well, no. We now think the fire was started deliberately, actually.'

'Good God.' I sat up, startled. 'By who?'

'By a child.'

'A *child*!' I stared in horror. My eyes darted from one face to the other. Both unmoving, impenetrable. 'No! Not Ben, Max—they wouldn't!'

'Ben, we believe.'

'*Ben!* But—'

'Mrs Fellowes,' he took a large open notebook from a slim leather case on the floor and flipped back a page. 'Where were you on the night of the 24th—yesterday evening? Sit down, please.'

I sat, ashen. 'I was—out. I was in a pub in Little Burchester.'

'With a gentleman by the name of . . .' he referred to his pad again, running his finger down to find the spot. 'Charles Fletcher?'

'Yes, but only for an hour or so. I left to go home.'

'Straight home?'

'No, I went to see a friend.'

'And her name?'

'His. Kit Alexander.'

'But wasn't it your intention, Mrs Fellowes, to be out for the entire night?'

I swallowed. 'Yes.'

'And you left the children with?' he swept on.

'Well, I left the children with their grandmother. Lady Fellowes.'

He frowned. 'Lady Fellowes said not. She gave a statement in hospital, before she died, saying that you had never asked her to look after the children. That you'd simply gone off, with your boyfriend, and left them alone at the barn. She said that she'd no idea what you'd done until she saw the barn on fire and raced down there while the staff phoned the fire brigade.'

'No! I would *never* have left them! I asked for Trisha but she said Trisha was too busy, so she said she'd look after them up at the house.' My voice was rising hysterically now.

'Was anyone with you? When Lady Fellowes said that?'

I thought back frantically. 'Well—no. No, we were alone.' And now she's dead, I thought in panic.

'But presumably you told Ben the plan?'

I stared at him. Felt numb. 'No. I—I forgot.' I felt my throat constrict. 'You see, I was in such a terrible rush that day. And Ben got the wrong end of the stick. Thought he was sleeping in the barn.'

'So . . . they put themselves to bed without an adult? Is that usual, Mrs Fellowes?'

'No!' I looked up sharply. 'No, it's not, and I don't know why! I've asked, but . . . well, he's too upset to tell me.'

'And did your son know where you were?'

I hung my head. 'No. I said—I would be in London, with a girlfriend. I didn't want to—well, hurt him. Say I was seeing—a man.'

'I see. Did you leave them during the day?'

'No,' I whispered, aghast. 'No! Max is only four, for Christ's sake!'

'How about the time,' he flipped the notebook open, 'he fell in the river and was only saved by the quick thinking of Lady Fellowes's nephew, mid-morning, while you were still in bed? Or the time Lady Fellowes said she found you drunk, lying comatose on a sofa, smashed bottles on the floor, the children playing with the bits of glass? Or the time—'

'Stop, stop!' I gasped. 'No! I mean—yes, OK the first bit, the river, but comatose on the sofa—that's a blatant lie!'

'So—when he fell in the river, did you know where he was?'

I stared. His eyes were not unkind, but focused, direct.

'She told you all this?' I whispered. 'In hospital?'

'Wrote it down over the course of a few months. This is her notebook. There are pages of it, Mrs Fellowes.' He flipped through to demonstrate. 'The children left alone for days on end, no food, so coming up to her for meals. She said she was worried about their welfare. Began to document the neglect.'

'Neglect?'

'We have to verify it, of course, but we've already done that to a certain extent. Dates and times have been confirmed. Sometimes, naturally, Lady Fellowes was the sole witness, so it's difficult—'

'Difficult because she's dead!' I shrieked. 'And she's lying!'

'Mrs Fellowes,' he cleared his throat. 'We also talked to Ben when we arrived. He did confirm he started the fire.'

'No! Ben . . . no!' I stood up, trembling. 'Why?'

The blonde girl spoke for the first time. Her voice was soft and silky. 'Who knows? But children do all sorts of things when they're unhappy. It's often for attention, we find.'

I swung round to her. 'Who are you?'

'I'm from Social Services. Mrs Fellowes, your husband is dead, isn't he?'

'Yes,' I whispered, horrified.

'And so you're a one-parent family. We do sympathise. We do know how hard that can be. Nevertheless . . .' She glanced at the man and they both got to their feet.

'I'm afraid I'll have to advise your parents to temporarily care for the children. We won't make an immediate care order if your parents can act *in loco parentis*.'

'*In loco*—but I'm not absent!'

'But not effective,' she said softly. 'I'm sorry, Mrs Fellowes, but someone has died as a result of your son's actions. He is under age, but the crime is nevertheless arson. We also believe his actions to be a direct result of yours. I must ask you not to remove your children from this house, Mrs Fellowes, and, for the present, to give your parents full control. We'll go and speak to them now. You'll be visited later on today by the local Social Services. We'll be in touch as soon as a full report has been made. Good day, Mrs Fellowes.'

And leaving me standing there, white-faced and shaking, they left.

Maisie crept in some time later, white-faced, and knelt down beside me, taking my hand.

'Have they gone?' I muttered.

'Yes, they've gone.'

'It's not true, Maisie,' I whispered, finding her eyes. They were huge and frightened. 'I wouldn't leave them alone, you know I wouldn't.'

'I know that, I know,' she soothed. 'It's all been a terrible mistake, and it's all going to be fine.'

'It's not going to be fine, they're going to take my children away!'

'No, no, they just said for us to look after them, at the moment. In the interim.'

'You think they'll take Ben into care, because of what he did? Oh God, tell me that won't happen!' I shrieked hysterically, standing up now, tears streaming down my face.

'No, no, of course they can't, darling, of course not!' She reached up and seized my hands, her lip trembling, eyes desperate. 'But why would Rose say those things? Why would she lie?'

'I don't know,' I wailed in despair. I paced around the room. 'I don't know why she'd do it. Did she hate me so much? I mean, Christ, she was the one who got me down there in the first place, wanted me right there on her doorstep, so I just don't know why—' I suddenly stopped by the bay window. 'Yes, I do.' I swung round to face Maisie. 'She wanted my children. Without me. She wanted them for herself.'

'But she was so kind to you, took you in. She wouldn't be that wicked.'

'Oh, but she would, Maisie,' I breathed. My mind was on fire, spinning like a kaleidoscope, shedding scattered shards of light. 'She wanted them on her terms, up at her house, Netherby, not down at the barn with me.' I paced the room again, working it through.

'Her grandsons, Ned's boys, to bring up as she saw fit. That's what she'd wanted all along. She was clever, too. The things she wrote in that book *were* lies, but sprinkled with grains of truth . . . Now that she's dead, no one will know the truth.' I sank down into the sofa, appalled.

I thought back to when Ned had died. Rose, always on the phone, pushing me to admit that I couldn't cope. Couldn't cope with the boys. She'd wanted custody way back then.

'Ben!' I sat up suddenly, startling my mother with my gasp of inspiration. 'I must talk to him.' I darted out of the room into the kitchen. But the kitchen was empty. Deserted. I spun round in terror.

'Maisie, where are the boys? *Ben!*' I bellowed, tearing back into the hall. 'Maisie, they haven't taken them, have they? They haven't—'

'Lucy, it's all right.' She came running out of the sitting room. 'Lucas took them out to the park, for an ice cream. It's fine, now calm down!'

I put my face in my hands and sobbed. She put her arms round me. Helplessly, I let her guide me into the kitchen, let her sit me down, weeping, at the table.

'They'll be back in a minute,' she said quietly. 'You can talk to Ben then. And we must stop panicking,' she said firmly. 'That's not going to get us anywhere. Getting hysterical is not going to help our case.'

'No.' I looked at her, wide-eyed. Horrified I had a case to answer. 'The fire was probably just a little prank that went wrong, don't you think? I mean, surely—'

'Of course it was,' she said staunchly. 'Little boys and matches—Oh!' She stopped as the doorbell rang. We stared at one another.

'Oh, Maisie. It'll be them again.'

'Just answer truthfully. It's all going to be fine.'

She went down the hall to answer the door. I waited, numbly, at the table. I thought of the times in London, when I'd felt myself slipping into that quicksand. How many times could these people have called then, and found me in a heap? Legitimately have had cause to worry about my children? Yet now, four years on, when I'd battled through . . .

Maisie opened the kitchen door to show them in. It was Jack and David.

'Oh!' I stood up, relief and confusion flooding through me. Glancing at Maisie's face, I realised she'd already briefed them on the doorstep.

'Lucy,' David quickly crossed the room and took my hands. 'Ghastly for you. I'm so sorry you've had to go through this.'

'But—but it won't happen, David, will it?' I babbled. 'You—you both know me,' I dared to look at Jack, 'and you'll tell them, won't you, what Rose did—'

'Sit down, Lucy,' said Jack gently, interrupting my gibbering and pulling a chair up for me.

I sat, and realised I was trembling. I held on to the table, gripped the oilcloth top, as he sat beside me. Maisie and David perched opposite.

'Lucy, David and I know Rose tried to frame you, gave false statements to the police.'

'You do?' I gasped. 'For sure?'

'Oh, definitely.'

'Oh, thank God!' I flopped back in my chair. Stared at him.

'She wanted to show you up as an unfit mother. And to that end she kept a detailed log. If they were left in her care, she'd pretend she wasn't consulted. Or if she'd lent you Trisha, she'd call her back unexpectedly, which left the boys alone in the barn, and then she'd go and get them. And write it all down.'

'Christ! Did she?'

'And when you and Charlie met at her party, she couldn't believe her luck. She gleefully tracked your progress, waiting for her chance, waiting for you to spend the night with him. And she was delighted when you went out, forgetting to tell the boys where they were sleeping. For some reason—and we still don't know why—the boys went to bed on their own. That's when Rose crept down and started the fire.'

'*Rose* started it!'

'Oh, yes, definitely. In the kitchen, apparently, in a rubbish bin. Just a small fire, with some comics and matches, something she could easily have put out later and reported to the authorities.'

'Hang on, hang on.' I clutched my head. 'She *said* she started it? You mean she told you all this?'

David nodded. 'Just before she died. Some time after her previous, fictitious statement to the police.'

'Oh!'

'Anyway, she started the fire, making it look like the boys' doing, but as she was making her way back to Netherby to raise the alarm, she looked back and saw to her horror that there was already smoke billowing out of a downstairs window. Horrified, she ran back, and found that the plastic lining of the bin had gone up with a whoosh, and caught the banisters behind. She started to throw buckets of water around, but it was no good, it was out of control. Panicking, she ran upstairs, grabbed the boys and ran back with them to the staircase, but by now the fire had really taken hold. It was quite impassable. They holed up in the boys' bedroom, huddled behind the bed, terrified, with no plan of action, except, apparently, Rose started to pray.'

'Christ,' I muttered. 'David, are you telling me that that's how badly she wanted custody of my boys? That she'd go to those lengths?'

David hesitated. 'It went wrong, of course, disastrously wrong. But yes, she wanted them at all costs.'

'Without me?'

'Well, no, not initially. But she was nervous you wouldn't stay. She had it out with you—remember? She was desperate for you to stay on at the barn, but it seemed you might be moving on, taking her precious boys with you. She thought bitterly of all the plans she'd made, how she'd planned to educate them, the important families she'd introduce them to, and now, just on a whim, it seemed she could lose control. Control was so important to Rose. And family, of course, was everything.'

'As it is to me, too!'

'Yes, but we're talking family with a capital F, here. Ben was heir to Netherby,' said Jack.

'Ben?'

'Of course. Hector had gone, for ever in Archie's eyes, Ned was dead, Ben was the eldest male. But what Rose *didn't* know,' said Jack quietly, 'is that Archie would never have let Ben inherit.'

'Why not?' said Maisie.

There was a silence. Jack looked at David.

'I think you know, don't you, Lucy?'

I didn't, but as I gazed at David, the wheels of my mind whirred like a propeller starting up. I gazed at this handsome, elderly face before me . . . at his high brow, his kind mouth, that nose . . . not the eyes, necessarily, too grey, but his hands, definitely. So familiar. I nodded, slowly, amazed. Amazed it hadn't occurred to me before.

'Yes, I see. Ben wouldn't inherit,' I said slowly, 'because he's not a Fellowes. Ned wasn't Archie's son.'

'He was my son,' said David quietly. 'Rose and I, well, we had a long love affair, many years ago. Ned was the result.'

'You and Rose!' Maisie gasped.

'Yes, me and Rose.' He hesitated. 'Or Rose as she was in those days. The most beautiful woman imaginable. And I was potty about her, for a long time. Because she was full of fun and damned good company. I'd known her for years in that vein, but when we became close—well, all the fun had gone out of her life and she was just very sad and lonely. Archie wasn't interested any more. He'd moved on. To younger models.'

'Did Archie know?' I whispered. 'About you and Rose?'

'Oh, yes.' He looked surprised. 'He asked me once, over cards, straight out. And I told him straight back.'

'How did he take it?'

'Oh, on the chin. As his due, I think.' He rubbed his cheek reflectively. 'He said, "Saw her going over the edge, eh? Brought her back. Glad you did. Glad it was you. Couldn't face it myself."'

'But—Pinkie came later?'

'Yes, I think Archie was peeved at being sidelined, so they had another child, and our affair came to an end.'

'But—he never told Rose he knew about Ned?'

'Lord, no. Chap's got his pride. No, nothing was said. Rose had no idea he knew.'

I remembered Archie, mumbling, 'Couldn't let Rose have that . . .' Couldn't let Ben inherit, that's what he'd meant. Not when Ned wasn't his son.

'And what about Ned?' asked Maisie, quietly. 'Did he know?'

'No!' I blanched. 'He'd have told me. I'm sure he would. And yet—well, he always . . .' I hesitated. 'He was always so wary of them. Certainly of his mother.'

I remembered how adamant he'd been that they wouldn't attend our wedding. 'They've screwed up most of my life,' he'd shouted angrily, 'they're not going to screw up this!' And I remembered Rose's letter, too, telling me how Ned had rejected her, in his teens. Had he guessed?

'And you never . . .?' I glanced quickly at David.

'No, I never said. It wouldn't have been fair, separating him from his family like that. But I hope I always looked out for him.'

'He always liked you, David,' I said truthfully. 'He said so, often.'

Something flooded David's face at this. Love? Relief? He must have been itching to acknowledge his son all those years. It explained why Ned had so little of the Fellowes character, explained his brains, his easy, relaxed manner. All David. I looked at him almost gratefully. Pleased for my boys. Not Felloweses. Felt a guilty rush of relief.

A silence ensued as we were each prey to our own private thoughts. As we digested the lies, the lust, the love and the deceit over the years.

'So, she told you all this, David?' asked Maisie, eventually.

He nodded. 'Yes. At the end, in the hospital. Archie came to find me. Said he didn't think she'd got long. That she was asking for me. Asked if I'd like some time with her.' I realised his eyes were watering. 'I went to her, and sat with her. Stroked her hair, like I used to . . .' He paused, in difficulties now. We all glanced at our hands to give him a moment. He cleared his throat. 'And—well, I had wondered about the fire, so I asked if she had anything to tell me. She knew she was dying, knew the fight was over, so she told me everything.' He gave a wan smile. 'I'm no priest, but I imagine that's what absolution does for you. Gives you some sort of comfort. I hope so. At the end, she asked you to forgive her, Lucy. She asked God, too. And then she died in my arms.'

I caught my breath, imagining Rose asking me to forgive her. I gulped and felt a wave of revulsion. I'd think about it later, but not when I'd just gone through the most appalling hour of my life.

'But why didn't you tell me all this this morning?' I rounded suddenly on David. 'Why didn't you tell the *police* then? Christ, you could have spared me all of this.'

'We knew the police were on their way to interview you,' Jack said impassively. 'Ten minutes earlier I'd taken a call. At that stage I didn't have the faintest idea what was going on. David was on the point of telling me, but hadn't, and I got the impression from the police that you were in deep trouble. I wanted to give you time, so I simply said I hadn't seen you, which was perfectly true, and why I didn't turn round when you came to the gunroom door.'

'And I wanted to tell Archie and the girls what Rose had done without the police being there,' said David quietly. 'Wanted to get rid of them. Which meant seeing you off the premises, since it was you they were after. I owe you an apology, Lucy, but I'm afraid I made Archie and the girls my priority.'

'And do the police know the truth now?' I asked, suddenly fearful.

'I've let them know I have a statement to make and I'm on my way back to Oxford right now,' he glanced at his watch, 'to do just that. I just wanted to explain to you first, though. In person.'

'Thank you. And d'you think they'll believe you?' I asked anxiously.

He smiled. 'Don't worry. There was a ward sister on hand behind the curtain. She heard everything.'

I nodded. Breathed a sigh of relief. After a while, he sighed too.

'I must go,' he said wearily, making to get up.

'But what I still don't understand,' Maisie stopped him a moment, her fingers on his arm, 'is why Ben said he started the fire?'

We all turned at a noise down the hall. The front door slammed, then the kitchen door opened. Jack stretched out his hand.

'Let's ask him, shall we?' he said gently. 'Because here he is.'

'Ben?' I got up.

He stood there in the doorway, then came slowly into the room, his dark eyes lowered, glistening. He wouldn't look at me. Down the hall, I saw Lucas usher Max into the sitting room with his dripping lolly.

'Ben, darling, this is important.' I crouched down beside him. I noticed he still kept a tight hold of Jack's hand. 'Ben—why did you tell the police you started the fire?'

'Because I did,' he said obstinately, staring at the kitchen floor.

'But that's not true, is it? Granny told David she started it.'

'Granny did?' He looked up, startled. 'Why?'

'To frighten us, I think, because I was out, and—well, complicated reasons, but not to burn the barn down. It just got out of hand.'

'But she said you did it!' he blurted out. 'When she ran up to us, I

142

screamed, "Granny—the house is on fire!" And she said, "Yes! Yes, I know, Mummy left the gas on! The kitchen's caught fire!" I thought you'd go to prison!' he cried, eyes brimming. 'So I said it was me, because they don't send children to jail, do they!' He was crying now.

'Oh, darling!' I hugged him, but his little body was like rock. I held him at arm's length, knowing there was more.

'But why were you and Max down there in the first place? Didn't Granny say you were sleeping at the house?'

'No, she didn't,' he gulped, 'and I had an argument with Granny, anyway.'

'Why?'

'Because when you'd gone, she came and found us in the garden. She said, "Well, your mother's really done it this time!" And when I said why, she said that you were staying the night with your boyfriend. So I said that wasn't true, and she was lying, 'cos you didn't have a boyfriend and she said yes it was, and I said, "Well, anyway, Mummy said Trisha's coming down to baby-sit so we're not staying here with you, we're going home!" ' He caught his breath. 'And I ran off!'

'I see,' I breathed. 'And she didn't come after you?'

'No, no one came. We just went to bed. It felt really odd.'

'Have you got a boyfriend?' said a little voice behind us. Max had escaped Lucas's clutches and crept in for some drama.

I turned to look at him. Shook my head. 'No. No, I haven't. But I *was* going to meet someone that night. But—it didn't work out. He wouldn't have been right.' I struggled. 'For any of us,' I whispered.

I was aware of Jack's eyes on me while David and Maisie tactfully contemplated the tablecloth.

'You can have boyfriends,' went on Max generously. 'We don't mind, do we, Ben? But we'd like to know, wouldn't we?'

Ben nodded, scuffed his toe. 'I think the truth's important.'

I took a deep breath. Regarded my own shoes. A silence ensued.

'Well,' said Maisie, breaking it briskly. 'I think what we all need now is a very large drink. With plenty of gin. I certainly do, and then some lunch. Lucas and I had planned to make pizzas, so if you boys want to help choose your toppings, you'd better come out to the pantry with me.' She opened a side door and disappeared.

'I'll come!' Max was off like a rabbit.

Ben followed, but he stopped at the door. Turned. 'Sorry, Mum.'

'For what?' I swallowed. 'Trying to keep me out of prison?'

He shrugged. 'Doubting you, I suppose. Like Thomas.'

'Hmm?'

'In the Bible.'

'Ah.' Furiously blinking back tears, I nodded as he left the room.

David stood up with a great sigh. 'And now, I really must go. But, Lucy,' he paused at the kitchen door, 'I know you think she was a wicked old woman and she got what she deserved, but—if you can understand the sort of life she led with Archie . . .'

I followed him silently down the hall, opened the front door for him.

'I think that you must have loved her very much, David.'

He looked down at his shiny brown brogues. Nodded. 'Yes. Yes, I did. Never stopped. And blindly, perhaps, but that's how it is, isn't it?'

I looked into his kind, sad, grey eyes. 'David, you know, I'll want the boys to know, when they're older.'

He smiled and his eyes brightened for the first time that day. 'I'd like that very much,' he said softly.

I reached up and kissed his thin, weathered cheek. 'Bye, David.'

I watched him go, pensive. Turned to find Jack, standing behind me.

'A nice man,' I murmured.

'And a good man, too.' We watched as he got into his car. I was very aware of Jack's presence. Close to me. I wondered what he was thinking. About last night? Surely we both were.

He cleared his throat. 'Well, I've said my goodbyes in the kitchen, Luce. I'll just pop in on Lucas, then I'll be on my way too.'

'Oh! Really?' I turned, panicky. 'Where are you going?'

'To collect my car, which for various complicated reasons is still in another part of London, and then—I'm not sure. Back in a mo . . .' He slid off sideways, into the sitting room.

I saw Lucas through the crack in the door standing up to embrace him in his continental way, Jack responding and picking up the book Lucas was reading, asking if he normally read such tosh. 'I mean, look at the cover, Lucas, come on!'

My father roared with laughter. 'Lurid, I agree, but readable tosh, and makes a refreshing change from some of your earnest oeuvres!'

And so it went on, the bantering and the teasing, with me thinking, with a sinking heart, that my parents could behave in this light-hearted, easy manner with this man, while I was standing foolishly by, incapable of joining in, because of some ghastly barrier I'd erected between us. But then, he'd done so much for me, I thought eagerly; hiding so he could tell the police he hadn't seen me, and then coming all this way with David to give me the good news, behaving . . . well . . . Like a brother. But like a lover? That was ridiculous. I bit my lip. Don't get excited. No. And yet that kiss, I thought, as hope resurged. Oh

God, that kiss! He reappeared, at my elbow. 'Right. I'll be off then.'

'Can I come with you?' I gasped wantonly.

He looked surprised. A smile played on his lips. 'Of course.'

See? Quietly amused. Quietly guffawing. But I just couldn't let him go like this. I dashed down the hall to tell Maisie and the boys I was off.

My feet felt as if they had wings on as I shut the door behind me. I felt reckless now. Exhilarated. My ordeal was over, and I was a normal human being again, on an ordinary London morning, when the worst crime I could commit would be to make a fool of myself in front of an old friend. I sighed with pleasure as we stepped out into the sunny streets.

'Isn't this wonderful?' I sighed, sniffing the air.

'You mean the carbon monoxide?' He sniffed too. 'Yes, I must say I'm rather partial to it, but then you and I have always been city slickers at heart, haven't we, Luce?' He smiled down.

You and I. Those sweet, delicious words. Totally innocuous, of course, but nonetheless, they crashed over my head like a tidal wave.

'Yes!' I agreed, coming up for air. 'Yes, definitely. Can't bear the country actually.' Why was I so nervous? 'I mean, no, the country's lovely, but—'

'D'you want to get that bus?' he interrupted. 'It could take us ages to get a taxi. Come on, it's a nice big red one and we can even go upstairs. If you're a good girl I'll buy you some sweets when we get off, too.' He hustled me aboard and I clambered upstairs, giggling stupidly.

'Any idea where we're going?' As if it mattered.

'Of course. Come on, right down the front. You can pretend to drive.'

I laughed some more. This was fine. He'd got the merry banter going and we could hide behind it, in the lurching conviviality of a London bus, until we found our feet. As we sat down on the front seat I concentrated hard on the meandering crowds ebbing and flowing on the pavements beneath us, all seen through the leaves of rustling plane trees that brushed the windows. I sighed with pleasure.

'A very big sigh. Happy to be back?'

I smiled. 'Very. This feels like home to me. The boys feel it too, I know.' I gazed down. 'Not that I have anywhere to house them in this splendid city, of course, but I refuse to think about that just yet.'

'Talking of houses, I spoke to Lavinia this morning. Now that the male line has been exhausted, she'll get Netherby.' He smiled. 'No more handsome rectories.'

'You mean—'

'Well, she doesn't have to get married now, does she? And I don't think she ever wanted to, really. It was the thought of having no stately pile that was driving her to all those dates. When Archie dies, she'll be mistress of Netherby. In fact, *before* Archie dies, if you ask me. Oh, she'll run that place like an oiled watch, take over where Rose left off.'

'She'll love it. Although don't be so sure about there being no man beside her. A certain Roddy Taylor set her pulse racing the other day.'

'Roddy?' He raised an eyebrow. 'Nice chap. I was at school with him.'

I smiled. 'I'm pleased for Lavinia. She'll certainly do a better job than Hector would. Although, maybe she'll offer it to him? When Archie dies?'

'She's already said as much, but Hector turned it down.' Jack's mouth twitched. 'No, he and Rozanna are setting up in a cottage in Cornwall.'

I grinned. 'Good for them. And good for Lavinia. She's the best man for the job. She'll be in heaven.'

'No doubt. She sent her love, by the way. When she heard what Rose had done, she said she'd like to come up and apologise for her mother.'

'She doesn't have to do that,' I said slowly, 'but I'd like to see her, anyway. I don't want,' I struggled, 'well, I don't want to cut the boys off entirely. One day, I think I'll tell them about David, but Netherby's still their grandparents' home. D'you think that's right?'

'I do,' he said. 'But I also think you'll find Ben and Max will make up their own minds about who they want to see. I would just tell them the truth and let nature take its course. We need to get off here.'

I glanced up, surprised. We were by the river in Chelsea. I followed Jack downstairs. He jumped off and set off down a little backstreet.

'Jack, where are you going?' I yelled, jogging to catch up.

He stopped. 'Oh, didn't I say? This is where I left my car. Over there.'

At the end of the road was his ancient Mercedes, parked outside the pretty blue mews house, the one with the cascading window boxes full of lobelia. My tummy churned. Pascale. This was Pascale's house.

Chapter Seven

I SWALLOWED AND GLANCED around in panic, desperately wanting to be able to jump back on that bus.

'Um, Jack, look, now I'm here, I might, you know, peel off. Do some shopping or um—go and see Teresa.' I tried to sound cheerful, willing my disappointment not to show.

He turned, looked surprised. 'You're not coming in? Oh.' He looked disappointed. 'I wanted to show you around.'

I blinked. 'Around Pascale's house?'

He frowned. 'Pascale's? This isn't Pascale's house, this is my house.'

'*Your* house!' I stared. 'You *live* here?'

'Well, no, not yet, but I intend to, soon. It's only just been finished. Only just got rid of the builders.' He took a key out of his pocket.

'But, hang on—when I picked you up that day you didn't say it was *your* house!'

'You didn't ask.'

'Yes, but—I mean . . .' I gazed up again, astonished. 'Well, a mews house in the heart of old Chelsea must have cost a flaming *fortune*!' I gaped. 'Have you been selling your body? Become a proper gigolo?'

He grinned. 'Nope. But, heavens, how impudent of you to enquire as to how I have the means.' He raised an eyebrow in mock surprise.

'Well, gosh, *sorry*, Jack, but the last time I visited your gaff it was a two-roomed, fourth-floor affair in Earls Court, with mice behind the fridge. How come you've migrated to a place like this!'

'I had no idea my penury was so apparent,' he mused. 'How distressing. And you're quite right,' he conceded with a sigh, as we reached the door, 'this isn't my house at all. It's actually Jason Lamont's.'

'Jason who?'

He ushered me in and I gazed around, marvelling, as we stood in a pretty cream hallway, walls covered with watercolours. An archway led off to a sunny sitting room with sandy wooden floors, pale green sofas and dusty rose curtains, while another arch led to an airy kitchen.

'Jason Lamont,' he said as he marched off kitchenwards. 'He's a writer,' he informed me helpfully as he made for the French windows. With one hand he reached up to unbolt them, and with the other, delved into a box, which seemed to contain about a dozen identical books. He plucked one out. 'Here!'

'Oh!' I caught it. Stared at the cover. 'Hang on, this is the one you and Lucas were both reading.' I opened the cover and read the flyleaf.

Jason Lamont was born in Oxford. Little more is known about him, save that he is unprolific and has a penchant for fly-fishing, the former, quite possibly, being a direct result of the latter. He lives in London, with his conscience.

Suddenly it dawned. 'You're Jason Lamont,' I said, looking up.

He grinned. 'Good name, don't you think?'

'I know this book,' I said slowly, turning it over in my hands. 'The hardback was a best seller last year. And now they're making a film out of it, with Tom Cruise and Julia—'

'Roberts, that's it,' he said.

He strolled out into his leafy garden, humming, clearly unable to keep a huge smile at bay.

I, in turn, seemed unable to retrieve my jaw. 'God, you sneaky . . .' I stood watching as he studiously arranged some teak chairs round a small table in the middle of the lawn. Then I hastened after him.

'Jason bloody *Lamont*, Jack! Why didn't you tell me?'

'Oh, come on, Luce. Much more fun to be incognito, and, anyway, I wasn't entirely sure how penning a trashy blockbuster would go down with the university, or my literary poetry publishers. Actually, I needn't have worried. My poetry editor thinks it might help sell the poems. Hope so,' he scratched his chin. 'That's my real pride and joy.'

'So,' I swung round the garden, waving my arms incredulously at the tasteful, leafy enclosure, 'that's how come you bought all this?'

He shrugged. Thrust his hands in his pockets. 'I needed somewhere to live, and the money was suddenly in the bank. This was in the right location, so—'

'Right location for what?'

'Oh, I don't know. '

'For Pascale?' I said suddenly. 'Is she close by?'

'Pascale?' He gave a hoot of laughter. 'Pascale's my decorator.'

'Your *decorator*?'

'Or should I say my interior designer. She did this place up for me. I just gave her a "light and airy" brief and let her get on with it.' He glanced back into the house. 'She's done quite well, don't you think? D'you like it?' He sounded almost anxious.

'Oh, yes!' I breathed, gazing back into the creamy kitchen, admiring the bright Turkish rugs on the wooden floor. 'Yes, it's lovely.' I was warming to Pascale, too, now that I knew she was just the decorator. Clever girl, I thought—

'Oh!' I swung abruptly back to Jack. 'When I picked you up, you know, that day when I'd been—'

'With Charlie,' he said grimly.

'Well, yes, OK. You two were hanging out of an upstairs window like a couple of lovebirds, billing and cooing and looking like you'd just—'

'Made love? Excellent. That was entirely the impression I intended to give. In fact, we'd just been choosing the carpets for the bedrooms.'

I stared. 'But why would you . . .'

'Want to make it look like a love nest?' His blue eyes widened. 'Why, because that's where you'd just emerged from, my dear Lucy. All tousled and rumpled from the steamy, sensual arms of your lover. I couldn't let you think I'd merely been comparing the Axminster with the Wilton all morning, now could I?'

'But, hang on, why would you want to . . .' I stared, confused.

'Make you jealous?' He scuffed his toe. 'Didn't work, did it?' He grinned down at the daisies.

'But why?' I persisted. I stepped forward. We were close now. Very close. His eyes came up from the grass to meet mine. 'I need to know.'

The silence that followed was highly charged. At length he went on in a low voice.

'Well, I should have thought that was obvious. I love you, Lucy. I've always loved you. Surely you know that?' He regarded me gently, his eyes soft. Vulnerable, even. I knew at once it was the voice of truth.

'No,' I whispered. 'I didn't know that. God, Jack, *always*?' I was stunned. So stunned I sat down, on a convenient chair. He pulled up another and straddled it backwards.

'Pretty much,' he decided thoughtfully. 'Right from day one.'

'Day *one*! But you never said!'

'No, that bastard Ned got in before me.' He folded his arms across the top of the chair, rested his chin on them and smiled ruefully. 'The deal was, you see, that when we went out together, on the pull, I'd comman-deer the bar and give the girls a bit of banter as they lined up for their spritzers. His job was to organise a couple more bar stools and follow through with some more intelligent chat. And there we were, Ned and I, propping up the college bar as usual, when in you walked. You asked the barman for an orange juice. And then Ned, in a very un-Ned-like way, butted in and offered to buy it for you. I couldn't bloody believe it. He'd never offered to buy the drinks in the past. Anyway, we spent the next hour or so chatting at the bar, the three of us, remember?'

'Of course I do,' I said slowly. I was staring at him, stunned. He loved me. He'd *always* loved me.

'I can still remember very clearly the impact you had on me. How I felt when you looked at me with your clear, blue-green eyes. How my heart buckled up when you smiled, talked so naturally and so unaffectedly.

'And then you said you had to go. And I was on the point of coolly offering my services, when Ned suggested he walk you back to your house. Well, I waited, teeth gnashing, and half an hour later he returned, looked straight at me, and said, "You know, Jack, I've just met the girl I'm going to marry." '

I gulped. Couldn't utter.

'I hoped, prayed, that he'd forget. Not bother to get in touch with you. But the next day—there you were. Having coffee with him in the window of that steamy café we used to go to. And then, a year later, you were married. It was all over.'

I stared, astonished. 'But, Jack,' I struggled, 'no one would have known. I mean—you never gave an inkling.'

'Of course not. Last thing I wanted was to look like some love-struck git who fancied his cousin's wife. Especially since Ned was my best mate too.' He narrowed his eyes thoughtfully. 'Glad it didn't show. Always wondered. Nice to escape with a few tattered shreds of pride.'

'But, Jack . . .' I struggled, 'so *many* women! I mean, surely one—'

'So many, but never the right one,' he interrupted brusquely. 'I couldn't have you, so I tried as many other varieties as possible. And very pleasurable it was too. And I was nothing if not optimistic, either. I kept thinking one might eventually cut the mustard. But not one of them, to my mind, Lucy, came close to you. Not one.'

He looked at me steadily. It seemed to me the garden went very still for a moment. The trees stopped their rustling, the birds paused in their singing.

'And when Ned died . . . You never showed your hand, Jack.'

'I couldn't, Lucy. You weren't ready. I kept thinking you nearly were, but your grief was—so huge. So . . . humbling. Seeing you sob at that kitchen table, night after night, there was no point at which I could have said, "Ah well, never mind, Luce. Ned's gone, but I've always fancied you, so how's about it?" And how could I compete with a ghost? A ghost I loved and mourned, too?'

'And then I got it together. I polished up my act, and then—'

'Then?' He was watching me intently.

'Well. Then I met Charlie.'

'Would you like to tell me about that?'

Something in his tone made me look up. I sighed. 'I was attracted to him for obvious reasons. Sexy, gorgeous, handsome etc. Jess thought I wanted him because I couldn't have him, because he was unavailable, but—there was more to it than that. I wanted him because he was married, and a father. It was what I'd lost, you see. A married man with a child. I didn't want anything else. I wanted the same again. He was irresistible. Awful.' I shuddered.

Jack shook his head. 'Not really. This amateur psychiatrist would say it made perfect sense.'

'And yet . . . Well, things have a way of coming full circle, don't they? It's almost as if I had to go through all that. The grief, the guilt, the

depression—and then afterwards, as I came up for air, I remember feeling so elated, as I chased around after Charlie. It was another kind of
madness. The high after the low.'

'And now? At the top of the circle? Where the two lines meet?'

'Now,' I spread my hands carefully on the wooden table. 'Now you're
all I want, Jack. All I want.' I looked up.

We regarded each other and it seemed to me his eyes devoured every
fibre of my being. And mine his. My heart swelled. How well I knew
him, I marvelled, and how strange that only recently I'd known myself
to be in love with him. Or was that so? Why had he always had the
capacity to rattle me, to force me to view myself from unflattering
angles—often with guilt and shame—if I hadn't cared?

So much I'd seen of him, but so little I'd known, understood. The
strings of girls, the wayward life, all, if I'd really stopped to think about
it—not Jack. Not in keeping. He wasn't a shallow man, I knew that, his
poetry told me that. Why hadn't I spotted that there was a huge gaping
hole in his life, which he wrote about constantly but couldn't fill?

'Jack—I'm so sorry.'

'Don't be.'

'So stupid. No idea.'

'Just as well. You were married. A married woman.'

He grinned and I gave a weak smile in response.

'And, Jack—this house.' I stood up, glanced around. 'I mean, was it—'

'For the boys. And you, of course, but mostly for Ben, so he could go
back to school. Be among friends, have the security he needs.'

I appeared to have a lump the size of an Elgin marble in my throat.

'To—live here? With you?'

He straightened up from his chair. Scratched his head awkwardly.
'Well, yes. With me. Sorry. You see, I suppose what I'm asking, in a fairly
inarticulate way, is whether,' he licked his lips, 'whether you'd do me the
honour of becoming my wife.'

'Your wife?'

'Quite a step, I grant you,' he went on hurriedly, 'but—I missed out
the first time by being too slow, and I've waited and watched you ever
since—can't hold back any longer. Lucy, you look so shocked. I'd
hoped, imagined, that you might feel, well . . .'

I took his hands. His eyes were anxious, but I couldn't speak, couldn't
reassure him. I felt totally overwhelmed, as tears inexplicably choked my
throat. You see, I'd never expected happiness to come like this again. It
was something I'd once had, had never cherished enough, and had
never expected to have back again.

'Yes,' I breathed when I could. 'Yes, Jack, I do feel the same. I love you. I know that now and I think—well, I think I've known for some time. So,' I took a deep breath, 'to answer your question, yes. I will marry you.'

We stood for a moment, smiling at each other. Then he took me in his arms and kissed me in the middle of that leafy London garden, under the gaze of a pure blue sky. And as he did, a feeling flooded through me that had a pretty good claim to be called pure joy. When we finally parted, he stepped back, took my face carefully in his hands. Cradled it. I could see the desire streaming out of his eyes. Our hearts pounded together, thumping away in proximity.

'In the end,' he whispered, his eyes searching my face, 'I went for the pale blue Axminster.'

'Did you?' I gasped.

'I did. It's a short, tufted pile, and I'm told it's very hard-wearing— what the salesman called Top of the Range. Would you like to see it?'

'Nothing,' I murmured, as he took my hand and led me back towards the house, 'would give me greater pleasure.'

CATHERINE ALLIOTT

On a wonderfully bright, crisp autumnal day I drove to St Albans to meet Catherine Alliott at St Michael's Manor, a hotel where we had met once before just after her previous novel, *Olivia's Luck,* was published. When Catherine arrived, looking poised and elegant, she seemed slightly worried. 'I think my car might have a flat tyre,' she declared. 'People kept pointing to it and mouthing "flat tyre" all the way here, but I'm sure all it needs is just a little air. Let's have lunch and I'll worry about it later.'

As we sat in the hotel's conservatory, overlooking a beautiful lake glittering in the midday sunshine, we talked about her writing and where the ideas for her novels come from. 'I'm really not sure,' she told me with a smile. 'You know, it's funny, but my two daughters are constantly coming home from school with English homework that requires them to write stories using just their imagination. I find that extremely hard to do. I need to start with my own experiences of life and only then can I let my imagination flow. All I can say is that when I'm writing I spend my time either laughing or crying, which I hope is a good thing!'

Catherine Alliott writes a novel every two years and is currently in the planning phase of her next one. 'I'm having a rather nice time at the moment,' she told me. 'I finished *A Married Man* in April and since the revisions were finalised I've been taking some time out—though it does

make me wonder how I ever find the time to write! But once Christmas is over, and the children are back at school, that's when I will take up my pen and paper again.'

A Married Man is Catherine Alliott's sixth novel and she recalls how her first success changed her life irrevocably. 'I wrote my first book, *The Old Girl Network*, under my desk while I was I working as a copywriter and about to go on maternity leave. Once it was published there was suddenly enormous pressure to write another. Almost overnight I had changed persona from copywriter and mother-to-be to novelist, and I have never looked back. Writing has now become one of my obsessions—along with worrying about whether the duvet matches the curtains and silly things like that—and obsessive behaviour is one of the themes I enjoyed pursuing in *A Married Man*, especially Lucy's crush on Charlie. Everyone believes that crushes are only for the very young but, if we are totally honest, we all know that they're not!'

After a most enjoyable meal and a good gossip, we went to check on Catherine's tyre, which was now as flat as the proverbial pancake. It was obvious that 'just a little air' was not going to do the trick. Luckily, the AA came to her rescue, and I left Catherine in the capable hands of a knight in shining yellow. As I drove away, I wondered if he might feature in her next novel!

Jane Eastgate

HIDDEN
TALENTS

ERICA JAMES

Each member of the Hidden Talents creative writing
group has a different reason for seeking refuge in
the written word.

There's Dulcie Ballantyne, founder of the group, coming to
terms with her married lover's heart attack; Jaz Rafferty,
seventeen years old and desperate to be taken seriously by
her rowdy Irish family; Beth King, a widow with a teenage
son, looking for love; Jack Solomon, recovering from his
wife's infidelity with his best friend; and finally, Victor
Blackmore, a man with little talent but an enormous ego.
They are a diverse group but, as they meet week after
week, a powerful friendship grows between them.

Chapter One

DULCIE BALLANTYNE HAD MADE a lifelong habit of not making a drama of the unexpected: for sixty-three years silver linings had been her stock in trade. Yet it wasn't a trouble-free life that had given her the ability to cope no matter what, it was a wealth of experience. In short, life had taught her to deal with the severest catastrophe.

But as she sat at the kitchen table, waiting for the day to fully form itself, tearful exhaustion was doing away with the last remnants of her self-control and she was seconds away from making a terrible mistake. Desperation was pushing her to ring the hospital to find out how Richard was. As his mistress, though—even a long-standing mistress of three years—she had no right to be at his bedside or have his condition explained to her. 'Are you family?' the nurse had asked her on the telephone late last night, when she had almost begged to know how he was. She should have claimed to be a relative, but shock had wrenched the truth from her and she was informed politely that Mr Richard Cavanagh was still in the coronary care unit in a stable condition.

Stable. She hung on to this thought, closed her eyes, and willed the man she loved not to leave her. How often had Richard said that to her? 'Don't leave me, Dulcie. Life would be intolerable without you.'

'I'm not going anywhere,' she had always told him. She had meant it too. Her affair with Richard had been infinitely better than any other relationship she had known since the death of her husband twenty-two years ago. Before she had met Richard, there had been a series of liaisons

157

and one or two men had almost convinced her she was in love, but mostly they had proved to her that she enjoyed living alone too much to want anyone with her on a permanent basis.

She swallowed hard, ran her fingers through her short, dishevelled hair, and only just kept herself from crying, 'No, no, *no!*' She had changed her mind. She wanted Richard to stay in her life for ever.

She heaved herself out of the chair and set about making some breakfast. She hadn't eaten since yesterday afternoon when she and Richard had met at their usual restaurant for lunch—a hotel at a discreet distance from Maywood. It was while they were discussing the creative writers' group she was forming that he had grimaced, dropped his cutlery and clenched his fist against his chest. Horror-struck, she had watched his strong, vigorous body crumple and fall to the floor.

It had been so quick. One minute they were chatting happily, the next they were in an ambulance hurtling to hospital. She had behaved immaculately: no distraught behaviour that would give rise to the suspicion that they were lovers. She had called Richard's home on his mobile and left an anonymous message on the answering machine for his wife, just saying that Mr Cavanagh had had a heart attack. Half an hour later, though it was the hardest thing she had ever done, she had left the hospital before people started to ask awkward questions.

Now she wished she had stayed. Why should she worry about anyone else's feelings but her own? Yet she *did* care about other people's feelings. Richard had once said to her, 'You care too much sometimes, Dulcie. You're too understanding for your own good.'

'No I'm not,' she'd said. 'If I was that saintly I would think more of Angela and call a halt to this affair. It's very wrong what we're doing. It's selfish to be happy at someone else's expense.'

He'd held her tight. 'Don't say that. Don't even think it. Not ever.'

She had always thought that his need for her was greater than her need for him. Now, however, she wasn't so sure.

Rousing herself, she cleared away her untouched breakfast and went upstairs to dress. It was time to pull herself together and become the cool, composed Dulcie Ballantyne everyone knew her to be.

Once she was dressed, she looked down on to the walled garden from her bedroom window. Curved steps led down onto the lawn, which was edged with well-stocked borders; some, despite the onset of autumn, were still bright with colour. In the middle of June, Richard had helped her spread several barrowloads of manure over the rosebeds. His family had thought he was away on business, but he had been with her for a whole delicious two days—and they had spent the afternoon shovelling horse droppings. They had laughed about that afterwards.

Their love was founded on a strong understanding of each other's needs and a companionship that was both passionate and close, something so many married couples lost sight of. She seldom wanted him to talk about his marriage, but often Richard felt the need to explain, or perhaps justify, why he, an ordinary man (as he called himself), was behaving in the way he was. From what Dulcie knew of his wife, she was an anxious woman who depended on him too much.

Turning from the window, she glanced at herself in the full-length mirror and tried to see beyond the stocky roundness of her body and the burst of lines around her blue eyes, beyond the short fair hair she had dyed every six weeks because she knew it took years off her, and beyond the skin that had lost its firmness. Beyond all this, she saw a woman who was a chameleon. She had played so many different roles in her life, and was destined, she was sure, to play a few more yet.

Downstairs in the kitchen, while she was trying to summon the energy to go out and rake up the leaves, the telephone rang. She snatched up the receiver, her heart pounding. Richard.

But it wasn't. It was a young girl enquiring about the creative writers' group. She had seen the card Dulcie had placed in the window of the bookshop in town, and wanted to know if there was an age restriction.

Jaz Rafferty put her mobile on her bedside table and relished a rare moment of blissful quiet. Added to this was the knowledge that she had a secret. Secrets were great, especially if she could keep them from her brothers and sisters, who were the nosiest, most irritating bunch on the planet. Phin (short for Phineas) was the oldest at twenty-two, then Jimmy, who was twenty. Although they were both earning good money working for Dad's building firm—Rafferty & Sons—they still lived at home. 'Ah, it would break Mum's heart if we moved out,' they said. They were probably right. Mum loved and spoilt them to bits.

Pathetic.

At seventeen, Jaz was next in line in the family pecking order; after a gap of several years, Tamzin (ten) and Lulu (eight) had arrived. 'Sweet Moses,' her dad often complained, 'I'm overrun with women! What have I done to deserve this?'

More to the point, what had *she* ever done to deserve such a family?

From a very young age she'd had a feeling of being displaced. If it weren't for her colouring—so like her mother's—she would have believed she had ended up in the wrong family. She couldn't have been more different from her brothers and sisters, who all took after their

Irish father: heartily robust of build and temperament. Jaz would have put money on Tamzin and Lulu having been born with fists clenched, ready to take on the world and destroy it. In contrast, she herself was small and pale with annoying childish freckles across the bridge of her nose. Her hair was long, to her waist, and auburn ('Not red!'), and she preferred to think rather than yak like the rest of her family. When Tamzin was born, followed quickly by Lulu, Jaz accepted that she was destined to be the odd one out. Everyone but her was one of a pair: her parents, her brothers, and now her sisters. She withdrew and immersed herself in books, reading herself into other people's lives, happily escaping her own. With hindsight it seemed only natural that one day she would discover the joy of writing, that the simple process of putting words on paper—poems, short stories, rhymes, observations—would allow her to escape yet further.

She rolled off the bed, went over to her desk and switched on her computer. She checked that her bedroom door was shut, then opened the file marked 'Italian Renaissance'. She scrolled through the six-page essay she had written on Uccello's *The Hunt in the Forest*, and stopped when a block of blank pages had flicked by and she came to the words 'Chapter One'. After months of messing around with poetry she was writing a novel. She had started it last week but, what with all the homework she'd had, there had been little time to devote to it. Being at sixth-form college was great, but the workload was crazy.

Vicki, her closest friend from school, had moved with her to Maywood College last month, and there was no shortage of new students to get to know. There was one in particular Jaz wanted to get to know better. He was a year older than her and was in the upper sixth. His name was Nathan King and he lived near the park in Maywood. He was tall, wore his hair short, and was never without his long black leather coat. He looked as if he knew exactly what he was about, as if he had it all sorted.

Hearing feet thundering towards her room, she snapped forward in her seat and scrolled back to the start of the history-of-art essay.

The door flew open. 'Who were you talking to?'

'Tamzin Rafferty, get out! You too, Lulu. Can't you see I'm working?'

'You weren't a few minutes ago. We heard you talking to someone. Was it a boy? Have you got a boyfriend?' Her sisters looked at each other and began to giggle in that high-pitched tone that grated on her nerves. She moved calmly across the room to the bookcase and her CD player. She picked up the remote control, switched it on at eardrum-bursting level and watched Tamzin and Lulu take flight. They hated her music.

'Sweet baby Moses on a bike! Turn that racket down.'

Her father, Pat (or Popeye), stood in the doorway. Jaz switched off the music and he came in. 'Jeez, girl, how you can work with that rubbish playing, I'll never know.' He looked towards her computer, stooped slightly, and began to read aloud what was on the screen. '"Uccello was fascinated by perspective . . ."' He placed a hand on her shoulder. 'I've said it before, Jasmine, and I'll say it again, you owe it all to your mother. You get your brains from Moll. Never forget that, will you?'

She turned and smiled affectionately at him. He was always making himself out to be the ignorant partner in his marriage. 'You're not going to give me that old I'm-just-a-thick-Paddy spiel, are you?'

He gave her a light cuff round the ear. 'Cheeky madam. Now, get on with your work. I'm expecting great things of you.'

'No pressure, then, Dad?'

He was almost out of the room when he stopped, turned back to her and said, 'So, has my little Jazzie got a boyfriend?'

She rolled her eyes. 'Chance would be a fine thing.'

'Hmm . . . best keep it that way until you've got college sorted.'

She watched him go. As dads went, he wasn't bad. Sentimental at times, and scarily volatile, but she knew he was proud of her.

What he didn't realise was that his pride put unbearable pressure on her to perform. What if she let him down? And did he have any idea how trapped she felt by the restrictions he placed on her in his desire to see her do well? He was happy for her to go out with Vicki, but heaven help any guy who showed the slightest interest in her. She knew her father wouldn't tolerate the distraction of a boyfriend at this stage in her life. But who'd be interested in her anyway? She dismissed this line of thought and got back to the opening sentence of her novel. But it wasn't long before her thoughts strayed once more. To her wonderful secret.

Next week she would be going to the first meeting of Hidden Talents. Just think, a writers' group where she would be taken seriously. Where she could talk openly about her writing and not be laughed at. Because that's what her family would do if they ever found out.

She wondered what the others in the group would be like. The woman she'd just spoken to, Dulcie Ballantyne, had sounded really nice.

Beth King enjoyed washing-up—not for any strange, puritanical reason, but because the kitchen of the first-floor flat that she and Nathan had lived in for more than ten years overlooked Maywood Park. The view was a constant source of pleasure to her: there was always something different to watch—squirrels scampering across the grass, couples strolling arm in arm along the winding paths, mothers with prams, dogs, and children playing on the swings and roundabout—which Nathan had enjoyed when he was little. And then there was the ever-changing look of the park. Now that it was autumn, the trees were losing their coppery leaves and the fading bedding plants would soon be replaced with pansies tough enough to survive the rigours of winter.

The last of the lunch dishes rinsed, Beth dried her hands and reached for the tub of luxury hand cream her mother had sent her. Her parents were wonderfully generous and still went out of their way to make her life easier, as did her in-laws, Lois and Barnaby King. But while she was grateful for her parents' generosity, which came from 300 miles away—they had retired to the south coast—she found it difficult to feel the same enthusiasm for Lois's doorstep offers of help. Lois tried too hard and made Beth feel as if she were a charity case. 'Would you believe it?' Lois had said in April. 'I've stocked up at the supermarket and, without any warning, Barnaby's taking me away for the Easter weekend. You'd better have it, I hate to see good food go to waste.'

It would have been ungracious to refuse, especially as Beth knew Lois meant well. She always had. Ever since Adam's death, eleven years ago, she had committed herself to taking care of her son's widow and her only grandson. Occasionally Beth privately questioned Lois's motives, but she hated herself for thinking so cynically. She should consider herself lucky that she had such supportive in-laws. Nothing was ever too much trouble for them and, living just a few miles away in the village of Stapeley, they had always been there for her. Many a time Lois had dispatched Barnaby to fix a leaking gutter or sort out a rotting window ledge. 'Heavens! Don't even think of getting a man in to do it. Let Barnaby take a look for you. You—you know that's what Adam would have wanted.'

After all these years of living without Adam, it was difficult for Beth to know if Lois was right. Would he have wanted his parents to play such a central part in her life? Or would he have expected her to move on?

'Moving on' had become an irritating cliché to Beth. Everyone had served it up to her: her mother, her friends, her work colleagues—in fact, anyone who thought she should have remarried by now. 'You're not getting any younger, Beth,' her closest friend, Simone, had said only last month. 'You're forty-three, not twenty-three, in case it's slipped your notice.'

'Fat chance of that happening,' Beth had retorted, wishing that a sandstorm would engulf her friend's house in Dubai where she was currently living with her husband, Ben.

'Or are you working on the misplaced theory that the choice of eligible men increases with age?'

'No, I'm just being selective. I haven't met anyone who measures up to Adam.'

'Rubbish! You haven't allowed anyone near enough to see how they'd measure up. You're being a coward.'

Simone's words were uncomfortably near the truth. Fear and guilt had played a part in stopping Beth finding a new partner. She had hated the idea of being disloyal to Adam. In the aftermath of his death, she had thrown herself into taking care of Nathan, who had been only six. Within six months of the funeral they had moved from their lovely house in the country to this flat in Maywood. Money had been tight. Without her knowledge, Adam had taken out a second mortgage on their house and had invested what little savings they'd had in a business venture that had gone disastrously wrong. It had taken Beth some time to find work, but perseverance had paid off: she had landed a gem of a job at the recently expanded health centre in town.

Her social life had not been so fulfilling: on a receptionist's salary she couldn't afford to do much. She was always totting up the pennies—a modest trip to the cinema plus a baby sitter amounted almost to the cost of a pair of shoes for Nathan. Funnily enough, Lois had never offered to baby sit so that Beth could go out at night. Beth strongly suspected her mother-in-law didn't want her to meet anyone. To Lois, it was unthinkable that Beth could replace Adam.

But Beth's friends had had other ideas and before long they were dropping hints that it was time for her to start dating. Invitations materialised for her to meet unattached men at dinner parties. Simone had set her up with several highly unsuitable candidates, so she had started to turn down her friend's invitations, using Nathan as an excuse— 'Sorry, Simone, I have to give Nathan a lift somewhere that night.' Or, 'Sorry, Nathan needs me to help him revise for an exam.'

Simone was no fool. Eventually she had said, 'How much longer are you going to use your son in this shameful manner? What excuse will you come up with when he leaves home?'

Beth knew that Simone was right, she *was* hiding behind Nathan. Plenty of parents struggle to come to terms with flying-the-nest syndrome, but she knew that because she and Nathan were so close she would undergo a painful period of adjustment next year when he left for university. Common sense told her that she had no choice but to fill the void his absence would create.

In preparation for this change, she had taken an important step this morning, which she hoped would expand her horizons. She was joining a creative writers' group. She had always enjoyed 'scribbling', as she called it. It had started after Adam died: when she couldn't sleep at night, she had written down the thoughts that were keeping her awake. It had been soothingly cathartic and before long she had grown confident enough to turn the random scribblings into short stories. She now had a collection that no one but herself had read. Or ever would. Those clumsily put-together vignettes were about the past. Now she wanted to write something to reflect the new life ahead of her.

This morning she had told Simone about Hidden Talents.

'Good for you,' she'd said. 'Any men in the group?'

'I wouldn't know. We have our first meeting next week.'

'What else are you going to do to occupy yourself?'

'Isn't that enough to start with?'

'You tell me.'

'Goodness, you're giving me the choice? What's got into you? Has the sun fried your brain?'

'Crikey, it's time to come home to Cheshire if it has.'

For all Simone's bullying, she was a wonderful friend, and Beth missed her. She screwed the lid back onto the tub of hand cream and put it on the window ledge. Looking down into the park, she noticed a fair-haired man sitting on one of the benches; he had two little blonde girls with him. She was still staring at them when she remembered that she had promised to go downstairs to see her neighbour.

Adele—Miss Adele Waterman—had moved into the ground-floor flat a year after Beth and Nathan had arrived, which made them not just long-standing neighbours but good friends. To Beth's sadness, the old lady had decided, now that she was eighty-four, to move into a retirement home. 'I'm under no illusion that my nephew wants the burden of me. He can never spare any time to visit so I'm spending his inheritance the fastest way I know how,' she had told Beth, with a chuckle.

Beth hoped that when the time came, Nathan would treat her more kindly than Adele's only relative had treated her.

Jack Solomon switched off the car radio before Jimmy Ruffin's 'What Becomes Of The Brokenhearted?' could do its worst. The traffic light changed to green and he pressed his foot on the accelerator. It was a typically tedious Monday afternoon. It was also his birthday. He was thirty-six, but felt more like sixty-six, and he certainly wasn't in the mood to celebrate. The girls in the office had surprised him with a card and a CD and he had been touched by their thoughtfulness, but less so by the choice of CD. He had nothing against Britney Spears, but there was nothing worse than a middle-aged man trying to be hip. A wry smile twitched at his lips. He could have been describing that bastard Tony.

He felt the sudden tension in his shoulders and loosened his grip on the steering wheel. He mustn't dwell on Tony, he told himself. But it was futile. Tony Gallagher . . . the best friend he'd ever had. They'd grown up together, played and learned together. They'd shared practically every rite of passage. But Tony had taken 'togetherness' and 'what's yours is mine' too far and too literally.

Almost a year ago Jack had come home early from work one afternoon with a high temperature and found Tony in bed with Maddie. Turned out they'd been having an affair for the last six months.

Dumb old Jack Solomon, that was him. Too blind to see what was going on under his own nose, in his own home. Too in awe of his old friend to think he'd ever betray him.

But these things happen. Jack wished that every time some smug prat said this he could smack them in the face. 'These things happen' was supposed to make him feel better about losing his wife and becoming a part-time father, seeing his daughters only on alternate weekends.

On Saturday he'd taken the girls to the park in Maywood. Lucy had enjoyed it, but then she was only seven and still young enough to feed the ducks and play on the swings. Amber, though, was eleven and fast becoming too grown-up for such childish entertainment. While Lucy had flung bread at the ducks, Amber had sat on the bench with him and watched her sister disdainfully. 'Can we go now?' she had asked, getting to her feet and folding her arms across her chest. 'I'm cold.'

'But I want to play on the swings,' Lucy had pouted.

'Five minutes on the swings,' he'd said, 'and then it's Amber's choice what we do next.'

The peace had been kept and Amber's choice had been to walk back into the centre of town to have tea at McDonald's. During the weekend he'd sensed friction between the girls, and when he was putting the tray loaded with food onto the table where they were waiting for him, he caught Amber telling Lucy off. 'Hey, what's the problem?' he'd said.

'It's nothing,' Amber said matter-of-factly.

'It doesn't look like nothing to me,' he persisted. 'What's up, Luce?' He noticed Amber flash her a warning look and when Lucy began to cry, he said, 'OK, that's it. What's going on?'

'I only said I was looking forward to our holiday.' Lucy sniffed. 'Tony's taking us to Disney World for half-term. We're going to America.'

'That's nice,' he forced himself to say.

165

'Well, I'm not going!' Amber announced. 'I'm going to stay with Dad for half-term. I wouldn't go to America if you paid me.'

Atta girl! he wanted to cheer. But he didn't. Not when Lucy looked as if she was going to cry again. His heart went out to them both, caught as they were in an impossible situation. 'Is it definite?' he asked.

Lucy nodded. 'Tony showed us a picture of the hotel we're going to be staying in. It's huge. And there's a pool with a slide and—'

'Shut up, Lucy.'

'Amber, don't speak to your sister like that.'

She looked at him, hurt.

Damn! He wasn't handling this at all well. Poor Amber, she was only trying to be loyal to him. 'Sorry, sweetheart,' he said, 'I didn't mean to snap at you. How's your meal? Burger up to standard?'

He drove them back to Prestbury the following day, to where Maddie had set up home with Tony. Home for her, these days, was a modern pile of impressive proportions with six bedrooms, three bathrooms, a sitting room the size of a football pitch and a sauna to sweat away the day's troubles. Well, yippity-do, hadn't Tony Gallagher done well for himself? Tony had set up his own business importing Oriental furniture; he now had a string of shops throughout the Northwest.

Tony opened the door to him and it took all of Jack's will-power not to smear the smug devil's brains right across his expensive wallpaper.

'I hear you're off to Disney,' he said, with false bonhomie.

'Yes,' said Tony. 'Some sun to cheer us all up.'

'You do surprise me. I thought you had everything you could ever want to make you happy.' His caustic tone rang out discordantly and Maddie materialised. As if sensing trouble, she placed herself between the girls, a hand on each of their shoulders. Even now, despite the bitterness that consumed him, he was reminded of the intense love he'd once felt for her. She was as slim as the day they'd met, and just as pretty.

'Everything all right?' she asked with chilly briskness.

'Oh, everything's hunky-dory, Maddie. Nothing for you to worry about. Although it might have been nice for you to inform me about your plans for half-term.' Then, in a less acerbic voice, he said, 'Good night, girls. I'll see you when you get back.'

He moved forward to kiss them goodbye, but Amber wriggled free from her mother and said, 'You can't go yet, Dad. Lucy and I have something for you.' She shot upstairs and was back within seconds. She handed him a present that must have taken ages to wrap, judging by the amount of Sellotape and the bulky edges of the paper around it. 'Happy birthday for Monday, Dad.' She gave him a fierce hug. When she stepped away, she narrowed her eyes and gave Maddie and Tony a pointed look.

He drove home that afternoon, close to tears. All he could think of was the harm that had been inflicted on his children by his and Maddie's separation. Poor Lucy, so guilty and upset because she was excited about going to Orlando, and Amber defiantly refusing to go, but knowing she would have to. And how long had she been rehearsing the little scene when she had given him his present in front of Tony and Maddie?

Jack knew he had to come to terms with what had happened. He had to find a way to resolve his anger and bitterness.

He parked outside 10A Maywood Park House, where Miss Waterman lived. A shame it wasn't the whole house he'd been instructed to sell, but a flat in this area would be easy to shift, so long as Miss Waterman was realistic about the selling price. Fingers crossed that the old lady didn't have any greedy relatives manipulating her behind the scenes.

He gathered up his clipboard and tape measure from the front passenger seat and locked the car. He examined the small front garden with a professional eye: it was well tended. Then he took the three steps up to the front door, which had its original lead-and-stained-glass fanlight. Again this was a good sign. There were two bells—one for 10A and one for 10B. He pressed the former, straightened his tie and tried to imagine Miss Waterman. He pictured her in a high-necked frilly blouse with a string of pearls, a pale mauve cardie and an embroidered hanky.

The door opened. 'Er . . . Miss Waterman?' Either his client had undergone thousands of pounds' worth of plastic surgery, or this was a relative who had been called in to check out the potentially scurrilous estate agent. She was an attractive woman with wavy fair hair, collar-length and tucked behind her ears: a tousled look that suited her bright, open face. She looked vaguely familiar.

'No, I'm a neighbour,' she said. 'I live in the flat upstairs, which is where Miss Waterman is. I'm afraid her boiler's conked out and I insisted she stay in the warm with me. Luckily I had the afternoon off. You must be Mr Solomon. Come in.'

Inside Flat 10A he was pleased to see that most of the original features were still intact. He stood for a moment to take in the proportions and features of the sitting room: the bay window, the fireplace, the high ceiling and the intricate cornice.

'I've been instructed to stay with you,' she said, observing him from where she stood next to a baby grand piano.

'Quite right too,' he said. 'I could be anyone, after all.' He slipped a hand into the breast pocket of his suit and pulled out a business card.

She read the card and said, 'Well, Mr Jack Solomon of Norris and

Rowan the Estate Agents'—her voice was playful—'I've also been instructed to give you some tea when you've finished. Miss Waterman was most insistent on that. I should point out, though, that she'll drive a hard bargain with you over your commission. Be warned.'

And you'll see that she does, he thought. He found himself warming to Miss Waterman's helpful neighbour. Dodging the clutter of antique furniture, he pulled out a length of the tape measure and hooked the metal end into the edge of the carpet. 'And what do you do when you're not looking after your neighbour?' he asked.

'I'm a receptionist at the medical centre in town.'

Ah, so that's where he'd seen her.

Soon he was being led upstairs to meet Miss Waterman. When he stood in the hall, inside 10B, the warmth wrapped itself around him, as did his new surroundings. There was a homely smell and feel to this flat, which Miss Waterman's lacked: hers was too formal and prim for his taste. He thought of his own rented modern town house and acknowledged that he didn't much like it. It wasn't a home, merely a stopgap. When Maddie had left him, he'd sold their house almost straight away, finding it too painful to live there alone.

When he entered the main room of the flat, L-shaped and clearly used for sitting, dining and cooking, he almost stopped in his tracks at the sight of his client. Unbelievably, he'd pictured her perfectly. How extraordinary! One—nil to his vivid imagination.

'Goodness, Mr Solomon, you look like you've seen a ghost.'

Smiling, he stretched out his hand. 'Not at all, Miss Waterman. It's good to meet you at last.'

While he and Miss Waterman discussed the marketing of the flat and the thorny issue of commission, he was conscious of his client's neighbour moving quietly at the other end of the shabby but charming room, where she was making a pot of tea and arranging some cake on a plate. Out of the corner of his eye, he saw her pick up the tea tray. He got to his feet. 'Here, let me do that.' He took it from her and noticed, for the first time, the view from the window. He wondered if she had seen him on Saturday in the park with the girls.

'That was delicious,' he said, after he'd eaten two slices of cake and drunk his tea, 'but I really ought to be going. I wish all my appointments were as convivial.' He meant it.

It was when he was driving back to the office that he remembered it was his birthday and Clare, his girlfriend—*girlfriend*: even after five months he wasn't used to that expression—was cooking a special meal for him. He wished now that he hadn't eaten so much cake.

From the garden, Dulcie heard the telephone. She threw down the rake and rushed to the house.

It was Tuesday morning, four days since Richard's heart attack, and for all she knew the unthinkable might have happened.

She snatched up the receiver. Before she could say anything, a man's voice she didn't recognise said, 'Hello? Who am I speaking to?'

'This is Mrs Ballantyne,' she answered, irritated by the pompous voice at the other end of the line. 'And who am I speaking to?'

'My name's Victor Blackmore and I'm calling about the writing group. Is it serious or an excuse for people to chat over cups of coffee?'

'There'll be coffee on offer for those who would like it,' she said coolly, instinct telling her that this man would not be an asset to Hidden Talents, 'and doubtless there'll be a lively exchange of views and opinions. It will be as serious as its members want it to be.'

'Mmm . . . So what can you tell me about the other people who have signed up for it? I don't want to get involved with time-wasting cranks.'

Bristling, Dulcie said, 'I'm not sure that's a fair question, Mr Blackmere. It rather depends on your definition of the word "crank".'

'Black*more*. Victor *Blackmore*. Perhaps I'd better explain. I'm working on a novel and I'm keen to find an expert appraisal. What are your qualifications for running a writing group?'

It was time to get rid of this ghastly man. Under no circumstances did Dulcie want him joining Hidden Talents. 'I have absolutely no qualifications whatsoever, Mr Blackmore. It sounds to me as though our little group wouldn't suit you at all. Have you thought of submitting your novel to a publisher for a professional appraisal?'

'Publishers! What do they know?'

So he'd already been down that route and had his work rejected. She decided that her only course of action was to be firm. 'Oh dear, I must go, there's someone at my door. Goodbye, Mr Blackmore, I hope you find what you're looking for.' She replaced the receiver with a smile. It was the first time she had smiled in days and it felt good.

Back out in the garden, she resumed her leaf-raking. She was picking up the handles of the overflowing wheelbarrow to push it down to the compost heap when she heard the telephone once more.

'Mrs Ballantyne? Victor Blackmore again.'

Her heart sank.

'I wanted to go over a couple more points with you.'

'Does this mean you'll be joining us?'

'Let's just say I'll give you a try and see how it works out. Now then, what will the format be?'

'Format?'

'I presume you've thought of that? If there's no order or structure to the classes, I can't see them working.'

Fifteen minutes later, her patience pushed to its limit, Dulcie managed to get rid of him. She wished now that she had never come up with the idea of forming a writers' circle. What had she been thinking of? And what if more people like Victor Blackmore wanted to join? So far he was the third person to make a definite commitment to Hidden Talents—there had been other enquiries, but they had come from people looking for something to do during the day. 'I'm afraid our meetings will be in the evening,' she had told them. 'Otherwise people who work will miss out.' Some of the enquirers had been surprised that the group wouldn't be meeting in a public room, and again this had been deliberate on Dulcie's part. A small gathering would encourage members to relax and express themselves more openly—essential if the fragile buds of creativity were to blossom.

It was raining now. Dulcie abandoned her gardening and decided to write instead. She went through to her study—like the kitchen, it overlooked the garden. The previous owners of 18 Bloom Street—a Georgian town house in the centre of Maywood—had used this room as their dining room, but Dulcie had known straight away it would be her study. It was beautifully proportioned and very elegant.

She picked up a pen and began to read through what she had written before Richard had suffered his heart attack. When she had told the boorish Victor Blackmore that she had no qualifications to lead a writing group, she had been a little economical with the truth. For years now she had had modest success with writing short stories for magazines. She had also picked up the occasional prize for her literary endeavours. She had always written, even as a child. She had played with words—like others played squash or tennis to amuse themselves—bouncing them around on the paper until they formed just the right pattern. It was immensely satisfying. However, it had been a sporadic hobby. Marriage and children had been her priority but, once Kate and Andrew had left home, she had been able to devote more time to it. Before then, and while the children were young, she had nursed her husband for almost six years until his death. Parkinson's disease had turned him into a chronic invalid, but he had borne the debilitating illness with great dignity. Sadly for him, he had been a doctor and had known his future better than anyone. She would never forget how brave he had been, or how hard he had tried to lessen the effect his illness had on them as a family. But his death created a haunting emptiness in their lives, especially hers. Dulcie had known she must do something positive, so she had moved from south Manchester to Maywood with the children to be nearer her closest friends, Prue and Maureen, and formed her own business, a relocation company.

It had been many years later, when she had been on the verge of selling the business and retiring, that she had met Richard. A company move from Wiltshire to Cheshire put him and his wife in contact with Home from Home. Initially Dulcie dealt with Angela, who made it very clear she was moving north reluctantly. 'My friends and family all live in Wiltshire,' Angela had lamented, over the telephone. 'I don't know what I'm going to do without them.' She flitted rapidly from one line of conversation to another, but eventually Dulcie managed to note Angela's requirements. 'We don't want anything modern, or anything that needs a lot of work doing to it. We want to be out in the country, and we'll need five bedrooms. We have two grown-up children, Henry and Victoria, living in London and they will be frequent visitors. And we have another two still at home, Christopher and Nicholas. I'll need your help in finding them a suitable school . . .' Dulcie had formed a mental picture of her client: she foresaw a long haul.

Two weeks later, with a string of viewings arranged, Dulcie drove to the Maywood Grange Hotel on the outskirts of town to meet her clients. Richard Cavanagh was waiting in the hotel lounge. He rose to his feet and shook hands warmly. 'Would you like some coffee before we set off?' He indicated the sofa, where he'd been sitting, and took a hard upright chair for himself. He was older than she had expected, but attractive with it. His eyes were blue and his hair silvery grey; it curled boyishly into the nape of his neck. He passed her a cup of coffee. 'My wife sends her apologies. Our youngest has chickenpox.'

As the day wore on—and with six houses viewed—Dulcie discovered quite a lot about Richard Cavanagh. He was charming and quick-witted, and appeared a thoroughly nice man. But, and it was a colossal but, he was married, and therefore out of bounds. End of story.

Yet she allowed herself to be drawn in. He invited her to join him for dinner that evening. 'Don't let me suffer the ignominy of dining alone,' he said. 'I'll have everyone feeling sorry for me.'

'Nonsense! All the waitresses will rush to keep you amused.'

'I'd rather *you* kept me amused.'

They were sitting in her car in the hotel car park, and he'd turned to face her as he said this, his gaze as direct as his words.

She didn't answer him, but she didn't need to. He knew she would accept, just as she knew what the consequences would be.

That had been three years ago, and now she was in love with a man who . . . who, for all she knew, might be dead.

She put down the pen she had been holding—a fountain pen Richard had given her on the first anniversary of their meeting—and lowered her head into her hands, when the telephone on her desk rang.

It was Richard. At the sound of his voice, she burst into tears.

'Dulcie?'

'Oh, Richard, I've been so scared.'

'Ssh, my darling, I'm fine. Well, fine for a man who's recovering from his first heart attack. Oh, Dulcie, I'm so sorry to have put you through this. How are you bearing up?'

'Oh, you know, not bad for a mistress whose lover has suffered his first heart attack.'

'Don't speak like that. You know I hate that word. You're not my mistress, you're the woman I love. Oh, hell, I can see a posse of nurses and junior doctors heading in my direction. I'll ring you again as soon as I can. I love you, Dulcie.'

'I love you too. Take care.'

After she had put down the phone, Dulcie went outside and stood in the rain, her face turned up towards the sky. It was the maddest thing she could think to do. She was so unbelievably happy that nothing but an act of sheer lunacy would satisfy her.

By rights Jack should have been looking forward to the evening—he'd had some excellent news during the afternoon, and that, combined with seeing Clare, should have made him feel a whole lot happier. But last night he and Clare had argued. It wasn't the first time, but the nature of the exchange had made him feel awkward about seeing her again. He would have preferred to reschedule this evening's dinner, arranged for him to meet Clare's parents.

The cause of their row still rankled. Clare had accused him of being obsessed with Tony or, more specifically, with what Tony had done. 'Just get over it,' she'd said. 'What's done is done. My husband left me for someone else, but do you hear me banging on about it?'

'Banging on?' he'd said in disbelief. 'Is that what you think I'm doing?'

'Face it, Jack, you've done nothing but moan about him this evening. I'm bored of hearing you complain about your soon-to-be-ex-wife who, allegedly, is stopping you seeing your children. We have so much going between us, but I can't compete with Maddie and the girls.'

'I don't want you to.'

'That's how it feels.'

Exasperation made him say, 'I have enough problems of my own without taking yours on board.'

'Frightened of the truth, are you, Jack?'

'What truth would that be?'

'That you haven't moved on. It's time you accepted that Maddie and the girls are making a new life. Because if you don't, you'll end up lonely and miserable, an embittered man whom Lucy and Amber won't want to see. Is that what you want?'

He hadn't stayed the night, as they'd planned. Instead he drove home, wondering why the hell he was bothering to be in a relationship with Clare. They had met through mutual friends. 'Clare's great,' Des had told him, during one of their boys-only curry nights at the beginning of May. 'She's one of Julie's work colleagues, a friend too. She's recently divorced, but prepared to give the male species the benefit of the doubt. You'll hit it off, I'm sure.' Des ran the Holmes Chapel branch of Norris & Rowan, and Jack had accepted the offer of dinner with cautious interest. Much to Des's satisfaction, Jack and Clare had hit it off.

So tonight, five months on, Jack was meeting Clare's parents. 'It's no big deal, Jack,' she'd said. But he knew it was.

He drove in through the gates of the Maywood Grange Hotel and parked his car in the last remaining space. He switched off the engine, drummed his fingers on the steering wheel, and wondered why he had allowed himself to be manoeuvred into this situation. 'Come and meet the folks' was tantamount to saying, 'Do you fancy a finger buffet or a sit-down meal at the reception?' The thought sent a chill through him.

Mr and Mrs Gilbert—oh, please call us Terry and Corinne—tried hard to be nice, but their eagerness for their only daughter to remarry—and doubtless provide them with grandchildren—was shockingly obvious. And when they started asking after his own children, he found their manner disturbingly intrusive. He changed the subject abruptly and said, 'Clare, I forgot to tell you, I had some good news today—'

'Oh, yummy, look at that,' she said, eyeing the sweet trolley. 'Sorry, Jack, what were you saying?'

He fixed a smile to his face and said, 'It's OK. I'll tell you later.'

But later didn't come. After the goodbyes, Clare had squeezed his arm and said, 'There, that wasn't so bad, was it?' Then he had driven home alone. Except he didn't go home. He put the car into the garage then went for a walk to get his bad mood out of his system.

What he had tried to tell Clare during dinner was that he had been invited to become a partner. His reaction to her lack of interest—not to tell her—now seemed more akin to the behaviour of a petulant child than a grown man. Why was he behaving so badly?

If he was honest with himself, he hadn't wanted to share his good fortune with Clare. Which, he supposed, spoke volumes about his feelings for her. He had to end it, he knew. He had met her too soon after his split with Maddie, when he was still vulnerable, and had thought her to be the answer to his loneliness and hurt pride. And although she might never admit it, Clare had probably viewed him as the means to get herself back on-line with her plan to be happily married with children. He didn't begrudge her that—after all, a family had been what he and Maddie had most wanted, for they had both experienced fragmented family life while growing up: Maddie's parents had divorced, and his had died in a car accident. Children would give them security, stability and continuity. And they had, until Tony had intervened.

Tony had never married. 'I'm too busy to settle down,' he had claimed in the past. But not so long ago, in a moment of drunken self-pity, he had confessed that he envied Jack. 'You have everything I've ever wanted. A beautiful wife and two children who adore you.'

'But you're the one with the Porsche and a different girlfriend for every night of the week.'

'It means nothing,' Tony had said. 'Take it from me, it means absolutely nothing unless you feel you can't live without that woman.'

And, if Tony was to be believed, that was what he now felt about Maddie. 'I'm sorry, Jack,' he'd said, after Jack had found them in bed, 'but she means the world to me. I can't live without her.'

'Neither can I!' Jack had roared. Landing a direct hit on Tony's jaw, he'd knocked him to the floor. 'She's *my* wife and you're not having her!'

If he had thought violence was going to put an end to the affair, he had misjudged Tony. And Maddie. That very night she had taken the girls and moved in with Tony. One minute Jack had been a happily married man, the next he was alone in Dumpsville.

The streets were busy now: it was chucking-out time. Sidestepping a passionately kissing couple, he crossed the road and turned into the main street of Maywood. He passed Turner's, an old-fashioned department store, and went on towards Novel Ways, the town's only bookshop. Last year the owner had acquired the next-door premises—Jack had been in charge of the sale—so that he could knock through to provide his customers with a coffee shop.

Before Clare had appeared on the scene, Jack had often browsed the shelves before sitting down to a latte and a quiet read. Nostalgia made him cross the road to look in the window. He saw that the latest Harry Potter was out and made a mental note to pop back tomorrow and buy it for

Amber and Lucy. But what if Tony bought it for them before Jack could?

He gritted his teeth and was about to walk away when a piece of paper caught his eye.

> *Ever thought of writing a book, or penning a few lines of poetry? You have? Then why not join a writing group, where, among new friends, you can discover those hidden talents you never knew existed?*

He read it through one more time and thought of all the song lyrics he had written as a teenager. Writing again might be an outlet for all the anger and bitterness he didn't know what to do with.

Without giving himself time to change his mind, he wrote down the contact name and phone number on the back of his hand.

Chapter Two

IT WAS THE LAST LESSON OF THE DAY—double English with Mr Hunter—and Jaz was impatient for it to be over. At last it was Thursday. Her parents thought she was going round to Vicki's for the evening and, as long as all went to plan, they would think the same every Thursday night. She didn't like lying to Mum and Dad, but the alternative, in this instance, was unthinkable. Better to keep quiet than put up with the teasing from her brothers and sisters.

At three forty-five the bell rang. Books and files were slapped into bags. Outside in the corridor, Jaz caught up with Vicki. They usually walked home together, unless one of them had an after-college activity. Vicki had just landed the role of Gwendolen in the drama department's production of *The Importance of Being Earnest*; from next week she would have rehearsals on Mondays and Wednesdays, leaving Jaz to walk home alone. More crucially, Vicki, with her enviably sleek long hair the colour of jet and her flawless skin, would be spending all that time with Nathan King, who was playing Algernon.

Jaz had debated with herself whether to let Vicki know that *she* had her eye on Nathan. Yesterday, she had confided in her friend.

'Nathan King,' Vicki had said, with a wide grin, 'I like your taste, girl. But you might need to take a ticket and get in line.'

'What? You mean you're interested in him?'

'I'm teasing. Billy the Kid is more my style.'

'Billy Kidswell?'

'Yeah. He's playing Ernest.'

If Vicki was considered to be the hottest date in the lower sixth, Billy the Kid was the fittest, most lusted-after guy in the upper sixth. Her friend's declared interest in him should have put Jaz's mind at rest. But it didn't. Of course Nathan King would fancy Vicki so there was little point in Jaz getting worked up about him. Never in a million years would he look twice in her direction.

'So tell me again about this writers' group,' Vicki said. 'Won't it be a load of frustrated old women writing about men in bulging breeches?'

Jaz laughed. 'It might be, for all I know. I'll find out tonight.'

Vicki stared at her. 'You're a strange girl, Jaz. Way too secretive for your own good. Whoa, hold up! Look who I see.'

Ahead of them, and standing within a group of other students, mostly girls, were Billy the Kid and Nathan King. Billy waved. 'Yo, my precious Gwendolen, how's it going?'

'Ernest, my love, how sweet of you to enquire. Truth to tell, I'm feeling quite faint and in need of a handsome Adonis to carry my bag home for me.' She tossed her shiny black hair with an exaggerated sigh. 'If only such a man existed.'

Jaz marvelled at her friend. How did she always manage to do and say the right thing?

Billy grinned. 'Then, my sweet, allow me to oblige.' He pushed a hand through his hair affectedly. 'Fancy a ride . . . home?' he drawled.

Vicki ignored the innuendo and said, 'Jaz too?'

Everyone turned and looked at Jaz. Including Nathan. Was it her imagination, or was he staring at her harder than the rest? She felt an excruciating flush creep up her neck. No! She wished the ground would open up and swallow her. 'It's OK,' she said, 'I'd rather walk—'

'You haven't got room, Billy,' Nathan interrupted her rudely, 'not with all the other groupies you've offered to drive home.'

She felt the sting of his words. So, she was just another groupie, was she? Well, she'd show him. In a gesture that Vicki would have been proud of, she tossed one of her long plaits over her shoulder. 'I'll see you, then, Vicki.' She walked away quickly, out of the college gate. Bloody Nathan King! Whatever had she seen in him?

'Do you always walk this fast?'

She spun round. Oh, hell! It was him. 'Yes,' she snapped. 'I find it preferable to hanging round people who don't have any manners!'

He fell into step beside her, his long, languid strides outpacing her. 'Would I be right in thinking I've done something to annoy you?'

'Yes. So leave me alone.'

'Oh,' he replied. 'Well, fair enough.' With his hands deep in his pockets, he sauntered beside her. 'Does everyone get this treatment, or have I been singled out specially?'

She shot him a furious look. 'You told Billy not to give me a lift home because he already had a carload of groupies to bolster his ego. I am nobody's groupie. Got that?'

'Listen, if you hadn't gone stomping off, you would have heard what I was going to say next.'

'I didn't . . .' She hesitated. 'What *were* you going to say next?'

'That rather than let you risk your life in Billy's deathtrap of a car, I'd walk you home.'

She looked at him suspiciously. 'Why would you want to do that?'

He thought for a moment, then smiled. 'I guess I must get some sort of perverse pleasure out of girls giving me a hard time.'

Beth felt as if she were a child again getting ready for the first day of the school term. A4 writing pad, Biros, pencil . . . What else did she need to take with her to the first meeting of Hidden Talents?

'How about a ruler? Or maybe a dictionary? Better still, a thesaurus.'

She looked across the kitchen. 'Don't tease me, Nathan,' she said. 'I'm nervous enough.'

He leaned back against the worktop, a picture of easy-going nonchalance. 'Keep it chilled, Mum, that's what you've got to tell yourself.'

She smiled. 'I'm not sure I like all this role reversal.'

'It's the future. Which reminds me, I'll see to your computer for you tonight. I want you hooked up to the Net and best friends with it before I leave home. How else will I be able to keep an eye on you?'

'By telephone?'

'Old ground, Mum. Email's much better, a piece of cake to get the hang of. Now I must learn my lines. Oscar's waiting for me in the bedroom.' He swept past her in a flourish of camp theatrical posturing.

It was ridiculous that she was so keyed up. She was only going to a writers' group. She was on a mission: to convince all those doubters, herself included, that she would be able to cope when Nathan flew the nest. She was a capable woman—as Simone frequently reminded her—now she had to learn how to enjoy exploring the unfamiliar. She wished she could be more like Nathan, who took everything in his stride: exams were a challenge, as was standing up on a stage and performing for an audience. She could never do that. His outward self-assurance came from his father. Nothing had seemed to faze Adam, which had made his untimely death all the more shocking. He had hidden his anxiety well. Too well. If only he had been more open she might have been able to help him.

She arrived at number 18 exactly on time. Bloom Street was the most sought-after address in town. Having said that, her own address had become almost as highly prized—if the asking price that the estate agent had put on Adele's flat was anything to go by. She rang the bell, admiring the window boxes at either side of the handsome wooden door. Dulcie Ballantyne had style, Beth decided.

To put everyone at ease, Dulcie had decided to offer a glass of wine before the meeting got under way. They made a small gathering, but an interesting one. That was the thing about writers' groups; they brought together a diverse mix of people who, on the face of it, had little in common. She, for example, wouldn't ordinarily socialise with a man like Victor Blackmore. It was patently obvious that he was a spanner in the works. She put him in his late fifties; he had thinning, sandy-grey hair, and was very pale with beady eyes tinged with pink. He was wearing a pair of seen-better-days trousers that were too short—an inch or two of shiny, hairless white shin was exposed—and he looked ill at ease as he sipped his red wine.

Nearest to Victor was Beth King, an attractive woman in her early forties. She wore no wedding ring, so was possibly divorced. She had a son and his name had already been mentioned several times. Dulcie wondered how dependent Beth was on him.

It was good to see that Victor Blackmore wasn't to be the sole man of the group. With a bit of luck Jack Solomon's presence would keep the dreadful man from thinking he could lord it over the rest of them. He was good-looking, if a little sombre, and cut a striking figure in his dark blue suit and silk tie. But she detected a sag in his shoulders and a tiredness in his eyes. He had apologised when he'd arrived for being so formally dressed, but apparently work had run on. It turned out that he had already met Beth King.

The most interesting member of the group was Jaz Rafferty: she would add a fresh and exciting dimension to the group. She was a delicate sprite of a girl and probably had no idea how pretty she was, with her striking auburn hair and charmingly freckled complexion. There was a delicious defiance in her manner—Dulcie had forgotten how fascinating and intense teenagers could be.

It was time to get things started, and Dulcie said, 'How would you all feel about playing a little game to get us in the right mood?'

'I haven't come here to play games,' Victor muttered.

The rest of the group was galvanised.

'Sounds OK to me,' smiled Beth, 'so long as it doesn't involve a Trivial Pursuit board.'

'Is it role-play?' asked Jaz doubtfully.

'No, it's not role-play,' Dulcie assured her. 'It's basic storytelling. We each take it in turns to add a sentence to the story. Victor, perhaps you'd like to set the ball rolling.'

'Very well.' He closed his eyes, steepled his fingers and inhaled deeply. He let out his breath and they waited for him to speak.

Nothing. Complete silence.

Someone—Jaz?—cleared their throat.

Victor's eyes remained shut. 'I'm thinking,' he said, in answer to the not-so-subtle prompt.

Another deep inhalation. And then it came. 'It was the best of times, it was the worst of times.' He opened his eyes and looked about him as though expecting a round of applause. Across the room, Dulcie was aware of Jaz stifling a snigger. She swallowed to stop one escaping her as well and said, 'Good start, Victor. Beth, your turn now.'

'It was the best of times, it was the worst of times,' Beth repeated slowly, her gaze focused on the clock on the mantelpiece, 'but no one could have been prepared for the awful calamity that struck, that wild, windy night, on exactly the stroke of midnight.'

With visible relief, she turned to Jack, who dived in straight away. 'Not even Gibbons, the one-armed gardener, who could never steer a straight course with a wheelbarrow, especially if he'd spent the morning in the potting shed savouring his favourite tipple of potato gin.'

'But despite his drinking habits,' said Jaz, 'and the loss of his arm during a fight over his prize-winning marrows, Gibbons was a crack shot, quite used to killing trespassers who came onto the master's land.'

It was Dulcie's turn next and she was glad to see that the game was working well and, with the exception of Victor, that the others were enjoying themselves. 'Now, the master was a curious man. Some said he had never been the same since the incident with the pitchfork . . .'

After several more rounds, which had them all laughing—the master, Jack told them, was a cross-dressing lap dancer—Dulcie pronounced an end to the game. She had decided that Jack was a quick-witted good sport, an asset to the group.

'And the point of that exercise?' asked Victor, drumming his fingers.

'To relax us,' Dulcie said. 'And to make us see how easy it is to slip into clichés and stereotypes,' she added, more seriously.

'First rule of writing,' Victor chimed in. 'Avoid clichés like the plague.'

Surprised at his ready wit, Dulcie laughed. Then, seeing the deadpan expression on his face, she stopped short. Oh Lord, the wretched man wouldn't know a cliché if it whacked him on the bottom. 'Right, then,' she said, careful to avoid Jack's eye, 'why don't we discuss what we each hope to gain from these sessions? Perhaps we could also share a few details about ourselves and say why we write. Beth?'

'Oh. Well, it's . . . Well, I've been writing for some time, um . . . since my husband died, eleven years ago. I suppose you could say it's been cathartic for me. Does that sound terribly like a cliché?'

'Not at all,' Dulcie said encouragingly. 'When my husband died I wrote frantically. Any spare moment I had that might leave me dwelling on Philip, I filled with words. Have you had anything published?'

'Oh no. I've only ever written for myself. I've never wanted other people to read my thoughts.'

'So what are you doing here?' They all looked at Victor. Dulcie could have slapped him. 'Surely that's the whole point of writing,' he continued, 'to know that one has a talent and share it.'

'That's a fair enough theory,' said Jack, leaning back in his seat and looking directly at Victor, 'so long as one is sure one has such a gift.'

'Yes,' agreed Jaz. 'No point in shoving a load of opinionated rubbish on people in the mistaken belief you can write.'

Good for you two, thought Dulcie. 'So, Beth,' she said, 'what would you like to get out of our meetings?'

'Oh, um, basic teaching, I suppose. Someone to show me where I'm going wrong. I know I'm not very good, and I'd like—'

'You can't teach people to write. You're either a writer or you're not.'

'That's an interesting point that we'll discuss another time, Victor,' said Dulcie smoothly. It was like dealing with a truculent child. 'I ought to say at this stage that every time one of us apologises for our writing, or says, "I'm not very good," a fifty-pence piece will have to be put into the Self-belief Box.'

Beth laughed. 'In that case, do you take credit cards?'

'How about having a Know-it-all Box?' muttered Jaz.

Dulcie was growing ever fonder of the youngest member of the group. 'Jack, how about you tell us a bit about yourself.'

'Not much to tell, really. I'm at a point in my life when I need to have a rethink, and, well, it was a spur-of-the-moment thing.'

'Any writing experience?'

180

'Nothing published, if that's what you mean. I wrote some rather poor song lyrics when I was very young. More recently I've been thinking of keeping a diary.' He turned to Beth. 'More catharsis for the soul.'

'And your expectations of the group?' asked Dulcie.

'I'm not sure I have any. I just wanted to try something new.'

Victor clicked his tongue. 'Unless we're all serious about writing and getting published, this group will be a waste of time.'

Dulcie saw Jack's hand clench. 'I don't think that's a helpful thing to say. For all we know, Jack may turn out to be the next Tony Parsons.'

'Tony who?'

Jaz rolled her eyes. 'Tony Parsons. He wrote *Man and Boy*.'

'Well, I've never heard of him.'

Dulcie intervened. 'We're not here to judge one another. We're here to offer support and helpful criticism. Jaz, do you want to take a turn?'

'OK.' She shot Victor a direct glance. 'I've just started writing a novel, so you could say I'm very serious about writing.'

'Was there a particular reason why you decided to write?'

Jaz paused. 'Hmm . . . I like doing stuff on my own. I suppose I like the power it gives me.'

'Yes,' nodded Dulcie, 'writing does empower you. It's just you and that piece of paper, and when you've filled it, you know no one else had anything to do with it. A nice point, Jaz. And finally, Victor, you're obviously a seasoned writer. How and why did you start writing your book?'

He squared his shoulders, ready to take the stage. 'It's a thriller set in a fictitious state, somewhere between Macedonia and Albania, and encompasses everything from drug trafficking to political intrigue. Two hundred thousand words and still going strong.'

'Goodness, how do you find time to write so much?' asked Beth.

'I'm very focused,' he replied, crossing his legs and revealing more white shin.

Later, when Dulcie was showing them out, having set a simple exercise to be completed by next week, she knew that as much as Victor had initially harangued the group, he would continue to grace it with his awkward and at times antagonistic presence. Doubtless he was secretly delighted that he had written more than anyone else in the group: it put him above the rest of them. Which meant that deep down, just like everyone else, he was hopelessly insecure about himself.

'Mother, I'm shocked! *Who* was that man I saw you with?'

Despite knowing Nathan was teasing her, Beth felt her cheeks colour. 'And what man would that be?'

He wagged a finger at her. 'Don't come the innocent with me, my girl. I saw the two of you, bold as brass out there in the road for all the neighbours to see.' He shook his head. 'I don't know, I've tried my best to bring you up properly and this is all the thanks I get.'

She squeezed past him and planted a kiss on his cheek. 'For starters you can put the kettle on and I'll tell you all about it.'

They sat at the kitchen table with their mugs of tea. 'So, first off, who was the guy in the Beamer?' asked Nathan, his bare feet stretched out towards the log-burning stove.

Momentarily distracted by Nathan's long legs—she never failed to be surprised by the size of him—she said, 'Jack Solomon. Coincidentally, he's Adele's estate agent and is really quite nice.'

Over the rim of his mug, Nathan raised an eyebrow. 'How nice?'

She swatted him with one of the cork table mats. 'Not in that way. He's much too young for a decrepit thing like me.'

'Oh, Ma, give it up! I bet you were easily the best-looking woman there. And the youngest to boot.'

'Wrong again. There was an interesting girl about your age. You might know her, she goes to Maywood College.'

'Name, rank and number?' He pulled out an imaginary notebook from his pocket and pretended to flick through it.

'Jaz Rafferty and she lives on—'

He looked up. 'Marbury Road,' he finished for her. 'I walked home with her after college today. Did she know you were my mother?'

'Why? Are you worried I might have told her the truth about you and put her off?'

'Now, Mum, don't let this fiction business go to your head.'

Later that night, soaking in a scented bath, Beth took stock of the evening. It had gone well. She had enjoyed herself more than she'd expected to, and felt a sense of achievement. She put this down to Dulcie Ballantyne: she had led the group firmly but not autocratically. She had given encouragement without resorting to patronage. It was just a pity they had had to put up with Victor. She thought about Jaz Rafferty. Had she imagined it, or had Nathan shown a little too much restrained interest when she'd mentioned the girl's name?

A knock at the door interrupted her thoughts.

It was Nathan. 'Will you test me on my lines?' He came in and settled himself in the creaking wicker chair beside the bath.

'Go on, then. Pass me a towel.' After she'd dried her hands she took the script from him. Assuming her best Edith Evans accent, Beth began to read the part of Lady Bracknell. '"It really makes no matter, Algernon.

I had some crumpets with Lady Harbury, who seems to me to be living entirely for pleasure now."'

"'I hear her hair has turned quite—"', Nathan broke off. 'What is it? What's wrong?'

'Quick, fetch me a pen and a piece of paper.'

He returned within seconds and watched her scribble in large block capitals the words, LIVING FOR PLEASURE.

'What do you think?' she said. 'Good title for a book?'

'Not bad.'

Beth went to bed happy that night. The homework Dulcie had set the group had been to think of a suitable title for a novel, and to put together an opening page. 'You need a hook to grab the reader's attention, a sense of time and place, and the general tone of the story.' Well, she'd stumbled across the title. Now all she had to do was write the necessary 300-odd words.

Chapter Three

ON SUNDAY MORNING Jack woke with one of Clare's arms draped over his chest. He lay for a moment without moving, his eyes fixed on the narrow gap in the curtains: rain was pattering against the window. Another wet, miserable day, he thought. Thousands of miles away, Amber and Lucy would be enjoying sun-drenched days in Florida.

Today he and Clare were meeting Des and Julie for lunch at the Italian in town. It had been Clare's idea to celebrate him becoming a partner, but Jack didn't feel comfortable at the prospect. He knew that Des had expected to be offered the same promotion, but nothing had materialised for him, and this would rub his nose in it. What was worse, a step up the career ladder would have been a welcome break for Des: six months ago his wife had given birth to Desmond Junior. But Clare had arranged it behind Jack's back.

He had finally got round to telling Clare about his partnership on the day of the writers' group's first meeting. They were speaking on the phone, late afternoon, and she had suggested they go out for dinner. 'Sorry,' he'd said, 'it'll have to be another night, I'm busy this evening.'

'Oh? Got something or some*one* better lined up?' Her words were playful, but beneath them he caught an edge of jealousy.

He hadn't wanted to tell her about Hidden Talents and had said, 'Now I'm a partner there'll be even more late nights I'm afraid, regular meetings I'll be expected to attend.' As soon as he'd said this, he'd realised he'd given himself a plausible alibi for every Thursday evening.

'Oh, well,' she'd replied, more happily, 'that's the price of success.'

He slid out of bed, dressed and went downstairs. The kitchen looked over the river. When he'd viewed the property this had been its one redeeming feature. He didn't like modern houses—an opinion, in his line of work, that he kept to himself. But what he wouldn't give to live in Bloom Street or Maywood Park Road.

Making himself some toast and a cafetiere of coffee, he envied Beth King and Dulcie Ballantyne. They were both widowed, but they seemed to have coped and got on with life. Perhaps if he got to know them better, he might learn something from them. How long, he wondered, had it been before Beth King had sorted herself out? Dulcie too.

It had been interesting seeing Beth last Thursday evening: she had seemed quite a different woman from the one he had met a few days earlier: less sure of herself. Maybe she had thought the same of him. He had told the group he was thinking of writing a diary, and after he'd driven home that night—having given both Beth and Jaz a lift—he had made his first entry on his laptop.

The rain was coming down harder now. It wasn't the kind of day that induced one to go out. He'd prefer to spend some time writing. He had that exercise to do for next Thursday evening. Trouble was, he didn't want Clare to know what he was doing. He wanted to have something that was his, and his alone. He chewed his toast, and reflected that this was why he and Clare had no future together. She wanted too much of him and he wasn't ready, not so soon after Maddie.

During lunch, Jack drank too much and found himself drifting in and out of the conversation. Once or twice he made eye contact with Clare, and in return she rubbed her foot against his leg. He almost wished he could make it work between them. She was intelligent and attractive. Any number of men in his shoes would leap at the chance to have her. Why couldn't he?

Because he didn't love her. And never would. It was as simple as that, and she deserved better. The sooner he ended it, the better.

'Hey up, Jack? What's thee dreamin' of?'

He shook himself out of his reverie. 'Nowt you'd understand, Des, my lad.'

Julie groaned. 'Oh, they're off again, Clare, speaking int' northern tongues.'

'Let's leave them to it and go to the loo. We can talk about them behind their backs,' Clare said, with a smile.

When they were alone, Des topped up their glasses. 'You OK, Jack? You're very quiet. Everything all right *chez* Solomon?'

As he looked at Des's concerned face, Jack was tempted to confide in him. Maybe that was all he needed to do. Perhaps it was nothing more than a case of cold feet that was making him back away from Clare.

'Nothing's wrong,' he said. 'What the hell could be wrong with my life? I've got it made, haven't I? A fantastic girlfriend and a partnership thrown in for good measure. What the hell could be wrong with that?' His voice was sharp and much too loud.

Still holding the bottle of Valpolicella, Des stared at him. Then, 'You tell me, Jack.'

'Watch out for the cyclist, Nathan.'

'Relax, Mum, I saw it way back.' He indicated and overtook the cyclist, ignoring his mother's right foot, which twitched on an invisible pedal. He knew it was difficult for a parent to be a passenger, but at least Mum let him drive whenever they went anywhere together. It would be great to have his own car, like Billy, but they couldn't afford it. He didn't mind. When he'd got his law degree and was in London, things would be different. It would be a hard slog to get there, but he'd do it.

Nathan had the next five years of his life carefully worked out—as long as he got the right grades next summer he hoped to go to Nottingham—and he was determined that nothing would spoil his plans, least of all a relationship. He preferred to be friends with everyone; it kept things from getting messy or complicated. Even so, he couldn't deny his interest in Jaz Rafferty. There was a spiky independence about her that appealed to him, and he liked the distinctive way she dressed and spoke. But he suspected that her huffy manner, when he'd walked home with her on Thursday, had had nothing to do with his apparent snub, but everything to do with her fancying Billy.

He drove through the gates of Marsh House and Grandpa Barnaby opened the door to them. He was wearing an apron and a wide smile. 'Good-oh,' he said. 'Now that you're here Lois will let me have a drink. I was so worried you'd be late. Come on in. Lois is beavering away in the kitchen. Got all manner of delights in store for you.'

They followed him through the house, their shoes clattering noisily on the polished wood floor. In the kitchen doorway, Grandpa Barnaby said, 'Look who I've found, Lois! A charming couple bearing gifts of the horticultural variety.'

'Ah, Beth dear, there you are. And, Nathan, look at you in your smart leather coat. Very dashing. What a fine young man you've become. So tall.' Lois sighed and Nathan knew what was coming next. 'The spitting image of your father.' They'd been in the house less than two minutes and already the first comparison had been made.

Although he had promised himself he wouldn't react, Nathan clenched his jaw. He hated having to keep up the pretence that had become an absurd reality for Grandma Lois. This whole day—his father's birthday—was a mockery, and he no longer wanted to be part of it.

'Another roast potato, Nathan? Perhaps a parsnip?'

'No, thanks, Grandma.' His grandmother was a great cook, but she always overdid it. To deflect her, he said, 'Did Mum tell you I'm in the college play?'

'Ooh, are you? How exciting. Which one?'

'*The Importance of Being Earnest.* I'm Algernon.'

'The best part, of course. Adam was the same. He could always land the lead in a school production.'

Irritated, Nathan said, 'It's essentially an ensemble piece. I think you'll find Lady Bracknell steals the show once or twice.'

But Lois seemed not to hear him. 'Barnaby, do you remember the time Adam played Puck in *A Midsummer Night's Dream*, and afterwards everyone kept coming up to us saying what a natural he was and that he ought to consider a career on the stage?'

Nathan stood up abruptly, knocking his plate askew. He caught his knife before it fell to the floor. 'Shall I clear away for you, Grandma?'

From the other side of the table, Beth also got to her feet. 'Yes, Lois, you sit down and rest. Nathan and I will tidy up.'

'Sorry, Mum,' he whispered, when they were alone in the kitchen, 'but I can't stand it when she goes on and on about him.'

'I know, Nathan, but it's only for today. It's her way of coping with it.'

'But she's *not* coping with it. She's simply denying everything that really happened. Is that what Dad would have wanted?' He turned and stared out of the window, his resentment growing. 'I can't tell her anything without her comparing me to him. Sometimes I just want to shout at her, "I'm *me*, *Nathan* King! Not Adam King, the deceased golden boy of Lois and Barnaby King."'

'Look,' Beth said softly, 'this isn't the moment to talk about it. For now, let Lois remember her son the way she needs to. OK?'

A brief silence passed between them. The rage inside him began to subside. 'We're trapped . . . defined by what happened to Dad. You'll always be the widow and I'll always be the orphaned grandson.'

She frowned. 'Excuse me, but you're not an orphan. You have a mother who loves you very much. And if you weren't so keen to drive us home, she'd suggest you had a drink.'

He made an effort to smile. 'It's come to something when my own mother's encouraging me to hit the bottle.'

'How do you think Barnaby gets through the day?'

His father's death seldom got to Nathan, these days. He had been six when his mother had told him his father was dead. There had been tears. Lots of them. Once he'd realised that she was crying, he'd been scared and started to cry with her. And then Grandma Lois had appeared in his room. She had one of her cardigans draped round her shoulders and seemed sort of hunched. Older suddenly. In a chilling voice he had never heard her use before, she said, 'Beth, stop this at once! You're frightening Nathan. That isn't what Adam would have wanted.' He could remember vividly how his mother had looked as though she had just been slapped. But, then, that had been his grand-mother's intention, to bring his mother to her senses. In Lois's world you didn't admit to sadness or loss. You gritted your worn-down teeth and got on with it. As a result, his father's death was never referred to directly at Marsh House. Instead, he was revered and held up as the per-fect son, the perfect husband, the perfect father.

Just once, Nathan would have liked someone at Marsh House to tell the truth so that his remaining memories—the honest ones—of his father could be treasured, not tainted with Lois's deluded portrayal of a man who had only ever existed in her mind.

When Nathan and his mother went back into the dining room with the desserts, Grandpa Barnaby groaned and clutched his stomach. 'Oh, Lois,' he said, 'you'll be the death of us all.'

Nathan winced. In any other household a remark like that would have meant nothing, but Lois shot her husband a look of total horror. 'I really don't think it's appropriate, today of all days, for you to use me as the butt of your stupid jokes.' She walked out of the room.

'Oh Lord,' muttered Barnaby. 'Do you think I ought to go after her?'

Already on her feet, Beth said, 'How about I go and talk to her?'

'Would you? I'd be eternally grateful.'

Nathan watched his mother leave the room. The Beth King he knew was strong-willed, determined and fun to be with. When Lois was on the scene, she lost some of her confidence, became diminished.

Sometimes Lois went too far and trampled over his mother's feelings. On the few occasions when there had been a hint of a man in Beth's life, Lois had been quick to stamp on it. On one occasion he had overheard her say, 'What are you thinking of? The man's clearly only after one thing. And what kind of a stepfather would he make for Nathan?'

Her voice hesitant, his mother had said, 'But, Lois, we've been out for dinner twice, that's all.'

'You must be careful, Beth. Nathan's at an impressionable age. Mothers have to be above reproach.'

Oh, yes, thought Nathan. Lois could be cruelly manipulative. But she could also be extremely generous—yet even that was not without its own agenda. While she was paying for things—driving lessons, school trips—she had a hold over them. His mother would never admit it, but he knew she didn't like the situation. That was why, when he had passed his GCSEs, he had insisted on leaving the private school Lois and Barnaby had paid for since he was seven. Instead, he'd opted to go to Maywood sixth-form college. 'I need to spread my wings,' he'd said, when his mother had asked him why. They both knew the truth though.

Beth found Lois upstairs in her bedroom. She was sitting on the bed, crying. When she saw Beth, she gave her eyes one last stoic dab then pushed the handkerchief inside her sleeve. 'Silly of me, I know,' she said, her voice frayed with edgy cheerfulness. 'Barnaby's such a fool.'

'He probably thought he was helping to make light of the day,' Beth said.

'Well, he failed badly,' Lois said. She stood up, and moved away from the bed. 'I don't suppose he's thought to put the coffee on, has he?'

She was past Beth now and standing at the door. The moment to talk, really talk, about Adam and how Lois still felt about him was gone. Perhaps a stronger woman would have taken her by the scruff of her neck and made her confess, but Beth would never be able to do that. When the two of them were together, she became a coward.

She followed her mother-in-law down the wide staircase, and they had their coffee in the sitting room. And just as she and Nathan had known would happen, Barnaby was assigned the task of setting up the old projector and screen. For the next hour they sat in semi-darkness watching jumpy images of a skinny, dark-haired boy grow into a handsome teenager. Then they turned the pages of Lois's photo albums. Beth knew that Nathan was finding this annual ritual more of an ordeal than ever, and her heart went out to him.

It was dark and raining when they left Marsh House. Nathan was driving faster than Beth would have liked and she told him so.

'Worried I might put us out of our misery by killing us both?' he said savagely.

Horrified, she did not reply. How could he have said that?

'I'm sorry,' he said, some minutes later when he'd dropped his speed. 'That was a shitty thing for me to say.'

'Yes, it was.' Then, with false brightness, she said, 'And, anyway, an accident would result in a dreadful mess in the boot.'

He groaned. 'How much stuff did she off-load onto you this time?'

'Oh, just the usual amount. Two puddings, the remains of the joint of pork and half a cauliflower.'

'Doesn't it ever get to you, this constant supply of leftovers and hand-me-downs?'

'Of course it does, but I also recall how grateful I was in the early years when keeping you in socks and shoes was a constant worry. You've no idea how fast you grew then, or what an expensive liability your feet were.'

The rain came down harder and Nathan flicked at the switch to make the wipers go faster. After a few minutes, he said, 'I know it hasn't been easy for you, Mum, but I do want you to know that—that my enormous feet and I are very grateful for all you've done.'

In the light cast by the streetlamps she could see that there was now a softness to his face. 'I'm glad to hear it.'

In bed that night, Beth thought of Nathan's anger in the car. Never had he spoken with such bitterness before, and it scared her. She wished he didn't know the truth about his father's death. If he hadn't overheard her conversation with Simone all those years ago, he would have believed it was a tragic accident. But he knew the truth. That his father had gone out that night and deliberately killed himself. He had stopped off at the local off-licence, bought a bottle of cheap whisky, drunk half of it then driven into a tree. He had died instantly.

And that was what Lois had spent eleven years refusing to accept. She simply would not admit that Adam had been so depressed he had taken his own life as a way out of his problems.

Beth had always believed that the reason behind Lois's denial was her inability to forgive her son for being less of a man than she had thought him. Poor Adam. And poor Lois.

Des couldn't sleep. And if Jack knew what he knew, he doubted his friend could either. He turned over and gazed at his wife in the semi-darkness. He didn't know what he would do if he came home one day and found Julie in bed with Paul, his oldest and closest friend.

Outside, rain lashed against the window. He thought of what Jack had said at the restaurant: how he knew he had to break it off with Clare but was scared of hurting her. And of what Julie had said when they were driving home. 'Guess what Clare told me in the loo. She's not a hundred per cent sure, but she reckons she might be pregnant.'

Des wondered who would confess first—Jack, or Clare. Either way, they were both in for one heck of a shock.

The older Dulcie became, the more she believed that it was the simple things in life that provided the most pleasure: the sun on one's face and a happy heart. It wasn't much to ask for, was it? It had rained all day on Monday and for most of Tuesday, but this morning the sun was shining and the sky was a brilliant blue. She pedalled her bicycle along Bloom Street, feeling that nothing could take the shine off her day.

Richard had been discharged from hospital yesterday and he had phoned her earlier this morning to give her the good news.

Despite the brightness of the sun, the day was cold, but Dulcie glowed with an inner warmth. She pedalled on to Churchgate, locked her bike to the railings of St Cecilia's, unclipped her basket and went to do some shopping before meeting Prue and Maureen for lunch.

Every three weeks she and her friends got together for lunch and a gossip. Although they were close and had known each other for many years—they had children of roughly the same age—she had never confided in them about Richard, believing that the fewer people who knew about her affair, the less chance there was of it becoming known.

She called in at the delicatessen for some cheese for supper and a large tub of black olives, shiny with oil. With these purchases, and knowing she had a bottle of excellent red wine at home, she looked forward to the evening ahead.

It was one of the nicest things about living alone: she could eat what she wanted without having to consider anyone else. She had devoted most of her life to others—Philip and the children. Now it was time to pamper herself a little. She would never have dreamed that she would be so suited to living alone. She had turned into a most self-contained person: a good book, a glass of wine and she was content. And it was only now, at sixty-three, that she had discovered that if she demanded nothing of another person no demands were made of her.

It was this philosophy that was at the heart of her relationship with Richard; it was why it worked between them. Given the immovable parameters of their affair, neither could be possessive of the other. Few people would understand, and fewer condone, what she was doing, but it suited her to have an affair with a married man: it meant that she could retain her singleness yet feel as if she were part of a couple.

Next she called in at Novel Ways to see if the book she'd ordered last week had arrived. It had and she handed a ten-pound note to the girl on the till. While she was waiting for her change, she heard a voice behind her: 'Come on, Nicholas, do hurry up and choose what you want.' There was something disturbingly familiar about the thin, careworn voice. She turned her head, cautiously, and her suspicions were confirmed: it was Angela. She was hovering over an angular boy with a sensitive face and in her hands was a pile of paperbacks; the latest Ian Rankin, a Robert Harris thriller, and two John Grishams. Books to occupy Richard while he was convalescing? Dulcie thought of the sweet book of poetry he had given her—a collection of love poems from which he often read to her.

With a trembling hand, she took her change and fled.

By the time she slowed her pace, she was standing outside St Cecilia's, her heart thudding painfully, her legs shaking. She felt sick, panicky and guilty. And weepy. The happiness that had filled her only a short time ago had gone. Now her heart was heavy.

Dulcie closed her eyes. She considered how an affair was generally acknowledged to be a roller-coaster ride of out-of-control emotions. But it hadn't been like that between her and Richard; she had never put herself through the he-loves-me-he-loves-me-not game. Grounded in her own sense of who she was, and the fulfilling life she led, she had been perfectly content with what they had.

She had never harboured the hope that he would leave Angela: he had made it very clear that he wouldn't. 'I couldn't,' he confessed. 'It would destroy her.' Also, there were the two younger children to consider—they had been eleven and nine at the start of the affair, and Dulcie knew that Richard loved them dearly. To leave his wife would be to leave his sons, and he simply wasn't that kind of man.

When he'd told Dulcie that he had never been unfaithful to Angela before, she believed him. In the early stages of their affair, he had been overwhelmed by guilt. But right from the day they had met, in the lounge of the Maywood Grange Hotel, there had been a spark between them, and the first time they had kissed, Dulcie had known it was only a matter of time before they slept together. When their lips had touched, it was as if they had both waited a very long time for the moment.

Prue and Maureen were on fine form, which was just what Dulcie needed to lift her spirits. Where would we be without our friends? she thought, as they ordered their lunch and got down to discussing

Maureen's impending holiday in the Algarve and how she was going to avoid playing golf morning, noon and night with her husband, Geoff.

But just as the waitress appeared with their plates of quiche and salad, Dulcie caught sight of someone else approaching their table. For the second time that day, she felt wrong-footed and panicky.

It was Angela. From the expression on her face, it was clear that she had just recognised Dulcie and was coming over to say hello.

Upstairs in her room, Jaz switched on the computer. She wanted to read through what she would be taking to the writers' group tomorrow evening. All Dulcie had asked them to do was produce the opening page of a novel (with title), which, of course, she'd already written, so she hadn't had much to do. It was based on her brothers and sisters, and the more she wrote, the more empowered she felt. Every jibe they made about her was a point they scored against themselves. Oh, revenge would be sweet. She clicked on PRINT, and wondered how the others had got on. Being with a group of adults had been more fun than she had thought it would be. Jack and Beth were a laugh, and it had been kind of Jack to drive her home. So that she didn't give the game away with her family about where she'd spent the evening, she'd asked Jack to drop her on the corner of Marbury Road. Hurrying home, she hoped he hadn't thought her ungrateful. She also thought how weird it was that she had spent the evening with Nathan King's mother when she'd talked to him for the first time that afternoon.

She had thought a lot about Nathan since that day, but couldn't decide what to make of him. Why had he walked home with her? She had decided that, close up, he was even better looking and would be no more interested in a girl like her than Billy would. She would have to be careful when half-term was over and she was back at college. Not for a minute must she let him think she had ever been interested in him.

A knock at the door had her clicking on CLOSE.

Her mother was the only person who respected the sign on her bedroom door that read: 'Private—Please Knock Before Entering.' She was eight years younger than Dad, and Jaz had always thought her beautiful. Nothing was too much trouble for her. She could always be relied upon. But not so much, these last few weeks. Most of the time she seemed lost in a world of her own.

'What's wrong?' she asked, when both of her parents came in. They only ever put in a double appearance if it was something important.

Suddenly a huge grin appeared on her father's face and, after exchanging a look with her mother, he said, 'Jaz, we've got brilliant news, and your mother wanted you to be first to know. She's pregnant.'

Nothing could have surprised Jaz more. They were both grinning at her now. Oh, this was terrible. 'You're kidding,' she stammered. *Oh, please, say you're having me on. I couldn't stand another brother or sister.*

'And what's more,' her father said, putting a hand on her mother's shoulder, 'we've hit the jackpot. It's twins.'

Chapter Four

IT WAS THURSDAY EVENING and the group was listening to Victor, who had just summed up his *magnum opus*—*Star City*—and was now giving an over-the-top reading of his opening page.

'Thank you, Victor,' Dulcie said, when at last he paused. 'What a lot you squeezed into one page.' They all knew he'd read out at least twice the specified amount.

He nodded and leaned back into his seat. 'That, of course, is my objective,' he said. 'I want to hit the reader right between the eyes.'

'An ambitious opening such as that requires skilful handling to pull it off. Anyone else want to make a comment? Jack?'

Dressed in jeans and an open-necked shirt, Jack was looking less formal than he had last week, but he didn't appear to be any more relaxed. He looked tired and drawn. 'Ah,' he said carefully. 'To be honest, I got confused. There seemed to be a great number of characters.'

'I thought that too,' agreed Jaz. 'And they all had foreign names.'

'That's because they *are* foreign,' Victor said waspishly.

'I think the point they're making,' Dulcie said cautiously, 'is that you gave a tad too much information. Perhaps you could cut back on some of the characters. And was that second explosion really necessary?'

Victor cleared his throat. 'Essential.'

'You don't think it weakened the effect of the first?' suggested Beth.

Before Victor exploded, Dulcie said quickly, 'Good point, Beth, and one we should all bear in mind. Who's going to be brave enough to go next? Any takers? Jaz, how about you?'

'Mine's called *Having the Last Laugh*,' she said, then launched into reading her work in a clear, confident voice. When she'd finished, she looked at Dulcie for her verdict. 'What do you think? Was it OK?'

Dulcie smiled. 'Jaz, that was more than OK. It was brilliant. My only quibble is that you stopped when you did. I wanted more.'

'I have a couple of quibbles,' Victor said, clicking his Biro. 'What's a head-mash? Doesn't using modern-day parlance limit your audience and date the book before it's even published?'

A protective motherly instinct made Dulcie want to come to Jaz's aid, but she needn't have worried.

'A head-mash is when you've scrambled your brains trying to work something out,' Jaz said levelly. 'I expect you get that a lot, Victor, don't you?' He looked at her uncertainly and she smiled sweetly at him. 'I know I do after a long day at college and then three hours of homework.'

Dulcie went next, and then Beth took her turn, a little nervously, but with an amusing central character called Libby, an insecure self-confessed self-help junkie. And then it was Jack's turn.

'It's called *Friends and Family*.' He cleared his throat and fiddled with the neck of his shirt. '"By their friends shall ye know them. That's what I'd been brought up to believe, and believe it I did. Until now. Now I know differently. Friends are rarely what they seem. Friends come and go. Like chameleons they change their colours to suit the moment. I once had such a friend. But, there again, I once had a wife."' He swallowed, straightened the papers on his lap, then continued, his voice low.

Dulcie listened intently. She saw the profound sadness in Jack's face. Poor man, she thought. When he'd finished, the room fell quiet. Nobody rushed to speak. Not even Victor.

'Sorry,' Jack murmured, 'was that a bit too much of the Misery Joe's?'

Both Jaz and Beth reached for the Self-belief Box at the same time and rattled it in front of him. It broke the tension in the room and Dulcie suggested they discuss his opening page over a cup of coffee.

Out in the kitchen, while she waited for the kettle to boil, Dulcie listened to Victor telling Jack that he needed to lose some of the introspection and liven his opening page up with a bit more action. Dulcie sighed. What with? A couple of car crashes? The man didn't know the words 'subtlety' and 'sensitivity'. Horribly patronising too.

Not dissimilar from how Angela had treated Dulcie yesterday.

'I thought it was you,' Angela had said. 'How are you? Still running your little business?'

Dulcie had bristled to hear her livelihood dismissed as no more than a hobby. 'No,' she'd said. 'These days I'm a fully fledged lady of leisure.'

'Oh, good for you. I wish I could say the same, but with Christopher and Nicholas to chase after, my leisure time is non-existent. And now I have Richard at home. He's just recovering from a heart attack. He gave us all a dreadful scare. I've been on at him for years to slow down, but you know what men are like, they never listen, and the next thing you know, you're a widow passing round the sherry at a funeral.'

Dulcie had cringed at Angela's overly jolly manner. Or was she simply trying to hide her concern for a husband who had nearly died?

'You must give him my best wishes,' Dulcie had said.

'Thank you, I will. But I doubt he'll remember you. He has the most shocking memory. Anyway, I must press on.'

And then she was gone. After talking to Angela, Dulcie might have expected to feel guiltier about her affair with Richard but, perversely, the reverse had happened. Angela's offhand manner—as if his heart attack had resulted from his own carelessness—had irritated her, and she believed that Richard deserved the happiness she could offer him. Any pangs she had experienced outside St Cecilia's had vanished.

Now, pouring boiling water into the mugs, she thought of Jack. There was no doubt in her mind that what he had written was autobiographical. How would she feel if she was in his position? Or, more to the point, in Angela's shoes? When she took the coffee into the sitting room, she found herself unable to meet Jack's eye.

After a relatively wet but mild October, winter arrived at the back end of November with icy mornings and bitter winds.

Maywood Health Centre was always busier when the weather turned cold and, on this particular Monday morning, it was teeming. Beth had a theory that the first note of a piped Christmas carol was the harbinger of medical doom and gloom. As she listened to the endless coughs and sniffles, Beth knew that most of the patients weren't as critically ill as they claimed. She felt sorry for the elderly, those who suffered in silence, who would not dream of troubling their overworked doctor.

Only a couple of days ago, she had called on Adele Waterman and found her in a terrible state. She had immediately called out the old lady's doctor who diagnosed pneumonia. Beth and Nathan were taking it in turns to keep an eye on her, ferrying down food and drink at regular intervals. Beth would miss Adele when she moved. According to Jack, if all went well with the sale, she would be leaving in the New Year.

Thursday nights had become part of her routine, and Beth looked forward to seeing the group each week. Apart from Victor, who never spoke of his life outside Hidden Talents, they were learning about each other. It had occurred to Beth that, without exception, they all had a raw spot. As open as Jaz was, she refused to speak about her family, but she wrote amusingly, perhaps tellingly, about a fictional family from hell. Jack, clearly going through a painful divorce, wrote in poignant detail about the break-up of a marriage. Dulcie was the most reserved, somehow managing never to tell them what she'd really been up to.

But the really good thing, as far as Beth was concerned, was that she was gaining in confidence with regard to her writing. *Living For Pleasure* was growing fast. Dulcie had encouraged them to have a go at entering a short-story competition, and it was the group's homework. They had two weeks to complete the task.

Late that night, after Nathan had gone to bed, Beth poured herself a glass of wine and switched on the computer. Nathan had bullied her out of her technophobia, and now she was hooked and did all her writing on it. The best part was that she was in daily contact with Simone by email. She spent more than twenty minutes replying to Simone's latest message, then hesitated before she switched off the machine. Last night, she had done the craziest thing: she had visited a chat room. She blamed Simone: it had been her suggestion. At first Beth had been dubious about doing it. 'What if I get chatting to some pervy anorak type?'

'Not everyone using the Internet is a raging weirdo,' Simone had emailed back. 'Of course, if you're not sure how to go about it . . .' There had been something in Simone's tone that had made Beth want to prove to her friend, and herself, that she could. To her surprise, not only had it been straightforward but there were several chat rooms specifically for writers. She had picked one at random and was soon reading messages in the 'meetings' room. It all seemed innocent enough: critiques wanted, word-processor services offered, listings of workshops.

She hadn't plucked up the nerve to respond to any of the messages, but tonight one message in particular caught her eye:

> I'm new to this, and as someone once wrote, 'One should always be a little improbable,' so I'm giving it a whirl. I've had one of those days, and to quote again from the same source, 'I am sick to death of cleverness.' Anyone on the same wavelength? Mr Outta Laffs.

After a brief tussle with the warning voice in her head, Beth typed:

> I know what you mean, Mr Outta Laffs. 'Everybody is clever nowadays. You can't go anywhere without meeting clever people.' BK.

A few seconds passed. Then another message appeared.

> How refreshing to find someone who knows their Oscar Wilde so well. Bravo! Are you a fan?

My son is currently rehearsing *The Imp of Earnest* for his sixth-form college.

As soon as she clicked on SEND, she regretted it. Even in a chat room she had resorted to mentioning Nathan.

I'm a parent too [came the reply]. My daughter once played Gwendolen and after spending weeks helping her learn her lines, I became hooked on Oscar Wilde. By the way, if I may be so bold, you sound like you're a woman. Am I right?

She hesitated before answering, suddenly picturing the perve in the anorak hunched up over his keyboard. Quoting Oscar Wilde again, but this time from *An Ideal Husband*, she typed:

'Questions are never indiscreet. Answers sometimes are.'

Point taken. But let me assure you, I'm a respectable man, whose only vice, thus far, is to have come on-line (for the first time) to chat, instead of getting on with my novel. I seem to be stuck. Any advice?

I find a glass of wine helps.

Way ahead of you. Onto my second. What's your preferred drug of choice? In terms of writing, that is! Which genre?

I'm very much a novice. A history of unpublished short stories behind me, but now I'm trying my hand at a novel. And you?

Oh, novels primarily. What's your book about?

A self-help junkie.

Autobiographical?

NO!

I'll take that as a yes. Title?

Living For Pleasure.

Aha, do I detect more overtones of Mr W?

Guilty as charged. Time for me to go. Good night, Mr Outta Laffs.

Well, thought Beth, whoever Mr Laffs was, he had taught her that chatting on-line was as easy as pie. She went to bed wondering what he was like. For all she knew she had just spent fifteen minutes in the presence of a dead ringer for Victor. As was her habit before giving in to sleep, she read for a quarter of an hour. Beside her bed was her inspiration for writing *Living For Pleasure*: a stack of self-help books Simone had given her over the years. Her current favourite was *Feel the Fear and Do It Anyway*. She'd certainly done that tonight.

When Clare had told Jack she was pregnant, he had been poleaxed, as though the world had crashed in on him. 'Are you sure?' he'd asked, once he could think straight enough to string a sentence together.

'Yes,' she'd said, 'I've done a test.' And then she'd smiled, a smile that told him just how she felt about the situation. He thought he would never forget that look on her face. Or the sense of being trapped by it.

'But I thought you were on the pill, that that was all taken care of.'

Her gaze didn't quite meet his. 'I'd been having trouble with the pill,' she murmured, 'so I was using something else.'

'What? Hope?' She'd done this deliberately, he knew it.

'What's got into you, Jack? You love children, you told me that.'

He stared out of the window, onto the small fenced garden of her modern estate house. He had never felt so confined before. He pushed a hand through his hair. 'I was talking specifically about my own children, Amber and Lucy. Not every Tom, Dick and Harry's children.'

'This child is yours, Jack, not Tom's, not Dick's or anyone else's.'

He made no response, and they were quiet for a long, threatening moment. Until Clare said, 'Thank you for making your feelings so clear. At least I know exactly where I stand. I think you'd better leave.'

She started to cry. He went to her and put his arms round her, then led her back to the sofa, where she clung to him. 'Oh, Jack. I know what you're thinking. That I was deliberately careless. I wasn't. Please believe me. And please don't go. Don't leave me. I love you.'

He held her tightly, moved by her need for him. He knew he was caught. It was too late now to walk away from her and the baby.

No matter how much he wanted to.

The phone rang on the desk in his office, making him start. Mr Mitchell was on the line. He was withdrawing his offer on Miss Waterman's flat. They were back to square one again. Damn. He decided to deliver the bad news in person. Just once, he'd leave early.

He joined the stream of early-evening traffic. It was almost dark and the shop fronts along Bridge Street were brightly lit. By next week he wouldn't be able to move for twinkling lights and sprayed-on snow.

The thought of Christmas depressed him. Maddie still hadn't let him know when he would see the girls—apparently Tony had some grand notion about taking them skiing.

Jack parked outside Maywood Park House. When he rang the bell for 10A, Beth answered the door. 'Hello,' she said. 'Is Adele expecting you?'

'No. I've called on the off chance, with bad news, I'm afraid, which I thought I'd impart face to face.'

'Oh, that's the last thing she needs. She's in bed with pneumonia.'

'I'm sorry to hear that. I could always ring tomorrow.'

She hesitated, as if weighing up the options. 'Hang on. I'll go and have a quick word with her. Go through to the sitting room.'

The flat was a lot warmer than it had been on his last visit and he found himself liking it more. He felt awkward for intruding, though.

'Adele says you're welcome to see her, as long as you behave like the perfect gentleman and don't look too closely at her.'

Miss Waterman was propped up with several pillows behind her, the bedclothes decorously drawn up to her chin. She indicated a chair. 'Why don't you give me your news. It's bad, I presume.'

He told her about Mr Mitchell withdrawing his offer. 'Of course, as soon as you're feeling better, we'll get people viewing again.'

'What about the others who viewed and were keen?' asked Beth.

'I'll chase them first thing in the morning.'

'You look tired, Mr Solomon,' Miss Waterman said. 'Are you working too hard?'

He smiled. 'Please, it's Jack. And, no, I can't admit to working too hard.'

'Well,' Miss Waterman eased herself into a more comfortable position, 'you look nearly as bad as I feel, Jack.'

'A few personal problems at the moment,' he said lightly. 'Nothing that will get in the way of me selling your flat.'

'The flat be damned,' she said, with surprising feeling. 'You look as if you need a good hearty meal to build you up. Beth, as Nathan's out this evening, why don't you invite Jack for supper?'

It was difficult to know who looked more astonished, Beth or Jack.

'I think Adele might have been trying her hand at a little matchmaking,' Beth said to Jack later that evening when he was helping her to lay the table. 'I hope you weren't embarrassed.'

'Not in the least.'

She gave him a handful of cutlery. 'But she's dead right, Jack.'

'Do I really look that awful?'

'To be brutally honest, and speaking as a friend, yes.'

While Beth took a small plate of supper downstairs to Adele, leaving him to open a bottle of wine, Jack was struck again by how comfortable he felt in Beth's flat. It had an almost magical ability to make the rest of the world and its troubles disappear. He didn't even feel guilty that he was in the company of a woman Clare had no knowledge of. And, anyway, there was nothing going on between him and Beth. But since she had told him about the baby, Clare had become increasingly possessive. She had wanted to move in with him, but he had held off, using Amber and Lucy as an excuse, claiming that he didn't want to unsettle or alarm them. Clare's possessiveness also stretched to her badgering him about his regular absences on Thursday evenings. He still hadn't let on about the writers' group. Sometimes he thought it was only his new-found passion for writing that kept him sane. Whenever he sat down in front of his laptop to write his diary or his novel, the words tumbled out of him, an unstoppable outpouring from the heart.

'I'm under orders to feed you till you burst,' Beth said brightly when she came back, 'and to get to the bottom of what's troubling you.'

They sat down to eat, and before long he found he was telling her everything. About Maddie and the girls, Tony and Clare, and now the baby. He sighed heavily. 'I've only myself to blame. I shouldn't have rushed into things with her as I did. I've been bloody stupid.'

'Don't be too hard on yourself. You haven't said, but presumably Clare wants the baby?'

'Very much so. And I wouldn't want her to do anything . . . well, you know, anything drastic like get rid of it.'

'I'm probably letting the sisterhood down, but you mustn't marry Clare if it means the pair of you will end up hating each other. You have to be sensible. Look long-term, Jack. You have a duty to the child, but also to be true to yourself. And there's Amber and Lucy to consider. If you're unhappy, think what that will do to them.'

He was no nearer to solving his problems, but spending an evening with someone who was straightforward and easy to talk to had cheered him. Thank goodness for Beth.

Richard Cavanagh knew he was taking a risk. Driving a car so soon after a heart attack wasn't advisable, but he simply had to see Dulcie.

With nothing to do while he'd been recovering from his heart attack, he'd thought a lot about his life and what was important to him. Before it was too late, he had to make the most of what was left to him.

He squeezed the accelerator, enjoying his moment of freedom. With

Angela taking his convalescence so seriously, he had been kept a virtual prisoner in his own home. Ever since Angela had told him how she and Nicholas had bumped into Dulcie, his heart had hardened towards her. 'I expect you can't remember what she looks like, but I don't recall her looking so old,' Angela had gloated. 'And I'd bet a pound to a penny she's put on weight. It would explain why she's still a widow.'

With his hands forming fists under the duvet, he'd said, 'How do you know she hasn't married again?'

'She wasn't wearing a ring, of course.'

He couldn't say with any certainty when or why he had stopped loving Angela but, like middle age or a change in season, it had crept up on him. At times he felt choked by her neediness, yet she was a wonderful mother: she gave her all to the children. It was he who was at fault. He had forced too much upon her. He had chased a good promotion at work to satisfy his own needs and uprooted Angela and the younger children. She had never settled: she felt cut off from all that she knew, became ever more dependent on him.

Dulcie heard the front-door bell and stopped mid-sentence. Annoyed at the interruption, she reluctantly went to see who it was.

'*Richard!*'

They held each other tightly, kissed, and cried with the sheer joy of being together again. It was a while before either of them could speak.

'You've no idea how much I've missed you,' Richard said. 'I had to see you. I thought I'd go crazy if I didn't. I can't stay long, though.'

'I know. I understand.'

'But one day I will. If you'll agree, I'd like to stay for ever.'

She looked deep into his eyes and saw the conviction in them, and the love. But still she doubted what he'd said. His place was with his family. They both knew it. For now, though, none of that mattered.

Billy slid into the passenger seat of the car and gave Nathan one of his classic lazy-eyed looks. 'So what's the score between you and that cute little redhead, *Jasmina* Rafferty?'

Keeping his expression inscrutable and concentrating on the road, all Nathan said was, 'Her name's Jasmine. Jaz.'

It turned out that Nathan had got it wrong about Jaz being interested in Billy. She'd been horrified when he'd suggested as much. Scornful, too. 'Oh, please,' she'd said, 'credit me with more sense. Billy's so into himself he's in danger of vanishing up his own bum.'

He was glad that she was smart enough to see through Billy. He and

Jaz only saw each other at college; occasionally they walked home together. They talked about the kind of books and films they enjoyed and her writing. She was different from most other girls he knew, more serious and intense. Occasionally she gave him a contemplative smile, but more often than not her manner was defensive and prickly. He had wondered if it wasn't an act she put on for his benefit. If so, why?

Nathan and Billy arrived at the party to find the usual suspects present but no sign of Jaz. Disappointed, Nathan stared round the sitting room and wondered where she was and what she was doing.

Jaz was furious. How could her parents do this to her? Why was it always her who had to baby-sit Tamzin and Lulu? And what did they think they were doing having more children? They were past their sex-by date. She tried to block the nightmarish thought from her mind, but was distracted by an almighty racket from downstairs.

She found Tamzin and Lulu in the sitting room, the television blaring and crisps, peanuts, and feathers all over the carpet. A small table lay on its back and one of Mum's china ornaments lay broken among the chaos. Her sisters stared at her, out of breath with hysterical laughter.

It was a surreal moment, and when her scream came, she gave it full vent. She was still yelling when she heard the doorbell ring.

'That'll be the police,' she said, blurting out the first thought that came into her head, and went to answer the door. She did a double take when she saw who it was.

Nathan stood hesitantly on the doorstep. When Vicki had told him Jaz had had to baby-sit her sisters, he'd come up with what he'd thought was a brilliant idea to surprise her and see if she fancied some company. But from the drawn brows and the arms pinned across her chest, she plainly didn't want him here. He was all set to leave when she seemed to change her mind: 'Look, you can come in, if you like, but you'll have to put up with my awful sisters. Hey, would you do me a favour? Could you pretend you're a policeman and that you've come to arrest them? You'll understand why when you see what they've done.'

He laughed. He was already having more fun than he'd had at the party. 'Anything to oblige, miss.'

With the collar of his leather coat pulled up and an authoritative swagger, Nathan walked into the middle of the sitting room and tried to look every inch the plain-clothes detective as he surveyed the damage. It was awesome. How could two kids create such devastation?

'I told you it was bad, Officer,' Jaz said, switching off the television.

'Strikes me that I came in the nick of time.' He stepped towards the pair. 'What do you have to say for yourselves, then?'

The smaller of the two girls took a step behind her sister, but the bigger one held her ground. 'How do we know you're a real policeman? Where's your badge? You could be a piddyfile for all we know.'

Nathan was taken aback. When he was their age, he'd never heard the word 'paedophile'. He ignored her request to see his badge. 'Seeing as it's a first offence,' he said, 'we'll say no more about it. But I'm warning you, you've committed several serious offences here tonight. Now, don't do it again. Do you hear? And it's high time you were in bed.'

They nodded and disappeared upstairs. When Jaz and Nathan were alone, she closed the door, leaned against it and groaned. 'You see what I have to put up with? Please don't judge me by their awfulness.'

He had taken off his coat and was crouched on the floor picking up the broken china. 'Hey, it's OK, no comparison made.'

They worked together, binning, scrubbing and hoovering, until the place looked as it should. 'After all that, the least I can do is offer you a drink,' she said. 'Or would you like something to eat?'

Out in the kitchen, she made some hot chocolate and two fried-egg sandwiches. They kept their voices low, so as not to bring her nosy-parker sisters down again. She was glad now that she'd invited him in. Her initial reaction had been of acute embarrassment, but this was great, it was as if they were proper friends. She was relieved that he didn't fancy her. It meant they stood a chance of developing a friendship that might last—he was good company.

She took a bite of her sandwich, then ran her tongue over her lips to catch a dribble of melted butter and egg yolk. She noticed he was staring at her. Self-conscious, she said, 'What? Have I missed a bit?'

He shook his head slowly, his gaze still on her lips.

'You're beginning to spook me. What is it?'

He brushed some breadcrumbs off his fingers and cleared his throat. 'I was just thinking how much I'd like to kiss you.'

Stunned, she wiped her mouth again. But instead of thinking how much she might enjoy him kissing her, she was suspicious. Suppose Vicki had told him at the party that her parents were away and he had come here with the express intention of taking advantage of her being alone . . . of trying to get her into bed? She had a horrible vision of Billy, and everyone else at the party, urging him to do exactly that. She drew back from the table sharply. 'I think you should know there's absolutely no chance of you getting me into bed. Got that?'

He frowned, looked genuinely perplexed. 'Well, I'm glad we've got that sorted out.'

She was saved from having to respond by the sound of a door slamming upstairs. Grateful for the distraction, she excused herself. How could she have made such a fool of herself? Of course he hadn't been trying to jump her. All he'd asked her for was a kiss. It was no big deal.

When she'd taken out her embarrassment on Tamzin and Lulu, she went back to the kitchen and found Nathan ready to go.

She'd blown it. Now they wouldn't even be friends.

There was a very relaxed atmosphere among the group that evening. Victor hadn't turned up.

At Dulcie's suggestion last week, they were trying something new. To encourage a greater level of participation, they were taking it in turns to lead the group. Jack had risen to the challenge and volunteered. He was now explaining what they had to do.

'It's an exercise to teach us the importance of fair-minded characterisation. To kick off with we have to create a character in no more than fifty words that no one in their right mind would like. Don't hold back, make him or her as nasty as you want. OK?' He pointed to the clock on the mantelpiece. 'We have precisely ten minutes to do that.'

They fell quiet and concentrated on the task in hand. Minutes passed before Beth wrote anything. Then, with the pressure on, she found herself caricaturing Lois—the archetypal interfering mother-in-law.

She had nearly lost her temper with Lois at the weekend. Lois had shown up unexpectedly at the flat and had gone round the houses before she got to the real purpose of her visit. She wanted to know all about the writers' group: Nathan had inadvertently spilt the beans about it on the phone. 'What kind of people would go to something so extraordinary? You're turning into quite a dark horse, Beth. How many more little secrets are you keeping from us?' Her light, tinkling tone barely disguised the brittle hardness of her words. 'I could scarcely believe it when Nathan told me what you'd been up to. I wouldn't have thought you'd have time, what with Nathan so busy in his final year.'

A flutter of anger released itself inside Beth. It was outrageous that Lois should use Nathan to manipulate her like this.

'Lois, Nathan is quite capable of taking care of himself while I treat myself to the odd night out.'

'But it's not the odd night, is it? It's every week, so I understand from Nathan. You know, if he fails to get the grades he needs, you'll never forgive yourself. I was always there for Adam. I always put him first.'

Beth stared at Lois, suddenly confronted with the shocking discovery that she was on the verge of hating her. 'I don't think you have any idea how offensive or hurtful you've just been to me. I've always put Nathan first. But that's not what's really behind this, is it?' Beth wanted to clear the air. It was time to confront the lies and pretence.

Lois's normally composed face twitched. A hand went to her throat and fiddled with a beaded necklace. 'I'm not sure what you mean. I'm sorry if I've offended you, but I was merely showing concern.' She gave a shrill laugh. 'Oh, did I tell you about Barnaby cutting his hand on a broken pane in the greenhouse?'

And that was it. In one of her classic manoeuvres, Lois had made her point then moved the conversation on so that it would appear churlish to retaliate or pursue the argument further.

Beth was about to put a line through what she had written when Jack called time. 'Right,' he said. 'We now have twenty minutes to create a believable scenario in which we can turn round our neighbour's character. We have to make him or her not just likable but redeemable. Now hand your pieces of paper to the person on your left.'

Beth handed hers to Dulcie, hoping that Dulcie wouldn't guess at the extent of her unkindness.

Later that night, Beth settled at the computer and tried to get on with Chapter Eight. She had set herself a goal of 1,000 words a day, and the more she wrote, the more convinced she became that an author often had little say over a character's input to a story. Apparently the most experienced writers suffered from this phenomenon.

Mr Outta Laffs had told her this. They had slipped into a nightly habit of emailing each other. She wasn't a secretive person, but she had decided to keep quiet about Mr Outta Laffs. She knew what people would say if they were aware of what she was doing: that he could be anyone—at best a saddo who still lived at home with Mother, or at worst, a serial murderer. But instinct—or was it misplaced hope?—told her that Mr Outta Laffs fitted into neither category. He seemed as concerned for his own safety as she was for hers.

How do I know you're the full shilling? [he asked.]

What made you think I was?

Clever reply, a bona fide madwoman would have gone to great lengths to convince me she was firing on all cylinders.

I could be double-bluffing you.

Shucks, I hadn't thought of that. So where does that leave us?

Watching our backs, I guess.

So far they had discussed little of a personal nature and had only broached the subject of their real names last night.

In the spirit of you show me yours and I'll show you mine, my real name is Ewan. Yours?

Beth. Short for Bethany.

Nice. Does anyone ever call you Bethany?

Not since I was a child.

Then I shall distance myself from the crowd and address you by your proper name. That's if you don't object.

She hadn't minded. Quite the reverse, in fact. It added an element of intimacy to their correspondence.

At midnight, and after Nathan had announced he was going to bed, Beth logged on, but there was no message waiting for her from Ewan, as there usually was. She felt almost as though she'd been stood up.

Ewan Jones gave the keyboard one last thump of frustration. But it was no use: no amount of coaxing was going to get the machine working again. The damn thing had crashed. For good. He would have to summon help first thing in the morning.

He turned out the light in his office and made his way to the kitchen, where he filled the kettle and plugged it in. While he waited for it to boil, he reread the letter he'd left on the table earlier that evening. It was from a publisher who had read the first three chapters of his novel, *Emily and Albert*. It was a love story set in the fifties and based, loosely, on the illicit relationship between his parents, a young schoolteacher and a married GP. For all sorts of reasons, his book was a secret project—only his daughter knew about it—and to his delight the publishers wanted to see the rest of the manuscript. All he had to do was finish it, which was why it was so irritating that his computer had chosen to give up the ghost. Still, as Alice would be the first to say, 'Stop moaning, Dad. Just bite the bullet and replace it.'

How easy life was for a twenty-year-old girl who possessed sufficient self-confidence to reduce Anne Robinson to a quivering jelly. Since Alice had left home for university, he'd missed her. They had always been close, but when Alice had turned nine her mother had left him and father and daughter had become inseparable. He was looking forward to her coming home for Christmas.

He was continually told by Alice that at the age of forty-six, he had to do something about his long-term single status. He sipped his tea thoughtfully, and wondered if an on-line friendship counted.

Chapter Five

IT WAS A FREEZING SATURDAY afternoon. A misty blanket of fog shrouded the whitened banks of the river and elegant willow branches drooped with brittle stiffness. In the warm, Amber and Lucy were decorating the Christmas tree. Jack had given the girls free rein on choosing the ornaments and consequently he was going to spend Christmas with the most kitsch tree this side of *It's A Wonderful Life*. But he was happy to let the girls go wild: to watch their eager faces as they worked together so industriously was reward enough.

'What do you think, Daddy?' Lucy was looking at him expectantly.

'It's the best I've ever seen. We'll be the envy of everyone.'

Giggling, Lucy pushed her face into his neck and kissed him. 'We'll need to put some presents around it,' she said. 'Have you got any?'

'Only yours.'

Lucy's eyes lit up.

Amber came and sat on the sofa next to Jack. 'Don't be stupid, Lucy, you can't have them yet. Christmas isn't for another two weeks.'

'And don't forget,' Jack said, 'you'll have lots of presents from Father Christmas too.' He knew Amber was too old to go along with such things, but he hoped Lucy was still a happy believer. She had been forced to cope so young with so much harsh reality and he wanted her to enjoy what innocence was left in her childhood.

'Will he be able to find us in France?'

'Of course he will.'

Maddie had finally informed him last week of the arrangements for Christmas and New Year, and it was just as he'd feared: the girls were going to France for a two-week skiing holiday. 'Good of you to keep me up to date,' he'd said drily.

'Please don't be like that, Jack,' she'd said, impatiently. 'We've only just decided what we're doing.'

'And I don't suppose it crossed your mind that I might like to make plans for Christmas?'

'If you can't be civil, Jack, I'd rather not speak to you.'

It had been another disastrous conversation, and once again he had told himself that it would be their last angry exchange. He would swallow his pride. And his bitterness. Except he didn't seem able to.

'Who's for a mince pie?' he asked. 'Amber?'

'No, thanks. I'm on a diet.'

Convinced he'd misheard, Jack said, 'Come again?'

'It's no big deal, Dad, I just don't want to get fat.'

Appalled, he pulled her onto his lap. 'Listen to me carefully, Amber. You're perfect as you are. Girls of your age don't need to diet.'

'But, Dad, all the girls at school are doing it.'

He stroked her cheek lovingly. 'Maybe that's because they're not as beautiful as you.'

She didn't say anything, but she leaned back into his embrace and he was reminded of all the times he'd held her as a baby and a toddler. He suddenly thought of the baby Clare was carrying and, to his sickening shame and dismay, he couldn't imagine feeling the same strength of love for this new child that he'd always felt for Amber and Lucy.

The next day, Jack drove the girls to have Sunday lunch with Clare. They were meeting her for the first time. He was on edge, as were they.

'If she's just a friend, why are *we* meeting her?' Amber had asked, her eyes weighing him up shrewdly.

'Well, I suppose she's a special friend and I'd like you to meet her.'

There was a pause.

'Are you going to marry her?' asked Lucy.

'There's a chance I might one day. But that's a long way off.'

'Why do you want get married again? Don't you love us?'

'Love you? I'm mad about you. You'll always come first with me.'

He could tell they weren't buying it. They spent the rest of the journey bickering and as Jack parked in front of Clare's house, he had a feeling that things were about to get worse.

Straight away Jack could see Clare was tired. It was also clear that she had put a lot of effort into creating the perfect lunch for Amber and Lucy—spaghetti bolognese, then apple crumble and Hägen Dazs ice cream. But as the four of them sat at the table, Amber and Lucy just picked uninterestedly at their food.

'There are bits in the sauce,' Lucy complained.

'Bits?' Clare repeated. 'That's a mushroom.'

Lucy pulled a face. '*Ugh!* I don't like mushrooms. They're slimy—and they might be toadstools. Toadstools are poisonous, aren't they?'

'I promise you they're harmless, from the fruit and veg counter in Tesco's. Why don't you cover them up with some Parmesan?'

'Can I have some proper cheese, please?'

'Lucy, I don't think—'

'It's OK, Jack,' Clare interrupted. 'There's plenty of Cheddar in the fridge. It won't take me two seconds to grate some.'

He watched her leave the dining room, then turned to his daughters. 'Eat as much as you can, girls,' he said quietly. 'Clare's gone to a lot of trouble for you.'

Neither of them said anything, and when Clare came back into the room, he noticed she was frowning. 'You OK?' he asked, taking the dish of cheese from her. 'You look tired.'

She smiled unconvincingly. 'Knowing my luck, I've got that bug that's doing the rounds at work.' She sat down heavily.

Ten minutes later, when it was apparent that Amber and Lucy weren't going to eat any more, Clare said, 'You can leave that if you want. Next time I'll check what you like first, shall I?'

An indifferent shrug was all she got in answer. Jack was about to reprimand them when Clare stepped in before him. 'Hasn't anyone told you it's bad manners not to answer a question?'

Amber looked up sharply. 'Hasn't anyone ever told you to shut up?'

In the silence that followed, Clare stared at her across the table, then at Jack, who was as shocked by Amber's rudeness as Clare had been. 'Amber, what on earth's got into you?' he said. 'Apologise this instant.'

'Why should I? I didn't want to come here and I certainly didn't want to eat this!' She raised her hand to point at her unfinished lunch, misjudged the distance and the plate, plus its contents, flipped over. Amber began to cry. 'I hate you,' she cried, looking straight at Clare, 'and I wish you'd drop down dead and leave my daddy alone.'

Jack got up abruptly. 'Amber, that's no way to speak to Clare. Clare, are you all right? *Clare?*'

He watched her try to stand, but she swayed towards him. He grabbed hold of her and held her firmly. 'What's wrong?'

'Bathroom,' she whispered. 'You'll have to help me.'

'Is she going to die?' asked Amber.

His daughter's voice was so faint that Jack had to strain to catch it. He held her hand and squeezed it. 'Of course not,' he replied, keeping to himself that for most of the hair-raising journey to the hospital he had been terrified by the same thought. All the while, Clare had been dipping in and out of consciousness, alternating between gasps of pain and frightening silences. Everything told him that she was losing the baby, but that this was no ordinary miscarriage.

'I didn't mean it when I said I wished she'd die,' Amber murmured. 'I'm sorry, Daddy.' Tears filled her eyes.

Jack hugged his daughter. 'None of that matters, sweetheart. Everything's going to be all right. Clare knew you didn't mean it.'

On his other side, Lucy said, 'But what made Clare be so ill? Do you think it was those mushrooms? Maybe they *were* toadstools.'

'I don't know,' he lied, unable to meet her gaze.

It was the day before Christmas Eve and Dulcie stared in disgust at the amount of food she had just lugged in from the car. If it weren't for her children's nostalgic fondness for a traditional Christmas with all the trimmings, Dulcie would have been happy to kiss goodbye to the whole wretched business. She made a pot of tea, ignoring the beds she still had to make up. There was plenty of time. Kate and Andrew—plus unknown friend—wouldn't be arriving for another three hours. She had offered to drive across to Crewe to meet them off the London train, but they'd insisted they would catch the connecting train to Maywood. It would only add another forty-five minutes to their journey.

Andrew had been curiously secretive about his friend, saying only that he was bringing someone he was keen for her to meet. Which, naturally, added to Dulcie's speculation that she might soon be on the verge of a new role, that of mother-in-law. She liked the idea. She had asked Kate on the telephone what she knew, but Kate had replied, in what Dulcie recognised as evasive tones, 'Hardly anything, Mum, only that the pair of them seem ideally suited to each other. I don't think I've ever seen Andrew so happy. Have you put the tree up yet?'

'Yes. And before you ask, I've bought chocolate money for you and several kilos of brazil nuts, which will still be here for Easter.'

'But you can't have Christmas without brazil nuts.'

'I know, darling—but just once, I'd like someone to eat them.'

At half past four, just as he'd promised he would, Richard telephoned. He was back at work now, part-time, and that meant he was able to call Dulcie more regularly. They had even met for lunch. He was looking much better, and Dulcie grew more confident that he would soon be his old self. But his opening remark had her clutching the receiver in panic. 'Dulcie,' he said, 'you don't have to agree to this, but we're throwing a

Christmas drinks party and Angela wants to invite you.'

'*Me?* Why? Oh, my goodness, does she know?'

'Darling, calm down. It's nothing of the sort. Ever since you met that day in Maywood she's wanted to show off the house to you. If it means we can be together for a few hours, wouldn't it be worth it?'

Dulcie couldn't believe what she was hearing. 'Are you saying *you* want me to come?'

'Yes, I do.'

'You're crazy!'

He laughed. 'Only for you. So I'll see you on Boxing Day?'

'But Kate and Andrew will be here.'

'Bring them. The more the merrier. I'd like to meet them. Listen, Angela will call you, so do your best to sound surprised.'

'That won't be difficult.'

It was dark and raining hard when Dulcie drove to the station, but her spirits were high. On reflection, and despite the risk she was taking, she was pleased that she would see Richard over the Christmas period.

When she drew up outside the station she spotted Kate and Andrew before they saw her, and she pipped the horn to attract their attention. She was just wondering where Andrew's girlfriend was when she caught sight of a dark-haired, strikingly handsome young man.

I don't think I've ever seen Andrew so happy.

Dulcie drew in her breath and hated herself for feeling shocked. Why had Andrew never told her? She went round to the other side of the car to hug and reassure him: he looked strung out. She had to make it clear that she was delighted to meet his friend.

Miles proved the perfect house guest and Dulcie liked him enormously. Throughout supper he had been amusing and helpful, and had further endeared himself to her by insisting that he and Kate would tidy the kitchen so that she and Andrew could have a quiet chat. 'Here you are,' he said, pulling a bottle of port out of a bag Dulcie hadn't noticed before. 'Take it with you to the sitting room.'

Watching her son move nervously about the room, she poured two glasses of port and waited for him to speak.

'I'm sorry, Mum,' he said at last. 'I should have told you, but the time never seemed right.' He turned slowly and met her eye. 'Are you OK about this, or are you putting on one of your famously brave faces?'

'Oh, Andrew, how well you know me, but how little too. Of course I'm all right about it. Surely you never doubted my reaction?'

He smiled. 'Telling your mother that you're gay isn't easy.'

'I like Miles. Kate told me she'd never seen you so happy. Is that true?'
He nodded. 'It feels right with Miles.'

Thinking of Richard, she gazed into the flickering flames of the fire. 'I know exactly what you mean.'

'Is that what it was like between you and Dad?'

Dulcie was about to agree, when she changed her mind and decided to share her own secret life with her son. 'This might come as a surprise, Andrew, but I've been having an affair with a married man for the last three years. We're very much in love.' It was remarkably satisfying to see the shock on his handsome young face. Especially when he smiled.

Lois sighed for the second time. 'Barnaby, do we have to have the television on?' she asked irritably. 'It's so antisocial. We ought to be playing a game. Anyone for Scrabble?' It was Christmas Eve and they were in the sitting room at Marsh House. Over the years, Beth had tried several times to wriggle out of this annual duty, saying her parents wanted her and Nathan to spend Christmas with them. But Lois had no hesitation about playing her trump card: 'Since we lost Adam,' she'd say, in a small, wavering voice, 'you're all we have. If it weren't for you and Nathan we wouldn't bother with Christmas.' Other than wilfully upsetting her, Beth could see no way to change the situation.

'Scrabble it is,' Barnaby announced.

As usual they let Lois win, and as usual they went to bed with strict instructions not to mind Lois getting up early on Christmas morning. 'No, no, Beth, there's no need for you to help. You make the most of a well-deserved lie-in.' Beth had taken her at her word one year and poor Barnaby had spent most of Christmas Day being subjected to mutterings that no one had offered to help.

Beth switched on the bedside lamp and reached for her book. Ewan had recommended it and she was enjoying it immensely. Their correspondence, which was always a lively and entertaining exchange of views and opinions, had moved on considerably. She knew now that Ewan was forty-six, that he was divorced and had a twenty-year-old daughter called Alice. She had also discovered he lived in Suffolk, on the coast—it sounded idyllic: a writer's paradise with views out to sea—and he ran his own public relations business:

> My job is to make people suspend their disbelief and accept what
> they wouldn't ordinarily go along with. It's all in the spin.

She still hadn't told anyone about the mystery man in her life, as she now thought of Ewan, and she knew that it was dangerous to become fond of someone she had never met. But naive as it sounded, she was convinced that if they met they would get on.

She had acknowledged that part of the attraction for her was that Ewan was safe. Because he wasn't 'real' she could allow herself to like him and not feel disloyal to Adam. No one needed to tell her that this was absurd, that after all these years she was at liberty to have a relationship with another man, but with Lois's determination to keep Adam's memory alive it was often an uphill struggle to believe it.

Nathan woke to the sound of his grandmother singing 'Once in Royal David's City'. He buried his head under the pillow. 'Happy Christmas, one and all,' he muttered.

At least he was having a break from college. It had been a busy term, what with *The Importance of Being Earnest* and applying for a place at university. Exeter had made him an offer, as had Sheffield and Hull; he was still waiting to hear from his first choice, Nottingham.

The play had gone well. Lois and Barnaby had had front-row seats on the last night. Jaz had been in the audience, too. He'd hoped she might come to the end-of-show party, but she hadn't.

They hadn't spoken since the night he'd gone round to her place and stupidly asked if he could kiss her. She couldn't have made it any more obvious that she didn't fancy him. The memory still made him flinch.

Christmas Day wore on tediously with vast quantities of food. After the Queen's speech, they were given the go-ahead to exchange presents. 'Nathan, dear,' Lois said, 'before you give me anything, I want you to find a present for yourself. There's a special one for you.'

He held up a long, thin package. 'This one?'

He was suddenly the focus of the room. Dreading what he'd find, and preparing himself to look pleased, he sat next to his mother. The wrapping paper dispensed with, he held an old velvet jewellery box. He opened the case and saw a watch inside. It was a Rolex, old and scratched, but he knew its significance.

'It belonged to your father,' Lois said unnecessarily. 'Go on, put it on.'

But he couldn't do as she asked. Burning from within, he felt an uncontrollable desire to grind the watch under the heel of his shoe. Very carefully, he put the watch back into its box and gave it to his grandmother. 'Thank you,' he said, 'but I don't want it.'

She stared at him, as if not understanding what he'd said.

'Didn't you hear me? I said I don't want it. I want nothing from my father.' Nathan could see that he was hurting everyone, but he didn't care. 'If Adam King was such a fine man, why the hell didn't he sort out the mess he'd created? Why did he have to dump us in it by killing himself? He was a coward and I hate him for what he did to Mum.'

He heard his grandmother start to cry, but he didn't hang around. He slammed out of the house, threw himself into his mother's car, started it and hit the accelerator.

Beth stood on the doorstep and watched her son narrowly miss colliding with one of the gateposts. Near to tears, her arms locked round herself, fear flooded her. What if history repeated itself?

Consumed by a frightening anger she had never known before, Beth went back into Marsh House. Lois was going to pay for this.

Nervously drumming her fingers on the steering wheel, Dulcie wondered if it wasn't too late to back out. She must have been mad to accept Angela's invitation.

'Wakey, wakey, Mum, the lights have changed.'

She looked at her daughter. 'What? Oh, silly me.' She drove on. 'I hope you won't be too bored at this party,' she said.

'It's always good to broaden one's horizons,' Kate said. 'And, anyway, didn't you say that they have an eligible son?'

'I never said he was eligible, or that he was a bachelor,' Dulcie said, disconcerted. 'He'll probably turn out to be thoroughly obnoxious.' She exchanged a look of concern with Andrew in the rearview mirror. Having shared her secret with him, she had made him promise not to tell anyone about her affair with Richard, and she knew from his expression that he was thinking as she was—that it would be disastrous for Kate to form an attachment with Richard's eldest son, Henry.

Richard was on his way to the kitchen when he heard the doorbell ring. His heart leapt. Dulcie? He opened the door and saw, to his delight, that he'd been right. He smiled the smile of a congenial host and shook hands with Dulcie. 'Mrs Ballantyne, how lovely to see you again.'

He ushered them all in, hoping he appeared to anyone observing him as good old Richard getting drinks for a group of new arrivals, not as a man who was cheating on his wife and had had the audacity to bring 'the other woman' into the family home. Yet as contemptible as his behaviour might seem to others, it didn't feel so awful to him. What's more, he wanted to put an arm round Dulcie's shoulders and declare to everyone that this was the woman he loved. He was so sure that this was the woman with whom he wanted to spend the rest of his days, that he knew the time had come to tell Angela.

Much as he was tempted to devote his time to Dulcie and her family, he couldn't. There were other guests to see to, drinks and food to organise.

From across the room, Dulcie caught him looking at her. She gave him one of her half-smiles and his heart swelled. He raised his glass to her and wandered off into the conservatory, to find Angela. She was nowhere to be seen, but he discovered that this was where the 'young people' were hiding. They seemed to be getting along well enough. 'Sorry to barge in,' he said. 'You all OK for drinks?'

'Fine, thanks, Dad, though some food wouldn't go amiss.'

He smiled at Henry. 'Give me a hand, then, and we'll get you sorted with some supplies.'

Back in the kitchen, while Richard was loading up a tray of dips, crudités and canapés, Henry said, 'Between you and me, Dad, I'm rather taken with the lovely Kate.'

'Kate?'

'Your memory going, Dad? Mrs Ballantyne's daughter. I think if I play my cards right, we'll be seeing each other in London. Often, if I have anything to do with it.'

Richard slowly absorbed what his son was saying. He pushed the tray of food at Henry. 'I've just remembered something I was supposed to do.' He hurred back to the sitting room to find Dulcie. He had to tell her that under no circumstances could *his* son and *her* daughter become involved with each other.

Intolerable: insufferable, impossible, from hell, insupportable . . . Jaz closed the thesaurus with a weighty slap. None of those words came close to expressing the horror of living with her family. When had she become an outsider in her own home, so out of step with everyone else?

She went to lie on the bed. It was proving the longest, most boring Christmas known to mankind. She'd done all her homework and was all revised-out in readiness for her mock exams. There was nothing else to do, no one to hang out with: Vicki was away and, because of her idiotic overreaction, she had lost Nathan as a friend. She would give anything, right now, to have his company. Oh, she'd made such a mess of it. It was a pity the writers' group wasn't meeting during the holiday—at least that would have given her something worthwhile to focus on.

Bored, and restless with frustration, she decided to go for a walk.

Nathan was standing at the kitchen window. There was no mistaking the solitary figure in black jeans and knee-length baggy sweater that came into his field of vision from the right of the park. It was Jaz.

He watched her play with one of her long plaits as she settled on a wooden bench, and thought how much he missed her company. Perhaps he should apologise. He decided that there was no time like the present, took the short-cut route to the park and made his way over to where Jaz was sitting. 'Hi,' he said casually.

She looked up, startled. 'Oh. Hi.'

'OK if I join you?'

She slid along the wooden seat to make room for him. 'Good Christmas?' she asked.

'You don't want to know. I stirred up World War Three.'

'Who with? Not your mum, surely?'

He shook his head. The look on his mother's face when he'd arrived home late on Christmas night—he'd known she would be at the flat, just as she'd known he wouldn't go back to Marsh House—was one that would stay with him for ever. He had put her through seven hours of hell. She had been convinced that he was lying dead in the wreckage of their car. But she hadn't lost her temper, as he'd expected her to. 'I was too relieved that you were alive to be cross with you,' she'd admitted later. 'Besides, I took out my anger on Lois. I'm afraid that we won't be welcome there for a long time.'

Aware that a silence had settled on them, and that he hadn't given Jaz a proper answer to her question, Nathan turned and saw that she was looking at him intently, but when his gaze met hers, she lowered her eyes. He couldn't work her out. 'Do you want to walk?'

They wandered down towards the pond. When a boy riding a bike much too big for him came careering in their direction, Nathan instinctively pulled Jaz out of harm's way. 'Sorry,' he said. 'That's an even blacker mark against my name, isn't it? Rough-handling in the name of safety probably goes down as well as asking for a kiss.'

She stared at him, her brows drawn together. For a nasty moment she looked so furious that he thought she was about to thump him. But then, just as he noticed a snowflake land on top of her head, her face broke into a tentative smile. Once again, he had the urge to kiss her. This time, though, he didn't ask permission, simply leaned in and pressed his mouth gently to hers. Her lips were icy cold, but he sensed no coolness in her. 'Just for the record,' he murmured, 'I have no immediate plans to drag you off into the bushes for a mindless shag.'

She stiffened within his arms. 'Please don't tease me.'

'I'm not,' he said. 'I'm trying to put your mind at rest.' He felt her relax and kissed her again. And, as the snow fell slowly around them, he felt strangely at peace. Holding Jaz made the rest of the world disappear. No more Lois. And no more Adam King.

Chapter Six

FOR FIVE CONSECUTIVE YEARS Des and Julie had thrown a New Year's Eve party, but this year they had agreed to give tradition a miss and settle for a low-key evening with a bottle of bubbly. But, to Des's disappointment, at the last minute Julie had insisted Clare couldn't possibly spend New Year's Eve alone—'not after all she's gone through'—and she had arrived yesterday afternoon to stay the night. When she wasn't berating Jack for being such a bastard, she was begging them, as the wine flowed, to make him see sense.

It didn't matter what he or Julie said, Clare wouldn't listen: 'He cares for me, really. I know he does.' In the end, so that they could go to bed— it was nearly four in the morning—Des had promised to talk to Jack.

Now, at five past seven, while he was giving a perky little Desmond his breakfast, Des knew it wouldn't do any good. Jack had made his decision. OK, maybe his timing might have been better—telling Clare it was over while she was still recovering from an ectopic pregnancy hadn't been the most sensitive way to handle it—but the upshot was that Clare had to accept she and Jack were finished.

Lost in his thoughts, he didn't hear footsteps coming into the kitchen. Clare, her complexion green, rushed past to the downstairs loo. Poor girl. A hangover as well as a broken heart. Hardly the best way to start the New Year. He wondered how Jack was feeling this morning.

Jack was in the spare room doing the one thing that kept him from dwelling on Clare. So long as he focused on the troubles of his characters, he could block out the events of the last few weeks.

But not entirely. He would always feel responsible for putting Clare through such a painful ordeal. The guilt he'd felt while she had been undergoing the emergency operation to remove the tiny foetus that had caused one of her Fallopian tubes to rupture had been unlike any he had ever known. When he had been told that the operation had been a success, he had almost wept with relief.

Shortly afterwards, and he knew it had been unthinkably selfish, he remembered that he'd had a lucky escape, and that he had to act on it . . .

as soon as Clare was over the worst. But decisive action came sooner than he'd intended. While she convalesced, Clare started talking in earnest about how much she wanted Jack to move in with her. He couldn't lie to her or give her false hope. He'd found himself telling her it was over between them, that if she were honest, she would admit that she had known this for some weeks too. He'd held her hands and looked her straight in the eye as he'd spoken, knowing he would never have been able to forgive himself if he'd done it any other way.

'You bastard!' she'd murmured, withdrawing her hands from his. 'Couldn't you at least have waited until after Christmas?'

The irrationality of her question hadn't struck him till he was driving home: it summed up how superficially Clare viewed him.

He leaned back in his chair, his hands clasped behind his head. It wasn't just writing that calmed him, it was knowing that he was starting the year on a positive note. He had made an important decision on the stroke of midnight. He intended to make an offer on Miss Waterman's flat. A new start in a real home was just what he needed.

At what he considered an appropriate time to call, bearing in mind that it was New Year's Day, Jack phoned Beth to enquire after Miss Waterman. 'She's well on the mend,' Beth said, 'much more her old self. Why? Have you got good news for her about the flat?'

'I might have,' he said carefully. 'Do you think she'd mind if I give her a quick call?'

'I have a much better idea. Why don't you come here for lunch? Adele's joining us. As is a friend of Nathan's. Someone you might know.'

The streets were empty as he walked to Maywood Park Road, his footsteps echoing along the deserted pavements. At bang on one o'clock, he rang Beth's doorbell. 'Happy New Year,' he said, and passed her a bottle of champagne.

She took it from him with a smile. 'How very kind of you.'

He followed her upstairs and through to the sitting room, where Miss Waterman was resplendent in what had to be a 'special occasion frock'. From behind him, he heard a familiar laugh: Jaz! So this was the 'someone' Beth had mentioned on the phone. Following hot on Jaz's heels was a tall lad whom Jack took to be Beth's son.

It was during lunch that Jack brought up the reason for his visit. 'I've found you a buyer, Adele,' he said, 'and one I have every reason to believe will be a dead cert.'

'Really?' she said. 'How wonderful. This is good news.'

'Hang on a moment,' Beth said. 'No one's been round to view Adele's flat for ages. Who's made an offer?'

'Ah,' he said, amused by her sharpness, and her continued protectiveness of the old lady. 'Time to come clean. It's me. I'm making an offer.'

'Is that ethical?' asked Adele.

'It is if he's divvying up the full asking price,' said Beth.

'Yes, I am,' said Jack. 'What's more, I'll pay for you to have the property independently valued, so you'll know I've priced it correctly.'

'Well,' Adele beamed, 'I'm delighted with the news. I can't think of anyone I'd rather have moving into my flat.' She raised her glass. 'To you, Jack. I hope you'll be very happy living in Maywood Park Road.'

Beth topped up Jack's glass. She welcomed the prospect of having him as her new neighbour, but she would now have her work cut out convincing the mischievous Adele that there was nothing going on between her and Jack. He was just a friend, a good platonic friend.

But her neighbour's misplaced determination to bring about a romantic union for Beth was the least of her worries. She hadn't seen Lois since Christmas Day. Each time she had telephoned Lois had cut her dead. 'I have no wish to talk to you, Beth,' she had said. 'You've turned my only grandson against me by filling his head with lies about Adam. I shall never forgive you for that.'

'But, Lois, you know as well as I do that Adam committed suicide. The coroner's verdict was—' She got no further.

There had been many moments when Beth had regretted her outburst at Marsh House on Christmas Day. 'You stupid bitch!' she had yelled at her mother-in-law. 'Have you any *idea* what you've done to my son? Nathan despises you because you've refused to accept that his father was anything but perfect. He was a normal human being, Lois. A man who, when the chips were down, couldn't go on.'

It was then that Lois attacked. 'If you had been a better wife Adam would never have been so depressed!'

'It was you who brought him up to believe that no member of the King family was allowed to fail.' Beth pointed her finger. 'You made him do it, Lois. You made Adam so ashamed of failing that you might as well have handed him the bottle of whisky and car keys yourself.'

Lois swallowed hard, and held her head high. 'I want you to leave, Beth. I want you out of my house. Now.'

Beth had been left with myriad feelings of guilt, anger and confusion. Not so long ago, if faced with a crisis, she would have looked automatically to Simone for advice and support, but this time she had turned to Ewan, telling him everything that had happened. By sharing the problem with an outsider, she felt less disloyal to Lois. When she had mentioned this to Ewan, he'd said:

It's loyalty to Lois that's helped to create this mess. How about a bit of loyalty to your own self-respect? Sounds to me as if Lois has tried systematically to diminish you, Bethany.

Ouch. And double ouch. Are you always this blunt?

Only with . . . those who I care about.

Flummoxed by his comment, she hadn't known how to respond. A further message appeared on her screen.

Strike that disclosure from the record if you'd prefer.

No [she'd typed, after another brief hesitation]. It was nice. It took me by surprise, that's all.

An OK-ish surprise?

Yes.

In that case, I have a favour to ask. How do you feel about exchanging pictures of ourselves?

Whenever Ewan was anxious, frustrated or under pressure, he opened a bottle of wine and made bread. On this occasion he had turned to the flour bin for solace because he was having second thoughts about exchanging photographs with Beth. They had agreed to do the deed at midnight, and as the time grew nearer—it was eleven thirty-six—he couldn't shake off his rising doubts. Would it be a mistake?

The stupid thing was that he was genuinely bothered by what Beth might think of him. In his opinion, he was just an ordinary middle-aged man with lines fast developing and grey hairs aplenty. Who the hell are you? he'd think, when he looked in the mirror. Where's that energetic young man I used to be? Alice said he was too hung up on his age.

While his daughter had been at home for Christmas, he'd confided in her about Beth. 'Are you out of your mind, Dad?' she'd cried. 'What was it you used to lecture me about? I wasn't to talk to strangers.'

'This is different,' he'd said defensively, all too aware it wasn't.

'Different?' she'd said. 'Like hell it is! For all you know this "Beth" could be a man getting off on some weird sexually perverted game.'

As he stared into her stormy face, all he could say was 'Some risks are worth taking.'

'I would have thought there were easier ways to pull.'

'I'm not on the pull!'

'Then perhaps you should be. You have a lot to offer, Dad. You're intelligent, funny, and not bad-looking. The only downer is that you're as rich as Midas. But, hey, nobody's perfect.'

It was now eleven forty-five. He kneaded the dough some more and pondered his feelings for Beth. Despite all of Alice's warnings, he really did view Beth as a friend he wanted to get to know better. It was obvious that their correspondence meant a lot to both of them; but by taking this step, were they running the risk of spoiling what they had?

At eleven fifty-two he covered the dough with a damp tea towel, poured himself another glass of wine, and approached his office.

Beth clicked on OPEN, closed her eyes, held her breath and waited for Ewan's picture to materialise. It was the most excruciating moment. Would Ewan turn out to be the greasy-haired, bespectacled, nerdy anorak she'd always hoped he wasn't?

She opened a cautious eye and saw a face that . . . that she liked the look of. Reflected in his relaxed expression was the humorous warmth she had come to know through her exchanges with him. His hair, short and grey—no hint of a centre parting!—was receding. She hoped that her photograph was being equally well received in Suffolk.

Ewan's first thought was that Beth was just the kind of woman he would look twice at. It wasn't only the fair hair or the slim body that appealed to him, but the brightness of her smile.

His second thought was that he wanted very much to meet her. It was in his head for no more than a nanosecond before he squashed it flat. It was the dumbest thing he'd ever come up with. Or was it?

It was the first Thursday of the year and the first time the group would be together since halfway through December. There had been no word from Victor—not even a Christmas card in return for the one she'd sent him—and Dulcie decided to give him a call. Using the phone in the kitchen, she tapped out his number, but the doorbell interrupted her and she replaced the receiver.

Richard was standing on the doorstep. 'What a lovely surprise,' she said. But straight away she could see that something was wrong. 'What is it, Richard?' she asked. 'Is it Angela? Does she know?'

He put his arms round her shoulders and held her to him. 'No. But it's what we dreaded. Henry and Kate are seeing each other.'

221

'No!'

'I'm afraid it's true. Henry phoned last night. They've met up regularly since they got back to London. Oh, Dulcie, there was something so . . . so upbeat in his voice. He's mad about her.'

Dulcie tried to think straight. When Richard had first warned her at the party that Henry had hinted he was taken with Kate, she had been as shocked as he was. But what could they do? She made coffee and they went into the sitting room and settled on the sofa. 'So what's to be done?' she asked.

He stared across the room, through the French windows and out onto the terrace. 'I'm damned if I know,' he said.

She reached for his hand, and as her fingers touched his skin, she saw how things stood. 'You want me to warn Kate off, don't you? I have to tell her about *us* and the inappropriateness of there ever being a Kate-and-Henry?'

Slowly he faced her. 'You do see that it's the only way, don't you? I can't possibly tell Henry. I'd have to tell him why.'

'I thought you no longer cared what others thought,' she said, her voice flat. 'I thought you were on the verge of telling Angela about us.'

Suddenly he looked very tired. 'But this would be too brutal. I couldn't do it to her. Surely you understand that?'

Dulcie understood only too well. The world was full of women who had to carry out other people's dirty work.

It was official. Jaz Rafferty and Nathan King were an item, but she didn't want anyone in her family to find out.

'Are you embarrassed about me?' he'd asked.

'No. I just like to keep certain areas of my life private,' she'd said, not admitting that it was the rest of the Raffertys who embarrassed her. To her shame, she was lying even more to her parents, telling them she was at Vicki's whenever she was with Nathan.

When college was over, Jaz walked home with Nathan. He wanted to call in at Novel Ways, and they decided to have a drink in the coffee shop. 'We'd better not stay too long,' she said. 'It's my writers' group tonight and I've still got some revision to do.'

'No sweat. Hey, who's so interesting you can't tear your eyes off him?'

'Sorry, I've just noticed someone from the writers' group. His name's Victor. He's the biggest pain going.'

He followed her gaze across the coffee shop to where Victor was tussling with a sugar sachet. When at last he managed to rip it open, sugar scattered over the table and several sheets of handwritten notes. Jaz could see exactly what was going to happen next and, sure enough, Victor promptly knocked over his cup. A puddle of brown liquid flooded the papers and dripped onto his trousers. There was something so pathetically hopeless about the man that Jaz felt sorry for him. She went to the woman behind the counter who gave her a handful of paper towels. 'He's one we could do without. Every day he sits there scribbling, and he's as tight as they come. He makes a cup of coffee last an hour.'

'There you go, Victor,' Jaz said. 'Are your papers OK?'

He narrowed his eyes at her, and she saw recognition dawn. He muttered something unintelligible. Jaz left him to it. What an ungrateful weirdo, she thought.

She was still thinking this when, later that evening, she rang Dulcie's doorbell and recalled what the woman who worked in the coffee shop had said about Victor always being there. If that was true, why wasn't he at work? The obvious answer, she decided, was that he was on holiday.

From as early as Victor could remember, life had dealt him a rotten hand. As a child his hard work was never rewarded as it should have been. It didn't matter how hard he tried at school, his reports rarely reflected the true worth of his endeavours.

It was no better when he left school at sixteen and started work as a junior clerk in the local council offices. From day one he was expected to be the general dogsbody and the butt of everyone's jokes.

He'd found his niche at last in the accounts department of J. B. Reeves, an office supply company. He had been a loyal, trustworthy employee with a keen nose for sniffing out irregularities on expense claims. Which was why he felt so aggrieved when, just before Christmas, he was called into the senior manager's office and informed that he had been made redundant. 'Streamlining' was what head office was calling the loss of jobs. Bullying was what it amounted to. But he'd show them. Now that he had time on his hands, he'd finish his novel, get it published and revel in its success. He'd prove to the whole damn lot of them that Victor Blackmore was a winner.

He had programmed himself to say this, aloud (if he were alone), every half-hour. 'Victor Blackmore, you are a winner,' visualising *Star City* displayed in the window of Novel Ways. It was this belief that got him out of bed every morning. He wasn't going to bother with that absurd excuse for a writers' group any more. He'd known it would be a mistake to join them and he'd been proved right. Hadn't his late mother always said that the only person one could trust was oneself?

His love of books had come from his mother. She had read to him from as early as he could remember, and every Saturday morning they had gone to the library together. Before long he was writing his own stories, tales of escape and heroic adventure, always in private, to blank out the daily grind of school and the bullying he had to endure.

He pictured the writers' group sitting in that smug woman's front room doing nothing more constructive than playing silly word games. What was the point in that? Writing. That's what it was all about. Head down, words on the page, nothing to distract the focus. He worked upstairs in the smallest bedroom at the back of his terraced house. He'd removed the bed, the chest of drawers, the carpet, even the light bulb. He now had nothing but a desk and a chair. During the day, when he wasn't writing in the coffee shop, he worked there, and at night he lit the room with candles. He allowed himself no form of heating, other than a small Calor Gas burner, and there was no danger of being interrupted by the telephone: he'd had it disconnected.

By depriving himself of any comforts he hoped to dig deep into his creative soul and produce his best work. The thought that he might be taking things too far never crossed his mind.

Dulcie woke with what was now a familiar sense of foreboding.

It had been more than two weeks since Richard had told her about Kate and Henry. As she'd promised, she had called her daughter. But on hearing the happiness in Kate's voice as she had talked so enthusiastically about Henry, Dulcie couldn't bring herself to burst the bubble of her daughter's euphoria. All she could hope for was that whatever was going on would fizzle out. Kate bored easily.

She had told Richard this over lunch the day before yesterday. Sitting in the kitchen, with the low January sun streaming brightly through the French windows, there had been a tension between them that she had never known before. 'I disagree,' he'd said, when she'd explained how she felt. 'I'm convinced that Henry wants something to come of this relationship with Kate. He'll pursue her until he gets what he wants.'

Out of bed now, she went downstairs to see what the postman had brought that Saturday morning. Her heart gave a tiny jolt when she saw a large, buff-coloured envelope with her own handwriting on the front.

> *Dear Dulcie Ballantyne,*
>   *I am delighted to inform you that your short story 'Young At Heart' has won first prize in our annual creative-writing competition . . .*

Paperclipped to the back of the letter was a cheque for fifteen hundred pounds. Her earlier mood was immediately replaced with a burst of pure happiness. Nothing matched the thrill of having one's writing accepted. Her happy mood stayed with her for the rest of the day. Until the phone rang early that evening.

'Hello, Kate. How are you?'

'I'm fine, Mum. Well, better than fine.' Girlish laughter—which Dulcie rarely heard from her daughter—echoed down the line. 'The thing is, I'm ringing to let you know that I'm moving in with Henry. He's everything I want in a partner. Oh, Mum, I really think he's the One.' There was more girlish laughter and Kate went on to list Henry's finest qualities. Only half listening, Dulcie closed her eyes. It was just as Richard had feared.

'Mum are you listening to me?'

Rallying herself, Dulcie said, 'I heard every word. And I'm very pleased for you.'

It was dark by the time she got off the phone and, sitting in the study in a pool of soft light cast from the lamp on her desk, Dulcie lowered her head. As a mother, she could not deny her daughter the chance to be happy, which meant she had to sacrifice her own happiness. If there was to be a Kate-and-Henry, there could not be a Richard-and-Dulcie. She had no choice but to end her affair with Richard.

It had snowed heavily during the night. As Jack pulled back the bedroom curtains, he squinted at the brightness that met his eyes. Everything was covered in a blanket of sculpted whiteness. Along the riverbank, branches drooped under the weight of snow and, from a crystal blue sky, the sun shone. Lou Reed's 'Perfect Day' came into Jack's mind. He had the whole weekend off, the girls were with him, and this afternoon he was taking them to see what would soon be his new home. Theirs too, albeit on a part-time basis.

Almost a month had passed since he'd made his offer on Adele Waterman's flat and the purchase was going through without any delay. If his luck held, he'd move in during the second week of February.

They arrived at 10A Maywood Park Road late, damp and out of breath. They had left the car beneath its duvet of snow and walked across town, Amber and Lucy throwing snowballs at each other and shrieking at the top of their voices. Their enjoyment was infectious; he couldn't remember the last time he'd felt so happy and relaxed.

Adele welcomed them in and asked if they would like to take off their wet things. 'Let's see if we can have them dry by the time you leave.'

It didn't take them long to explore the flat, and Jack brought their tour to an end in what was to be the girls' bedroom. Like all the other rooms, it was crammed with treasured possessions.

'Will all this furniture be here when you move in?' asked Lucy.

'No. It belongs to Miss Waterman and she'll be taking it with her.'

'Where's she going to live? Will it be as nice as this?'

'She's moving into a retirement home.'

Amber turned from the window where she had been looking onto the garden and the park. 'I think she'd be happier staying here. This is her home. It doesn't seem right that you're pushing her out.'

'Your father is doing no such thing,' said a firm but kindly voice at the door. Adele came into the room and stood next to Amber. 'I've been very happy here. Now it's time to let someone else enjoy it.'

They had tea in the sitting room, in front of the old-fashioned gas fire that hissed and fascinated the girls. When Lucy started to fidget, Adele asked if they would like to go outside and play. 'You could build a snow-man for me,' she said, making it sound as if they would be doing her an enormous favour.

After the girls had bundled themselves up in their warmed coats, Adele let them out and made a fresh pot of tea. 'They're lovely girls, Jack, you must be so proud of them.'

'I am,' he said simply. 'They mean the world to me. Nearly losing them when Maddie took off, well, it sharpened my focus.'

She handed him his cup. 'You sound bitter, Jack.'

He swallowed. 'I am. Sorry if that sounds petty.'

'And your wife, she's now with your oldest and closest friend. Please forgive an old lady's impertinence, but may I ask you something extremely personal?'

He shifted uncomfortably in his seat. 'I probably don't have much choice in the matter, do I?'

She smiled and took a sip of her tea. 'Think back to when Tony was your best friend. If anything had happened to you, who would you have wanted to help Maddie take care of Amber and Lucy?'

Unable to meet her piercing stare, he looked beyond her, to the garden where his two precious daughters were playing in the snow. He didn't know if the old lady was psychic, but years ago he and Maddie had had it written into their wills that if anything happened to both of them, Tony would not only be the executor of their wills but would become Amber and Lucy's legal guardian.

'I don't think that's a fair question. The circumstances have changed.'

'Indeed they have . . . but I would imagine that Tony would want only the best for those two delightful girls. You might be surprised by how much peace of mind that thought could give you.'

Chapter Seven

IT WAS RARE FOR BETH to have an entire day to herself, but on this particular Sunday, early in February, she was entirely alone. Nathan had borrowed the car and driven Jaz to Nottingham University for the day to show her where he hoped to be studying, come the autumn. He had been delighted when he'd been offered a place.

It was time to treat herself to an afternoon of uninterrupted writing. Before losing herself in her novel, she would check her emails. There was one from Ewan. She smiled and clicked on OPEN.

> Hello, Beth,
> How about this? I'm all wired up with the latest in mobile phone and laptop technology. It means I can keep in touch while I'm away from home. I'm currently down in deepest Cornwall, showing my face at a conference, and while I'm hanging out at an undisclosed address I feel brave enough to ask you something important.
> Bethany, p-p-please . . . (huge intake of breath here, maybe even a drumroll) . . . p-p-please . . . c-c-can we meet?
> Your stuttering with nerves, humblest of lowly humble servants,
> Ewan Barefaced-cheek Jones

Beth laughed, and was all set to reply when the doorbell rang. What timing! She clicked on SAVE, rushed downstairs, opened the front door and found Barnaby on the step.

'Am I welcome?' he asked.

It was almost six weeks since she had last seen Barnaby and the sight of him standing hesitantly at her door moved her to tears.

His eyes were moist too. 'I would have come sooner, only I didn't know how I'd be received. Didn't want to walk into hostile territory.'

They sat at the table with mugs of hot chocolate. 'How are things at Marsh House?' Beth asked. 'How's Lois?'

'Oh, don't you go worrying about Lois. She's keeping her spirits up by rapping me over the knuckles when the mood takes her. My day wouldn't be complete without a good scolding.'

She admired Barnaby for his apparent indifference, but Beth knew that he wouldn't be there unless he was upset about the situation in which they found themselves. 'Barnaby,' she said, 'we can't let this go on. Lois has to understand that while I'm genuinely sorry for what happened there was a lot of truth in what I said. What's to be done?'

He leaned forward. 'I have a plan. I'll need your help. Nathan's too.'

Nottingham was busy with rush-hour traffic and Nathan wasn't taking any chances. He had no intention of arriving home with a crumpled bonnet. His mother had enough to cope with already.

Lately, though, he had noticed that his mother's confidence was growing. He'd put it down to the writers' group she had joined. She was smiling more these days. Several times he had caught her staring out of the window, looking as if she was on the verge of laughter. 'Something amusing you, Mum?' he'd asked yesterday at breakfast.

'Oh, not especially,' she'd replied, her face inscrutable. If he didn't know better, he'd suspect she was keeping something from him.

He turned this thought over in his head, surprised by how much it bothered him. He and his mother had always been so close, they had seldom kept things from each other. It made him wonder how he would react if that was to change. He explored this thought further, and a disturbing realisation crept up on him: he understood the root cause of his grandmother's problem. Her overbearing behaviour stemmed from a basic need to be close to him and his mother. By trying to stop things changing, by denying the truth, she had hoped to preserve the safe little world she had invented for them all to live in.

A world that he had nuked ruthlessly on Christmas Day.

For the first time, he felt a wave of shame and regret.

'Dulcie, please, I beg you to reconsider. Don't do this to me . . . to us.'

'My mind's made up, Richard. Please don't make this any more difficult than it already is for me.'

Hearing the terrible finality in Dulcie's voice, Richard passed a shaking hand across his face. He had never felt more shocked. He had come to have lunch with Dulcie and from nowhere she was telling him it was over between them. He placed a hand on her shoulder and turned her gently towards him. Tears filled her eyes and he saw his own pain mirrored in them. 'Dulcie, this is madness. We can't inflict so much pain on ourselves.' He took her in his arms and held her close.

'Please, Richard, I love you, and probably always will, but it's over between us. It has to be.'

He let go of her, bewildered. Angry too. Angry with Kate and Henry.

His head pounding, despair welled up inside him. 'Explain to me one more time why and how you can justify what you're doing.'

She looked at him sadly, her face wet with tears. 'I'm not thinking of us. I'm thinking of your son. If you ever leave Angela for me, you put Henry in an impossible situation with his mother.'

'But, Dulcie, what they feel for each other is nothing compared to what we have. Our love is worth infinitely more than theirs.'

'How can you say that?'

'They're young. They're—'

'They're not that young, Richard. And if you loved your son as much as I love Kate, you'd want to give him the benefit of the doubt.'

He drew in his breath sharply, as if she'd dealt him a physical blow. 'That's unfair, Dulcie. Who gave you the monopoly on familial love?'

In response, Dulcie's shoulders sagged. 'This isn't doing either of us any good,' she said. 'Please, let's finish it by being civil.'

'No!' he argued wildly. 'I won't give you up. I love you, Dulcie, and stupidly I thought you loved me. Perhaps . . .' he went on, more slowly, knowing he was being cruel, '. . . I've been wrong all this time. You were never really committed to me, were you? Maybe that's why you didn't warn Kate off before it was too late.'

She turned on him, eyes blazing. 'I don't think you're in any position to speak of commitment. You're a married man who's been sneaking around having an adulterous affair.'

He knew when he was beaten. He covered his face with his hands and wept. 'I'm so sorry,' he mumbled. 'Forgive me, please.'

She stroked his hair, a gesture that was so evocative of their being in bed together. He shuddered, knowing, and now accepting, that he would never experience that pleasure again.

Dulcie marched through the park gates. Already breathless, she increased her speed, as if to convince herself that her heart wasn't breaking. But it was futile. She had just made the ultimate sacrifice, had given up the man she loved for her daughter's happiness. She felt no virtuous gain for what she had done, only the deep ache of loss. She lowered her head, and let the tears flow. What did it matter if anyone saw her? But she changed her mind when, coming towards her in the distance, she recognised Victor Blackmore. He was zigzagging between the trees in a bizarre fashion, glancing over his shoulder every now and then, or stopping to tie a shoelace. How very odd.

Victor was in character. He was Irving Hunter, special-ops agent, the protagonist of his novel *Star City*. Peering furtively over his shoulder, he was checking the trees, bushes and litter bins for CIA agents.

He had started work on Chapter Ninety-six at five o'clock that morning, but the words had failed to flow. The situation hadn't felt real to him, and without further delay he'd left the house and thrown himself into acting the part of Irving Hunter. He'd found the experience exhilarating and exhausting. His feet ached and were wet from the rain, but a little discomfort was a small price to pay. All the great writers suffered for their art. If only he could find a publisher who had half a brain and the wit to take on his book, he knew *Star City* would be a huge success.

He took in his surroundings, not sure how he'd got there. This was happening to him more and more. A swivel of his head informed him that he was in Maywood Park. And there, a few yards in front of him, was Dulcie Ballantyne from the writers' group.

Dulcie braced herself. 'Hello, Victor.' She took in the shock of Victor's appearance. He'd lost weight and his bloodshot eyes had a strained, slightly manic look. Perhaps he was working too hard? Her compassionate nature got the better of her. 'Victor, I'm chilled to the bone. I don't suppose you'd join me for a cup of coffee at Novel Ways, would you?'

A downpour of sleety rain hastened their departure from the park. Dulcie didn't know what surprised her more—that she had made such an invitation, or that Victor had accepted it.

Everyone was getting on with the exercise she had set them and, in the silence of their intense concentration, Dulcie was regretting her decision to go ahead with tonight's meeting. But she hadn't been thinking straight today. Why else would she have encouraged Victor to join the group again? It was all too easy to laugh at people like Victor, but her own vulnerability that day had given her an empathy towards him and it was clear, even in her dazed state, that he was depressed. She hadn't been able to turn her back on someone so obviously in need.

With fifteen minutes left in which to complete the writing exercise, Dulcie focused her thoughts. Her own piece of writing wasn't going well. But how could she even think of writing when all she wanted to do was crawl upstairs and hide under the duvet for the rest of her life?

'Time's up!' declared Victor, so loudly that Dulcie jumped.

The evening progressed with everyone taking a turn to read out their work. All except Dulcie. 'Sorry, everyone,' she apologised. 'I wouldn't inflict my attempt on my worst enemy.' And before anyone could shake the Self-belief Box, she suggested it was time for coffee.

'I'll give you a hand,' offered Beth, quick to get to her feet.

No sooner were they in the kitchen than the telephone rang. The kettle almost slipped out of Dulcie's hands when she heard who it was.

'Dulcie, just listen to what I have to say.'

'I'm . . . I'm afraid I'm rather busy at present.' Her voice sounded cold and stilted. She saw Beth shoot her a curious glance. 'Goodbye.' Hating herself, she dropped the receiver onto its cradle with a clumsy clatter.

Then she burst into tears.

Beth was instantly at her side, a hand on her shoulder. 'Dulcie, whatever is the matter? What can I do to help? Shall I get rid of the group?'

Unable to speak, Dulcie leaned into her and sobbed. Minutes passed, and to make things worse, Jack appeared. 'Don't suppose I can hide out here—' He stopped short. 'Anything I can do to help?'

'Yes,' said Beth, taking command. 'Tell the others Dulcie isn't well.'

'Leave it to me. I'll run Jaz home. Then I'll come back for you. Do you have anything stronger than coffee in the house? You look like you could do with a stiff drink.'

'There's nothing seriously wrong with her, is there?' asked Jaz, as Jack pulled away from Dulcie's house.

'I hope not.' And, making light of the situation, 'Maybe it was the shock of having Victor back in the group.'

He turned into Jaz's road and stopped the car on the corner. 'See you next week. And fingers crossed everyone's feeling better.'

She was just unbuckling her seat belt, when a P-registered Rav-4 stopped just yards from where they were parked. The two men in the front turned round and looked down at Jack, then at his passenger.

'Oh, hell!' Jaz cursed. To his astonishment, she flung open the door and marched away down the road in the pouring rain. Puzzled, he watched her go. The driver of the car scowled at him with such menace that Jack had to look away. And then they were gone, tyres squealing.

The evening was getting weirder by the minute.

He turned the car and drove back the way he'd just come to Bloom Street. Beth opened the door to him. 'How's Dulcie?' he asked.

'Come and see for yourself.' Dropping her voice, she added, 'She hasn't let on what's troubling her.'

Dulcie was still in the kitchen. On the table in front of her stood a bottle of whisky, a pot of tea, some mugs and a large plate of toast and honey. 'Comfort food,' she said, with an attempt at a smile. 'Beth's idea.'

'Excellent. OK if I join you?'

'Of course. And I can't apologise enough for my loss of control.'

He sat down. 'If you apologise any more I'll have to fetch the Self-belief Box.' This elicited a proper smile from her. 'You would say if there was anything I,' he glanced at Beth, 'or we, could do, wouldn't you?'

She patted his hand. 'That's very sweet of you, Jack, but I shall be fine. Now, then, who's going to help me polish off all this tea and toast?'

The three of them sat round the table talking about anything that was neutral; Jack described the incident when he had dropped Jaz at home.

'Goodness, how peculiar,' said Beth. She looked thoughtful. 'They must have been her brothers. I'm sure Nathan once said something about a couple of brothers and how she can't stand them.'

But Jack wasn't satisfied. If the two men had been Jaz's brothers, why had they looked at him so threateningly?

They had moved on to Victor, when the shrill ring of the phone made them all start. Jack saw the frozen expression on Dulcie's face and registered also that she made no move to answer it. It rang three more times.

'Erm . . . shall I answer that for you?' he offered.

'No,' she murmured, tightlipped, 'let it ring. He'll give up.'

So that was it. The poor woman was being plagued by a nuisance caller. Jack said, 'Dulcie, how long has this been going on?'

'I'm not sure that's any of your business,' she said primly.

'If someone I know is receiving obscene phone calls,' he said, 'I think it is my business. How long?'

'He's right, Dulcie,' said Beth. 'There's no need for you to put up with it. BT can do all sorts of things nowadays to track down these people.'

To their combined amazement, Dulcie smiled. 'Oh, you two wonderfully concerned people. I suppose it won't do any harm to tell you. Today I told the man I love that I couldn't see him any more. That was him, probably. As it was earlier this evening.'

'But if you still love him, why stop seeing him?'

'Because—' Her voice cracked and she blinked hard. 'Because he's married, and now my daughter's fallen in love with his son. A tangled web, wouldn't you say? Sounds like a novel.'

'The problem I have, Jaz, is that on the one hand I'm led to believe you were at Vicki's for the evening, and the next I'm hearing from your brothers that last night they saw you getting out of some man's car. I don't know how long you've been sneaking off behind our backs seeing this—this man, but let me tell you, if he's so much as laid a finger on you, I'll—I'll bloody kill him!'

Jaz gasped. When she'd been lying in bed last night worrying about whether her brothers would say anything to their father, she'd been concerned about him finding out about the writers' group. She hadn't considered he'd make such a mind-blowing assumption. Jack was old! OK, he made her laugh and could write like a dream, but he was *old*! 'Dad, you've got it all wrong. Jack's a friend. He gave me a lift home.'

Her father banged his fist on the breakfast table. 'Oh, a friend, is he? So maybe it's time he started hanging out with *friends* of his own age, instead of preying on a girl young enough to be his daughter!'

'Look, Dad—'

'Don't give me any of that "look, Dad" stuff, you lied to your mother and me. You told us you were seeing Vicki when all along you've been seeing this man. And if you weren't seeing him, why the lies?'

Jaz stared at her father. She knew if she told him about her writing and how important it was to her he'd want proof. Only trouble was that the contents of her novel, *Having the Last Laugh*, would make everything worse. If he read a word about the Clacketts and sussed that she had been making fun of her family behind their backs, he would go ballistic. Weighing up the odds, she decided she'd be better off keeping quiet. If she said nothing, her precious writing would be safe. So what if they thought she'd been having secret assignations with a bloke as old as Jack?

At first Jack thought he was imagining it, but after several miles of driving along country lanes he had to admit that his imagination wasn't playing tricks on him. A black Golf was following him. He decided to flush it out. He lowered his speed to twenty-five miles an hour, which he knew would infuriate the driver of the Fiesta immediately behind, and sure enough, the Fiesta accelerated past, leaving Jack a clear view of the Golf. To his amazement, in it were the two men he'd encountered in the Rav-4 last night. But what in hell's name were they up to?

The Golf shot in front of him, then slammed on its brakes. His heart in his mouth, Jack skidded to a halt. The next thing he knew he was being hauled from his car and bundled into the Golf. 'What's this all about?' he asked, more shocked than scared.

The young man on his right spoke first. 'We're gonna make this as simple as we can, mate. So listen up. You so much as set eyes on our Jaz one more time and we'll tear you apart. Got that?'

Jack stared, open-mouthed. 'Does this mean you *are* Jaz's brothers?'

Now it was the turn of the man on his left. 'Don't play dumb, Jack. We saw you last night so we know exactly what you've been up to. We know all about you. It's amazing what you can find out about a person once you've got their car registration. The internet's a wonderful thing. I expect you use it a lot, don't you? Men like you do: perverts who can't keep their hands off girls half their age. But we're here to let you know that nobody messes with our little sister.'

What they were accusing him of was preposterous. 'Look,' he said, 'you've got this all wrong. There's nothing going on between Jaz and me. I was giving her a lift home from our writers' group.'

There was a pause. 'Writers' group?'

'We meet on Thursday nights. But surely you must have known that. We've been meeting since October last year.'

At this, the two men exchanged looks. He saw doubt on their faces. 'Outside,' the first man instructed his brother. Both doors were slammed shut so Jack wasn't able to hear what was being said, but the gist was plain. They had realised they'd cocked up and were now reviewing matters. Jack knew he was within his rights to threaten them with police action but, bizarrely, he respected them. Who was he to hold a grudge when they'd only been looking out for their sister?

The door was yanked open. 'Seems like we . . . Well, how about a drink, mate? We could throw in some lunch, if you want.'

'Is that your way of apologising?' Jack asked, when he was helped out of the car. He smoothed down his suit jacket. 'I'd love to, gentlemen, but I have lunch planned already. Something a little less physical.'

Perhaps he should have been more shocked by what had happened to him, but the more Jack thought about it, driving away, the less surprised he was that Jaz had kept Hidden Talents from her brothers. *He* hadn't let on about it to Clare, or even to Des and Julie.

When he had told her brothers that he already had a lunch appointment, he hadn't been lying: he'd arranged to meet Maddie. Talking to Adele Waterman had set him thinking. For the sake of the children, he wanted to put things right between them.

Maddie came across the restaurant towards him, hips swaying in that unconscious way he'd always loved. 'I'm glad you came,' he said, rising to his feet. For an awkward moment, neither knew how to greet the other. They settled for a wary smile and a bob of the head.

They had just one course because Maddie said she couldn't stay long: pasta and salad. Maddie pointed out that the waitress had forgotten the mineral water. 'In America you never get such sloppy service.'

'I wouldn't know. I've never been to the land of plenty.'

She looked at him sharply. 'Don't goad me, Jack.'

'I'm not.' He tried to relate to the irritable woman sitting opposite him. Where had the happy-go-lucky girl gone? 'Maddie,' he said, 'I want to talk seriously about the children and their future.'

Her expression changed. Gone was the sharp defensiveness, and in its place a softening. A softening he knew so well. His heart ached that she could still have that effect on him. She said, 'And I wanted to discuss that with you too. I've got something important to tell you. Tony's got a new business venture that's really taking off in the States. Nothing's definite, but we're considering going to live in California. It would be a fantastic opportunity for the girls.'

Her words knocked the breath right out of him. Along with all his good intentions. He sat back in his chair. 'Over my dead body. That bastard is not taking my children anywhere.'

Several times during the morning Vicki had asked Jaz what was wrong. By the end of the day Jaz had relented and confided in her. Vicki lapped up every word. 'So your family reckons you're seeing some old guy on the quiet? How awesome is that? You're not, are you?'

'*No!*'

She looked almost disappointed. 'Hey, this might not be a bad time to tell your parents about Nathan. Your dad'll be so relieved you're going out with someone your own age, he'll think Nathan's an answer to a prayer. Which, let's face it, he is.'

Would that be such a bad idea? Yes, it would. Jaz could picture the scene perfectly: her father demanding to meet Nathan so that he could interrogate him and her gloating brothers preparing to embarrass him. And what would Nathan think of them and, as a consequence, of her?

No sooner had she set foot out of the college gates than Jimmy's black Golf appeared: checking that she wasn't slipping off for another assignation with her middle-aged lover.

Jimmy lowered the driver's window. 'We met a friend of yours this morning,' he said. 'What was his name, Phin? Was it John?'

'Nah. It was Jack. Jack Solomon.'

Jaz froze. Her brothers had spoken to *Jack*? But how had they found out who he was? She chewed her lip. Phin and Jimmy had both learned to box and once, much to Mum's horror, they'd been involved in a late-night brawl in Manchester. Someone like Jack—a man to whom they were determined to teach a lesson—wouldn't stand a chance. 'What have you done to Jack?' she yelled, when she'd got into the car. 'If you've hurt him, I'll make sure he goes to the police.'

Jimmy grinned at her in the rearview mirror. 'Cool it. Jack's fine. Why don't you tell us what you've really been up to?'

Did this mean what she thought it did? Were they onto her writing? Or did they know about Nathan? What had Jack told them? Trying to deflect them, she said, 'How did you find Jack?'

'Easy as pie,' crowed Jimmy. 'Number plate.'

Jaz's heart sank. 'You're nothing but a pair of loathsome yobs.'

At home, her mother was cooking tea. 'Hello, Jaz,' she said. 'I see the boys found you. Supper's nearly ready, so go and get washed.'

Jaz moved uncertainly towards the door. 'Where's Dad?'

'In his snug. Oh, he did say he wanted a word with you.'

Avoiding her brothers' eyes, she went to find her father.

'Ah, there you are, Jaz,' he said, as she stepped into the room he called his snug. 'Close the door after you,' he added ominously.

'Jaz,' he began, 'out of all our children, your mother and I always had you down as the most sensible. The one with the brains we could trust. But now'—and she could see the disappointment in his eyes—'you've let me down. I think that's what hurts the most, finding out that you had it in you to deceive us all these months. You probably know by now that your brothers have spoken with your so-called friend, Jack Solomon, and if we're to believe him, you've been sneaking off to some kind of group where you sit around writing.' He paused. 'Is that true?'

So, he and her brothers knew that much. 'You make it sound like a subversive activity, Dad.'

He widened his eyes. 'Well, pardon me, Miss Hoity-toity, but why lie to us about it if it was so innocent? And what, I want to know, is the effect of this group on your college work?'

'I've always put college first, Dad.'

'And you'd better be telling the truth over that.' He let out his breath. 'But you still haven't explained why you acted the way you did.'

She swallowed. The truth, she decided, was the only way to satisfy him. 'I couldn't face Phin and Jimmy going on and on about me kidding myself I was a writer, and Tamzin and Lulu forever nosing around in my room trying to find what I'd written.'

He looked at her as if he hadn't understood.

'Dad, you don't get it, do you? I have no privacy in this family. Everything I do is made fun of. I don't fit in. Is it any wonder I keep things to myself?' She lurched to her feet, tears welling. 'I'm sorry I lied to you, and that you're disappointed in me. But you'd better prepare yourself for more disappointment because I'll probably never be the brilliant success you expect me to be. Why don't you save that honour for the next load of babies Mum's having?'

Shaking, she fled the room. She heard her father call after her, but she stumbled up the stairs, threw herself on her bed and sobbed.

Richard stalked into the centre of the village, knowing that his behaviour had been unforgivable. He should never have shouted at Angela like that. She didn't deserve to be on the receiving end of his ill humour.

Ill humour! Could going half crazy really be described so simply?

It was three agonising days since Dulcie had ended their relationship. He couldn't sleep, couldn't eat, couldn't concentrate. If he didn't see Dulcie again, he wasn't sure he could continue living. Every day was torture. The thought that she was able to carry on her life without him made the pain more excruciating. How could she?

He continued towards the church and the footpath he had often used during his convalescence. He took the steep incline slowly; anger alone wouldn't propel him up the slope—it might even kill him.

But who would miss him if he had another heart attack and died?

Angela would miss him as a provider, but not as a husband or a lover. As for the children, Nicholas and Christopher would mourn his passing, but the older ones were sufficiently established to get on perfectly well without him. And Dulcie had cast him out of her life easily, proving that she could not have felt the same for him as he did for her.

Filled with a desperate urge towards self-destruction, he began to walk faster, rage and despair quickening his step, his breath coming fast, his chest aching.

Chapter Eight

BETH WAS FULL OF ADMIRATION for Barnaby. His plan to get Lois back on speaking terms with Beth and Nathan was to whisk away his wife on a luxury cruise. He hoped that after three weeks on the high seas she would feel like a new woman and would be receptive to an extended olive branch. While the two of them were exploring the Caribbean, Beth and Nathan would look after Marsh House.

'I shall tell her I've got an agency taking care of things, then present her with a fait accompli on our return.' Beth gave Barnaby full credit for being so brave. Railroading Lois was not for the faint-hearted.

After supper, Beth went downstairs to see Adele. She was moving out the day after tomorrow—Jack was moving in on Friday—and Beth had promised to help her pack.

Adele looked tired and flustered when she opened the door and, when she stepped inside, Beth realised why. A balding man and a thin woman in an unflattering leather skirt were unhooking a pretty Victorian watercolour from the wall above the radiator. Beth knew that it was a particular favourite of Adele's and she couldn't imagine her friend wanting to part with it. 'I'm sorry, Adele,' she said, 'I didn't know you had visitors. Shall I call back later?' She had no intention of leaving, but she had to make a show of courtesy.

'No, please, don't go.' A hand was placed insistently on her forearm. 'This is my nephew, Vernon, and his friend Sheila.'

'*Sylvia*,' the bald man corrected her. 'And you might be?'

'Oh, Vernon, don't be so pompous. Beth is my neighbour from upstairs. She's always looked after me so well.'

Beth smiled at Adele, but she saw Vernon's grey eyes grow sharper. She didn't much care for the look of him. Or his skinny friend. This was the first time in ages he had called on his aunt; his showing up like this smacked of opportunism, and Beth was having none of it.

The telephone rang and while Adele went to answer it in the sitting room, Beth said, 'Be careful with that picture. It's extremely valuable.'

'Do you really think so?' Vernon took it from Sylvia.

'Yes,' said Beth. 'I'd go so far as to say it's practically priceless . . . to your aunt. So why don't I put it back where it belongs?'

The grey eyes were boring into her, but Beth held her ground. 'Are you staying to help Adele pack, or do you have to rush away?'

Vernon looked as mad as a hornet. He opened his mouth to speak, but was cut short by Adele reappearing in the hall. 'That was Jack,' she said to Beth. 'Just wanting to reassure me that everything's going like clockwork. Oh, not stopping, Vernon?'

'No,' Vernon said briskly. 'We'd better be making tracks. You obviously have it all sorted here.' He threw Beth a hostile glance. 'Well, good luck with the move. Call if you need anything.'

'Thank you, Vernon. It was nice of you to drop in.' Adele had relaxed. 'You must come and see me in my new home. You too, Shirley.'

'It's *Sylvia*.'

'Of course it is, Vernon. Whatever was I thinking? It must be my age.'

They stood on the doorstep waving off the scavengers. Out of the corner of her mouth, Beth said, 'You wicked woman. You knew perfectly well what her name was, didn't you?'

'How could you think such a thing? Oh, I'm so glad to see the back of them. Seeing Vernon sizing up my possessions so blatantly brought it home to me that I'm on borrowed time and the vultures are circling.'

Later that night, Beth felt weary of spirit. Before the move business had taken root, Adele would never have spoken like that. To cheer herself up, she switched on her computer. There were two emails. The first was from Simone, complaining about how hot it was and that if she wasn't careful she'd soon be able to get a job as a Mother Teresa lookalike. The second was from Ewan.

Her heart stepped up a gear or two, as it always did when she heard from him. It had taken a lot of courage on her part to agree to meet him. He'd promised to leave her to decide when. She clicked on open.

BAD NEWS, I'VE BEEN REJECTED!

The publisher, who seemed so keen, has now read the whole manuscript and thinks, and here I quote, 'Blah, blah, blah . . . not quite what we're looking for . . .'

Oh, to have one's fragile spirits soaring one minute only to have them dashed upon the rocks of one's shattered dreams! Are you getting the hint that I'm feeling sorry for myself? No? Well, believe me, there's plenty more self-pity at my disposal.

But something good did come my way today—the opportunity to attend a writers' conference at Norton Hall. It's a week-long residential course near Harrogate where wannabe writers get the chance to meet agents and editors and attend talks and workshops.

The thought has occurred to me, that maybe—just possibly, at a pinch . . . erm . . . that you might like to . . . erm . . . attend said course as well. You'd be completely safe, surrounded by so many other people. Granted I can't vouch for their sanity, and let's face it, writers are not the sanest lunatics in the asylum, but at least you'd have plenty of folk to protect you, should a full moon appear and I turn into a madman.

Write back soon and tell me something to cheer me up, Ewan X

Beth smiled and began typing.

You're mad, Ewan Jones! One little rejection and you go to pieces. Get a grip, man! Seriously, though, I'm sorry to hear you've had such a horrible knockback. Remind yourself that you haven't written a bad book, you just sent it to the wrong publisher.

Now then, and don't fall off your chair with shock, I think the writers' conference sounds a good idea. But you'll have to give me more information before I commit myself . . .

Forever cautious, Beth X

She still couldn't believe she was conducting such an enjoyable relationship via the Internet. She was utterly charmed by Ewan's ability to poke fun at himself, even when he must have been feeling low.

With the three removal men now gone, Jack surveyed the mess they'd left behind them. There didn't seem enough space for all his belongings.

He poured himself a large glass of single malt whisky, stood with his back to the dining-room door and faced the fireplace. When the original house had been divided into two flats, this room had suffered: space had been taken from it to provide a kitchen. As soon as he had the flat organised, but before he got too comfortable, he would get a builder in to open up the rooms. The kitchen needed a complete revamp too. He wanted to create a stylish room to be the focus of the flat, somewhere Amber and Lucy would feel at home. If they didn't go to America.

His throat clenched and he tightened his grip on the glass. Maddie's words from last Friday came back to taunt him. *It would be a fantastic opportunity for the girls.*

'And what about the fantastic opportunity of seeing their father?' he'd thrown at her, once he was able to speak without resorting to swearing.

'Keep your voice down, Jack,' Maddie had hissed. 'People are staring.'

'Let them! But it's good to see that you're more concerned about what people think of you in public than the welfare of our children.'

'Oh, for heaven's sake, stop it!'

'You just don't get it, do you? You don't understand that there's nothing worse you could do to me. You sleep with my best friend, you leave me for him, and you limit the amount of time I can see our children. Then you expect me to sit back and keep my voice down while you inform me that I'll be lucky to see them again!'

She stood up. 'I feel sorry for you, Jack. You've allowed yourself to be blinded by your bitterness. Perhaps it would be better if Amber and Lucy did see less of you. I'd hate the girls to see you like this. It would harm them far more than anything Tony or I could do to them.'

The unfamiliar ring of his doorbell interrupted his thoughts: Beth. 'Hi,' she said. 'I've just got in from work and wanted to make sure you hadn't forgotten you were having supper with us tonight.'

Smiling, he said, 'It's only been the thought of a decent meal to look forward to that's got me through the day.'

'It'll be fine,' she said. 'Every move is the same—you'll soon have it together. I could give you a hand tomorrow. Now, I'd better get my skates on or there'll be no supper tonight. Eight o'clock suit you?'

As it turned out, Beth had time to set the table and grab a quick soak in the bath. Afterwards, while she was slipping a pair of pearl studs into her ear lobes, she heard Nathan talking on the phone in the kitchen.

It was half-term, and to Beth's knowledge he hadn't spoken to Jaz all week. She had wanted to ask him if everything was all right between them but, respecting her son's privacy, she had held off probing. After all, she had her own need for concealment.

Jack arrived promptly at eight o'clock, bottle of wine in hand. Beth thought he looked more cheerful than he had earlier, and was glad she'd invited him to dinner. They were clearing away the main-course plates when Jack asked Nathan if he'd ever met Jaz's brothers.

'No, but I get the feeling she isn't too keen on them. Why do you ask?'

He looked at Beth, with a strange half-smile. 'Well, OK, I'll tell you, but I don't want this to get back to Jaz. Her brothers followed me last Friday, bundled me into the back of their car and threatened me. They'd seen her in my car and they thought I was carrying on with their little sister. Very laudable behaviour on their part, you could say.' He glanced at Nathan. 'And for the record, I'm *not* up to anything with Jaz.'

'Her family know that Thursday night is her writers' group night,' said Nathan. 'Why didn't they assume you were her legit ride home?'

'Ah, well, for reasons best known only to Jaz, it appears that she's kept her family in ignorance of that one important fact.'

'Do you suppose that means she's been lying to them?'

'Almost certainly,' said Jack.

'Which would mean,' Nathan said thoughtfully, 'that if she's been caught lying, she's probably been grounded.' Suddenly he smiled. 'Thanks, Jack, you've cleared up a mystery for me. Well, folks, I'm off out now. Don't wait up.' He left the flat whistling.

Beth saw the puzzled expression on Jack's face, and said, 'I think you've just solved what's been bugging him. There hasn't been a peep from Jaz. Now he knows why. Dulcie told me yesterday that she couldn't contact Jaz to tell her she was cancelling last night's meeting. Perhaps her parents have punished her by taking away her mobile.'

'How did Dulcie seem when you spoke to her?'

'No better, really. Tired and subdued.'

'I would never have thought her capable of deliberately moving in on a married man to break up his marriage.'

Beth knew how sensitive Jack was about the breakup of his own marriage, and chose her words with care. 'I don't think these things are ever deliberate. Besides, she hasn't broken the marriage up, has she?'

'She certainly wasn't strengthening it.'

A silence fell on them, until Beth said, 'You OK?'

He sighed. 'Just as I think I'm getting my act together, another load of crap falls into my lap. The latest news from Maddie and Wonderboy Tony is that they want to go and live in California. It would mean I'd never see the girls.' His voice broke and he turned away.

For an awkward moment Beth didn't know what to do. Instinct told her that he needed physical reassurance, a gently placed hand, or a hug. But years of hiding her own emotions and keeping herself to herself held her back. She resorted to words. 'Oh, Jack, I'm so sorry. That's awful. Is there anything you can do to stop it?'

He kept his eyes from hers. 'I've spoken to my solicitor and he says all I can do is appeal to their mother's better nature.' His cynicism rang out in the quiet of the kitchen and he turned to face her. 'And I stand as much chance of doing that as I do of winning the Booker Prize.'

'Stranger things have happened,' Beth said softly. Why couldn't she just give him a hug? She hadn't always been like this. Before Adam had died she had never been afraid of physical contact. It was as if the woman inside her had withered and died too. Inexplicably she felt like crying. But more inexplicable was the anger she suddenly felt towards Adam. How dare he still have the power to do this to her?

She got up abruptly to fetch another bottle of wine. While she opened it, she asked Jack about the plans he had for the flat.

Plainly relieved to talk about something else, he apologised for the inconvenience he would soon be causing. 'I hope you won't be disturbed too much when the builders arrive,' he said.

'I'm sure it will be fine. I'll be out at work when they're here.'

It wasn't long before Beth had drunk too much, but she didn't care. Her anger had now given way to giggling mellowness. Jack, too, was laughing more than usual and together they sat on the sofa, finding whatever the other said absurdly witty and amusing. When she offered to make them coffee, Jack pulled her back with a clumsy tug. 'Coffee's for wimps,' he said. 'How about another glass of that excellent malt?'

'Adam used to like whisky,' she said, mournfully. 'He drank half a bottle of it the night he died. You mustn't tell anyone I said that.'

'Why?'

'Because it would be very, very, *very* disloyal to Adam.'

He leaned back on the sofa, put his arm round her. 'And you're a very loyal person, aren't you, Beth? Is that why you haven't remarried?'

'In part.'

'Which part in particular?'

'The part other beers cannot reach.'

He joined in with her laughter. 'But have you really never been tempted to get married again? You must have had offers.'

'Nobody's asked me.'

'Is that because you've had the drawbridge up?'

'It's not a crime to be discerning,' she said, defensively.

'It *would* be a crime if you ended up depriving yourself of a happier life. But, then, who am I to talk? Look at the mess I made of things.'

Hearing a maudlin tone creep into his voice again, Beth said, 'I have a secret. A whopping great secret no one knows anything about.'

His face broke into a wide smile. 'What, precisely?'

'A man. His name's Ewan Jones.' She laughed, then waited for the room to stop spinning. 'He's a little older than me and has a great talent for making me laugh. He's also a writer. Not published, but hopeful.'

'So where did you meet him?'

She hesitated. 'Um . . . we haven't actually met.' She told him how they'd 'met' on-line, even about the possibility of meeting Ewan at the writers' conference. 'I suppose it all sounds silly to you, doesn't it?'

He squeezed her close to him. 'I think it's brilliant. How else should a writer meet his or her ideal partner but through the written word?'

'But what do you think about me meeting him? Tell me honestly.'

'Go for it, Beth. You know deep down you want to. So why not?'

'He might turn out to be—'

'A roaring nutcase,' he interrupted her. 'In which case you need a chaperon.' He paused. 'Hey, I've just had the best idea of the night. Why don't we all go? Hidden Talents—Dulcie, Jaz, Victor, you and me. Just the thing to spur us on with our writing and at the same time we'd be checking out your bloke for you. What do you think?'

'I think you're a genius, Jack Solomon.'

'And to prove my brilliant idea isn't a one-off, here's another. Let's email your cyberspace boyfriend the good news right now. What's more, let's spice up the message and give him a taste of the real Beth King.'

She looked at him doubtfully, but he laughed and pulled her to her feet. 'Don't come over all wimpish on me, Beth. We're going to make him even keener to meet you in the flesh.'

It was a mark of how drunk she was that she allowed Jack to drag her across the room to her computer. 'I hope you're not going to make me do something I'll regret,' she said.

The following morning, in Suffolk, Ewan went for a brisk walk along the beach. A blustery wind blew off the North Sea, sending waves crashing in. It was an invigorating start to the day, and he felt better for it. One way or another, he'd had a lousy week. The rejection of *Emily and Albert* had hit him harder than he'd thought it would.

Back home, while he was cooking his breakfast, he thought of the dinner party he would be going to that evening: yet another attempt by some of his well-meaning friends to partner him off. That was the trouble with the happily married: they hated having a single person loitering untidily about the place. He hoped the woman he'd be seated next to tonight would have something interesting to say. The last woman at one of Phil and Susannah's dateline parties had been an intensely bitter divorcee—an English lecturer and a foaming-at-the-mouth feminist to boot. 'What in God's name did you think we'd have in common?' he'd asked Phil the next morning.

'Susannah thought you'd enjoy the intellectual challenge,' Phil had said. 'Not forgetting the literary connection.'

'Oh, yes. What was it she said about popular fiction? It should be strangled at birth.'

Afterwards, he went through to his office, pretending, as he always did, that he wasn't eager to see if there was a message from Beth. There was. He read it twice, and hoped she wouldn't regret having sent it. It was a gem. Written, he presumed, while she was under the influence of something a little more intoxicating than a mug of Ovaltine.

Beth knew that something was terribly wrong even before she opened her eyes and found that the light penetrating the gap in the curtains was burning the back of her eyeballs. As she recalled the events of the night before, she drew her knees up to her chest, assuming the foetal position, as though it would protect her from the shame of her behaviour.

Drunk. Oh, horribly drunk.

She remembered Jack kissing her goodbye and leaving, and Nathan arriving home to find her bent over the toilet. 'I don't think I'm very well,' she'd whimpered, thinking of the countless lectures she had given him on the evils of alcohol. 'It must have been something I ate.'

'Yeah, that would be it, Mum,' he'd said, helping her into bed.

Then she remembered something else: the email she and Jack had sent Ewan. 'Oh, let the world end now,' she murmured.

Dulcie had thought she was covering up remarkably well, but under the full glare of her friends' gaze, the last of her defences crumbled.

'I'm not going to beat about the bush,' Prue said, after their waitress had brought them their baked potatoes and salads, 'but what on earth is the matter with you, Dulcie? Are you ill?'

Maureen said, 'She's right, Dulcie. You don't look your normal self.'

How had she thought she could ever convince them that all was well? Everything was slipping away from her. She'd had to cancel the writers' group last week and didn't think she'd be able to cope with it tomorrow evening either. And all because of Richard. Of what she had denied herself. With each day that passed, the pain grew worse. He phoned her every morning, trying to make her see sense. This morning he'd sobbed, 'Don't do this. I'd rather be dead than not see you again.' She'd replaced the receiver with a trembling hand. The pain of hearing his anguish, knowing that she was the cause of it, was too much.

She had loved Philip, and had gone on loving him long after he'd died, but losing him hadn't been as painful as this, because she had played no part in causing her loss: there had been no guilt to deal with.

She looked up suddenly and saw that both Prue and Maureen were hunting through their handbags. When Maureen handed her a small packet of tissues, she understood that the game was up. She wiped her eyes, blew her nose and said, 'I think I ought to go home.'

While Maureen sat with Dulcie on the sofa, Prue poured three cups of coffee. When they were all seated, Dulcie told them the whole story. She started at the beginning, with the day she had met Richard—the day he had changed her life. She told them how easily she and Richard had fallen in love, and even what a wonderful lover he was. 'He really was the most perfect man,' she murmured.

'Except for being married,' muttered Prue.

'Yes. Except for being married,' echoed Dulcie. Then she told her friends about Kate and Henry. Which shocked them.

'Is that why you've ended it with him?' asked Maureen.

Dulcie nodded. 'I had no choice. If there's a chance of those two young people being happy, I couldn't stand in their way.' She drained her cup and placed it carefully on its saucer. 'Anyway, it's all over now. And it's time I pulled myself together.'

Her friends looked at her doubtfully. Prue said, 'Dulcie, you need a break. You should get right away from Maywood. Why don't you go to London and stay with Andrew?'

What her friend suggested wasn't so silly. London was out of the question: she would inevitably end up seeing Kate and, very likely, Henry. But time away from Maywood would do her good. And Richard wouldn't be able to ring her. That evening she unearthed her stock of holiday brochures. The one on the top of the pile caught her eye— *Italian Escapes*. She took it downstairs to the kitchen and made herself a sandwich. What would best suit her current frame of mind? The dramatic scenery of the Amalfi coast? Or the hills and valleys of Umbria?

She poured herself a glass of wine—Italian, as it turned out. An omen? She opened the brochure and flicked through the glossy pages, seeing images of rustic hotels nestling in rural idylls, of piazzas, palazzos and stunning waterfronts, of perfectly ripened tomatoes, basil and creamy white mozzarella sprinkled with black pepper and drenched in olive oil. For the first time in days, Dulcie felt hungry and she bit into her sandwich. Delving further into the brochure, she stopped at the section for city breaks. A photograph of St Mark's Square stared back at her.

Venice? Oh, surely not. Venice was for couples taking magical moonlit gondola rides along the Grand Canal. How could she consider rubbing salt into such a raw wound?

But how long was she going to allow herself to wallow in self-pity?

She read on, looking for a hotel that appealed. The Hotel Isabella was described as an oasis of tranquillity and refined charm reminiscent of a bygone era, five minutes' walk from St Mark's Square. It sounded perfect. She bent back the corner of the page to mark the place, then realised that she'd finished her sandwich. It was the first meal that she had managed to eat in days. Her friends would be pleased. 'You must eat,' they'd told her. They had left her with hugs of sympathy and repeated instructions that if she needed them she must ring.

There had been no criticism of her affair, which was what she had feared. Married people tended to take a dim view of others who appeared to ride roughshod over the sanctity of marriage.

How long, she wondered, before she would rid herself of the guilt? Not just for being party to Richard's betrayal of his marriage vows but for the pain she was now causing him. She told herself that Richard was as culpable as she was. But men were different. Guilt slid off their consciences so easily. Jaz had once said: 'Show me a woman who feels no guilt and I'll show you a man.'

How extraordinarily mature and perceptive Jaz was, despite her age.

With a terrible feeling of déjà vu, Jaz listened to her mother.

'Now, Jaz, there's plenty of food in the freezer. I expect I'll be home by the weekend, so everything will be back to normal then.'

It was Thursday, almost two weeks since her father had found out about Hidden Talents. Jaz had come home from college to find her mother packing a bag. 'What's going on, Mum?' she'd asked.

'Oh, nothing to worry about. My blood pressure's sky-high so the doctor's ordered me to have a few days' bed-rest in hospital.'

Jaz's heart had plummeted. 'Where's Dad?' she asked.

'He's on his way with Phin and Jimmy. They'll be here any minute and then your father will take me to the hospital.'

'But if there's nothing wrong, Mum,' Jaz persisted, 'why the rush?'

She didn't get an answer because just then they heard the back door nearly crashing off its hinges: it was Tamzin and Lulu.

'You will be patient with them, won't you?' her mother said.

'I'll try, Mum, but they act up even more when you're not around.'

Her mother stroked her hair. 'I'm sorry about how things seem to fall your way, Jaz.' Her expression turned serious. 'Now, I don't know what's going on between you and your father because he won't tell me. I just want you to know that if you need anyone to talk to, please don't think I haven't got time for you.'

How tempted Jaz was to spill it all out there and then in the hope that her mother would take her side.

Her father's punishment hadn't been as bad as she'd thought it would be. She was allowed out now, but he'd banned her from Hidden Talents. 'It's for your own good, Jaz,' he'd said. 'You've got a lot on your plate at college and the last thing you need is a distraction.'

It had been great when half-term had ended and she'd been able to see Nathan at college again. Explaining what had happened and admitting that she was being treated like a child had been mortifying, but Nathan was fantastic about it. He said he knew better than most that families could be weird.

Billy had said she should stand up to her father, and Vicki had asked, 'Why not talk to your mum? Mine's great for getting round my dad and making him do what we want.'

But Jaz knew, as she stood on the landing, looking at her mother's tired face, that she couldn't confide in her. Not with her going into hospital. 'I'm OK, Mum, really. You mustn't worry about me.' She peered over the banister towards the front door. 'Sounds like Dad's back.'

She was right. Her father burst through the front door like a member of the SAS. He flung down his jacket and called, 'Moll, where are you?'

At their mother's insistence, no one but their father was to go with her to the hospital and, waving them off, Jaz realised that her father loved her mother very much and would do anything to keep her safe. What would he do if the unthinkable happened and something happened to Mum? She buried the thought deep. Nothing was going to happen to her mother. She was pregnant, not ill.

Never in the history of Most Embarrassing Moments had Beth experienced such head-hanging shame. What had she been thinking when she'd sent Ewan that email? And what must he have thought of her when he'd read it? Oh, he'd been pleasant enough about it in his response but, deep down, he must have been quietly reviewing his opinion of her. What else could he have done in view of what she'd suggested she might like to do with him and a bar of chocolate?

Top tip, Beth [he'd emailed back]. Be sure to melt the chocolate first. But for the sake of clarity, would that be Galaxy or Cadbury's? I'm rather partial to a bar of Fruit and Nut, if my personal preferences ever need to be taken into account.

It was now March, and nearly two and a half weeks since the night she and Jack had got so thoroughly plastered. The embarrassment should have passed by now, but it hadn't.

The next day Jack had apologised to her when she'd summoned the energy to go downstairs and help him with his unpacking.

'I'm struggling to piece together the exact details of last night,' he'd said. 'I didn't let the side down too much, did I?'

'I don't think so,' she'd murmured, 'but if you could lower your voice, I'd be eternally grateful.'

They didn't get much done in the first hour but, after drinking several glasses of water, they made some headway on the boxes in the kitchen. 'For a single man, you have a surprising amount of stuff,' she'd said.

'That's because Maddie didn't want any of it. I think she fancied the idea of taking Tony by the scruff of the neck and starting from scratch with him. Women like to do that, don't they?'

'I wouldn't know.'

'OK, point made,' he said, 'I'm condemning the whole of womankind based on the actions of one woman. I retract the statement.'

And that's what Beth wished she could do with Ewan—retract that drunken email. Despite his reply, she hadn't had the nerve to correspond with him again, and wondered if she ever would.

After work that evening, Beth drove to Marsh House to help Barnaby pack—Lois was at her South Cheshire Women's Group. First thing tomorrow morning she was being whisked off to Manchester airport to fly to Miami where she and Barnaby would embark upon their cruise.

Upstairs on their double bed was a large suitcase. 'I've put a list together of the clothes I think Lois will need,' Barnaby said, 'but I want you to choose shoes and jewellery, and . . .' he lowered his eyes 'those all-important undergarments. I'll be downstairs making us a drink.'

It was strange sorting through Lois's clothes, especially when it came to selecting her underwear, which caused Beth to see her prim mother-in-law in a different light. Here was a woman who indulged herself in exquisite lingerie. Beth was astonished by the amount of silk and delicate lace. In comparison, her worn-out chain-store bras and knickers would never pass muster. I've let things slide, she thought.

She looked at her reflection in Lois's dressing-table mirror. Her hair needed cutting, but otherwise she didn't think she was totally beyond redemption. With a lick of paint here and there, she'd almost get away with it. Whatever *it* was. Her figure wasn't too awful either: she was still a size twelve and could wear the same clothes from years back. It was a boast she shouldn't be proud of, she realised. Those old clothes should have been thrown away a long time ago.

She held one of Lois's lacy suspender belts against her and decided that one day she would like to spoil herself with something as pretty.

'Here we are then, coffee. Oh . . .'

She whipped round from the mirror to see Barnaby looking almost as embarrassed as she was. She smiled awkwardly. 'I—I was just thinking how lovely all these things are. Lois has exceptionally good taste.'

For a moment Barnaby looked as if he didn't know what to say. Then he chuckled. 'It's a little weakness of hers, and one I'm rather fond of.'

'You sweet man.'

They stood in silence, staring at the open suitcase. Then: 'I've never said this before, Beth, but you're a very attractive woman, who ought to have remarried by now. A nice man, to make you feel complete.'

She laughed. 'There are women beyond these four walls who'd pluck out your nose-hairs for saying that.'

He squared his shoulders. 'Yes, and they doubtless live alone and will never know the joy another person can bring into their lives. I know Lois and I don't always give the impression of being in accord, but for the most part we've been happy. I suspect you and Adam would have been the same. You *were* happy, weren't you?'

Smiling, she said, 'Oh, yes, extremely so. If we hadn't been, then perhaps I *would* have met someone else.'

'You won't leave it too late, Beth, will you? I understand the pressure you've been under from Lois. She's never fully recovered from Adam's death, and I doubt she ever will, but one day I pray that she'll accept you have every right to move on and fall in love again.' With his free hand, he put his arm round her. 'You're the daughter I never had, Beth. And I'll move heaven and earth to see you happy. Hence the drastic measures.' He indicated the bed with its half-packed suitcase.

Unable to express her gratitude in words alone, she leaned into him and buried her face in the warm softness of his woollen sweater.

It was almost nine o'clock when Jack came off the telephone. He'd just been talking to Dulcie, who, after much apologising for letting down the group again, had told him she was going away for a brief holiday. 'Jack, I know this is a terrible imposition, but I'd feel inordinately better if you could keep the group going while I'm away.'

'Is it worth it, with so few of us able to attend?' he asked. 'Jaz still can't join us and Victor doesn't seem keen.'

'Even if it's just you and Beth who get together, I'd feel better about it.'

'OK, then,' he conceded. 'But how long are you going to be away?'

'A week or two. Now, tell me about your new flat. How's it going?'

'I'm gradually getting it sorted. Which is stupid because I'm going to mess it all up next week—I've got the builders coming in on Monday. They're knocking through from the kitchen to the dining room.'

'Oh, I wish you luck. The dust will be horrendous. If it all gets too bad for you, you're more than welcome to stay here. In fact, you'd be doing me yet another favour, house-sitting for me. Shall I let you have a set of keys, just in case?'

While he heated up a microwave meal for one, Jack wondered why Dulcie had asked him to lead the group. Why not Beth? But he didn't have time to waste musing: he wanted to do some writing as well as get the girls' bedroom ready. He was picking them up tomorrow morning and he wanted the flat to look its best for their first proper stay.

There had been no more talk from Maddie about California, but he didn't think that was because the threat had gone away. It was all he could do to contain his anger, some of which he used in his writing, venting it late at night in controlled bursts of passion. On a more practical level, he had instructed his solicitor to write to Maddie's, asking her to think about what would be most beneficial to Amber and Lucy, stressing the obvious basic need for them to see their father regularly.

On the other side of town, Victor tried to ignore the person who was knocking on his front door. Why couldn't people leave him alone?

At last the knocking stopped. But the intrusion wasn't over. He heard the sound of metal on metal: the letterbox was being opened.

He pushed himself to his feet unsteadily, feeling light-headed. He took the stairs slowly, wondering why he couldn't move faster.

There was no one at the door when he reached it, but on the floor was an envelope. With shaking hands he ripped it open. It was a handwritten note from Dulcie Ballantyne. What did she want *now*?

He read it, then tore it up in disgust. She was going away: in her absence that jumped-up estate agent would be in charge of Hidden Talents. Why hadn't she thought to ask him if he'd lead the group?

He dragged himself back upstairs, his skull throbbing with the headache he'd had since he woke that morning. He yanked the page he'd been writing from his typewriter and inserted a fresh piece. Then he hunted for the notes he'd made earlier, remembering, ten minutes later, that he'd written them on the wall behind him. This was a new technique he'd adopted to keep his notes safe.

Shivering, he went over to the Calor Gas burner to make himself a drink. But when he tried to light the gas, it spluttered, hissed, and the flame slowly died.

Silently, and not knowing why, he crouched on the bare floorboards, covered his unshaven face with his hands and wept.

Chapter Nine

DULCIE WAS GLAD she had taken Prue and Maureen's advice: without question, Venice was the perfect tonic. From the moment the water taxi had dropped her off in the Castello district, she had felt at peace. Walking the short distance to her hotel, she had marvelled at the early-evening sky, a glorious infusion of fading blue and subtle shades of pearly pink. Tourists had buzzed around her, but she had ignored them, continuing to drink in the still, magical atmosphere of the lagoon as day surrendered itself to the dusky mist of twilight.

Enchanted, she had reluctantly torn herself away and, armed with her map, had wheeled her suitcase in the direction of the family-run three-star Hotel Isabella.

This had been two days ago, and her love of the city was growing with each hour. 'Today,' she told herself, 'I will not walk too far.' She made the promise as she helped herself to a sweet pastry and a bowl of fresh fruit from the breakfast buffet in the small hotel dining room. Such was the temptation to explore every square inch of Venice, lest she miss some gem of architecture, yet another Tintoretto or spectacular reflection of light on water, that she was in danger of wearing herself out.

Putting on her most comfortable shoes, she set out for another day of adventure. She left the hotel behind her, turned into the Calle della Pietà and stopped in front of the church of Santa Maria della Pietà. There was a board outside advertising a concert for that evening. Making a snap decision, she climbed the steps. There was a small ticket booth at the entrance and, the transaction quickly made, she left the church looking forward to an evening of Vivaldi.

It was a beautifully warm March day and, arms swinging, she headed for the *vaporetto* stop for the waterbus that would take her to the Dorsoduro district and the Guggenheim.

The *vaporetto* was packed and, not for the first time, Dulcie wondered how the rickety diesel-run motorboat kept afloat. Ahead of her, at the entrance to the Grand Canal and bathed in brilliant sunlight from a sky of powder blue, was the magnificent Baroque church of Santa Maria della Salute. It was true, Dulcie thought, that every way you turned in Venice there was a breathtaking view. Who needed physical love, when the senses could be touched so satisfyingly with this perfection?

The same thought struck her again that evening. It was irrelevant that *The Four Seasons* had become such a cliché; to hear it played in a church where the great composer himself had written and directed performances of his own work was an experience she would never forget.

During the interval, she looked across the nave and recognised an American couple from the hotel. They came over and introduced themselves; they were an engaging couple and Dulcie took an instant liking to them. Their names were Cathe, pronounced Cathy, and Randy Morris.

'How're you enjoying the concert?' Randy asked.

'I'm loving it. It's the perfect end to a perfect day. Have you visited Venice before?'

'We sure have. We came here for our honeymoon. We're doing a kind of re-enactment twenty-two years on, you could say.' The man put his arm round his tiny wife and looked deep into her eyes, in a gesture so loving that Dulcie was reminded of Richard. She caught her breath.

She spent the rest of the concert trying not to allow memories of Richard to intrude, forcing herself to focus on Venice and how much better she was feeling and what she had planned for tomorrow.

Jaz perched on the edge of her mother's bed. For once she was glad that her father had money: Mum had a private room.

'So how's everything at home?' her mother asked.

'Oh, I've got the girls well under my thumb,' Jaz said breezily. It was a lie, but she didn't want her mother to worry. She'd been in hospital for a week now, and her blood pressure was still too high for her to come home. There were other complications with her pregnancy too, so, no, she could not tell her mother that Tamzin and Lulu were as out of control as they had ever been. The good news was that, at Mum's insistence, Dad had got in touch with an agency and now Mrs Warner came in every day to cook, clean and do the ironing. She was a godsend.

They had visited Mum every day, but this evening Dad, Phin and

Jimmy were out on the town in Liverpool: it was St Patrick's Day and they probably wouldn't be home until the early hours. Friends, whose parents presumably hadn't met them, had invited Tamzin and Lulu for a sleep-over, so, for one fantastic night, it was just Jaz and her mum.

'Is anything bothering you, Jaz?'

'No. Why would you think that?'

'Your serious expression. How's college?'

'It's great, really.'

'So what *is* troubling you? Come on, Jaz, spill it all out. I want to know what's been going on behind my back. If you're worrying about upsetting me and sending my blood pressure off the chart, don't. There's no better place I could be for receiving bad news.'

Worn down by her mother's gentle insistence, and the need to talk to her, Jaz explained everything: about Hidden Talents; her reasons for her secrecy; and Dad's ban on her attending the group. 'They're a really nice bunch of people, Mum. There's nothing weird about them. Dulcie lives in a lovely house in Bloom Street where we meet, and she's the one who's in charge. And then there's Beth . . .' She hesitated, thinking of Nathan. 'I'll tell you about her in a minute. Jack's great, he's an estate agent in town and a really cool writer. Only trouble is, Phin and Jimmy jumped to the conclusion that something was going on between us.'

Her mother's eyes widened.

'There isn't, Mum. It was because Jack always gave me a lift home and they saw me in his car. How're you doing? Blood pressure OK?'

'Go on. I'm fine. Tell me more about the group.'

'Well, the only other person is Victor, and he's seriously cranky.'

'I thought you said there weren't any weirdoes?'

'He's the exception. Delusional too. He reckons he's writing the book of the century. God, Mum, he couldn't write a shopping list.'

Her mother laughed, reached out to Jaz and hugged her.

'What's that for?' Jaz asked, when her mother released her.

'For making me laugh. For taking my mind off being pregnant.'

'You're not angry, then?'

'I'm cross with your father for overreacting. So typical of him. Trouble is, he judges others by his own standards and mistakes: he was a terrible tearaway before he met me.' She sighed. 'But if that's the height of it, I'm sure I can sort it with your father. Leave it to me.'

But Jaz wanted to have everything out in the open. 'Um . . . actually, Mum, there is something else. Something I haven't told Dad. I've been seeing this really nice guy from the upper sixth. His name's Nathan King and his mother is the woman I mentioned earlier, Beth.'

'So what's wrong with him? Why keep him hidden from us? Is he covered from head to foot in tattoos and body piercings?'

'No! Nothing like that. He's great. But . . . but I didn't want anyone to know about him. I thought Phin and Jimmy would scare him off.'

Her mother gave her one of her soft, knowing looks. 'He wouldn't be much of a boyfriend if he was that easily put off. It's you he's interested in, not your brothers.'

Jaz took a moment to consider what her mother had said. She was right. Jaz had told countless lies because she had been convinced that the slightest thing would frighten Nathan away. But it wasn't just her insecurity that was to blame: pride had clouded her vision and caused just about the entire mess she now found herself in.

'Did you hear what I said, Jaz?'

'I'm sorry, Mum. I was thinking. But, yes, you're right.'

'Good. Now, when do I get to meet Nathan? Don't look so horrified. I ought to meet the young man so I can put Popeye's mind at rest.'

Jaz flung her arms round her mother. 'Oh, Mum, you're the best.'

Jaz rode home in the back of the taxi happier than she'd been in a long time. She let herself into the house and stood in the dark hall.

Instinctively she knew something was wrong. The burglar alarm wasn't on. Her mouth went dry and her heartbeat quickened. She walked nervously towards the sitting room. Holding her breath, she pushed open the door and switched on the light.

It was difficult to be certain, but it looked as if anything that had been worth taking was gone: hi-fi, telly, video player, silver ornaments, pictures. Worse, the place was trashed: sofas turned over, cushions ripped open, curtains pulled down, lamps and the glass-topped table smashed, walls and carpets smeared with God knew what.

'Don't worry, I'll be there in seconds. Just hang on.'

Nathan switched off his mobile and looked at Jack and his mother's concerned faces. 'Sorry to break into your two-man writing group, but Jaz's been burgled. I'm going round to make sure she's OK.'

'Is she on her own?'

He was already out in the hall pulling on his coat. 'Yes.'

'In that case,' his mother glanced briefly at Jack, who nodded, 'we're coming with you.'

Jack drove, and when they got there they found a police car in the drive and lights blazing from every window of the house. A WPC opened the door to them, and after they'd explained who they were, they were shown through to the kitchen, where Jaz was pacing the floor.

Nathan went straight to her. 'Dad'll kill me when he finds out,' she cried, holding him tight. 'He'll say I didn't put the alarm on. But I did.'

Another police officer joined them in the kitchen. He held a pair of wire cutters. 'The alarm's been tampered with. They broke in through the French windows in the dining room.'

It wasn't until the two police officers had gone, just after midnight, that Jaz managed to get an answer from her father on his mobile. 'It's OK Dad,' she said, when he allowed her to speak. 'I'm fine. I've got some friends here with me. Look, the place has been trashed. It's awful . . . every room . . .' When Jaz started to cry, Beth took over.

'Hello, Mr Rafferty. You don't know me, but I'm a friend of your daughter's from the writers' group. I'm here with my son and Jack, who's also from the group . . . Oh, thank you, but there's no need. Jaz is shaken but, on the whole, I'd say she's doing pretty well . . . No, there's nothing more to be done. The police have been and gone and Jack's boarded up the broken pane of glass. What I was going to suggest was, rather than you come rushing home, Jaz could stay the night with Nathan and me . . . OK, I'll hand you over to Jaz.'

'Thanks, Mum,' Nathan said, when they were back at the flat. Jack had gone downstairs and Jaz was in the bathroom, getting ready for bed.

'What for?'

'Being so nice.'

'Nice doesn't come into it. I wouldn't have dreamed of leaving the poor girl on her own. And there was no way her father could drive home. He and everyone he was with sounded as drunk as skunks.'

He was helping his mother to make up a bed on the sofa for Jaz when she appeared self-consciously in a pair of oversized Winnie-the-Pooh pyjamas. 'Don't you dare laugh,' she warned him.

'It never crossed my mind.'

'And if it does, you have my full permission to pinch him hard,' his mother said. 'Anyone for a drink before we turn in for the night? No? In that case, I'll wish you both sweet dreams.'

'I'm sorry I was a bit of a headcase earlier,' Jaz said, when they were alone and she was curled up beneath the duvet on the sofa.

'When was that? I must have missed it.'

She nudged him with her foot. 'Don't patronise me.'

'I wasn't.' He stroked her face. 'Anyway, how could I do that to someone wearing such a colossally cute pair of pyjamas.'

She laughed, and he moved in to kiss her. But she frowned and pushed him away. 'It's OK,' he said, 'I'm not going to do anything silly.' He smiled. 'Certainly not with my mother in the next room.' The frown vanished and she put her arms round him. He lay down next to her and closed his eyes. Before long they were both asleep.

In the morning, Beth found them lying on the sofa, her son fully dressed and wrapped in Jaz's arms. Who was protecting whom?

For a man who had to be nursing a monumental hangover, Jaz's father was hiding it well. As were her brothers, Beth suspected, handing round cups of coffee as if she was perfectly used to entertaining at this time of day: it was five to eight with college and work to get to. 'You must have been up early,' she said to Mr Rafferty. 'Sugar?'

He helped himself to three spoonfuls. 'I couldn't sleep for worrying. The boys and I hit the road at seven.'

'Have you been to the house yet, Dad?'

'No. I wanted to make sure you were OK first.'

'I'm fine.'

Her voice sounded tight and edgy and Beth could see that Jaz's main concern this morning had nothing to do with the burglary, but every-thing to do with Nathan being in the same room as her father and broth-ers. She hadn't so much as glanced at Nathan since her father's arrival.

Stirring his sugar-laden coffee, Mr Rafferty returned his attention to Beth. 'Look, Mrs King—'

'Please, it's Beth.'

'Well, Beth, I just want to say how grateful I am for what you and your son did last night. And this Jack bloke, I need to thank him as well. Holy Mother of God, what the sweet Fanny Adams is that?'

From beneath them came the noise that Beth had grown used to: Jack's builders starting work. They were a shambles. They arrived incon-veniently early and left shortly after lunch—Jack knew this because he'd seen their van driving past his office on Tuesday. Beth explained about Jack living downstairs and the work he was having done.

'Who's he got in to do it?' Mr Rafferty shouted, above the racket.

'I don't know their name. They're a small outfit, I think.' She told him how unreliable they were.

All three Rafferty men rolled their eyes. 'Bloody cowboys. If he needs someone decent, tell him to get in touch. I owe him.' Mr Rafferty handed Beth a business card. 'Right, then, are we set?' This was to Jaz.

'It's OK, Dad, I've got all my stuff for college. I'll walk with Nathan.'

'Don't be an eejit, Nathan can have a lift too. That OK with you, lad?' Nathan nodded. 'Thank you. I'll just get my things.'

While he was gone and Beth was clearing away the cups, she heard Jaz's father whisper, 'Nice boy that, Jaz. You could do a lot worse.'

With his track record for cocking things up, Jack should have known better than to court disaster by getting any building work done. The builders had done a runner, leaving the job half done and his flat practically uninhabitable. Beth told him to get in touch with Jaz's father. 'I got the feeling he'd do it for a good price as a favour to you. I received a gorgeous bouquet of flowers from him and he's had a change of heart regarding Jaz and Hidden Talents. Having seen for himself how normal I am, he's decided she can come back.'

That had been yesterday morning, Saturday, and since then things had moved apace. Jack had spoken to Mr Rafferty, feeling slightly guilty for bothering him at the weekend, and had arranged for one of his men to visit on Monday—tomorrow. Then he'd moved out of the flat to take up Dulcie's offer, having rung her in Venice to check it really was OK. 'Of course, Jack.' She'd asked if he'd got the group together on Thursday evening. 'What about Victor? What's the latest on him?'

'I tried ringing him as you asked, but the number doesn't work. If I have time during the week, I'll call on him one evening.'

He'd also told her that Jaz was allowed to join the group again, and about the writers' conference. Dulcie thought it was an excellent idea. He'd then gone through a few domestic details, finally saying goodbye, conscious that she had a holiday to get on with.

It was now eight o'clock and an age away from the Double Mac and fries he'd had for lunch with Amber and Lucy before driving them back to Prestbury. He started to fix himself some supper with the intention of getting down to Chapter Thirty-five afterwards. He reckoned he only had another five to do before *Friends and Family*—his first book—was finished. He liked the sound of that: his *first* book. He had a feeling that, now he had started, nothing would stop him. Writing was addictive.

He grilled some sausages and buttered some slices of soft white bread, adding a squirt of ketchup—which he had been surprised to find in Dulcie's kitchen—then sat down to eat his culinary masterpiece, but a ring of the doorbell stopped him mid-bite.

'Is . . . is Dulcie in?' the grey-haired man on the step asked awkwardly.

Jack hedged: 'Um . . . not just at the moment.'

Suspicion passed across the man's face. 'Can you tell me when she'll be back?' His voice was scarcely polite now.

'Sorry but I can't.'

'Look, I don't know who you are but, please, go and find Dulcie and say that Richard wants to speak to her. Please, do that much for me.'

Jack hadn't considered that while he was in Bloom Street the man from whom Dulcie had run away might turn up. There was something so desperate about him that Jack said, 'I think you'd better come in.'

Richard's hopes soared. At long last he was going to talk to Dulcie face to face. But when the stranger led him into the kitchen and he saw no sign of Dulcie, hope drained out of him. 'What's going on?' he demanded. 'Where's Dulcie? And who are you?'

'I'm a friend of hers,' the man said calmly. He held out his hand. 'Jack Solomon, a member of the writers' group.'

'And Dulcie?' Richard prompted, ignoring Jack's hand. 'Where is she?'

'She's away, and I'm house-sitting for her. Beer?'

'Away? Where?'

'On holiday.'

'Look,' Richard exclaimed, 'do you know who I am?'

'I know exactly who you are. You're Richard Cavanagh, Dulcie's ex-lover. Now, before you get any more uptight, why don't you just accept that until Dulcie returns from her holiday you won't be able to speak to her? Perhaps you should go home to your wife and children.'

The direct words brought Richard up short. 'How dare you?'

'A bit of straight talking too much for you?'

'Who the hell are you to judge me?'

'I'm a man who knows what it feels like to wake up one morning and find that his wife has been sleeping with someone else.'

Richard winced. He passed a hand across his face. Oh, hell. What could he say? 'I don't suppose that offer of a beer is still on, is it?'

They both drank in an awkward silence.

'This feels very peculiar,' Richard admitted.

'I know what you mean. And I'm sorry for coming on so strong. It's really none of my business what you and Dulcie have been up to.'

'I'm not making excuses, but I've never loved anyone the way I love Dulcie. I don't expect someone as young as you to appreciate that love is just as exhilarating and wonderful at my age as it is at yours. Dulcie means everything to me,' he said simply.

'Still? Even though she's finished with you?'

'I'll go on loving her for ever. Where's she staying, Jack?'

'I'm not sure she wants you to know. That's the point of her going away. She needed to put some distance between the two of you.'

Richard nodded. 'I understand. But she's got it wrong if she thinks a holiday will solve anything. I'll still be here when she comes home.'

'And your wife and family? Where will they be?'

He felt the stab of Jack's question. 'I've told Dulcie that if she wants to make a go of it, I'm prepared to bear the full brunt of the consequences.'

Jack fixed him with a disdainful stare. 'I have two young daughters who are currently bearing the full brunt of their mother's choice, so I know what I'm talking about when I say it's never the straightforward business you think it will be. How old are your children?'

Richard swallowed. This wasn't what he'd come here for. 'Please, if you don't mind, I'd rather not discuss my children.'

'No, I guess not. Another beer?'

'No, thanks.' Richard watched Jack help himself from Dulcie's fridge. He was about to try once more to get out of Jack where Dulcie was when a mobile rang. 'Excuse me a minute,' Jack said. 'Hi, Des, how's it going?' He wandered out into the hall.

Left on his own, Richard relaxed. Dulcie's house-sitter was a nice enough man, but there was something disturbingly judgmental about him. Richard glanced at Dulcie's noticeboard. On it was the name and address of a hotel in Venice. He looked out to the hall and, seeing that Jack was still deep in conversation, grabbed a pen and a square of paper and scribbled down the details. Just in time, he pocketed the scrap of paper as Jack came back into the kitchen.

'Sorry about that,' he said.

Richard waved aside his apology with a smile. 'No, it's me who should apologise. I'll leave you in peace now.'

Jaz and Nathan both had a free period so they were able to leave college early that Tuesday afternoon to go to the hospital.

When Jaz had asked Nathan if he'd like to meet her mother—'the sanest and nicest member of my family'—he'd agreed.

To Jaz's horror, her father was now encouraging her to go out with Nathan. 'He looks a regular decent boy to me,' he'd said at breakfast only that morning. 'Smart, too. I could do with a tame lawyer in the family. Think of the fees I'd save.'

'Dad!' she'd remonstrated. 'I'm only seventeen. I'm not thinking of marrying anyone, let alone Nathan King.'

'Aw, get away with you, girl. I'm looking to the future.'

Blushing to the ends of her toenails, she'd made a hasty exit. It was difficult to decide which was worse: her father taking a hard line with her or being too interested in fixing her up with Nathan. But at least he'd given her the go-ahead to rejoin Hidden Talents; Beth and Jack's kindness after the break-in had won him round.

But her father had much more to think about than Hidden Talents.

He had taken one look at the house and moved them lock, stock and barrel into the Maywood Grange Hotel. Jaz had never seen her father so angry, or so upset. Apart from Mum's jewellery, he wasn't bothered about the stuff that had been taken. 'That can all be replaced,' he'd said matter-of-factly. It was the damage that had been done to the house that incensed him. 'I built that house for your mother,' he'd said. 'It was her dream home. Now it's a friggin' nightmare.'

It had been a crazy few weeks, what with worrying about her mother being in hospital and the burglary, but the experience had forced Jaz to get things into perspective. As a result, she had come to see that *Having the Last Laugh* had been a cruel parody of her family. It had had its funny moments but, overall, it had been childishly spiteful. Where had been the depth and integrity she so admired in other writers?

Once her father had overcome his anger, he had pulled out all the stops to get the house put right. An army of professional cleaners had worked round the clock, and now the decorators were doing their bit. When they had finished, every carpet was to be replaced. And all so that Mum would never know the worst of it.

At the hospital, Jaz reminded Nathan not to say a word about the burglary to her mother. He took her hand as she poked her head round her mother's door. She was relieved to see that her mother was looking better. 'Hello, Mum, how are you?'

'All the better for seeing you.' She put down the magazine she'd been reading. 'Ah, now you must be Nathan. Close the door and come on in.'

They drew up two chairs and Nathan handed over a prettily wrapped box of chocolates. 'I thought you might like these,' he said. 'That's if they're allowed.' He glanced at the large basket of fruit on the other side of the bed.

'They'll make a welcome change from the healthy stuff I'm being forced to eat. This morning I woke up starving.' She took the box from Nathan and thanked him. 'We'll have one right now, shall we?'

Jack could think of any number of ways he would rather spend his evening, but he'd promised Dulcie he would call on Victor.

He knocked at the door. Knocked again.

Nothing. It had been the same when Dulcie had tried to call on Victor. 'But I felt sure he was in,' she'd said. 'Don't ask me how, I just felt it.'

Jack felt it too. Standing back from the house, he looked up at the windows, which were thick with grime. Was it his imagination or was there a flicker of light coming from one of the upstairs windows? He decided to see if he could get round to the back.

He walked along the rear of the properties until he drew level with Victor's. Looking up at the back of the house, he realised that what he'd thought to be a softly glowing light was a fire. Victor's house was on fire.

He phoned for the emergency services on his mobile, then tried the gate. It was locked. He threw his weight against the rotting timber, burst through it and stumbled into the small back yard. The door into the house was locked, but he seized a wooden broom and swung it at the kitchen window.

Once inside, he called to Victor as he peered into the dining room, then the sitting room. He got no response so he went back to the kitchen, grabbed a tea towel and shoved it under the cold tap. When it was soaking, he took a deep breath and made for the stairs. On the smoke-filled landing, with the wet cloth pressed to his face, he braved the room where the source of the fire was. Thick smoke stung his eyes and made them water. He forced them to stay open, and saw a body on the floor: flames were licking over and around it. He pushed himself forward, grasped Victor under his armpits, and dragged him from the room. Out on the landing, he took off his jacket, wrapped it around Victor's apparently lifeless body to snuff out his smouldering clothes. Then he heaved him down the stairs, to the hall, where he laid Victor on the floor, and allowed himself to catch his breath. Just as the shock hit him of what he'd done, and what might happen if he didn't get out of the house fast, he heard the high-pitched wail of a siren. Jack fumbled with the front-door lock and carried Victor to safety. Within seconds a team of firemen were on the scene.

Jack rode in the ambulance with Victor to the hospital. His own injuries were superficial—a raw soreness in his throat and chest, a few burns—nothing that wouldn't heal within a week or two. But Victor looked like he'd be damned lucky to live.

Chapter Ten

WITH THE CURTAINS DRAWN BACK, Dulcie lay in bed looking at the surrounding jumble of rooftops and chimneys. She was thinking what a perfect way it was to start the day.

She had been in Venice for over a week now. She had never felt so settled in a foreign place as she did here, and her writing was flowing effortlessly. The muse's reappearance was a sign that she was almost back to normal. It meant that she could think of the future and getting on with her life without Richard.

She had thought hard about the writers' conference Jack had mentioned on the phone, and had concluded that it would be a marvellous opportunity for them all. If it was well run there would be interesting guest speakers to learn from, tutors on hand to give advice, and possibly one or two agents and editors to talk to. She hadn't said anything to Jack, but she harboured a real hope that he might be 'discovered'. He wrote so compellingly, with such incisive honesty, that she was convinced *Friends and Family* was publishable. What she liked most about Jack was that he had no inkling of the extent of his talent. Too often would-be writers had an overly inflated view of themselves and their work. Would-be writers such as poor old Victor. Any dislike or critical views she had once held for Victor had now been subdued by her concern that something was terribly wrong with the man. She hoped that Jack had found the time to call on him.

A glance at her travel clock on the bedside table told her it was time to get up. She was having breakfast with Cathe then going on a trip to the islands in the northern lagoon with her. Randy had opted to forgo the excursion, saying he had some important phone calls to make.

They paid for their tickets and joined the chattering group of tourists who had already climbed aboard the boat and taken their seats. Last to get on was their guide for the day, an exceedingly handsome Italian man of about the same age as Dulcie.

Murano was their first stop, and their guide, Antonio, filled them in with some background information. His English was excellent and he explained how Murano had been the centre of the glass-making industry since the thirteenth century. 'Here,' he told them, 'mirrors were made a long time before anyone else thought of it. And spectacles too. It is thought that they were also invented here. It is truly a marvellous and creative place. Come, I take you now to see some glass-blowers at work. And then I invite you to join me in the showroom to see the many splendours on offer for you to purchase and take home.'

Following Antonio, Cathe said, 'Don't you just love the understated way they try to relieve us of our dollars?'

Most of what was for sale—stunning handmade chandeliers and exquisite sets of wineglasses—was wildly expensive; both Dulcie and Cathe settled for some modestly priced scent bottles. Next the tour moved on to the island of Burano. 'This is the prettiest of the islands in the lagoon,' boasted Antonio, handing out maps. 'Nowhere else will you find such a collection of colourful houses. But before all that excitement, we stop for lunch.' He smiled broadly. 'Where I promise you will taste the best fish in the best trattoria on Burano.'

Everyone laughed, by now used to Antonio's gilding of the lily.

'Sì,' he exclaimed, 'I know this restaurant to be the best because it is my youngest son Giorgio who runs it. I will meet you there in thirty minutes.' He offered his hand to Dulcie, who was last to get off, and said, 'You permit me to invite you to join me for a drink before lunch?'

Dulcie was so taken aback that she nearly lost her footing. He held her firmly. 'Was that such a dreadful shock to you?'

'Yes,' she said, flustered. 'I'm afraid it isn't possible. I'm here with a friend and it would be rude of me to abandon her.'

But Cathe had gone on ahead, a grin on her small elegant face.

'It looks to me as if you are the one who has been abandoned,' he observed, with a smile. He took her to a bar in a shady square and ordered two Bellini cocktails.

'You look surprised,' he commented, when the waiter brought them.

'I am,' she said. 'It doesn't look the kind of place that would serve a cocktail. Or do they keep a bottle of Prosecco here specially for you?'

He laughed and raised his glass. 'Here is to many more surprises for you during your stay in Venice. How long are you here for? But wait, before you answer that tell me your name.'

She swallowed a refreshing mouthful of sparkling wine and fresh peach juice. 'It's Dulcie, and I've been here for just over a week.'

'Dulcie, that is an unusual name, is it not?'

'I suppose it is. It comes from the Latin *dulcis*, meaning—'

'Sweet,' he finished for her. 'Yes, I am a man of education. The name suits you. Is there a husband for the sweet-natured English lady?'

'No.'

'Divorced?'

'Widowed.'

'Ah. I am sorry. Did your husband die recently?'

'No.'

He drained his glass. 'One-word answers, they tell me to mind my own business. You are here on holiday to enjoy yourself, not to be interrogated by an Italian man with too much curiosity. Come, it is time for us to join the rest of the group and your American friend.'

Dulcie hurriedly finished her Bellini. 'Thank you for the drink,' she said. 'I enjoyed it.'

'*Prego*. I almost believe you.' He slipped his sunglasses on, making her feel as if he'd pulled down the shutters on their conversation.

'Look,' she said, feeling as if she owed him an explanation, 'it isn't anything personal, I'm just quite a private person.'

He led her across the square. 'And do such private people ever risk having dinner with men they hardly know?'

'It's only dinner,' Dulcie had to keep reminding herself later, waiting for Antonio in the hotel foyer, as arranged. Then why did she feel that she was being disloyal to Richard? It was ridiculous. Richard was a married man whom she'd sensibly shooed off back to his wife, where he belonged. Now she could do as she pleased. She was a free agent.

She didn't have to wait long: Antonio appeared through the revolving door almost at once. Steering her out of the hotel, he said, 'I have booked a table at my favourite restaurant near the Rialto Bridge.'

Dulcie soon discovered that Antonio was known to nearly every local they came across. 'I have lived in Venice all my life,' he explained, when they were sitting down with a ringside view of the brightly illuminated Grand Canal, 'apart from a brief time in London when I was a student.'

'What were you studying?'

'I was a medical student, training to be a doctor.'

'Really?'

'Aha, once again I have surprised you! Yes, the simple guide turns out to be more than you thought.'

'That's not fair,' she said defensively. 'My husband was a doctor. I was merely thinking of the coincidence.' She took the menu their waiter handed to her, wondering why on earth she was here being goaded by this monstrously egotistical Italian. 'So what kind of doctor were you?'

'An excellent one!'

'You're impossible.'

He said, 'I was an eye surgeon at the local hospital here in Venice, but I retired two years ago, not long after my wife passed away.'

'And you became a tourist guide?'

'No, I became an *excellent* tourist guide.'

He was incorrigible, but he was amusing company, she decided, and felt herself relax into the evening. The spotlight soon turned away from Antonio and onto her. He wanted to know why she was travelling alone. In the end she told him much more than she had intended.

'So this Richard from whom you are running, you still love him?'

'Yes.' The admission was out before she could stop it.

He topped up her glass. 'I do not understand this need you have to punish your heart so cruelly.'

'It's for the best. For Kate and Henry, for Richard's wife and his sons.'

'But not the best for Dulcie. Or Richard, I would dare to suggest. To have pestered you so intensely before you came away shows the strength of his love for you.' Suddenly he leaned forward in his seat. 'Dulcie,' he said, 'permit me to be straight with you. I believe you have made a terrible mistake. To be blunt, at our age we have to grab the chances that come our way. Let the young people, Kate and Henry, sort themselves out. If they truly love each other they will find a way to continue their relationship.' He held up a hand to stop her interrupting him. 'Please, I know what you are going to say, but you are wasting your time protecting Richard's wife. By being honest about your love for Richard, you will give his wife the opportunity to find her own happiness and she will stop clinging desperately to a man who loves another. There, I have finished. It is now your turn to speak.'

But Dulcie couldn't. She was literally struck dumb by the man's audacity . . . and maybe by the sense of what he'd said.

Dear Beth,

I have the distinct impression that you are hiding from me. Is it something I said? Did I push you too hard over the writers' conference? Just because I'm a writer, it doesn't mean I'm any good at subtexts. If I've done anything to offend you, please don't hesitate to show me the error of my ways.

Yours, confused-and-disappointed-of-Suffolk, Ewan

Beth finished reading Ewan's email, then, without giving herself a chance to change her mind, she clicked on REPLY and started typing fast.

Dear Ewan,

Please, please, PLEASE don't berate yourself. My silence had nothing to do with you, but everything to do with me. Or, rather, everything to do with being so embarrassed. I'm ashamed to say that when I last emailed you I was disgustingly drunk. Truly, I am the most temperate of souls, and please believe me I wouldn't dream of sending such an outrageous message in a more sober state.

She went on to tell him about the Raffertys' house being broken into and of Jack staying at Dulcie's while she was away in Venice recovering from the end of her affair with Richard.

But more dramatic than any of this is, was that Jack called round to see Victor, only to find his house on fire. Jack had to smash a window to get in and rescue Victor, who is now in hospital recovering from the most awful burns. It looks as if the fire was started by a candle falling onto a pile of papers. When Jack and I visited him, we had to break the news to him that his manuscript had perished in the fire and he doesn't have a copy of it. It was heartbreaking to see him cry, Ewan. Poor man, he was utterly devastated. He doesn't seem to have any friends or family, and from what the nurses tell us, we're his only visitors.

Well, that's about the height of it this end. Oh, only to add that my in-laws are away on their cruise and Barnaby emailed me from the ship (such technology!) to say that all was going very well. I've also been to see my old neighbour, Adele, who's enjoying the retirement home she's moved into. Nathan is at the cinema with Jaz, which leaves me with a quiet evening to do some writing.

Best wishes, Beth

PS I've decided to take the plunge and go to the writers' conference. Jack's coming too, to act as my chaperon.

She clicked on SEND, then logged off. There, she'd done it. She'd put the humiliating incident behind her and committed herself to meeting Ewan. Anticipation outweighed any last remnants of her embarrassment, and happiness swelled inside her.

It was a long time since she had experienced the butterfly sensation in her stomach at the prospect of meeting a man, but there was no denying that she felt it now. Having decided to go to Harrogate, her next hurdle was telling Nathan about Ewan. She didn't have to, but she felt she should. Trouble was, she knew what his reaction would be: 'After all those lectures you gave me about not talking to strange men in public loos, you've struck up an email relationship with an unknown man?'

It was gone eleven when she finished writing and, knowing that Nathan would be back soon, she logged on to see if, on the off chance, Ewan had responded to her email.

Do my eyes deceive me? Or is this really an email I see before me from my sweet maiden in Maywood? Gadzooks, it is!

And what an extraordinary time you've been having. That poor guy Victor has my full sympathy.

I'm polishing my shoes in readiness for meeting you at the conference. I know all too well that women judge men by their shoes: you know you won't find me wanting in that oh-so-crucial department.

Now to a tricky problem. Since your last email, I've been stock-piling bars of chocolate, but now it appears I won't have a use for them. Any ideas what I should do with two dozen catering packs of Fruit and Nut? Time to dash for the bunker. I feel a Scud missile heading this way from Maywood.

Yours, so-very-glad-to-hear-from-you, Ewan X
PS Please don't waste any more energy worrying about THAT email.
It will be wiped from the memory banks, as of now.

Hearing Nathan's key in the lock, Beth logged off hurriedly and decided that now was the time to tell him about Ewan.

The pleasing rhythm of Dulcie's stay in Venice had changed subtly.

Cathe and Randy had left for home first thing in the morning; already she felt their absence. And home was somewhere *she* would have to return soon. Antonio's words during dinner, two nights ago, had had an effect on her. Was there a chance he had been right? If so, could she really put her own happiness above anyone else's?

'Trust me, these things resolve themselves, Dulcie,' Antonio had said as he walked her back to her hotel that night. 'If only we let them.'

Now it was just gone two o'clock and she had been wandering the labyrinth of alleyways in the San Marco district. Finding herself in the Campo San Stefano, she decided to stop for a late lunch. While she ate, she took out her notepad and pen and continued with the short story she had started yesterday. Before she knew it, two hours had sped by. She paid her bill and set off for the *vaporetto* to return to the hotel.

As they approached the landing stage, Dulcie shaded her eyes from the glare of the afternoon sun. For the craziest moment, she thought she saw Richard among the blur of tourists. She strained her eyes. Yes, unbelievably it *was* him. Her heart thumped wildly as she willed the boat to stop. At last she was off. On the waterfront, she almost broke into a run. She feared now she would lose track of Richard, but, amazingly, she caught sight of him again. He was side on to her, his gaze fixed rigidly on the rows of gondolas gleaming in the sunshine. He didn't hear her approach until she said, 'It's a stunning view, isn't it?'

He turned, did a double take, then flung his arms round her. The strength of his embrace was so great it nearly knocked her off her feet.

'Oh, Dulcie, don't be cross with me,' he said, clasping her hands in his. 'Don't be angry that I followed you here. Just let me talk to you. Hear what I've got to say, then I'll go . . . if you want me to.'

She took him back to the Hotel Isabella. Smiling broadly, Alberto handed over her key. 'And, Signor Cavanagh, *your key?*'

Dulcie glanced at Richard as he took it. He looked shamefaced. 'It's a long story, and I'm aware how devious I must seem. Forgive me?'

'Nothing to forgive,' she said, still dazed with shock that he was here. She let them into her room. She stood for a moment at the foot of the bed, acknowledging that words could wait: now she wanted to feel

Richard close to her. She wanted to lie beside him and feel the tender warmth of his hands on her body. But if she allowed that to happen, as she knew she would, she would never let him go.

Behind her, she heard him moving. She felt his breath on her neck as he gently pressed his lips to her skin: oh, he'd always known the effect it had on her. He turned her round and kissed her. They made love in silence, with an intensity that left them both exhausted.

All thoughts of a concert that evening were abandoned, and as Dulcie and Richard lay in bed, he explained how he'd found her. 'I went to see you, and found myself confronted by a strange man who refused point-blank to tell me where you were staying.'

'So how did you find out where I was?'

'It was on your notice board in the kitchen. I wanted to book the first flight available, but I had to wait for things to calm down at work. I was convinced, the way my luck was going, that I'd arrive too late.'

She ran her fingers over his chest and said, 'What happens when we go home, Richard?'

He took her hand and raised it to his lips. 'I do what I should have done a long time ago. I tell Angela the truth. I've been a coward and I'm not prepared to go on hurting either of you the way I have till now.'

'Are you sure you want to do this, Richard? The ramifications will go on for the rest of our lives.'

'I know, but I love you, Dulcie, and while I won't be able to offer you all that I'd like to in the way of financial security, I must see Angela and the boys established—'

She removed her hand from his, stopping him short. 'Richard, I don't care what money you may or may not have. All I expect you to bring to our relationship is commitment and honesty.'

After dinner, arm in arm, they went for a stroll. It was a perfect night wrapped in moonlight and gently lapping water. I shall always remember this night, Dulcie thought, as beneath a starry sky they lingered on a tiny bridge overlooking a narrow waterway of shimmering inky blue.

Standing behind her, his arms round her, Richard said, 'One day, when we're married, we'll come back here and stand on this same spot and I shall tell you that you've made me the happiest man alive.'

'Not before then?'

'No.' He turned her round to face him. 'I want us to be married as soon as we can. I wish it could be tomorrow, but I'm afraid we have to be patient.'

She shushed him with a kiss. 'One step at a time.'

Victor was sick of people telling him how lucky he was to have survived. Would any of those infuriating nurses feel lucky if they were going through this pain? The worst of his burns were around his neck, chest, right shoulder, arm and hand, and there would have to be skin grafts. His throat and lungs were still suffering from the effect of smoke inhalation; he could only speak in a hoarse whisper.

He didn't remember a thing about the fire. Jack had explained that he'd found him on the floor and had carried him downstairs. He'd also told him that there was no sign of his manuscript in the room where the fire had started. To his shame he had cried when he'd heard this. Both Jack and the policeman had said the damage to his house was confined to just two rooms. But were they telling him the truth? To be honest, he didn't want to go home. What they didn't know was that the insurance company wouldn't pay up. Because of his redundancy, he'd let the monthly payments slip. If his throat hadn't hurt so much, he would have cried out his frustration.

The next morning brought a troupe of trainee doctors to gawp at him. Lunchtime came and went, followed by a bossy nurse who spent an age fiddling with his dressings and made him cry with the pain. Hours later he woke to find a girl staring down at him.

'Hello, Victor, how's it going?'

He closed his eyes. 'I'm tired. I just want to sleep.'

'That's OK. I'll sit here and eat my way through these grapes.'

He forced his eyes open. 'You're that lippy girl from the writing group.'

Jaz grinned. 'Nice one, Victor. How are you?'

'How do you think I am?'

'Well, for a man who's gone through what you've been through, I reckon you don't look so bad. The sexy voice is an improvement.'

'If you've come here to mock me, have your fun, then go.'

'Now why do you think I'd do a thing like that?'

'Why else would you be here?'

'To see how you are. Oh, and I brought you these.' She delved into a small rucksack, pulled out a newspaper and a box of chocolates. 'There's an article about you and Jack. Because of you, he's a hero.'

'I thought you said something about grapes.'

'I was kidding. Of course, if you'd rather have the vitamin C, I could take the choccies away and bring you something healthy instead.'

'No,' he said. 'I'll make do with those.'

She laughed. 'Good to see you've not lost your touch, Victor. You're still a miserable old goat.'

He stared at her, incensed. 'How dare you talk to me like that?'

'I dare because you're stuck there in bed unable to do anything about it. Now, when are you going to start writing again?'

'That's none of your business.'

'Yes, it is. We're members of a writers' group. We're supposed to support and encourage each other.'

He sighed. His voice was growing weaker and the pain in his throat was getting worse. 'I doubt I'll be able to hold a pen for months.'

She looked at him solemnly. 'Is it very bad?'

He swallowed, and to his horror tears filled his eyes. With an effort that sent waves of unbearable pain shooting through him, he turned his head. 'I'd like you to go now.'

To his immense relief, he heard her get to her feet. But the relief was short-lived. 'I'll see you tomorrow, Victor. Take care, won't you?'

Jack had said he would visit Victor during the afternoon, between clients and, with Beth working late, Jaz had said she would do the evening slot. It fitted in well with seeing her mother first.

Jaz had been warned by Beth that Victor looked awful, but nothing had prepared her for the sight of him. He was straight out of a horror movie. She'd done her best yesterday to hide her shock and had chatted to him as though nothing was wrong, even being rude to convince him she wasn't there out of pity. When he'd started to cry, she hadn't known what to do or say—other than to go, as he'd requested. But she was back to see him today, as she'd said she would be.

Victor was lying in exactly the same position as he'd been in yesterday, flat on his back, staring up at the ceiling.

'Hi, Victor,' she said. 'What's new?' She noticed that the box of chocolates she'd given him yesterday had been opened.

'Nothing's new,' he whispered morosely.

She sat down next to his bed. 'I've just been to see my mother—did I tell you she was here? She's expecting twins . . .'

She rambled on, chattering, telling him about the burglary and the house being wrecked. 'They messed up all my college work, but I've managed to sort it out.'

A flicker of something, possibly understanding, passed across his face and he said, 'What about your writing?'

'Ah. Long story. I decided to ditch it. I'm waiting for inspiration to hit me so I can start something new. What will you do next?'

'I'll give up.'

She was shocked. 'You'll do no such thing,' she said. 'If I can start again, so can you.'

'I think we can safely say our circumstances are very different.'

'And that's where you're wrong. We have one very important quality in common with each other: we're writers. And once a writer, always a writer. You just need to get going again. Once you start using your brain again, you'll soon be feeling less sorry for yourself.'

'Sorry for myself?' he echoed, in a hoarse whisper. 'Next you'll be telling me to pull myself together.'

She smiled. 'I hadn't thought of that. It's not a bad idea, is it?' What spurred her to carry on talking to him in this no-nonsense way was the hope that, while she had his attention, he wasn't thinking about his injuries. 'OK, that's me done here. I've got a stack of homework to get through this evening.' She stood up. 'Shall I come again tomorrow?'

She had to hide a smile of satisfaction when, in a tired, strained voice, he said, 'Perhaps you could bring me a book to read.'

'Consider it done.'

Despite knowing what he would have to face when he and Dulcie returned home, Richard had never enjoyed a day more. For a brief period he and Dulcie had been an ordinary couple. There had been no fear of a chance encounter with someone who knew them. And this was how the rest of their lives would be, once the initial horror of telling Angela that he wanted a divorce had passed. They were returning home tomorrow. Returning, paradoxically, to the future. *Their* future.

While Dulcie was in the bath, he checked his mobile to see if there were any messages—there was only one, from Juliette at the office.

'Sorry to do this, Richard, but I needed to get hold of you. I thought you ought to know that I've just spoken to your wife and, well, I had no idea you were on a course in Bristol. I thought you were on holiday. Hope I haven't caused any problems. Speak to you soon. Bye.'

Oh, hell. It had started.

It was raining when they landed at Manchester Airport. The dirty grey sky and the strong gusting wind that met them were a far cry from the beautiful weather they'd enjoyed in Venice.

As she held Richard's hand, Dulcie's heart went out to him. Shortly after he'd listened to Juliette's message, Angela had phoned. 'Exactly where are you?' she'd asked. 'Because I know you're not in Bristol.'

'Angela, please, I'll be home tomorrow. We can discuss it then.'

'I want to discuss it *now*. You're . . . you're having an affair, aren't you?'

'Angela—'

'Please tell me it isn't true,' she had cried. 'Tell me I've got it wrong.'

'I'm sorry, but it is true.'

She had ended the call. Ten minutes later Richard had tried ringing her back, but the line was engaged: either she was speaking to someone else or she had taken the phone off the hook.

It was still raining hard as Richard drove home. He was thinking of the day he'd first met Dulcie. Until then he had never believed in anything as rhapsodic as love at first sight. But it had happened. He hadn't intended it to: he had always dismissed men who embarked upon affairs, but he'd been unable to withstand the force of his attraction to this unusual woman. With her sense of fun and independence, her uncomplicated love of life, she made the world seem a better place. Oh, if only they had met in their twenties. What a rich and fulfilling life they would have had together.

He swung through the gates and came to a stop in front of the garage. Inside the house it was eerily quiet. He put down his case at the foot of the stairs and called to Angela. No reply.

Without removing his raincoat, he went through to the kitchen. No sign of her there either. But, on stopping to look out of the window, he saw her sheltering beneath an umbrella at the bottom of the garden. His heart thudded. He walked over the lawn and called softly, 'Angela, what are you doing out here?'

She turned, slowly, as if she had been waiting for him. He could see that she'd been crying. His heart thudded painfully.

'Oh, Richard . . . why? Why have you done this to us?'

'I'm sorry,' he said, 'more sorry than I'll ever be able to say.'

'I don't understand. I thought we were happy.'

'I . . . I changed. I became someone different. I didn't mean to.'

Tears flowed down her cheeks. She said, 'I suppose it's some young girl from the office. A pretty bit of ego-boosting fluff half my age.'

'Don't do this, Angela.'

She sniffed defiantly. 'Why not? Why shouldn't I be allowed to know who you've been with? Is she very pretty? Is she—' Her voice faltered and she began to cry in earnest, her sobs loud and choking.

He stepped forward, took the handle of the umbrella and walked her back to the house. He sat her in the kitchen and knelt on the floor at her side. And still she cried. 'I'm sorry,' he said. 'I never meant to hurt you.'

She lifted her tear-soaked face to his. 'Tell me about—about this other woman. I want to know. I *need* to know.'

'It's Dulcie. Dulcie Ballantyne.' He heard her sudden intake of breath. And then, unbelievably, he heard her laugh. It was a cruel, mocking laugh, which he'd never heard from her before.

'But she's *old*! She's not even remotely beautiful,' Angela said. 'My God, Richard, is that the best you can do?'

'You don't have to resort to being spiteful,' he said.

'Oh, that's wonderful. That woman can wreck my marriage but I'm not allowed to say a word about her age or her crabby old looks.'

Richard kept his face impassive. 'I know you're upset and angry, Angela, but if we're going to sort this mess out, we need to remain calm.'

'Right, so what happens now?' Angela said. 'Do I make you promise never to see her again and we carry on as if nothing has happened? Or do I, for the sake of the boys, have to accept that there'll always be this . . . this third person in our marriage?'

His heart slammed against his ribs. 'I'm afraid neither of those options will work, Angela. I want a divorce. But I want you to know that nothing here will change. This will always be your home. You won't have to worry about money. I'll see to all that.'

'A divorce? You can't be serious.'

'I'm sorry, but I am. I—I want to marry Dulcie.'

She shook her head. 'No. No you don't. You're having a silly mid-life crisis.' Her voice had reached a high hysterical pitch. 'It's because you had a heart attack, isn't it? So, when did the affair start? After our Boxing Day party?'

He knew the truth would hurt, but she had to know he was serious about Dulcie. 'Since I first met her, when we were house-hunting.'

Angela's mouth dropped open, a small cry escaped her, and then she fled from the room, crashing the door after her.

Chapter Eleven

THE FLAT WAS LOOKING less like a bombsite now and more like the airy, comfortable home Jack had envisaged. He had Rafferty & Sons to thank for that. The men Patrick Rafferty had organised to do the job were one hundred per cent reliable and planned to finish the job next week.

Now, as Jack stood in the soon-to-be demolished kitchen beneath the harsh glare of a fluorescent strip light, he went through his mail. The only envelope of any interest was from the organisers of the writers' conference in Harrogate. They had sent him several copies of the programme with some application forms. He slipped the pieces of paper back into the envelope and took it upstairs with him. Yet again Beth was bestowing more neighbourly generosity on him.

Nathan opened the door. 'Hi, Jack. Mum's just getting changed, she won't be long. Jaz and I have nearly got supper ready. Don't look so worried, we washed our hands before we started.'

'That's not worry on my face, Nathan, it's awe. Hello, Jaz. What's cooking?'

'Chilli con carne.'

'And pudding?'

Banoffee pie.'

'Now I *am* impressed. Anything I can do to help?'

'Absolutely not,' said Nathan. 'We promised Mum a night off, and we're not going to be accused of being incapable because we've taken on extra help.'

Beth joined them in the sitting room. 'Aren't they sweet, Jack? I'm racking my brains as to what they're after. The car? Money?'

During the meal they caught up with each other's news. Anyone observing them, thought Jack, as they laughed and joked, would think they were a regular family. The thought made him sad: he wished Amber and Lucy were there too.

Shaking off his thoughts, he said, 'How was Victor when you saw him yesterday?'

'Actually, Jack,' Jaz replied, 'he's being almost polite to me.'

'And she's being too modest to sing her own praises,' said Beth. 'Against all the odds, Jaz has got Victor writing again.'

'No? How?'

'She was downright rude to him, from what I can gather. Shook him by his singed shoulders and told him to stop whinging,' said Nathan.

'You're all making too big an issue of it,' said Jaz. 'He asked me to take in a book for him, so I gave him a notepad and pen as well, just in case anything came to him in the middle of the night.'

Beth passed her the basket of garlic bread. 'I think you've been brilliant. You even got him to admit that he'd been made redundant.'

'I just gave him the opportunity to talk. It must have been hard on him, losing his job like that, after so many years.' She bit into a piece of garlic bread. 'Do you want to know what my latest plan for Victor is? Now that Dulcie's back, I think we ought to start up the group again and hold our meetings at the hospital so that he can join in.'

Jack looked at Beth. 'Can we do that? Will the hospital allow so many of us to visit at the same time?'

'I don't see why not, so long as we don't make too much noise and only stay for the specified time.'

'And who'd have thought we cared enough about him?'

Beth glanced at the burns that had almost healed on his hands. 'There speaks the hero who risked his own life to rescue Victor. And talking of Dulcie, how do you think she's faring? I did ask her to join us tonight, but she said she wasn't in the mood for company.'

It was four days since Dulcie had returned from Venice and they'd learned that her affair with Richard was now back on and out in the open. As for what would happen next, Dulcie had refused to comment.

'I haven't a clue,' Jack said, in answer to Beth's question. 'She doesn't give much away, but when I called round last night to thank her properly for letting me use her house, she seemed OK-ish.'

'I still can't believe that Dulcie's been having an affair,' said Jaz, scraping up the last of her dessert. 'She just doesn't seem the sort.'

'Why's that?' asked Beth, with a wry smile. 'You wouldn't be casting aspersions on her age, would you?'

Jaz missed the implied criticism. 'There is that. But, well, she seems so nice and normal, not the man-eater type. The opposite, in fact.'

'I didn't know adulterers had a certain look. What would it be? A lascivious leer?'

Jaz rolled her eyes. 'Don't be obtuse, Nathan.'

While Beth made the coffee, Jack pondered this thought. Had he demonised Maddie and Tony because of their actions? Weren't they really just two people who had fallen in love?

From across the kitchen, while she waited for the kettle to boil, Beth watched Jack's face growing ever more solemn. She could guess what he was thinking of. How long, she wondered, would it be before he could think of Maddie and Tony without it hurting?

To lighten the mood for his benefit, she said, 'You wouldn't believe what I've had to put up with these last few days, Jack. I told Nathan about Ewan and it's been nonstop innuendoes, warnings and advice.'

'Honestly, I teach her how to use the Internet and the next thing I know she's cosying up with some bloke. Irresponsible or what?'

'Oh, give your mother a break, Nathan. I think it's *so* romantic.'

Beth blushed. 'It's not like that, Jaz. We're just friends. How could it be anything else when we haven't met?'

'But that's about to change,' said Jack. '*Voilà!* Application forms for the writers' conference. What's more, Beth, you and I are going to sit here this evening and fill them in, ready for posting tomorrow morning.'

Late that night, Beth switched on her computer hoping there would be a message from Ewan. There was.

Dear Madly Teased of Maywood,

Oh, how I feel for you! There's nothing like the brutal teasing of one's offspring to make one squirm. I wish I could reassure your son that my intentions are perfectly honourable, but I fear I'll be whistling in the wind. If he's anything like Alice he'll have made up his mind that you're incapable of making a reasoned decision for yourself. It's called love, Bethany. Don't be too hard on him. Because of your circumstances, he's had to grow up very quickly (as Alice did) and has assumed responsibility for you.

Anyway, I must away and do some writing. If you don't hear from me over the next couple of days, worry not, it'll be a hectic schedule that's kept me from getting in touch, not a moody turn.

All the best, Ewan X

Nathan came and stood next to her. She sensed he wanted to say something important.

'Mum? You will be careful, won't you?'

'I know what you're saying, but do you have any idea *how* careful I've been all these years? I'm tired of being so circumspect. Everyone else is allowed to have some fun and take the occasional risk. Why can't I?' She sighed. 'Can we call a truce? No more lectures?'

'Maybe just the odd one. To counter the hundreds of warnings you give me every time I go out in the car.'

She reached up and, just as he often did to her, ruffled his immaculate hair. 'Touché.'

Fourteen days after they'd flown home from Venice, Richard moved in with Dulcie. He brought with him clothes, a selection of his favourite books, a small album of photographs, some files, and a heavy heart. Seeing him so downcast, so worn down and wretched, Dulcie had doubts about what they had done. 'You don't have to do this,' she told him, as she watched him hang his clothes in the wardrobe she'd cleared for him. 'It's not too late to change your mind.'

'Is that what you think is going through my head?'

'You wouldn't be the man I love if you weren't wondering whether you were doing the right thing.'

He tossed the remaining clothes onto the bed and came to stand with her in front of the window. He stroked her cheek. 'Thank you,' he said.

'For what?'

'For always allowing me to be me. For giving me the space to doubt and yet not be doubted.'

In the days immediately after Richard had told Angela the truth, the phone seemed never to stop ringing. The first person to ring her had been Richard, to say that Angela now knew everything.

'It's going to take a while, Dulcie. She's going to need a lot of help to recover from the shock. I can't just walk away immediately.'

'I understand. Believe me, I do. However long it takes, Richard.'

The following morning Kate had phoned her. It was the call Dulcie had dreaded most. Disbelief, anger and horror were at the top of Kate's agenda and Dulcie could say nothing to appease her daughter.

'Oh, Mum, you of all people! How could you?'

'I don't see what makes me any different from anyone else.'

'But with a married man! And young children are involved.' Kate's voice was shrill with condemnation and righteous disgust.

'I'm well aware of the situation, Kate. Are you sure your view of me isn't coloured by the delicate position in which you now find yourself?' Dulcie enquired, with an edge to her voice.

It was then that she felt the full force of Kate's wrath. 'I'm in no such position, Mum. For your information, and because of your sordid goings-on, Henry's dumped me. How does that make you feel?'

'How very shortsighted of him,' Dulcie said drily, recalling Antonio's advice in Venice: if Kate and Henry loved each other they would find a way round the problem.

A four-letter expletive she'd never heard Kate use hurtled down the line followed by, 'How can you be so bloody insensitive? You've wrecked two relationships in one go. I don't know how you can justify what you've done. And I can't believe you've been seeing Henry's father for so long. Why didn't you say anything?' She drew breath, but not for long enough to give Dulcie time to speak. 'And what was going through your mind when Henry and I started seeing each other? Why didn't you stop me? You could have saved me all this pain.' She started to cry, and at once Dulcie's animosity towards her daughter vanished: she longed to take Kate in her arms and make everything right for her.

'I'm sorry, Kate,' she said, 'but there's nothing I can say or do to make amends, I know that. I just hope that one day you'll forgive me.'

The phone went dead and Dulcie replaced the receiver.

An hour later Andrew phoned. Without preamble, he said, 'I've just had Kate ranting and raving on the phone, Mum. How're you doing?'

'Coping. Just.'

'It'll sort itself out in the end,' he said pragmatically.

Dulcie said, 'I wish I had half your certainty.'

'She'll be OK, Mum. Trust me. I might be the gay one, but we both know that Kate's the real drama queen.' He paused. 'That was a joke, by the way. You were supposed to laugh and feel better for it.'

'Oh, Andrew, what would I do without you?'

'Shall I see if I can get some time off and come up?'

'That's sweet of you, but there's no need. I'm just reeling from the shock of Kate's anger.'

'Look, I can't speak for long now. Shall I call again this evening?'

And so the days had progressed, with Kate phoning regularly to take out her anger on Dulcie, and Andrew to pick up the pieces.

Then one day, around lunchtime, Angela phoned. There was reproach in her voice, but skittish desperation too. 'Why can't you leave him alone?' she cried. 'He's my husband, the father of our children.'

'I don't think this conversation is a good idea,' Dulcie had said. 'I can't say anything that will help—other than that I'm sorry.'

Her apology had been flung back at her. 'Don't patronise me with your smug sympathy. I don't need it.'

Dulcie went out into the garden, thinking of Richard and what he was doing upstairs, and felt an even bigger weight of guilt and sorrow towards Richard's wife.

Richard, his unpacking interrupted again, was sitting on the edge of Dulcie's bed—*their bed*—talking to his eldest son. Henry had just heard that his father had moved in with Dulcie.

'Henry, there's no point in going over the same ground again. At some stage you have to accept that this is the decision I've made.'

'But, Dad, it's so not you.'

'What? Being happy?'

'No. Being such a bastard to Mum. Do you have any idea what you've done? Mum says Christopher and Nicholas won't stop fighting, they're turning into a pair of hooligans. And all because of you.'

'Credit me with sufficient—'

Henry cut him dead. 'Right now, Dad, I can't credit you with anything but gross stupidity. For God's sake, all marriages go through a rocky period, but most couples pull through and get on with it.'

Losing patience, Richard said, 'And what would you know about marriage? You, whose idea of commitment is to remember a girl's name after you've bedded her!' He heard his son gasp. 'I'm sorry,' he said hastily. 'That was out of order. I shouldn't have said it.'

'Why not, if that's how you feel about me? It's good to get these things into the open and know where we stand with each other. But I'd like you to know that Kate—yeah, how about that? I can remember her name!—Kate and I thought we had a future. You've put paid to that.'

'It needn't be so.'

'Get real, Dad. How can I possibly go on living with her when you, to use your own choice expression, are *bedding* her mother? You might not have any principles, but I do. I wouldn't hurt Mum in so vile a manner.'

Richard sagged beneath the vicious onslaught. 'We're not getting anywhere, Henry, so I suggest we say goodbye.'

'Suits me. I only called to let you know that Victoria and I will be up at the weekend to stay with Mum. I thought it might matter to you.'

No, thought Richard, when he'd rung off. You called, Henry, because you still can't accept that your boring old father has dared to do this dreadful thing. He's chosen love over staid security.

'Family,' announced Popeye, beaming round at his, 'that's what it's all about. You can't beat it.' Five hours ago Jaz's mother had unexpectedly gone into labour and given birth to two healthy babies, a girl and a boy. Although premature they were a good weight, and Jaz was relieved that her mother's difficult pregnancy was over.

It was weird how they had all started to get on better with each other since Mum had gone into hospital. In a funny kind of way the break-in had also brought them together. The news about the house was good. The decorators had finished and so had the carpet-fitters. Dad was planning for them to move back in tomorrow. Which was perfect timing because Mum and the babies would be home at the weekend. Between now and then he was going to tell Mum about the burglary. Jaz had the feeling that her mother would be so preoccupied she wouldn't have time to worry about the damage. As Dad had said, it was family that counted. And as none of them had come to any harm, what did they have to complain about? When she thought about Victor, alone and in pain, the Rafferty troubles paled into insignificance.

It was the weekend and Richard was driving home. Or, as he corrected himself, to his former home. Last night he had decided to accept Angela's invitation to join them all for Sunday lunch. Respecting his new status, that of a guest, he rang the bell.

Victoria opened the door. She looked at him for a moment or two, as if sizing him up as friend or foe. 'Why didn't you use your key?'

'It didn't seem appropriate.'

She brought her eyebrows together in a frown of disapproval—she had done it so often as a young child, usually when confronting food that was green and described as good for growing children. The memory made him put out his arms. 'How about a hug?'

The frown vanished and she slipped into his embrace, burying herself inside his coat. 'Oh, Dad, why have you left us?'

He held her tight. Finding it difficult to speak, he breathed in the sweet smell of her freshly washed hair. 'I haven't left you,' he murmured. 'I'll always be there for you, you know that.'

'Ah, so it was you I heard.'

It was Angela, and to Richard's consternation, Victoria almost leapt out of his arms. She now stood with her hands behind her back against the radiator. To hide his awkwardness, he took off his coat and hung it in the cupboard under the stairs. 'What can I do to help?' he asked Angela.

'Oh, nothing,' she said airily. 'It's all done. Henry's opened the wine and the boys have set the table. Lunch is ready.'

In the dining room Richard found himself at the head of the table. 'I've sharpened the knife for you,' Angela said. In silent concentration, he sliced the pork with slow, deftly precise movements. He wondered how he could appear so calm before his family after all that he'd done to them. Angela blew her nose, then excused herself.

Victoria asked Christopher to pass the plates round, and by the time Angela reappeared, with a jug of apple sauce, a stilted conversation had sprung up. But Henry looked as if he wanted to kill him, Victoria was quiet, and the boys were more interested in a noisy contest over whose jaws could accommodate the largest roast potato than in answering any of his enquiries about school or their friends. Opposite him, Angela was firing off random statements that bore no relation to the reality of the situation. His being here was a mistake. It was too soon.

'So, Dad, when are you going to stop this nonsense and come home?'

'Henry, I don't think this is the time or place to—'

'I would have thought it was exactly the time and place.'

'Henry—'

'Mum, one of us has to drill some common sense into Dad's befuddled head. What he's doing to you, to us, is wrong.'

'I really don't want to discuss it now,' Richard said calmly, conscious that Christopher was banging a foot against the table leg and Nicholas was biting his nails, which he'd never done before.

'When, then?' Henry's voice was querulous and demanding.

'Henry, I'm not prepared to answer you when you're behaving with scant regard for anyone's feelings but your own.'

'Me behaving with scant regard for other people's feelings? Oh, that's good. And where does that leave you, I wonder?'

'Please, Henry,' said Angela, 'don't spoil what's been a perfectly pleasant lunch. Simmer down and pass me the gravy.'

Henry switched his gaze from Richard to his mother. 'Are you completely mad, Mum? No one in their right mind would describe the last hour as having been pleasant. Wake up and smell the divorce papers!'

'Don't you dare speak to your mother like that.'

'It's all right, Richard, Henry doesn't mean it. Do you, darling? He's just upset. Nicholas, stop biting your nails and, Christopher, please don't keep kicking the leg of the table. How would you like it if—'

'I don't give a shit about the table.' Christopher lashed out with a vicious kick. 'And if you'd cared more about Dad, he wouldn't have needed to go off with some other woman. It's all your fault.'

Angela's face turned white. 'Christopher!'

'Oh, shut up, all of you!' cried Victoria. 'Can't you see that none of this is helping? The simple truth is that Dad no longer loves Mum, and no matter how much she or we pretend otherwise, he's not coming back. He loves someone else and all we can do is accept that and get on with it.' Her voice wavered, and she added, 'Painful as it may be.'

'Nice one, Victoria, that really hit the spot,' muttered Henry when Angela had slowly risen from her chair and walked out of the room. 'I'd better go and make sure Mum's all right.'

'Stay where you are,' instructed Richard, scarcely able to keep his fists from pounding the table. '*I* will go and see how your mother is, but not before I've said this. While I have to take full responsibility for what I've done to your mother, I will *not* tolerate any of you speaking to her like that. None of this is her fault. Do you understand that? Christopher?'

Christopher chewed on his lip and nodded.

He found Angela upstairs in what had been their bedroom. She was on the bed, sobbing. 'Leave me alone,' she said. 'Go back to the woman who means so much to you.'

'What can I do to help?'

She turned over and looked at him through swollen, tear-filled eyes. 'There's nothing. Can't you see you're doing more harm than good by being here? Haven't you humiliated me enough? Go, Richard. *Go!*'

Beth fiddled with the vase of tulips she'd arranged, while Nathan checked Ceefax to see if Lois and Barnaby's flight was on time. She was convinced that their presence at Marsh House when the Kings arrived home would not be met with the forgiving acceptance Barnaby was hoping for. When they heard the sound of a car at the front of the house, Beth steeled herself to open the door. Smile fixed firmly in place, she said, 'Hello there, you two, welcome home.'

To her relief there was no hostility in Lois's face, just confusion, followed swiftly by alarm. 'Beth, what are you doing here? And you too, Nathan? There's nothing wrong with the house, is there?'

Barnaby cleared his throat. 'Beth and Nathan have been keeping an eye on things, Lois. At my instruction, I might add.'

'Everything's absolutely fine with the house,' Beth said. 'The kettle's on. I'll make the tea and let you settle in.'

She beetled off to the kitchen. She was just pouring boiling water into the teapot when she heard footsteps behind her. Lois.

Beth put the lid on the pot and turned round. When Lois didn't say anything, she gave in, her heart sinking fast. 'Please don't be cross with Barnaby. He thought he was doing the right thing, that this would help. If you'd rather we left, just say the word.'

Lois raised a hand. 'It's all right, Beth. It's me who should be making the apologies. I'm so very sorry. If you could find it in your heart to . . .' She trailed off.

'Oh, Lois, there's nothing to forgive. Really there isn't.'

But Lois disagreed and, with great stoicism, she met Beth's eye. 'I've given the matter a lot of thought these last few weeks and I'm left with the conclusion that I could have treated you and Nathan a lot better. And I'm not just talking about Christmas. It . . . it goes a long way back. Perhaps we could have a proper talk some time.'

The next day Lois came to the flat. It was Saturday and Nathan was out with Jaz, Billy and Vicki and Beth had a good feeling about her mother-in-law's visit.

They sat at the kitchen table, sunshine streaming in through the windows, lighting the room with a golden warmth.

'Beth,' Lois began, 'you've been a part of my life for more than twenty years, and yet, in all that time, I've seldom been truly honest with you.'

This didn't come as a shock to Beth. She had always suspected that Lois had wanted someone a little more top-drawer as a daughter-in-law; a younger version of Lois, perhaps. In those far-off days, Beth had been a carefree and independent young woman who regularly threw caution to the wind, who had lived her life as she wanted to.

'You see,' Lois pressed on, 'I'm not one of those people who would survive on their own. I've always admired you. You coped so well with Adam's death. Alone, and with a young son to bring up, you stood there as solid as a rock. While I floundered hopelessly.'

'It always felt the other way round to me,' murmured Beth. 'You seemed so strong. So in charge.'

'I shut down, Beth. I closed off my emotions. Whereas you, you didn't hide your grief. To me, that showed real strength.'

'But I only kept the show going because of Nathan. And because of your and Barnaby's help. I felt I owed it to the three of you. And, of course, there was Adam. It was as if I had to keep going for his sake.'

Lois looked up. 'Yes, there was always Adam, wasn't there?'

'That's been the problem, Lois. He's haunted us for too long. We can't go on living in the past. It's not fair to any of us. Especially not Nathan.'

'I know, and I'm truly sorry that poor Nathan has suffered as he has. I had no idea of the harm I was doing to him. But let me finish saying why I admired you so much for coping on your own. You see, I'm frightened of being alone, of losing those I care for most. If anything happened to Barnaby, or if he left me, I don't know what I'd do. And I know what you're thinking: why do I give him such a hard time? It's my way of trying to prove to myself that I don't need him as much as I do.'

'So when you lost Adam . . . when he killed himself,' Beth said gently, 'you were confronted with one of your worst fears?'

'Yes. I couldn't accept the way he'd died. How could he have taken his own life when he was surrounded by people who loved him? How could he possibly want to leave you and Nathan? And his own mother. I don't think I'll ever understand why he did that.'

'For what it's worth, I don't think I will either. I've made myself accept that he simply wasn't the Adam we all knew and loved on the night he died. He hid his unhappiness well . . . just as we all do,' she added.

'But, Beth, it was only money he'd lost. He could have come to us.'

'He chose not to.'

Lois frowned. 'Doesn't that ever make you angry? That he deliberately made the wrong choice?'

'It used to. Now I'm more concerned with making the right choices for myself. And for Nathan. Of course, these days, he's making his own.'

They both fell silent, until Lois said, 'Aren't you frightened of being alone when Nathan leaves home?'

'I was. But now I'm just beginning to discover the wonderful opportunities that await me. What's more, I've come to the conclusion that I deserve a little fun.'

Lois sighed. 'I wish I had half your pluck.'

'But you do, Lois. You just haven't got round to using it.'

'Maybe you're right. I've lived in a state of fear too long. When Adam died I was terrified I'd lose you and Nathan as well. That's why I tried to keep things as they were, making sure you stayed close to me.'

'Oh, Lois, a caged bird thinks of nothing but flying away.'

Lois nodded. 'I dreaded the day you'd fall in love with another man and not need Barnaby and me any more. I was terrified of losing our only grandson. Watching Nathan grow up was almost like having Adam all over again. The most precious gift I had been given.' She wiped away a tear and Beth reached out a hand to her.

After a minute's silence, Lois said, 'Goodness, you must be wondering what's brought this on.'

Beth said, 'I'm assuming it has something to do with Barnaby.'

For the first time since she had arrived, Lois's expression relaxed. 'One night when we were away, we were sitting on the verandah of our cabin watching the sun go down and I suddenly realised I was happy. And happier than I could remember being in a long time.' She smiled unexpectedly, looking almost young. 'And that was when Barnaby told me that if I didn't apologise to you and Nathan when we arrived home, I would lose you both for ever. He also said he would never forgive me if that were to happen. He didn't say as much but it was implicit in his tone, that if I didn't do as he wanted, I might lose him too.'

Beth was shocked. Who would have thought he had the nerve? Three cheers for good old Barnaby.

That evening, when Nathan came home, Beth told him about her conversation with Lois. 'I don't think we should hold out for a miraculous change in your grandmother,' she concluded, 'not right away, but let's do all we can to help this dramatic change of heart. By the way, I've invited them to spend Easter Sunday with us. Is that OK with you?'

'Fine. But won't you be busy preparing to meet the Chosen One?'

The writers' conference was the day after Easter Monday, hence Nathan's comment. Apart from Victor, who was still in hospital but making a surprisingly good recovery, everyone in the group was going, although only for the first three days of the week-long course—Jaz couldn't spare any more time away from home as she had exams, and Jack hadn't wanted to use up too much of his precious holiday entitlements. He'd kindly offered to drive, which had come as a relief to Beth, since her car had been playing up recently. The only aspect of going away that she didn't like was that Nathan would be on his own. While she trusted him she felt guilty leaving him on his own to revise for his exams. 'It's fine, Mum,' he'd said, when she'd started backing out of the trip, 'I'll get far more done without you here.' He'd also accused her of trying to find an escape route. 'It's too late now to use guilt as a means to avoid the Chosen One.'

Victor was looking forward to something, and he couldn't remember having done so in a long, long time. The days of mourning his manuscript were behind him. Now he was really onto something. That extraordinary girl, Jaz, had set him on this track. 'I've brought you something else to read,' she'd said. 'I thought it would cheer you up.'

He'd taken the book from her reluctantly. 'But it's for children.'

'Get real, Victor. Harry Potter's for everyone. That's half his charm. I bet you a shiny pound that when I see you next you'll have finished the book, and if you're really nice to me, I'll bring in the next in the series.'

To his astonishment she'd been right. He'd read *Harry Potter and the Philosopher's Stone* in a day, finding it both gripping and strangely comforting. He'd scrounged a pound from one of the nurses and put it on his bedside locker next to the book ready for when she next visited.

Smiling, she'd handed over the next instalment.

'Of course, it's nothing but money for old rope,' he'd said. 'Simple enough idea that anyone could have dreamed up.'

She'd nodded and agreed. 'It's always the simplest ideas that are the best. Now, I can't stop long today, I promised Mum I'd take care of the twins so that she can run Tamzin and Lulu to their gymnastics class.'

'Oh,' he'd said, trying not to show his disappointment. He never told her as much but he looked forward to her visits.

The day after that he'd had the surprise of being visited by Hidden Talents en masse. 'We thought we'd hold the meeting here with you tonight,' Jaz had told him.

'We checked with the top brass,' said Jack, 'and were told that, so long as we keep the noise down, nobody will mind.'

'A pity you didn't think to check with me first,' he'd said peevishly. He didn't like it when people started organising him.

'Quit whinging,' snapped Jaz, 'or I'll cut off your Harry Potter supply, and where will you be then? Trawling the streets for a new dealer.'

Jaz had promised to bring in the third Potter book for him, and he'd decided to tell her this evening that his next novel was going to be along similar lines. Obviously his would be better, but it would appeal to children and adults. To get started, he needed Jaz to buy him a new A4 pad and a fountain pen. He was able now to sit up for longer periods and writing would kill the hours of boredom.

But as the clock in the ward ticked away that evening's visiting session, there was no sign of Jaz. Feeling depressed and very alone, he closed his eyes, pretending to anyone who might glance his way that he was asleep and in no need of a visitor. Minutes passed.

'Sleeping on the job again, Victor?'

He recognised the voice instantly. He opened his eyes. 'You're late.'

'And you're a miserable old devil, but I try not to let that get in the way of our special time together.'

He smiled. 'Have you brought me the next book?'

'Would I ever let you down, Victor?'

'Everyone else has. Why should you be any different?'

'First, I *am* different. That's why I go to all the trouble to visit you and deny myself an evening with my gorgeous boyfriend. And second, you can switch off the self-pity tap. Any more of that and I'll spill the beans about what happens in *The Prisoner of Azkaban* and spoil the ending.'

Later, he asked her why she kept coming to see him.

'Didn't I tell you? It's my care-in-the-community work. I'll get a nice gold badge to wear when I've got you back on your feet. See you.'

He watched her go. What *was* in it for her?

The Rafferty builders had finished work on Jack's flat, and now that it was just how he'd wanted it, he felt a growing desire to tidy up the loose ends of his life. This Easter Sunday was destined to be a turning point.

An excited cry from Lucy, who had her nose pressed to the window, made him look up from the garlic he was crushing. 'Dad, they're here!'

First to arrive was Julie with Desmond Junior who, on seeing Jack, grinned from his car seat, reached for a foot and proudly pulled off his sock. Des brought up the rear with what looked like enough survival gear to aid a party of ten to the top of Mount Kilimanjaro.

In the crowded hall, Amber and Lucy stepped forward, their interest not in Des and Julie but in the smiling Desmond Junior, whom they'd not met before. 'Look, Dad.' Lucy was itching to play with a real baby. 'He's eating his sock.'

'Hey,' said Des, moving into the middle of the large room and giving it a professional once-over, 'this is great. Must make the hassle with those cowboy builders seem almost worth it.'

'Oh, don't remind me.' He helped relieve Des of his load. 'Now, who's for a drink?'

Leaving Amber and Lucy to watch over Desmond Junior, Des and Julie followed Jack to the far end of the L-shaped room and into the kitchen. 'Now, this I do approve of,' observed Julie. She ran her hand over the polished granite work surface.

'How in hell did you manage to get it done so quickly?' Des exclaimed. 'I thought these jobs dragged on for months.'

'I guess I was lucky,' Jack said. He almost added, 'For once,' but didn't. During the last week, he'd come to the conclusion that he was luckier than he'd ever realised. He had two beautiful daughters, a relatively secure job, a great roof over his head, and a circle of friends that now included those who shared his passion for writing. He handed round the drinks. 'I'd like to propose a toast,' he said.

Des raised his eyebrows. 'Oh, yes? That sounds ominous.'

'I finished *Friends and Family* last night.'

'Come again?'

He smiled, enjoying the look on his friends' faces. No one outside Hidden Talents knew about his writing. 'I've written a book.'

Des looked incredulous. '*A book?*'

'Yes, one of those strange objects with rows of letters covering the pages. You must have come across one at some time.'

'Ha, ha, *ha*. How long has this being going on?'

'Since last October.'

'But you never said anything.'

'Sorry, Julie. Don't be offended, it wasn't personal.' He frowned. 'Or maybe that's the point. I've found the whole exercise extremely personal, and I couldn't bring myself to tell anyone.'

'So, what's the book about?' Des asked. 'Is it a saucy exposé of the world of estate agents? Any car chases in it?'

'Ignore him, Jack, he's a philistine. Who's it aimed at?'

He thought about this. At length he said, 'People like us,' then added, 'With the exception of Des, perhaps,' and grinned.

Des tipped his nose in the air. 'In that case I'm taking my beer and going to mix with more congenial company.'

They watched him join the children. A moment passed and Jack said, 'Thanks for burying the hatchet, Julie. I really appreciate it. I upset you over Clare, and I'm sorry for that.'

'That's water under the bridge now. Clare is only too happy with the way things are currently shaping up.'

'Yes, I'm intrigued to meet the new man in her life.'

Less than five minutes later, his curiosity was satisfied when the sound of the doorbell heralded the arrival of Clare and Colin. Inviting Clare for lunch had been, he liked to think, the first step on the road to his very own glasnost. 'Of course you can bring him,' he'd said, when she'd mentioned a new boyfriend. 'The more the merrier.'

Colin, an accountant, had a good sense of humour, and before long they were having a classic battle of estate agents' versus accountants' jokes. 'Right, then,' said Des, rolling up his sleeves and getting into the swing of it. 'Why were estate agents invented?'

'Don't know. Why?'

'To give accountants someone to look up to!'

They all laughed, and Jack asked, 'Now, who's for dessert? We have a choice of M and S's finest crème brûlée or their equally fine lemon tart.' He started to gather the plates, noting that Amber had eaten more than she had of late. He took it as an encouraging sign.

That evening, a few hours after the lunch party broke up, Jack drove the girls home to Prestbury, Amber perfectly still, her eyes closed.

'Have you really written a book, Dad?'

He looked at Lucy in the rearview mirror. 'Yes, Luce, I have.'

'What's it about?' This was from Amber, her eyes open now.

Keeping his eyes on the road, he said, 'It's about a family who, one minute, is happy, but then everything starts to go wrong and . . . and the parents split up because—'

'Is it about us?' interrupted Lucy.

'In some ways, yes, but in other ways, no.'

'What happens in the end?' Amber's voice was cool. 'Do the parents get back together?'

'No. But they promise each other never to do anything that would hurt their children.'

'And do they keep their promises?'

'In the end, yes.'

Chapter Twelve

'THERE'S NO NEED for you all to see me off,' Jaz said.

'I agree,' her father said, 'absolutely no need to do anything half so daft, but we'll do it all the same, if that's OK with you, you silly eejit.'

Jack, Beth and Dulcie were coming towards the house when Jaz broke free of her father's hug and escaped outside. While she put her bag in the boot of Jack's car, a round of handshaking ensued.

'Don't worry, Mr and Mrs Rafferty,' Beth was saying, 'we'll take good care of your daughter.' Jaz noticed that her brothers were talking to Jack, a little apart from the rest of the group. She crept up behind them, and tuned into what they were saying. None of it made any sense: Jack was laughing and saying something about treating the whole thing as a joke.

'All the same,' muttered Phin, his face oddly serious, 'fair play to you for taking it so well. The flat OK?'

'It's great. I wish I'd come to Raffertys' in the first place.'

'Anything else you need doing, give us a bell. It's the least we could do.'

. . . the least we could do. Something was going on. Over the coming days in Harrogate Jaz planned to get to the bottom of it.

The mood in the car—the excitement and anticipation—as they headed towards Harrogate reminded Dulcie of long-ago school trips. Feeling relaxed, and enjoying the music that was playing on the radio, she closed her eyes and gave in to her tiredness.

Richard had been tense all last night, and at half past three they had gone downstairs for some tea. With his head in his hands, he had groaned, 'My children hate me.'

'Give it time,' she had said soothingly, hating to see him so wretched. 'Let them be angry for a while, and eventually it'll pass.'

And wasn't that exactly what she was doing with her own daughter? The angry telephone calls had stopped, and instead there was now a stony silence. Kate was refusing to speak to her, and it hurt.

Half an hour before Jack had come for her that morning, Richard had left for work, his face ashen from lack of sleep and worry. 'Why don't you take the day off?' she'd said, concerned how drained he looked.

'I can't,' he said. 'I have two important meetings to chair.'

She had kissed him goodbye and warned him not to overdo it.

Unlike Dulcie, who was now asleep, Beth was wide awake and fidgety, her mind racing. The prospect of meeting Ewan was tipping her over the edge of reason. She had fully intended to go to bed early last night but she'd been up until two, dithering over what clothes to pack.

When the last item of clothing was at last neatly folded inside the bag, she had quietly switched on her computer. Ewan had promised to send her one last message.

Hi Beth,

Glad to hear things have been resolved between you and the in-laws. Barnaby sounds like a veritable saint. And you mustn't worry about leaving Nathan on his own to do his revision—from what you've told me of him, he sounds motivated enough to get the work done.

Here's me telling you not to worry, when I'm down to the very beds of my nails at the thought of meeting you. What if she doesn't like the colour of the anorak I've bought specially for the occasion? And what if she doesn't go for a man who keeps his small change in a handy little purse?

These questions, and many more, have kept me awake at night

over Easter. All I ask of you, is to be gentle with me. Looking forward
(it goes without saying, but feel it would be an appalling omission if
I didn't) to meeting you. Travel safely.

    All best, Ewan X

Apart from a brief hitch near Cambridge, where a lorry had jackknifed,
Ewan had had a good run. He was now skirting Leeds and reckoned
he'd arrive at Norton Hall earlier than he'd anticipated. He cruised along
at a blistering speed, then eased off the accelerator when he spotted a
police car. All around him the traffic slowed as they played Grandma's
Footsteps, trying to slip past the police car without being seen. The
games we play, he thought.

And the game he was playing with Beth, he reminded himself, had
every chance of backfiring on him. While he hadn't actually lied to Beth,
he had been less than straight with her. He hadn't meant to mislead her
for as long as he had, but before he knew it, he had been caught up in a
mire of his own making and unable to admit the truth. It seemed easier
to wait until they met and she could take the facts at first hand, then
decide what she thought of him. And the reasons for his deviousness.

As Jack unpacked his bag, he looked out onto the grounds of Norton
Hall. Some early arrivals were already sitting on benches dotted around
a croquet lawn, others were sprawled on the grass enjoying the afternoon sunshine, and in the shade of a large oak tree, a woman dressed in
what looked like a caftan was sitting cross-legged with her palms
extended, as if checking for rain. Dulcie had warned them that writing
courses tended to attract a rich and varied mix.

A knock at the door made him start. He opened it and was confronted with yet more proof of Dulcie's theory: a gangly man with
copper bangles on both wrists and a golf-ball-sized crystal on a leather
thong round his neck, wearing a pair of scruffy green slippers.

'Hi,' he said. 'Zed Wane. I'm next door. This your first time?'

Jack nodded.

'Aha, a Norton Hall virgin. Thought I didn't recognise you. I came last
year, and the year before that, so I could show you round, if you like.'

'Er . . . I want to unpack first. I'll catch up with you later,' Jack said,
judging it prudent not to become Zed's best new buddy too soon. He
closed the door and wondered if he was going to regret coming.

At three o'clock, as arranged, he knocked on Beth's door. Dulcie and
Jaz had got there ahead of him, and they set off for a cup of tea. They
tagged on to the end of a small queue and Jack noticed that Zed was at

the front of it. 'Someone to watch out for,' Jack told the others, in a low voice. He explained about his friendly neighbour.

Beth laughed, but Jaz said, 'You're sure he said his name was Zed? It wasn't Ewan, by any chance, was it?'

'Well, he did say something about a pseudonym . . .'

'Jack,' warned Dulcie, with a smile, 'Beth's going through enough turmoil as it is. Behave yourself. You too, Jaz.'

A hubbub of voices filled the high-ceilinged room, and it was obvious that many of the delegates knew each other from previous conferences. Unlike Zed, if their dress sense was anything to go by, they gave the impression of being relatively normal. But Zed wasn't alone in his eccentricity: grouped around a sofa in the far corner of the room was a noisy crowd of men and women sporting identical black T-shirts with the name Jared Winter emblazoned across them. Jack knew him to be a well-known science-fiction writer. Or was he a fantasy writer? The distinction had always been lost on Jack. Jared Winter was one of the guest speakers at the conference, and Jack decided, from the look of his devotees, that the man was in for some serious hero-worshipping.

At four o'clock they made their way to the main conference hall and listened to the formal introductions made by the committee, then they set off for a workshop on characterisation. The session was to be led by a formidable woman with a face plastered in make-up; chunky rings adorned all but one of her fingers. Her name was Dorothy Kendall.

The first half of the session flew by, and Beth soon had several pages of useful notes. They were given a five-minute break, then in the second half of the workshop, they were paired off and after a ten-minute conversation they had to write a 100-word description of the other person. 'And don't insult me by going for the obvious,' Dorothy Kendall barked at them, 'such as the colour of hair. I want you to look out for interesting mannerisms, turns of phrase, and use them to give a fresh, cliché-free character sketch. Whoever comes up with the worst offering has to buy me a drink in the bar tonight.'

Beth concentrated as if her life depended on it: she didn't fancy spending time alone with the awesome Dorothy Kendall. Later, relieved to survive the workshop without being humiliated as the class dunce, she slipped out of the room. 'I had no idea it would be as scary as this,' she said to Jack. 'I hope the rest of the course tutors aren't like her.'

'Come on, I'll see if I can rustle up a strengthening cup of tea.'

'Bugger that! I need something stronger. Lead me to the bar!'

Jack laughed. 'Beth, hush your mouth! Whatever would Nathan say? Still no sign of the elusive Ewan Jones?'

'I told you before, he said he wouldn't be here until supper-time.'

They squeezed through the throng, heading in the direction of some comfortable chairs. When they were almost there, Jack said, 'You go ahead, I need to make a trip to the little boys' room.'

It was a full ten minutes before he returned, and when he did, he was grinning from ear to ear. 'I hardly dare ask what you've been up to in the gents' loo to make you smile like that,' she said.

He sat down next to her, still grinning. 'I've just had the pleasure, as it were, of standing side by side with Felix McCallum. You know—the editor I have an appointment to see tomorrow.'

'The one who's giving you a critique on the chapters of *Friends and Family*?'

'The very man. He saw my badge and asked if I was the one who'd sent him the stuff about a bloke whose marriage goes belly up.'

'Good with words, is he?'

'Don't nit-pick. It's what he said next that's important. He said he hoped I'd brought the rest of the manuscript with me because he was very keen to read it.'

'Jack, that's brilliant. Well done, you!'

Jaz was furious. During the car journey up here, she had asked Jack what he and her brothers had been discussing before they'd set off for Yorkshire. He'd refused to tell her at first, but had then relented, concluding that it didn't matter now. But it did! She felt so ashamed. How could her brothers have done that to him?

Suddenly she smiled: her dimwit brothers had inadvertently given her the means to get Victor's house sorted for him. When she got home she would blackmail them into doing the job; she knew they wouldn't want Mum and Dad to find out what they'd done.

She locked her door and went to meet the others in Jack's room. Before they joined the queue for dinner, they scanned the conference notice board, and Jaz was delighted to see that a short story she had submitted had been short-listed for a prize.

Dinner was surprisingly good—pork in green peppercorn sauce with glazed carrots and creamed potatoes, then lemon cheesecake. When coffee had been served they were told that there would be a fifteen-minute break before Jared Winter took the floor in the main conference hall for his talk, 'The Perception of Honesty in Novel Writing—What You Can and Cannot Get Away With'. A loud cheer went up from his fans and, as one, they scraped back their chairs and made a noisy exit. 'Wow,' said Jaz, 'they're eager to get front-row seats, aren't they?'

The rest of the audience trickled into the hall more sedately, and Jaz insisted they sit in the back row. 'Last thing we want is to be associated with a bunch of crazies. Polo mint, anyone?' She passed the tube to Jack, who passed it to Beth—who froze. Up on the podium, taking his seat beside the conference chairman, she could see a man wearing a navy-blue anorak holding, of all things . . . a small purse. Ewan?

'You lied.'

'I'm sorry.'

'But you *lied*. And you did it all the time. Every exchange we had was a sham. You conned me.'

'Are you going to let me try to explain?'

'Why? So you can fool me with yet more lies?'

'Please, Beth. I'm guilty of keeping things from you, but not of lying to you. If you don't believe me, it's all there in the emails I wrote.'

Enraged, she said, 'So now you're saying I should have been more clued-up and read between the lines?'

He shook his head. 'No.' A group of delegates was approaching, including the conference chairman. 'Look,' he said, 'I can't talk now. I've got to sign some books. Will you meet me later? In the bar?'

She gave in with bad grace. 'Oh, all right. But don't expect me to be falling over you like all those adoring fans of yours.'

'That's exactly the point, Beth.'

'You look like you could do with an extremely large drink,' Jack said when she joined the others.

The bar wasn't as busy as they'd expected, and the lad who served them said it was always the same when a popular author was signing.

'So just how popular is he?' asked Jaz.

'Don't tell me you've not heard of him.'

'I'm not into science fiction.'

'Strictly speaking, he's fantasy.'

Beth snorted. 'I'll say he is.' She couldn't get over how shocked she had been when she'd recognised Ewan. Frightened he'd spot her, she'd sunk down in her chair. Jack had asked her if she was OK. 'It's him,' she'd hissed. 'It's Ewan.' Jack had glanced at the people around them.

'No, up there. Jared Winter is Ewan.' She'd only ever seen the one photograph of him, but she knew she wasn't mistaken.

'You're kidding?' exclaimed Jaz, who'd overheard.

There was no time to say any more: the chairman was telling them how honoured they were to have Jared Winter with them. 'What some of you may not know is that Jared got his lucky break on a writers' conference just like this one, and he feels it's important to put something back into the system. Ladies and gentlemen, Jared Winter.'

More applause followed and Jared—Ewan—rose to his feet. 'You might be wondering why I'm dressed like this,' he began, as he put the purse into his anorak pocket, 'and the answer is twofold. The theme of my talk this evening is honesty, or its perception as carefully orchestrated by the author. The way I'm dressed is to prove how easy it is to manipulate the reader. Put a character into an anorak and show him sorting through his loose change in a purse, and you've created a shy mummy's boy. More sinisterly, he might be a shy mummy's boy by day, but a potential serial killer by night. According to convention, what he isn't—based on those two simple details—is a red-blooded Adonis with a taste for fast cars and even faster women. Or is he?' He waited for the laughter to die down. Then, scanning the rows of faces, he said, 'And the other reason for my turning up like this is that I'm sharing a private joke with a friend in the audience.'

At this, Beth had sunk even lower into her chair.

His talk was self-effacing, entertaining and informative, and had it been delivered by anyone else Beth would have enjoyed it, but she was stunned by the depth of his deviousness.

'Well?' said Dulcie, as they sipped their drinks, while around them the number swelled at the bar. It was impossible not to notice that a good many paperbacks bearing Jared Winter's name were now in circulation. 'I think it's obvious why he lied to you, Beth.'

'Yes,' agreed Jack. 'He was seeking anonymity.'

'It doesn't help,' Beth said. 'I feel as if he's made a fool of me. If I'd known who he was I'd never have kept up the correspondence.'

'And he probably knew that,' said Jaz.

Three pairs of unblinking eyes stared at Beth.

It was another hour before Ewan reappeared. Beth saw him searching the bar for her. 'He's here,' she said to the others.

'In that case, we should go,' said Dulcie. 'If there are apologies to be made, he deserves the right to make them in private. Good night, Beth. Come on, Jaz. You too, Jack.'

Ewan looked tired as he came over to Beth. 'Have I scared your friends away?'

'No. They're being diplomatic and giving you the benefit of the doubt.'

'And are *you* prepared to give me the benefit of the doubt?'

'That depends on how convincing you are.'

He leaned forward, but just as he was about to speak, a woman in tight black leather trousers tapped his shoulder: she wanted him to sign a book. He obliged politely, but Beth could see that he was frowning. No sooner had she thanked him than another appeared.

'Could we go somewhere else?' Ewan asked, when they were alone again. 'Somewhere quieter?'

They ventured outside. In the darkness, he pointed to a bench across the lawn and led the way. 'Are you warm enough?' he asked.

She nodded.

'OK, then, time to start the grovelling. But you must have sussed now why I did what I did.'

She nodded again.

'In which case, you must have also sussed that I'm the most extraordinarily attractive man you've ever set eyes on.'

She turned and looked at him incredulously.

'Aha! At least that elicited more than a passing nod.'

'Don't play games with me. You've done enough of that already.'

'OK, I admit I kept things from you because I'm sick of meeting people, women in particular, who think of me as Jared Winter. Believe it or not, that bunch in there is pretty typical.'

'And how many other women have you conned in this way?'

'None. I swear it. You're the first.' He groaned. 'That didn't come out right. What I meant was, I've never chatted with anyone on the Internet before. The night I met you was the first time I'd tried it. And, you have to admit, we hit it off. If we hadn't, we wouldn't be sitting here now.'

'But I feel as if I wasn't chatting to the man I thought I was. Who are you, really? Jared Winter or Ewan Jones?'

'I'm Ewan Jones. JW, as I think of him, is a pseudonym. He's not even an alter ego.'

'Why didn't you tell me before now? All right, not at the start, I can see that. But why not once we'd got to know each other?'

'I had to be sure.'

'Of what?'

'That it was me, boring old Ewan Jones, you wanted to get to know better, not JW, the zany fantasy writer. You should see some of the mail I get from my female readers. The things they say they'd like to do to me . . . Well, let's just say it's reading those letters that's turned my hair grey.'

She laughed, but stopped when she remembered her email and what she'd suggested she might do with several bars of chocolate.

'It's not funny,' he said.

'I'm sorry. But just for a minute, you sounded like the Ewan I know.'

He leaned back on the seat. 'Thank goodness for that. Here, you're shivering, have my jacket.'

'You should have hung on to that ghastly anorak.'

'I suppose that joke fell flat, didn't it?'

'As a pancake. But you spoke very well. You had the audience hanging on your every word.'

'But not you, I suspect.'

'I was in shock.'

'And now?'

'Mmm . . . coming round, slowly.'

'Excellent. So tell me what you've done today. Which workshop did you attend?'

'"Characterisation" with Dorothy Kendall. Is she always so fierce?'

'Legendary for it.' He lowered his voice. 'I met her years ago at a similar writers' conference and I was so struck by her I used her in my next novel. Trouble was, the readers loved her as she strutted about in her shiny thigh-high boots. She had to become a regular turn in all the subsequent books.' He smiled. 'I owe it all to that woman.'

'I'm afraid I haven't read any of your books,' Beth admitted.

'I was hoping that might be the case.'

She turned to him, remembering something important. 'You *did* lie to me. You said your book was rejected.'

He shook his head. 'Sorry, but that was true.'

'But how? If you're so successful, why—'

'I wanted to write a novel that was totally different.'

'Wouldn't the Jared Winter name sell it anyway?'

'I wanted it to be accepted in its own right, so I submitted it under another name.' He smiled ruefully. 'And I experienced a healthy dose of rejection, just as I did before I started writing as JW.' He paused. 'Any chance that I've been forgiven yet?'

'I'll let you know in the morning.'

Next morning, drawing back his curtains and seeing that the warm spring weather was holding, Ewan felt refreshed. He was looking forward to the workshop he was leading. And to seeing Beth again.

He'd known all too well the risk he'd taken with her, and had anticipated her reaction right to the last accusation. All he could hope for was that she had calmed down since last night and was prepared to carry on as before. Unless she was disappointed with him in the flesh—hair too grey, waistline too full, wrinkles too many.

There hadn't been any disappointment on his part: Beth was just as attractive as her photograph had led him to believe.

Washed, shaved and dressed, he went down to the dining hall.

Taking care to avoid eye contact with anyone, he sought out Beth and her friends. Eventually he located them and went over to their table.

In for a penny, in for a pound. If she'd decided he was *persona non grata*, he was about to find out.

The afternoon went slowly for Jack. His mind kept straying to his manuscript, which had been with Felix McCallum since yesterday evening. How much of *Friends and Family* had he managed to read? And had he liked it? Jack knew he would have to wait until after dinner, when he had an appointment with Felix, to find out.

'Can you believe we're nearly halfway through our time here?' said Jaz, during dinner.

'I know what you mean,' replied Dulcie. 'The time is flying by. Are you glad you came?'

'Oh, yes. I'm having a fantastic time. How about you, Beth?'

Caught with her thoughts elsewhere, Beth said, 'Mmm . . . sorry?'

It was Jack who was brave enough to ask, 'So, have you forgiven Ewan for wanting you to like him for *who* he is not *what* he is?'

She had been thinking of the conversation she'd had with Ewan after lunch, when once again her friends had left them discreetly alone. 'I think we've reached an understanding.'

'And?'

'And nothing, Jack.'

As the conversation returned to the afternoon's workshops, Beth's thoughts wandered again. Ewan had invited her to go for a drive tomorrow. 'I don't know this area of the country, and I'd like to explore. I wondered if you'd come with me.'

'Only if you promise not to wear that appalling anorak,' she'd replied.

'I think I could agree to those terms.'

They had then chatted happily while they finished their coffee. When they left the dining hall together, Beth saw two of Jared Winter's groupies looking daggers at her.

Dulcie was bursting with pride and happiness: Felix McCallum had read Jack's novel, liked it, and wanted to make an offer for it.

Late last night, while they'd been celebrating in the bar, Ewan had advised Jack to find himself an agent and offered to ring his own agent in London and put him in touch with Jack.

'I'm so proud of you,' Dulcie said to Jack. 'But didn't I say all along that you had that magic touch publishers are on the lookout for?'

In an uncharacteristic display of emotion, he'd thrown his arms round Dulcie, Beth and Jaz, and said, 'But I couldn't have done it without your encouragement and support.'

'Just you remember that when you're rich and famous,' Jaz said.

Dulcie had wanted to share the good news with Richard, but decided not to bother him so late. Now, with a few spare minutes before breakfast, she tapped in his number on the tiny mobile he'd given her.

'Richard, Jack has a publisher interested in his novel!'

'That's marvellous! Give him my best wishes.'

'I will, darling. And how are you?'

'Oh, OK. Missing you.' The line crackled noisily. 'Are you still there, Dulcie?'

'Yes. The line's awful. Where are you?'

'On the M6 heading for Worcester. The traffic's horrendous.'

'Well, just you make sure you drive carefully. I'd better go now, the others will be waiting for me. Take care.' She rang off, inordinately happy for Jack, and for herself, for the deep commitment that existed now between her and Richard.

Beth was glad she had agreed to take time out from the conference to see some of the local countryside. The first surprise of her expedition was Ewan's car: a slinky black Porsche.

'I make no apology for being a big kid who likes a flashy motor,' he said, opening the door for her. 'You any good with a map? I fancied going up to Brimham Rocks.' He leaned in towards her, and pointed them out on the map. When he looked up she noticed the colour of his eyes for the first time. Blue.

The rock formation was enormous, much larger than either of them had expected. Leaving the car, they set out to explore. The view was spectacular and, beneath a cloudless blue sky, they could see for miles.

'It's beautiful,' she said. 'Stunning.' When he didn't respond, she turned. He wasn't looking at the view. 'Ewan?'

'Sorry, I allowed myself to be distracted by a far more interesting sight.' He groaned. 'Tell me I didn't say something so clichéd. Dorothy Kendall would flay me alive!'

When he suggested they walk on, it seemed perfectly natural that he should take her hand. Quite at ease in his company, Beth said how much she was enjoying herself.

'Good,' he said, 'because I am too. Thank you for coming.'

'Thank you for the invitation.'

'And thank *you* for being so polite.'

'Are you making fun of me?'

'Just a little.'

'Well, don't, unless you don't object to me getting my own back.'

'How will you do that?'

'I shall tell La Kendall about the gratuitous clichés.'

He burst out laughing. 'Ooh, straight to my Achilles' heel.'

From Brimham Rocks they followed the road back towards Norton Hall, then took the route to Harrogate. 'We can't possibly come to this part of the world and not experience afternoon tea at Betty's,' he told her. 'I hope you're a cream tea person or there'll be no hope for us.'

They ordered a selection of sandwiches and cakes. When their food arrived, Beth looked at Ewan in horror. 'Did we really order so much?'

He shrugged. 'That's just yours, mine will be along in a minute.'

They tucked in. 'I hate to be so picky,' Beth said, 'but I've just thought of a whopping great lie you told me in one of your emails. You said you ran your own public relations business.'

'Correct. To be a writer who sells well these days, you have to get out there on the road and do your share of PR work. I've been doing it for years, showing my face at writers' conferences, signings, interviews, meeting booksellers. You name it, I've done it.'

'That's cheating,' Beth frowned. 'But tell me about the book you had rejected. The other night you said it was very different to a Jared Winter novel. In what way?'

'Confession time. You see before you a man who is trapped by his own success. I've written twelve fantasy books now and I've reached the point when I'd like nothing better than to switch horses mid-race.'

'You mean try a different genre?'

'Yes. I wrote a love story; about my parents. Back in the righteous fifties, they scandalously fell in love. Dad was already married but they persevered and despite the stigma of living in sin, which really meant something then, especially as they had a child, me, they were immensely happy. Until sadly my father died.'

'What an interesting story. Will you try again with it?'

He smiled. 'Eventually, when my bruised ego has recovered.'

'So what's wrong with the books you're so successful with?'

'I'm bored with them. I need to do something different. But I have a plan. I write phenomenally fast and I'm hoping to stockpile a few, then take a break from JW and write something else.' He helped himself to another egg and cress sandwich. 'Well, does that satisfy you? Are you convinced now that I haven't lied to you?'

Respecting him for his honesty, she said, 'You did lie to me, about something else.'

'Go on?'

'You played down how nice you are.'

She could see from his expression that for a split second she'd wrong-footed him. But then a slow smile worked itself across his face.

All in all it had been a good day. The meeting Richard had driven to Worcester for had gone well. He was now on the M6, not far from Maywood, but the traffic was heavy and slow. Knowing that he was bone-tired, he wound down the window and decided to stop at the next service station for some strong black coffee.

He pulled into the car park, found himself a space, and switched off the engine, tempted to take a short nap. As he turned the key, a pain shot through his left arm. He let out a cry, drew his fist to his chest and clutched his shoulder, waiting for the pain to subside. But it didn't. He fought for breath, trying to keep calm, knowing that he was having another heart attack. He fumbled for his mobile but another spasm of pain shot through him and he jerked his head back against the head-rest. 'Oh God,' he gasped, 'this is it . . .'

His last conscious thought was of Dulcie. Of never seeing her again.

Chapter Thirteen

DULCIE WAS WORRIED. It was unlike Richard not to answer the messages she'd left on both his mobile and the telephone at home in Bloom Street. The obvious solution was to call Richard at work, but it had been one of her many golden rules throughout their relationship that she never rang him at his office. However, he was openly living with her now . . .

She put off phoning until lunchtime, two hours before they would be leaving Norton Hall. The weather was so warm and bright that she went outside to make the call. The telephone in Cheshire was answered by a young girl with a singsong voice, whose tone changed immediately when Dulcie asked to speak to Mr Richard Cavanagh.

'Oh—I'll—I'll just put you through to someone who can help you.'

Dulcie had expected to be put through to Richard's secretary, and was taken aback when she heard the resonant timbre of a man's voice. For no real reason, anxiety twisted into the piercing stab of certainty. Something *was* wrong. 'Is Richard there, please?' she asked.

'I'm afraid not,' the man said. 'May I ask who's calling?'

She noted his cautious tone. 'My name is Dulcie Ballantyne and I'm— I'm a close friend of his. I've tried his mobile but I can't get an answer.'

'I see.' He cleared his throat. 'I'm sorry to be the one to tell you, but Richard died yesterday.'

Her hand flew to her mouth, held back a cry of disbelief. *No! Oh, no!* 'Hello? Are you still there?'

She uncovered her mouth and tried to speak. 'Yes, I'm still here. When did Richard . . .?' Her voice broke. She tried again. 'How did . . .?' But her throat was clenched and nothing would come out.

The man came to her rescue. 'At the moment the only information we have is that it was another heart attack. He was on his own, driving back from Worcester yesterday afternoon and—'

This time she couldn't stop the cry escaping. 'No! Not on his own!' She ended the call and held the phone to her chest. She sobbed aloud, her whole body shuddering with the shock. Above her, a cloud passed over the sun and she felt as if the whole world had just gone dark.

While Jaz and Jack finished their packing, Beth volunteered to look for Dulcie. When at last she found her, her head was bowed and she was weeping silently. She didn't notice Beth until she had put her arms round her. 'Is it Richard? Has something happened to him?'

It seemed an age before Dulcie raised her head from Beth's shoulder. 'He's dead, Beth. Another heart attack. I—I should have been with him.'

Beth held her tightly again. 'Oh, Dulcie, I'm so sorry. So very sorry.'

Shivering, Dulcie pulled away from her. 'I can't believe I'll never see him again. And just as we'd begun to plan a real future for ourselves.'

Reminded of her own grief when she had been told Adam was dead, Beth blinked away the tears that were pricking the backs of her eyes. She held Dulcie's hand: it was icy cold. 'Come on, Dulcie, let's get you back to your room. I'll ask Jack to rustle up something for you to eat.'

'No. I want to go home. I want to be nearer Richard.'

Dulcie could remember little of the journey home. She must have dozed at some time because when she next opened her eyes they were back in Maywood and turning into Bloom Street. Beth helped her out of the car and Jack took Jaz home. When he reappeared the three sat at the table, which reminded Dulcie of the night she had first told them about Richard and how she had just ended their relationship. The memory was too much and she buried her face in her hands and wept for the man she had lost, for what she had done to him and the effect it must have had on him. 'This is all my fault. If it wasn't for me causing the stress in his life, Richard would still be alive, his heart wouldn't have—'

'You can't know that. And that way madness lies so clear it from your mind. Now.'

She had never heard Jack speak so severely and it helped. She stopped crying. They sat with her for the rest of the afternoon and late into the evening. Beth had suggested she stayed the night to keep her company, but Dulcie wanted to be alone.

Except she wasn't alone. In the silence of the night as she lay in bed, she felt Richard's presence. The smell of him was still on the pillow and sheets and the book he'd been reading was at his side of the bed. Next to it stood a silver-framed photograph of the two of them in Venice—it had been taken by a tourist, a man who had slipped briefly into and out of their lives and unwittingly provided Dulcie with a keepsake she would always treasure. She fell asleep lying on her side, her hand resting on the space where Richard had once been.

Since they had returned from Yorkshire, Beth and Ewan's email correspondence had tailed off. It was more common now for them to phone each other: they had swapped telephone numbers and addresses.

'I don't suppose I've convinced you I'm not a serial killer with a penchant for bumping off fellow writers, have I?' he had asked, as they took a late-night stroll during Beth's last night at the conference.

'You might have. Why?'

Coming to a stop, he said, 'OK. I'd like to ask you two questions. The first is this. Can we stay in touch, and not just by email but by that antiquated device known as the telephone?'

She had no hesitation in agreeing. 'Yes. I'd like that very much. And your second question?'

'Crikey, not so fast, Beth, it took all my courage to get that one out. I need to psych myself up for question number two.'

He started walking again, but this time with his arm round her shoulders. She could smell his aftershave, a fresh citrus fragrance that she knew would always remind her of this moment.

Plenty of other people were taking advantage of the mild night, and after several women—die-hard Jared Winter fans—had stared openly at Beth, she had suggested he might like to remove his arm. 'Your book sales are going to plummet if you don't,' she added.

He surprised her by leading her towards the middle of the floodlit croquet lawn. And there, for all to see, he said, 'This is my last night with you, and even if I have to spend the rest of my life dodging looks that could kill, it's a price I'm prepared to pay.' He took both of her hands in his. 'Prepare yourself, Bethany King, here comes question number two.' He coughed. 'Would it be too much of a liberty to ask if a lowly wretch such as I would be allowed one small kiss? And to hell with the book sales!'

She had laughed. 'For that, I'll grant you a colossal kiss.'

And she had. A kiss that was so perfect that even now when she recalled it—thought of his lips moving slowly against hers—her legs went weak. Suddenly a loud cheer had gone up behind them. They hadn't noticed the crowd of onlookers who had spilled out of the bar.

Laughing, Beth and Ewan had slipped away to a less visible spot in the garden, and after he'd apologised for sullying her good name, he held her close and kissed her again, tenderly, lovingly. 'Thank goodness our children aren't here to witness such appalling behaviour,' he joked. 'I'd be grounded for at least a month if Alice knew what I was up to.'

That was what she liked so much about Ewan: his sense of humour. He could make her laugh and was sexy too—a winning combination!

But it didn't feel right to be so happy when Dulcie was torn apart with grief. It was heartbreaking to see, especially as Beth knew how it felt.

She had been touched that Ewan had sent Dulcie a card of sympathy: he was as sincere as he was generous. He'd kept his word about speaking to his agent on Jack's behalf; Jack had sent a copy of *Friends and Family* to London and was now waiting to hear what kind of offer Felix McCallum would make. It was all very exciting. She was glad that Jack had been the one to find success with his writing; he richly deserved it.

Back in October, when she had plucked up the courage to respond to the card in the window of Novel Ways, she had hoped it would provide her with an opportunity to meet new people and explore a shared interest. To her delight, it had given her a whole new lease of life: with a new circle of friends and revitalised self-confidence. Nathan's leaving home in the autumn didn't look half so daunting now.

On top of that, and to her amazement, there was also the potential for romance. She was going to stay with Ewan in Suffolk in a couple of weeks' time. Secretly, like a child waiting for Christmas, she was ticking off the days on the calendar.

The other day Simone had phoned, and howled with laughter when Beth had told her what she'd been up to all these months. Ben had recently discovered Jared Winter's books. 'And you know what an infuriating laugh Ben has—he's like a pressure cooker about to explode. Tell your new friend to stop writing such off-the-wall books or I'll be citing him in my divorce petition. Is he as quirky as Ben says the books are?'

Since coming home Beth had read several of Ewan's novels, so she could answer her friend's question from an informed standpoint. 'Not really. He's funny, but never at the expense of anyone else.'

'Does he remind you of Adam?'

'No.'

'Good. Adam took life too seriously. That was why he killed himself. Now, go and have some fun, Beth.'

As a consequence of her improved relationship with Lois, Beth had decided to tell her and Barnaby about Ewan. 'I thought you ought to know, not that there's much to tell, that I've met a man I'm quite fond of. He lives in Suffolk, so there's no danger of . . .' She lost her nerve.

'No danger of what?' prompted Lois, her faded blue eyes blinking.

She summoned her courage by reminding herself how Ewan had made her feel when he'd kissed her so publicly. 'Of making a fool of myself or getting too involved too soon.'

Barnaby said, 'It's high time you threw caution to the wind and got involved with a man, Beth. Wouldn't you agree, Lois?'

'Does he make you happy when you're with him?'

The question was so unlike any other Lois had asked her that Beth responded with equal candour. 'We haven't had the opportunity to spend much time together yet, but yes, he does.'

'Well, then, what else is there to say? Does he have a name? And what does he do?'

'Ewan Jones. He's a writer.'

For a moment Beth waited to hear Lois exclaim, 'I knew all along that you had an ulterior motive for joining that writing group!' But she didn't. She smiled stiffly and said, 'That's nice. At least you have something in common. Something on which to build.'

Jaz stood back to admire their handiwork. Not bad.

For the last week she and her brothers, with help from Nathan, and even, occasionally, from Billy and Vicki, had been secretly working on Victor's house. She had seen the house for the first time when Victor had asked her to have a look at it, then report back to him. She had been relieved to see that things weren't as bad as she'd thought they would be. What also came home to her was that if Jack hadn't been the kind of man he was, Victor would be dead. And as far as she knew, only she, Jack, Beth and Dulcie would have been upset by his death. She thought of Dulcie and the state she'd been in since they got back from Harrogate, and hurriedly pushed away the thought of death.

Victor was very much alive and would soon be back home.

Now, with only the replastered walls in the bedroom to be painted when they'd dried out, the small terraced house was habitable again. She couldn't wait to see Victor's face. It would be almost as interesting as her brothers' faces had been when she'd impressed upon them the reasons why they had to help her. 'Boys,' she'd said, not long after her return from Norton Hall, 'I have a job for you.'

'Oh, yeah, little sis,' said Phin. 'What's that? You need a hand counting your winnings?' Everyone at home had been amazed when she'd received the letter from the conference committee telling her she'd come second in the short-story competition and had won fifty pounds.

'No,' she'd said, 'but I'd like your assistance with something I know you can do.' She'd explained about Victor's house and they'd laughed at her. Until, that was, she'd said, 'Do you think Mum and Dad will laugh when they hear what you did to Jack?' They gave in.

Standing alongside Phin and Nathan in Victor's hall, she clapped her hands. 'We've done it, boys. Well done.'

Nathan said, 'Happy now?'

'I will be when Victor sees what we've done.'

'You're sure he'll approve? Won't he accuse you of interfering?'

'He'll be as ungracious as he always is, but inside he'll be OK about it. He just won't know how to express his gratitude. I get the feeling he hasn't had much experience in that area.'

Nathan took Jaz home, then drove to the health centre to pick up his mother. It was Adele Waterman's birthday today and they were treating her to dinner. It seemed ages now since she had moved out, but that was the funny thing about change, he supposed; once it had happened, the new became the old. The same would be true once he left home for college. Last year he'd been worried how his mother would cope on her own, but not now. With Jack living in the flat downstairs, he knew help would be on hand, should she need it, and with Ewan on the scene, he was sure she would soon start to live her life quite differently from the way she had since his father had died.

Thinking of his father, he was glad that things had been resolved with his grandparents, and that he no longer had to compete with the distorted memory of a man he could scarcely remember.

Change, he'd come to realise, happened all the time.

Once again Victor was being told how lucky he was, and he was almost tempted to believe it. He was being allowed home next week.

It was the endlessly chatty WRVS woman who was currently telling him how fortunate he was. 'We'll miss you when you've gone, Mr Blackmore,' she was saying. 'You're a lucky man to have recovered so quickly. It must be the combination of the excellent nursing care and your devoted little girlfriend who visits you so regularly.'

He looked up from his A4 pad, horrified. 'My devoted what?'

She smiled. 'The pretty redhead.'

'For your information Jaz doesn't have red hair, she has *auburn* hair.' For a split second he wondered why he'd said this. Then he remembered Jaz telling him that she hated anyone describing her hair as red.

The woman's smile broadened. 'You're the envy of every man here.'

'But I'm old enough to be her father—her grandfather!'

She threw a glance at the rest of the patients. 'That's what's driving them mad. They want to know what your secret is.'

'That's disgusting! There's absolutely nothing between Jaz and me. We're . . .' he sought to find the right word. Acquaintances? No. They were more than that. 'Friends,' he said, surprising himself with the admission. 'And I take great exception that you should think otherwise.'

'Calm down, Mr Blackmore, I'm only teasing you.' The woman, who was about the same age as Victor, clicked her tongue. Then, just as he thought she was moving away, she said, 'Oh, I hope you don't mind me saying, but I really like what you're writing.'

He eyed her suspiciously. 'And what would you know about that?'

'I've read it. It's very good.'

'When have you read a single word of what I've written?' he demanded, outraged.

'Ssh—don't get so worked up.' She gave a faintly embarrassed shrug. 'Perhaps I shouldn't have done it, but, well, there we are, I did. You left your notebook on your bed. I thought you wouldn't mind.'

'It's an invasion of my privacy. I'm going to report you.'

She looked alarmed. 'Oh, please, don't do that. The trouble was, once I'd read the first couple of pages I couldn't stop. I wanted to know what would happen next. I felt so sorry for the poor little boy, I just had to know if he'd get his own back on those rotten bullies.'

'You wanted to know what would happen next?' he asked. 'Really?'

'Oh, yes. I was hooked.' She lowered her gaze, shamefaced. 'I don't suppose you'd let me read the rest when you've finished it, would you?'

Victor's annoyance disappeared. 'I'll think about it,' he said. He watched her trundle her trolley along the row of beds and returned her wave as she left the ward. He made a note to find out her name. An objective opinion from someone with such a refreshing view of his writing might prove invaluable. The thought occurred to him that she might also help him after he had been discharged next week. He would need the odd errand running for him, and she seemed pleasant enough.

All the members of Hidden Talents had said they'd lend a hand when he went home, but it was Jaz's offers of help that had surprised him most. She had always been rude to him, but he liked her because she was so remorselessly plain-spoken with him. That was why he'd trusted her to look at his house. Anyone else would have tried to put a gloss on the state of it to spare his feelings. Jaz hadn't done that. 'Well, Victor,' she'd said, 'there's a mess, but I reckon you've been lucky. Tell you what, why don't you leave it to me to get it sorted for you?'

'But it must be worse than that? It has to be.'

'Victor, would I lie to you?'

'Mmm . . . maybe not. How will you get it sorted, though?'

She'd tapped her nose with a finger. 'I have contacts. Don't forget, I come from a family of builders. If you want, you can settle the money side of things when you're back on your feet.'

Victor closed his eyes and thought over the last six months of his life. The shame of being made redundant seemed lost in the mists of time, as did those depressing days and nights of sitting, cold and alone, in the spare room writing *Star City*. He knew now that he'd made himself ill doing that, had very nearly lost his life. But how could he ever have believed he would produce his best work by writing in that stifling vacuum? Nowadays, and because he was used to having company twenty-four hours a day, he felt a hundred times more creative. As soon as he was well enough, he would start looking for a new job and attend Hidden Talents more regularly. And he'd go on a course like the one everyone else from the group had gone on.

Jack was finding it difficult to concentrate at work. His mind was constantly elsewhere, as he waited to hear the latest news from London. Nick Ellis—Ewan's agent in London who had read *Friends and Family*—had said, 'Leave it with me, Jack, but I think we can safely say you should get in a bottle of your favourite drink. You're going to need it. I don't suppose you've started on the next book, have you?'

'Are you joking?'

'Get to it, Jack. Publishers like to know there's more of the same in the offing. I'll tell Felix you're well on your way with book number two.'

Jack had the feeling that literary agents could knock spots off estate agents when it came to wholesale flannel and brass-necked cheek.

At five thirty, he left the office and drove to Prestbury to fetch the girls, his thoughts switching to the rehearsing of the script he'd put together for tonight. If only he knew that the others concerned would stick to the lines he'd written for them, he'd feel a whole lot happier.

Maddie answered the door. She looked anxious, probably wondering what it was he wanted to discuss.

'Is it OK if we talk in the kitchen?' she said. 'Tony's in the middle of cooking supper.'

'I'm experimenting with vegetarian cuisine,' Tony said. 'Lentils. Glass of wine?' He reached for an opened bottle of Merlot.

'Just a small one,' Jack said.

The wine was poured and glasses were handed round.

'Look,' said Jack, needing to clear the air, 'I haven't come here to fight or make a point. I just want to talk to you.' He took a sip of his wine. And another. 'The thing is, I doubt I'll ever feel totally happy seeing the pair of you together but, for Amber and Lucy's sake, I have to learn to appear that way. To achieve that, you two have to help me.'

'How? Every time I try to discuss anything with you, you fire off at me,' Maddie said defensively.

'I know. But sometimes . . . sometimes it's as if you deliberately fail to see things from where I'm standing.'

'That's what you always say. What you don't realise is—'

'No, Maddie,' Tony intervened gently. 'There have been occasions when Jack's been right and we've been wrong.' He turned to Jack again. 'Would saying sorry help?'

The unexpectedness of Tony's suggestion, its sheer simplicity, brought Jack up short. He crossed the kitchen to look out of the window, giving himself time and space to think.

'Jack?'

He turned his head, and saw before him . . . not the man he'd come to hate, whom he'd vilified for everything wrong in his life, but his boyhood friend. Memories of their glory days flashed before him. Until this moment he had thought that writing *Friends and Family* would be the last word in catharsis, but now he knew differently. He had to hear that Maddie and Tony were genuinely sorry for what they'd done.

'Would it help, Jack?' his old friend pressed.

'Yes, Tony,' he murmured, his voice shaky. 'I think it would.'

Tony passed a hand through his hair. He glanced briefly at Maddie. 'I've known you nearly all my life, Jack. What I did to you was wrong. I was a shit for falling in love with Maddie, but I did and I can't change that. All I can say, and I'll say it for the rest of my life if it helps, is that I'm sorry. I'm sorry for wrecking everything between us, and to prove it there'll be no more talk of California. I just couldn't do that to you and the girls.' He glanced again at Maddie. 'Sorry if you're disappointed.'

She shook her head. 'Far from it.'

'But I thought you wanted to go?'

'I only went along with it because I thought you wanted it so badly.'

Tony groaned. 'Oh, the great unsaid. It must be responsible for nearly all the world's troubles.' He put his arms round Maddie and held her.

Jack stiffened, then forced himself to relax. Maddie caught his eye and slipped self-consciously out of Tony's embrace. She moved towards Jack and, in an elegant gesture that reminded him of when they used to dance together, she held out her hands. 'I'm sorry, Jack. Truly I am. Please don't hate me for what I did. I couldn't bear it.'

'I don't hate you,' he murmured. 'I never have. And never will.' Then, unbelievably, he took her in his arms.

Back at the flat with Amber and Lucy, he played his answering machine messages. There was only one: from Nick Ellis. 'Give me a call, Jack, I've got great news for you. I'm in the office till late, so you'll catch me here until about eight thirty.'

While the girls helped themselves to a drink, Jack dialled Nick's number in London. The phone was answered instantly

'Oh, hi, Jack. How are you?'

'Fine. Actually, better than fine. I'm over the moon. I've just had some excellent news.'

'It must be your lucky day. How does a two-book contract for a six-figure sum sound to you?'

His heart racing, Jack said, 'Depends what the six figures are.'

'I was thinking of a cool one hundred and fifty thousand pounds.'

Jack swallowed. 'Did I hear right?'

'You did. Felix loved the book, he said it was amusing and poignant and straight from the hip. Or did he mean heart? Whatever. I've told him I had to OK the offer with you. It's a good one, Jack.'

Laughing, Jack said, 'You don't have a clue how good.'

'I do, actually. Shall I say yes to Felix?'

'Affirmative. You might like to add on a thankyou from me.'

'Steady on! Let's not give him ideas above his station. And don't be surprised if he wants you to change the odd thing here and there. From what you've told me, you wrote the book at lightning speed, so there's bound to be some rewrites on the cards. But it'll be a breeze. Now, go and do the sensible thing and celebrate.'

'Do you fancy going out for supper?' Jack asked the girls, when he came off the phone. 'How about Chinese?' He hugged them both. 'We're celebrating two mega-fantastic events in my life. One, you're not moving to America, and two, against all the odds, I'm suddenly the happiest man in the whole wide world!'

Dulcie was driving to Maywood station to meet Andrew and Miles. They had wanted to come up sooner so that they could make a fuss of her, as Miles had put it so sweetly, but work commitments had dictated that this was the earliest they had been able to get away. She was looking forward to their company—not that she'd spent much time on her own. Prue and Maureen, Beth and Jack had seen to that. With their kindness, which was sometimes gentle, sometimes firm, depending on her state of mind, they had ensured she wasn't left to her own devices for long.

It was a fortnight since Richard had died, and nothing could keep her thoughts from him. Their time in Venice would always be special to her. She would never forget the beauty of the moment when they had stood on the small bridge in the twinkling darkness of the night and he'd said that one day they would return as man and wife.

Occasionally she tortured herself by questioning whether she had made Richard happy. If they'd never met he would not have had to endure the pain of choosing between his wife and her. She still couldn't rid herself of the thought that it was her fault he'd died.

She wasn't alone in thinking that. Angela had written to her, a letter of vengeful cruelty blaming Dulcie for Richard's death. 'You caused the stress that ultimately tore his heart apart,' Angela had written. 'I just hope you never know a moment's peace for what you did.'

Jack and Beth had been firm with Dulcie when she'd shown them. 'You're not to believe a single word of what she's written,' Beth had said.

Jack had been more forthright. He'd taken the letter from Dulcie and ripped it up. 'We all understand why she felt the need to write it, but it helps no one. Least of all her.'

Even now the letter, though it was long gone, still hurt Dulcie. But it didn't hurt as much as not being able to attend Richard's funeral. She had accepted that she had no right to be there. Another woman might have sent an anonymous wreath, but Dulcie planted a climbing rose against the back of the house where she and Richard had often sat. Patting down the soil, she spoke aloud as if Richard was there with her: 'I once promised you I would never play the part of a possessive lover, my darling, and now I'll make you another promise. I will do my best to grieve for you quietly and lovingly. I will think only of the good times we shared. Just as you'd want me to.'

The following day she had a surprise visitor. Richard's daughter.

'I haven't come here to make a scene,' Victoria said. 'I just want to talk to you. But I'll go away if you'd rather.'

'No. Come in. Please.' She took her through to the sitting room. 'I suppose you've come for his things.'

Victoria frowned. 'What things?'

'All the things he brought with him.' She was thinking of his clothes and books upstairs, and more importantly, his papers and documents.

The frown was still on Victoria's face—reminding Dulcie of Richard—and she said, 'That's not why I've come.'

'Why, then?'

'I need to understand why you meant so much to him. It was so out of character what he did. I still can't accept how he could do it.'

'You probably won't believe me, but we felt the same ourselves. Neither of us felt proud to be deceiving so many. I don't expect you to condone what we did, but we loved each other. I didn't throw myself at him, didn't trick him into an affair. It was love. I'm sorry if that hurts, but it's the truth.'

Dulcie watched Victoria chew her lower lip, and then, to her horror, the poor girl started to cry. Dulcie went to her. 'I'm sorry,' she said, 'perhaps I shouldn't have said that.'

'No, it's OK. In a way it's what I came to hear. I wanted to know that Dad was happy before he died. The last time I saw him he looked so sad. I hated seeing him like that. Henry was bullying him into coming home. He caused an awful scene. I knew then that Dad would never come back. I felt as if we'd lost him. As if *we* were lost to him.'

'Oh, no. He loved you. You four children meant the world to him. He was terrified you'd stop loving him. It was why he stayed as long as he did. He was a devoted father. You must never doubt that.'

She left an hour later, after Dulcie had given her the documents she felt belonged to his family rather than to her. They had parted with a handshake, which was more than Dulcie felt she deserved. But, that night, she had slept peacefully for the first time in days. She had woken in the morning with a sense of calm.

She had been waiting for no more than five minutes when a stream of people emerging from the station caught her attention. She looked for Andrew and Miles. When they appeared, she saw they weren't alone. Kate was with them, a tentative smile on her lips. Dulcie's heart soared. To be reconciled with Kate so soon was more than she could have hoped for.

Dear Beth,

I've just heard the news from my agent about Jack's book offer.

Please pass on my best wishes. I know exactly how he'll be feeling, as if he's won the Lottery ten times over.

Now, knowing what a worrier you are, I'd like to put your mind at rest. I want you to know that when you come to stay here next weekend, there won't be a trace of the bars of chocolate I'd stockpiled in the garage. I will be the epitome of the perfect gentleman during your visit. Only trouble is, I've eaten the aforementioned chocolate and have ballooned into the size of a humpback whale. Hope this won't put you off coming to stay.

Lots of love, Ewan X

PS Be warned. Alice will be putting in a brief appearance while you're here, to give you the once-over!

PPS How about I nip out and buy us the one bar of Fruit and Nut? Just in case . . .

Dear Ewan,

I have a sweet tooth, better make it two . . .

Love, Beth

ERICA JAMES

For many years, writing was just a hobby for Erica James and, like her characters in *Hidden Talents*, she joined a writing group, took courses and attended conferences. 'It's something I would warmly recommend any other would-be writer to do,' she told me. 'Of course, there are always those, like Victor Blackmore in my novel, who are convinced of their talents, but don't let them put you off. I was usually the one sitting at the back of the group feeling horribly intimidated and hiding behind the know-it-alls. But I made copious notes and absorbed everything I thought was useful. And when it all paid off, that was pure magic. I can still remember my agent ringing to tell me that my first novel, *A Breath of Fresh Air*, had been accepted by a publisher. I was sitting on the bed writing everything down so that my sons, Edward and Samuel, could understand what was going on. They were ten and eight at the time. When they got the gist of it, they went and fetched some streamers they'd had in their bedrooms and showered me with them. An amazing moment!'

Writing has now become a way of life for Erica, but even though she has become a best-selling author, she still feels apprehensive whenever one of her novels is published. 'I guess it's because I am a closet writer— I love to write but hate anyone to read what I've written. Please don't ask

why I put myself through such an ordeal! Probably because, purely and simply, I just love to write.'

When Erica is not busy writing, she enjoys travelling. 'My favourite place in the world is Venice and I couldn't resist having a few chapters of *Hidden Talents* set there so that I could, mentally, spend time wandering the maze of little alleyways. But this summer I took my youngest son, who is now sixteen, to Japan because he is learning the language. It's the most amazing country, culturally extraordinary, and everyone is so courteous. I can't imagine what Japanese tourists who come to Britain must think of us! And Japanese women are so elegant. *And so tiny.* I'm a size eight but the clothes I bought in Tokyo were labelled large!'

For Erica James one of the biggest rewards of being an author is the correspondence she receives from her readers. 'Some of the things people say are very humbling. Just recently, a reader got in touch with me to tell me that as a result of reading my previous novel, *Precious Time*, in Reader's Digest's *Of Love and Life*, she had sold her house, bought a camper van (just like my heroine in the story) and was taking to the road!' Spurred on by *Hidden Talents*, there are bound to be a handful of Erica's readers who will soon be trying their hand at writing a novel!

Jane Eastgate

Summertime

Liz Rigbey

For three generations the women in
Lucy's family have witnessed the loss of
their baby sons—firstly her grandmother,
then her mother, and lastly Lucy herself.
Why has such sadness hit one family?
Were all three women unfit mothers,
as Lucy fears? Or is there a simpler
but far more sinister explanation?

One

My MOTHER TOLD my sister and me this story many times. How it took days for the train to cross Russia and how, by the time they reached the border, it was clear that the baby was dead.

The father had known for some time. His three daughters, one by one, understood. The other passengers told each other with silent, shocked looks. Only the mother seemed incapable of comprehending what had happened to the child locked into her arms.

From the moment the Andreyev family boarded the train the baby cried—the full, insistent cry of a six-month-old. Everyone in the car told themselves that it would soon stop crying and, anyway, the three girls took up little space. Each car was oversubscribed and each passenger wore a thick coat, hat, scarf and gloves. Baggage was piled high over the heads of the travellers, on the floor, on laps.

When, far later than expected, the train pulled out of the station, the other passengers confidently awaited the silence that would come as soon as the child felt the lulling rhythm of metal wheels on metal rails.

But the silence did not come.

The train cut its way out of the city, past factories and apartment blocks. The passengers sat listening to the endless circle of cries. Each tiny gap of silence when the baby drew breath was followed by a roar of such misery that it seemed the child was voicing the sadness of everyone.

As Moscow retreated behind the train, the travellers were at first glad to see the countryside. It was good to peer, through the dirt that obscured the window, at the snowy landscape. They soon tired of it.

Hour upon hour of flat land, unbroken by trees or roads or hedges, any variation in its colour or crop obscured by the snow. When forests came they were disappointing, dark slabs of uniform conifers. And as night gathered outside the train, still the baby cried.

'Can't you stop it, for God's sake?' a young man yelled at last. But all the mother could do was shrug and shake her head.

The father ignored the child and his wife but sat still, hard-mouthed, his eyes running over the faces of the passengers. Four, yes four children, with each of the girls well-dressed and carrying a small leather travelling case on her lap. It was clear that Andreyev had done well. His menacing air of officialdom prevented many a protest at the baby's cries.

After the first few hours the train stopped. There was no station, no apparent reason. Only when the first pearly light fell on the grey faces of the travellers did the train shudder into motion. And still the baby cried.

But then, hours after everyone had given up hope that the noise would ever stop, the gaps between the baby's cries grew longer and the angry edge to its roars disintegrated. Passengers exchanged hopeful looks. They peered at the scarlet-faced bundle in the mother's arms. It was scarcely whimpering now. The baby was falling asleep.

When at last silence fell, satisfaction stole round each passenger, and everyone, except the mother, fell asleep. Some slept a long time, others only in snatches. From time to time those who were awake glanced at the baby and a suspicion gradually became a conviction. It was white now, and they detected no movement at all. The baby was dead. The three girls watched horror register on the faces of the passengers. No one spoke. The woman continued to cradle the bundle in her arms.

As soon as he opened the door of the Andreyev car, the guard detected that something was wrong. It was too silent. Everyone looked up at him. They seemed to be waiting for him to notice something. Only one person did not watch him, a tired woman with a sleeping baby.

He reached out to the child's small, white face. Cold. Colder than stone. He lifted the baby's hand and tried to bend the fingers but they would not move. The baby had been dead for hours.

The guard said, 'You will have to give the baby to me. It is dead and can travel no further.'

'No!' cried the mother. 'No, no, he's asleep.' She was sobbing now.

The father stood up suddenly. 'Give him to me,' he ordered, and the woman allowed the stiff bundle to be removed from her arms. Watched by his three daughters, he handed the baby to the waiting guard, who took it gingerly.

The woman clutched at the guard's shabby uniform. 'Please, please,

please, promise me that my child will be given a proper burial!'

The man could give no such assurance; indeed, he was even now wondering how to dispose of this inanimate baby in a swift and trouble-free manner, and the possibilities did not include hours of pickaxing at the frozen ground. He left the car carrying the baby and was heard descending from the train.

The mother cried silently and ceaselessly for the rest of the journey.

My mother knew this story well because she was the youngest of the three daughters on the train and the sobbing woman was my grand-mother. It was a story I heard all through my childhood but when, in my teens, my mother moved into a clinic for the mentally ill, it slid from my mind along with her other stories like a shoal of small fish sliding through a crack in the rocks. Only when I gave birth to a son myself did the fish dart back again, flashing silver at me when I held my baby in my arms. When he died and was taken away by a woman in dark clothes that might have been a uniform, I sat in our house in California and it seemed that the woman who had sobbed in the train in the snow in Eastern Europe more than sixty years ago was me and I was her.

It's a spring day, cold, but each time I cross a street the sun appears at the end of it like some advertising billboard. I cut through the park. I watch the babies sitting in their buggies. It's three years since I held a baby. It's almost exactly three years.

Click clack, click clack. My new shoes on the sidewalk, scraping a little against my heel. Occasionally, when the Manhattan traffic hushes unex-pectedly, it seems to me that my left foot hits the pavement harder than my right. I try to balance my weight, but your walk's like your mother or some other relative you didn't choose and can't change. *Click clack.*

The lobby of our building is a towering, glassy atrium. Some of the bushes that grow here are like the trees my father grows in his garden back in California, only here their shape is more perfect. The elevator doors close and there is that light-headed feeling as it ascends. When Daddy stayed with me in New York, just that once, more than two years ago, I brought him into the office on a Saturday morning. As the elevator started to catapult us up the building, Daddy was so shocked by its sud-denness and power that he staggered backwards. I reached out to steady him, but he had turned his face into the caricature of a grimace and pinned his body to the wall in a comic shape of mock horror. I smiled, a little relieved. We don't acknowledge Daddy's age and if he shows signs of frailty we ignore them. He isn't allowed to grow old or get ill.

I move fast along the hallway. 'Hi.' 'Hi.' 'Hi.'

Heads bob round the screens in our office, registering my presence with a deference that acknowledges that it's a big deal day and the deal's mine. It's only three months since Gregory Hifeld appeared at my desk and told me about his son. George has a drink problem and no business sense. A man unlikely ever to take over Thinking Toys from his father.

'You're sixty-eight, that's not so old. And you look strong and fit to me,' I told Gregory. Not so strong and fit as Daddy but then, nobody is. 'Why do you need to do anything about the business right now?'

He bowed his head. 'I'm tired and my wife is ill. We'd like to enjoy the time we have left together.'

Soon, George Hifeld was sitting where his father had sat, yellow fingers and the tremor of a guy who needs a cigarette but thinks it might start the fire alarms. And finally, Mittex. Keen to buy Thinking Toys but trying not to show it. Dark suits, nodding white heads like vultures. Their CEO-in-waiting, Jay Kent, asking questions, slicing through figures as professionally as a chef slicing onions. Today, they will all sit at the boardroom table together for the first time and maybe, by the end of the day, we'll know whether Mittex will buy Thinking Toys.

When the boss arrives, I have my fingers wrapped round my second cup of coffee. Jim Finnigan is bald. He's obese. When I started working here he was just fat but he takes the train in and a guy at the station sells hot cinnamon buns, dripping with butter. Jim has three every morning. He tells his wife, June, that he has only one.

'Jeez,' says Jim, pulling up a chair. 'You're going to have a tough time in the boardroom this afternoon. I was thinking about it at the station and I had to have an extra cinnamon.'

'The first time you ate four?' I ask.

He shuffles his feet. 'Well . . . actually five.'

'Ji-im. You've been eating four every day?'

He nods miserably. 'Only for a month or two. Don't let me eat anything more today, OK? And don't tell June.'

'Of course not.'

Jim looks at me twinkly-eyed. He says, 'So how you planning to handle Kent up in the boardroom?'

'He isn't my client, Jim. The Hifelds are my clients.'

'Precisely. So how are you going to handle Kent?'

Jay Kent, not tall but as slim and quick as some metallic weapon.

'He wants you, Lucy,' says Jim and his words make me start because they're just the words Jay Kent used, sitting in the Michigan restaurant.

Jim manoeuvres his feet into their favourite place on the garbage bin. 'Has anything happened between you two?' he asks.

'Of course not.'

'Nothing?' asks Jim, searching my face.

'We talk a lot. On the phone.'

'Like, pillow talk without the pillows?'

'Friend talk.' Mostly Kent talks and I listen. He doesn't know a lot about me and I like that.

Jim studies me for signs of insincerity then he says, 'June thinks you only get yourself into relationships where you can't have a real relationship, for example with a guy like Kent who's married and has a kid.'

I imagine Kent's kid, a wriggling blade of a baby, surrounded by plastic, blaring Mittex toys.

'The kind of relationship I have with Kent is limited for professional reasons,' I say briskly.

Jim doesn't seem to hear me. As he gets up he asks, 'What did you do this weekend?'

'Oh, just visited friends.'

'Uh-huh.' He shambles off and there's something dissatisfied in the hunch of his shoulders. He turns and says, 'Lucy, I'm hungry. I want you to know I'm hungry but I'm not eating anything.'

My sister calls. It's not seven o'clock yet in California. She's due to leave for the hospital any minute and she sounds clinical, hurried.

'We've been trying to get you all weekend, Luce.'

'I was away . . .'

'Good! I hope you were having a good time and not moping about.'

'I moped a bit.'

Her voice softens suddenly. 'Oh, Luce, are you OK?'

'Yeah.'

'I took Daddy up to Stevie's grave. We left some spring flowers.'

'Thanks, Jane.'

It should have been me driving Daddy up to the children's section of the big cemetery. Supporting him as we walked to the place that marks Stevie's brief sojourn in this world.

'It doesn't seem like three years,' she says.

If I let myself think about it, Stevie's death seems like now to me. That moment when I found my son's body lying white and motionless in his blue crib like something small floating on the surface of the ocean. I wish I could erase that moment but all I can do is turn away from it.

I say, 'I did call Daddy a few times at the weekend but I guess he was out. Is he OK?'

She hesitates. When she speaks her voice is kind. 'Of course he was low on Saturday, but who's going to be ecstatic visiting their grandson's grave? Afterwards we had lunch with Scott and we thought he seemed a little better this year than last, and Daddy was pleased with that. Larry says you should use anniversaries to accept the alleviation in your grief. I mean, celebrate the fact that you're getting better, not feel guilty about it. Daddy agrees with him and I guess he should know.'

Daddy never talks about it directly, but he also lost a son. My brother. I don't even remember him. He died in some kind of accident when he was a small baby. When Stevie died Daddy still didn't talk about it but he understood. He knew, and he knew better than anyone.

'I hope . . .' Jane is cautious, so it's half a question, 'that there's been some alleviation in your grief.'

I don't want to talk about grief. I say, 'How's Daddy's hip?'

Jane's voice is reassuring. 'It doesn't seem to slow him down. He's seventy-two, Lucy, and he's fitter than a lot of people half his age. As for his memory, well, we were remembering some field trip we took years ago and he said he could recall practically every rock we found.'

'Which field trip?' Each field trip is a discrete memory. There was always something that happened, something we found, someone we met. Only the rocks seemed the same.

Quietly, Jane says, 'Arizona.'

I remember that trip. I can feel its heat now. 'Arizona,' I echo.

'Daddy never says so, but I'm sure he'd really like to see you, Luce. I know he was half looking forward to this weekend, because he thought maybe you'd come home. He even said he thought Mother might benefit from seeing you. Since I doubt she'd even recognise you, that may have been Daddy's way of saying he'd benefit from seeing you himself.'

'I have some big negotiations happening, Jane, I wouldn't want to leave town right now. But when it's all over, maybe I'll come.'

Jane takes my concession for confirmation. She says how pleased she is. I remind her, 'I only said maybe.'

In the early afternoon, when I've completed my preparations for the big meeting, I take my coat and go down onto the street. People are still eating in sidewalk cafés. I go into a diner and eat a cream cheese bagel.

Suddenly I glimpse Daddy, peering at me through the window. In an instant I realise that the sky outside has blackened and my own reflection is looking back at me. Dark hair, dark eyes, actually green but not in this strange snapshot, prominent bones. I never understood before now how people could say I resembled my father.

'Most beautiful women,' Jay Kent told me, 'have uninteresting faces. Your beauty is intriguing.' His tone was dispassionate.

The coffee the diner serves is so strong and bitter that it makes my mouth curl just the way Kent's mouth curled that cold morning in Michigan. Day two of the Mittex trip to Thinking Toys in Michigan and it was still snowing. The workers were arriving in their cars, their voices ringing in the frosty air as they greeted one another cheerfully across the parking lot. Most were overweight, some were obese, but they had an aura of rural contentment as they waddled in for their shift.

'Santa's happy little elves.' Kent's cheeks were hollow with cold.

'Not even a small part of you would want to live out here and be one of them?' I asked him. I thought everyone had a rural dream buried somewhere inside them. Kent pulled his lips back over his teeth.

Then, later, wrapped in warmth at the restaurant, he said, 'Neither could you be one of those guys. Don't kid yourself, Lucy.'

'Actually I used to be sort of like them, Kent.' No one calls him Jay. Except possibly his wife.

He raised his eyebrows at me.

I said, 'When I worked in private banking in California I used to plod across the parking lot into work just like one of Santa's elves.'

'Private banking? In California?' The lips turned down.

I was defensive. 'I had some very big clients, mostly Pacific Rim.'

'You were wasted there. I assume this is when you first started out?'

No, it was right up until I moved to New York, devastating my husband, disappointing my family. It was just three years ago. But I wasn't going to tell Kent that. He watched me, waiting for my reply. I studied the menu. Finally I said, 'Well, it all sounds like roadkill to me.'

That's when he straightened his back and said, 'I want you, Lucy. I don't know what to do about it.'

I knew I should look at him. It took a moment and when I did his eyes were waiting for me, invulnerable despite his words, as he explained that his interest in me was not restricted to his company's possible acquisition of my client.

I answered, 'We have to respect professional boundaries. We're working across the table from each other in some delicate negotiations.'

Fast, too fast, he said, 'You can have a professional boundary and a personal relationship at the same time. If that's what you both want.'

I looked down at his wedding ring and then at my own. Occasionally I think of taking it off but something stops me, perhaps the thought of Scott still wearing his. I said, 'Maybe.'

As I leave the diner, I wonder how it will be today, negotiating with a man who knows me the way Kent does.

Back at my desk on the eighty-third floor, Gregory and George Hifeld arrive. I sniff George's breath for liquor as we talk about airplanes, George's passion. He has two antique airplanes and a landing strip outside his father's house.

When Fatima announces that Mittex are in the boardroom, we get in the elevator. No one looks at anyone else.

As I walk into the boardroom I know that Kent has been waiting for me. When he greets me his eyes have a shine that shouldn't be there. He looks at me a moment too long before he looks at the Hifelds.

I greet Kent's colleagues and introduce our analyst and the Hifelds. I see Gregory as Kent must see him. Correct. Tall. His back erect but his face tired and his eyes sad. He doesn't want to be here, talking to fast, incomprehensible young men about selling the company he's spent his life building. George sits next to him, grinning too broadly, dishevelled despite the new suit.

'So, George,' says Kent abruptly. I jump a little. George jumps too.

'Tell me, George. What can you do? What place could we find for you in the new Thinking Toys?'

George brushes hair out of his eyes in a sweeping gesture he probably established in boyhood, only now there isn't any hair. 'Um, well, I don't want to run it,' he says unnecessarily.

Kent smiles at him but his eyes glitter and I know he's going to be merciless. 'Oh boy,' he says, stroking his chin. 'I wonder, George, how you'll deal with the changes we have in mind for Thinking Toys . . .'

Kent explains that Mittex think Hifeld productivity is too low and wages too high. That 1,000 employees is too many employees, too many by 1,000. Gregory's face is frozen.

I clench both fists but feel the deal slipping away from me.

Gregory looks at Kent. 'Your world,' he says, and his voice trembles a little, 'is plastic. Maybe you don't understand that high-quality wooden products are labour-intensive. Our labour is second to none.'

Kent smiles. 'Mr Hifeld, Gregory, I know the welfare of your work force has been a priority for you and I admire everything you've done. But at Mittex we don't have the same allegiances. We believe we can make your products to as high or higher a standard in the Far East. We see no reason to manufacture in Fullton, Michigan, for twice the price.'

'The Far East?' echoes Gregory.

'Most of our manufacturing facilities are located in Malaysia.'

'The Far East . . .' Gregory repeats. 'It would make your figures look good but the price in human terms would be incalculable for Fullton.' I know how much he must hate Kent. At this moment, I hate him too.

There is a knock on the boardroom door. An interruption. This wasn't supposed to happen and I assumed everyone knew that. The door opens and Fatima inches in. The whole room watches her in silence although she's trying to edge towards me as if no one's noticed. When she reaches me her face is red as she hands over a piece of paper. On it is Jim's big, sloppy writing, *Emergency. Come now. Sorry. J.*

I stare at the paper. No emergency is enough of an emergency to pull me out of this meeting. Anything could happen with me out of the room.

'Please, now, Lucy,' Fatima whispers.

'Excuse me,' I say, turning to Gregory and then to Kent. 'Could we take a break for five minutes? I can't imagine what this is about.'

From Fatima's face it's easy to see this is no negotiating ploy and Kent nods at me. 'Sure,' he says, 'we'll take a break.'

The Hifelds nod, George too vigorously. Everyone watches me leave, Kent most intently. I give an apologetic shrug as I edge out of the door.

In the hallway I look at Fatima for an explanation but she says, 'Can you go into Jim's office? He's waiting for you. Oh, Lucy, I think it's bad news. I'm sorry, I'm so sorry.'

We walk to the elevator and go down nine floors and get out together and we don't speak. My mind doesn't even begin to examine the possibilities. There's a numbness where fear or panic should be.

Jim, behind his desk, his feet propped on the edge of the wastepaper bin, is expressionless. When I walk in he struggles up, circumnavigates his desk and puts his arms round me. I see that he's crying.

'Jim?' I say.

'Sorry . . .' His voice is strangled. 'I'm crying because this shouldn't happen to you, Lucy.'

I still don't ask any questions. I like not knowing.

'You want to sit down?'

'No. I want to get back to the meeting.'

'Lucy, it's your father. He's dead.'

I am silent. I wait for some rush of pain or emotion but none comes. I feel nothing. I say, 'But he can't be. Jane saw him at the weekend . . .'

'He's dead, Lucy.'

Stevie's small body, lifeless in his blue crib. The five of us standing round him, gaping in disbelief. Daddy, me, Scott, Larry and Jane. I lift Stevie from the crib and he feels heavier than usual, a dead weight. His face is white and perfect. His eyes are closed. One hand is raised a little, but as I lift him it rolls lifelessly downwards. Jane said, 'He's dead, Lucy.'

'I don't know the details,' says Jim. 'But it's not straightforward. Your sister wants you on a plane as soon as possible. Lucy . . . as I understand it . . . it appears your father may have drowned. In the ocean.'

I look at Jim and I am brisk. I say, 'Are you sure about this?'

Jim says, 'The police need to interview you. You want to call your sister so she can explain?'

'No, Jim, not right now.'

'Fatima's already booked you on a flight west this evening. Seven o'clock. You should get home and pack. You can't go alone . . .'

I hear a distant voice. Some woman dressed as me says, 'I don't understand the hurry, Jim. If Daddy's dead there's no point rushing.'

Jim moans. 'It hasn't hit you yet. When it hits, it's going to hurt.'

'OK, I'll fly tonight,' says the woman, 'but I want to see this deal through before I go.'

She leaves the office. Back in the elevator she is surprised by the ghost of a man, a big man but a man who is growing old, who is so shocked by the elevator's velocity that he staggers back against the walls.

'Daddy's dead,' the woman says as she walks down the hallway, but the words don't mean anything and she doesn't break her stride.

The boardroom feels warm. Most people are standing. There's some desultory chatter. Silence when they realise the woman is back. People are quick to return to their seats.

'Is everything all right, Lucy?' asks Gregory.

'Well . . .' For the first time, she hesitates, this woman. Then she says, 'My father just died in unusual circumstances. I'll be flying out to California tonight, so I'd appreciate the concentration and cooperation of everyone in this meeting right now.'

You should not have been in there,' says Jim, as I unlock the door to my apartment. 'You should have been talking to your sister on the telephone. She's distraught.'

'My sister's a doctor; she's never distraught.'

'Well, she's very worried about you. Will you call her with your flight details so she can meet you?'

'I don't want her to meet me.'

'Call Scott, then.'

'I'll be fine alone.'

'I'm not letting you get on a plane unless someone's meeting you off it. Who's it going to be?' He hands me the phone. 'Jane or Scott?'

I sigh. 'I don't want to stay with either of them.'

'Just let them take care of you. Jane wants to do that, I can tell.'

Jane has always taken care of me. She was my doctor long before she was anyone else's. When I was a kid I had the kind of ill-health that needed managing and it was my big sister who managed it. Less exercise.

More exercise. Less excitement. More food. Less food. It's three years since anyone's cared about me as much as Jane. But I don't say that to Jim. I say, 'I've escaped from all that now, Jim.'

He looks upset. 'When did you last speak to your sister?' he asks.

'This morning and before that a few weeks ago. We call each other sometimes and it's very civilised but she just can't forgive me for going away and neither can Larry and neither can Scott.'

'They'll forgive you when you tell them you're coming home.'

I say, 'I'm calling Sasha.'

'Who's she?'

'He. Alexander.' I search for Sasha's office number. 'My mother has two sisters and the nicest is Aunt Zina and Sasha's her son. He's the same age as me. They live in the Russian quarter of town.'

Jim lets me dial.

A man's voice: 'Planning and Development, Eastern Europe.' It makes planning, development and Eastern Europe sound beyond tedium.

'Sasha, is that you?'

At once his voice changes. 'Good God, who can be calling me Sasha and speaking English to me with an American accent. Americans have always called me Alex.'

'Not this one, Sasha.'

'Let me think . . . Aha. I have the answer. My American cousins, Jane and Lucy. You're probably Lucy, no, certainly Lucy. Am I right, Lucia?'

'Yes, Sasha, you're right.'

'How delightful. How very delightful to hear from you.'

'But I'm calling you because . . . I'm calling with bad news.'

'Oh,' says Sasha. And that oh is thick with the knowledge that our lives are built on the shaky foundation of our own mortality and that of our loved ones. 'A death,' he says. 'A death in the family, I fear.'

'Yes, Sasha, a death. In the family.'

'Oh Lucia, is it your poor mother . . .?'

Fleetingly, bitterly, I wish I was calling to announce Mother's death.

'It's Daddy. He drowned. There was some kind of accident in the ocean. I don't know more than that, don't ask me more.'

'Oh God. I offer you heartfelt condolences. But where are you now?'

'I'm in New York and flying west tonight. I know this is short notice. I know I haven't seen you for years. But would you meet me at the airport?'

'Of course. Will I take you to your sister's? Or Scott's?'

'Actually, I can stay at Daddy's house. Probably it shouldn't be left empty.'

But Sasha is quick. 'No, Lucia, that would be too melancholy and, besides, it would please me very much if you would stay with us. And my mother, of course, would be delighted.'

'Are you living with Aunt Zina again?'

'Certainly.'

'Aren't you still married to Marina?'

'She informs me that I am not. But this is no time to talk of such things. Please stay with us, it would make us very happy.'

I try to protest but he continues, 'My dear Lucia, I have many warm memories of your father. He was a good man. Such a great loss.'

Everyone seems to feel Daddy's death more acutely than I do. 'Thank you, Sasha.' I give him details of my flight.

'All arranged?' asks Jim, as I end the call.

'Yup.'

Jim is ambling around looking at the shelves. 'What are all these rocks, for God's sake?'

'They're Daddy's. He's a geologist and he's always giving people rocks.'

'I thought he was a professor or something.'

'A professor of geology.'

Jim strokes the rocks. 'They're sort of beautiful. If you like rocks.'

'I collected the stripy ones myself. I used to go with him on field trips.'

'Where did you get them?' Jim cups his palm round one of the striped rocks and rolls another in his fingers. He passes one to me.

'Arizona.' I run the pads of my fingers over the rock's stripes.

'So, how come they have this pattern? Did your dad explain that?'

I slip the stone into my pocket. 'If he did, I've forgotten.'

'Why don't you put the phone down, Lucy?' asks Jim. I'm still cradling it against my shoulder.

'It just told me there are messages.'

I already knew that. They piled up over the weekend, five of them. I didn't listen to them. Now I realise that one of them might be from Daddy.

Jim's thinking the same thing. He says, 'Better retrieve them, kid.'

Two from Jane. One from Scott. And two from Daddy. The first just registers his attempt to contact me. The second is different.

'Lucy, I've tried calling you already. Now it's Saturday night and I know this has been a hard day for you. If you're there and you're sad and you're just not answering I want you to pick up.' As the silence grows longer my heart aches at my own absence, at my silence.

'OK, then, I'll just say this.' His voice is big. My big, blustering Daddy. 'I know how much you're suffering, how much you've suffered. But don't lock up your grief like some wild beast. Open the cage and let it out. It will never go away but it won't be so fierce again. And let's use this anniversary to take stock. You've been away almost three years, Lucy. I never argued with you for going. I'm not arguing if you want to stay. You can even marry some unsuspecting fool in New York but, whether you do or not, just release Scott because he's a good guy and he's still waiting for you here. And, by the way . . .' A hesitation. A small note of vulnerability. 'Don't worry about me. I'll be all right.' His hip. His age. The inevitability of his death. All the things we never talk about, it's as though he used a moment's silence to shout about them. I swallow.

Daddy's voice drops. 'I don't want you to be sad, Lucy. Please don't be too sad.' A long pause. And then his voice again, thick with emotion now, 'Take care of yourself, my little Lucy. Please take care.'

I save the message and play it again. It makes my body prickle all over, as though a cloud of small insects just landed on me.

'Are you OK?' asks Jim. He's watching me. 'Lucy?'

'I'm OK.'

I save the message and then find a bag and open it on the bed. Jim sits in the adjacent room while I pack. I open the closet and pull out some old but comfortable shoes. They close gently round my battered feet. I throw the new ones into the bag and start to fold a nightdress.

'Did you tell the meeting about your father?' Jim asks from the living room. 'Or did you actually pretend everything was normal?'

'I told them. It strengthened my position. They all turned into lambs, even Kent, and acquiesced to virtually all my suggestions.'

'Which were?'

I summarise the problems that arose and the solutions I proposed.

Jim sounds impressed. 'Good. You did real good.'

'And there's more. George is going to fly a company jet.'

'What?'

'Well, maybe. He sat there saying he couldn't run a toy company, couldn't participate in management, research, marketing . . . Kent got more and more scathing. Then I asked about the Mittex jets. Whaddya know, there are three of them. Three jets and George air force trained. The answer's obvious, so long as he can stay off the liquor.'

Jim says, 'No one's going to travel in a jet George Hifeld's flying, I mean, not without their own parachute.'

I giggle. 'OK, I'm all packed.'

He stands up and looks right at me. 'Lucy. Your father's dead,' he says.

And this time I gasp at the pain. My heart is crushed in my chest, my breath is short. I feel the heat of my tears. He's dead and no one else will ever love me so much. He's dead and the knowledge and wisdom inside his head counts for nothing. He's dead and the house he lived in and all his things and the people he knew and the places he went are still there, but there without him. And when enough tides have washed in and out then all evidence of his life will have vanished too. I sob into his void. But he's dead, and he can't answer my sobs.

Two

I'M GOING HOME.

On the flight it seems to me that Daddy's death and Stevie's death and the death of my brother, name unknown, features forgotten, all roll up into one huge ball of sadness and grief. I turn the rock from Arizona in my pocket over and over. Daddy said that the stripy stones were worthless, abundant, geologically uninteresting, but I liked them and took them anyway. They were my only souvenir from that terrible trip.

It began right after my brother died. I guess Daddy thought it would be good to get Mother away from the house. It was a subdued vacation, but something in the primitive landscape touched us. Daddy liked clambering through the red canyons until the rock dust had turned his dark hair red. Jane was seven and she followed him, I was only four and I followed Jane. We followed on one white-hot day I will never forget. Mother refused to come, choosing to sit in the car, sizzling, despite the open doors and windows, on the lonely blacktop.

Daddy moved fast. He climbed dried riverbeds with firm steps and jumped between rocks without hesitation. Jane and I soon fell behind. Ahead of us we could hear the ringing of Daddy's hammer or his voice, 'C'mon, girls,' echoing round some rocky corner. When we reached the corner, he would already be distant. We never seemed to catch up.

After the fall, when my arm had become one vast, throbbing temple of pain and the rest of my body, thought, feeling, everything, had disappeared inside it, Jane emptied the rocks we had found from our canvas bag and turned it into a sling. Then she left me and went to find Daddy. I watched her scramble along the bone-white trail of some absent river, growing tiny until she disappeared behind a pillar of rock.

Alone in the canyon, I understood why Mother had chosen to fry in a car. In the car you could look in front of you and see the blacktop rolling far ahead, while here in the canyon the rocks and cliffs pressed in on you like a silent crowd. The silence was so intense that it seemed to tumble down the canyon sides like great boulders, crushing the life out of me. It was unbearable. I knew I had to move.

I stumbled when I left the shade as though the sun had slapped me. Some vicious fingernail of rock had scored the skin off one leg, and the light and heat impeded my progress. I limped slowly, stopping frequently, learning not to lean on rocks that would burn me. When the silence was broken I thought at first that it was by the shriek of some angry bird. Instinctively I looked up and searched the sky. When the sound came again I recognised it. A woman's voice. A woman's voice so forceful and high-pitched that it eventually collapsed, but within seconds it had recurred, this time with even greater strength and higher pitch. I recognised the voice's craziness and I shivered despite the heat. I had thought we were alone in this wild country and now it seemed some other, crazy person had joined us.

The woman's words, long forgotten now, echoed round the canyon. I watched a lizard scuttle up a rock and disappear into a crevice. And then, my legs weakened by fear, I stumbled towards the source of the noise.

I emerged from between the canyon's rocky teeth to find myself by the road. The canyon was a semicircle and a quarter of a mile away, on the blacktop, the car seemed to waver in the heat. Standing next to it, also wavering, as though this wasn't the desert but some underwater place, were Daddy, Mother and Jane. No crazy stranger, just my family.

I found the stripy stones in my pocket later, when I was waiting at the hospital for X-rays. I kept them on the floor of the car and when Daddy drove us home they slid from side to side. And, although it had been set and plastered at the hospital, each time he flung us round another bend and the rocks slid, my arm throbbed with pain. Daddy's face and knuckles were white. Maybe he guessed that the woman he found when he walked out of the canyon was not the same woman, would not ever be the same woman, we'd left behind on the blacktop in the hot car.

We seldom spoke on that journey, except for Mother of course. When she lapsed into long silences we sank into them with her, relieved, wanting them to last all the way back to California, and Daddy would accelerate, as though speed would put more ground between Mother's last outburst and the next. Jane and I assured Daddy that we didn't want lunch, we didn't need the bathroom. We didn't want to stop because we didn't want Mother to get out of the car. And maybe we thought that when we got her home she might be the same Mother she was before.

IT IS SOME YEARS since I last saw Sasha and I have an irrational fear that I won't recognise him. But his wide face, his mouth stretched right across it, is first in the group of faces clustered at the gate. He is shorter and broader than I remember him. His face has grown fleshy, his hair thin.

I put down my bag and at once he flings his arms round me, pushing his bristly cheek to mine. He smells of cigarettes, leather and chocolate.

'My dear Lucia, I don't know whether to be happy to see you or sad at your loss. I must allow myself to experience both emotions simultaneously.' He picks up my bag. 'Don't you have any more than this?'

'No.'

'How different from my wife for whom no trip is complete without an excess baggage fine.'

'Are you and Marina divorced?'

'Let us say that I regard her as my excess baggage fine in life's journey. Follow me, please.'

I am content to trail behind Sasha's round, leather-jacketed back into elevators and across the dim parking lot to his car. The last time I saw him was four, perhaps five years ago, at the clinic. A birthday celebration for Mother at which she behaved badly. I remember how angry I was that he seemed to find the whole event comical.

We reach his car and Sasha turns to me. He asks, 'Lucia, what have you been told about your dear papa's death?'

'Just that he drowned in the Pacific. I don't even know where.'

'At Big Brim beach, as I understand it.'

'Big Brim?' A line of sand dunes by the coast road, the beach invisible.

'You know nothing more? You are unaware of police involvement?'

'Oh, the police. I think someone mentioned the police.'

Sasha's face folds itself with concern. 'Lucia, you look so tired that I can hardly bear to tell you . . . Instead of driving you now to our apartment where Mama and Aunt Zoya are waiting, I must take you at once to your father's house as you originally requested. Your sister called us—'

'But I didn't tell her I was staying with you.'

'She was aware of it all the same. Sisters are like that. Jane called to say that you must go directly to Uncle Eric's house. She explained that this is at the request of the police.'

Shaking my head with incomprehension I climb into the car. As we drive through the pay station, I remember how Jim said that Daddy's death was not straightforward.

We drive east. Until Sasha winds up his window I breathe the air in deeply. I recognise in it the balminess and saltiness of San Francisco.

Sasha says, 'Now, Lucia, you will need a car.'

'My colleague's having a hire car sent over in the morning.'

'Good gracious. A hire car actually delivered to our house. Your humble Russian relatives may find this somewhat intimidating.'

I redden, then say, 'How about you, Sash? I was surprised to contact you on the same number.'

He sighs, 'I, too, am surprised at this. But whenever I think of leaving the foundation, my salary expands enough to keep me there. Perhaps you feel horrified that Sasha is living with Mama as he used to. But the ease with which one can resume the rhythms of one's past is astonishing.'

For an instant it seems to me that the car's momentum has nothing to do with its engine. We are being dragged back into the past.

From the moment we cross the bridge, I find myself reliving another journey along this route, my family's return from Arizona many summers ago. The other road-users were lost in their own dreams and we hoped they would hardly notice the crazy woman bouncing and yelling on the front seat of our car. As we reached the bridge, Mother seemed to understand that we were close to home but this did not calm her. 'You murderer!' she shrieked at the surprised man in the toll cabin. Jane and I sank lower in the back seat. 'God, yes,' she snarled, 'I see it in your eyes that you also have killed! Oh, I know all about you.' Daddy apologised and we took off rapidly like a boat blown on by the wind.

When we turned into our drive Mother quietened suddenly. She stared up at the house with something like meekness and Jane and I exchanged grateful glances. We were home and Mother was better. Daddy stopped the car and we got out slowly. We stretched, blinked and staggered a little with the knowledge that we were no longer in motion. Mother sat in the front seat of the car without moving. Gently, Daddy opened her door. Mother still did not move. Daddy said softly, 'Tanya, let's go inside, you'll feel better.' We gathered round the car door, not too close in case there was a sudden arm-waving ambush of crazy recriminations. But Mother spoke quietly. She said, 'I am not getting out of the car. You treat me like some piece of cargo to be pulled across the world, some battered old suitcase left at the quayside. Well, now you cannot leave me anywhere because I do not intend to get out of the car.'

We stared at her. Ever since the canyon we had attempted to restrict her movements; now she was doing this herself when it was least appropriate. 'Do you hear me?' she yelled so loudly that I jumped.

'Tanya, you can't sit here for ever . . .' Daddy began, but his voice disappeared beneath her screams.

'I am not . . .' Her face was swallowed into a massive black hole of mouth, tongue and teeth. 'I am not getting out of the car.'

We waited and waited for her, motionlessly. Then, reluctant to leave her alone, we went into the house. It got dark. Daddy brought her food, which she ignored. He spoke to her with soft kindness. From the kitchen window I saw his helplessness when she closed the car door on him. He was big enough to force open the door, lift her, drag her into the house but he didn't try that. He didn't even shout.

She stayed there all night and most of the next day and Jane and I remained indoors. We looked at her from the kitchen window sometimes and it seemed to us she didn't move at all. Occasionally, oppressed by the strange silence, we sat on the deck that looks out over the valley. It felt good to have the whole house between us and Mother. Then Daddy, apologetically, sadly, told us that he would have to call for help. His shoulders were bent and he looked smaller. Two men and a woman came. The one in a suit had a hushed conversation with Daddy in the kitchen, while his colleagues tried to talk to Mother through the car window. She did not wind it down or give any indication that she heard them. It was evening when they took her away. When I could bear her screams no longer I ran down into the garden. I sat in the furthest corner with my fingers in my ears where I wouldn't hear any more of her yelling ('So! You are murderers! He has sent you to kill me, now I understand it!'). Finally there was silence and when I crept back round the barn I found a new emptiness. The car and Mother were gone.

Sasha and I travel in silence. The lights of the city behind us have dissolved in the darkness. When we reach the undulating hills I am lulled by their rhythm. My eyes close and fatigue sweeps over me.

'Are you asleep?' asks Sasha suddenly.

'I'm not sure if I'm asleep and dreaming or awake and remembering.'

'How close to the turning are we?'

'It's over the top of this hill and down a bit.'

Sasha slows and swings right. We ride high along the valley's steep sides, bouncing in and out of craters in the dirt road. I know that over to the left, when the bushes clear, the valley can shock you like a vast eye, open and glaring. But now there is nothing out there but the dark.

We near Daddy's house. My heart speeds, my breath shortens.

'Don't I recognise this one?' asks Sasha, pausing before a break in the foliage. Our headlights fall across a drive, snaking into the fold of the hill.

'No, that's the Holler house.'

'Friends of yours?'

'I used to play with Jim Bob Holler. I thought I was in love with him when I was nine and he was eleven.' I start at the sudden memory of Jim Bob, blond crew cut, his body nut-brown, running at the edge of a pool.

334

'Aha,' says Sasha, driving on slowly. 'Nine and eleven. Was there perhaps a juvenile undercurrent of sexual awareness?'

'I didn't know about that stuff when I was nine.'

'And later? When you did?' He is peering along the sides of the dirt road looking for the next break in the foliage.

'Jim Bob wasn't around by then.'

'Now, I'm sure it's on that bend,' says Sasha, leaning forwards.

A distant mailbox glints in the headlights. 'No, before it. That's the Zacarro house up by the bend.'

'And were the Zacarros good neighbours?' murmurs Sasha.

'OK, I guess. Mr Zacarro had a limp.'

Suddenly Daddy's drive seems to jump out at me. I draw back.

'This is it,' I say.

No sooner has Sasha turned the wheel than he must halt the car. Red and yellow tape is threaded between bushes so it hangs right across the drive. On it the words POLICE DO NOT CROSS are repeated like a mantra.

Suddenly there is light bouncing off my face, pouring into all the car's dark crevices. We turn and the beam of a flashlight diverts a little to reveal a rectangle of uniform. Sasha winds down his window.

A policeman leans towards us. 'I can't let you drive any further.'

I stare at him. 'I live here,' I hear a voice say. 'I mean, I used to.'

The officer looks across Sasha at me. 'Maybe . . .' he suggests, looking down. The light follows his eyes. 'I have your name here on this list.'

I give him my name and he nods.

'Oh. Oh, OK. You're the other daughter.' He looks at Sasha.

I explain, 'This is my cousin who just met me at the airport.'

The man shines his light on the clipboard again. 'OK, well, leave your car this side of the barrier. It's getting pretty congested up there.'

Sasha reverses into the dirt road.

'Be careful,' says the man when we duck under the police tape. 'Those rocks are dangerous in the dark.'

Sasha takes my arm and we stumble towards the house. The policeman shines his light for us but as we step beyond its beam there are a few minutes of darkness. I close my eyes. Despite the sound of Sasha puffing and cursing at my side, I experience the deep peace of my last moments of ignorance. Soon I'll know everything.

'I believe,' says Sasha, 'that Jane and Larry are here waiting for you.'

Up the incline and round to the right and I open my eyes. I stop at the sight of the big house. In my dreams, I remember it as it was when I was small, surrounded by slender trees and sparse bushes. I had forgotten how choked by growth it has become, how the trees now press against the windows, how creepers suffocate the porch.

'Lucia? Are you all right?'

I nod. The doors of the house and barn are open. The scene, lit by a police car, flashes at me in red then blue then white. Alongside the flashing car are others, two of them police cars.

I look up at the big, flashing house. Its gables have sinuous woodwork and the porch posts have candy-cane twists. It should be cute as a gingerbread house but it isn't. It looms right over you like a big bully. It mocks me and it mocks the beating of my heart.

As I climb the steps, another police officer emerges from the house, faceless in the artificial light. 'Name or ID, please.'

As a child I'd spend hours on this porch and the swing where I sat is still in the same spot by the door. I reach for the swing and my fingers find a crust of rust. At first Mother sat next to me, telling stories as we rocked back and forth. Then I sat here with Lindy Zacarro, my giggling blonde-haired friend. Finally, I sat alone, hunched in the corner, as though their absence was so massive it took up the rest of the swing.

'Ma'am, would you please identify yourself?'

A new softness in the officer's tone makes the back of my eyes sting. My legs feel weak and I sit on the top step of the porch and watch hot, salty tears fall onto my lap. The man leans over me.

'You have some connection with the decedent?'

I say, 'Daughter.' The word sounds odd.

He disappears and the screen door slams. Sasha sits down next to me, one plump arm across my shoulders. We sit together on the top step of the porch while police officers shuffle past, up or down the steps.

And then a voice says, 'Luce?' and I jump up and there is Jane.

We stand facing one another, staring, and then she holds her hands out and I step towards her. She wraps her arms round me as though I am still a small child.

'You're too thin,' she chides me.

I'm supposed to pull away from her now but I can't. I was OK until she used that big sister voice. Her hug tightens. I smell her perfume, the faint aroma of crushed flowers. It smells good. At last I stand back, sniffing, rubbing the tears from my eyes with my arms.

'Oh, Luce,' she says softly. She takes my hand and strokes it as though she's trying to dry it. 'Luce, you don't know how much I've missed you.'

There's no one in New York who would ever speak to me so sweetly. I experience again how it feels to be loved as Jane puts an arm round me and holds me close. She has never left me in doubt of her love. As a child, she was always there to compensate for Mother's absences and inadequacies. Once she saved me from drowning at the local swimming pool. She stayed with me at the hospital after the car crash with Robert Joseph in the valley. Then, years later, when Stevie died, Jane sat with me for hours, maybe days, talking and in silence, knowing what to do when everyone else, even Scott, was frightened or upset by my grief.

She pulls back to look at me. 'If only you'd called us we would have met you at the airport . . .' The gentlest of reproaches and from someone entitled to be angry. My departure from San Francisco was as painful as it was incomprehensible for Jane. And now I have hurt her again.

I flounder. 'It's been so long . . . I didn't know how you'd feel about me just arriving . . .'

'Pleased is how we would have felt. We've waited three years for you to just arrive.' Her generosity is simple and unquestioning.

Sasha steps forward and shakes hands with Jane. There is a formality in the condolences he offers and a formality in her acceptance. 'The time must have come,' he says, 'to ask the precise manner of Uncle Eric's death.'

Suddenly Jane's older, more tired. 'The police think . . . I wish there was a way of saying this that didn't sound so awful.' She takes my hand. 'The police are working on a theory that Daddy's death wasn't accidental.'

I nod. I'm pretending to understand.

'They think . . .' asks Sasha carefully, 'that he intended to die?'

'That's ridiculous,' I say. I hear myself. Weak, small, as though all the air has been squeezed out of me. 'Suicide. That's absurd.'

'Lucy,' Jane says carefully, 'the police are treating Daddy's death as homicide.'

Sasha echoes, 'Homicide . . . Surely not. Surely not Uncle Eric.'

My voice is stronger now. 'The police think someone killed him?'

'They're waiting for a full autopsy report but apparently the initial examination indicates—'

'Killed him? They're saying someone killed Daddy?'

'Shhhh, Lucy.'

'Is that what all this is for? The tape across the drive and guys with clipboards? They're here because they think someone killed Daddy?'

Jane's voice is quiet. 'Luce, I know it's a shock but you have to remember that it may not have been violent or painful or—'

'But who would kill Daddy? No one would have any reason—'

'Shhhh. Stop shouting, Luce.'

'Daddy was a university professor, not some kind of thug. Good, decent people like Daddy don't get murdered!'

I am yelling into the darkness, but within an instant the thick night air seems to absorb my words as though I had not spoken.

JANE SLIPS INTO THE HOUSE. Sasha follows her, holding the screen door open for me, but on the threshold I stop to inhale the old house, its special smell. Oil and rugs and wood and coffee. When I was small and Mother was well, the house aroma always included a little of her perfume and the scent of lemon furniture polish and sugary cookies.

'They've asked us not to go anywhere but the hall and the kitchen,' Jane is telling us from down the hallway. She puts her head into the den. I hear her say, 'My sister's here.' The reply is indistinct.

In the hallway a man walks past me. 'Please don't touch anything,' he murmurs.

I go into the living room and stare around me. Daddy's chairs, books, photographs. And rocks. Round, smooth rocks in a pile by the fire like an exhibit in a gallery. Specimen rocks on the shelves. Rocks of startling formation or colour. Rocks wedging open the door or used as paperweights. Rocks as sculpture. Rocks as pictures.

'Has much changed?' asks Sasha from the doorway.

I do not turn round. 'No, nothing's really changed.'

I go to the big sliding doors and open them slowly. They growl back at me. Then I cross the deck and lean out over the valley. It is a plate of darkness stretching on for ever. Tiny sets of car lights glitter, two, maybe three, moving slowly. Occasionally a cluster of lights indicates a house or a farm. I search, from some old habit, for the long, straight stretch of blacktop where the car I was riding in with Robert Joseph turned upside-down. But there is nothing out there but stillness and silence.

Sasha is waiting at the door, but inside the room now are the man who passed me in the hallway and a woman whose hands are covered in latex. In one hand the man carries a collection of small plastic bags.

'Ma'am, we haven't completed our work in here yet,' the man says. 'I must ask you to vacate this room until we give you clearance to enter.'

I lead Sasha past the den. It is a small, near-windowless room full of paper and rock. A uniformed woman and two men in suits peer at Daddy's blinking computer screen. They do not look up.

Larry is making us coffee in the kitchen. When I walk in his eyebrows shoot up and he smiles at me then embraces me. I can feel how his body has expanded and when he pulls back I can see it. Even his features have thickened so that his nose is less prominent and his tidy beard looks too small for his chin. 'Lucy, it's good to see you,' he says. 'Despite the circumstances.' He sounds as though he means it.

Larry greets Sasha and Jane passes us coffees. I look around. It never occurred to me before how shabby the kitchen is. I never noticed that the sink is stained and battered or that the doors of some units don't fit.

I say, 'Jane, did you put sugar in this coffee?'

'Just a little.'

'I stopped taking sugar years ago.'

She smiles. 'I know. But you looked like you needed something.' And although I resent the sugar I also enjoy its sweetness.

The officer from the living room appears noiselessly. 'Kirsty'll be with you in a minute. I have to take your prints,' he says.

I realise he is talking to me. 'My fingerprints?'

'I have to. You opened the door to the deck and held the deck railings. Did you touch anything else?'

'No.'

The man has laid out a small attaché case on the table in front of me. 'Please remove your wristwatch and jewellery,' he says mechanically.

I submit my right hand to him. He takes one finger, pressing it onto the paper, rolling it harshly. He does this with each finger in turn, and the same with my left hand. Then he rolls each hand in ink and onto the paper, the fingers and then the palms.

'Now you,' he tells Sasha.

'But I haven't touched anything.'

'I need to take your prints just in case.'

'I prefer my prints not to be lodged for ever on some vast computer.'

Jane says, 'For heaven's sake, Alexander. They took my prints too. They took Larry's. They took Scott's. They took them from everyone who's been in the house today.'

Sasha looks at her stubbornly. 'Allow me, Jane, to indulge my Russian paranoia.'

Jane's voice is taut with irritation. 'You've lived here all your life. You didn't suffer under the Soviet system. Paranoia is for people who did.'

Sasha is wounded now. He and Jane stare at one another wordlessly. Larry is about to intervene when we hear voices. The woman I saw in Daddy's den is right outside the kitchen. I can't see the man she is talking to, only his elongated shadow. Then he disappears and the woman turns to us, looking from face to face.

'What's the problem?'

She is about my age and height, with short, dark hair. I see now that she is not wearing a uniform but her dark clothes have the simplicity of a uniform.

'I need to take a set of elimination prints here,' snaps the officer. 'But this guy's refusing to allow me.'

Sasha shrugs. 'The procedure is unnecessary. I have touched and will touch nothing outside this room.'

339

The woman says, 'Who are you?'

Larry and Jane introduce me and Sasha and the woman nods.

'I have not seen my late uncle for perhaps four years,' Sasha informs her frostily.

'OK,' she says. 'So long as we can contact you if we need to, we'll leave your prints tonight.'

The fingerprint man closes his briefcase and melts out of the room. I wash and dry my hands while the woman explains that she would like to interview me and asks Sasha, Jane and Larry to sit out on the porch.

Jane pauses. 'Kirsty,' she says. 'Could this interview wait until tomorrow or the next day? Lucy's tired and very shocked. Her health has never been good and she really shouldn't get too stressed.'

These words touch and embarrass me. Although I was sick a lot as a kid, I now thrive on stress.

The woman turns to me. 'What do you think, Lucy?' she asks.

I say, 'Oh, thanks, Jane, but you don't need to worry. I'll be fine.'

Sasha follows Larry and Jane out of the room. When we are alone, the woman gestures me to sit down at the table with her.

'Just relax, Lucy. At this stage I only have a few informal questions.' She places a notebook in front of her. 'I need some basic details like name, date of birth, address—'

I say, 'Can you tell me what's going on?'

The woman looks at her notebook. 'After a preliminary view of your father's body the medical examiner has some concerns. The full autopsy is tomorrow but at this stage it's our job to respond to the ME's first analysis.'

'And what is that analysis?'

Her brown eyes meet mine. 'The decedent was found by a fisherman floating off the coast at Retribution. At first he was assumed to have drowned but the medical examiner believes that in fact he was dead before his body entered the water.'

Her voice echoes inside my head. *He was dead before his body entered the water.* Finally I say, 'How did he die?'

'That's not clear yet. His clothes were found, folded in a pile, at Big Brim beach. His car is missing. We believe that the killer attempted to make it seem like your father went for a swim and died in the water.'

'But . . .' I protest. 'No one would have a reason to kill Daddy.'

She is silent and her face does not move.

I say, 'It must have been some crazy person on the beach. The kind of maniac who stabs joggers for their radios.'

The woman's look is not unkind but she says, 'No, Lucy. This doesn't look like that kind of death.'

'What kind of death does it look like?' My voice is loud.

'The kind where the victim knew his killer. In fact, we may have reason to believe he knew his killer well.'

I wait for the reason but she doesn't offer it.

'You think it was someone close to him? A friend? Someone . . .' I swallow. 'Someone I might know?'

'Probably someone known to you or your sister. But maybe not. Your father may have had parts of his life you were unaware of.'

I blink at her. There is fatigue standing between me and comprehension. I ask, 'When did he die?'

'We're waiting for more information on that. Probably he died early on Monday. Lucy, I have to ask you where you were on Sunday night.'

'At home.'

'Monday morning?'

'I got to work before eight. I had a big meeting I needed to prepare for.'

'I have to confirm that. Please give me the name, address and telephone number of your employer.'

She writes down these details.

'Now, your sister already explained that you were staying with friends at the weekend. Where was that?'

I feel my cheeks begin to burn. 'That's what I told Jane . . .'

She raises her eyebrows. 'You weren't staying with friends?'

'Well, no.'

'So where were you?'

'In my apartment. I barely left it after I got home on Friday evening.'

There is a silence before she speaks again. 'Did you talk to anyone? Visit anyone? Call anyone?'

'No. I was working. I had a lot of preparation for Monday . . .'

'Are you sure no one saw you? Not a doorman or a neighbour?'

I shake my head. 'New York's not that kind of place.'

'So no one saw you all weekend,' she states quietly.

I say, 'That doesn't mean I wasn't there.'

Her eyes are shrewd. 'Why did you lie to your sister?'

'Because I didn't answer the phone. I didn't want her to know that I wasn't picking up on her. I didn't want to hurt her.'

'I see. When were you last in California?'

'Almost three years ago.'

'Was that the last time you saw Professor Schaffer?'

'No, he visited me six, nine months later in New York.'

'And you didn't return to California at all in the last three years?'

'No.'

'When did you last speak with him?'

I tell her about the messages Daddy left on my phone on Saturday.

'But why didn't you answer these calls?'

'When I work at home I don't pick up; it's the only way to get anything done. Probably I would have if I'd known Daddy or Jane was calling.'

'Did you save the messages?' she asks.

'Yes.'

'I'd like to hear them. As soon as possible.' She stands up. I jump up too as though she just unhandcuffed me.

'You look tired. I have further questions for you but they can wait until tomorrow morning. I assume you're staying with your sister?'

My cheeks were just cooling and now they're hot again. 'I figured I could maybe just stay . . .'

'In this house?' There is a note of alarm in her voice. 'Forensic won't finish for a while, but in any case you'd be unwise to stay here alone.'

'But I'll be fine . . .'

'Lucy, until we know what happened to your father and why, we can't be sure of your safety. His keys weren't found on the beach. We don't know who has them.'

As she leads me down the hallway she pauses. 'We're having difficulty accessing some documents on your father's computer. You don't, by any chance, know his password?'

I shake my head.

'Any guesses?'

'Hmm. Probably a rock name . . . obsidian, quartz, pyrites . . .'

She smiles. 'I'll look in a rock book. Lucy, I'd like to see you back here tomorrow morning. Is nine thirty OK?'

'Sure.'

'Keep this in case you ever need to contact me.' She hands me a card. Her name is Kirsty MacFarlane. She is a senior detective in the police department's homicide division.

I say, 'You see homicide everywhere because it's your job. It's your life. But it just doesn't occur in an ordinary family like ours.'

The woman doesn't reply. She opens the screen door. From the hall-way I could hear the voices of Larry, Jane and Sasha chatting. Now I see Larry on a porch seat and Jane on the swing. A smoke ring wafts between us. Sasha, on the porch steps, watches me as he exhales.

Jane turns to me. She looks cold and tired. 'Are you OK?'

I nod.

Sasha says, 'Come, Lucy, let me take you home at once. Mama will be waiting for you.'

Jane and Larry exchange concerned looks and then Larry speaks. 'There's a bed ready in our apartment.'

I think of their city apartment, of its white chairs and white surfaces.

'Mama has already prepared a bed for you,' insists Sasha, 'and she will be most disappointed if you don't sleep in it tonight.'

I look at Jane and she nods her permission but when she hugs me farewell she says, without confidence, 'Will you come to the beach house tomorrow? Larry and I are going at lunchtime and Scott would sure like to see you. Or . . .' She looks away, ready for rejection. 'Or maybe you don't want to see any of us? If you don't, we'll try to understand.'

I am reproached by her kindness. I say, 'Jane, I want to see you all more than anything.' And as I say this I know it's true.

Her body relaxes and she smiles at me. 'Including Scott?'

Foolishly, secretly, I've imagined my reunion with Scott many times, and always as a joyful occasion at the beach house on a warm day thick with the scent of ocean and pines.

I say, 'I'm looking forward to seeing Scott.'

Sasha drives us back to the city. He tells me to try to sleep and then is silent, but my eyes don't want to close and I stare at the road ahead.

As we approach Aunt Zina's apartment building I am overtaken by emotions for which I am unprepared. Aunt Zina has occupied the apartment since Grandma's death and for years I visited here regularly with my mother. Now, that part of my childhood, like a dog that has been waiting patiently, leaps up to greet me, knocking me over with its weight. The shabby building, its underlit lobby, the juddering elevator, daubed with graffiti in Russian, the smell of cabbage, the unchanged patina of my relatives' lives combines with my grief to overwhelm me.

When the elevator doors slide open on the third floor to reveal my aunts, I am too tearful to speak. Aunt Zoya, a long, thin broom of a woman, and the smaller, bustling Aunt Zina engulf me at once in a tide of love. They bear me across the hallway to the apartment, where the air is dense with the smell of Russian cooking.

'But your poor papa,' they say as the door closes behind us. 'Why did he drown? What do the police say about such a thing?'

I tell them all I know and the aunts cluck and shake their heads.

'Surely no one would harm your dear papa,' they say miserably.

'He was a kind man,' Aunt Zina informs me. 'He had an instinct to give. He would give his time, his attention, his money . . . many husbands would have turned their back on Tanya but Eric was a man with a sense of right and wrong. He adhered to what was right.'

Their words warm me. The way the detective spoke about Daddy dehumanised him. He was reduced to a homicide case, renamed The Decedent. Now my aunts are giving me back the man.

'No one could wish to kill such a one as your papa,' they assure me. 'It's impossible and the police will find they have made a mistake.'

I look to Sasha for agreement but he is busy pouring a pale liquid into small glasses to celebrate my arrival and does not catch my eye.

'And your husband?' they ask. 'Is he still at the university?'

'Yes. And his book's been published.' I know that because I turned on the TV late one night, and the small New York apartment was suddenly filled by Scott's voice. I crouched in front of the TV, staring as Scott stroked his chin, watching him thinking, listening to his voice. When the programme finished I switched off but remained in front of the TV, and the silence in the apartment was acute.

'But,' ask my aunts, 'are you still married to him?'

'We haven't discussed divorce . . .'

'Does he love you?' they cry. 'Do you still love him?'

'I think so. But . . .' I flounder and Sasha rescues me.

'Mama, Aunt Zoya, for heaven's sake, let us toast Lucia instead of grilling her.' And he clinks his glass against mine.

I am purred over, stroked, fed. I listen to stories of relatives, confused by the half-remembered names. Finally, inevitably, they speak of Mother.

'We visit weekly,' Aunt Zina assures me. 'Even Sasha comes sometimes.'

Sasha, relaxed now in an armchair, raises his glass in confirmation.

No dereliction of duty by me is implied but I am nevertheless stung. I telephoned Mother at the clinic a few times when I first left California, but the conversations were difficult and I allowed them to peter out. At Christmas or on her birthday, and sometimes in between, I send her small, colourful cards. I spend a long time selecting them. A picture of a brown dog like the one she used to own. Something abstract in which her colour, blue, is dominant. Cards from a Russian exhibition showing peasants in felt boots pulling sledges through the snow. These thin, colourful pieces of card bear our whole relationship these days.

As if sensing my feelings, Aunt Zoya throws up her arms. 'Such beautiful pictures you send her! She saves them all, and speaks of you often.'

Aunt Zina darts. 'Yes, yes. Your return will bring her great pleasure.'

I know my face is crimson. I wish they wouldn't talk about her as though she were sane.

Sasha looks at Aunt Zina. 'For God's sake, Mama,' he says. 'It is five in the morning in New York and Lucia learned only hours ago of her father's death. Do you think it is fair to talk to her when she should be sleeping?'

Aunts Zoya and Zina agree quickly and lead me to my room. It was once Grandma's and is little altered. It seems to me that even Grandma's scents of candy and medicine linger here. I lie in her bed, glimpsing by occasional carlight the accumulation of mementos that, at the close of each day, furnished Grandma's world. In the living room I can hear my relatives murmuring the music of the Russian language. It is Daddy's death, I reflect, that has brought me, in the space of one day, from an eighty-third floor in New York back into the heart of my family's past.

Three

I AM WOKEN by a strange quality to the light. A yolky yellow bathing my eyelids, wrapping itself round me as though I'm inside an egg. Or maybe I'm at home and I left the lamp on all night. Then I remember that Daddy is dead and I'm back in California. Once again, shock, sadness and grief, physical sensations, as violent as the cartoon books I read as a kid. *Bif! Bam! Phoof!* First my belly, then my chest, then more blows around my temples. I open my eyes and there is sun in them.

In the kitchen, Aunt Zina is flitting from fridge to oven and back like a hummingbird. I am struck by her similarity to my mother. So this is how Mother might have looked one day if she were sane. The movements swift and precise, the eyes bright.

'Aaaah,' she cries when she sees me, a cry of pleasure. She produces coffee, toast, kasha, jelly, blinis, juice, and as soon as one sample is consumed, begs me to try another.

I smile. 'You haven't changed a bit,' I tell her.

She hands me a large photograph in a new frame. 'Since when? Since then?' She giggles.

I recognise the three sisters, Zoya, Zina and Mother, seated shyly with their parents. The father, bones standing high in his face, his mouth proportioned without generosity. Grandma, eerily young, younger than I am now, unsmiling but beautiful, her eyes penetrating.

'Zoya discovered this old picture and had it made big for my birthday,' Aunt Zina informs me. 'It was taken soon after we arrived in America and Papa took his first job. Zoya is perhaps fourteen, I am twelve. Your mother is nine, no, ten years old. Even then she was beautiful.'

I stare at the smallest of the girls. She is not smiling but receptive to the camera's stare, her blonde hair curving round her cheeks, the bones of her face prominent like her father's, her eyes dazzling, although in the photograph they are grey. The girl who grew up to be Mother.

'We were poor but still Papa paid for this picture. He understood how the ordinary is fascinating when time has left it behind.'

'You weren't so ordinary, any of you,' I tell her, still staring at Mother.

When Mother and Daddy decided to marry, only Zina offered no opposition. Grandma and Grandpa presented alternative candidates from the Russian community. Zoya pleaded for longer consideration. It was true that it had been a whirlwind romance. Daddy was a professor in the university's geology department. Mother worked in the Russian department as a secretary. One summer her boss went on vacation and she had nothing to do, so, when the geology department advertised for people on campus to help them move premises, she volunteered. She worked for Daddy for three weeks and at the end of it they were married.

I've liked that story since I was a small child. Mother told it well. She described how she helped Daddy catalogue rocks. How he labelled each rock gently and handled them with care while she listed them. She said, 'I knew then that for Daddy rocks are not lifeless the way they are for most people. And I knew that a man who had enough love for rocks must have a little to spare for me!' She beamed and her face, which could look unhappy in repose, was another face, the face of the beautiful woman who catalogued the rocks, who married the professor.

'God!' I exclaim involuntarily. 'Where did that woman go?' The woman who married Daddy. The woman who told us the story of how she married Daddy. The woman who looked as though a light had just clicked on inside her whenever she smiled. One day I walked into a canyon and when I came out she had become another woman completely.

'Sometimes,' Aunt Zina informs me, somehow understanding my thoughts, 'it is possible to find a little of the old Tanya, even today.'

But it is many years since I stopped looking for my mother amid the human wreckage at Redbush Clinic. Silently I hand back the picture. In exchange, Aunt Zina passes me a key.

'For your shining new hire car.' Her eyes glitter. 'It was delivered this morning by a young man in a uniform after Sasha left for work. He took Sasha's space. These old apartments have a lack of parking places.'

'Tonight I'll park in the lot where Mother used to leave the car.'

'No, Lucia, it is two blocks away. Sasha can park there.'

I have no intention of taking Sasha's parking space but it is eight fifteen and there is no time to argue. I explain why I must leave at once.

Aunt Zina snorts. 'Why should the police interview you so urgently? It is impossible that you can be of any assistance to them. They are simply wasting their own time and yours.'

In the parking lot I climb in my hire car. It gleams with newness.

When I arrive at Daddy's house, I find the tape and the uniformed officers gone. I still have a key to the front door. In the three years I was away I didn't take it off my key ring. I place it in my palm and walk beneath branches to the porch. The dead bark and sharp leaves of the eucalyptus trees crackle beneath my feet and overhead the foliage releases a medicinal aroma. At the threshold of the house I pause to accustom myself to its smell, its coolness, its darkness. Its absences. Impossible to believe that I won't find Daddy here.

'Hi!' calls a voice. The detective. She is advancing towards me, briefcase in hand, dark under the dark trees. 'What a beautiful day. It's only March but it feels like summer's here,' she says cheerfully.

Together we go into the house. We stand at the door to Daddy's den and she tells me that she has taken Daddy's computer. She wants me to sign for this and for the paperwork she removed from the den.

'What paperwork?' I ask curiously.

'Oh, financial stuff, like bank statements. We need a full picture of your father's finances.'

I wonder why, but sign the documents she gives me without asking the question.

'I've copied it all, but you still need to sign for it,' she tells me, putting piles of papers on Daddy's desk. 'Scott's going to need these originals.'

'Scott?'

'He's your father's executor.'

'Scott?' I echo incredulously. 'Daddy appointed Scott executor?'

She looks at me. 'You think Professor Schaffer should have asked you?'

'Well . . .' Of course he should have asked me.

'After all, you're the banker around here,' she adds, watching me.

She's wondering why Daddy didn't trust me to carry out his wishes. I'm wondering too, but I shrug. I wish she'd stop looking at me.

'I guess he had his reasons,' she says at last.

I am grateful when she suggests that she interview me out on the deck and I can turn my back as I lead us across the living room.

'You're the beneficiary,' she says. 'You and Jane. Did you know that?'

'I sort of assumed it.' I pull back the sliding doors. I prepare myself for the shock that is the valley but even so I have to pause a moment to absorb its immensity and flatness, its tidy productivity. We sit down.

The detective draws her notebook from her briefcase. 'I'm hoping,' she says, 'that by now you've thought of someone who can confirm you were home all last weekend.'

I shake my head. 'There isn't anyone.'

'You worked the whole time? You didn't leave the apartment?'

'I took some short breaks for food.'

'Is work what you usually do at the weekends?'

I hesitate. 'It's what I do all the time,' I say at last.

The detective raises her eyebrows. 'Do you know anything about your father's movements over the weekend? Did he talk about any plans?'

I omit mentioning Daddy's visit to Stevie's grave. I say that I knew he intended to spend Saturday with Jane and Larry and Scott.

'Do you recall your father mentioning that he expected company on Sunday? Or was there someone who visited him most Sundays?'

I shake my head.

She says, 'His car's still missing. Do you have any idea of somewhere he might have driven it early on Monday?'

'Well, he might have intended to take some kind of exercise with his friend Seymour. They sometimes did fitness things together.'

The woman does not respond and I see that Jane's already made this suggestion and Seymour has been contacted. She asks me more questions about Daddy, about his habits and his character. I find them hard to answer. I've never analysed what sort of a man he was.

The detective persists. 'When you were small, when you went to other kids' houses . . .'

I tense. We didn't much go to other kids' houses because it meant the kids would sooner or later demand to visit our house and that was not OK, at least not until later when Mother was in the clinic.

'Did you meet their fathers? Do you remember thinking that your father was similar or different?'

I nod. 'Oh, yes. Other people's fathers were scary. They'd shout a lot.'

'Your father didn't shout?'

I shake my head. Daddy was always kind. I wonder now at how even and unchanging he was. Did he ever feel mad at us and not show it? I try to recall Daddy getting upset or emotional, even a tiny bit. I can't. I can't even recall him laughing the way other people sometimes laugh, red-faced, shaking, head thrown back.

The detective says thoughtfully, 'Jane's told me about your mother's problems. I guess Professor Schaffer had to play both mother and father to you. That must have been hard. Did he leave you alone a lot?'

It seems to me that, once Mother was trapped on her private, hellish treadmill of psychosis, I was always alone.

'Well, there was my big sister,' I remind her. 'She did a lot of the stuff Mother should have done.'

'You and Jane were close as kids?'

I look out across the valley. 'I don't know what would have happened to me if it hadn't been for Jane,' I confess. 'I mean, I was her first patient. I was always sick and she took care of me.'

'Maybe that's why she went into medicine,' suggests the woman.

'Well, maybe. There was this car crash in the valley when I was just out of high school and she helped me a lot then, too.'

I look down at Sunnyfruit Orchards, to that long, straight stretch of road where the car I was riding in with Robert Joseph turned right over. The first person I remember being there was Mrs Joseph, with a friend who happened to be in the house. The friend told me not to move and held my hand, talking to me kindly. Someone must have called the house because Jane, just home for the summer, arrived soon afterwards. She stayed by me and Mrs Joseph's friend seemed to evaporate. Then the ambulances came. They lifted Robert's body slowly through the open doors, the stretcher moulded around his shape. Jane said, 'No, Luce, he isn't dead, he really isn't.' In the hospital I learned that he was crushed along one side and that maybe they would remove a leg. They released me that same day with a couple of minor fractures in one foot, and when I came home I could see Robert's father's car still down in the valley. It lay crooked at the side of the road, upside-down, like a dead insect on its back. It was another whole day before the Josephs had it moved. And now, all these years later, I'm staring out across the valley and searching for the car again as if I just graduated from high school and am in love with Robert Joseph.

'Lucy?'

I look back at the detective. She's asked me something but her voice got lost years back. She repeats the question. She wants to know whether there were any arguments within the family, what Daddy's relationship was like with Scott and Larry, whether he had enemies.

I shrug in answer. 'Everyone gets along,' I say. 'Nobody hates anyone. Daddy didn't have enemies; he wasn't that kind of a man.'

Her voice is sharp. 'Lucy, why did you leave California?'

'Career reasons,' I tell her quickly. 'I was a personal banker but I wanted to move into investment banking. There were better opportunities in New York.'

She looks at me, waiting, as though she already knows there is more. She waits so long that finally the words come stumbling out of me.

'We had a baby but he died. Sudden Infant Death Syndrome.'

'Your baby's death played a significant part in your decision to leave?'

'Yes. I left soon afterwards. It was exactly three years ago. That's why I stayed home all weekend. That's why I didn't answer the phone.'

Kirsty closes her notebook. 'That's all I have right now. Thanks for your help.' The notebook won't fit back into her briefcase. 'I was expecting my colleague, Detective Michael Rougemont, to join us this morning, but I guess he's been detained elsewhere. He'll want to talk to you soon.'

I rise but she is still reorganising the contents of her bag. After a moment, I realise that she's stalling while she thinks about something else she wants to say. Then she stands up suddenly and her eyes are level with mine. She says carefully, 'The death of a parent can bring the past right up close. Have you already felt that?'

I nod, acknowledging the past's new clarity.

'Maybe when you went to New York you thought you could leave everything here behind,' she adds. 'But now you're back you could just decide that it's time for you to stop running; time to turn round and look at whatever it is that's been chasing you right in the eyes.'

I watch her car disappear down the drive. Then I walk round the house to the steep hillside, and edge along the base of the deck. I skirt the sunken garden, overgrown now, and at the Holler orchard I cut back up through the trees towards the barn. I'm watching the ground. Not far from the orchard I find a rock. Its shape is familiar. I pick it up. It is not a rock but a shoe heel. I examine the heel and pocket it, but before I can move on up the hill I hear a sound. *Crack*. I am seized by a new knowledge. I am not alone. *Crack*. The snap of a dry, fallen branch underfoot.

I reel rapidly round. The branches, the leaves, the grass seem to stare back at me, as though surprised into motionlessness. I swing to the right and left, staring through the trees. A few trunks are thick enough to hide a human figure. I stand so still that I don't breathe. There is no sound, but way back, through the Holler orchard, a shadow flickers that could be a man moving fast or a tree shuddering in the far breeze.

I go back up to the house. I turn round twice more before I get there, but see nothing. When the screen door has slammed behind me, I find my bag and tuck the shoe heel into one of its compartments. I snap it shut. The snap echoes into the silence like the twig that snapped out in the garden, snapped beneath someone, face unknown, intent unknown.

Out on the deck the silence persists. I lean on the railings and keep a constant vigil across the garden. I'm looking for movement but, apart from the occasional bird, there is none. Gradually the valley claims my attention. My eye meanders over the usual landmarks.

I feel the hairs on my neck stand up. At first I don't know why. Then I see that, far below me, cutting slowly across the valley floor, glinting like a silver fish, is a tow truck. From here it is no bigger than a toy. When it reaches the intersection it turns north. I watch until it disappears.

As I drive away from the house, heading for the coast and my family, Lindy Zacarro surfaces again in my memory. I haven't thought about her for years and then yesterday I remembered her presence on the creaking swing. I recall her face. Round, pretty and pink. Pink tongue, pink lips, invariably pink clothes. The prettiest, pinkest girl in the class.

Once Mother came out of the clinic, we didn't play at my house any more. I had hoped that when Mother was finally discharged she might be the way she used to be, before she went crazy in the canyon. But after Daddy took us to visit her in hospital, I knew this was impossible. Mother sat in her room and regarded the three of us with distaste. I waited for her to recognise me and put her arms round me. I thought if I could touch her maybe Mother would break out from inside this strange shell and start to make cookies and tell stories. But when I advanced across the room towards her she looked shocked, and Jane pulled me back. As we filed out, Mother began to cry. Daddy gestured for us to wait in the hallway but I lingered a few minutes, watching him crouch as close as she would allow, talking softly, reassuring her. I hoped his words would coax Mother out from inside this stranger.

When at last she came home I could see that she was trying to resume her old self, her old life. She tried hard but now this was a mask. When she laughed it was too loud and when she told stories they were strange, jumbled narratives. When she attempted physical affection she either clutched me to her, suffocating me, or her touch was so light it felt like insects. She found small practicalities, like cooking, almost impossible. Cookies emerged from the stove smelling right but with the consistency of rocks. We pretended to eat them while we hid them in our pockets. We pretended, to Mother and to each other, that she was normal.

'Luce, maybe it's not a good idea for friends to come home with you right now . . .' Jane warned me sagely.

'But Mother's better,' I said. I was playing real hard at normal.

'Sure. We know she is . . . but other people may not see it.'

'Sure they will,' I insisted. What she meant was, other people couldn't be trusted to join in our make-believe, but I didn't understand that. 'I mean, maybe just Lindy can come here,' I added, cajoling, not pleading.

Jane's face wrinkled. 'Not even Lindy,' she told me quietly. 'I'm saying this to protect you. I know what could happen.'

I was mad at her. I was often mad at her, and I see now that this was

351

the sort of anger children feel whenever their parents prevent them from doing something that jeopardises their safety. To the uncomprehending child the parent appears to be using their authority arbitrarily, issuing prohibitions in their own interests and not the child's.

About twenty minutes south of Scott's house, I stop at a place where you can pull off the road and park right by the edge of the cliff with only a thin safety barrier between you and the sea. This place is called Seal Wash but there are no seals visible today. I switch off the car's engine and I can hear the sea hammering against the rocks below.

I take the shoe heel from my bag. I get out and stand close enough to the cliff to look down on the massive body of water pressing against the land like a threatening crowd. I look up at the coast road, winding along the land's edge. When there is no car in sight, I fling the shoe heel as far out to sea as I can. It bounces back against the cliff face beneath me before it disappears into the hissing water.

After Seal Wash there are a couple of sandy bays, then Big Brim. My heart beats fast and I try to slow down, but the other traffic, seeing the sudden straight stretch, accelerates. There is a parking lot on the right, and, on the left, high sand dunes mask the sea. In a moment the coast-line is rocky again and the road winds round it once more.

When I reach Needle Bay and see the gentle curve of the beach where I lived with Scott, I am almost overwhelmed by emotion. Instead of swinging down the track to the beach house, I stop at the hilltop park-ing lot. I revisit that inner landscape of loss, empty after Stevie's death.

The little wooden cottage is invisible among the tree tops but the beach screams white and beyond it the sea stretches away for ever. I have been here many times in my dreams and now that I am back I feel a sort of relief. There is even nostalgia for that brief period when we moved here, right after Stevie died, when my grief was fresh. Life was straightforward then. It consisted of grief. There was nothing else to do but relive, tirelessly, relentlessly, the night of Stevie's death.

Stevie was asleep when I showered and dressed, probably because he had woken many times in the night. Then, just before I was due to leave for work, he woke. I fed him and changed him but he started to cry with a dogged determination that meant he had no intention of stopping.

'Go,' Scott said. 'Just go. He'll be fine.'

As I drove down the pretty street where we lived, I could hear Stevie's protests echoing inside my head and mostly what I felt was relief. I was going to a job that I was good at and leaving behind a situation that was completely outside my control.

I spent the day with a client. I didn't think about Stevie all morning, but during the afternoon I experienced sudden flashes of longing and by the time I returned to the house I just wanted to smell him and feel his small, soft body in my arms. Larry's car was in the drive and so was Daddy's Oldsmobile. I parked on the street and, the moment I switched off the engine, I heard the sound that had followed me down the road that morning. Stevie was crying again.

Inside, the house was filled by his misery. Scott appeared from the kitchen and gestured helplessly up the stairs. 'We fed him, we changed him, we distracted him but he won't stop. Jane's up there with him now.'

'Has he been crying all day?'

'Nope, he saves it up for you.'

It was hard not to take Stevie's tears personally.

I didn't go straight upstairs. First I looked into the living room where Larry and Daddy were playing chess, oblivious to the sound overhead.

'Hi, Lucy,' Daddy said to me. 'Check,' he told Larry.

Larry turned and gave me a conspiratorial nod, trying to suggest he was letting the old man win.

I climbed the stairs and the noise increased with every step. Jane was sitting by the window holding the baby against her shoulder.

'I tried everything,' she said when she saw me. 'And in the end I just gave up and let him cry.'

I took Stevie from her, very gently. He turned his wet face to me and, for a moment, it unscrewed itself. His eyes widened and it seemed the noise would cease. But when I placed his body against mine his back arched and he lifted his head and roared with renewed vigour.

'Thought you'd done it for a moment there,' said Jane.

I shook my head. 'He was crying when I left. He's crying when I get home. What am I doing wrong?'

'Nothing. He just needs to cry; some babies do.'

'Why am I such an incompetent mother?'

Jane was firm. 'You're not.'

The noise was increasing in intensity. The meal was ready. Jane and Scott tried to persuade me to leave Stevie in his crib.

'Holding him isn't helping and you need to eat,' Jane said.

'He's sure to fall asleep soon,' Scott assured me, but I knew that he didn't like leaving our baby alone either, shrieking in anguish.

When they had gone downstairs I shut the door and incarcerated myself with Stevie's noise. I sang and opened the window and closed it again and shook rattly toys in his face. But still he cried. Finally I sat and waited and eventually there was silence. I looked at Stevie's tiny face, battered with the effort of his protests. He was once more that creamy, lovable baby he was supposed to be. I laid him gently in his blue crib, pulled the blanket up and gazed at his perfection for a few moments before joining the others downstairs.

After the meal I went upstairs to check on him. I knew the moment I opened the door that something was wrong. The room had a special silence, and my skin bristled. I switched on the light and ran to the crib. I pulled back the blanket.

I held my own breath as I waited for his. I looked for breath, I listened for breath. I scanned his chest, hands, face for movement. I pulled at his hand so it would curl back. But there was no movement in the stiff, cold fingers and I knew that here was a lifeless effigy of my Stevie and that he would not breathe again.

The silence that had been hanging over the room descended, weighty and stifling. My throat constricted and then stretched, my voice emitted a long, high noise.

When the others came in, breathless, their eyes big, nobody spoke. They pressed against the blue crib, their faces contorted with horror. Scott, his lips blanched and his skin translucent. Jane, next to me, eyes burning in a white mask of a face. And Daddy, his mouth open, like a swimmer who has just surfaced after too long, gasping for air, his eyes full with the weight of the shock, looking up from Stevie's body into my eyes and then sliding off me as if the weight was too much to bear.

When I lifted Stevie out and held him to me and he failed to curl his body against mine, to press his head into my shoulder, it seemed to me that the silence in the room was deafening.

'Sit down, Lucy,' said Larry firmly.

'Calm down. Calm down now.' Jane this time. But I did not understand their tone or their words. I thought I was already calm in the face of a vast inevitability, but Larry seemed to arrest me, trapping my arms against my body. Jane took the baby in a rapid, authoritative movement.

'Stop, Lucy,' said Larry, holding up his hand. And the silence, which I now realised I had been covering with a blanket of screams, thinned.

Jane and Larry laid Stevie's body on the changing table and pulled at his clothes. Larry felt for a pulse, Jane listened at his chest and they looked at each other. Then Jane shifted her weight over Stevie and drew her elbows up and laid her hands on his heart, one on top of the other.

'No point,' said Larry. His voice was gruff. 'Too cold.'

'We should try,' Jane insisted, but when Larry only shrugged she dropped her elbows and I moved in to pick Stevie up and make him warm again, to stop the last heat from leaking out of him.

Larry said, 'I'll call the police.'

There was a roar, so loud that I instinctively covered Stevie's head, his ears, with a protective hand.

'The police! What do the goddamn police have to do with anything?'

'Shhh, Daddy,' said Jane, but Daddy looked at her and his mouth stretched into shapes I did not recognise. Tears ran down his cheeks as he looked at Jane for the support we all rely on.

'Daddy, it's routine,' Jane said in her hospital tone. 'A baby's died and the police have to come.'

I saw Scott flinch at these words. He was still frozen by Stevie's crib. He hadn't moved at all since he first came in.

When the police arrived, Scott was holding Stevie, wrapped in a blanket. He carried Stevie upstairs and the officers followed him.

I was interviewed by a white-haired man. I said, 'It's my fault.'

The man, who had thought the interview concluded and was leaving the room, paused and looked down at me. 'Pardon me, ma'am?'

'It's all my fault. I'm to blame.'

He sat again. 'Now,' he asked. 'Now, how is this your fault?' His eyes were large with something more than compassion. Suspicion.

'The blanket must have been too heavy. Last night was so cold, I put the big blanket on him but it was warmer tonight, I should have fetched a lighter blanket, maybe just a sheet . . .'

The detective wrote something in his notebook and said, 'We'll find out if there's a cause of death. But with SIDS there's usually no cause at all. Mothers always blame themselves. They try to find something they did wrong just to explain it. But there usually isn't any reason.'

'It's all my fault,' I said.

The white-haired detective left the room.

Jane came in and sat down beside me. She took my hand but did not speak. Much later, Scott brought our dead baby in. He lay in Scott's arms, the blanket folded back to reveal the small, still face.

'They're going to take him,' Scott said. His voice cracked and broke into a thousand pieces. Tears gushed down his cheeks as he handed me the unyielding doll who used to be Stevie.

A man and a woman stood in the doorway, the light behind them. They wore neat, loose uniforms of dark blue, almost black. I turned from them with hostility.

'Take your time, sweetheart,' said the woman.

I grasped Stevie for this leave-taking, holding his inelastic body against mine, studying him greedily. When I turned back, the woman moved forward and held out her arms to receive him. As the couple left with my son I felt a loneliness beyond anything I had ever known.

When I looked up, I saw Daddy. His face secreted misery. Our eyes met in acknowledgment of each other's wound and his filled with tears.

'There is . . .' He tried to speak. His voice was husky. He restarted his sentence several times before he was able to complete it. 'Lucy, there is no escaping the immense pain that lies ahead.'

I nodded. I opened my mouth to speak but my voice was like a blunt knife that could not slice the words.

The tide at Needle Bay is going out. While I have been sitting here at the hilltop it has left a perfect fingernail of damp sand along the edge of the beach. The sun, where it catches the ocean, blanches the blue water.

I start the car and begin my descent through the pines. The car tyres squish against the damp track. Then, a clearing in the trees, a carport, a car, and beneath me the little wooden cottage appears, squatting on the beach, sand lapping against the porch.

I get out and pine needles roll beneath my feet. I am halted by their intense scent and by the brightness of the sea only a few hundred yards away. The back of the cottage lies low, as though someone planted it in the sand and it didn't grow. I go down the steps and round to the front.

Scott is on the porch, sitting looking at the sea. A book is open on the table in front of him and he fingers a coffee cup. When he sees me, dragging my feet through the sand, my shoes in my hand, his face rearranges itself. When I reach the top step he stands up and puts a hand on the railings. We stare. There is three years pressing between us and a sort of shyness. And then I walk right through those years and right up to him and he puts his arms round me and it feels like slipping into old clothes that long ago moulded themselves to your shape. He holds me hard against him and then he shudders and I know that he's crying. I stay wrapped in the warmth of his body and the security of his arms.

Finally we sit down at the table together and I hold his hand and stroke his big, shaggy head while he cries. It's like stroking a lion. I move the book so it doesn't get wet. I whisper that I'm sorry.

'Are you apologising for going away?' he asks, his voice strangled by tears, not like his real voice.

'I'm not sure.'

'Then why are you sorry?'

'I feel as though it's all my fault.'

He turns to me and looks right at me, his grey eyes red now and his face swollen. 'What? Stevie? Your dad?'

'Everything. Everything that makes you cry.'

He sits up and puts his arm round me and we both look out to sea like the couple who moved in here together, four years after meeting, three years after marrying, two weeks after Stevie died.

I say, 'Are you angry? Are you real mad at me?'

'I've been mad at you for three years, Luce. In my head I've yelled at you. And now you're here . . . I don't want to yell, I just want to cry.'

When he's cried some more he says, 'I can't believe Eric's dead. He was sitting right here on Saturday. I loved that guy more than my own father.' His voice breaks and I move closer to comfort him.

'How was Daddy on Saturday?' I ask.

'Oh, quiet. Because it was Stevie's day, I guess. Quiet and sad. I've been thinking all day about how much sadness there was in his life.'

'No!' I protest. I don't want Daddy's life to have been sad.

'Sure it was sad. He married this beautiful woman and it turns out she's not fascinating because she's Russian, she's fascinating because she's crazy. That's sad. And his baby son died. Then his grandson. Then you went away. That's all goddamn sad, but it brought me closer to him because we both missed you so much and because he understood about Stevie. I can only completely relate to people who understand about Stevie.'

It occurs to me that in New York I don't relate to people at all.

'The police interviewed me yesterday,' Scott is telling me. 'Just like I was a goddamn suspect. I tried to explain how much I loved Eric but she ignored it, like I was saying something embarrassing.'

'Who interviewed you?'

'A woman detective. There was a man there too, an older guy. He didn't say anything but he nodded a lot and I think he understood. The woman asked all the questions. I kept thinking I'd seen her before. Then this morning I remembered. At our old house on Lalupa. I think she came the night Stevie died.'

I stare at him. 'What do you mean, Scott?'

'There were so many of them, going in and out. It seemed like the entire police precinct was there. But I'm certain she was one of them.'

'No,' I say. 'No, no, I didn't recognise her at all.'

Scott asks, 'Have you been to Stevie's grave yet?'

I shake my head. 'I know you sent me that picture of the headstone but I still remember it as a little mound covered with flowers.'

'Want me to go with you?'

'Yes.'

I haven't heard a car so when two figures round the house I am unprepared. Jane embraces me as warmly as she did yesterday.

'Hi, Lucy,' says Larry, standing behind her, puffing.

Scott delivers cold drinks and we sprawl around the porch talking, just the way we used to. I look away from my family to the restless sea. I hear their voices without listening to their words.

'I mean, did he actually mean to go to the beach to swim? Or was he coerced into going?'

'He and Seymour were doing some new fitness programme. It did involve a lot of swimming.'

'Listen, Big Brim is renowned for its crosscurrents. If he wanted to swim he'd have gone somewhere safe, like here. Eric was lured to Big Brim, or forced there against his will.'

'The point is that he could have died anywhere. They didn't have to kill him on the beach.'

'You're saying . . . it could have happened right at his own home?'

'Maybe.'

'But then why is his car missing?'

'I'll tell you. It didn't happen at his home. He drove it somewhere and then died there. Maybe he witnessed something he shouldn't have seen. They killed him on the spot and hauled him to the beach. Something like that. When they find the car, it'll probably be right where he died.'

'But, Larry, who's going to do any of it? Who would want to kill Eric?'

There is a silence into which a wave crashes. A phone rings.

Scott gets up and goes inside. We listen to his tone as he answers the call, guarded at first. 'Where?' he asks, anxiety in his voice. We look at each other, then at the doorway. In a moment, Scott's big frame fills it.

He says, 'The police have found Eric's car.'

His words make me jump. Jane goes inside to take the call. When she emerges again, her face is pale. She sits down and Larry strokes her hand.

'They found Daddy's car about five miles away. A place called Lowis . . .'

'I know it,' says Scott. 'It's not far from Bellamy, right where you come off the freeway to go into the San Strana Valley. So how come . . .?'

Jane shrugs. 'The police don't know how come yet. They've done all the forensic tests they need to do on the Oldsmobile. They asked me whether they should tow it back to Daddy's house. I said OK . . . Now I'm wondering if I shouldn't have just told them to tow it to a scrapyard.'

'I'm glad it's going back where it belongs,' I say. There's something pleasing about the idea of Daddy's house with his own car right outside.

Larry shakes his head at me. 'This is a time of change, Lucy. Nothing's going to be back the way it was, ever. You should understand that.'

Later, when Jane and Larry have left, Scott and I sit on the porch in the late-afternoon sun.

Scott says, 'It seems right that Eric died around the anniversary of

Stevie's death. Because he was devastated when Stevie died and I'm not sure he's been exactly the same guy since then. I mean, you could always see he was a man with burdens. But it was like it was one burden too many for him . . . Oh, Luce, I didn't mean to make you cry.'

I sob, 'I should have been here. I should have been here for him.'

Scott wraps himself round me and the porch envelops us both. The beach is deserted except for two swimmers, far away, walking slowly into the sea. Soon they are two tiny heads on the ocean's surface.

I ask, 'Do you ever think of moving from here?'

'There soon won't be a choice.'

'Does the owner want it back?'

'The ocean wants it back. Next month the tides are going to be exceptionally high and if the weather's bad too . . . well, I should probably get out for a few days.'

I imagine a big wave tipping its burden of water right into the cottage, smashing it to pieces.

'At the highest tides last year,' says Scott, 'a window got smashed.'

I stare at him. 'Were you here?'

'Yes. It was scary but it was only spray. Next time, it might not be.'

'Was it at night?'

'In the middle of the night. When we went to sleep the ocean had seemed pretty quiet.'

It was the middle of the night and someone else was here asleep with Scott. I feel something in my stomach contract.

'Who was here sleeping in the middle of the night?' I ask, too quickly.

Scott turns to me and his tone is aggressive. 'Why do you care?'

'I'm sorry I asked. I have no right to care.'

He says, 'I have a girlfriend. She teaches French on campus. She lived in France for many years. She has a son who lives in France with her ex-husband. Right now she is spending a semester with her son. How about you, Luce? Do you have some guy who matters in New York?'

I get up to go. Scott gets up too. He stands right in front of me.

'No,' I say, walking round him. 'I don't.'

'So. So now you know about Brigitte you're leaving.'

'I'm leaving because I want to get to Big Brim beach before it's dark.'

He looks troubled. 'Don't go alone, Luce. It will make you feel lousy.'

'My father's died and I already feel lousy.'

He sighs and his eyes search mine. 'Then,' he says at last, 'I guess you should hurry before it gets dark. Wait . . . I have something for you.'

We go inside the cottage and the little living room seems to jump at me. In my dreams, the faded red furnishings were never so vibrant.

'Here!' Scott yells from the bedroom. He wants me to go in. 'You can't keep wearing those city clothes. I still have your old ones.'

He is bent into the closet. Inside it, I see a few women's clothes hanging with Scott's shirts. They could be Brigitte's but no, I recognise them as my own, my California clothes, not the kind I wear now.

'I'm not sure I want to wear that old stuff . . .'

Scott puts them in a bag, a swimsuit on top. 'Take them. It's getting too warm for city suits now and they're forecasting a heatwave.'

'In March?'

'That's what they say.'

He walks me round the cottage to my car and stands watching me until there are so many pine trees between us that they seem like one enormous tree. When I reach the coast road I can see him far below on the beach, walking towards the sea. I wish he would look up but his eyes are fixed on the ocean. Brigitte. I wish he hadn't told me about her.

I pull in at Big Brim's parking lot. Although I know from the intensity of the light that the sea is nearby, it is masked by the mountain of sand that runs alongside the road. Traffic zooms past, rocking the car. I cross the blacktop as soon as I can and start to walk up the dune.

At the top the ocean is still invisible behind two more dunes and only when I have climbed these, sweating now, does the flat beach sprawl beneath me. I sit down, breathing heavily. I try to imagine Daddy walking these dunes. He was fit but not so fit he could climb them without stopping frequently for breath. Did he choose to swim at this beach? Did he walk this way with someone he believed to be a friend? Or behind him, next to him, was there someone he was powerless to resist?

I run down the last dune until I feel the damp sand by the water's edge firm beneath my feet. The sea is the colour of blood, stained by the swollen sun. I stand ankle deep, lifting the hem of my skirt. The ocean is icy. It is deceptive here. It rocks quietly, beckoning you to walk out into its calm depths, but Scott says its crosscurrents make it the most treacherous place to swim in this whole stretch of coast.

The beach is empty now except for a couple of people, and one of them is heading back to the road. The other, a large man, is marching, almost running, along the tideline towards me, a small white dog trotting a few feet behind him. When I turn my back on the Pacific and follow my footprints up the beach, I see that the man and his dog have halted nearby, collecting something, driftwood, perhaps, or clams.

I reach dry sand and sit down. The sun is disappearing. I see a figure heading towards the ocean. It gets closer and I see that it is the tall, thin figure of a man, incongruous here in a suit and necktie.

The tall figure is framed by the fiery sky. It seems he is walking towards me. Soon I can see his face. It is cadaverous. Hollow cheeks, prominent nose, immense mouth pulled clownishly downwards.

'Hi,' he says in a reedy voice. 'Forgive me for disturbing you. Is it Lucy? Lucy Schaffer?'

I stare at him and my astonishment answers his question. The mouth splits his face in two. He is smiling.

'I'm Detective Michael Rougemont. I'm involved in the police investigation into your father's death. I live not far from Professor Schaffer's house and I knew him a little. I'd like to express my condolences.'

I nod my thanks. I remember the elongated figure I took for a shadow talking to the woman detective in the kitchen doorway. And this morning she named some colleague who had questions for me. He flashes an ID, which I ignore, because my surprise has turned to anger at this intrusion. The way he walked right up to me, on this vast stretch of beach, suggests that he knew I would be here. I look away from him out to the darkening sea.

He sits down next to me. 'I hope you don't mind me talking to you. I was passing and I thought that, in the circumstances, I'd like to take a look at this place again.'

'You've been here before?'

'Many years ago now, more than thirty.'

I am flippant. 'And has it changed much, Mr . . .?'

'Rougemont. But call me Michael.' He looks along the beach. 'Well, I don't remember that guy being here,' he says, gesturing to the pear-shaped man strolling back along the beach, his dog behind him. Rougemont's face cracks into the broad smile again. I do not smile back at him.

He looks suddenly serious. 'Your father was a rare man, the kind people trust. I'd like to hear you talk about him, Lucy, and not his recent history. I'd like to know about him right from the beginning.'

'You're investigating the end of his life, not the beginning, Mr Rougemont.' I have no intention of calling him Michael.

That awful smile again. 'Oh!' he says, and it is an exclamation of pleasure. 'Well, the two are often connected. It reminds me of a toy I played with as a kid. I used to line up little tin soldiers. If you pushed the first they'd all fall down one by one. You knew it was inevitable but it was fascinating anyway. Oh hell, Lucy, but you never had any little tin soldiers. You had soft toys which you hugged a lot, furry things, like a dog.'

I stare at him in surprise but he isn't looking at me. He's watching the sea. I don't want to give him the satisfaction of knowing that he's right. I did like soft toys and I remember now that my special favourite was a brown dog with floppy ears. His name was Hodges, I don't recall why.

'What do you want to know about my father?'

'Anything you can remember. Stories about himself, his family, his youth. He must have said something about his past.'

'Daddy left his past behind a long time ago.'

Rougemont chuckles. 'Oh, Lucy, forgive me. But you can't lose your past any more than you can lose your shadow.'

I shrug. 'Then he dissociated himself from it.'

There is a silence. We both look out to sea as he waits for me to speak. And to my surprise, I do speak. I tell Michael Rougemont about Daddy's strange beginnings in a small religious community high in the mountains in Utah. The community was dominated by its religious elders, one of whom was Daddy's own father. Daddy hated it. Too smart for open rebellion, he worked as a carpenter and mechanic. He learned to fix almost any machine. He looked like he was praying a lot but mostly he was planning. He was planning his escape.

A man with a truck came once a week in summer to buy the fish that the community caught in the mountain lakes. One visit, the truck broke down, Daddy spent most of the evening fixing it. When the truck drove away, Daddy was in the back with the fish. He had three dollars and a hunk of bread and, although the driver let him into the cab when they were halfway down the mountain, Daddy already smelt awful. When they got to Salt Lake City, the driver took Daddy to a hostel. He lived there and found a day job and enrolled in night school. His native community gave him a lifelong aversion to organised religion and the lifelong love of mountains and rocks that became his career.

'Uh-huh,' says Michael Rougemont, grimacing, nodding his big head. 'Uh-huh. That's very interesting. Who told you all that?'

'Daddy.'

'Did he tell you he ever went back?'

'It wasn't that kind of place. If you left, you never could go back.'

'When did he come to California?'

'Well, I don't exactly know. He was certainly here by the time he was in college, but I'm not sure how old he was.'

'When did he meet your mother?'

I tell him but the chasms in my knowledge gape at me. Years and years, Daddy's years, between high school and meeting Mother. Now Daddy is dead those years are lost. 'Was she a good mother?' he asks.

I eye him in the half-darkness. He must already know the answer to this. 'My mother's schizophrenic.'

'She's always been that way?'

'Eventually she was diagnosed as an episodic schizophrenic. She has periods between psychotic breaks but they get shorter and shorter. By the time I was fourteen she pretty well lived at the clinic.'

'When she wasn't psychotic, she was at home looking after you?'

I swallow. 'Well, she was at home. I wouldn't say she looked after us. Her behaviour was unusual and it got worse. By the time I was in second or third grade I hated her leaving the house because she was guaranteed to do something embarrassing.' Like, laughing uncontrollably during the Pledge of Allegiance at school open day. Or stopping the car to accuse some shocked pedestrian of following her.

'But, Lucy, your mother wasn't always sick. Was there anything that triggered it, the first time it happened?'

I don't tell Rougemont about the trip to Arizona we took right after my baby brother died. I say, 'I was just a small kid. I don't remember. It took years for them to diagnose her as schizophrenic but when they did we understood a lot more. It's a chemical imbalance of the brain; it doesn't need an emotional trigger.'

'It was all pretty tough on you, Lucy,' remarks Rougemont. The sand, which was dry when I sat down on it, has absorbed some of the ocean's dampness now and the night air is thick with moisture. I stand up.

'Luckily, I had Jane. Why don't you talk to her about all this?'

'I already did. But no one knew Eric Schaffer the way you did. No one. Not even Jane.'

I say, 'I'm staying with my aunt. I should go back there now.'

Rougemont nods. Between sitting and standing there is a moment of stiffness and of pain, then his face clears. We collect our shoes and without speaking make our way across the sand. The constant fretting of the ocean grows fainter. As we cross the dunes, Rougemont puffs and his breath heaves. He falls behind. When we reach our cars, the traffic that swishes past illuminates Rougemont's face and I see it is wet with sweat and the lines around his mouth look long and deep. I realise for the first time that he is old, not so old as Daddy, but not so very much younger.

I unlock my car.

'Thank you, Lucy,' Rougemont wheezes. 'I appreciate the help you've given me. I'll be seeing you real soon.'

'Goodbye, Mr Rougemont.'

I reverse the car and swing south. In the headlights I capture a large sign by the side of the road. It reads, BIG BRIM BEACH. DANGER, SWIMMERS! CROSSCURRENTS!'

363

The apartment is thick with the smell of cooking. Aunt Zina urges me to kick off my shoes in the living room and relax while she makes the evening meal.

'Oh.' She has seen the small piles of sand that spill from my shoe. 'You have surely been to Big Brim beach. Did it bring you closer to your papa?'

'No,' I admit, easing off the other shoe.

'There was a telephone call for you,' she tells me. 'A man. I think he was calling from New York where people so often speak like machine guns. I was unable to understand a word, not even his name. No doubt he will call again.'

'Jay Kent?' No one sounds more like a machine gun than Kent.

'It might have been that name,' she says, going back to the kitchen.

A little later, Sasha comes home. He offers me a whisky and smiles benignly when I accept. 'I'm very glad, Lucia. Whisky is the perfect relaxant.' He hands me a drink and watches as my face curls when I sip it. 'Your quality of life would greatly improve if you could acquire a taste for whisky.'

'It sort of burns my mouth.'

'Then I shall make it more palatable.' He disappears and returns with ice in the glass, clinking like money.

Settling himself in his chair, his leather jacket and the chair both creaking, he asks, 'Lucia, when is the funeral?'

'I don't know. I saw Jane and Larry and Scott today at the beach but we agreed to talk about the business stuff at Daddy's house tomorrow.'

'Will Aunt Tanya be there?'

'To be honest, Sash, I hope not. In case she does something awful.'

'Lucia, Aunt Tanya should certainly be at her husband's funeral. I offer, for myself and for my mother, to undertake all necessary care on that day. We can pick her up, look after her, take her back to Redbush.'

'But supposing she . . .?'

'She has great physical frailty these days. However, to please you, I will walk with her arm in mine. I have an iron grip.'

'She used to scream and shout sometimes.'

'At the first hint of such behaviour I will remove her from the room.'

'Well, thanks. I'll ask Jane . . .'

'No, no,' Sasha insists. 'I want you to make the decision. The way you make decisions in New York.'

I hesitate. Then I accept his offer.

Sasha sips his whisky and licks his lips. 'I believe that to be the right decision, Lucia.'

Four

THE NEXT MORNING I drive out to Daddy's house wearing a sleeveless blue dress I found among the clothes Scott gave me. Aunt Zina threw up her hands with approval when she saw it.

'Beautiful, and, you know, you look very like your mama in it. She also wore blue dresses.'

I said, 'She's crazy, Aunt Zina, I don't want to look like her.'

Aunt Zina slipped an arm round my shoulders. 'Before Tanya was crazy, she was beautiful, and often still is,' she said. 'You do not share your mother's illness, Lucia, but her great capacity to love.'

I pulled back and looked into Aunt Zina's watery blue eyes. 'Love?'

'This surprises you? Her illness certainly took her away from you but in your early years she loved you as fiercely as any woman ever loved her child. And you her. Indeed, you were inseparable.'

I tried to remember my mother's love. I tried to remember a time when loving her didn't lead to disappointment.

'Will you visit her today?' asked Aunt Zina.

I explained that I had arranged to meet the others at Daddy's house, to organise the funeral and other formalities. 'Maybe tomorrow,' I said.

Driving now towards Daddy's house, I try to remember that other mother, not the one I dread visiting at the clinic but the engaging, exciting mother from whom I was inseparable. But she cannot be reached.

I swing up the drive and there, parked right in front of the barn where Daddy used to leave it, is his old grey Oldsmobile. It is rusted in places and there is a noticeable dent in its front fender but I warm to its familiarity. Since I am first to arrive, I take the space right next to it.

Heat swells the air here and when I get out of my car the blue dress seems to float around me. I finger the Oldsmobile's battered paintwork. Daddy liked the car's oldness. He fixed worn machines compulsively. In the barn is a tractor he was fixing for years; before that there was an ancient printing press, a pick-up, a motorbike, a generator.

I try the driver's door. I am not expecting it to open but it does. I sink into the driver's seat and close the door. It seems to me that, very faintly, I can smell him in here. That sweet, soft, oily smell that clung to his overalls. For a moment, Daddy is in the car with me, a pencil behind his ear, his square fingers oily, thinking hard about some machine.

When I unlock the house the heat inside it bounces out at me like an excitable dog. I pin back the door and walk right in, and the first thing I notice is that there is light where there should be shade. The light in Daddy's den is on. I shrink back into the dark edges of the hallway. Who has been here since I locked the house yesterday and left for the coast? I conclude that the police must have come inside to leave Daddy's car keys, and I am looking for them when I hear a voice.

'Morning, Lucy,' says Kirsty MacFarlane. 'I came to check that the car came home all right.'

'I think someone's been inside,' I tell her. 'There are lights on.'

'Maybe Jane?' she suggests, but we are passing the living room now and I have halted in the doorway.

'The sliding doors! They're open!'

She walks across the room. A space about two feet wide gapes between the doors. Through it, I can feel a slight breeze from the deck.

'Are you sure you didn't leave them open yesterday?' she asks, examining the catch. 'There's no sign that this has been forced.'

I watch the drapes tremble. 'Well, pretty sure . . .' It seems a while since I've been sure about anything.

The detective checks the front door too but there is no sign that this has been forced either.

'Daddy's keys . . . is it possible that whoever . . . whoever was with him at the end . . .?'

She nods. 'Yes, that's a possibility. I suggested to your sister that she change the locks as soon as she could. Have you taken a look round to see if anything's missing?' she asks.

'I just arrived.'

'Let's do it.'

First we glance into the den. It looks just how it looked yesterday but the detective goes in and surveys the piles of papers on Daddy's desk. She rearranges one of them. 'Have you or your sister taken a look at this stuff? Or Scott, since he's executor?'

'I didn't look at it. And no one else said they were coming here.'

She frowns. 'I'm sure I left the will and the insurance policy on the top. I thought they'd be the first things you guys would need to see.'

'Have they gone?' I ask, staring at her.

'No, but they're underneath the bank statements and some letters.'

Downstairs everything seems normal. The detective goes upstairs. Like the rest of the place, it is a repository of the past. At the bedroom door I try to say something, some routine pleasantry, but my words disappear.

Kirsty watches me. Finally she says, 'Want me to go first?'

'No.'

I close my eyes and walk right in. Behind me, I can sense the woman's movement, involuntary and sudden as the shying of a horse. She suppresses it with professional rapidity. That's the effect the bed has, even when you've seen it before. A fairy-tale concoction of swaggers and loops and bows, it hangs over the room like a big blue castle.

'My mother made this bed,' I explain. 'Like her, it's completely crazy.'

Kirsty nods and I guess that she has already tried to interview Mother. I ask, 'Did you get any sense out of her?'

'Well, she did speak back. In Russian.'

'In Russian! That's a new one.'

The detective says, 'You know what this bed reminds me of?'

My body goes taut like a rubber band.

She says, 'Your baby's crib.'

After a moment's silence I realise my mouth is open a little. I close it.

'Oh, I forgot to tell you—but maybe you already realised. We've met before.' She waits for me to speak. Finally she says, 'It was three years ago. I mean three years on Saturday.'

The back of my neck feels cold. I cross the blue rug and sit on the edge of the bed. I look up at the canopy and see a deep blue sky.

The detective says, 'Of course, I met your whole family that night, including your father. Isn't that something? There aren't many homicide victims I've met when they were alive. Professor Schaffer was shocked by your son's death. You all were, but I recall his grief in particular. When we were doing all the things we had to do, your father was sitting alone, in the corner of your living room, crying quietly to himself.'

I didn't know this. The world contracted to my own shock and grief that night. I don't like to think of Daddy crying quietly in the living room.

'I've seen a lot of tears,' Kirsty is saying, 'but your daddy sitting crying so quietly was one of the worst.'

Scalded by her words, I jump to my feet. Then I am awkward. Suddenly I have too much body and I don't know what to do with it all.

'Did you buy that beautiful crib for your baby because it reminded you of this bed?' asks the woman, watching me.

'Well, no, I don't think so.'

When I was round and still with the sense of anticipation of late pregnancy, Jane told me she wanted to buy the baby's crib. She admitted that she had given up hope of having children of her own and that she wanted to be a good aunt, a special aunt, to my baby. We went to all the

big stores and the expensive little ones and when we saw the blue crib
with all those ruffles and frills we just had to have it. I looked at the
price tag and hid my face. But Jane insisted. When they delivered it, I
wasn't sure I even liked it. I thought of sending it back to the store but I
couldn't hurt Jane's feelings. It became Stevie's crib and, when everyone
admired it, I came to admire it too. Then Stevie died in it and I hated it.

'If somebody broke in last night, they certainly would have taken
those silver boxes,' says the woman, gesturing to the vanity. 'Were there
any other items of value in this room?'

I shrug. 'I don't think so.'

We resume our tour of the dusty house. The detective wants to know
which room was mine and which Jane's. Both are full of old boxes now.
And there is the room where Grandma slept on her occasional visits, or
Daddy did when Mother was ill.

'Whose was this?' asks the detective when, at the end of the hallway,
we open the door onto a small room, painted pale blue. It smells musty.

'Daddy used it as a study before he moved his desk to the den.'

'And before that? Could it have been your brother's room?' she asks
and for the second time this morning her words halt me and I am
speechless. She adds, 'You did have a brother, right?'

I nod. 'But he died when he was just a baby.'

'Was this his room?'

'I don't know.'

'You don't remember him?'

'I don't remember anything about him.'

'That's surprising,' she says, turning and leading me away. 'You were
just about old enough to remember something so dramatic.'

I don't ask her how she knows this. I don't say anything. The death of
my baby brother is seldom, if ever, mentioned.

Going downstairs, the detective says, 'Well, the dust up here hasn't
been disturbed for a while. If there was an intruder anywhere, he was
probably in the den. But since nothing's gone let's just hope that you left
the lights on and the doors open last night.'

I nod despondently. Let's just hope that. She looks at me. She is
despondent too. Then she turns and starts to walk out to the porch.

'Your father's Oldsmobile was found at a place called Lowis,' she says,
when the screen door has slammed behind us. It was in a new housing
area. Big homes. A lot of kids. Did your father ever mention Lowis?
Maybe he visited a friend there?'

'No . . . We could look in his address book . . .' I suggest.

'I have that copied and I already looked. Local folk differ in their opinions but most of them think that the car had been there since Monday afternoon, probably since Monday morning, and a few are claiming it was there all weekend.'

'Didn't anyone see him leave it?'

'No, Lucy. No one saw a damn thing.' Her tone is resigned.

'But were there any fingerprints?'

She sighs. 'Someone took a lot of trouble to wipe the car completely clean. We managed to pick up a few old prints, a few stray fibres, but they were pretty much all your father's. Some from Jane but you'd expect that because he drove her to your son's grave on Saturday.'

'Can I have the address where it was found?'

'OK, if you think it might help you remember something useful. I'll check in my notebook and tell you the exact address,' she says.

She stoops to examine the big dent on the Oldsmobile's front right fender. 'Did your father ever mention this?'

'No.'

'It looks pretty fresh. But forensic didn't have anything interesting to say about it.' She straightens.

The sun feels oppressive today. The weight of its heat seems to pin me to the drive. When I duck into shade it brings little relief.

'There are so many questions about this case, Lucy,' the woman says. 'Over the next few days I'll be interviewing everyone who knew your father well. I'm hoping people will start remembering things they've forgotten. You and Jane especially.'

I don't know why I blush at her words.

'My colleague Michael Rougemont,' she continues, 'has this amazing memory. He can recall details from cases over thirty years ago. So it frustrates him when other people forget everything.'

I know my face is red. It feels as though it is swelling in the sun.

'For instance, Lucy, you and Jane both say you can't remember a thing about your brother's death.'

I swallow. 'I was very young . . .'

'Sure, but the loss of a sibling has a huge impact on a family. I'd expect one or two images to have survived. And I'd expect considerably more than that from Jane.'

'Larry would say we've buried the trauma.'

'Sure he would. And that would explain why you don't remember a thing, why you don't even remember your brother when he was alive?'

I say, slowly, shakily, 'I remember that I loved him. That's all.'

'Didn't anybody ever talk about it in your family?' she asks gently.

'Never.'

'I mean, when your son died, didn't your father talk about it then?'

'Not directly. It was referred to as a loss and Scott and I always knew he had a special understanding. But Daddy never discussed it.'

She sighs. 'Do you even know how the child died?'

'Oh yes.' I am prompt. 'I know that. In an accident.'

She waits for me to say more and then sighs again. 'Do you have any idea where that accident took place?'

I shake my head.

'At Big Brim beach. He drowned there. You really didn't know that?'

I stare at her.

'Oh, Lucy,' she murmurs, her tone at once intimate and despairing.

Scott arrives before Larry and Jane. He's pleased to see the Oldsmobile back in its usual place.

'You're here, the old car's here, I can kid myself that things are going back the way they used to be,' he says when we're sitting out on the deck.

'Larry doesn't approve of that,' I remind him.

'Of course, things can't ever be the same. But is it so bad to make-believe for a few moments?'

I smile at him.

He tells me how his book went into a new edition, how he was even interviewed about it on TV.

'I saw you,' I say.

'You saw me on TV?' I nod but he is quick. 'So you switched right off.'

I look at him until he finally lifts his big head and looks back at me. I say, 'No, Scott, I didn't switch off.'

When we hear an engine we go round the house to the barn. Larry and Jane have arrived and Larry is first out of the car.

'Sorry we're so late,' he says. 'We've been visiting your mother.'

I feel colour creeping up my neck.

'How was she?' Scott asks.

Larry and Jane wrinkle their faces as though the sun is shining in their eyes, although they are now standing in the kitchen lifting packages from a big brown deli bag.

'Well, she was subdued,' says Jane at last.

'Does she understand about Daddy?'

'She seems to comprehend that something sad has happened,' Larry says. 'She may not know what that is.'

'She fluttered a lot,' adds Jane. 'You remember how she sort of flutters when she gets upset?' She waves her arms and wiggles her fingers in a half-comical gesture I recognise at once.

I say, 'It's when she feels helpless.'

'And distressed,' Jane agrees.

'The most she ever fluttered was when I nearly drowned at the pool that day. It was because she wanted to do something but couldn't, or didn't know how, and she just had to stand there while you saved me.'

We were at the local swimming pool and I was learning to snorkel when I breathed water instead of air. My eyes and nose and mouth were full of water and the passages that link them were swamped by water too. Above me the sky was more deep blue water, stretching on for ever. I stopped struggling and submitted to the beauty of the pool's infinity. Then, suddenly, a powerful mixture of flesh and muscle gripped me under the chin and I felt the rhythmic strength of the swimmer's stroke as I was pulled to the edge. When I opened my eyes I was on the pool's hard paving, kids crowded round me, Jane pumping me, banging at me, until I threw up all the liquid and my body became solid again. I remember Jane's serious face, rapt in concentration, and beyond it, Mother, her blue dress flapping, her fingers flying.

Larry stops taking interesting food out of the deli bag and puts an arm round Jane. He has always liked the story of how she saved me. 'And she's still saving lives,' he says, his voice both proud and foolish.

After that the day is businesslike. We look at the will first. Daddy left everything divided equally between Jane and me. That is no surprise. Only his appointment of Scott as executor causes a ripple, with Scott first disbelieving and then shocked and then pleading for my help.

'I haven't done personal finance in a long while . . .' I protest but he yelps like a dog someone just stepped on.

'You have to do it for me, Luce. You just have to.'

'How long are you staying, Lucy?' asks Larry.

'I have to get back right after the funeral.' I feel a movement of disapproval ripple round the group. I add, 'Well, I can't stay past the end of next week. I have a big deal that might collapse if I'm not around.'

Larry speaks, his tone serious. 'Lucy, there's a lot to do after a death. A lot of decisions, a lot to sort out . . . you can't leave it all to Jane.'

I hope Jane will contradict him but she is silent.

'Will you have time to sort out the executor stuff for me before the funeral?' asks Scott helplessly.

'Probably,' I tell him. 'If I work hard enough.'

'When do we want the funeral?' asks Jane. 'How about next Tuesday? And have we informed everyone we need to inform? Let's get things sorted out.' She reaches for a notebook and pen. I watch her affectionately. Jane is retreating into the detached efficiency of the clinician where she feels safest. She learned to do that in childhood when Mother made life impossible and now she uses the same professionalism every day. Dealing with bereaved relatives is a routine part of her work. The extraordinary is routine for Jane. Routinely she has to tell patients that they are going to die. I know that she never stalls or avoids the terrible truths. She delivers the news with her usual unbending directness.

'OK,' says Larry, adopting her businesslike tone. 'I suggest that next we look in Eric's diary and cancel any appointments he made.'

We fetch the diary. We look at each other, not wanting to make the first call. It seems Jane is about to offer when Scott surprises us.

He says, 'I'll do it. Give me the numbers.'

We can hear him in the study, breaking the news to people. Some seem to know already but they have questions, about the police, about Daddy, about the circumstances. We hear Scott struggle to answer them, knowing that most are unanswerable.

While Larry makes coffee, I point to an entry in Daddy's diary. 'Daddy saw Mr Zacarro on Sunday night,' I say. 'Isn't that peculiar? One of the last people to see him was Mr Zacarro.'

'Oh, he'd got real pally with Mr Zacarro and Mr Holler,' Jane tells me. She is thumbing through Daddy's address book, making lists of names, and she doesn't look up.

'Daddy? And Mr Zacarro? And Mr Holler?' They were neighbours, not friends. I haven't seen either of them for many years and Daddy certainly never mentioned them.

'I really didn't like it, but what can you do?' says Jane absently.

'You didn't like it?'

'They weren't good for Daddy. He'd stay over at the Zacarro house real late, talking and drinking beer.'

I want to question her further but now Scott comes back in, red-eyed.

'Joni Rimbaldi was real shocked,' he says. Joni was Daddy's secretary in the geology department for many years. 'She was getting her make-up on to meet Eric for lunch in town today, and I call to say, hey, Joni, lunch is off, Eric's dead and he's not just dead he's murdered. What a call.'

'Maybe we should phone in an hour or two. Make sure she's OK,' suggests Jane and we all nod. That is certainly the right thing to do.

Over lunch, Larry says, 'Lucy, I guess you must agree that the house should be cleared and sold?'

I look at him.

He explains, 'The choices are renting it or selling it. As I assume none of us is going to live in it.'

'Sell it,' says Jane rapidly.

'Either way,' Larry points out, 'we take what we want and the rest has to be cleared.'

'I know that, Larry,' I say quietly. 'But it'll take months, because there's a right person and a right place for everything . . . I mean, some tractor enthusiast who'll want the old tractor. Some geologist who'll want the rocks. A gardener who—'

'It would take years to dispose of everything that way,' Jane tells me. 'And a lot of the stuff here is junk.'

Larry and Jane keep their apartment free of clutter and dust. Jane doesn't like to receive beautiful ceramics as gifts. The white apartment is designed so she has nowhere to put them. I watch her as she discusses, with clinical seriousness, the disposal of our past. Hostel for the homeless always needs furniture. Geology department to value the rocks.

Later, as I turn the car back up the drive, her words rattle around in my head like gravel in your shoe.

Next day I am walking up the Zacarro's drive to ask Mr Zacarro about Sunday evening when I am ambushed by a powerful memory.

Over the years storms have washed away much of the drive's surface. I trip in a pothole and brush against a plant. Its pink flowers are dusty, its leaves are sticky. My eyes fill with tears.

It was early morning as I walked up this drive to ask about Lindy. I had gone to bed anxious and woken anxious. I felt shy but I had to go because I had to know that everything was OK. I walked slowly at the side of the drive, knowing the touch of my leg would release a sweet aroma from the pink flowers that Mrs Zacarro had planted alongside the asphalt. I walked with one leg trailing through them, so by the time I was within sight of the house I was dizzy from the sun and the cloud of perfume, and I didn't even feel astonishment when I looked up and saw Mother emerging from the Zacarro house. Although I knew this was astonishing. At that time Mother seldom left our house and never alone.

As she drew closer I saw horror on her face. When she saw me she said, 'You can't possibly go in there.'

I didn't need to ask why. I knew they'd found Lindy.

Mother didn't pause but walked right on past me.

The whole class went to the funeral. Lindy had been the prettiest girl and that was a reason for some people to dislike her when she was alive and for everyone to cry some extra when she died. Except for me. I couldn't cry at all. I tried but no tears would come.

Slowly, I stumble on up the broken asphalt towards the house, inhaling the plant's vanishing perfume. I've thought about Lindy more in the last couple of days than in all the intervening years, but I still excluded her death. She died when we were eight. The next few years were informed by her death. Eventually I determined never to think about her at all. I was so successful that when Sasha asked me whether the Zacarros were good neighbours, all I could recall was Mr Zacarro's limp.

When I reach the top of the drive I see a car facing the garage. I notice that its trunk is closed with three enormous metal padlocks.

I ring the doorbell. I wonder how Mr Zacarro feels about old friends of his daughter. I wonder if he hates them for still being alive.

There is no responding sound from inside so I wander round the house. At the side gate I see a pool. In the pool a large brown body floats motionlessly, back down, arms and legs splayed. There is no movement on the water's surface. A floating armchair is moored to one side.

I let myself in quietly through the gate but when it clicks softly behind me the brown body at once folds itself and raises a hand, breaking the water's smooth surface.

He bellows, 'Is it Jane or is it Lucy?'

'Lucy.'

'Good!' he yells disconcertingly.

I stand closer to him now but he continues to roar at me. 'I'm real glad you came, Lucy. I want to say how sorry I am about your daddy and I want you to tell me what's been going on over there. Want a beer?'

'Well . . . thanks.'

I remember Mr Zacarro as a large man and when he heaves his body up into the floating armchair in a practised manoeuvre around the pool steps I see that he is still large. His head is almost hairless now.

He instructs me, 'Just on the porch there's a fridge and it's full of cold beers. Bring me one too, will you?'

The porch. When Lindy and I weren't on the swinging seat over at my house we were here in the porch playing with our little toy horses. Lindy's favourite was a sweet-faced chestnut. It had a soft coat and legs you could bend. His name was Trigger and Lindy used to say that when she was older she'd have a real horse that looked just like him.

I take the beers outside and pass one to the floating man. He gestures for me to sit down at a poolside seat.

'So, Lucy Schaffer,' Mr Zacarro yells. 'I guess I've glimpsed you since you grew up but I remember you best playing out back with the kids.'

I swallow. I don't want to be the first to mention Lindy. 'How are Davis and Carter?' I yell back. I've worked out that he must be deaf.

'You don't have to shout. I'm not deaf. Davis and Carter are doing just great. They're busy so I don't see them too often. But they call me.' He gestures to the telephone nearby. I look around for the first time and realise that the back garden is furnished. There are the usual poolside couches and chairs but there is also a dressing table, a chest and a TV. By the side of the pool is a small, neat pile of rocks. Some are round and consist of interesting seams, others are crystalline.

Mr Zacarro watches me. 'Your daddy gave me those rocks. He often brought me rocks and I put them all right there.'

'What's that one?' I ask, pointing to a rock that lies behind the rest, larger and flat-faced. Words are inscribed on it.

He smiles. His smile is crooked. 'It's a headstone.'

The headstone is way down at the shallow end. I get up to take a closer look. I read: REMEMBER DEATH. JOE ZACARRO ALWAYS DID.

'There's a space underneath for my dates,' he explains. 'Do you like it?'

I nod, returning to the vast body, sprawled in its floating armchair. 'Did you see Daddy on Sunday night, Mr Zacarro?'

'Joe. Yep, he came over here, so did Adam Holler.'

'Do you know whether he saw anyone else on Sunday?'

He shrugs a big shrug. 'Didn't say so.'

'What time did he go home?'

'I don't know. He was here an hour or two.'

I see small goose pimples appear across his chest. 'Aren't you cold?' I ask. 'Can I get you a towel?'

He smiles and I guess that my solicitous tone has pleased him. And then something sad flits across his face and I know that he's just wished he still had a daughter to ask him if he's cold and needs a towel.

'Well, Lucy, I don't feel the cold these days,' he yells. 'At first it was hard, in the winter, but I just don't feel it any more.'

'You swim all year round?'

'I don't do so much swimming now. I float a lot.' He drinks some beer and then slips it into a can-shaped crevice in the arm of the chair.

I look around again. 'You . . . you live out here? In the pool?'

'Oh, sometimes I go inside the house. But it hurts, see. When I'm up on land I lumber around like some big old moose. I got one leg shorter than the other so I've always been a moose. Don't you remember that about me? I always thought it must be the one thing people noticed.'

Mr Zacarro limping. Mr Zacarro chasing after Davis and Carter, shouting with fury, and Davis and Carter laughing, knowing he could never catch them.

I say, 'When did you build the pool?'

'Boys were teenagers I guess. I got so I came home every night and had a swim, winter and summer. I can move how I want in the water. I guess I just spent more and more time here so now I hardly leave it.'

'But you'll come to Daddy's funeral?'

'Sure. I get dressed sometimes, I go to the store, fill the freezer. Since Gracie left I've pretty well eaten out of the freezer. Lucy . . .' He paddles his chair round with his hands so that he is facing me. 'Did I say I'm real sorry about your daddy? He was a great guy. Clever. Funny. Loved you two girls a lot. But what were the police doing at your place? Adam Holler had it from Bernard Dimoto that he drowned at Big Brim beach. Did he drown or didn't he? Will you tell me what's going on?'

I'd like to evade his question but can think of no way to do so.

'Daddy's death . . .' I flounder, then borrow the phrase Jim used back in New York. 'It wasn't straightforward. The police say it's homicide.'

There is a silence and then Mr Zacarro gives a long, low whistle. 'Homicide! Oh, Lucy, Lucy, that's just garbage. Homicide's garbage.'

There's a long pause. His lips form the word homicide again and again.

'Can you think . . . is there anyone you can think of who might have some reason to kill Daddy?'

'No one would kill Eric!' he roars. 'What are the forensic geeks saying?'

I shrug. 'That he didn't drown. He died first and then his body some-how got into the water.'

'Oh shit, shit, this is awful.' His lips form more silent words.

'Daddy's clothes were left at Big Brim beach. But no one knows how he got there. His car was found over at San Strana. Lowis, to be precise.'

He stares at me. 'Lowis?' he bellows.

'Did he know anyone there?'

'No, no, no, he never mentioned anyone up at Lowis.' He shakes his head. His lips move in silent conversation with someone.

'Did he say on Sunday what he planned to do on Monday?'

'No, no, no . . .'

'Did he say he was worried about anything in particular? Did he seem like a man who worried a lot?'

'Eric, nah. He wasn't worried.'

I say softly, 'Joe, there's a big dent in the front of Daddy's car . . .'

'There is?'

'I thought the dent might already have been there.'

'Never mentioned it.'

'Did he have any car problems?'

'Yeah, one big problem called an Oldsmobile.'

'Did it break down recently?'

'He never would have told me because he knew I'd have said, Get rid of that heap of garbage.'

'Did anyone tow it recently?'

Joe shakes his head. He is not looking at me.

I get up to go. 'I guess the police will probably be interviewing you soon. Mr Holler too.'

His big, doughy face studies mine sadly. When I leave he calls after me, 'You come swimming here any time, d'you hear? Whether I'm home or not, you swim here and not on some goddamn dangerous beach.'

I try not to look at the padlocked trunk of Mr Zacarro's car but now I've seen it I can't pass it without remembering Lindy, stroking the toy horse that she said would be just like her real horse one day.

Larry and Jane suspect that someone visited Daddy's house again last night. I find them in his bedroom, removing everything valuable.

'I'm furious that the locksmith didn't come yesterday like he promised,' Jane tells me, examining a small silver box.

'Even with the locks changed we should take this stuff away,' Larry says, 'Lucy, will you check the den to see if it's just the way you left it?'

I spent several hours working in Daddy's den yesterday afternoon, sorting out files for Scott.

'You think someone was in there last night?'

'We think someone was in the house because Jane double-locked the door and this morning it was only single-locked. But we can't find any other place they've been.'

I am relieved to find that my tidy piles of paperwork are arranged just as I left them. But when I examine the files closely I find small discrepancies in their organisation. Inside the drawers, two files have been removed and replaced back to front. Jane was right. Someone has been here.

I go back up to the blue bedroom. 'They tried to put it back just the way it was but they didn't get it exactly right,' I tell Jane and Larry.

'Are you sure nothing's missing?' asks Jane. 'They're obviously looking for something. They could have taken any of this silver, but they didn't. There's some kind of a file or a document that's worth more to them.'

'I looked at most of the files yesterday and, apart from a few I took back to Aunt Zina's with me, I can't immediately see any are missing.'

I continue working in the den. Two men arrive wearing red shirts on which are emblazoned the words *Buddy, you're safe with us.* I can hear their voices and the rasp of their tools as they change the locks. Afterwards they tell Jane how vulnerable the house is to intruders.

'We can't possibly do everything they're suggesting,' says Jane when they've gone, sinking onto the chair in the den. I look up at her. I am working on the floor now, files all around me.

377

'Like what?'

'Oh, alarms and CCTV and automatic gates. Let's just empty the house and sell it fast and leave whoever buys it to worry about security.' She gets up and picks her way across the floor through the files. 'You're sure making progress here.'

'Those are all closed,' I say, pointing to the big green files that she has just stepped over. 'I've informed anyone necessary of Daddy's death and finished all the paperwork. I should be able to close these by tomorrow. The files on the desk and in the drawers will take a little longer.'

'Is everything straightforward?' she asks.

'Daddy had a good system here. There's just one minor anomaly so far, but I'm sure I can sort that out with a few telephone calls.'

'What is it?'

'Oil well stuff. Maybe I was too tired when I was working on it last night at Aunt Zina's. I'm going to take another look today.'

'Oil?' Jane asks.

I nod. Daddy did oil-exploration work in the vacations sometimes. Before he married and then again many years later, when I was still home and Jane had gone to college.

'But he hasn't done any of that kind of work for years.'

'When he did he was smart enough to take a part of his payment in royalties. He was entitled to his percentage as long as the wells he found were producing. Believe it or not, a couple of those wells are still active.'

'He was still taking an income from the oil companies? Was it much?'

'I haven't checked the most recent statements but certainly until a few years ago it would have been enough to live on, if he lived frugally.'

Jane whistles. 'And he never even mentioned it!'

'I've tried to work back from his bank and other statements to the oil revenues. And I can't find them. Not so far.'

She looks at me in surprise. 'What did he do with it?'

'He collected the earliest payments, the ones that go way back to before we were born. Then, suddenly, after a few years, he stopped.'

'Were these regular payments?'

'Annual.'

'And every year it just sort of . . . disappears?'

'Well, I haven't found it yet.'

She looks thoughtful. 'I'll bet Seymour can help.' Seymour, Daddy's closest friend, was a retired petroleum geologist.

'I'm going to call him,' I agree. 'He'll probably explain it right away.'

'Don't forget to tell him that the funeral's on Tuesday,' she says over her shoulder.

I open the desk drawer to look for Daddy's address book so I can call Seymour. The address book isn't there, just a lot of the kind of junk you keep in your desk drawer. I withdraw a browning newspaper cutting. The typeface of the *Valley Gazette* is instantly recognisable: *Wedding News*. Curiously, I unfold the cutting and flatten it on the desk. It reports the marriage of Robert Joseph to Karen Sylvester.

Although I haven't been in love with Robert Joseph for many years, the article seems to bubble and swell. I stare hard at the grey picture. His hair is shorter and his face thinner but the groom is unmistakable.

I search for a date, do not find one, then read the report. The groom is a doctor. The bride is a banker. The bride wore antique lace. The bridesmaids wore yellow. There is a list of guests.

I go out to the deck and look down at the quiet order of the valley. My eye rests on the right angles of the intersection.

The bride is a banker, just like me. And Robert, who wanted to be a movie director, became a doctor. Maybe spending so much time in hospital and nearly losing his leg changed his ambitions. For me he stopped being at eighteen but since then he grew and changed and married and probably had children and I am just a tiny grain of his history.

If I look south, I can fool myself that I see the Joseph farm, a speck of vivid green, although I know it's only visible from further round the dirt road. You can fry down in the valley but the aqueduct runs right by the Joseph farmstead and their garden is an oasis, green and cool and shady. That summer I spent with Robert Joseph we lay together in a hammock swinging beneath two stout trees, talking about everything and being in love. Teenage love. Easy to ridicule afterwards but it felt real at the time. And all that talking. Robert's mother said she liked to hear our voices buzzing away in the hammock. She was nice and she had nice friends. I sometimes wished she was my mother and then felt guilty about it.

Back in the den I find Seymour's number and he answers the phone right away, as though he's working at his desk.

'Lucy, hey, Lucy, good to hear from you,' he says but his voice cracks suddenly. 'Boy, do I miss Eric. I miss him already and he's only been dead a few days. This morning I tore something out of *The Rock Hammer* that I knew would make him real mad. I was chuckling to myself at how mad he'd get and I put it in an envelope and wrote his address on it! Can you believe that? Glad I realised before I bought a stamp.'

I smile. In Seymour I can capture a little of Daddy. It's like finding a photo of the beach house right after the ocean has washed it away.

We talk a little about Tuesday's funeral. Then I tell Seymour about Daddy's oil royalties.

'Simms-Roeder still producing, eh? Well, I'm jealous. What a great find that was for Eric.'

'But, Seymour, I can't find any record of the money. Where it came in and where it went out. There's just the oil company's statement that it was paid. Did Daddy ever tell you what he did with it?'

'Nope. It must show on his bank statements, Lucy.'

'It doesn't show on any statements anywhere. I called the oil company and they were unhelpful . . . Do you have any contacts there now?'

'Oh boy. Most of the people I knew there have retired. But I could try. Let me work at it. Will you come by for the answer?'

I promise to stop by at Seymour's on Friday evening.

Hours later, when I look up and see that the square of sky beyond the small overhead window has turned the inky blue of late afternoon, I wonder why Daddy cut out the article about Robert Joseph's wedding. Did he intend to give it to me, then forgot, or did he change his mind?

The two detectives, Kirsty and Rougemont, arrive. Rougemont greets me as though we know each other well, smiling too broadly. Jane is friendly. She and Larry make coffee and she tells how we think the intruder came again last night.

'I really don't like it. I'm relieved the locksmith's been,' she says. 'Sometimes I get the feeling we're being watched.'

I look at her in surprise. It's hard to imagine anyone less inclined to paranoia than Jane.

'I've seen this guy outside our apartment,' adds Larry. 'He doesn't seem to be doing anything. Just sort of hanging around out there.'

'Uh-huh,' says Rougemont. 'How many times have you seen him?'

'Well . . . just twice,' admits Larry.

Jane smiles as she passes round the coffees. 'We're getting nervous and it's making us imagine all sorts of things,' she says.

'Someone with a spare set of keys has been here,' Kirsty says. 'We'll put a couple of officers in the garden tonight and see what happens.'

Rougemont drinks some of his coffee in gulps. Then he says he'd like to wander round the house.

'What are you looking for?' I ask him.

'I'm an old dog who likes to sniff around houses,' he says, loping off. Mother had a brown dog when I was real small. He liked to sniff around. He liked to hide and then leap out, barking and scaring me.

Kirsty asks if Scott's here.

'He's teaching today,' I explain. 'Plus he doesn't need to be here so often since I'm doing all his executor stuff.'

'Why do you think your father didn't appoint you in the first place?'

she asks and I recoil from the sharpness in her question.

'That's obvious,' says Jane quietly as she pours more coffee.

I look at her in surprise.

'You've left California, right? Daddy respected that decision. He didn't want to give you responsibilities that would drag you back, even though he knew you'd be the best person. It was a generous, loving gesture.'

I know she is right. Jane has detected my pain and relieved it, the way she always does. I glimpse Larry, too, looking at her with admiration.

She asks the detective, 'Any news from the ME?'

'We're now sure your father died close to eight in the morning. Death occurred very shortly before immersion. That's all.'

We consider the significance of this.

'So,' says Larry cautiously, 'he didn't die anywhere near the place his car was found.'

'I guess not,' Kirsty agrees wearily. 'Lowis is at least thirty, forty minutes from Big Brim.'

Jane asks, 'Did the ME get any closer to finding out how Daddy died?'

'She's consulting Charles Rossi, a professor of forensic pathology.'

Kirsty pulls her notebook out of her bulging briefcase. 'I have an unusual question to ask you . . . It's about a tow truck.'

I stare at her.

'I realise that it seems impossible. But could your father have been driving one the night before he died?'

Jane and I look at one another and pull faces. 'Well, no,' we say.

'We put out a request for any information that might help us locate your father on Sunday night/Monday morning and a highway patrolman contacted me. He says he spoke to the driver of a tow truck late on Sunday night on the big freeway into town about nine miles inland from Big Brim. He recalled your father's name and described him accurately.'

Jane sounds incredulous. 'He thinks Daddy was driving a tow truck?'

'He's adamant about it. Does that make any sense to you at all?'

I shake my head. 'I can't imagine it.'

'Why did the patrolman pull it over?' Larry asks.

'The truck had stopped by some kind of a wreck at the side of the road. Officer Howie asked to see the driver's licence and now he thinks it had your father's name on and that the driver fitted the description we issued. Unfortunately, he didn't write any of this down at the time, not even the number of the truck.'

'Was the tow truck picking up the wreck?'

'It was trying to but there was something wrong with the winch and the driver said that he was waiting for someone to come and sort it out.'

'Was the driver alone?'

'No. There were two other men with him.'

Rougemont comes in. I thought he'd been inside the house but he smells of eucalyptus. He sits down at the table. Kirsty tells him that Jane and Larry and I don't know of any reason Daddy should have been driving a tow truck on Sunday.

Larry says, 'He just wasn't that kind of guy.'

'Oh,' says Rougemont, putting his big head on one side. 'He sure used to be that kind of a guy.' We all stare at him while he sips cold coffee.

'What do you mean?' Jane demands.

'Well, I think I told you that I used to know your father a little, many years ago. He certainly had a tow truck then.'

'A tow truck?' echoes Jane. 'No, not Daddy.'

'Sure. He even kept his driver's certificate updated. Although that doesn't mean he drove one recently.'

I ask, 'When did he have this tow truck, Mr Rougemont?'

He narrows his eyes. 'Hmm . . . you were a small girl then, Lucy. You might not remember; I thought maybe Jane would.'

'Why would a geologist need a tow truck?' Larry asks sceptically. But I know the answer. The tow truck is already inside my head and it didn't just drive there. It has always been there, I just had to draw back the drapes and find it, standing behind them, sparkling in the sunlight.

'He was fixing it,' I say. 'Like the tractor and the printing press and the Oldsmobile . . . He used to lie underneath it with spanners, fixing it. It seemed enormous. And it was chrome, I guess, because it was silver and shiny. In front there was a sort of face. I mean, headlamps for eyes and this big fender that looked like a monster mouth.'

'You remember!' says Rougemont with admiration. 'You were only four, Lucy, and you remember! Of course, I don't know when he got rid of it. You may have been five or six or seven by that time. However, since it sometimes seems no one in this family can remember anything, well, I'd say you've shown definite progress!'

Kirsty agrees enthusiastically and they both look congratulatory. I glance at Jane. Her pale skin is glowing pink.

'Listen,' she says icily. 'When people can't remember, sometimes it's because their memories are so painful that they don't want to remember.'

'Sure, sure,' Rougemont agrees, nodding his head in his strange elastic way. 'But how can remembering a tow truck be so painful?'

There is silence, and then into the silence comes the unhappy voice of a very small girl close to tears.

She says, 'Because that's how they towed her away.'

Everyone swings round to face the girl. They are looking at me.

'When Mother wouldn't get out of the car . . .' I'm talking to Jane but she's staring down at the table top. 'You must remember when Mother wouldn't get out of the car?'

Jane says nothing. She thinks this is a betrayal, but I can't stop now.

'When we got back from Arizona and Mother was psychotic but we didn't know that's what it was because it was the very first time . . . well, she wouldn't get out of the car. When they came for her, two men and a woman still couldn't get her out of the car. She nearly defeated them. Except, there was a tow truck, parked right outside the barn. It must have been one of Daddy's old wrecks. So they used it to tow her away. I mean, the car. With Mother in it.'

The silence that follows is painful. The two police officers watch me keenly. Larry is startled, his air of detached observation temporarily abandoned. Jane's face is red and when she speaks, her voice is scarcely more than a whisper.

'We couldn't leave her sitting there in the car for ever.'

'We could have waited. Until she was ready.' I'm speaking softly too. 'I think she would have got out when she was ready.'

Jane looks at me, her head thrown back a little as though I'm a bright light that could dazzle her. 'She wasn't eating. And you were in tears the whole time. It wasn't an easy decision for Daddy but he did it for you as well as Mother. Are you saying he did the wrong thing?'

I shake my head rapidly, because I know that Daddy always tried to do the right thing. 'No. I'm just saying it was horrible.' I turn to Rougemont. 'That's probably why neither of us wanted to remember the tow truck.'

Five

BELLAMY IS A PRETTY COASTAL TOWN. Behind the shops and cafés and boats that the tourists see is the California Highway Patrol headquarters. I arrive at eight forty. When I called from Aunt Zina's last night, they told me that Officer Howie begins his shift at nine. I find a uniformed officer in the lobby and persuade him to intercept Officer Howie before he leaves the precinct. A few minutes later a handsome, immaculately uniformed patrolman appears. He looks at me doubtfully.

'My name's Lucy Schaffer. My father died recently and I understand that you may have been one of the last people to see him alive . . .'

He stares at me.

'On Sunday night you inspected a tow truck he was driving. On Monday morning he was dead, not so far from the place you saw him. He was a homicide victim and it's possible he was killed by one of the other people who were in the truck with him.'

He looks over my head, remembering Sunday night, Daddy, the tow truck. 'Oh jeez . . . A detective already asked me about that. Detective MacFarlane. She seemed real doubtful that it was the same guy but I recognised the picture. Plus I recalled the name. Yeah, Schaffer.'

'How sure are you?'

'Completely sure. And there were two other guys with him.'

'Can you remember anything about them? Anything at all?'

'I didn't get a good look at them. They stayed quiet the whole time.'

'Did my father get out of the tow truck?'

'No, ma'am. He wound down the window and explained that he'd come to take this wreck away that was right by the side of the road, but he had a winch problem. He said someone was on their way to fix it.'

'Officer . . . did my father appear distressed in any way? Or anxious?'

He smiles. His smile is white and symmetrical. 'Most people are anxious when they get pulled over by the California Highway Patrol.'

'I mean, was he especially unhappy? So ill at ease that it's possible he was being held in the tow truck against his will?'

The man pauses and thinks. 'Nah. He was nervous but not that nervous. There's nothing I could have ticketed him for but he sort of looked as if he thought I was going to anyway.'

'And the accident . . . what had happened?'

'Accident?'

'The wreck they were trying to tow away.'

'Oh, now. Now we're talking weird. I just came on duty and the wreck was right at one of our worst black spots. I assumed there was a crash there earlier in the day. The car was completely burnt out. I mean, unidentifiable. But you know something? I just found out yesterday that there was no accident. There were no reported incidents on that part of the coast road last Sunday. Nothing.'

'So . . .' I say slowly. 'So, how do you think the wreck got there?'

'I guess they were towing it from somewhere else and they stopped and unhooked it because they were having trouble with the winch.'

'Did they get the winch fixed?'

'No, ma'am, they did not. That wreck stayed by the side of the coastal highway causing big traffic problems on Monday morning.'

'It blocked the highway?'

'It doesn't have to block the highway to cause problems. People slow down to rubberneck and that delays everyone for miles back.'

'Just a couple more questions. Can you describe the tow truck?'

'Well, I'd say it was real old, almost antique. I guess your father had it a long time.' His statement is half a question, which I ignore.

'Can you remember anything else? Anything that was said, anything about the other people in the cab? Anything that didn't seem right?'

'No, ma'am. It was just a routine check for me.' He has hardly looked at me all the time we've been talking but suddenly his eyes meet mine. 'Ma'am, I understand your father was a homicide victim, but why are you asking these questions?'

'When your father's killed it makes you ask questions.'

From Bellamy I drive down the coast a little way. The road follows all the twists and turns of the tortuous coastline, but the traffic speeds up when it reaches the long, straight stretch by Big Brim. This must be the least popular beach in the area. The parking lot where Rougemont left his car right by mine is almost empty. Only two cars and a tow truck.

A tow truck. At Big Brim. Antique in appearance, chrome-covered, its silver arm pointing skywards like a shark's fin. I brake and swing round in a U-turn. The driver behind me honks and so does the car behind that.

I pull in by the tow truck and, rocked by the wind of each passing car, I walk round it twice. Far from monstrous, it seems to me small and battered with age. Its chrome sparkles in the sunshine. The network of crane and winch piled onto its back has the solidity of another era. The make of the truck is obscure because so many letters have fallen from its name. Diver or Divine, maybe. The remnant of a garage name is almost visible on the driver's door. The truck is so aged that I suspect it is still on the road only through good luck and constant tinkering.

I find a map in the hire car and on the back of it write the shadow names and the truck's number. The truck is harmless without its driver. The driver is powerless without his truck. My heart beats fast as I look across the road at the dunes.

During a pause in the traffic I dart across the blacktop. I take off my shoes and my feet are rapidly submerged in sand. It resists every step. I move on resolutely, my whole body leaning forward, and drag each foot towards the sea. All the time I am looking for the driver of the tow truck.

When I reach the third dune I look across the beach. The pear-shaped man and his little dog are here again. Two women, jogging. A mother with a gaggle of children surging round her. A few dogs in the sea, their owners watching them. And then I see him. He is alone on the dunes, perhaps a quarter of a mile away. A man, tall, dark, probably young. He is heading towards the road and is already nearing the top of the first dune. At its pinnacle he pauses and something makes him turn. We stare at one another across billions of grains of undulating sand. I know he knows I am looking for him. Then he turns again. He has only to descend one dune and walk along the roadside.

I run back down the dune I just climbed and start to ascend the second. The sand seems to suck at my legs, my feet are weights. When I reach the top of the dune nearest the road, my heart thumping, I look at once at the parking lot. I am already too late. The dark figure had only to run along the road and he would have reached his truck before I was down the second dune. I imagine the monstrous growl of its old engine, the whine of the transmission, the roar as he accelerated into the traffic.

I sit down on the baking sand. I stare at the place the tow truck stood. It was an answer, an explanation, and now there is only a void.

I slowly retrace my route across the dunes, feeling the sand scorching the soles of my feet. I run down the last dune to the beach and, when the sand is firm and damp underfoot, I put down my shoes. The sea is docile here, like a blue lagoon. I walk up to the water in a straight line and pause when I feel the ice of its touch at my toes.

'Hey!' shouts a voice. 'Hey, you, yes you!'

I turn. A large, amorphous shape is half running towards me, his tiny dog racing alongside him. He carries some driftwood under his arm. When he reaches me, he is too breathless to speak.

I stand with my hands on my hips. 'What's the problem?'

'I need to warn you. Point A. The tide comes up real fast. When it comes. Right now it's going the other way. Point B. This looks like it might be a good place to swim. Gently shelving. Calm waters. But there are these currents, caused by the sand spits at each end. It means this beach is not safe for swimming. I just thought you should know that.'

'Thanks. Actually, I already knew. I heard about a baby who drowned here a long time ago.'

'Oooh, that's too bad.' The man looks at me uncertainly. 'Is that why you came here today, lady?'

I make patterns in the sand with my toes, like ancient hieroglyphics. The sea breeze ruffles my hair. 'You've made a mistake.'

He looks at me wide-eyed.

'You thought I intended to commit suicide. Right?'

He studies the sand bashfully. 'It's the way you put your shoes down and then walked towards the ocean in a straight line. That's what they generally do.' He looks back at me. 'I mean . . . weren't you?'

'No. My father was found dead in the water a little way down the coast. He left his clothes right here on the beach.'

The man throws his head back as though he's been burnt. 'Oooh, gee. That guy. The one they're saying was a homicide. He was your father?'

'Did you see him?'

His rubbery features remodel themselves into contours of unhappiness. 'Nah. I didn't see anyone. That's how I know he wasn't here.'

'He died last Monday morning. The police think he died at eight.'

'Uh-huh. He didn't die here.'

I stare at the man. 'What do you mean?'

'I'm generally on patrol by seven,' he explains. 'No one was on the beach that morning. I already told the police.'

'But his clothes were found here.'

'No clothes here at eight o'clock. I mean, I didn't walk right down the beach but I'd have seen them. I live at the other end.'

'Who found his clothes?'

'Me 'n' Cinnamon.' The dog, which has flopped onto the nearest dry sand, looks up when it hears its name and then flops back down. 'I went home at eight thirty for a cup of coffee and I came out at nine thirty just like today and that's when I saw the clothes. I called the police and they came. Boy, they sure hate coming over the dunes in their uniforms.'

'So someone put my father's clothes here after he died,' I say at last.

The man nods. 'Or the medical examiner got the time of death wrong. If your father died on this beach while I was having my coffee then . . . I'm sorry.' And when I look up his mouth is pulling in all directions. 'I sure wish I could have saved your father but I really don't think he died at Big Brim.'

'You don't?'

'Nah. My money's on Seal Wash.'

'Why?'

'An informed guess. Your dad was found off Retribution. There are currents from here but there are also some that go right there from Seal Wash and the road there runs real close to the clifftop.'

Daddy's body plummeting from the clifftop into the depths of the blue ocean beneath. A splash. A splash that would be loud enough in a swimming pool but here in the ocean it would seem nothing more than the crash of a small wave on a small rock.

'Are you OK?' asks the man.

387

I nod.

'That's only a theory. Maybe I made myself that theory because I feel so bad to think I could've missed him. I only miss a few.'

I stand up and dust off the sand. 'Thanks. You've been very helpful.'

He looks up at me doubtfully. 'You OK now?' he asks.

'I didn't come here to kill myself. Really.'

'Oh sure,' he agrees, but I can tell he still believes that I did.

When I return to the car, hot and dishevelled, I sit sideways in the seat, my feet hanging out. I remember copying the number of the tow truck, and the letters on the door, onto the back of the map. I thrust the map onto the passenger seat before I ran across the road to the dunes. But there is no map on the passenger seat. It is neither on, under or behind the seat and it is not in the glove compartment.

At Seal Wash the sea is restless as a hungry animal. The black rocks that jut from the ocean's depth look more menacing than they did on Tuesday and the water sloshing against the cliffs throws spray high into the air.

You could park a car so that the passenger side was almost at the edge of the cliff and you could dump something inanimate, a bag of rocks, a human body, right into the ocean. Neither the splash nor the spray would be remarkable and the object, that is, the bag of rocks or the body, would soon be lost in the vast, deep blueness.

There is the crash of an immense wave and a few moments later I feel the ocean's damp cloth on my face.

Or maybe Daddy got right out of the car, Daddy and his killer, someone he knew, with whom he was relaxed. When Daddy looked away, the killer acted. If you pushed someone off the cliff here, you couldn't be sure they would die. The sea looks fierce but a strong swimmer might get to the safety of a nearby rock. No, as the medical examiner said, Daddy was dead when he hit the water. Did his killer watch the body topple down the cliff, listen for the splash? Or did he get back into the car and drive to Big Brim beach? Few people were around. He dumped Daddy's clothes. Then, did he return to his car and drive away?

'I know what you're thinking and I agree with you,' says a voice.

I spin right round and a long arm is extended to steady me. Michael Rougemont grasps me with his bony fingers.

'Don't get too close to the edge!' His eyes are wide.

'Are you following me?' I demand, stepping inland. His grip loosens and his arms drop. I see his car parked on the other side of the clifftop.

'I'm probably here for the same reason you are. You're thinking that your father died at Seal Wash and I agree with that.'

The ocean crashes beneath us. 'Mr Rougemont, yesterday you said you knew Daddy when he had a tow truck. How did you know him?'

He pauses, then speaks carefully. 'I met him when your brother died.'

I turn to look at his battered old face. 'When my brother died?'

'I was the investigating officer.'

'Why were you investigating?'

'A baby dies, it's usual. When your baby died, Kirsty investigated.'

'It's an incredible coincidence,' I say, 'that you two are both working on Daddy's case too.' He doesn't reply and I realise it isn't a coincidence.

'Of course, you have no memory of your brother's death,' he tells me. 'No.'

'Although yesterday it seemed that your memory was starting to work.'

'I don't remember anything at all about my brother. Except that he existed and I loved him.'

'I've been wondering if you can remember something much more recent. Can we get into your car?'

It feels good to shut out the spray and the crash of the rocks. I sit behind the wheel. Rougemont adjusts the passenger seat for his long legs. Then he asks me when I last saw my father.

'Your colleague already asked me that,' I say. 'I told her he visited me once in New York, about two and a half years ago. But we spoke often.'

'When was the last time you saw him in California, Lucy?'

'Just before I left. Almost three years ago.'

'What did he say when you told him you were leaving?'

'He didn't challenge my decision. I didn't ask for his permission but he gave it to me anyway.'

Rougemont asks quietly, 'Was it hard saying goodbye?'

'Yes, it was hard.' I don't tell him how Daddy cried.

'But you said goodbye,' continues the detective. 'And, except for that brief time in New York, you didn't want to go through the pain of saying it again. So when you came to California last weekend, maybe that's why you didn't tell anyone you were here.'

His words burn my ears.

I hear him say, 'You were here in San Francisco last weekend. Right, Lucy? You flew out on Sunday night. Shortly before your father died.'

I wind down a window. The car is filled by the sound of the sea.

His voice softer, Michael Rougemont says, 'It's all right. I'm not going to tell them. Your sister, your husband, I'm not going to say anything. But why didn't you tell me, or Kirsty? Why did you lie to us?'

I do not reply.

'What did you do here last weekend, Lucy?'

A slab of sunlight slants in through the windshield onto my lap. I watch the car's clock slowly change figures.

'Lucy, if you were here last weekend it won't take me long to find out what you did. Save me a day and just tell me because I need to know.'

But when I shake my head and the silence has stretched on longer than any silence should, then Michael Rougemont opens the car door.

'OK,' he says amiably. 'If you won't help me, I'd better get to work.'

As soon as I am back in Daddy's den I dial New York. I'm calling Mittex. Not only is Jay Kent in his office today but his secretary has clearly been told to put any call from me right through to him.

'Lucy! Good to hear from you!' he says. 'I tried to call you, but I got some woman I couldn't understand . . .'

'My Aunt Zina. She couldn't understand you. She said you sounded like a machine gun.'

Kent laughs his machine-gun laugh. 'How are you, Lucy?'

'I'm OK. What did you think of Gregory Hifeld?'

'I admired him a lot. But, Lucy, he didn't like me. He won't sell to us. He wants to play Santa to his little elves. He doesn't want mean ol' Mittex waving balance sheets around in Toyland. But I don't want to talk about this, Lucy. Have you found out what happened to your father?'

'Well, yes . . .' I say. 'It was homicide.'

'Homicide?' And for the first time his voice loses its certainty.

'That's what the police say.'

'But do you have any idea . . . have the police . . .?'

'No, Kent, but they know about last weekend.'

'What?'

'A detective told me that he's found out about last weekend.'

Kent is cautious. 'How much does he know?'

'At the moment, just that I was here.'

His voice rises. 'Oh, he'll find out. These guys find things out.'

'He says that by the end of today he's going to know where I was and who I saw and what I did . . .'

'For Chrissake, Lucy!' I hear his anger, his fear. 'What did you tell him?'

'Nothing. When they interviewed me I said I was home all weekend.'

'You've lied to the police! You've made a false statement! Shit, Lucy.'

'I'm trying to keep you out of it, Kent, that's why.'

But he's shouting now and doesn't hear. 'Lucy, they're going to get you and then they'll find their way to me. This could blow everything.'

'But what can I do? Now I've lied I can't change my story.'

'Nothing.' He breathes heavily. 'You can't do anything. Just sit tight and don't say anything if you can help it. I have to go now.'

Kent slams down the phone. There is electronic groaning on the line.

When I put down the phone the house feels sticky and silent. No one else is here today. Scott offered to help but I told him to stay on campus because everything in the den is under control. Larry and Jane have also gone to their offices. They have now removed any items that look valuable and are close to completing the arrangements for the funeral.

'You should be safe enough by yourself here in the daytime now we have the new keys,' Larry told me. 'Just be sure to lock the door.'

I followed Larry's advice, but right from the moment I walked in I knew that the house was too hot to remain closed. The walls inhale the day's heat with more stamina than they exhale it at night.

I fling open the sliding doors to the deck and a hot breeze blows in.

When we were kids, we used to flip through the railings onto the deck at one end, where the sloping ground and the deck almost meet. Now that there is no one here to see me, I scramble down to the slope, reach for the railing and take my feet off the ground. I swing myself once, twice, and then flip onto the deck with a practised movement. My body is hurled into its own trajectory, and then I am landing squarely on both feet. Satisfaction. The whole manoeuvre has taken a couple of seconds and my body's memory of it was perfect.

I go back to the den and call Jim Finnigan.

'Lucy, oh gosh, Lucy, I was just thinking about you. How're things? How're you feeling?' He is loud and fast, he is New York.

'It's good to hear you, Jim.'

'Life's pretty bad, huh? When's the funeral?'

'Not until Tuesday.'

Jim probably has his feet on the wastepaper bin. 'Well, don't hurry back.'

'Ahem, Jim. You're supposed to tell me you can't manage without me.'

'Well, I can. So take your time.'

'What about Hifeld–Mittex?'

'Don't worry about that. I'm doing whatever needs to be done.' Despite his words I hear that his voice is bumping along the bottom of some riverbed. 'Lucy, the police contacted me yesterday. About you.'

'What did they want?'

'Oh . . .' he exhales loudly. 'Some guy's flying out here to talk to me.'

'A guy? What's his name?'

'Er . . .' The rustle of paper. 'Rougemont. He'll be in the office on Monday. I have to produce a schedule of the hours you spent here in the ten days before your father's death. That kind of stuff.'

'Oh.'

Jim's voice rasps a little. 'Lucy . . . was your father really killed?'

'The police think so.'

'That's terrible. Do you have any idea who would—?'

'There just isn't anyone, Jim. Daddy was a nice guy who never would have given anyone a reason to hurt him. Did Rougemont ask you anything else over the phone?'

'He wanted to know how you spent the weekend. You said you were visiting friends and I told him so. He also wants to talk to Fatima. And he's asked for the tapes of your telephone calls for the last two weeks.'

I am silent, first with shock, then because I am thinking. Wondering what I said to Kent or he said to me over the company phone.

'Hey, Lucy? Are you there?'

'What did you tell him, Jim?'

'I said no because the tapes contain sensitive banking information. He persisted. I had to refer it up to Semper in the end.'

'Semper! Oh, shit, Jim. This could bring my career to an abrupt halt.'

'Yeah. It's like . . .' Jim swallows. 'Well, it's like you're some kind of a suspect.' He adds hastily, 'I'm sure you're not. But it sort of looks that way when the police start checking on your movements.'

'Will Semper give them the tapes?'

'Not without telling you first. But if you have a lawyer who—'

'Jim, I don't need a lawyer, I haven't done anything wrong. There's nothing in the tape the police shouldn't hear. It's just kind of a . . . an intrusion. A violation. That's all.'

'Yeah. This is awful, Lucy.' He swallows again. 'But at least you don't have to worry about Gregory Hifeld. Just leave him to me. You forget about us and spend this sad time with your family.'

I try to call Jay Kent again but his secretary has obviously now been instructed to intercept me. Humiliated, I wrap myself in the small print of Daddy's life, his files, his letters, his financial statements. Occasionally there is the flutter of drapes in the living room, otherwise nothing breaks the house's thin membrane of silence.

I slide open the desk drawer and guiltily, as though it's a slab of chocolate, withdraw the newspaper cutting. *Wedding News*. The groom is a doctor. The bridesmaids wore yellow.

After the car crash I was sent home swiftly from hospital. I spent the long summer months waiting for Robert to call or write. He didn't. I hoped maybe his mother would contact me. But she didn't either. I could only find one explanation. Robert and his family must blame me for the crash. He was after all stretching one arm across to me when it should have been on the steering wheel. Had I encouraged or, worse, demanded this near-fatal attention? His silence seemed to suggest that I had and in my heart I have always believed the accident to be at least partly and probably wholly my fault. At the end of the long summer, we both went our different ways to different colleges. When, later, someone told me that Robert kept his leg but had a terrible limp and wouldn't play sports again, I felt more remorse than compassion.

Immersed in these thoughts, I become aware that I am not alone.

I know someone is here not because they make any noise but by a sensation of movement. The movement is at the door of the den and I don't see it, I feel it. The hairs on the back of my neck stand up and I leap to my feet. The doorway is empty and the door still, but I perceive that someone stood there, or at least passed by, just a few seconds ago.

I get to the deck fast. My nerve ends are sizzling as I lean over the railings. The sun glares. Leaves shift uncomfortably in the breeze. Otherwise, the hillside is motionless. The valley bakes like a hard, brown loaf. I wait, holding my breath. Then I go back inside the house and search every room downstairs and, although the door was locked, I go out to the porch. The barn, the car, the drive. Nothing moves.

Back to the deck and this time, far to one side, amid the dappled shade of the trees beyond the house, I see motion. Probably a man, running. He must have crouched under the deck with the old lumber and machines, right under my feet, until I went back inside the house. Then he escaped. The shadow is at the edge of my vision. I fix my eyes on the spot, but he is gone. I am staring at an empty landscape.

I jump down from the deck and retrace the intruder's route. There are some large footsteps in the earth that could be his, or they might belong to the police or to Larry. I skirt round the house and walk over to the dirt road. There's a gap in the foliage where he must have escaped.

I turn back to the house. I stop at the sunken garden, looking, listening. My heart fills my ears with its thumping. The garden is sheltered by trees and half-blanketed by ivy. Nothing has been disturbed here for a while. And then, I miss a breath. Peeping between the shrubs is something alien. The angles are wrong. It shouldn't be there.

I brush aside the foliage and cautiously descend the stone steps. Propped against one wall, I find a gravestone. At first I take it for some very late, overblown monument to Mother's dog, who was buried around here. But when I have stared at the words long enough I read, REMEMBER ME. REMEMBER DEATH. ERIC SCHAFFER.

The headstone is grey, and rougher than the stone I saw at Joe Zacarro's and, although the words are similar, their style is less ornate.

There is a gap at the bottom for dates. It sits, with an absurd suggestion of jauntiness, askew on the uneven rocks that line the sunken garden.

I walk back to the steps. Daddy built this garden from round, sea-washed rocks. Beneath it is buried Nickel Dog, a brown mutt adored by Mother. The sunken garden should have been a good place to do your homework, but it never was because the sun, trapped like a bear here, was doubly aggressive. I don't remember ever sitting on the stone seats.

The old swimsuit Scott returned to me is in the car. I pick it up and am locking up the house, sliding shut the doors to the deck, when some instinct pulls me outside again to stare over the valley. The place where Robert Joseph's car turned over. The long, grey, straight road that leads to the intersection and along which, tiny, silently, a toy tow truck is now travelling. It points right to the heart of the valley and then, with the flash of bouncing sun, it turns north. I watch it until it is out of sight. Then I leave the house for Joe Zacarro's.

Joe is out. There is no reply to my ring at the bell or my yell and the car with the padlocked trunk is missing. The pool is empty except for the plastic armchair, moored by the steps. I walk right over to his headstone. REMEMBER DEATH. JOE ZACARRO ALWAYS DID. Different script but probably chiselled by the same craftsman.

I change into my swimsuit and climb into the pool. I swim rapidly, up and down, up and down, the water streaming each side of my face. My mind lulled by the rhythm of my swimming, I continue, I have no idea how long, until, abruptly, I stop, mid-pool. I climb out and wrap the towel round me. I have washed away hours and perhaps days.

'You sure needed that,' says a voice. Under an umbrella, in a swimsuit, sits Mr Zacarro. He pushes an iced coffee towards me. 'It took a while to make this; I didn't think you'd still be swimming by the time I finished.'

I sip the coffee and enjoy its sweetness. Joe rests his short leg up on a chair. I tell him about the intruder at Daddy's house.

He listens and thinks and finally says, 'You came right over here. You did good. You're safe at Joe's, you remember that.'

'But the intruder may still be around.'

Joe frowns. 'He ran away,' he reminds me. 'If he'd wanted to hurt you he could've done it when you were alone in the house.'

I nod. I'm pretty sure the intruder has already left in his tow truck.

'OK,' says Joe seriously, 'let's get this straight. He used a key. Twice. Until you got the locks changed.'

'Last night the police hid a couple of officers in the garden in case he came back to try again. But he didn't.' Jane had called me earlier in the day with this news. She had sounded disappointed.

'So either he knew or guessed you'd changed the locks, or he'd found what he wanted. Except, today he walked right in from the deck, saw you and ran right out again.'

'I guess he ran when he saw me. I don't know why else he would run.'

'So he's not planning on introducing himself.'

'I think he wants something. Something in the den.'

'Well, what's in there?'

'Just Daddy's papers.'

Joe gets up and walks distractedly into the pool. There's a huge crash and water explodes everywhere. He swims a couple of strokes under water with a natural, easy grace and then turns over onto his back.

'Gotta get in the water if I want to think,' he explains as swimming pool cascades down his face. He tilts back his head and, a lot further down the pool, his toes appear. He floats. He closes his eyes.

'I also have a theory . . .' I begin hesitantly. 'I think he drives a tow truck.'

Joe opens both eyes. 'This guy who keeps coming to the house? You seen him drive a tow truck?'

'No. But on the two occasions when I sensed he was around, I looked down into the valley, ten, maybe fifteen minutes later, and I saw a tow truck driving east. Then it turned north at the intersection.'

Joe closes his eyes again. 'If you only saw it twice then it's probably a coincidence,' he says.

'Did Daddy know anyone with a tow truck?'

The water is almost calm now. The waves Joe created have just enough movement to turn his body through a few degrees.

'I'll have to think about that,' he says at last. 'I mean, if you drive a goddamn heap of garbage like Eric did, you're going to need a number to call when it breaks down on the freeway . . .'

'I've already looked in his address book but there's nothing obvious.'

'Hmm,' he says. 'I gotta think.'

'There's something else I wanted to ask you.'

'Uh-huh.'

'I found Daddy's headstone.'

He sits up in the water, creating small waves all over the pool. 'You did? Down in that pit in your garden?'

'The sunken garden.'

'Fancy garbage name.' He pulls himself up and, as he scrambles into the floating armchair, curtains of water run down his skin.

'So you knew the headstone was there?' I ask.

'Sure. Didn't Eric mention it in his will?'

'I don't think he mentioned it anywhere.'

'Well, you probably noticed it's sort of like mine. Adam Holler's too. That's because we all got our stones from the same place.'

'Were they on special offer? Three for the price of two or something?'

Disconcertingly, Mr Zacarro flings back his head and roars with laughter. The armchair bobs around in the water.

'Economics didn't come into it, Lucy. We wanted our headstones that way so we figured we should get them carved ourselves to make sure.'

'Remember death? Isn't that kind of strange?'

'Not so. People have been saying that for centuries. I mean, it's a modern, industrialised nation sort of thing to ignore death and think it's never going to happen to you. But if you remember that you're going to die some day then you live your life in a different sort of a way. Not necessarily better, but probably better. Different, that's for sure. We believe that. We all agreed on it, me and Eric and Adam.'

'I don't recall Daddy ever talking about his own death.'

'Didn't mean he wasn't aware of it.'

I swallow. 'Was he scared to die?' I ask.

Mr Zacarro sighs and I see the sigh slip along his whole body. 'Oh sure, he was scared as any of us. We don't know how death's going to come or how much it's going to hurt and that's frightening. The only thing we know for sure is that it will come.' His voice has thickened.

I look at him quickly. 'Are you OK, Joe?'

'I got interviewed this morning,' he tells me. 'Nice gal from the police department. Wanted to know if Eric had an enemy or a reason to be scared of someone. In other words, do I know who killed him?'

'What did you say?'

His face is big and sad. 'The very dumbfool idea made me laugh.'

'What else did she ask you?'

'Well . . .' His jaw lengthens suddenly, his mouth turns down and he rubs an eye as if an eyelash, at this very moment, fell right into it. 'It was the damnedest thing,' he says. I wait for him and finally he turns back to me and I see that both eyes are red and there was no eyelash. In a voice creased and used as an old rag he says, 'She asked about Lindy.'

'Lindy!' I echo. And for a moment I feel angry with the detective, smiling her cold-eyed smiles, stabbing at people's pasts with her pen.

Sobs shake Joe Zacarro's big, brown body. His face is soon wet with tears. He scoops up some pool water then pulls it across his cheeks.

I reach out for his arm and he immediately puts a hand over mine, both trapping and protecting it.

'She asked me how Lindy died. Everything I could remember about that day. As if I ever could have forgotten one goddamn second of it.' He looks up at me. His chest heaves and he presses my hand tighter against him. 'Do you remember? Do you remember when my Lindy died?'

It was summer vacation and all the neighbourhood kids were playing hide-and-seek. There had been some kind of argument, a trivial, child-ish difference probably, and my friendship with Lindy had cooled. But we still sometimes joined in with the other kids on the hillside during vacations. When it was Lindy's turn to hide no one could find her. We looked and called and finally it felt late and we just drifted off home in our different directions. Mrs Zacarro hadn't been too worried at first, but when Davis and Carter got hungry and there was still no Lindy, Mrs Zacarro knew something wasn't right. She took the car and drove round the neighbourhood, looking, calling Lindy's name. She came to our house, but Mother, who had been ill, was resting and Daddy was out. We could see that Mrs Zacarro was angry with Lindy but now her face was starting to hollow with worry. She didn't know that the whole time Lindy was right there in the trunk of the car and had scratched off her fingernails trying to get out. The police said that the temperature in the trunk was so high she would have died within a half-hour.

'I don't understand,' says Joe. 'Why was this woman asking about my little girl after all these years?'

I pause. 'I've been thinking about Lindy a lot since I came back here.'

His face breaks into an indulgent smile. 'Yeah, you two were big pals. She would have grown into a lovely young woman. Like you, Lucy, just beautiful like you.'

When I'm back in Daddy's garden I go right to the sunken garden and stare at the headstone. REMEMBER ME. Didn't Daddy know that he occu-pied a place in the lives of those around him as solid as this big slab of rock? Didn't he know that we'd always remember him?

I hear a car. The air has the calm maturity of late afternoon now. The day has lost its heat, like a fever that has passed.

'Hi, Lucy,' says a familiar voice. I don't turn round. I'm annoyed, maybe because, without thinking about it, I've been waiting for him. He said I had given him a day's work. Now, at the end of the day, here he is.

'Hi, Mr Rougemont.'

He sounds friendly. 'I sure wish you'd call me Michael.'

I shrug. I hear him scrambling into the sunken garden, his big feet slipping a little on the steps. I remember how he appeared on the night of Daddy's death as a shadow, talking to Kirsty outside the kitchen. Even in the flesh he is the shadow of a man, impossibly thin and taller than I remember. His long head is turned to Daddy's headstone.

'Looks recent,' he says. 'How long have you known about it?'

'Not long. A neighbour and friend of Daddy's, Joe Zacarro, has one too. So does another neighbour.'

'Well, isn't that interesting?'

I shrug. 'It's nice in an odd sort of way. I like feisty old men.'

Rougemont smiles. 'What is this place anyway?' he asks, sitting down on one of the cracked slabs of stone that Daddy set in the wall as seats.

'The sunken garden. Daddy built it as a nice, private place to sit. And Mother's dog is buried here. He was called Nickel Dog because Daddy bought him for a nickel from some guy who didn't want him.'

'Did you like him a lot?'

'I was very small . . .' I close my eyes and for a moment sense something brown and yappy brushing past me. The sensation of wrapping my arms round a warm, yielding creature, which could have been my toy Hodges or Nickel Dog. 'Jane told me he used to jump on me and scare me but I'm not sure if I remember that. I'm not sure if I remember him at all. It could be that I just remember Jane talking about him.'

'Oh yes,' agrees the detective, 'oh yes, it's easy to confuse what actually happened with things you've been told and things you've dreamed. It's good that you recognise how unreliable memory is. But the sort of thing you could remember is Nickel Dog dying. I mean, feeling upset. Your mother's unhappiness. Someone, I guess your father, burying him.'

I try to remember the demise of Nickel Dog, Mother weeping, Daddy looking grim with a spade, Jane white-faced, but the dog's death is as elusive as his life.

Rougemont asks, 'Did you ever sit here when you were a kid?'

'Occasionally. But if I wanted to escape it was to the porch at the front of the house.' As soon as the words are out of my mouth I want to reach out and grab them back.

He quivers a little. 'What were you escaping from, Lucy? Or should I ask, who?' He stretches out his legs as he waits for my reply.

'You're probably wondering what I found out today,' he says at last. 'About your weekend.'

I am silent. I fix my eyes on Daddy's headstone.

'It would sure make my life easier if you'd talk to me, Lucy.'

When I maintain my silence he says, 'I don't just mean I want you to talk about the weekend, although I sure wish you'd clear that one up. No, I'd like to hear about the stuff you don't normally tell people because they're not interested. A lot of people just do not have any interest in anyone but themselves. Let's take, for example, Mr Jay Kent.'

I don't let myself react. Not stiffen or move any part of my body.

'Now, Mr Jay Kent is clearly one helluva businessman. But, no matter how intimate he gets with someone, I'm prepared to bet that he shows no interest in their past. Asks nothing about their childhood, reveals little about his own unless asked. But I'm different from Jay Kent, Lucy. I like to know about people and I'd especially like to know about you.'

I remain silent but a heat from within is spreading up my body and soon it will reach my face and he will see it.

'I spoke with Mr Jay Kent on the phone not long ago,' he continues.

Evening in New York. Did Rougemont contact Kent at the office or at home where Kent was with his wife and baby? I catch my breath.

'He wasn't entirely surprised to hear from me although I wouldn't say he welcomed my call. However, he wanted to be helpful. I'd even say he was anxious to help. Answered my questions without the smallest hesitation. See, Lucy, I've asked a lot of people a lot of questions and I've noticed that often they hesitate. Maybe they hesitate because they're formulating a lie but, in my experience, more often it's because they want to check it's OK for them to tell the truth, to establish what the consequences might be, for themselves or others, of revealing that truth. Jay Kent had no such concern, Lucy. He just knew that if he answered my questions, he'd get me out of his life fast. So he didn't hesitate, not once.'

Rougemont looks at me closely, so closely that I turn away. 'You're not in love with him, Lucy. Reassure me that you're not in love with him.'

I find myself giving the smallest of half-shrugs.

Rougemont takes this to indicate my indifference to Jay Kent. He sits back, nodding. 'That's good. I believe you already knew how little he cares for you. He's an acquisitive guy, in my opinion. You met him because you have a company that's looking for a buyer. But you aren't for sale, Lucy. You're not the kind of woman a Jay Kent sort of a guy can acquire.'

I look straight into his grey eyes. I say, 'Mr Rougemont, for someone who's supposed to ask questions, you sure answer a lot.'

He guffaws. 'OK, Lucy, I'll start asking. I'll ask you about last Sunday. Jay Kent was looking around stores with some *Untermensch* from his empire. What did you do?'

When I am silent he delves into the large black bag he was wearing on his shoulder until he sat down. When his hand re-emerges, it holds a shoe. He waves it at me. 'Wait, wait, just a minute. I can improve on that.' He delves a little more. 'Yes . . . yes . . .' He produces another, its twin, although this second shoe has no heel.

'So, here's my question. Do you recognise the exhibit?'

I am still standing by Daddy's headstone. I reach out for its coolness. I look at the shoes. They are women's shoes in soft black leather. Expensive, medium heel, ruined by contact with the wrong sort of ground. Red-brown earth has insinuated itself into the leather inside and out.

'Hmm . . .' says Rougemont, examining them. 'They're kind of dirty. But do you think they might just fit you?'

I shrug.

'Would you try one? Just to see if it fits?' When I remain silent he answers for me, 'Sure you will.'

He gets up and, when he's standing right by me, drops to a crouch. The headstone beneath my fingers supports my weight as he lifts my right leg a little. With great gentleness he pulls off the shoe I'm wearing and inserts my foot into the shoe in his hand.

'Aha,' he says. 'I'd call that a fit! Wouldn't you call that a fit, Lucy?'

I yield to his pantomime without participating in it.

'And this shoe I took off . . .' He holds it up to eye level, twisting it to right and left. 'The heel is worn a little more on the right side than the left. That's because your weight isn't distributed evenly when you walk, sometimes we favour one side of the foot, often we favour one leg.'

Click clack, click clack.

'For example, this shoe I just tried . . .' He wedges it off me in one deft movement and replaces it with my own shoe. 'Yes, this other one is also worn in the same place but perhaps a little more, not much. So the owner of this shoe also favours the outside of her foot. What a coincidence! Unless . . .' He looks up into my face and rolls his eyes comically. 'Unless of course . . . these shoes all belong to you.'

He stands up so he's towering over me. I grip the headstone hard.

'Shame about this one,' he sighs, holding up the heel-less shoe. He sits down. His voice cuts through the early-evening air with a new crispness. 'You're a snail, Lucy. You aren't too experienced at covering up your trail. Late Sunday morning you hired a car, drove out of the city and came up here to see your father. You left the car somewhere it wouldn't be seen. You didn't want anyone to know you were here. I don't know what you did but your shoes sure had a tough time. Walking over some pretty rough ground. Walking through earth. Maybe even running. When you got back to town they were ruined and you needed new shoes. You bought a pair at the department store a block away from your hotel. It was a Sunday, the store wasn't busy, the assistant remembers you. You put the old shoes in the box she gave you and threw them away in the hotel. The room maid took them home, intending to clean them up, get a new heel put on, have herself a nice pair of designer shoes. Luckily, she didn't do any of that yet.'

He lowers his voice now, because he knows how hard I'm listening.

'I could hand them over to Forensic and ask them whether the earth comes from this immediate area. But I won't need to do that, Lucy, if you tell me what happened here last Sunday. I need to know what time you were here. I think it was early afternoon. Am I right?'

When I am silent he sighs theatrically. 'I'm a generous guy, Lucy, and I'm going to give you a few days because tomorrow I'm leaving town for a short while. And when I get back I'm going to ask you to tell me what you were doing here at your father's house right before he died.' He gets up and puts the shoes carefully in his bag. 'I'll see you when I get back.'

I don't move until I have heard the hum of his car on the drive. I sit down on the cracked slab of the seat warmed by Rougemont and I remember Nickel Dog's death. I remember Mother's sadness distilled into a high-pitched and unnatural wail, Jane's pallor, Daddy holding with both hands the stiff bundle that was Nickel Dog wrapped in a blanket. And then I was running, past the old tow truck, round the bushes, in and out of trees. I ran until I reached a den we had made in the far corner of the garden under an overhanging bush. An old rug, some soft toys, and there, in the den, a friend waiting for me. Lindy.

Seymour pours pale brown liquid from a teapot into china cups. 'This is Lemon Rose Pouchong,' he explains. 'The tea club selection for March. The woman from the police department liked it.'

Seymour is a small, bald, wiry man who played baseball back in the days when he had a full head of hair. Once he played against Joe DiMaggio. It's a tale he has dined out on ever since. Daddy said he'd heard it at least fifty times and it was a little bit different each time and Seymour said, 'Well, I wouldn't want to bore you, Eric.'

The tea is too hot to drink. I inhale its flowery aroma. 'Did you tell the detective about the discrepancy in the oil well payments?' I ask.

'Well, no, I didn't. But I think that maybe someone should.'

'Why?'

'First, let me explain what I found out. Simms-Roeder is still producing. Eric tied the company up in a watertight royalty agreement and, believe me, if they could get out of it, they would. You're right that the money didn't go directly to Eric. It gets paid into another account.'

'Where is that account? Do you have any details on it?'

'Only the name.'

Seymour gets up and goes to the bureau. He pulls a piece of paper from beneath a carved African figure. He reads, 'The Marcello Trust.'

I stare at him. 'The what Trust?'

'Marcello.' He hands me the paper then sits back down.

'What is it?' I ask.

He shrugs. 'I hoped you'd know. Because I surely don't. Have you spoken to Eric's accountant?'

'Sure. He knows nothing about the oil well revenues. I'll ask him about the Marcello Trust, though. And I'll look in Daddy's address book. I'll look in the phone book . . .' I pause. I'm thinking.

'Have you heard the name before? Is it sounding familiar now?'

I shrug. 'I think I heard it recently. But everything sounds familiar if you think about it long enough.'

'Recently?' Seymour is surprised. 'Not from way back?'

'No, recently . . .' I drink some tea. I grope through my memory looking for the name, a first name or a surname, of Marcello.

Seymour looks at me. 'It's probably all straightforward and you'll find some obvious explanation, but there's one other possibility. You won't like it, Lucy. But maybe you should discuss it with that detective.'

I wait. The china cup in my hand feels absurdly fragile, as though I could crush it between my fingers.

Seymour says, 'Have you thought about blackmail?'

'Oh c'mon,' I say briskly. 'People can only be blackmailed if they have something terrible to hide.'

'Maybe he had,' says Seymour evenly. 'We all did things when we were a lot younger that we wouldn't be proud to own up to now. It's your father's high standards of morality that would make him a good target for blackmailers. If there was anything in his past he was ashamed of.'

I say, 'There wouldn't be.'

'The police need to get to the bottom of this. You should tell them about the Marcello Trust.'

I reply without looking at him. 'If Daddy had a secret, I'd keep it. I wouldn't have the police, or anyone else, investigate it.' I get up, saying that I'm going home to call all the Marcellos in the phone book.

'Sit down,' says Seymour, 'and I'll take turns with you.'

In the phone book we find eight Marcellos scattered around the Bay area. We make the calls. All the Marcellos who answer say they know nothing about a trust in their name and have never heard of Eric Schaffer.

'So,' asks Seymour, 'now what are you going to do about this?'

'Later I'll call all the Marcellos who were out. Tomorrow I'll search the den, ask the bank, phone the accountant. I have to sort this out.'

When I leave Seymour's I drive to the cemetery where Stevie is buried. I am surprised by the human traffic here at the end of the day.

Small groups, women walking alone, an elderly couple hand in hand.

As I approach Stevie's grave, I see a figure standing motionless in the dusky light. 'Scott?'

He swings round. When he sees me his face lightens. 'Luce!'

'I meant to come with you but we didn't get round to arranging it . . .'

'I thought the flowers we left on Saturday must be looking pretty dry by now,' he says. 'I just stopped by to tidy up a bit.'

'How often do you come?'

'Once a week, sometimes more.'

We stand before the grave in silence and I look around. Most of the small headstones in the children's cemetery are carved joylessly with nursery images. A teddy bear, a puppy, the man in the moon. Stevie's little headstone reveals only his name and dates.

Scott has been waiting for me to comment. Now he prompts me. 'Luce? Do you like it?'

'Yes,' I say. 'I'm glad you kept it simple.'

I stare at the grave. I know Scott wants me to cry. I try to cry. I am unmoved. This unyielding monument to Stevie's existence has nothing to do with the kicking, squirming baby I remember.

Scott says, 'Are you starting to get over Stevie? I am. It's not that I forget him or it doesn't hurt any more, but for a long time the grief was sort of physical, like something heavy on my back, and that's lifted now.'

I squeeze his arm. 'I'm not sure if I've laughed since Stevie died.'

'You mean, since he was born.'

I turn to look at him and he squares his shoulders defensively.

'It's a stage in the grieving process, Lucy. The stage when you become completely honest about the decedent. I've reached it. I admit that I loved him a lot but I didn't enjoy Stevie. Not at all. Right from the beginning it was a shock for both of us. Nothing prepared us for the sacrifices and losses of having a child. That's when I lost you. When he was born.'

When I'm driving home I admit to myself that Stevie's six months was six months of madness. Nothing happened when it was supposed to. I forgot things. I lost things. I arrived late. I arrived on the wrong day. And all the time Stevie voiced his objections. I rocked him and it made no difference. I sang to him and it made no difference. Eventually I'd stand there while he just filled me up with his noise as though I was an empty beaker. And after he died, I slept for twenty-four hours.

It is late when I finally drive across the bridge and back into the city towards my Russian family.

Aunt Zina has already gone to bed, but in the kitchen I find a light on.

'Lucia!' Sasha is raiding the cookie jar. 'I just got home and thought you must already be asleep. What have you been doing today?'

I sink down into a chair near him. Suddenly my legs are weak with fatigue. 'Mostly Daddy's paperwork. I also found his headstone.'

'Good gracious, wherever was it?'

'In the garden. It says "Remember Death". His two pals have similar stones. They think you live your life differently if you remember that you could die any minute.'

'The Remember Death Club. I love it. Perhaps your father's death leaves a vacancy and they will allow me to join. Wait here, please.' He disappears from the room and returns with whisky and two glasses.

'Oh no, Sash, it's too late for that and I'm tired.'

'The best talks are tired talks.' He pulls the stopper from the bottle. 'And is adding columns of figures so very exhausting for a banker?'

'Adding isn't. Thinking is.'

He fills one glass with ice and pours whisky over it. Then he pushes the glass towards me and lifts his own. 'A toast to Lucia, beloved cousin.' He touches my glass with his. 'And what have you been think-ing about so hard, Lucia?'

'I think I know who killed Daddy.'

He rubs his hands and sits down across the table from me. I sip the whisky and feel its heat run through my body, even to my toes.

'Have you shared this information with anyone else? That charming detective who was supervising on Monday night, for example?'

'I can't tell her. I can't tell anyone.'

'Except for your adoring cousin. How flattering.'

'Sasha, I've lied to everyone. The police, Jane, Scott, even you.'

He raises his eyebrows. 'Sasha will keep your secrets, Lucia.'

'I've told everyone I haven't been to California for three years. But I have. I was here last weekend. Here in San Francisco.'

I didn't enjoy it. I didn't enjoy any of the weekend. Kent was so on edge he didn't even sit next to me on the flight. And from the moment the plane landed I was anxious that some relative or old schoolfriend might see me. Later, he looked my naked body up and down without warmth and with no indication of admiration and then he pulled me onto the bed. Sex with him was single-minded, pursued by both of us with an energy and determination that excluded love and even lust. Afterwards we lay still, our bodies touching without connecting. A deep loneliness fell across me. I looked at Kent and wondered if he felt it too.

Whenever the phone rang, he answered it and I leapt up and into the bathroom and turned on the shower because it might have been Mrs

Kent calling. Mrs Kent with the baby cooing in the background. When the call was over he would switch off the shower and say, 'You can come out now.' He wrapped me in one of the big, soft hotel towels and I took this manoeuvre for affection. Only now, sitting in Aunt Zina's apartment, do I recognise that here I am loved. I am loved by Aunt Zina and Aunt Zoya and Sasha and Jane and Larry and Scott. I am wrapped up in their love like a bug in a curling leaf and I know I never should have chosen to mistake hotel laundry for affection.

Sasha raises his eyebrows. 'Why did you do this thing with this man? Do you care for him?'

'No. I couldn't come back here with him on the third anniversary of my baby's death if I did. And it's an unprofessional relationship. We're negotiating a deal and my clients' interests, not my sexual needs, are supposed to come first. And Mittex fosters a clean family image. That's why I told the police I was home all weekend. But it wasn't the only reason.'

Late on Sunday morning Kent left to spend the day with a regional manager. As soon as he had gone I hired a car and drove to the cemetery. When I reached Stevie's little grave, I sobbed at the stone's simplicity, its smooth perfection. Small bouquets were arranged lovingly around it. I sobbed as I placed one pink rose at the base of the stone. I sobbed as I walked back to the parking lot. I sobbed as I drove to Daddy's house.

I could have called him. I wish now I had called him and visited in the normal way, except nothing was normal that day. Daddy would have asked about Kent, expected to meet him, begged me to stay. He might have called Jane and Larry and Scott and invited them over. After three years my return would have been an event.

'Your reluctance to see Uncle Eric is understandable, Lucia. Please stop trying to justify it.'

'But, Sash, I had to see him. Whenever I spoke to him or to Jane I felt there was something they weren't telling me. Or maybe, I knew I hadn't listened to them. Occasionally they'd mention his hip. Or Jane would say casually that he was getting forgetful. Or I'd think his voice was rasping or notice that his handwriting was sort of shaky. And then I wouldn't think about it any more because it was too painful. So when I drove out to the house on Sunday, I just wanted to look at him. I just wanted to reassure myself that he was still OK.'

'You planned to see him without him seeing you?'

'Does it sound crazy?'

'No.'

'I parked my car way down in the valley in case any neighbours were about and I walked up an old trail we used when we were kids, up through the Holler orchard. It was damp and dirty and overgrown and by the time I decided to give up I was almost there so I carried right on. I sneaked round to the back of the house and flipped through the rails onto the deck just the way I used to when I was a kid.'

'Lucia, Lucia, you are so smart. What seemed the whim of a bereaved daughter on Monday night—to stare across the valley from her father's deck—was an act calculated to mislead the police fingerprint expert.'

I blush.

'Daddy was in the living room. But he wasn't alone. There was someone with him and the other guy's voice was raised and he was standing right over Daddy in a threatening way.'

'Who was he?'

'I don't know. He was tall, a little younger than me, jeans, dark hair. I didn't get much chance to look at him because this guy saw me within a few seconds. He came right after me without a moment's hesitation. I jumped down from the deck and ran round the barn. I could hear him looking for me, shouting. It was terrifying. I thought my heart was going to burst. I ran the heel off my shoe. He went round the other way and I slipped along the bushes by the drive and down by the Holler orchard while he was still running round the sunken garden, yelling as though he wanted to kill me. It wasn't until I got back to the car that I realised I wasn't a criminal and didn't have to behave like one. I mean, it's my father's house for heaven's sake. But I felt like a hunted animal.'

'And, your papa?'

Daddy, a moving figure half glimpsed through the sliding doors.

'I hardly saw him. Mostly he looked shocked.'

'Perhaps by the intrusion?'

'Or by this guy, yelling at him, standing right over him. Oh, Sash, if I'd called him and visited in the usual way, I would have seen him before he died. I might have saved his life.'

Sasha reaches out and covers my hand with his. 'If your supposition is correct that this young man's anger threatened Uncle Eric's life. Is there no way of identifying him?'

'When I was running away I saw something out of the corner of my eye parked outside the barn. I'm almost certain it was a tow truck, an old, chrome one. It must have been his. That didn't give me much to go on, until the woman detective arrived talking about a tow truck . . .'

I tell him about Officer Howie and how I discovered the old tow truck at Big Brim. How its driver, a man, tall, dark-haired, knew himself to be followed, and escaped. 'I think he ran away twice today. The second time was at the house. He sneaked in, saw me there and took off.

A little later, I saw a tow truck driving away through the valley.'

Sasha strokes his chin. 'Did you take the number of the tow truck?'

'I wrote it on the back of the map the hire-car company supplies. But that guy, the tow truck driver, he stole it.'

'Well, if you had the number of this truck then I would suggest you handed it over at once to the police for tracing. But since you do not . . .'

'I couldn't hand it over without telling them about last weekend. Except now, one of them has found out.'

I tell Sasha about Rougemont. How he confronted me with my shoes.

'You lied to them not just to protect Kent but to protect your family from the knowledge that you visited San Francisco without seeing them. Your untruth looks suspicious but, apart from allowing yourself to be seduced by an unfeeling brute, you have done nothing wrong.'

I look at him and he seems to be dancing. I realise that Sasha is still, but my eyes are losing and regaining focus.

'Sasha, when someone dies, should you keep their secrets?'

'Most certainly every attempt should be made to maintain privacy. But this is seldom possible. Do you suspect that your papa had secrets?'

'The tow truck driver was sort of a secret. Daddy knew him but he didn't tell me about him. He didn't tell Jane.'

'You think he had some significance in Uncle Eric's life?'

'I don't know. But if I set the police onto him, Daddy's secrets could come spilling right out.'

Sasha sips his whisky and rolls it over his teeth with pleasure before swallowing it. 'So, you prefer to clarify the situation yourself. Well, Lucia, proceed if you must. But I advise you to proceed with caution.'

Six

JANE CALLS ME EARLY on Saturday to say that the police want to see us at Daddy's house. 'Kirsty wants to see all of us, Scott too. She's asked to meet us at ten. Apparently Rougement's away so he won't be there.'

When I arrive at Daddy's house, Scott's car and Larry's are already there, side by side. Scott is pleased to see me. He has already thumbed through the letters I left on Daddy's desk for him to sign.

Jane puts an arm round me and kisses me lightly on the cheek. 'Sorry I couldn't get here yesterday. I hope everything was OK.'

If I tell her that there might have been an intruder who might have driven a tow truck then she'll ask questions and make calls and lift the whole situation right out of my hands. I say, 'Everything was fine.'

'What's cooking?' I ask Larry, sniffing the warm, spicy air.

'Paella,' he says modestly. 'This recipe is supposed to take twenty-four hours and I'm doing it in three so don't expect too much.'

'What's this?' asks Scott, picking up a yellowing newspaper cutting from the desk.

I try to pull it away from him. 'Nothing really, I found it in Daddy's drawer . . .'

But Scott has opened it out and is already reading: *Wedding News.* Marriage of Dr R. D. Joseph and Miss K. K. Sylvester.

Jane shoots me a rapid, penetrating look. 'Did you know?' she asks.

I shrug. 'No, but why should I care? I haven't spoken to him for years.'

By now Scott has recognised the groom's name. I see his jaw clench.

'We thought it was better not to tell you,' Jane says.

While I'm still deciding whether my reply should be aggressive or defensive, Larry asks, 'Who is he?'

'Robert Joseph, Lucy's teenage heart-throb,' Jane explains.

'The one she always wished she'd married,' adds Scott bitterly.

I made the mistake once of telling him how much Robert had meant to me. It was soon after I met Scott, when we knew we were embarking on an important relationship and thought we should tell each other about all the other important relationships.

'I wish I could take up the space Robert Joseph takes up in your heart,' Scott said then. 'But I never will.'

'That's ridiculous!' I told him.

He made the same observation several more times, even after we married, and, although I always denied it, a small part of me agreed with him and Scott somehow knew that.

He has turned away from me now and is heading out of the den saying something about coffee. I want to ask Jane how old the newspaper cutting is, but I cannot now betray an interest.

Larry has been watching us all keenly, stroking his beard. He seems about to comment when there is a voice at the door. Kirsty is here.

We lead her to the kitchen and she pauses for a moment.

'Wow, something smells good,' she says.

Larry is apologetic. 'It won't be ready until lunchtime. But if you're still here, then please join us.'

'I sure wish I could,' she says.

She is about to tell us why she's here when Larry says, 'Kirsty, there's something I'm still worried about . . .'

Kirsty looks at him evenly, without any sense of anticipation.

Jane groans. 'Larry, you're wasting Kirsty's time.'

'No,' insists Larry, 'I think this is important. The guy I told you about. He was there again last night. I think he's hanging around outside our apartment. He could be following Jane.'

'What makes you think that?' asks Kirsty.

'Last night she drove over to the caterers' to check that everything's OK for Tuesday. The guy disappeared when Jane left. Then, when Jane came back, he came back.'

'How late did he stay? All night?'

'Well, I'm not sure what time he actually went. But of course he was gone in the morning.'

Kirsty pulls out her notebook and asks Larry to describe the man. Tall, dark-haired, generally unshaven, maybe twenty-five or thirty.

'OK,' agrees Kirsty. 'We'll take a look.' She reaches into her bag and pulls out a small plastic sack.

'You've found Daddy's keys!' Jane exclaims.

The woman nods. She pulls them out of the sack and lays them on the table. 'Take them. Tell me if you think they're all here.'

Jane spreads the keys out evenly on the table round the ring. 'I don't recognise them all,' she says, 'but this is the door, car, barn, our apartment . . . Did he have a key to your house, Scott?'

'Uh-huh, since I went to France last Christmas. It's right here . . .' Scott points at the key to the beach house. I didn't know he'd been to France. I guess he went with Brigitte.

Jane continues, 'Not sure about that one. Or that one, but that one must be the tractor. Well, as far as I know, nothing's missing.'

'Where did you find them?' Scott asks the detective.

'With the kids who took the Oldsmobile from the Big Brim parking lot on Monday morning.'

'Kids stole Eric's car?'

'Nice kids who live in Lowis and never stole a car before. One of them had a little brother who told. It wasn't too hard to extract the keys. They couldn't give us the note, though. They hadn't kept that.'

We look at her, waiting.

'Note?' says Jane at last. 'What note hadn't they kept?'

'I can show you. We actually have our own copy.'

She reaches into her notebook and pulls out a sheet of paper with a few lines printed on it. She reads, '"To my daughters . . ."' I hear her voice as though I'm under anaesthetic and can feel no pain. '"To my daughters. I'd like you to remember me as a strong man, not old and helpless. So I've chosen to leave you now and I hope you'll see that this is an act of great love. Jane, Lucy, I love you both very much. If I've done my job properly you should be fine without me. Lucy, when you feel very alone, I know Jane will be there for you. With much love, Daddy."'

I look around at the shocked, pale faces. I guess I must be shocked and pale too. Jane's fingers play some silent tune on the table top. Larry holds his beard tightly in one hand. Scott is motionless.

'We should have known about this letter before,' says Larry at last.

'The copy in the stolen car was lost and we've only just accessed it on the professor's computer.' Kirsty looks from face to face. 'So, what's your reaction to this letter? Does it sound like the Professor Schaffer you knew?'

'Well . . . I guess so . . .' says Jane.

Larry nods gravely. Scott is silent.

I take the paper from her and study it. 'No,' I say.

The detective turns to me. 'You don't think he wrote it?'

'No.'

'What makes you so sure?' Kirsty watches me keenly.

He would have written us separate letters. I would have received a note with my name on it which was only for me, signed, *Daddy*.

'Is it the words? The way he uses them?'

I study the letter. 'He didn't write it,' I say stubbornly. 'This isn't how he would have done it.'

She turns to Scott. 'What's your reaction?' she asks.

'Lucy hadn't seen Eric in a long time,' he says. 'Maybe the Eric she left behind wouldn't have written this but the Eric he became . . . well, sometimes he didn't say a lot. You didn't know what he was thinking. Maybe this is what he was thinking in all those silences.'

I shake my head but Scott does not look at me.

The woman turns to Larry. 'You have a certain professional insight here, I'd be grateful for your comments,' she tells him.

He moistens his lips a little with his tongue. 'This letter has the kind of balance I'd expect from Eric. He's perceptive about each daughter. He anticipates that Lucy will need extra reassurance and that Jane will be there to provide this. He doesn't dwell on the doubts or fears he must have experienced facing death, because the note is designed to alleviate his daughters' suffering. I'd say the letter is the selfless, well-reasoned work of a selfless, reasoning man and therefore I think it's genuine.'

'Thank you. Jane?'

Jane stares at the letter with red eyes. She opens her mouth to speak but instead she starts to cry. I watch, fascinated and shocked. I have never seen her cry like this. Sobs shake her body like electric shocks. When she throws her head back the tears run into her hair and ears. I want to jump up and hug her but Larry already has his arms round her.

The detective watches dispassionately. 'Are you crying,' she asks, when the sobs begin to subside, 'because you believe he really killed himself?'

'Isn't this proof?' Jane says, her voice strange and tremulous.

'Oh no,' says the detective, looking sharply around at all of us. 'No, it isn't. I don't believe Professor Schaffer wrote this note or knew of its existence. It was the last document stored in his computer and it was stored at four oh-eight on Sunday afternoon. After analysing the keyboard, our forensic department said that whoever used it last wore ordinary domestic rubber gloves. We think it unlikely your father would have typed his suicide note wearing rubber gloves. So probably, although not necessarily, whoever killed Professor Schaffer was here, at this house, at four oh-eight on Sunday afternoon.'

There is a silence. Kirsty looks around at us to gauge our reactions. There is no reaction. No one moves.

'Didn't anyone see anything on Sunday?' asks Scott, his voice hollow. 'A neighbour, a friend . . .?'

Kirsty looks at all of us but perhaps particularly at me when she says, 'If they did, no one's telling us about it.'

I look at my watch, involuntarily, to calculate what time I hid on the deck on Sunday. Kent left the hotel at eleven, I went to the cemetery, drove to the valley, walked up the hill . . . maybe one thirty. Less than three hours before Daddy's killer. At four o'clock, the killer, displaying detailed knowledge of his victim's life and family, was right here in the den typing a fake suicide note. I dig my fingernails into my palm.

Kirsty continues, 'You've asked me a few times how Professor Schaffer died. Well, we have evidence that he was electrocuted.'

'Oh!' says a woman, her voice half a breath, half an exclamation. Did the 'oh' belong to Jane or me? I look at Jane and she is staring intently at the detective. Kirsty seems to be inside my head, saying over and over, He was electrocuted. We have evidence that he was electrocuted.

'Electrocuted,' repeats Larry, and the word seems to reverberate around the room. Jim Bob Holler who lived next door was electrocuted. He was only fourteen. His father didn't wire the swimming-pool lights properly and he died when he dived into the pool.

'How sure are you of this?' asks Jane.

'The ME and Professor Rossi are prepared to stake their reputations on it. Tissue analysis of a small blister on your father's neck seems to indicate that it was the site of a massive electric shock. Professor Schaffer instantly had a heart attack.'

Kirsty reaches into her bag and produces a small black box. She lays it flat in the palm of her hand and holds it out to us.

'You've probably seen this kind of thing. It's a taser. You can buy one over the counter for self-defence purposes. You only have to touch someone with the probes and you can override their central nervous system. Their muscle tissues contract uncontrollably and for maybe thirty minutes they can see, hear and even feel but they're incapable of controlled movements. Tasers have a one hundred per cent drop rate.'

We stare at the taser. It looks like an electric razor. 'So,' says Larry, 'Eric was touched with one of these things and left in the water to drown.'

Daddy, plummeting down the rocks at Seal Wash, hearing the roar of the sea getting closer, the water closing over him, powerless to swim.

'No,' says Scott, 'that's what his killer intended. Eric's death would have looked like suicide. But the taser gave him a heart attack. Before he hit the water. That's how you know it's a homicide.'

Kirsty nods assent. She looks at each of us in turn. 'Do you have any questions?' she asks. She smiles, not a broad smile but a receptive one.

I don't know how my face got covered with my fingers. I have to move them now to ask, 'Does it hurt?'

Before Kirsty can speak, Jane says, 'Oh, Lucy, probably electrocution isn't too painful. And you know, death, any death, is almost certainly a pleasant experience. Imagine slipping away into total relaxation.'

Larry says, 'You'd probably be too stunned to feel pain.'

'Maybe not,' Kirsty tells him. 'Certainly people report that tasers cause pain to the point of nausea.'

I close my eyes.

'Do you have any more questions?' Kirsty repeats.

We shake our heads. We don't have any more questions.

When the detective has gone she leaves a silence in the house that is like a blanket. We work and eat and talk, but the silence never fully goes away. It makes us edgy. We glance out of windows frequently, jump at sounds and ask ourselves if that was really just the house creaking.

'Does anyone know anything about the Marcello Trust?' I ask at lunchtime. They shake their heads.

'Did Daddy know anyone called Marcello?'

Jane thinks and then shakes her head. 'Doesn't mean a thing to me.'

'Try his address book,' suggests Larry. Even he is subdued.

'I have. I've tried the bank, the accountant, the phone book, a list of charitable trusts, Daddy's files . . .'

'Sorry. Can't help,' says Jane.

Larry passes round more paella. We all compliment him on it again. I drop a fork. Everyone jumps.

All afternoon we work in different rooms. The front door is double-locked. Larry sorts out boxes upstairs and, if they have rocks in, he pulls them onto the landing for Scott to move to the barn, where the geologists Jane has invited from the university can inspect them. Jane won't let Larry lift rocks because he has back problems. She has started to sort through all the stuff in an upstairs bedroom near him.

When I'm tired of bending over files in the den I make everyone a cold drink. I find Larry busy marking rock boxes with a red pen.

'Thanks, just leave it there,' he tells me.

Jane has closed the door of her old bedroom. I pause outside, watching the ice circling in her drink. When we were kids I was only allowed into Jane's room if I knocked or if she asked me. I knock. I don't open the door until I hear Jane's voice. She is standing among columns of fat cardboard boxes as though she's lost in a forest. I squeeze in shyly.

'I closed the door because of the dust,' she explains.

'What have you found?' I ask, passing her the drink.

'Nothing but junk. Old high-school yearbooks, diaries with no entries past January 6th, dolls with broken arms, clothes you couldn't throw away, clothes you never wore, photos of people you don't remember, a leash that must have belonged to Nickel Dog . . . junk.'

'What are you keeping?'

'Nothing.'

'But won't we want something to remind us? Just a few things?'

Jane puts down the drink and begins to shuffle through the contents of the box in front of her. 'I don't need anything to remind me. There's already too much of it inside my head.'

'I know what you mean. Stuff from the past, things that happened, it keeps jumping out on me like some crazy dog. Like Nickel Dog.'

Jane giggles. She's often told me how Nickel Dog used to jump on me. 'He'd knock you right over but mostly he was being affectionate.'

'I think I remember when he died.'

'You do? I'm not sure how old you were.'

'What happened?'

'I just found him on the porch steps dead one evening and Daddy said he'd been poisoned. The Carmichaels were having big coyote problems and they'd put down some poison so we assumed . . .'

I speak quickly. 'I remember that, Jane. I remember Mother crying. Daddy had Nickel Dog all wrapped up in a blanket. He was carrying the body to the sunken garden. And I ran down the garden to some den that I'd made with Lindy Zacarro. And Lindy was right there, too.'

Jane smiles apologetically. 'You've imagined that, Lucy. We didn't let you see the body, not even wrapped up in a blanket. And Daddy buried him when it was dark, after you were asleep.'

'But I remember! Daddy was carrying the blanket down the steps . . .'

'Sure you remember. You remember the way you imagined it.'

Rougemont said: It's easy to confuse what actually happened with things you've been told and things you've dreamed. It's good that you recognise how unreliable memory is.

'I guess you're right,' I say. Nickel Dog's death was no memory but a tapestry I wove from recent events. It had the colour and texture of memory but it was nothing more than a fabrication.

When I step off the porch and out from under the trees the sun ambushes me. Scott is in the barn now. He has bolted the small door from the inside. I bang with my foot.

'Who's there?' he yells. He sounds nervous. When he unlocks it I stare into the barn's great blackness. 'Bolt it behind you,' he instructs me. I can hear his words retreating with him into the body of the barn.

'Scott, where are you? I can't see . . . Why don't you turn the light on?'

'I have! It's so bright outside you have to wait for your eyes to adjust.'

The tractor is the first thing to materialise. 'Oh boy,' I say, shaking my head as gradually everything else appears. Sacks and logs, tools and nails. Old bed frames, parts of machines, planks of wood and wheels. Boxes, some labelled with rock names. Scott is surrounded by them.

When I hand him the drink I see he is dusty and wet with sweat. He gulps it greedily.

'I can't believe you still get mad about Robert Joseph after all this time,' I say. He doesn't stop drinking but he grimaces at me over the top of the glass. 'I mean, you go off to France with Brigitte and you still get mad about some boyfriend I haven't seen since I was eighteen.'

He puts down the empty glass and gasps for air. 'It was the strange way it ended with that Robert guy,' he says. 'Inconclusively. You never were able to slam the door shut on the way you felt about him.'

'I haven't thought about Robert for years and years.'

He shrugs and bends over a box. 'Then why did you fish out the report of his wedding?'

I pick up the glass and mutter something about sorting through Daddy's desk, finding all kinds of things.

'Whenever we made love,' says Scott, 'it was like you weren't really there. Not all of you.'

I am surprised and hurt. 'But I thought you enjoyed it. I thought it was good!' I protest.

Scott's voice softens a little. 'Luce, we had great sex but not the greatest. Because a small part of you just wasn't there.'

I think of lying in the downtown hotel with Kent, crying silently into the dark while he slept. When Kent and I had sex, neither of us was there.

I say, 'I don't know what you're talking about.'

'Sure you do, Luce. There was always something missing. And Robert Joseph had it. You gave it to him years ago and you never asked for it back. That's why I still get mad about him.'

Later, much later, when the square of sky over Daddy's den has deepened to black, I stretch and yawn. The house is still because the others are all out in the barn now, organising rock boxes.

I straighten the desk. In one corner is *Wedding News*, where it has lain haphazardly just as it was left this morning. I take one last glance at it. The bride's antique lace. Robert's hand, just visible on her shoulder. And then, something from further down the page leaps out at me. Marcello. The name I have been looking for is right here. When Seymour first gave it to me there was a familiarity about it, I'd read it here, in the list of wedding guests. B. Marcello.

Someone walks past the open door of the den. I put *Wedding News* hastily away. I thumb through the phone book but none of the Marcellos is a B. A possibility occurs to me that makes my heart beat faster. I could drive down into the valley and ask Mrs Joseph about B. Marcello. Maybe she'll even have heard of the Marcello Trust.

I go out to the deck. I look across the long, dark ocean that is the valley. A couple of car lights. A few farmhouses.

A rustle close by makes me jump nervously. Then I see that Jane is already here, sitting on a wooden chair with her feet up on the railings.

'It sure is a warm night,' she says. 'I mean, it would be a warm night in the summertime. In March, it's ridiculous.'

I sit down next to her and we stare out into the darkness.

'I wish you could stay here a while after the funeral,' she says.

'I can stay until the end of next week. But no longer, Jane. There's this deal and I'm losing it fast . . .'

'Sure,' she says quickly, quietly. 'Of course, Luce. It was selfish of me to ask. It's just I'm tired and when I'm tired I allow myself to get overwhelmed by all there is to do.' Her voice is helpless, sad.

'No, I'm being selfish, not you,' I say. 'I'll try to come back real soon.'

I see the lights of an airplane flashing. I cannot hear the drone of its engine as it begins its high journey across the valley.

Jane breaks the silence. 'Lucy . . .' she says quietly. 'I saw you reading that report of Robert Joseph's wedding just now in the den.'

'Jane, for Chrissake I was just looking at the names of the guests!' I say defensively. 'It so happens that one of them is Marcello and I've—'

'Have you read it over and over?'

I sigh. 'Maybe. It was an important relationship for me because it was the first that Mother couldn't wreck. She was safely in the clinic by then. And I guess . . .' I hesitate. 'I guess the first time you fall in love it means a lot. Actually, his whole family meant a lot.'

The Joseph oasis in the valley. Mrs Joseph, involved in her sons' lives without controlling them. Laughing at their jokes. Enjoying their small successes. Mr Joseph was older but he was jovial, he joshed with his sons and admired their girlfriends. He and his wife took time to talk together, although their home was always full of people. There was Ralph, Mrs Joseph's brother. There were friends, cousins, friends of cousins. It was hard to be alone there sometimes, but I liked that. I came from a house where it was hard to be anything but alone.

After the Josephs rejected me, so emphatically, so long ago, could I really just drive down there and ask questions about B. Marcello?

Jane points out, 'He wasn't so wonderful. He nearly killed you down in the valley.'

'I wasn't badly hurt.'

'You could have been; he was. And the car was such a mess, it really scared me.'

Jane, arriving soon after Mrs Joseph and her friend, minutes before the ambulances, her eyes gleaming as though she might cry any minute, surveying my body for damage with a doctor's cool professionalism although it was years before she qualified.

'You didn't show it.'

'I had to be calm so you wouldn't get frightened.'

I turn to her. I can see her eyes shining in the dark.

'I owe you so much, Jane. I know we both want to leave most of the past behind but it's you I have to thank for the good things. Not just for taking care of me when I was sick or saving me in the swimming pool. But all the other stuff. Helping me choose the right clothes. Say the right things. Act the right way. I don't think Mother brought me up at all. It was all you, and I'm . . .' Inexplicably and embarrassingly, my voice breaks for a moment. 'I'm grateful to you. And especially . . . when Stevie died. How you supported me.'

So now I've said it. Without any preparation, without knowing I was going to say it. For years I've been aware that I should express acknowledgment and appreciation, that Jane was entitled to expect this. But, for reasons I don't understand, I have withheld it from her until now.

Her reply is delayed and when I glance across at her, despite the darkness, I see that tears are leaking from her eyes. 'Oh, Lucy. Oh thank you. I mean . . . it sometimes seems like you don't remember.'

'I do remember,' I assure her. I can feel tears making a hot, wet, thin line down my own face. 'I know just how much I owe you. And I never thanked you. I just went away. Without saying a word.'

This is not the kind of conversation we have. Crying this way is not the kind of thing we do. We don't look at one another but throw our words, quietly, urgently, over the railings and into the valley. When we are silent we stare out across its infinite darkness, sniffing occasionally.

When Scott and Larry appear, smelling of the barn, we struggle to make our voices normal, but they detect that something significant has passed between us and look at us searchingly. I watch a pair of car lights move sluggishly through the darkness. Suddenly it seems essential that Jane and I shoulder our weighty burden of memories together. I think, for the first time, that maybe I'll move back to California.

On Sunday morning, I leave with Sasha and Aunts Zina and Zoya for Redbush Clinic. I am relieved that I won't be visiting Mother alone but Aunt Zina explains, 'It's not good for Tanya to have more than one visitor so we will wait while you see her.'

'But what will you do?' I ask.

They shriek with laughter. 'Talk!' they cry.

Redbush is thirty minutes north of the city. It has high walls and security cameras, and looks more like the estate of some movie star than a clinic for mental illness. Sasha pulls up to the security guard at the gate. The guard asks for proof of everyone's identity. He examines our cards and hands them back. We drive into the grounds. The grass is decorated with a pattern of perfect misty triangles. When the sun catches them they seem to throw out small rainbows.

'Ah, even the sprinklers are beautiful here,' sighs Aunt Zina.

'Such a peaceful place,' Aunt Zoya agrees. 'Look at the trees. Look at the flowers.'

I enter the low, red building with exactly the feelings of despair and helplessness I felt entering Redbush as a teenager. In those days, anything could happen. Mother might be all charm, welcoming me as an honoured visitor, asking me polite questions. Or she might sulk and refuse to talk to me. Gradually, as she aged, she mellowed into silence. Visits became more of a chore than an ordeal.

Sasha, as if detecting my mood, puts a plump, leathery arm round me. 'Don't worry, you won't have to stay in there long,' he says.

A man in a loose uniform nods recognition to the aunts. 'Miss Schaffer? Hi, I'm Jonathan, Tanya's nurse.' He extends his hand, and holds mine firmly in a grip that must be useful for difficult patients. He says, 'Please come with me to your mother's room.'

I fall in behind him obediently.

'How long are you home from New York?' the nurse asks as we pad along the hallway. 'Your mother says you got a real good job there.'

'She said that?'

'Oh sure. She's proud of you. She talks about you a lot.'

'Mother talks about me? I thought she didn't speak much any more.'

The nurse smiles as he holds a door open for me. 'There are days when she's real talkative.'

'Have the police been back to interview her yet?'

'They came just once. They did say they'd be back next week some-time with an interpreter because Tanya just gave them one big lot of Russian, but I'm not sure they'll bother. I think they understood she wasn't going to be too much help.'

'When did Daddy last visit her?'

'Saturday.'

We are standing outside a door and the nurse opens it. An old woman sits huddled on a chaise longue, wrapped in a fluffy blue shawl.

'Your daughter's here!' says the nurse jovially.

'Hi, Mother.' I want my words to slip along easily but I sound tense. I stoop to kiss her thin skin then sit down some feet away from her. Mother is looking out of the window and does not acknowledge my presence. I say, 'So, how are you?' but to my relief she does not respond. It's going to be just as Jane told me. I'll chat to her a bit and sit with her in companionable silence and then, duty done, I'll be free again.

'She won't mind,' says the nurse to me, 'if you move closer. She may not see you too clearly way back there.'

I acknowledge his words but I do not move. I feel something like panic as he walks towards the door.

'I'll be back in around twenty minutes, but if you want to leave before, or you need me for anything, you can just push that button.'

The button is red. It is hidden discreetly by the drapes.

The door clicks shut behind him. We sit in silence. I study Mother's white skin. Despite the impression of great age, she is unwrinkled.

Her eyes are large and their blue is paler than I remember.

I start to talk, awkwardly at first. I tell her a little about the funeral, how Sasha and Aunt Zina will be taking her. Occasionally Mother's hands make tiny scratching movements and sometimes she blinks, otherwise she is still. I do not know if she is listening or if she can understand anything I say, but gradually I find her silence liberating. I start to talk about Daddy, how I miss him, until I almost forget the still, silent woman. I say, 'This grief is different from when Stevie died. I mean, it's another shock but after the shock, then the grief is different.'

Suddenly, Mother's face turns to me. She is nothing more than a ghost now but I recognise that she is the ghost of a beautiful woman. I fall silent. We stare at one another for more than a minute. When I realise that she is opening her mouth to speak, my heart beats faster. Gradually her face twists. I shrink back. The first time I saw her face twist this way was on the sweltering blacktop, when I emerged, limping, from the canyon.

I watch until her face is inhabited by a cruel, monstrous creature and involuntarily I brace myself against the back of my chair, ready for the beast to strike.

She speaks in a whisper, spitting with venom, 'Why did you do it?'

She waits for a reply but I have none. My heart is pounding and sweat is speckling my face and body like glitter. She is not small, old and helpless but a deadly snake and I am a little girl who is terrified of her. She leans forward. She hisses, 'Why? Why did you hate him so much?'

Involuntarily I jump up. My fingers scratch at the folds of the drapes for the red button. When I find it and press it a light flashes but there is a disconcerting silence. I hope it is working. I press it again.

When I dare to look back at Mother she says something incomprehensible in Russian. Then she turns away and her face unwinds. By the time the nurse arrives she has almost resumed her earlier vacancy.

'Everything OK?' he asks, looking at me and then at Mother. Whatever residue of her anger remains, he knows her well enough to detect it. 'Oh, Tanya, did you turn mean?' He is apologetic. 'Are you all right, Miss Schaffer? She was really looking forward to seeing you, I don't know why she had to turn mean.' He walks towards me and gently takes my bare arm. 'OK, Tanya, well, I guess your daughter has to go now.'

Mother ignores him and I do not say goodbye. As we make our way back down the hallway we can hear the aunts, giggling and gabbling in Russian, as we approach the conservatory.

'Sounds like you ladies are having a good day out,' says the nurse.

'Perhaps you think they don't see each other often,' says Sasha. 'They live, believe it or not, only one block apart.'

'Oh, but it's such a treat to go out together!' they protest loudly.

The two men try to stand at one side of the conservatory to arrange Mother's attendance at the funeral. They try to discuss whether the nurse should accompany Mother but Zina and Zoya refuse to be left out and interrupt constantly. Finally they agree that Sasha can manage with the help of only his mother and aunt. Mother will be taken to the funeral and she will return immediately afterwards without eating at the house.

'Boy,' says the nurse, backing off with mock exhaustion. 'Boy, I'm sure glad I only have one of you sisters to take care of.'

Aunts Zina and Zoya yell with delighted laughter.

As we leave, the aunts cluster round me.

'How did you find our Tanya? Is she very much changed?'

'Well, I guess she's a bit smaller and older.' My voice sounds hollow.

'Despite the difference in colouring, you look a little like her,' says Aunt Zoya.

'It's true, it's true,' agrees Aunt Zina.

I say, 'I don't want to be like Mother.' And in that moment, as we cross the parking lot, I hear again the *click clack* of my own walk, with its threat of imbalance, an advancing imbalance that cannot be controlled. The aunts, perhaps alarmed by my tone, are busy assuring me that only in the matter of great beauty do I resemble Mother.

But by the time we reach the car they have fallen silent and I am the subject of sidelong and significant glances from all three.

'Lucia . . .' begins Sasha. 'I fear your reunion was not a happy one.'

I look away from him across the green lawns. I am trying to dam my tears, dam them at a source somewhere lower than my eyes, somewhere almost as low as my belly.'

We drive south from Redbush Clinic. After about ten minutes the traffic slows and soon we are stationary.

'Construction?' suggests Aunt Zina.

'An accident?' suggests Aunt Zoya.

We inch our way forward, the aunts' heads bobbing in the back seat as they speculate on the reason for the tailback. Eventually we see flashing lights ahead. A police car passes us. When we reach the source of the delay it is clear that there has been a collision between a car and a truck. Both have swerved off the road.

'How terrible, how shocking,' cry the aunts.

'There is no reason for such a tailback,' points out Sasha as we finally accelerate away. 'The damaged vehicles, the police and the ambulances are off the blacktop in the field and the highway is in no way blocked.'

'Ah, but everyone slows to look!' says Aunt Zoya. 'Despite one's great reluctance, one is compelled to look at this horrible sight.'

'We look,' explains Aunt Zina, 'thinking that the crushed car could have been ours. We remind ourselves of our vulnerability.'

'Of our mortality,' agrees Aunt Zoya.

Joe Zacarro said, If you remember that you're going to die some day then you live your life in a different sort of a way. Not necessarily better, but probably better. Different, that's for sure.

Monday is even hotter than yesterday. When I open Daddy's front door the heat jostles its way past me like an angry crowd. I drink two glasses of icy water before setting off through the garden for the Holler orchard.

Our lot used to be four acres until Daddy sold two to the Hollers. I remember playing around the foundations of their house and then watching the bricks grow higher each day. Finally, the family arrived. Daddy and Mr Holler were neighbourly but they weren't friends back then. The friendship must have come much later.

Like many houses around here, this one is built into the hillside, so it looks two storeys high when you drive in and three if you turn back and stare at it from the valley. When I was a child it felt clean and cool and modern, with light, bright rooms and air conditioning.

I ring the doorbell and, after a long wait, Adam Holler's voice is heard over the speaker. 'Who is it?'

'Lucy Schaffer.'

'Lucy.' It is a statement. There is no surprise. 'I'm finishing my exercises, it'll be a minute before I can get to the door.'

'OK.'

I know little about Mr Holler except that he is a man who has had to live with the most hideous of mistakes, a guilt even his wife could not endure, because it was Adam Holler who had been installing the pool lights that day Jim Bob dived in and died.

Jim Bob was two years older than me, but when I was nine there was a vacation when we played together all the time. The Hollers' swimming pool was newly installed and we played in it every day. Then the new semester started and we hardly spoke to each other again.

Bolts draw back and keys turn and Mr Holler stares at me from behind dark glasses. The other man who remembers death.

'Good morning, Lucy,' he says. He holds out a dry-skinned hand to me. 'I'd like to offer you my sincere sympathy on the death of your father. He was a man loved by many. I will miss his company sorely.'

Now I recall Mr Holler's formality of tone. It masks an awkwardness, maybe a shyness that I always knew was there, even as a kid.

I say, 'Joe's probably told you that the funeral's on Tuesday.'

He nods and gestures for me to come in. He bolts the door behind us. 'I'm kind of slow,' he apologises, leading me through the hallway. 'Arthritis. In the back. And in most places now. I've had it for years.'

Arthritis. That was why the Hollers built their pool long before anyone else. Swimming was good for Mr Holler's arthritis.

'I turned on the air conditioning yesterday,' says Mr Holler as I follow him down the hallway. 'It doesn't normally go on in March but this is remarkable weather for spring and they say it's going to get hotter.'

I look around me. The sitting room hasn't changed. It still has a glass wall that looks out across the valley and a complex system of shutters so you can close off the view or any part of it when it gets to be too much.

'Sit down,' Adam Holler instructs me. But I am drawn to the window. Beneath it is the terrace. Beyond that are steps leading down to a glassy eye implanted onto the hillside. I stare into the blue iris of the pool.

'How are you coping, Lucy?' he asks, but his voice is hard.

I am remembering the summer I spent playing with Jim Bob. He was small for his age, his skin was brown and his blond hair crewcut. I just liked to jump in and make a splash. But Jim Bob was teaching himself to dive, belly-flopping at first, then gaining in grace and confidence. 'Watch this, Lucy, I can do it, watch.' He ran up to the pool, barely paused, and then was airborne, cutting through the nothingness in a perfect arc. A crash like shattering glass as his body sliced through the water. Is that how Jim Bob, years later, dived to his death? With a grace and skill that were almost lyrical?

'Why won't you sit down?' asks Adam Holler quietly and I hear a sort of fear in his voice. He knows I'm remembering Jim Bob. I'm remembering his great mistake.

I say, 'I haven't been here since I was a child.'

'Your whole family used to come over sometimes. We'd have half the neighbourhood here and Bunny cooked hamburgers.'

'The whole family?'

'Sure. All you Schaffers and the Zacs and the Dimotos . . .'

I try to remember the Schaffers, all four of us, at a pool party. The idea embarrasses me. Even when the clinic said that Mother was well enough to be at home, she dealt badly with any social situation. She either tried too hard and laughed too much or she sat in still silence.

'You don't remember? You don't remember how you nearly drowned in our pool once? Snorkelling?'

'I remember that . . . but I thought it was at the public pool.'

'It was here. You were snorkelling down at the deep end and you got into trouble. I'm not sure what happened. Possibly you took water in through the snorkel. I don't know. No one noticed, not even the other kids in the pool, because you didn't struggle, you just went limp. You didn't fight it at all. Only your mother saw something was wrong and she dived right in with her clothes on and saved you.'

'I remember nearly drowning, I remember being saved. But actually it was Jane who—'

'No. Tanya saved you.'

'But Mother never swam. She couldn't.'

'She dived in and pulled you out. She laid you down by the side of the pool and that's when Jane helped. She rolled you onto your side and then pulled you back again and sort of pumped at you until you threw up. I don't know how old she was, twelve maybe, but Bunny turned to your father and said, "Jane's going to be a doctor, you wait and see."'

'Mother never went in the water, because she couldn't swim, Mr—'

He raises his voice. 'Lucy, I saw it with my own eyes.'

It seems to me that those eyes are unreliable witnesses.

'So, Lucy . . .' He's wondering why I'm here. 'Is there anything I can do for you? Do you need any help over there?'

I say slowly, 'I guess the police have questioned you, Mr Holler . . .'

'Sure. A woman. She was about your age.'

'Did she ask you when you last saw Daddy?'

'Of course.'

'What did you tell her?'

'Sunday night, over at Joe's.'

'Mr Holler, what did you do on Sunday night?'

He gestures and the gesture is too large and too careless for a man whose movements are habitually so controlled. 'Well now . . .' he says. He's looking for that relaxed, throwaway style that Joe Zacarro has perfected. But he can't wear someone else's clothes. The words don't fit him. 'I mean . . .' he tries again. 'What do old guys like us ever do?'

I say, 'Remember death? Is that what old guys like you do?'

He twitches suddenly, the escape of a small movement. He looks at me in silence. His mouth is shut tight, the way mine was when Rougemont confronted me with my shoes.

I am still standing by the window. I feel the sun flooding the room from behind me. I say, 'On Sunday night you and Joe Zacarro and Daddy drove out to the coastal highway in an old tow truck. You dumped a wreck at the roadside where it would remind drivers the next morning how precious their lives are. They see a wreck and imagine how it would be if their lives just stopped abruptly, before they've done what they want to do. And for a while they slow down, drive carefully, live life a little differently. All thanks to you and Joe and Daddy.'

He says nothing.

'I'll bet you do it often. I'll bet you dump wrecks all around the area. And I'm not criticising you for that, Mr Holler. I admire you for reminding so many people to readjust their priorities. I think you and Joe should go right ahead with it even though Daddy's dead. I don't want to tell the police or have them stop you. I only want one thing. I want you to tell me who the other guy is. The one who owns the tow truck. I need to talk to him.'

His response jumps out of him. 'No, Lucy. No.'

'Someone has to talk to him. If not me, then the police. And I guess none of us wants that, Mr Holler.'

He grips the arms of his chair. 'Lucy, stay out of this one. It doesn't concern you. If your father had wanted you to know he would have told you. Just wind up his affairs, sell his house, take the money and go back east. That's all you need to do; that's all Eric wanted you to do.'

Anger shoots through me as though someone injected it into a vein. 'Daddy didn't die the way he should have, quietly, with his family round his bed. And I want to know why. I have good reason to connect the tow truck driver with Daddy's death. You can help me locate him.'

'No,' he says. 'I'm not going to give you any information your father didn't want you to have. I don't betray confidences. If you want to proceed, it will have to be with police help, not mine. That's my decision and Joe Zacarro will support me.'

I feel the tightening of my nerve endings. 'Listen, Mr Holler—'

He holds up a hand. 'I don't want to talk about this any more, Lucy.'

Leaning on a stick, he shows me out in silence. He is a man who has developed a whole style of still dignity to contain his humiliation. He killed his son by mistake. A hideous own goal. The smallest of errors, just the width of an electrical wire, with outsize consequences. He unbolts the door. I wish he would mention Jim Bob.

'Goodbye, Lucy.' His voice is as flat as the valley. 'Your father arranged things the way he wanted them. I hope you'll think hard about his wishes before you go any further.'

You wouldn't drive into the valley without air conditioning in weather like this. That would be crazy. Heat rises like a spirit from the asphalt, making the edge of the road look crooked.

I hope the Joseph home will look the way it used to. In my memory it is a blur of green light and green shade. I grip the wheel as I cross the aqueduct and turn into the drive. Immediately I experience again the pleasure I used to feel on leaving behind the sunbaked brown earth and arriving in this other country. The sweep of the lawn lifts my heart. The riot of flowers and shrubs delight me. I look for the hammock where Robert and I spent all that summer, but one of the old trees it swung from has gone, and the hammock too. I wonder if the tree fell down.

The big house, freshly painted, gleams where the sun slips through the trees. I park right outside. Nearby, a woman who has been bending over a flowerbed straightens to stare at me. She is wearing a broad-brimmed straw hat and it is impossible to see her face.

I stand uncertainly near the car, looking at the green, green garden and the woman, who is walking slowly towards me. The figure is close when I realise that this is a man wearing a long, faded, loose-fitting dress.

'Ralph!' I say.

The thin, white face breaks into a smile. He speeds up and takes my outstretched hand. His touch is light. He looks at me with bright blue eyes and an undiminished smile.

'Hi, Ralph. It's Lucy. Lucy Schaffer. I haven't seen you for a few years.'

'Hi, Lucy,' says Ralph happily.

Ralph is Mrs Joseph's brother. He isn't a transvestite but whatever brake stops most men from wearing a cool dress on a hot day isn't a brake Ralph knows how to apply. In a curious misdistribution, Mrs Joseph got all the genes for being quick, bright and capable. Ralph never would have been able to hold down a job or graduate from high school and Mrs Joseph made sure he never had to. When she married Robert's father, Ralph came too. During my summer with Robert, Ralph was always there, usually in the garden, planting, pruning, watering.

Ralph wanted to see what Robert and I did in the hammock and behind the rose garden. As he knew, sex is what we did. I had no sexual experience at all and Robert had less than he admitted to. We were technically incompetent. But the way he cradled me in his arms, his pleasure at my pleasure, his delight in my body, the love in his touch, was more exciting than split-second timing.

Somehow, wherever we hid to make love, Ralph always managed to find us. We sent him on wild-goose chases into the orchard, we turned on the TV for him but, when we looked up afterwards, there was Ralph watching us with unashamed curiosity, his gentle blue eyes wide.

'How are you, Ralph?' I ask now.

'Good,' he smiles vacantly. He doesn't recognise me.

'Is Mrs Joseph here?'

'No. She's staying with Robert.'

Something inside my belly contracts with disappointment. 'Oh, that sure is a shame. I was hoping to contact an old friend of your family. Someone by the name of Marcello . . .'

'Barbara,' says Ralph. 'Barbara died.'

More disappointment. The Marcello Trust and Barbara Marcello must be no more than a coincidence. I'm ready to thank him and get back in my car when I remember Barbara.

'Oh, but I knew her! She was Mrs Joseph's friend! She was real nice.' The friend who was there the day the car crashed, who held my hand and talked to me softly until Jane arrived.

Barbara was often at the Joseph house. She was tall with long hair which she wore loose. She had one son, a lonely, demanding boy. He was about eleven and he'd get upset when Robert and I made it clear that we were more interested in isolating ourselves than in playing football with him. Eventually, though, we'd look forward to the kid's visits because, when we escaped from him, he'd persuade Ralph to play cards and that way they'd both leave us alone.

'I think she had a son . . . I can't remember his name . . .'

'Ricky. Ricky fixes beautiful cars,' Ralph informs me.

'Ricky, that was it.' Then, for a moment, my heart stops beating, blood stops moving round my body. 'Ralph, did you say he fixes cars?'

Ralph nods. 'Up in San Strana.'

I start to move. I move quickly. It is so imperative that I drive to San Strana right away that I don't even ask about Robert. I thank Ralph warmly, shaking his hand again, edging towards the car.

'Shelley's home tonight,' he says as I slip behind the wheel. 'Come see her soon, she'd like that.'

I slam the door and he shouts something after me. I don't hear so I wind down the window for him to repeat it.

'Come back,' he instructs me. 'We've waited a long time for you, Lucy.'

He waves as I drive away.

Out in the hot valley where everything moves slowly, I'm fast. I drive fast. My heart beats fast. In my search for the Marcello Trust, in my pursuit of the tow truck, it never occurred to me that the two might be connected. The journey takes an hour but for all that time there is a tingling in my fingers. Anticipation. Only as I approach the San Strana Valley do I remember how much I fear this man. He was a strange and lonely preadolescent who barely touched my life and who I never imagined would re-enter it. All I know about him now is that he is tall and dark-haired, he wants something from our house and he was aggressive to Daddy.

I ask for directions to Ricky Marcello's garage in a tourist shop in

Cooper, San Strana's main town, and three people assure me that it is just a couple of miles away. First I'll reach a converted barn called the Marcello Gallery and a hundred yards past it is the garage.

I drive out of town through the green, wooded valley. The habitations that cluster round the river are old and shaded by great, bowed trees. Soon I pass signs to the gallery and start to slow. The garage has a sign but it is small and indifferent to the possibility of new business, COOPER ROAD GARAGE, E. MARCELLO. Ricky must be a pet name or a diminutive. I wonder what the E stands for.

There are no gas pumps, no posters advertising tyres. The garage is just some old sheds, a tow truck and a small collection of cars, most of them antique. It is too picturesque to be a serious business.

I drive past it again before I turn and pull off the road. Then I approach the garage quietly, on foot.

The shed doors are all closed. I stand behind the tow truck and listen, barely breathing. I am waiting for noises or smells to touch me. A clanging wrench. A whistling man. Hot oil. But I detect nothing. I stay in the shadow of the truck long after I have concluded that the place is empty.

I can see most of the cars from here. They are in different states of repair. A couple are complete wrecks. An old blue car, cigar-shaped, has white paint all round one light like a bandage. There are two vintage sports cars that seem in good condition.

A gravel path leads behind the sheds. I walk noiselessly on the grass beside it, then edge round the buildings. Behind them is a small field. A well-trodden trail leads to a house, barely visible through the trees.

I cross the field quickly. There is a bridge over a creek and then I am invisible among trees near the house. When I see movement on the verandah at the back of the house, I lie flat on the ground, watching. A woman, with a baby. The house is large and mellow with age. I see the baby crawl onto the verandah and then the woman follows and picks it up. She holds it high over her head for a moment. I can hear the baby's whoop of delight. I think suddenly, bitterly, of Stevie, who was never delighted by anything. Then the woman puts the baby down and walks into the house. The baby follows her. They leave a void behind them.

I want to cry but instead I stand up and walk back through the trees, across the river, across the field. I walk back between the sheds and slip round the tow truck and then, so suddenly that I don't have time to react, I feel an arm round my neck. Suddenly, my face is pressing against the chrome of the tow truck and the smell of oil fills my head. A voice is hissing right behind me, 'What the fuck do you think you're doing?'

I can't answer because the arm is jammed under my jaw. I move my eyes to the right and the left but I can't see my assailant. Then he swings me round, and his body is all power and I know that I cannot escape from his grip. Slowly, my eyes meet Ricky Marcello's. I know his face at once. Hirsute now but with the same gaunt, searching look I remember from way back when I was big and he was small.

'What the fuck are you doing here?' he demands again. His mouth is curled down and I know from his eyes that he is either very angry or crazy or both. I smell his body. Oil, sweat, rags, coffee, a garage smell.

'I'm looking for you,' I tell him. My voice doesn't want to continue but I make the words come. 'I have questions for you. What do you want at my father's house? Why were you shouting at him right before he died? You were yelling at him and the very next day—'

His face is livid. He swings me round so my back is against him and his hand is across my mouth. He's squeezing my lips against my teeth, his thumb against my cheek, pressing my nose so I can't breathe. I struggle for the first time, trying to prise his fingers away, fighting for air, but his fingers are clenched too hard against my face.

'I don't want you here,' he hisses into my ear. 'I don't want to see your goddamn face around my house, my family, my truck, my barn.'

I pull my right knee up sharply and stamp my foot down as hard as I can onto his. The hand over my face loosens and I gulp for air. Then his grip tightens and I know I've made him even madder. I lift my knee and push my foot down again, harder this time. As he relieves the pain by swaying onto his left leg, I force my body weight left. For a moment he topples. I struggle. If I'm going to escape it will have to be now. I fight his fingers, I kick backwards, I push my elbows into his ribs. But his grip hardens round my neck, across my mouth, my nose.

Gradually my legs weaken and then my arms. I stop fighting him. I stop fighting for oxygen. There is none. My body goes limp like paper and as it does so, amazingly, he releases me. I stumble forward, disbelieving, biting at the air as though it's solid.

'Get out now,' he yells at me.

I put my fingers to my mouth. It's bleeding. My cheeks feel raw.

As I stagger he shouts, 'Get away from here. And keep your goddamn accusations to yourself and your goddamn mouth shut so I don't have to shut it for good.'

I break into a run. I don't look back. When I get to the car I fall into it and drive away fast. Ricky Marcello is standing by the garage, hands on hips, watching me go.

I drive holding a Kleenex to my face, checking my rearview mirror nervously for the tow truck. When I am almost out of the valley I swing into a dusty parking lot. There are a couple of fruit stalls that have closed for the evening. I reverse between them. From this hidden place, I watch the road, waiting, hardly allowing myself to blink. When at last the traffic eases I steal glances at myself in the vanity mirror. I look shocked and white-faced and one lip is swollen. There is dried blood on my chin. I try to clean my face without taking my eyes from the road.

I'm waiting for the tow truck but when the blue car with the white bandage on its fender passes, my body responds instantly. I start the engine and edge out of the lot. I reach the road a second too late to pull out in front of a pick-up laden with oranges, which shudders slowly up the hill. Four cars trail behind it. I try to pass. There are bleating horns and I am forced to fall into line. By the time the road evens and I leave the pick-up behind, I know Ricky Marcello must be far ahead.

I slot into the southbound traffic on the freeway. I scan the road for the blue car. When I don't see it I accelerate until I'm breaking the speed limit, diving recklessly in and out of traffic. Remember death. I sigh and accelerate again. Darkness is gathering.

I don't see the blue car until we are almost at the bridge and then it appears so suddenly that I have to brake and fall into a lane of slower traffic to remain invisible. To keep it in sight I must drive closer than is comfortable.

When it leaves the freeway I notice in time to follow. My heart beats faster. This is the exit closest to Jane and Larry's apartment. From now on stoplights are a problem. Staying one intersection back would be hard enough in daylight and in the dark it's impossible. I am just a couple of cars behind Ricky Marcello.

Then I make a bad mistake. I follow the wrong car. The blue car I tail moves fast, and I hurry to keep up. When I stop at a light I realise that the car with the white fender is right beside me. I don't look at it, I don't look at the driver, but I feel the proximity of Ricky Marcello, sense that his face is turned to me and his angry eyes stare at me. The light changes and all the cars move forward. Ricky Marcello is right beside me. I still don't look at him as we cruise to the next light, but as we go through it I realise that he has gone, peeled off into the right turn only lane.

I drive round the block. Then I do a figure of eight. Soon I am in despair at the impossibility of finding one pair of taillights in a city full of lights. I head towards Jane and Larry's apartment. I look up their street from the nearby intersection. He's there. I glimpse the blue car pulling in by a parking meter across the road from the apartment.

I double back further up the steep hill and park. From here I have a view of the street to the apartment. I can't see the blue car but I will if it pulls out. The hill is well lit, and if Ricky Marcello tries to cross the street I'll see that too.

The white apartment is on the second floor of a town house. Someone is home because the lights are on. Probably Larry, polishing and practising the tribute he'll be reading at Daddy's funeral tomorrow. Possibly Jane too. She was at the hospital today but I guess that she'll be home early, confirming all the arrangements. There's a car down the street that could be hers. I don't want to get out to check.

For a long time nothing happens. The temperature drops and I feel stiff and dirty and cold, but I try to stay alert so I can drive away fast if Ricky Marcello walks up the street and sees me here.

My face starts to throb. When people ask me how it got bruised I'll have to say I walked into a door. I can't tell anyone about Ricky Marcello, not until I learn why he was one of Daddy's secrets. I try to remember the young Ricky I knew at the Josephs'. I recall only his frantic and often irritating pleas for attention.

At last, when my whole body is exhausted by doing nothing, something happens. The lights are turned out in the apartment. Sensible Jane, sensible Larry. An early night before the funeral. I feel absurdly grateful to them when I see the blue car slide out from its parking bay. I fall in behind it. Now that traffic is scarce we slip through the night, Ricky Marcello and then me, without difficulty. I see him as far as the freeway then turn towards Aunt Zina's. I ask myself what he could accomplish by sitting outside the apartment all evening but I am too numb to attempt an answer to this question.

Seven

WHEN I WAKE on the day of Daddy's funeral I do not feel rested. I look back on the night as a marathon of anger and tears but I cannot recall my dreams. I get out of bed stiffly as though my body is made of metal. When I stare at myself in the mirror, I am surprised to see that my face is unmarked by yesterday's encounter with Ricky Marcello.

I wear my New York clothes. They will be too hot but they are sombre. When I slip them on, my body is unyielding like iron. The suit seems to hang limply, without its usual fluidity. I am unable to eat any of the food Aunt Zina offers me and even the coffee tastes sour on my metallic tongue. I add sugar and it still tastes sour.

Sasha and Aunts Zina and Zoya have already left for Redbush when Scott picks me up.

'How are you, Luce?' he asks anxiously. His face looks white. He has slept badly and now is worrying about the tribute he will be reading.

I say, 'I wish it was all over.'

We climb into the car, and soon join Jane and Larry in the lobby of the chapel by the cemetery. Jane kisses me. She smells of flowers as usual and looks almost translucently beautiful.

Mourners soon gather. I recognise only a few of them but others introduce themselves and all murmur sympathy and something nice about Daddy. I try to thank them but this new tongue, hard, shiny, won't say the right words.

'Honey,' says a large woman putting her hand on mine. 'Grief is cumulative. Each bereavement brings back all the other losses. The cycle never ends but it does get better.'

I nod and store her words away to think about later.

Seymour arrives. He hugs me, but the warmth from his body does not penetrate my new hard surface.

I watch Joe Zacarro limp in. Adam Holler walks stiffly behind him. As soon as he sees me, water drips from Joe's eyes.

'Shit, Lucy,' he says, grasping my hand in both of his. 'When you get to the funeral and you know you're going to see a coffin then you really have to believe someone's dead. Except I can't.'

I watch him impassively. I know I should say something, reach out to him. Slowly, with an almost superhuman effort, I stretch my hand to his arm. He grabs it and smothers it with his own big, wet hand.

Mr Holler says, 'Lucy, your father was a damn intelligent man. Usually people with that kind of intelligence aren't people you can love. But he . . .' His voice cracks. He leans against Joe and then straightens. I pull a Kleenex from the supply in my bag and he takes it gratefully.

'Didn't think I'd be needing any of these,' he sniffs. 'You never can tell what feelings are going to come sneaking up on you.'

Grief is cumulative. Each bereavement brings back all the other losses. He's crying for Daddy but also for the son who died, for the wife who left.

I am soon passing Kleenex to other mourners until it seems that everyone but me is pressing tissue to their face. I am the only person in the room whose entire body is made of metal.

Almost late, but not quite, are the Russians. They arrive in a cluster

431

with Mother at its centre. Her arm is linked firmly through Sasha's. Although I have resolved to avoid her, when she walks into the room I am drawn to Mother's tiny, shuffling body.

Jane kisses her lightly and then melts back into the throng of people before Russian hands can pull her to them. The hands capture me and drag me right up to Mother.

'Tanechka, aren't you pleased to see your own Lucia?' cries Aunt Zina and, although she says it in Russian, her words inexplicably cut through linguistic barriers and I understand her with a crystalline precision.

Suddenly and surprisingly, through wisps of blonde, white, hair, the vacant eyes focus on me. There is a fluttering movement and Mother's face widens, her eyes grow bigger, her confusion leaves her and she is complete. For a sudden, haunting moment her beauty returns. She holds out a hand to me and I clasp it. A tiny bird rests in my hand and I do not let it fly away. Then, as though there has been some silent communication between them, the whole group moves on.

Aunt Zoya, her hair slipping from its clasp, catches me excitedly. 'How happy she is to know you are here,' she says.

Guests melt away before the wife of the decedent. Sasha leads her towards the doors of the hall and they are now thrown open. We all follow Mother, who walks slowly and with dignity into the hall.

At the sight of the casket there is universal grief. Jane trembles and her tears fall quietly; Larry closes his eyes and stands straight, his mouth twitching; Scott sobs unreservedly. During the music I look around and try to recognise people, but it's hard when their faces are buried in Kleenex.

Scott, as he predicted, is halted by tears during his reading. '"He took his big candle and went into another room I cannot find . . ."'

Everyone seems to break down with him. I turn to see Joe Zacarro and Adam Holler supporting each other, tears flowing freely.

Scott finds his voice again and somehow completes the reading.

At the back, right by the door, are Rougemont and Kirsty. They are dry-eyed. They are watching. My eyes meet Rougemont's.

After more music it is Larry's turn. He takes his place at the front of the room, near Daddy's coffin. He has prepared a series of cards to help him remember his speech but he does not look at them. I imagine him practising in front of the bathroom mirror last night.

'We've been telling each other what made Eric Schaffer special for us. I'd like to try explaining not how Eric was special, but why. Yes, I'm a psychiatrist, as most of you know, and my professional training is relevant to what I'm about to say. But don't worry, I'll waive my usual fee.'

There is a ripple of movement which could be amusement but Larry carries right on.

'If we want to understand people then we usually start with their childhood. Not easy in Eric's case, he almost never spoke about his early years. We know he came from a small religious community in the mountains. We can guess that his family was a loving one, because Eric was a loving man. Many of us benefited from his ability to give love and to receive it. He can only have learned that in his childhood.

'But Eric empathised with the suffering of others because he had suffered himself. We don't know how. As a child. When he left his family behind as a teenager and faced the world alone.

'We do know that his marriage brought him great happiness, but when his beautiful wife fell sick, he coped because he'd learned in his childhood how to endure suffering. When his son died, he suffered but he coped. When his grandson died, he suffered but he coped. When his daughter moved across the continent, he suffered but he coped. Most of us can recall some small, quiet act of kindness from Eric. These acts usually said, I understand your unhappiness because I first met unhappiness long ago.

'A lot of people have asked me, why did Eric die the way he did? Nobody knows the answer to that yet. It seems incredible that such an unobtrusive, sweet-natured man could be a homicide victim. But we're not here to talk about Eric's death and we shouldn't let the word homicide stand between us and the Eric we knew. Let's celebrate his life.'

Larry snaps his cards together and nods at the mourners and sits down to the opening bars of a Mozart piano concerto. For the first time I feel something breaking through my armour. It is not sadness but anger.

When the ceremony is over, family members file out behind the coffin. First, the Russians, Mother almost invisible at their centre. Then Scott and Larry and Jane and me. We are burying Daddy and the sky should be grey, the day gloomy. Instead I am dazzled by the sunlight. It bounces off the headstones and ricochets off the brass on Daddy's casket.

The earth that is to cover Daddy is without moisture. When the first handful lands on the coffin, a powder-fine cloud fills the grave. I anticipated that the sight of Daddy's coffin in his grave would make me weak with emotion. But while everyone else is doubled with grief, my new metal heart feels nothing. Emotions slide right off its shining surface.

Looking up from the grave I see Mother. A rose drops from her fingers and tears trickle from each eye. Like everyone else, she stares, motionless, down at Daddy's coffin. Behind her, at some distance, I sense movement. A bird, flying from headstone to headstone. I look for it and see that it is a man. I catch my breath. He is not too far away for me to see his face. Ricky Marcello and I stare directly into each other's eyes. I want to yell. I want to chase him and demand explanations. But I can only watch as he withdraws rapidly behind a headstone like a snake disappearing into long grass.

As we start to walk silently back up to the chapel, I am still looking for him. In the road on the other side of the cemetery I see something that could be the flash of chrome moving through the bright sunlight. A faraway roar could be a tow truck.

Michael Rougemont is standing right outside the chapel.

'Did you see someone?' I ask.

He looks at me and nods.

When we arrive at Daddy's house the mourners form a long, whiskery line up the porch steps. Mother has been returned to Redbush now and Jane and I shake many hands and receive sympathy. Scott and Larry are both congratulated on their tributes. Scott reddens at their praise but Larry accepts it routinely. He directs diners to the caterers' table out on the deck. In the far corner of the porch, obscured by shadow and foliage, are the two detectives.

Soon the house buzzes with the murmur of low voices. All the time I grew up there was never a party and seldom visitors. Apart from Mother's shouts, this is the noisiest I have ever known the house.

When Jane is helping an elderly mourner to a seat and Scott has gone to fetch him some food, Larry appears at my side.

I say, 'Larry, did you ever call the police about the guy hanging around outside the apartment?'

He looks surprised. 'Once. But it took them so long to arrive that he'd already left. I haven't seen him for a night or two; maybe he's given up.'

'Maybe he's hiding. Sitting in a car.'

'Maybe,' agrees Larry. 'It's not a nice thought.'

'Close the drapes just as soon as it gets dark,' I advise. 'Or leave them open but turn out the living-room lights like you're not home.'

Larry doesn't take advice from me on anything, certainly not security matters. 'I want to discuss this with Kirsty.' He sidles through the people towards the detectives. He engages them in intense conversation.

Kirsty listens to Larry while Rougemont's eyes wander over the room. From time to time he catches my eye but I do not acknowledge him and when he gives me one of his meandering smiles I do not smile back.

Later, he approaches me. He is looking even more like a shadow than usual in a dark suit and a dark tie. 'How are you feeling, Lucy?'

'Sort of peculiar,' I admit.

'Like, you're not feeling anything?' he asks. I nod and he nods too.

'Yes,' he says. 'Yes.' There is a silence. Then he says, 'Jim Finnigan is a good guy and he likes you a lot but he doesn't know you real well. Same with everyone I met in New York.'

I stare at him.

'You went there to be some other person. That's the Lucy they know. But the whole time the old Lucy was waiting back here for you. I sure wish you'd listen to her. Because that other Lucy, the old Lucy, the one you ran away from, she has all the answers.'

I regard him stonily. 'What are you talking about, Mr Rougemont? I'm an investment banker. I've taken two weeks' compassionate leave following my father's death, and on Saturday night I'm flying back to New York City to resume my job.'

'Uh-huh,' says Rougemont, and his mouth is pulled into a shape that could be a smile or a grimace. I turn away from him.

Jim has already called to announce that the bank has released tapes of my telephone conversations to the police.

'Do you need a good lawyer, Lucy?' he asked.

'Of course not, Jim. Is there any update on Hifeld?'

'Gregory Hifeld's decided not to sell the company and Jay Kent was downright rude when I tried to follow up with him. Says he won't be doing any deal that involves us again.'

'Oh boy.'

'Semper thinks your career doesn't look too promising right now,' Jim warned me. 'I did my best with him but a deal that turned so mean plus the police asking a lot of personal questions about you . . . well, it's sort of an unfortunate combination.'

'Am I fired?'

'You're not dead yet,' Jim said. 'But you're seriously ill. Sorry, Lucy. Things could have been different. They should have been different.'

When I see Adam Holler and Joe Zacarro standing alone, I go right up to them. I ask them, 'Well, are you two still going to Remember Death out on the highways? I mean, without Daddy?'

Joe's face breaks into a broad grin. 'Lucy, how the hell did you work out what we do? You must be real clever like your daddy.'

'There are at least two detectives here, Joe,' says Adam Holler. 'If you must talk about this, would you do it quietly?'

'Sorry!' roars Joe. 'I'm going to tell you our plan, Lucy.' He leans closer but doesn't lower his voice. 'Your daddy always intended to do the bridge. Can you believe that? Think of the chaos we can create if we dump a wreck on the bridge. It could be a sort of Eric Schaffer memorial dump.'

'Shhh,' hisses Adam Holler, dragging him away.

Joni Rimbaldi, Daddy's former secretary, tells me how she was about to leave the house to have lunch with him when Scott phoned to tell her Daddy was dead. 'And you know,' she says, 'when I opened the closet this morning, I didn't want to wear the navy-blue dress I keep for serious occasions. I took out the clothes I was wearing for lunch that day and I knew I just had to wear them instead. Isn't that kooky?'

She laughs but the laugh is anxious and I try to reassure her. Joni, with her cropped grey hair, is sensible and predictable and I can see it frightens her a little when she does this kind of thing.

'Is the jacket too bright?' she asks.

'It's fine, Joni. You look good. Daddy would have thought so too.'

'I guess I'll need to change into something warmer this evening. We're flying out to Maine. We were due to fly out yesterday but I just couldn't miss Eric's funeral. It would be like standing him up for lunch.' And she gives a watery half-smile.

When all the funeral guests are eating and there seems nothing left to say to anyone, a woman, tall, slim and white-haired, touches my arm.

'Lucy . . . I guess you don't remember me?'

I study the woman. Her white hair is pinned up loosely. Brown eyes, even features, a kind smile.

'Oh! Mrs Joseph!' I am a gauche teenager again. 'Oh, gee.' I feel my face go pink.

'My hair certainly wasn't white when you knew me.' She laughs ruefully. 'It's so good to see you. I'm sorry I wasn't home yesterday when you called. I've hoped for years you'd come and visit. We missed you so much after that terrible crash. I hope you've forgiven Robert now.'

When I can't find any words, she rescues me.

'It took him a long time to get over you. But he's been married a while and I think pretty well married. Their youngest child is eight months old. I've been staying with them in Virginia. I just got back last night.'

We talk about how Robert became a doctor after spending so much time in hospital after the crash. She describes how Mr Joseph died of a heart attack suddenly one morning, twenty-four hours after Robert had left to return to the hospital in Baltimore where he was working. Step is teaching and Morton, the eldest brother, is running the farm.

'But I should have told you how sorry I am about your father,' she says. 'I got to know him pretty well over the years and I was very fond of him.'

'You were?' I had assumed her presence here was neighbourly.

'Lucy, are you going to visit with Ralph and me real soon?'

'I'd like to,' I admit. 'But I'm leaving for New York on Saturday.'

'What are you doing after the funeral?' she asks. 'Oh, but I guess you should be with your family.'

I want to be with Mrs Joseph and for an embarrassing, confusing moment, it seems to me that she is my family.

'I can drive over to the farm later,' I tell her.

When I cross the aqueduct and turn into the Josephs' oasis in the valley, it seems as welcoming as home. The evening sun creates pockets of shadow across the lawn and covers the house in a subtle light.

Ralph and Mrs Joseph hear my car and come outside. A couple of dogs stroll at their side, tails wagging lazily. Mrs Joseph has changed into pale, loose clothes. Ralph is wearing overalls. He smiles while Mrs Joseph hugs me. Then he evaporates into the garden.

'Did you eat today?' she asks as she leads me indoors.

'No.'

'Are you hungry now?'

I am astonished to find that I am hungry and that, when she places an interesting salad in front of me, I can eat all of it. The big dogs watch me, waiting for scraps of bread.

'Good,' she says when she comes back into the room and sees my empty plate. She has been collecting pictures and she sits with them at my side. 'This is the first thing we should do,' she explains. 'I mean, deal with your curiosity about Robert.'

One at a time, with a brief commentary, she hands me photos of Robert, some from his wedding or earlier but most of them recent.

'He's just the same,' I say.

'Not exactly. His personality deepened and changed after the car crash and I think that soon showed in his face.'

'His wife's beautiful.'

'I think she looks a little like you. And, she's a banker too. Isn't that a coincidence? Now here's a very old one of you with all the boys.'

Three boys aged from about five to fifteen. They all have the same black curly hair and they are sprawling across a couch and each other. In their midst, sprawling like one of the boys, is a girl, aged maybe ten.

'But . . . what was I doing here?'

'Climbing trees, building dens, all the things kids normally do.'

I look at Mrs Joseph. 'I didn't ever come here when I was a kid.'

'Sure you did. Your mother wasn't around and your father had to go away a lot so you used to stay here.'

'Often?'

'Some years it was often.'

'Years? This went on for years?'

'You don't remember. That's a shame, we had some good times.'

'Oh, Mrs Joseph, I had some great times here but I thought they were all in one summer, I mean, Robert's summer.'

'Robert was a pal to you long before he became a boyfriend. That's probably why, when you both jumped, it was in at the deep end. You'd done the shallow end stuff for years.'

I sigh. Now I understand why this house feels like a home. I've contracted my memories and feelings about the place into one short summer.

'But . . . where was Jane?'

'Your father left her with the Carmichaels, I think. Or the Spelmanns. I'm not sure where she went. Now, recognise these two young folk?'

Mrs Joseph holds out a small photo. A young Robert, hair curling over his face. His arm is tight round a green-eyed, dark-haired girl who smiles not at the camera but at Robert. I stare at the girl as though I'm staring at my own ghost.

Mrs Joseph waits while I study the picture. 'What's intriguing you?'

'Her smile. I mean, my smile. I can't believe I ever was that girl.'

Mrs Joseph gently removes the picture and scrutinises it herself. 'Why not, Lucy?' she asks, handing it back. 'It looks like you.'

'I can't believe I ever was that happy.'

She gets up. 'Oh, sure you were.' She pushes the icemaker and it makes a gurgling and scrunching noise.

I lift my feet to the rung of the chair and hug my knees. 'I was happy here. I liked this house so much. The way it was always full of talk and laughter. I liked the way you and Mr Joseph spoke with each other, polite and intimate at the same time. It was so respectful. I never realised before that respect is an important part of love.'

She smiles. 'What did you think love was about? Control?'

I smile too. I feel strong now. Strong enough to ask, 'Did you blame me for the car crash?'

Mrs Joseph turns to me in surprise. 'How could anyone blame you?'

'Robert was driving with his arm round me.'

'Then if I blamed anyone, and I don't think I did, I guess I would have blamed Robert.' She puts two iced drinks on the table and sits down behind one of them.

'I didn't ask him to drive that way,' I add. 'But maybe something I said made him think he should. Then I would be technically responsible.'

She sips her drink. Her silence compels me to continue.

'I . . . I thought that was why Robert didn't ever call me again. Why you didn't try to contact me after the crash. Because you blamed me.'

Mrs Joseph looks away from me as she thinks. Finally she says, 'Did you call Robert after the crash?'

'Well . . . no.'

'Did you call me?'

'No. I mean . . . you didn't phone and I thought you were mad at me.'

'Maybe we thought you blamed us. When you didn't call.'

The sun is shining through the kitchen window, heating my face. 'Oh no, no,' I stammer. 'Of course I didn't blame Robert or you or anyone.'

She looks at me closely. Her smile is understanding. I wonder what it is she understands. 'Someone has to pick up the phone, Lucy. That's all I have to say about this.' She drinks some more. 'I'm sure you're not still the kind of person who sits around waiting for others to call you. Your father was real proud of how well you've done in corporate finance.'

'Investment banking, actually, not that Daddy ever appreciated the difference.'

'Maybe he was too busy suffering to think about it,' she says, and she giggles. 'I'm sorry, Lucy, but your brother-in-law's tribute to Eric really was too much; it's been irritating me all afternoon.'

I take secret pleasure in hearing Mrs Joseph disagree with Larry. I say, with some enthusiasm, 'I didn't like that tribute either. It made me feel terrible. When I think of the pain I must have caused him and how I wasn't here to alleviate his loneliness . . .'

Mrs Joseph shakes her head. 'Personally I don't recall your father as a lonely man at all.'

'But,' I say quietly, 'Daddy never laughed.'

'Oh, sure he did!' Mrs Joseph exclaims, opening her eyes wide.

'Not really. Not from his belly, not from his heart.'

'Sure he did! For heaven's sake, he's sat right where you're sitting now and laughed himself into helplessness.'

I look hard at her in disbelief but she's smiling privately. 'I've never known Daddy laugh himself into helplessness,' I say.

'Does it reassure you to know that he did?'

'I guess so.'

'Well, he laughed long and hard and often. And he had a good sense of humour and could make others laugh too.'

I say, 'How come you knew Daddy so well? I'd like to ask you about that. And your friend, Barbara Marcello. Can you tell me whether Daddy had any connection with her or her son?'

'Did he tell you of any connection?'

'No.'

'Then it was either non-existent, insignificant or private.'

'Daddy paid money annually into something called the Marcello Trust. I'm sure it has something to do with Ricky Marcello. Ricky certainly knew Daddy. When I tried to ask him about it he got real mad. He attacked me.'

'Oh, I'm sorry to hear that. Did he hurt you?'

'Well, not really. But he held me and threatened me.'

'Did you hurt him?'

When I admit how I tried to break Ricky's foot, Mrs Joseph laughs out loud and says, 'Lucy, it sounds like he came off worse in that encounter.'

'I had to do something,' I protest. 'I thought he was trying to kill me.'

'Sure you did. I can imagine Ricky's real scary when he wants to be. He's always had a terrible temper. Barbara used to worry about it but she had to admit that he'd never hurt a fly.'

She's not describing the Ricky Marcello I've been encountering lately.

'And he's been a kind friend to Ralph,' she adds. 'He takes him out driving in the automobiles he fixes up in San Strana. And occasionally, he sits up in the tow truck with Ralph and lets him drive it round the farm. Now that's heroic. None of us ever lets Ralph drive anything.'

I shake my head. 'I think Ricky Marcello has another side to him that you don't know about, Mrs Joseph.'

'Probably. Most people have.'

'It's a mean side. Real mean. To be honest, I suspect he was involved in Daddy's death.'

'Now, Lucy,' she says. I wonder if her brown eyes are sparkling with amusement or curiosity. But when she speaks her voice cautions me. 'Lucy, what evidence do you have to say a thing like that?'

It is late when I return to Aunt Zina's apartment. Sasha is reading the newspaper, small glasses perched on his broad face. Aunt Zina has her nose buried in a book. They are pleased by my arrival. They have been waiting for me, hoping to discuss the funeral.

I sink into a chair. 'Thank you for bringing Mother. And thank you for everything,' I say.

They know from my tone that I am about to announce my departure.

'I haven't booked a flight but I intend to leave on Saturday,' I tell them. They urge me to stay longer.

'I really have to get back to work or I won't have a job,' I insist.

'Then,' says Aunt Zina, already on her feet and heading for the kitchen, 'take another. Here in California.'

I tell her I've eaten and beg her not to feed me but she reappears anyway with plates of homemade cookies. We discuss the funeral, agreeing that Mother behaved impeccably today and that she brought a dignity to the occasion that was reminiscent of Grandma. They tell me Larry has aged and Scott is handsome.

'And Jane,' adds Aunt Zina, 'still has great beauty. More so, perhaps, than ever.'

'Mama, she always did look like Greta Garbo,' insists Sasha.

Aunt Zina shyly produces a small parcel, wrapped in tissue paper and tied with a faded pink ribbon. She says, 'I have undertaken a small work for you, Lucia. It will be completed by Saturday. I hope you approve.'

She hands me the package and I pull at the ribbon and it falls silently away. I peel the tissue paper. It crunches softly. Inside are letters.

'These are the letters of a mother to a daughter. They were written from Grandma to your dear mama. When Grandma died, your papa gave them to me, a thoughtful gesture. It is a humble project of mine to translate them for you. I only hope I have been equal to my task.'

I pull a thin, crisp sheet from its envelope. Across one side is bold Cyrillic script. Aunt Zina is milking these dry pages for something that a mother should give a daughter because, whatever it is, she knows my mother could not give it to me.

'Thanks,' I say quietly. 'I appreciate that.'

Sasha has taken the bundle of letters and is surveying them through his tiny glasses. 'Is the content interesting?' he asks.

'The letters are full of maternal advice that is of the utmost relevance to a young woman. Grandma did not like to use the telephone and preferred to write and it is good that she did so.'

Sasha peels away an envelope at random and glances through the letter it contains. 'Mama, Lucia hardly needs to learn how much flour to put in a pirog,' he says.

'Oh, I'd like to learn to make pirog,' I assure them quickly.

'The advice takes many different forms,' Aunt Zina says.

'Let's see,' Sasha says. 'This one is dated June 1st. "My dearest Tanechka . . ." hmm, ' His eyes scan the page. 'OK. "My dearest little Tanya, there are no words to express my sadness, sadness for myself and for your family and for the poor darling little Nicolai . . ."'

'Ah, I haven't yet translated that one. It is the last letter she wrote and it relates to the death of your brother, Lucia. After that, Grandma went to stay with your family for a long time.'

'" . . . but most of all, my little one, for you,"' Sasha continues. '"Only a mother who has lost a son can understand your grief. I will come and when you can talk you can tell me how this terrible . . . catastrophe, accident occurred and when you have told me you can tell me again.

Because you see, I will never forget my horror when I lost my beloved Pasha, the emptiness of my arms when the railway official had taken my son's body away. I wanted to walk up and down the train wailing, telling everyone of my loss, and again on the boat, and then I wanted to tell everyone in America about my son and how he had died . . ."'

Sasha breaks off and looks at me mischievously. 'To tell you the truth, Lucia, I think she did. We certainly had to hear about it often enough.'

'My mother suffered much at the loss of Tanya's son,' says Aunt Zina. 'She behaved as though her own son had died all over again.'

I say, 'I don't remember my brother, or anything about his death.'

Aunt Zina looks up and stares at me fiercely. 'Nothing?'

'No.'

'Come now, Lucia, you were small but so was I,' Sasha points out, 'and even I remember this cataclysmic event. Everybody crying. Aunt Zoya saying, "My poor dear Tanya," over and over. Grandma inconsolable. Lucy, I believe your brother gave me my first childish glimpse of death, no, perhaps not of death but of grief.'

A terrible catastrophe, accident. The whole family crying, Grandma overwhelmed by grief, rushing to Mother. The glassy surface of our lives shattered, maybe for ever, by the death of a baby boy.

I say, with a huskiness in my voice as though I just crawled up into some dusty attic, 'I don't even know his name.'

'Americans called him Nicky,' says Aunt Zina, 'but he was Kolya to us.'

'Kolya? Kolya.' I want to say it over and over, as though the name might lead me directly to the memory.

'Kolya is a common diminutive of Nicolai,' explains Sasha. 'Does the name Nicky, Kolya, sound at all familiar, Lucia?'

'I don't think so . . .' My throat clenches. It tries to censor my words. I could never ask this question if Daddy were still alive or if Jane were in the room. I say, 'What exactly did happen when the baby died?'

Sasha and Aunt Zina exchange looks.

'Well,' says Sasha, 'have you discovered the interesting coincidence that father and son both died at the same place?'

'Yes. I took it as just another indication that Daddy's killer knew him well. If he knew the baby died there, he probably thought Big Brim was a credible place to stage a suicide.'

'Indeed,' nods Sasha.

'Although,' I add, 'it could just be an extraordinary coincidence.'

There is silence. I persist, 'So . . . what happened at Big Brim beach?'

'Tanya set the baby down too close to the water's edge, thinking perhaps that the light and movement might amuse him. She heard the crash of a huge wave. When she turned, she saw her son dragged from the shore as the wave receded. She waded straight into the water but he was beyond her reach. He was soon pulled down beneath the surface.'

I stare at Aunt Zina. 'But she could have swum in . . .'

'Tanya was the weakest of swimmers,' states Aunt Zina.

I remember how Adam Holler said that Mother saved me in the pool. 'But she could—'

Sasha looks at me over his half-moon glasses. Aunt Zina cuts through my protests. 'She would have been quite incapable of saving him.'

'So . . . she saw her baby die?'

'He returned to the surface several times but finally he disappeared for good.'

'She saw him die,' I repeat.

Aunt Zina's head nods vigorously. 'Yes, yes, she saw him die.'

'The body,' adds Sasha, 'was never found.'

Aunt Zina asks, 'Is it any wonder that she went mad?'

The next morning I move fast through the city. I enjoy the early freshness. It is possible to move quickly, unimpeded by heat.

I soon reach the library. It is huge and cold like a cathedral. I ask an assistant for help and a few minutes later the newspapers I have requested appear on the desk in front of me.

My grandmother's letter of condolence was dated June 1st. I don't expect to find a report of my brother's death until May 31st or June 1st. I turn the pages. When I reach June 2nd and there has been no mention of the accident, I lose hope. I give June 3rd and 4th a cursory scan. Maybe the death of a baby wasn't considered newsworthy. Then, on the front page of June 5th, I see it, BABY DROWNED BY FREAK WAVE.

I bend over the story. It says, 'Eight-month-old Nicholas Schaffer was swept out to sea at Big Brim beach yesterday by a freak wave.'

The death occurred at 10.10am. Mrs Tatiana Schaffer had been playing with her two daughters, leaving her baby son at the shoreline, when a large wave carried him away. Dr Schaffer, a university lecturer, was fetching sweaters from the family's car across the dunes. Mrs Schaffer was a non-swimmer. She had, nevertheless, attempted unsuccessfully to reach the child. Coastguards had later joined in the search for the body, which had still not been found. No one else saw the wave carry the baby away, although there are quotes from someone who watched Mother's floundering rescue attempt.

'Dr and Mrs Schaffer are being interviewed by police,' the article concludes. 'Detective Rougemont declined to comment on the case.'

I walk back to my car. The sun is already bouncing off the hood. The steering wheel feels hot and hard like something baked in the oven.

I turn into Daddy's drive and see Jane standing at the top, opening the barn door. I feel bad that she has been alone and vulnerable at the house and apologise for arriving so late.

She is forgiving. 'It's too hot to feel scared today,' she says. 'And the geologists from the university will be here any minute.'

We walk inside the barn and linger at the door, seeing black, waiting for our eyes to accommodate the darkness.

I say, 'Jane. There's something I don't understand.'

She laughs. 'Only one thing?'

It is dark in the barn but not cool. My mouth feels salty dry. 'Jane, I've been learning about . . .' This is difficult. 'Our brother. His death.'

Jane swings round to me. 'How come?'

'Well, last night Sasha translated a letter from Grandma to Mother, saying how sorry she was about the baby's death. It doesn't make sense, Jane. The story of how he died doesn't fit the facts.'

She studies me in the diminishing darkness. 'What facts?' she asks.

I start to tell her when there is the moan of an engine. The geologists have arrived.

'I'll get them started,' Jane says, 'then we should talk about this.' And suddenly it seems urgent that we discuss our brother, as though our great silence has collapsed beneath the weight of its accumulated years.

The geologists emerge slowly from their car in the sticky heat. One of them reminds me of Daddy, tall and kind-faced, the other is bearded. I fetch them cold drinks while Jane leads them into the barn and explains how Larry and Scott have organised Daddy's vast rock collection. They're still talking when I take them their drinks.

I wander round to the deck to wait for Jane. A haze lingers over the valley. When the heat gets this intense, only a storm can drive it away.

Jane appears at my side. 'OK, they don't need us. Let's go, Lucy.'

I follow her back into the house and out through the porch. The screen door bangs and our feet clatter on the wood. We cross the garden and pick our way through the Holler orchard. Light and heat pour down.

'Where are we going?' I ask.

'Down to the valley where no one can overhear us. Remember that old trail we used to take?'

I remember the trail because I walked up it the day before Daddy died. The heatwave has dried the earth since then. In a couple of places I think I can see my own footsteps. Jane picks her way down the overgrown path, holding her arms clear of the leaves, her hips and long, slim legs

444

swinging with the terrain. Small clouds of powdery red earth circle every foot and fill our shoes.

Suddenly, we're at the bottom of the hill. The valley is eerily still, as though someone cast a spell on it. The sun dominates, searing into the trees, the ground, the rocks. Everything here must submit to its rule.

'Let's sit,' suggests Jane. There are rocks nestled into the base of the hillside. The rocks are hot but they are shaded by a slanting tree. We sit, taking a little relief from the light, smothered still by heat.

'OK,' says Jane. 'I'm ready. Tell me the facts about Nicky's death.'

I am amazed to hear his name used with such casual familiarity. I thought Jane, like me, had forgotten all about him.

I tell her the story of that trip to Big Brim beach when I was four and she was seven. How Daddy went back for sweaters when the freak wave came and Mother was unable to save the baby.

She nods. 'That's it,' she says. 'That's pretty much how it was.'

'You remember?'

'It was a trauma I relived a thousand times. I remember every second.'

'But why did you tell the police you'd forgotten?'

'Because Nicky's death doesn't have anything to do with Daddy's. I was appalled they kept asking me about it. I mean, it was a terrible, tragic thing to happen and it drove Mother literally insane. But Daddy and I found the best way of coping with it was to grieve and then put it right behind us. And you just forgot about the whole thing. Until now. So tell me, Luce. What are these facts you've found that don't fit?'

I swallow. 'I guess it's nothing,' I say at last.

'Please tell me. Please, Luce.'

'I thought it looked like they staged Nicky's death.'

Jane stares at me. 'Staged it?' she asks. 'God, Luce, what do you mean?'

'This freak wave that's supposed to have snatched the baby away. It's hard to imagine there could be such a thing at Big Brim . . .' My words have been edging down a steep hill. They gather momentum and start to tumble. 'That place is like a lagoon. There are almost no waves. It's not a safe beach but the danger comes from the undercurrents, not the waves. Then, this stuff about Mother not saving the baby because she couldn't swim. Well, she could. Mr Holler remembers her diving into their pool to save me once, you resuscitated me but she actually pulled me to safety. Why didn't she do the same for the baby? But the strangest thing of all is a letter Grandma wrote to Mother when Kolya, Nicky, died. It's dated June 1st. But, according to the newspaper reports, Nicky didn't die until June 4th. So Grandma wrote a letter of condolence three days before the baby died. Isn't that bizarre?'

I am out of breath and out of words. Jane has been watching me, large-eyed, her body tilted gracefully forward on her rock.

'How could they have staged his death?' she asks.

'I don't know. But if the baby had died earlier in some other way, they could have pretended that he drowned at the beach to cover it up . . .'

She sighs. 'You shouldn't read too much into the date on Grandma's letter. She could have got the date wrong, so could the newspaper.'

'What about the wave? Do you remember the wave?'

'No,' she admits. 'I don't remember it. None of us saw it.'

'What do you remember, Jane?'

She pulls her body back and puts the soles of her feet up on her rock. 'Every detail,' she says at last. 'The exact grade of grey in the sky. The colour of the beachball we were playing with. Mother kicked the ball to you and then turned round and realised Nicky was gone. He'd been sitting on the sand in that dumpy way small babies sit, and then he just wasn't there any more. She screamed and we ran up to her and we all stared at the sand as though, if we stared hard enough, he'd reappear. You dropped the ball and the little waves sort of grabbed it. When we looked in the water for Nicky we couldn't see him there either, just the beachball bobbing up and down. Mother started shrieking and flapping her arms. She probably thought someone had taken him because she ran up and down the tideline but there was no one close enough to have done such a thing. Then I saw his little blue hat. It wasn't far away and the beach there shelves gently so I waded in for it. Mother rushed into the water behind me, splashing and yelling, and grabbed the hat out of my hand and then she went in further until she was submerged waist deep and her skirt was floating behind her on the surface of the water.'

There is a long silence. It sucks all the oxygen out of the air. I say, 'Didn't anyone help? Wasn't there anyone on the beach who could help?'

'There were a few people and yes, they did come to help. Not for a while, though. It turned out that they thought we were trying to get the beachball. And anyway, soon Daddy was back.'

'And did you see the baby at all?'

'A little way out, flung around by the movement of the water. He was face down and I'm pretty sure he wasn't moving.'

'Why didn't Mother swim to him? Why didn't she try to get to him?'

'Daddy did. He tried for ages but he had to give up when the currents nearly pulled him under. We all knew by then that it was way too late.'

'But why didn't Mother get in the water the moment she realised that Nicky had gone?' I demand loudly.

I see that Jane is crying silently.

'Luce, I've never told anyone this. I never even discussed it with Daddy, but I think he knew it too. I suspect . . .'

I wait while she fights with her tears.

'I've always suspected . . . that Mother may have drowned her baby.'

I am powerless to move. The heat pins me to my rock. A lizard peeks out from underneath it, moves a few feet and then stops. It is motionless in the dust as though the heat pins it, too, to the earth's surface.

'Nicky was a problem for Mother,' says Jane. Her voice is a monotone. 'You and I had been easy babies but Nicky cried and cried. Mother loved him so much but she couldn't cope and Daddy had to take time off to help and the whole house was tense. Mother was highly volatile but, Luce, I've always hoped that she didn't plan on drowning her baby. I prefer to think it was more like a split-second decision not to save him.'

I am crying too now. The tears make hot lines through my dusty face.

'Don't judge her too harshly, Lucy. I know you'll understand.'

'I won't judge her,' I sob. 'How can I?'

Jane gets up and walks across the soft earth of the valley floor. She puts an arm round me. 'I guess you must know just how she felt. Because, although she was responsible for his death, she really loved that baby.'

I howl. Like an animal, like a wolf. The valley side echoes my cry until Jane and I are surrounded by a whole pack of wolves.

I remember how, when I had Stevie, love seemed to spill out of me. But it was a love to which Stevie seemed indifferent. He was dissatisfied with my inadequate attempts to nurture him and he showed his dissatisfaction continually. He cried and cried and, because he felt like a part of me, his wails seemed to express some great sadness inside me I didn't even know was there. He was expelling my misery for all the world to hear. And, when I pulled back the blanket and knew from his special stillness that he was dead, wasn't my first reaction, before the shock, before the suffering, simply relief that there was silence at last?

I say, 'It was my fault Stevie died, Jane. It was all my fault.'

When he was dead, when the police had gone and the woman in dark clothes had taken him away, I slept. I slept for twenty-four hours.

'Shhh,' says Jane as I sob onto her shoulder. 'I know. Shhh now.' She hushes me softly like a baby. 'It's all over now, Luce. Nicky's dead. Stevie's dead. We can put it all behind us.'

When I look up, I say, 'Mother got sick right after Nicky died. I understand now. Her grief was compounded by guilt.'

Jane nods. 'Probably we went to Arizona too soon after his death.'

'What a terrible vacation for her.'

Jane takes my hand and holds it fiercely in hers. She says, 'Luce, do you ever think about death?'

'I think about it a lot.'

'Are you scared of it?'

I sniff. 'Yes.'

'Sometimes I think it must be wonderful. All the things you worry about, the headlong chase for happiness, the suffering even wealth can't prevent, the knowledge that the second half of your life can only be a decline . . . I've watched people die and, no matter how much they dreaded death, they always seem to sink into it with a kind of relief. I'm telling you this because I want you to know, it really wasn't so bad for Stevie. It wasn't so bad for Nicky.'

I feel grateful to her. Her kindness is like the sun. I thank her. I stand up. Rows of big fruit trees stretch away from us to the misty horizon.

Knowing that, now Daddy is dead, we only have each other in the world and that we alone are guardians of our family's past, Jane and I lean on one another as we stumble back up the trail. The effort of climbing erases all thought until we get to Daddy's garden and then I become aware that I am dirty all over. The earth is inside my shoes, it clings to my legs and I can taste it in my mouth.

'We should shower,' says Jane hoarsely.

I gesture for her to shower first and while she is gone I step down into the sunken garden. I sit down by Daddy's headstone and think of the terrible burden he carried, the terrible burden of his knowledge.

'Hi, Lucy.'

I turn and see the bony features of Michael Rougemont. His grey eyes survey me sadly. Followed by Kirsty, he descends the stone steps and sits near me in dappled shade.

'You OK?' Rougemont asks.

'You look like you've been mud wrestling,' says Kirsty.

'I just took a walk down to the valley.'

'Oh, you must like it down there,' says Rougemont. 'You went the day before your father died. I had Forensic analyse the earth on those shoes and they said you'd been in the valley as well as this garden.'

I sigh. 'I parked in the valley, that's all.'

'Why did you come here that day?' asks Kirsty.

'I wanted to see Daddy. But the circumstances weren't right for a big reunion. I looked in through the sliding doors on the deck. He was in his chair. Then I went back down to the valley. Then I returned to town. I was probably here at about one thirty.'

'Uh-huh,' says Rougemont. 'Thank you for telling us that, Lucy.'

I look at his strange face. The stretched mouth, the big nose. For the first time I recognise his sharp intelligence. When he investigated Nicky's death, did he suspect the truth?

I say, 'I'm sorry I lied to you.'

'When you lie,' Rougemont says, 'it's generally to protect someone else, not yourself.'

Kirsty nods. 'You have to stop taking responsibility for other people, Lucy. It could be dangerous.'

I look at her in confusion.

'Where were you on Monday night?' she asks. 'After dark?'

'Monday?' Sitting in the car watching Ricky Marcello watching Jane. 'Oh, I just sort of drove around. Then I went back to my aunt's.'

'Uh-huh,' says Rougemont.

'I didn't get out of the car. Not until I was back at Aunt Zina's,' I insist.

Kirsty says, 'You didn't get out of the car. But you didn't drive around too much.'

'Uh-huh,' says Rougemont. 'You were right outside your sister's apartment all evening.'

I blush. I am fighting tears, the tears of a small angry child who wants to stamp her foot. I haven't told them about Ricky Marcello because he was Daddy's secret but now it seems that they've known all along.

'Oh, don't misunderstand us,' adds Rougemont. 'We think it's real nice of you to be so concerned for your sister's safety. But, Lucy, leave the police work to us. We know what we're doing. As you probably already realise, there's more than one homicide involved. We're hoping that this case will help us close a few others that have been open for a while.'

My heart slips down inside me like alcohol. I want to ask him about the other homicides but my throat is too dry.

'We'll do the police work,' says Kirsty, 'and you go back to New York. You'll be safer in New York where you're only responsible for yourself.'

They look at me. Covered in earth and on the edge of tears. Their looks are kind.

'Stop taking so much on yourself, Lucy,' says Rougemont. 'You've always done it, even when you were a little girl. No matter what questions I asked you, you'd cry. I never got anywhere with you. Your sister was different. She was barely seven but she described precisely what happened when your brother died. Your mother was so emotional she was incoherent. Your father had a sort of grimness about him. And then there was you, little Lucy, four years old. You cried and cried for your dead brother and said over and over that it was all your fault. You seemed to be accepting responsibility for your whole family.'

I am silent.

'Don't you remember any of that?' Kirsty asks me. 'Not any of it?'

My head feels heavy, as though there is a thick crust around it. I say, 'I've tried. I've tried real hard. But it won't come back.'

When the police have left and Jane has volunteered to stay late with the geologists, I drive back to town. The air feels cooler and thinner now. Maybe the heatwave is ending at last. On the way I detour to the cemetery where Stevie is buried. I stoop close to the tiny headstone to place some small, yellow flowers from Daddy's garden on the grave.

A tune thumps through my head with sudden and unexpected insistence. I pause to listen. It is a song of nursery simplicity and someone is humming it. I catch stray notes, then whole bars; finally a voice I recognise at once as my mother's sings the whole song through. The words are incomprehensible, but involuntarily I lift my hands to form the fluttering bird that flies away in the last bar. The music sails through my head a few more times and then, as I walk down the hill, it sails away.

When I get back to the apartment, Aunt Zina is out at Aunt Zoya's and Sasha is alone in the kitchen.

'Mama has left enough here for at least ten people,' he says, ladling food onto my plate. 'And I have already eaten half of it.'

'I'm not real hungry, thanks, Sash.'

'In our family, as you very well know, Lucia, that is considered a pitifully inadequate excuse for refusing food.'

When I am silent he looks at me closely. I showered at Daddy's but had no change of clothes and the orchard's earth still clings to them.

'Something's happened. What is it, Lucia?'

I look at him, his blue eyes full of concern. I say, 'The police investigating Daddy's death say that there's more than one homicide involved.'

'That doesn't surprise me.' He passes me the plate of food and fills one for himself. 'Did the police reveal anything about the other deaths?'

'Just that they happened years back. Sasha, I think they mean Nicky. I think they mean Stevie.'

Sasha stares at me. 'Your brother? And your son?'

'It can't be a coincidence they've hauled in old Michael Rougemont. He investigated Nicky's drowning all those years ago. And they're using Kirsty because she was there after Stevie died.'

He sits down. 'Lucia, neither can be regarded as homicide.'

'I think they know the truth.'

'Which is?'

'That Mother was responsible for Nicky's death. And that I was responsible for Stevie's.'

'Lucia, now what is this madness?'

'The madness of motherhood. It isn't the way it looks in TV commercials. It's an awful mix of great love and hatred. Babies never take their mother's needs into account and everything she gives they seem to swallow up and then demand more. You can't control them and you can't control your life and sometimes you hate them for it.'

'And so you kill them? For heaven's sake, Lucia.'

'There were times when I wished Stevie dead. That's enough.'

'Stevie died tragically but not unnaturally. There are many SIDS deaths each year. His was one of them. No one is responsible. May I suggest that until you can talk about him more easily, even tell the story of his death to a stranger on a park bench, you will not overcome your grief?'

'I don't want to sit in parks talking about Stevie!'

'We all need to tell stories. Once we massage life's traumas into a narrative form they become less destructive. The fact of Nicky's death may provoke uncontrollable emotions, but the story of how he drowned at Big Brim at least offers us a way of working through them.'

I consider this. 'Like the story of Grandma's baby on the train?'

'Precisely. That story has certainly played its part in the family's grieving process. Even though it is untrue.'

I stare at him. He picks up his fork and scoops up a mouthful of food.

'If you're interested, I'll tell you what actually happened.'

I nod for him to continue and he finishes his mouthful and then reorganises his broad body in the chair.

'When Grandpa, Grandma and their daughters came here, like many emigrants they chose to, shall we say, reinterpret their history.'

'You mean . . .'

'I mean not everything they have told you is true.'

I am speechless at this challenge to family mythology.

'The train ride . . . it's all nonsense. Probably they've eventually come to believe it themselves, so much detail does it contain.'

'But . . .' I protest lamely. 'There was a train journey. Mother was telling us the story of the train journey when we were still in diapers.'

'It was exactly that. A story.'

'But what about the baby? The baby boy who couldn't survive such conditions? And the official who took the body away and wouldn't look at Grandma when she asked him to ensure there was a burial?'

'No truth in it at all.'

I watch Sasha as he forks food into his mouth energetically.

451

'How do you know this?' I ask at last.

'Papa confirmed to me shortly before his death that it was all a myth and I have every reason to believe him.'

'Oh, Sasha. Why would they construct such an elaborate lie?'

'They needed a narrative to lend structure to life's chaos and, in their case, perhaps to cover the unpalatable truth.'

'Was there ever really a brother?'

'Oh yes. There was a baby brother who died. And if you're hinting that the story was concocted around his death you're absolutely right.'

'So how did the baby really die?'

'Well, there *was* a train ride. But only from Moscow to Riga. Grandpa was indeed sent to Latvia to head a trade delegation and the family travelled there by train. But it took perhaps only thirty hours, stopping often, and it was no great hardship. The travellers were Grandpa, Grandma and the three girls. No brother. In Stalin's Russia even a valued member of the NKVD could not be sent away without some guarantee against defection. One family member had to be left behind. Grandpa invited Grandma to decide who this would be. She understood that he planned to flee from Riga and therefore that the child she left behind in Moscow, and the relatives taking care of that child (her brother and his wife), would be removed to labour camps and almost certain death. What a terrible decision. We can imagine her sleepless nights as she tried to select which child would go to its death. She finally elected to pawn her baby son for their freedom.'

'But what happened to him?'

'The brother's family and the baby all disappeared as anticipated. We don't know what happened to them. But we can guess all too easily.'

'So . . . Grandma effectively . . .' My throat is dry. My words scrape against it as I force them out. 'She effectively killed her son.'

Sasha looks at me and blinks.

'And the escape?' I ask.

'Soon after their arrival in Riga they boarded a fishing vessel. Their father had bribed the fisherman to take them to Sweden. This manoeuvre was not without its dangers but once they were across the Baltic they were free. They took a liner to America. Their escape involved little hardship. At least not to themselves.' Sasha produces a cigarette, which he lights, something he is not supposed to do anywhere in the apartment but his own room. He smokes slowly for a moment.

'A story,' he concludes, 'they were perhaps wise to conceal. But despite the fact that our sweet-faced old babushka effectively, as you suggested, murdered her son, her grief was no less, and may have been greater.'

I am silent.

'Oh, Lucia,' he pleads. 'Stop, please stop, feeling responsible for your son's death and start telling stories about it. Because it really doesn't matter if they are true or false. If you tell them often enough, the trauma will become more manageable.'

The heatwave is certainly ending. Not only is the air cooler at Daddy's house but it is more energetic.

Jane is at the hospital today, the geologists are back and Larry is helping them out in the barn. I work in the den all morning on my executor chores for Scott. I use Daddy's printer for the last batch of letters. Then I close every file and start to stack them in the boxes I found in the barn.

When I get to the oil royalties file, I pause and open it. In Daddy's financial life at least, loose ends have been tied. Except for this one.

I review the oil file's long history. Daddy started by keeping his Simms-Roeder income. Then, a few years later, he stopped collecting it and had it paid to the mysterious Marcello Trust. I try to calculate how old Ricky Marcello was when his family started to receive these payments. I was about seven. That means Ricky Marcello must have been a baby, or not quite born.

When I step onto the deck the view has a new clarity. There is no haze and no mist. There is even an intimation of the hills on the far side. The straight lines and right angles of the valley order my thoughts.

'Where are you going?' Larry asks when I tell him I have to go out.

Larry and the geologists have rigged up a temporary lighting system in the barn. It illuminates all the corners that have remained dark for so long. The three men sweat beneath the lamps, Larry and the bearded geologist on boxes and taking notes, and the tall geologist on the dusty floor, surrounded by rocks, wearing a magnifier across his face.

I answer Larry's question without precision. 'There's just one file I haven't been able to sort out,' I say. 'But I'm going to fix that now.'

When I get to the Joseph house, Ralph is in the garden. He greets me and the dogs wag their tails. Ralph is wearing overalls again today.

'Is Mrs Joseph home?'

'Sure.'

'I'm leaving California soon, I came to say goodbye.'

He does not move so I walk over to the house and ring the bell and then Ralph joins me at the door. We stand there together like a pair of Mormon missionaries, waiting while Mrs Joseph unlocks it.

'Hi, Lucy. Hi, Ralph,' says Mrs Joseph as though she is equally pleased and surprised to see us both.

The three of us go to the kitchen, the kitchen where Mrs Joseph and Barbara Marcello used to spend so much time. Robert and I could hear their voices and their laughter when we passed, on our way up to the bedroom or out to the hammock. Now Barbara Marcello smiles down on us from high on the dresser, her long hair escaping from the scarf that secures it. The picture suggests beauty and strength but the detail of her face is obscured by shadow.

'When did she die?' I ask, gesturing to the photo, as Mrs Joseph supplies us with cold drinks. She's cooking today and the baking trays spread across her work surface have been half filled by something that might be brownie mixture. The kitchen smells of chocolate.

'I guess it's two and a half, no, almost three years ago now,' says Mrs Joseph. 'Ovarian cancer. They thought they'd caught it in time. But they hadn't. Barbara was calm about it and she worked hard on those closest to her to help them accept that she was leaving them. The end was peaceful. Of course, we all miss her. I miss her every day.'

An unobtrusive death. Barbara Marcello was an unobtrusive woman. We sit in silence, sipping our drinks, while Mrs Joseph pours the brownie mixture from a bowl into the pans.

I say, 'Ricky isn't Ricky Marcello's real name. Do you know what his real name is?'

'I've always called him Ricky,' says Mrs Joseph.

'I saw on the sign outside the Marcello garage that it begins with an E. I think it's Eric.'

Mrs Joseph is busy with the brownies, Ralph with his drink.

I say, 'Who is his father?'

Mrs Joseph puts down the bowl. 'I guess Barbara didn't make a habit of telling people,' she says at last. She opens the oven, slides the brownies inside and closes it rapidly. Then she takes off her oven mitt and sits down. She looks open, receptive, but her brown eyes are concerned. 'Are you still worried by Ricky Marcello, Lucy? Please don't be.'

'Ricky's my friend,' Ralph assures me.

'I'm sure he doesn't want to hurt you,' adds Mrs Joseph.

I say, 'I think he's my brother.' And when I hear the words, I know they are true from the way the silent room receives them.

'Now just because they have the same first name, you can't conclude that they're father and son,' says Mrs Joseph carefully.

'Oh, there's a lot of other evidence. Daddy stopped taking his oil well royalties and started paying them into the Marcello Trust around the time Ricky was born. He taught Ricky to fix things and gave him the old tow truck. He came here with Barbara and when he was with her he was different, he was happy, he laughed. It was through Barbara he knew you, right? And when he used to leave me here . . . was he going on field trips? Or was he going to stay with Barbara and Ricky?'

Mrs Joseph sighs. 'Your face is red, Lucy. You look angry, hurt.'

I glare up at Barbara Marcello. Smiling, half in shadow. 'I thought I liked her,' I say bitterly. 'After the crash, before Jane got there, she was so nice to me. I didn't know she'd stolen my father and given him to Ricky.'

Ralph looks so miserable that for a moment I feel bad. He says, 'Aren't you pleased your father was happy?'

I want to cry with the pain but I'm too angry. 'Why did we have to get the lonely, sad Daddy? Why couldn't we have him happy too? It makes me feel I didn't know him at all.'

Mrs Joseph is compassionate. Her face droops as though she's about to cry for me. 'We never can know all of someone.'

'I didn't know he was a liar and a cheat. I thought he always tried to do the right thing. I respected him, I measured others by his standards.'

Ralph and Mrs Joseph are silent. I become aware of the trees shaking in the new breeze outside. Shrubs tap on the window as though they're trying to clamber through it. Then, quietly, Mrs Joseph starts to talk.

'Through no fault of her own, whatever a husband is entitled to expect in a wife—companion, helpmate, lover, homemaker, friend— your mother couldn't deliver. Your father met Barbara soon after your mother got sick and soon after that they had Ricky. The relationship continued until the end of Barbara's life. It was close and it was happy. They were like man and wife but most of the time they didn't live together and it worked for them.'

'But . . . he was our father! Jane's, mine!' I protest. 'How could he have another family at the same time?'

'He only saw them once a week, occasionally more. He'd have vacations with them when you were away at summer camp or staying here. Having them didn't make him love you less. He was a big-hearted man.'

'He was a big cheat,' I mutter.

'He needed support and kindness. He was coping with your mother and bringing up two daughters alone.'

There's a sniff in my voice. 'But it was such a betrayal. He kept one whole part of his life secret.'

'He didn't want your mother to know because it would have upset her so much. But when you were old enough not to tell her, I thought he could have explained it to you. But he chose not to do that.'

'He came to stay with me in New York . . .'

'Right after she died. It was a good vacation for him, Lucy.'

'But he didn't tell me. He was grieving and I didn't realise.'

Daddy in New York. A man staggering and smiling in the elevator.

'I guess he'd trained himself to hide his feelings. He was adamant, even when Barbara was dead, that the two sides of his life should never meet. And that was hard on Ricky because he knew about you and Jane. But he promised his father that he would have no contact, under any circumstances. I think that added to his feeling that you were Eric's first family and he and Barbara were way back in second place.'

I get up and stand at the window. 'Did Ricky know?' I sob. 'When I met him here as a kid? Did Robert know?'

'No one knew except for me. And Ralph, of course.'

'I know everything,' says Ralph shamelessly. 'I eavesdrop. But I don't tell what I hear.'

'When did Ricky find out?'

'Oh . . .' Mrs Joseph thinks. 'He was eighteen or so. Barbara wanted him to understand and she thought she could trust him with the information. She told him on the condition that he had no contact with you.'

He kept the bargain. Nobody could have tried harder to repulse me than Ricky. I say, 'I think he hates me.'

'I don't agree. It did take him a long time to come to terms with the situation. He was always a difficult boy. Barbara had a lot of trouble with him when he was an adolescent. But he's married to a lovely girl called Martha now and they have the sweetest baby.'

'Baby Jordan,' Ralph tells me helpfully.

'Martha converted the barn into a gallery and she's doing real well. Ricky has inherited his mother's land and some capital and he can always earn money fixing things because he has gifted hands. He paints well too. I like him now, very much. He's spent a lot of time here.'

Ricky Marcello. He stole my father and then he stole the Josephs. All the years I was exiled, he was feeding off their comradeship.

I feel an arm slip round me, tender but timid. It is Ralph. He has stood up and crossed the room without making a sound.

'Are you going to forgive him, Lucy?' he says.

I sniff. 'Maybe.'

I feel the arm disengage itself and, when I next turn round, Ralph has gone. Mrs Joseph is alone at the table. She is watching me.

'There's no reason to be jealous of Ricky,' she says.

'How can I not be? When they were together they were like a real family. Two parents who loved each other and their son. I'm jealous of that.'

'You had a lot of love too. Your mother may not always have known how to express it or even show it but she loves you.'

'Poor Mother,' I say softly. 'Poor, poor Mother.'

Mrs Joseph asks, 'Will you go and see her before you leave?'

A warmth spreads over me when I think of the tiny figure dropping a rose into Daddy's grave. She is a victim of circumstances and of her own passionate nature. She lost Daddy years ago to Barbara but not all of him. He continued to visit her, to support her and, who knows, maybe to love her. Now, apart from Jane and me, she is pitifully alone.

'Will you go?' asks Mrs Joseph.

I say, 'Yes.'

I plan to go to Redbush Clinic at the end of the afternoon. Before that I'll go to the beach house and before that to the San Strana Valley. I have a small gift for Ricky Marcello waiting back at Daddy's house.

The gift is lying right on the desk.

Larry appears at the door of the den. He looks hot and tired.

I tuck the file under my arm and pick up the folder of letters for Scott. 'I have to go out again.'

'Why?'

'The file that's been worrying me. I've found out where it belongs. Then I'm going to give some stuff to Scott. Then I'm going to say good-bye to Mother.'

'I've made you a sandwich. Aren't you going to eat it before you go?'

'OK, thanks.'

I follow him into the kitchen. He slides the sandwich towards me and pours us water.

'It's too hot in that barn now we have the lights,' he complains. 'I don't know how those guys stand it, it's worse than the heatwave.'

We talk about how the heatwave is ending, and the forecasters are predicting rain tomorrow. Then we fall silent.

'So where are you going with that file, Lucy?' Larry asks at last.

'To the San Strana Valley.'

'Who are you seeing there?'

I hadn't planned on telling anyone but Jane but I guess Larry has to know sooner or later. I say, 'My brother. My half-brother, to be precise.'

It's nice to shock Larry. He has trained himself to control his reactions but now he freezes, sandwich in his mouth, his eyes wide, and I enjoy my brief power over him. As I tell him about Daddy's other life my words are punctuated by his incredulity.

'And we never guessed. We never even suspected . . . Have you ever seen the guy? Have you met him?'

I do not plan to reveal any of my recent encounters with Ricky

Marcello. Not until I understand them better. I say, 'I might have glimpsed him at the cemetery when we were burying Daddy.'

'That's sad,' says Larry. 'Real sad. He should have been a leading participant at his father's funeral, not skulking around in the graveyard.'

For the first time it occurs to me that maybe Ricky hangs around Jane's apartment because he shares something of the Schaffers' loneliness. Suddenly he seems no longer threatening but an isolated figure, seeking sisters then running away from them when he gets too close.

I stand up to go. Larry says, 'I don't know how Jane is going to react to this news. I'd like to phone her right now.' Maybe Larry is hungry for the same power he gave me a few minutes ago, the power to shock.

When I get to San Strana the garage looks closed again but the Marcello Gallery is open. I pull in like a regular customer. There is a gravel parking lot near the barn, ringed by bright garden flowers.

The gallery has large, modern windows but the rough timber and high roof of a barn. Inside, the sun fills it. There is a woman working at a desk in one corner. She smiles when I walk in.

'Hi,' she says. 'Feel free to wander around.'

I recognise her as the woman who picked up the baby and held it over her head. And sure enough there is movement at her feet and a baby, fat and dribbling, emerges from under the desk.

'Oh, he won't bother you,' says the woman, following my stare. The baby crawls towards me. I back off. I haven't held a baby for three years.

The paintings are mostly big and bright. There are a couple by Barbara Marcello. They contain a hundred shades of green. When the woman sees me studying them she approaches me.

'Are you familiar with the work of Barbara Marcello?' she asks.

'No. But these are nice.'

'This is where Barbara Marcello lived and worked all her life, her family farmed in the San Strana Valley. I'm trying to turn this gallery into a showplace for her work, but'—she grimaces—'they sell too quickly.'

Another picture attracts me. When I've looked at it for long enough I realise the attraction is recognition. It shows the view from Daddy's house. The valley, the orchards, the intersection.

I point to it and the woman says, 'That's by her son, Eric Marcello. You can see there's a similarity of style.'

'Is he here?' I ask.

She looks at me uncertainly. 'You want to meet Ricky?'

'I've already met him a few times.'

The baby approaches and tries to pull himself to his feet on the long skirt of his mother. She stoops and picks him up.

'What's your name?' she asks me as the baby curves against her, the way babies do, tucking its head into her shoulder.

'Lucy Schaffer.'

Her face has the beauty of perfect symmetry but I see it harden against me. She sighs. 'Why did you come here?'

'I have to talk to him. There are a lot of questions he can answer.'

'You don't need them answered. Go back to New York.'

The gallery door opens with a squeak and Ricky walks in. When he sees me he glares and lingers in the doorway.

'I thought I recognised your car. Would you just get the hell out of here?' He is aggressive but his tone is milder today, maybe because he has noticed the baby clinging nervously to its mother.

I hold out a thick green file. 'I'm leaving California. I brought you something you wanted.'

He takes it gingerly.

'It's Daddy's oil royalties. That's what you were looking for, right? You want it, so here it is.'

He glances at the file but only for a moment. His stare is fixed on me.

I say, 'I know you're my brother.'

The silence that falls in the room is penetrating. Eventually Ricky looks at the woman for guidance but she turns away from him. The baby holds out his hands and whines for his father. Ricky takes him, tenderly, into his arms. Satisfied, the baby smiles at me broadly.

'Listen,' says Ricky. 'Dad didn't ever tell you about us. That's because he didn't want you to know. And he made me promise never to make contact. I like to keep my goddamn promises but God knows he didn't tell me what to do if you kept sneaking around here.'

'You kept your promise as well as you could,' I say. 'Now you have to let me in.'

He looks to the woman again but she has turned her back and walked right away from us, shaking her head a little. She sits down at the desk and tries to look busy. A car pulls into the lot outside.

'You'd better come into the house,' he instructs me brusquely, and, with the baby still in his arms, walks into the house.

I recognise the disorder of the kitchen right away. Baby mess. Toys on the floor, drawers open, food all around the highchair, bottles, crusts.

'Here, Jordan,' says Ricky, putting the baby down on the floor amid his toys. Jordan ignores the toys and starts to examine a shoe. I peer at him jealously. Daddy's second grandson. I hope Daddy didn't love him more than he loved his first.

Ricky is busy in one corner. He still doesn't say anything. When he turns round I see he has made us both coffee. He pushes mine across the table to me and gestures for me to sit down.

'It's OK, it doesn't have arsenic in it,' he says. He sits back and almost smiles. 'The police interviewed me last week.'

'How did they know about you?'

'My fingerprints were all over Dad's house. And you have to give your prints to get your tow truck certificate. When that patrolman said he saw Dad in the tow truck he pretty well led them right to me.'

'They knew all about you?'

'Yup. And they knew I was there Sunday afternoon and that you were there too. I told them everything.'

I redden.

'So,' he says, stretching his long body. 'So, who told you about me?'

'I worked it out. You were right to go looking for that file; it was the only link between us. It showed that, around about the time you were born, Daddy stopped receiving his oil royalties from Simms-Roeder. When I was tracing them, I found you.'

He reaches for the file. He opens it and pulls out one sheet at random. 'Simms-Roeder put me through college and a lot else besides.'

'You probably hated us,' I say. 'I mean, Jane and me.'

'Yes,' he agrees amicably. 'When I learned that you were Dad's first family and that he'd fitted us in around your glee club gatherings and your summer camp, yes, I guess I hated you for that.' He pauses. 'But, I had this terrific mother and yours was locked-up crazy. So I think I didn't draw such a bad ticket in the big raffle.'

He is relaxed. His tone is lazy. I watch my coffee. I am irritated that he has access to my family history without any of its burdens.

When Ricky speaks again, his voice is kinder. 'I guess it was real tough on you having that kind of a mom. When did she go crazy?'

'Right after her baby died. I was four.'

Jordan crawls over to Ricky and he bends down and strokes his son's hair. Something in the gesture touches me. He looks up, waiting for me to say more.

'I was in a canyon in Arizona. Daddy and Jane and I went into the canyon to look for rocks and as usual Daddy got way ahead. I fell and hurt my arm and Jane went on to get help and eventually I made my own way out and there they were, Mother and Daddy and Jane, standing on the hot blacktop. And Mother was yelling. Crazy yelling.'

I try to remember her words. I close my eyes and I'm stumbling towards the canyon's mouth, my arm throbbing, and there's a voice, so loud and high-pitched that it seems to have been drawn from the fierceness of the sun. I look for her words. I try to intercept them but they escape.

'You mean . . . that was it?' Ricky asks. 'Just that?'

'I don't remember what she was saying. But the tone of her voice wasn't like any tone I'd heard before.'

Ricky rearranges himself a little. 'So, you went into this canyon and she was OK. And you came out and she was insane?'

'That's the way it seemed to me.'

'Something must have happened.'

'Her baby had died just a few weeks earlier. I guess her grief must have reached boiling point right out there in the sun.'

He shook his head. 'Sounds to me like something must have happened while you were in that canyon.'

He pushes some dirty plates out of the way so he can put his elbows on the table and cup his chin in one hand. He smiles suddenly, a lop-sided smile that seems to appear right out of his fingers.

'Well, at least we both had a great dad.'

I look into Ricky's dark green eyes. They are the same colour as my own.

'Why were you shouting at him?' I ask. 'That day I watched you?'

He sighs. 'I've regretted it every day since. I wasn't shouting, but I probably came on too strong. I was telling him it was time to leave that big mean old house up there on the hill and come and live with us. He could have had one whole part of the house here to himself and I'd have known he was safe. But no. He was too goddamn stubborn.'

'Safe? Did you think he was in danger?'

'Yeah, from daughters who sneak around his house.'

I stumble through an unsatisfactory explanation. He listens and then says, 'That the last time you saw him?'

I nod sadly.

'I last saw him when they brought back the tow truck late on Sunday night,' Ricky tells me. 'I know you know about that. They didn't mean to disturb us but I heard them so I went to see how they got along. They were agitated because they'd nearly been picked up by Highway Patrol.'

'How was Daddy?'

'Oh . . . very tired. He'd been driving the truck and had his licence checked and stuff. And . . . he was sort of sad.'

'Sad?'

Ricky speaks quietly now. 'Like he knew what might be coming. I mean, when I said good night, he walked up to me and . . .'

I stare at him. His voice has stopped as though it just ran right off the road. His face creases. He looks down at Jordan and suddenly sweeps him onto his lap, hugging him, placing the baby between himself and his grief. The child curls against his father's body but he cannot hide his father's tears. 'He hugged me and he said goodbye. Not good night. Goodbye. Like I wouldn't see him again . . .'

Ricky is crying hard now and the baby doesn't like it. He wriggles to get away. I stand up and, reluctantly, offer my arms to the squirming Jordan. He reaches out for me and I lift him. A baby, fitting its body to my arm, looking up into my eyes, stretching its fingers to my face. I feel an intense pleasure and an intense pain. I kneel down and put my other arm round Ricky. He is, after all, my brother.

'Oh no,' says a voice. Martha is frozen in the doorway. 'No,' she says. 'No, no, this is not allowed to happen.'

We all look at her and Jordan reaches for her. She walks right over and removes him firmly from my arm. I take a step back from Ricky.

'It's OK,' he tells Martha. 'She already knew everything.'

'So what? C'mon, Ricky, you gave your dad your word. No contact. Looks to me as though there's a whole lot of contact going on here.'

'Martha, she's my sister. Dad's dead now and—'

'You promised,' she says. 'He wouldn't have made you promise if he didn't have a good reason.' They stare at each other stormily.

Martha turns to me. 'Why do you have to keep coming here like this?'

'If you found you had a brother, wouldn't you want to know him?'

'You didn't need him before. You don't need him now.'

But, despite his hostility, despite everything, it seems to me that I've waited for Ricky all my life. The brother I loved was taken away from me as a tiny baby and now it feels that he's come back as this big, dark, angry stranger.

'You've made a mistake,' Martha says, returning to the gallery with Jordan under her arm. 'Your father didn't want his two families ever to know each other because he knew something bad would happen.'

'What can happen?' I ask her, but she swayed through the door and slammed it shut behind her.

'Why didn't Daddy want us to meet?' I ask Ricky. 'Why? Did he ever give you a reason?'

He shakes his head. 'Martha will come round, I guess. She can take a while to get used to things.'

I say, 'I have to go now. I have to meet Scott and then get to Mother's clinic. They don't allow late visitors.'

When we go outside, the house looks pretty. A house and a barn, Daddy's other house, his other barn. The warm, bright side of his life.

Standing by my car, Ricky asks, 'Well, are we going to meet again?'

I look at him. 'Do you want to?'

'Lucy, I'm kind of relieved. I think this may just be one of the good things to come out of Dad's death.'

And to my amazement he suddenly puts his long arms round me and hugs me to him, this stranger who is my brother.

Eight

A WIND FROM THE OCEAN is blowing Scott's hair around and he is looking out from the porch through binoculars. The wind feels so cold that Scott has given me an immense sweatshirt. Here on the coast, March is back.

'It could be a whale-watching boat,' Scott reports. 'The migration might have started.'

Apart from the funeral I haven't seen Scott much recently. I suspect that Brigitte is home from France. I hope she doesn't arrive while I'm here.

I place the big folder right in front of him. He picks it up.

'Is this executor stuff?'

'It's everything. Finished. Death certificate duplicated and enclosed where necessary. All you have to do is sign the letters and put them in the envelopes and get them to a mailbox. They even have stamps on.'

'Oh jeez, Luce . . .' He flicks through the papers. 'I don't know how to thank you . . .' He leans across the wooden table and kisses me. Not a long kiss, but long enough to show that, at the very least, he's grateful.

'When's your flight?' he asks.

'Tomorrow, three o'clock.'

'Can I come to the airport?'

'OK, but you may see me again soon anyway. I'm thinking of moving back to California.'

For a fraction of a second, I detect something like shock on his face. I wonder if things have already progressed too far with Brigitte for Scott to feel the State of California is also big enough for me. Then he recovers and smiles and there is genuine pleasure in his smile.

He reaches for my hand. 'That's terrific,' he says. 'How come?'

'Now Daddy's dead, maybe Mother needs me,' I say. 'And my family's here. Stevie's buried here. There are a lot of reasons to come back.'

'Luce . . .'

The wind has blown some colour into his cheeks. Or maybe he's embarrassed. I wait for him to speak then realise he's waiting for me. He presses my hand tighter. Beyond us the waves crash against the shore. When I stand to go the wind almost buffets me back down.

'I have to get to Redbush now so I can say goodbye to Mother.'

He releases my hand. We walk to the steps together.

'Lucy, the police don't seem to have any answers. I'm not sure we'll ever know what really happened to Eric. Can you live with that?'

Not knowing. I remember how, when Sasha and I arrived at Daddy's house that night, I relished my last few moments of not knowing.

I say, 'Sometimes it's better not to know. And in the last couple of weeks, so many other things have been resolved.'

He halts suddenly and, holding my shoulders, revolves my body so we're facing each other. 'You look good, Luce. You look terrific. So alive.'

I smile at him. 'I'm just beginning to feel good, Scott.'

Mother's big, smiling nurse is waiting for me in the conservatory at Redbush. As we walk down the hallway he says, 'I'm real glad you're back for another try. I didn't think you would be after the last time. I'm sorry you saw her mean side. She can be that way with your sister. I couldn't believe she did it to you when she hadn't seen you in so long.'

'Jane says Mother mostly doesn't know her.'

The nurse laughs. 'Oh, she knows Jane, that's for sure.'

He stops at Mother's door. My hands feel clammy. When I walk into the room I search for Mother's tiny body amid the ornate drapery, the cushions, the plush chairs.

'Wait and I'll get her. Her class is just over.'

'What class?'

'Ceramics. It finished five minutes ago.'

There is a blue felt folder lying on the bed, worn at the corners. When the nurse leaves I glance out of the window to make sure no one is watching me. Then I open it. The folder is full of photographs. Baby Nicholas. Me. Daddy. Grandma, the aunts. Me again. Daddy and me. Another baby, probably Nicky again. Me, gazing rapturously at Nicky in his cradle. Daddy standing outside the house. Along with the photographs are postcards, with my writing on the back. Postcards with abstract blues, a brown dog, felt-booted peasants in old Russia. Every postcard I have ever sent Mother is here, dogeared with use.

At the back of the folder there is one more picture. A class picture, three rows of smiling kids. *Cornington School, Second Grade*, says the small blackboard the teacher holds. First I see Lindy, blonde, pretty, and, next to her, me. I am smiling at the camera and cradling one arm against my body. It is encased in plaster. I look closer. I was six when I went into second grade. But I know I broke my arm years earlier, in the canyon in Arizona, because we took that trip right after my brother died and I was four then, I'm certain of that. I stare at the plaster arm in the picture, trying to persuade myself it is a white sleeve or paper, or even a joke. But the way I cradle it, protectively, is unmistakable.

I hear voices in the hallway. I rapidly replace the picture and close the folder. The door opens to reveal Mother, her arm in the nurse's. Today she wears glasses. Their severe frames make her seem less vacant.

I walk right over to her. I say, very softly, 'Hi, Mother, it's Lucy.'

'Lucy.' She reaches out and there is a small, warm tug at my hand. Carefully, gently, she embraces me. I submit to her maternal caress and the moment has a strange, isolated sweetness of its own.

'I guess I'll leave you two,' says the nurse. 'I'll leave you two right now.' I hear the door thud shut softly behind him.

I say, 'Mother, I've remembered a song. A song you used to sing me when I was little . . .'

She waits. She looks apprehensive. I hope the song will be there when I need it. I reach inside my memory to that strange, elusive place where music is stored. A few broken bars of the nursery song float out. I hum them and Mother's face breaks into a smile and her eyes shine. Then she picks up the tune from me and, uncertain at first, she begins to sing. I close my eyes while, holding both my hands, she sings gently. When we reach the closing bars, we both make birds with our hands and they fly away. We look at each other smiling, delighted.

I say, 'Mother, I want to talk to you about my baby. About Stevie and how he died. Just lately I've started telling about it a little but I want to talk to you, because you'll understand better than anyone.'

We go over to the window and sit down. Mother looks at me, waiting for me to speak, and I see her mind is fully engaged. There is clay in her hair, clinging to some of the strands.

I tell her how Stevie used to cry and cry. 'Each yell seemed to eat a little bit of me away. His unhappiness was my unhappiness. I loved him so much, but his demands, his dissatisfaction made me some other woman and, God knows, that woman wanted to smother him often enough. I just wanted him to stop. When he died, it felt inevitable. I had silenced him so many times in my head that I knew it must be my fault.'

I am crying now and Mother reaches out and wraps my fingers in her two small hands. When I look up, I see that she is crying too.

465

She says, 'It was my fault.'

I stare at her. I assess her eyes for knowledge, for coherence. She looks right back at me, tears falling, no longer silently but accompanied by a high-pitched wail I remember in my dreams. 'She did it again! It's my fault she did it again!'

I am alone in a sizzling landscape of towering red rocks and sun-baked earth. I am approaching the mouth of the canyon, my arm throbs and I hear a shrieking that at first I think is some angry desert bird. Then I know it is a woman and I know the woman is my mother. I listen and her words reverberate through the canyon. 'It's my fault, she did it again! She did it again! Oh God, she did it again!'

I say, 'Who did it again? Who?'

Mother holds my hand tightly, staring at me, waiting for me to know.

We were in Arizona two years, not two weeks after Nicky died. Jane and I went into the canyon. And Jane came out alone. That's when Mother started to yell. That's when her misery took her through the membrane between unhappiness and psychosis. That's why they all stopped and stared when I appeared, but it was too late for Mother. She believed Jane had done it again.

'Jane,' I say. Softly. Then louder. 'Jane.'

And Mother's whole body twists with distress.

'Jane,' I say. 'Jane killed Nicky.' The words come out so easily, I wonder how it is that they've been choking me since I was four years old.

I sit outside by the parking lot where I sat with Sasha and the aunts, staring out across the expanse of unnatural green lawn. When the nurse came in and Mother couldn't stop crying he told me I should go. Mother clung to me tightly and then planted a small, sad kiss on my forehead. I promised her I would come back soon.

Scott's sweatshirt is so big I can put my knees up inside it and hug them to me, but the new coolness in the air cuts through my clothes as though I'm naked. But I don't care. I don't care that I'm cold. I want to be colder still, until I'm completely anaesthetised.

The dead baby was wrapped in a blanket in Daddy's arms. Mother emitted high-pitched wails. Jane stood next to them, her face white. There was no remorse. Daddy went to the porch. He was carrying the unmoving shape inside the blanket that was Nicky. He was going down the steps to bury him. He was going to the sunken garden.

Rougemont said, when we were by the grave, that it's easy to confuse what actually happened with things you've been told. Maybe there never even was a Nickel Dog.

Mother and Daddy had decided not to tell anyone what Jane had done. Their beautiful, clever daughter, it was almost impossible that she would kill her brother, inconceivable that she would commit such a crime again. They foolishly, lovingly, fatally, protected Jane.

It was a secret. Maybe Rougemont guessed but nobody else knew how Nicky really died. Except for Lindy Zacarro. When Daddy left the house carrying the small body in the blanket, I ran. I stumbled through the yard, in and out of trees, round pungent bushes, until I reached the den we'd made under some branches. Inside was Lindy.

With Lindy, it wasn't so easy to disguise the facts by creating family mythologies about dead dogs. No, Lindy knew, and it seems to me now that as we grew older her knowledge turned acidic inside her.

I think of her curled in the trunk of the car, her blonde hair wet with sweat, her fingernails scratched right off her hands. I twist my whole body to avoid the thought but now Mother is emerging from the Zacarro house, hands fluttering like trapped birds. There is horror on her face.

Faces round the blue crib, contorted with horror. Stevie's body, motionless. Jane's eyes burning in her face. Daddy's eyes, full, brimming, slowly sliding off me. Off me and onto Jane, at my side. Daddy stared at her. He knew. She's done it again. She's done it again. His tears, his roar. 'The police! What do the goddamn police have to do with anything?'

I moan softly. I can hardly breathe for pain. I can hardly breathe for wanting to feel Stevie's soft body push itself up against me again. My howl seems to rip the green lawn like paper. I hear someone crying Stevie's name over and over, then muttering it. That person is me. I am powerless to silence her. Tears without end, grief without limit.

It's my fault, she's done it again.

I leap up from the bench as though it's on fire, and I run to my car. I drive fast. I break speed limits, weave through traffic, irritate truck drivers. Along the freeway, through Lowis, past fruit stalls, past farmsteads.

The Marcello Gallery, the house, the flowers, the trees all slumber. Out of the wind, everything here is still. Inside the barn I see Martha look up from her desk as the gravel protests beneath my car tyres. I park right outside, blocking the drive, and jump out. I fling open the door.

Martha isn't pleased to see me. She stands and puts her hands on her hips with a deliberate slowness, silently demanding an explanation.

'Where's Ricky?' I ask.

'Out.'

'Where?'

She starts her spiel about how Daddy didn't want us to have this kind of contact and I interrupt her.

'He was right, Martha, Daddy was right. I have to warn Ricky.'

She raises her eyebrows but her face does not soften.

'I think he's in danger. It's my fault. Please, please, where is he?'

She studies my face and sighs. 'He's taken Jordan to Tigertail Bay.'

'Tigertail?'

'Whale-watching. A woman called Joni something called. She used to work for Eric.'

'Joni? Joni Rimbaldi called you guys?'

'You know her?'

'She was Daddy's secretary for years and years.'

'Ricky recognised her name. She said that Eric told her all about us. Apparently he gave her some kind of folder with Jordan's name on it.'

I remember Joni at Daddy's funeral, worrying that her jacket was too bright. Was she nursing Daddy's secret all the time she spoke to me?

'She asked Ricky to go and collect the folder. She said to take Jordan because she lives by Tigertail and there's a load of whales around the bay there now. She's meeting them in a parking lot so they can watch.'

My heart thuds.

'Did Daddy ever say he told Joni? Did he ever say?'

The barn's high roof echoes. Before it has finished echoing I've remembered my conversation with Joni at the funeral. I've remembered that Joni's in Maine. She's not at Tigertail Bay. There are no whales.

I don't even say goodbye or thanks to Martha. I'm back in my car within seconds and I'm reversing into the Cooper Road and then I'm driving again, driving with the breathlessness and energy of a runner. Behind me once more, shocked faces, angry gestures, honking horns.

It seems a long way to Tigertail and as I roar along the road to the coast I feel the exhaustion and relief of a hunter who nears his quarry. I can see the rocks of the bay long before I can see the ocean. Then the Pacific is suddenly revealed as though it just blinked open one icy eye.

I drive between the clifftop parking lots looking for the tow truck, the blue car with the white bandage, any car at all with Ricky and Jordan inside it. I drive from lot to lot. I see a few cars, a couple of pick-ups, but no tow truck. No Ricky. No Jordan. No tow truck.

Defeated, I park facing the sea. No whales either, but I was already sure of that. I watch the restless water throwing itself against the rocks, flinging spray into the air. There is no beauty in the scene before me. Watching the water's ceaseless battle with the rocks, I am overcome by fatigue. I feel tears sting at my eyes. I realise I wasn't looking for Ricky or Jordan here, I was looking for Jane. It is her absence that now shows me where I must go and exactly what I must do.

By the time I reach Daddy's house the sun is easing itself behind the hillside. Night is already concentrating the air.

The big barn door swings open with a squeak. I wait for my eyes to accustom themselves to the dark then flick the old metal light switch. Avoiding the geologists' lamps I select a pickaxe and a shovel. I carry them along the winding paths that lead to the sunken garden.

I crouch down at the heart of the garden to examine the rocks I must remove. First Daddy's headstone, which I walk away on its corners. Remember death. Then I begin to work on the big, round rocks beneath it. They are set in dirt, not concrete, and they offer little resistance to the point of the pick. I lift them and stack them under a eucalyptus.

I shovel aside the first sandy layer and loosen the impacted earth beneath it with the pickaxe. I continue until I hit a rock. The shriek of metal on stone sounds angry and sparks fly. I shovel out the dirt I have loosened, then I jump into the hole to clear more loose dirt and some jagged, rotten pieces of wood along with it. I have pulled most of the wood free when I realise it is an indication that I am about to find what I am looking for. Some kind of a box.

Below me there is the sound of an engine and lights pick their way along the dirt road. I crouch, still and silent, until the car has passed.

I scrape with my hands now as well as the shovel. There are more pieces of wood and then my shovel taps against something that does not sound like rock or wood or dirt. It has a soft resonance of its own.

I peer into the dark hole and crouch to inspect the mottled object. It looks like old, dirty china and, ridiculously, I want it to be a doll or a small bowl but I know from its particular roundness that it is a skull.

I do not touch my find but gouge at the dirt around it. I dig fast. Nausea starts in my belly and then spreads to the rest of my body. Small balls of sweat catapult across my flesh. When I have uncovered about half of the skeleton I pause in the dim light to look at it.

The bones are not a dog's bones because there never was a dog. They are those of a tiny child. It lies preserved in small perfection.

I can feel the force of my sobs but I can't hear them. I remove the rest of the dirt to see the child in its entirety. Then I reach down and gently brush the last, loose covering of earth from the bones with the same care that I would turn back a baby's blanket.

A tiny rib cage, slender feet, the hands, curled slightly, the finger joints clogged with dirt. A boy, a small dead baby boy, laid in its grave by my father. It is my brother. It is Nicky.

Wearily I sit down on the edge of the sunken garden and listen to the approaching car. I hear it turn into the drive and park outside the barn.

Nothing surprises me now, nothing frightens me. I wait quietly in the dark. I hear the car door. The front door. The slam of the screen door. Silence. The screen door again. Silence. Finally footsteps.

I am a butterfly pinned to a card by the fierce beam of Jane's flashlight. It shines first on me and then on the pile of stones and then down into the hole I have dug and it ends on the tiny skeleton lying there.

Her voice is strange. It is cold. 'Luce,' she says. 'Oh, Luce.' Her use of my name is eloquent. Sadness, disappointment.

I say, 'It's all been inevitable, ever since Daddy died. Everything that's happened has been like those little toy soldiers we used to play with, the sort you stand in a line. You push one and then they all fall down.'

'We never had any toy soldiers,' she says.

'Then maybe someone else did.'

The flashlight is on me again. I am shivering. I want Jane to come out from behind her light.

'OK, Luce,' she says, 'it's time to go.'

We pick our way along the narrow paths and when we reach the drive, instead of turning up to the house, Jane steers me down towards the dirt road.

'Where are we going, Jane?' I ask. My tone is conversational. The answer doesn't much interest me.

'Swimming. At Joe Zacarro's.'

I am weak after my efforts in the grave and I stumble up the Zacarro drive, leaning heavily on Jane. She pulls me through the side gate and I can see the pool, looking like a black rectangle of polished obsidian.

She sits me down at the edge of the water and shows me something, a small black box.

'Are you OK, Luce?' she asks kindly.

'Yes. Thank you, Jane.'

'I hope this doesn't hurt too much. It wasn't clear from the literature.'

'I guess it's my turn.'

'It's been your turn a lot of times before but you always came bouncing back.'

'Yes, when you pushed me in the canyon all I did was break an arm. And in the swimming pool Mother jumped right in and saved me.'

'There were other times, too. But after Nicky went, Mother guarded you like a jewel. She hardly let you out of her sight.' Jane sighs. 'It hasn't been easy for me, Luce. You know this, I'm a very special person.'

'Oh yes,' I agree. 'You've always been very special to me.'

'Mother and Daddy understood that. They handled me with care. They worked hard to give me the right kind of encouragement, the right environment where I could flourish. Then it all changed when you came along. They were besotted with you.'

Jane's face curls in disgust. I've never seen her look this way.

'Then there was Nicky. It was too much. When he started sitting up and grabbing things and making sounds I knew it was time to stop. I've never regretted it. I just regret what I found out today. That Daddy betrayed me. He went off and adored some baby in secret and now the baby's grown and has his own baby. I wish I could have dealt with them today.'

'You pretended to be Joni Rimbaldi,' I tell her tonelessly. 'But when you got to Tigertail Bay you must have backed off.'

'Police in the parking lots. No uniforms but you can tell anyway.' She shrugs. 'I'll try some other time.'

I shiver.

'Are you cold, Luce?' she asks, looking at me, sounding concerned.

'Just a little.'

'I can help you with that.' She leans over and picks up the box.

'Lindy knew what happened to Nicky,' I whisper.

Jane smiles. 'She wasn't bright. I mean, it was almost too easy to tell her I knew this great hiding place.'

I am shaking now. 'Jane . . . I wish you hadn't hurt Stevie.'

'Oh, but I didn't hurt him. I just helped him to go. He really didn't suffer. He hardly struggled.'

'Did Daddy struggle?'

'No, he knew it had to happen and he sort of accepted it. I warned him he was spending too much time with those ridiculous old men . . .'

'You mean Joe Zacarro? And Mr Holler?'

'He was talking to them too much. I didn't like to think what he might say. I warned Daddy and he didn't listen but he wasn't surprised when I said it was time for him to go. He didn't struggle. Like you. Maybe he knew how nice it would be. I hope it's nice for you, Luce.'

She touches my neck with the box and pain explodes through my body like a bolt of lightning, a pain that blinds thought, a pain that cancels movement. There are sparks before my eyes. I topple backwards but Jane catches me before my head hits the paving.

'We don't want any bruises.' She lays me flat at the poolside. I can't move. I can't speak. I can see Jane only through a veil of sparks.

'I've tried to make life better for you. I've tried to look after you. You're not a strong person. You're ordinary. I know how hard it's been for you. Now I'm going to set you free from all the things that worry you. Those deals in New York you kid yourself are so important. That crazy mother of ours, hissing and snarling and yelling. Scott's reproaches. Larry's put-downs. Clingy Russians. All the sadness, Luce. And so many losses. From when we're tiny, life just feels like a series of blows and losses, isn't that right? It's thanks to me Stevie was spared all that. I'm sure that deep down you're grateful, Luce. You've been through it all once yourself; you didn't want to suffer watching him go through it too. All the things you thought mattered so much, I'm going to release you from them now. I think it will feel real good.'

Above us I see the stars. My short life span is insignificant in their universe, too small even to be measured.

'I'll be real sad when you're gone, the way I was real sad when Daddy went and Stevie and Nicky. But, Luce, I want you to know that, more than any of them, I love you.'

I'd like to thank her but my mouth won't open and anyway, my body is already plunging through the air. She has thrown me so forcefully that I feel my arms and legs scatter like a doll's. I hear an immense splash and then I am enveloped by cold water. I sink to the bottom of the pool, water fills my nose and mouth and ears and I wait to experience death.

Nine

I AM LYING ON A COUCH, wrapped in some kind of a robe, covered in a blanket. I don't move. I don't open my eyes. I listen to the voices. There are a few muttering softly nearby, but outside the voices are loud, mostly male, and sometimes they call to each other.

I open my eyes to admit a slither of light. The colours change constantly. Red, blue and then white. I open my eyes a little more.

'Lucy . . .' says someone. 'Lucy, you're opening your eyes.'

Adam Holler. I recognise the way he speaks, but he's invisible. If I moved my head I could probably see him but I don't want to move.

'Thanks, Mr Holler, I'd like to talk to her if she's receptive now,' says someone else. A woman, young, her voice even.

'It's Kirsty.' She moves into my line of vision and leans over me and her brown eyes search mine. She says, 'The paramedics are pretty sure they don't need to take you in to hospital. They're just waiting for a doctor to confirm that.'

I look at her without curiosity.

'Do you know what happened?' she asks.

I blink.

'Do you understand what happened?' she repeats, a little louder.

I make an enormous effort to speak. This isn't easy. Something's been clawing at the inside of my throat. I make an odd, strangled noise.

'OK,' she says. 'I realise it's hard for you.'

I try again. I'm trying to tell her that Jane will be here soon but the words sound like a braying donkey. She furrows her brow with incomprehension and then I try once more and this time the strange, cracking noises that come from my throat approximate to words. She looks up and I know she is looking at someone. Adam Holler? Or is there a third, silent person in the room?

'I guess,' she says sadly, 'you don't recall why you're here.'

'Sure,' I say. She waits while I croak slowly, 'It was my turn to die. Jane was helping me.'

She glances again at the silent person.

I explain, 'Nicky, Lindy Zacarro, my Stevie, Daddy . . . of course it had to be my turn.'

'You knew?' says another voice. Reedy, unmistakable. 'Lucy, you knew about your sister all along? And you pretended you didn't?'

'No, Mr Rougemont.' I wish he'd move closer so I can see him. Obligingly, he moves into view and I feel a surprising rush of affection for this shadow of a man. I say, 'I finally worked it out, too late. Then I realised that I'd known it all along.'

'I guess I knew it all along too,' he says sadly, 'but we couldn't do a damn thing about it. Except keep watching her until she tried again.'

'Where is Jane?' I feel a sudden rush of concern for her.

Rougemont's voice sounds strained. 'They've taken her now, Lucy.'

I don't like the way he says that. I don't like the finality of it.

'Taken her where? Mr Rougemont, she's a very special person . . .'

His grey eyes study me but he does not reply. There is a voice at the door. Kirsty disappears and Rougemont straightens with difficulty. There is a whispered discussion in some other part of the room. I hear cars backing and turning in the drive. The coloured lights disappear suddenly. A shout. More voices, loud, female, heavily accented. My Russian aunts, speaking simultaneously. With them are Sasha and Scott, sounding reasonable but persistent. Joe Zacarro roars, 'It's my house! It was my goddamn pool! I've been real cooperative with you guys, and now you won't even let me into my own porch. I mean, I'll only take a quick peek at her and say hi, that's all.' His voice is drowned by a crescendo of aunts.

I smile and close my eyes. I feel as though someone just threw an extra blanket over me.

When I next look around, Adam Holler is standing right by me.

'Lucy,' he whispers, leaning as far towards me as his stiff back will allow. 'Will you tell me? How did it feel to die?'

I whisper back. 'Did I die?'

'Sure. The police officer brought you back, don't you remember? You were dead, Lucy. Probably for a minute. How did it feel?'

I sigh. His pale skin pinkens a little.

He says, 'Lucy, do you remember Jim Bob?' The boy's name seems to leap out of him, a name thought of but perhaps unspoken for years.

I say, 'Sure I do.' A child's death and an unnatural one right in the next house. But Jim Bob's was not a death caused by Jane but by someone who loved him and has suffered every day since.

'Oh, Mr Holler, you want to know what he felt when he died. Right?'

I see tears at the corner of his eyes.

'I can put your mind at rest,' I tell him with enthusiasm. 'Don't torture yourself over it any more. Jim Bob didn't suffer, not one bit.'

When I hear him shuffle out there is a voice I don't recognise too close to my ear.

'You did good there, Lucy, real good.'

I struggle to see its owner.

'Hi, sis,' says Ricky Marcello. 'I sneaked in through the kitchen.'

'You're sure good at sneaking,' I tell him petulantly.

'Runs in the family.' He smiles broadly.

'What are you doing here? Have you been helping the police?'

'Only today. There was a whole crowd of us hoping to watch whales with her.' His face falls. 'Maybe too many because she backed off. Before today I thought I was the only one worrying about you.'

Ricky's blue car, sliding down the freeway at nightfall, waiting outside Jane's apartment.

'You didn't even know me. You hated me.'

'Not really true. And . . .' Ricky grins. Fleetingly, eerily, he looks like Daddy. 'And Dad loved you. So I knew I had to take care of you.'

'You were taking care of me?'

'Listen, you're my goddamn sister.'

The door opens and for a few moments the voices outside get louder.

'I'm going, I'm going,' says Ricky. 'I was just passin' through.'

The door closes again. Someone says, 'What a bunch! Are they press?'

'Relatives.'

'Well, they sure want to get in here.'

He introduces himself. He says he is a doctor and then asks me the name of the President of the United States.

I hear myself laugh, a strange, clear sound like a bell. I name the President and then tell the doctor, 'I'm thinking coherently. Probably more coherently than usual.'

Back at Aunt Zina's I sleep a lot. I am astonished at my ability to fall asleep as soon as I feel tired, sometimes right after I have woken or even while Aunt Zina is talking to me. The sleep is peaceful as pale light.

'What's the matter with me?' I say incredulously when I wake up again in one of Aunt Zina's armchairs and see her at my side.

'You are making up for lost sleep. Not the sleep of days or weeks but the sleep of years,' she tells me wisely.

I can drive but mostly Scott chauffeurs me. I know Brigitte is back and I expect him to say one day that he's busy and he can't come but he shows up frequently, his face anxious, watching me.

We visit Ricky in San Strana a couple of times. We sit on the porch drinking beers and trying to catch up on all the missing years. Sometimes we play with the baby. Scott likes Ricky and buys his painting of the view across the valley from Daddy's house.

Looking hard at it, I say, 'OK. I guess I'm ready to go there now.'

We climb up the steps to the porch and unlock the door and I stand on the threshold sniffing the smell of the place before I walk right in.

It is hot here. Although the faux summer is over, the house retains its residue like someone anxious not to lose their suntan.

'What are you going to do about it all?' asks Scott, gesturing at the clutter. Larry and Jane started the upheaval but everything is still here.

'I'm going to sort it out. I'll clear it. Then I'll sell the house.'

'I thought you seemed a little offended that Jane and Larry were doing it so soon after Eric's death. I got the impression you didn't want to help.'

'I don't feel that way any more. Now I want to do it myself. I'm coming back to California so I can deal with it.'

He stares at me. 'You're really coming back? You've decided?'

'I'm not running away any more, Scott.'

We have a small ceremony for Nicky. His remains are buried near Stevie's. Joe Zacarro and Adam Holler ask to come and they lean on each other weeping. I understand that they are crying for their own children as Scott and I cry for Stevie. Everyone has someone to cry for. Only Mother cries for Nicky. We stand looking down at his casket, our arms round one another, locked together in our grief.

'Does she understand, do you think?' Sasha asks me quietly as we walk back through the cemetery together.

'She understands too well and feels too much,' I say.

We drive Mother back to Redbush. When we have delivered her to her nurse, Sasha and I hover uncertainly in the parking lot.

'Well?' he says. 'Have you changed your mind?'

'No, Sash.'

Jane is incarcerated at Redbush too. Larry negotiated to have her bailed here to the secure wing. Larry has looked old and tired since Jane's arrest and now he has announced his retirement.

'The reunion cannot be a pleasant one,' says Sasha.

'I must go in; she's all alone,' I insist.

'Scott has refused to visit her and he is right. She killed his son, she is not entitled to his compassion.' Sasha lights a cigarette.

'No one could forgive her for that,' I say carefully. 'But you know, Daddy and Mother never should have covered up the first death. By protecting her, they exposed the rest of us to risk.'

'If they were wrong, they have paid dearly for their mistake; your mother with her sanity and your father with his life.'

I turn towards the secure wing. 'I have to go,' I say. 'Jane needs me.'

Sasha follows me. 'Must we really regard her needs as paramount?'

'She loved me and looked after me for years. Should I just forget that?'

'Loved you and looked after you.' He snorts. 'She presented herself as your protector when she was actually your controller, and everyone but you was aware of this. She diagnosed bogus health complaints that enabled her to regulate your life, she isolated you from your friends, she attempted to kill you on a number of occasions while appearing to save you, and she created a version of your past, a series of fictions about your childhood, which disguised her own destructive role.'

'But, Sash, we all create fictions about our past for our own ends. A couple of days ago you were recommending that to me,' I remind him.

'We structure our own past with narrative. We have no right to structure other people's.' He waves his cigarette at me. 'Since you are determined to defend Jane, let us visit her. But we can expect little thanks.'

Despite everyone's warnings, I imagine myself talking over recent events with Jane. I even believe she might offer some kind of explanation. I am convinced that at the very least she will be pleased to see me.

I am told that I may only speak to her through a grille. When it opens I peer through it like a visitor at the zoo searching for some particularly well-camouflaged reptile. Finally I locate her across the room. She sits, her body still, her face turned away, her hair like a curtain between us.

I call her name gently. I say, 'It's Lucy. Jane, it's Lucy.'

She does not look up or respond.

Sasha and I drive home in silence. When we are back in the kitchen and Aunt Zina is crashing pans around us, I ask, 'Sash, what did you mean when you said that everyone knew Jane tried to control me?'

'Exactly that. For example, your childhood visits to this apartment. It was clear to Grandma, Mother and me that she disliked your forming any relationship over which she could not exercise direct influence,' says Sasha. 'I imagine that she usually tried to dissuade you from visiting? And often succeeded.'

When Mrs Joseph came to see me she told me that, after the crash in the valley, Robert had called me many times. She herself had both called and written. Jane had intercepted each time, informing the Josephs I didn't want to speak to them again.

'If you'd had the confidence to pick up the phone yourself,' Mrs Joseph said, 'she never could have controlled things so effectively.'

'But unconsciously, Lucia,' says Sasha now, 'you knew about her. You escaped from her to New York and when you returned you chose to stay with us. I believe you knew it all.'

Scott takes me to the airport. He says, 'Am I allowed to ask exactly when you're coming back?'

'I just have to say goodbye to Jim and pack my apartment. I'll be home in a week.'

He smiles and picks me up as though I'm as small and weightless as a toy and then swings me round. 'Everything's lighter now,' he tells me.

I am walking away from him as he yells, 'Lucy, don't take three years about it this time. Or we'll come and get you. Me and your brother.'

As the plane nears New York I see Manhattan glittering in the distance. The cab driver informs me that the weather just changed. That heatwave they had in the west has worked its way right across the continent, he tells me, and arrived, weakened by travel, in New York City.

'It's great, it's summer!' he says.

'It's spring,' I remind him.

My key in the lock of the apartment, my bag over my shoulder, a stack of mail from the lobby under my arm. The lock feels a little stiffer than usual, but the door swings open easily enough.

Everything's as I left it. I sit down and enjoy the silence of my own place. One hour slips into another. I can hear the noise of the street outside, the airplanes overhead, distant music from my neighbours, but in here there is no noise unless I make it.

Eventually I stretch and fetch the mail I carried up from the lobby. I start to sort through it. One letter arrests me. Handwritten envelope.

Familiar writing. My hand starts to shake. Tears sting at my eyes.

I sit down and stare at the letter that was mailed to me in some other era and has waited for me to return from my long journey. I brace myself for the new reality it might contain. I prepare for another shift in my knowledge, after so many, and just when I thought I was home.

Slowly, reluctantly, I tear open the envelope. I unfold the letter.

My dear Lucy, I've tried calling, now I'm writing because it's clear to me that I won't be around so very much longer. I don't want to go, Lucy. I don't want to leave you. But when I do, please don't be too sad. Don't be too angry. Don't ask why unless you're ready for what you might find. Don't come back to California. Don't have any more children here, have them in some other part of the world, but for God's sake, have them, you were a good mother and don't let anyone tell you otherwise. Don't think too badly of your father, he loves you dearly. And don't you dare forget me. As long as you remember me, I'm still there. Daddy.

LIZ RIGBEY

'There aren't many certainties in life,' Liz Rigbey told me when we met at the Savoy Hotel in London, 'but one thing I've always known was that I'd be a writer, even though I didn't start my "real" writing career until I'd had a few interesting jobs along the way.'

Liz started out as a journalist on *Farmers Weekly*—'I've always been deeply interested in agriculture'—and went on to become a producer of farming programmes for the BBC. Then, in a wild leap of faith from fact to fiction she moved to the BBC Radio 4 series *The Archers* for three years. 'My favourite part of this immense job was scripting,' she admitted, 'and it became clear to me that I shouldn't put off my intention to be a writer any longer. I left that promising BBC career, with everyone saying I was quite mad, to write my first book, *Total Eclipse*. It took ages and I had to fund myself through it by doing some presenting on *Gardeners' World* for the BBC, which was totally different for me, but great fun.'

With writing now her prime focus Liz began work on her second novel. 'I got the idea for *Summertime* years and years ago when I read a newspaper article about a woman whose babies kept dying of some mysterious disease. She was certainly distraught at each death, although it was eventually proved that she'd been killing the children. I remembered that when I had my own first baby I loved him passionately, but I could

see that such powerful love had a darker side. That was the germ of the book but the plot soon spiralled away from the initial idea. I must have rewritten *Summertime* at least eight times over a six-year period. I'd had two children too, which is not the best point in one's life to write really! I enjoyed writing so much and, in the very limited time available to me now that I was a mother, I'd write frantically instead of plotting. That's hardly forgivable in someone who used to be editor of *The Archers*, where plotting and structure is everything.'

When Liz finally finished *Summertime*, she asked her agent to find her some ghost writing for relaxation. 'I know that probably the best way to relax is to do nothing, but that just didn't occur to me.' The ghost writing took her and her family to northern Italy, near Lake Garda, where they have lived for the past year. 'When we moved here none of us were able to speak a word of Italian and I can't pretend it's been easy. However, my daughter is now in nursery school, and my son in elementary school, and even I can stumble through most conversations. And the benefits of living in Italy are abundant—the food, weather and the genuinely warm and friendly people. Hopefully, living in this relaxed setting, my next novel should be the easiest one of all to write!'

Jane Eastgate

Printed and bound by Maury Imprimeur SA, Malesherbes, France

601-019-1